TELEMACHUS

by

BILL DUNBAR

volume I

anANNAL Publishing Co.
30 Harrow Road
Stanmore, NSW 2048

ISBN: 978-0-6450592-0-5 (hardcover)
ISBN: 978-0-6450592-1-2 (ebook)

Cover design by Quick Fox Editing

Printed in Australia by IngramSpark

Credits: Front + back cover: Heritage Auctions, HA.com.

TELEMACHUS

by

BILL DUNBAR

volume I

anANNAL PUBLISHING CO.

30, Rue de Harrow, 30

SYDNEY

2020

THIS EDITION IS OFFERED FREE TO READERS IN PDF AND E-BOOK FORMATS. PRINT COPY CAN BE PURCHASED VIA THE WEBSITE – TELEMACHUS.COM.AU. THE FIRST EDITION OF ULYSSES WAS LIMITED TO 1000 COPIES: 100 COPIES (SIGNED) ON DUTCH HANDMADE PAPER NUMBERED FROM 1 TO 100; 150 COPIES ON VERGÉ D'ARCHES, NUMBERED FROM 101 TO 250; 750 COPIES ON HANDMADE PAPER NUMBERED FROM 251 TO 1000.

The editor asks the reader's indulgence for typographical errors unavoidable in the exceptional circumstances.

J. C.

1.

"But, for the unquiet heart and brain,
A use in measured language lies;
The sad mechanic exercise,
Like dull narcotics, numbing pain."

– Tennyson, *In Memoriam*, Canto V, 5–9

2.

"And BILL, of course, Bill, abandoning himself, smiling,
laughing in every face, incurably romantic, sickeningly cynical –
vandalism, theft, alcohol, BEING YOUNG."

– David McComb, *Diaries*, 1982

3.

"The postmodern would be that which, in the modern,
puts forward the unpresentable in presentation itself;
that which denies itself the solace of good forms ..."

– Jean-Francois Lyotard, *The Postmodern Condition*, 81

4.

That's the story of my life / That's the difference /
Between wrong and right / But Billy said, / Both those words
are dead, / That's the story of my life."

– The Velvet Underground, *The Velvet Underground*, 1969

Table of Contents

List of Tables & Illustrations

I
Gods in Council

"Book 1 of The Odyssey *opens with an invocation of the muse, followed by an account of a council of the gods on Olympus at which Zeus decides that it is time for Odysseus to return home ..."*

— **Frank Gifford.**

Spoilt chimeras that cling to my imagination in quavering obscurity, must I call you into focus again, insert optics over my dying eyes, and trawl your nether lands for some weak explanation of this wilful, lucky life? Of course, I must or else these words will become just another sentence washed-up and forgotten on the fizzy blanking banks of Charon's Lethe. But what a different type of "sentence" they become if I continue: one of conviction ... to utterance. It is with a clear comprehension of the task ahead that I fix myself in my own era like a deep-set totem and will my mind to become anannal. Such a posture could be rendered thus: "]meaning[". These parenthetic ears burn like a gem-like flame as I step over the wall of books surrounding my desk and fit my body into the enclosed recess before the computer, encased in this pedagogical capsule like some stern Cosmonaut, reference books stacked to the left, diaries and notebooks on the right. I grope into the dark past seeking the familiar patterns of objects that will unlock fields of memory like fingers striking the worn-down keys of a broken keyboard. To grid the pale screen with words and scroll on, to think "space over, text progressed," that is success in life. Come closer then, sweet Memories, pile around me so that I feel half-alive in a sinking mass grave. Your cold swoll'n faces can now be observed with detachment as if gazing upon a pool of old vomit that you suddenly recognise as having once been part of you, and you parting of it, provoking heroic efforts of reprise – *das Ich* – from an otherwise annihilated intellect. It is certainly a thrill for my loam when you stir worm-style from the murky floor of my conscience like Milton's infernal army reaching up to Daylight. Love and Friendship shimmy out in coils entwined with Jealousy, Betrayal, Hate and the luckless Dead. Soon this Medusa's head of emotions is fixed firmly in my gaze. It projects a single foreboding image of us shackled together in a stiff semi-circle in the West Berlin sludge staring at the easel without acknowledgment or contact. Discarded books, tapes and drawings are spread like a soggy offertory over the hastily brushed foreground. Only our uniform black clothing suggests fidelity to a certain epoch, that itself can only be made tangible by its music: The Saints, Birthday Party, feedtime, the Velvet Underground, Joy Division, Tactics and always Bob Dylan. This relic congeals the Aristotelian PAST as if from a great height so that it appears almost comprehensible. But you might as well force goggles over the eyes of blind Oedipus as dredge up any expectation of definitive closure. That unbound period will never be resolved. It implodes in my mind like Brueghel's vast labyrinthine Babel, its receding chambers withdrawing momentary insights into the dim core of Being LOST. All that can be done in its aftermath is to raise a clouded glass of retentions, swish the echo around my mouth, and spit their gormless traces back at Time's unsmiling face. Come still closer then, dear Memories, until you have advanced to the window of my soul and I can watch from a deep armchair as you scrape away trinkets of frost from the brittle pane with dirt-stiffened cuffs and expose all my facets. Gaze inside on the glazed insides of my Being. Its opaque hide shines like copper crystals in the ebb as the warm air from my one-bar radiator rocks the Japanese paper lantern above my head. Slowly, I look up from a heavy stupor at your Shape presst against the thick aquarium glass. Your features are squasht out of humane proportion like one of Goebbels' anti-Semitic posters. [LOUD] "Can you still distinguish my voice," I ask. No reply. Pressured fissures pit the jellied glass. Secret punctures down the dim membrane. First seepthru. Bitter recollections begin passing out of me like sweat. Days long gone lost & o'er <u>STOP</u> You are scattered like so much fall pollen, my own dear deadens. SHIFT Only my angel from the end ("O") remains. So be it. *The Odyssey* is over. The Classical period has closed. And Telemachus has drifted out of orbit like some Bronze Age Major Tom. Yet I will go on alone post-Wormwood through the nullified Space that Time once measured until I reach the spot where the last star fell into the sea (Revelations 8:11) and there, as St Jerome in his study, a recumbent lion his only companion, so I, with language slumbering protectively inside me, contemplate the blank page. I've been planning this text for some time but I never expected to execute it, let alone in such straightforward fashion. I'd always intended to let the shards of your demise work their way out of my system like those fragments of shrapnel that burrow through the body of an ageing ANZAC until they finally push through the flesh in a blasphemy of birth. I felt your legacy would be more manageable that way. But just as Shelley's influence was apparently effaced from Browning's poetry at the superficial level of style, only to remain deeply entrenched in his forms, so you, too, infest every aspect of my being. Student, pedagogue, clerk, husband, father. I have rimmed the Ontology without ever being able to mainline myself into EXISTENCE. Not that I can really complain. I've finally arrived at what amounts to Elysium. Rebooted like Winston Smith. With the family I always coveted. Some sense of social utility at my back. Black suit blues on the bus each morning when I'm still too full of one final grin from my daughter all dimples gums forehead and gaze as she sucks her fist, gags on a carmine jumpsuit and whispers "coo coo." Soon she'll be crawling across the floor of her lamp-lit room like Huysmans' tortoise. At dawn, she stands in her cot, spreads her lower lip as tight as a drum and cries: "ning ning ning ning ning ning ning." Seven times. It's the longest sound she can make between gulps of air. It is my invocation to rise. Recalling it now fills me with deep feeling until I'm distracted by an old nurse working her way down the aisle. Nobody offers her a seat. I touch her sky-blue cotton work dress and rise. A private school pupil steals my place. I turn so as not to defy. I have delivered myself up to this point by sheer will to integrity. It's a warm safe ride through familiar country like touring regional Victoria in spring. Why would I want to put all of that at stake by dredging you out of the murky bed where you lie? We ought to fade into teeming human space together like Ulysses and Diomedes inside Dante's eighth circle. All this anguish makes it sound as if I've got nothing better to do than workshop the crazy stratagems which mutilated my youth. Nothing could be further from the truth. These days I am more interested in understanding things of which you were only the plastic manifestation. Not that I would ever underestimate you. Even reduced to the status of mere character, you are still capable of inflicting untold (or in this case "told") damage. At any moment you could surge through my proofs like some uncalculating tempest. All your scattered potency on display. It's an unpalatable sight. Writers often turn to metaphors of pollution and death to relay the power of such tropes. I tend to revert to the safety of my obscure studies. Indeed, I am surprised that it has finally come time for candour. The thin lips which zip my mouth shut are mute symbols of self-containment. Yet here I am as open and exposed as Isaac on the slab. Perhaps it's a Proustian reflection of the *zeitgeist* and all those relentless confessions which America broadcasts as a substitute for ethics. But who am I to criticise celebrity shrinks ... telemarketing ... chatrooms ... blogs ... gaming ... endep ... or any other form of escape for that matter? I have jacked-up and cranked-up on toilet seats right across Europe, staggered into the biting late night frost and droppt onto the footpath, pulling my grit-heavy overcoat around my face, suspended in saline and smack like some bottled museum piece. Bluddy needle puncture hanging out of ma swoll'n vein. Ichor surging through my cistem. The aperture into life closes. Mundane visions of insects and fleece. Dark shapes which blockt out all light in childhood. Pins and needles sizzling my wrist. Groggy attachment to the crap infesting our lounge room. Willing your touch. This is what Browning's Paracelsus called the "breath so light / Upon my eyelids, and the fingers warm / Among my hair." Quest to regather Time commences. Like Tennyson, I just want to rest my cheek against your denim-shrouded shoulder once more. To reach into your embrace in another airport. To curl my fingers through your slick mane. And hear your thick lisp again. *Putuwá*. My eyelids finally part on a silhouette set within streetlight halo. Just briefly I thought it was you. But the voice and its language were quite foreign. I closed my eyes and rolled over in the snow. The urine came hot and quick then cold. Only nausea finally compelled me to slide along the footpath like a wounded animal until some decent burgher assisted me into the warm foyer of his apartment building, propped me up in the landing, fed me strong filter coffee and gave me my S-Bahn fare home. Joyce was walking down a Zurich Street when the definitive attack of iritis hit him. The face of the stranger who carried him to a nearby bench remained blurred. He was never able to ascribe identity to this Good Samaritan. He saw halos around the streetlamps in rims of red, yellow and green. But this wasn't a sublime moment. I returned to Sydney soon afterwards to repair my junk-dependent cells. Not that I want to glamorise my insipid dalliance with the GEAR. It's taken me thirty years to achieve some kind of parity. I can blow into your image so that its pale ghost glows like Shelley's fading coal. It doesn't take much to reawaken you. And it doesn't take much to put you away. There's even some chance that I'll still abort this scheme. That's the way it is between the Gods and Man. I tend to shift between fragments – advancing each one by increment – shifting self-contained units of meaning like jigsaw pieces – allowing some duplication – finally installing a temporary text in which the line is subjugated to the page (no caesura no enjambment) – every sheet gridded with ink – a reticulated vehicle of expression – sheer prose. If the Modernist poem is like peering down a nocturnal coastline then prose is the vast electrified network of the contemporary city. It is process driven by computer program. The Internet has conflated language into a field of symbols and slogans – all transient – opening its mechanics to display. The book too must become BINARY like that. It must expose its HTML, drilling down discursive channels without closure. Samuel Beckett said that there's no finished works, only aborted ones. But he was vain about publication. Beckett despised quotation marks. He picked this up from Joyce, who called them "perverted commas". This is why he used the M-dash. Joyce wanted language to make smooth progress without distraction. It all became his own testament then, even slabs of conversation appropriated from cafes and pubs in Trieste and Zurich. Ultimately,

Joyce disliked characterisation being built solely through speech as per drama. He wanted to work through STAGE DIRECTIONS (see C7) and footnotes. He needed to probe the boundaries of parody and pastiche to delineate characters before they were finally called forth to make verbal utterance. We are both more comfortable transcribing events and dispositions from the fluctuating rhythms of narratorial perspective. Everything is up for grabs with this method. The logical conclusion of my approach is an endlessly amended chronicle of the manifold utterances which make up Self. Stitched thus, it acts as cipher. **CODE**. Every allusion plotted and matched. Cascading lists. A website full of dropdown boxes that unravel like a concordance. In words like weeds I'll wrap me o'er, as Tennyson said. Penelope stitching unstitching then re-stitching the weft. Driving inwards Berkeley-style. This is an enterprise best-suited to the unflinching resolve of figures like Shelley, Byron and Joyce. BUT I COULD NEVER AFFECT THE HEROIC MODE. For more than a few stanzas. As with Melville, call it self-deprecation. I am only ever Wagner to someone else's Faust. Fitting my puny sole inside the cast of Samson's footfall. NO AGON. Pressing against the pillars of the Canon as they close. AN INVERSE PRAXIS. No fidelity to form. Call it **TECHNICAL FICTION**. You're sent forward in the work. You're sent back. You get a sense of a work plaited by internal referencing, that sets itself against chronology. It's like the operations of the human mind. We look to the future, we go back; inhabiting our time casually. Approaching TMAC is like examining a model ship inside a glass bottle. It's a pure form erected by contrivance behind a sheer barrier. From different angles, you get different refractions: depending on the shape and thickness of the glass at any given point. I conceived the plan to commemorate your life straight after your death as a kind of Personification Allegory but kept postponing it until my memory was decontaminated (I should probably say "tinctured") by my essential human optimism. It seemed more manageable that way. But now all the done and undone things are equally out of reach. My parents are dead. I don't have to endure their imbedded disinterest anymore. I've abandoned the monograph on Pater because he was so obstinately bland that it started to read like Beckett's *Trilogy*. I had the idea to write a series of metaportraits updating his themes in *Imaginary Portraits*. I've inserted the latest draft right into the centre of this work like a key (see C5, E10). The next episode in ONE MILLION WORDS is called VAULT. See C8, Q&A4 for the full plan. It's now just a matter of execution as with M at the end of *DTP*. Nothing really stands in my way now except WILL. Never a strong point. And lately I've been flat out just coping. Paternity shuts you down like that. External events become like falling leaves in the ebb. Oh, I no that I shudd a(r)gue that there's flamy hardgem in my sowl yet – and there is!! – but then the telephone ratatattled and I pickt it up'n'sigh'd involuntary at the didactic mumbell of authority on t'ether end and I hanged up and ma eyelids just dropt w/out being voided n I went outside forgettent of goggulars an wandead parblind in a dayze ma grasp of the quotidian receding with ma faltering eyeslight till all replaced by John Donney outlines and touchness like sum skilless child fossicking through xmas gives. My mind turns easily to the uncanny perception of those long-gone days. O says I waste too much time dwelling in HISTORY. But the emblems of experience become more precious with age. Soon I'll be relying on them for atoms of retained meaning. Perhaps I should get it all down on tape like Krapp. I have to be careful not to scatter my small dividend. Not with the arduous process of revision still to take place. Ah, those days of desperate concentration, bent towards the computer screen pasting the fragments of my petty brain-waverings into new sequences. Luvox cooling my temper of all its manners so I can stay seated for a few minutes without pacing. But stuff never rolls out of my mouth in some neat chronology. I always start with a simple idea. Apparently unrelated images manifest themselves at the demand for sibilance or a vowel. Sometimes I seem merely the medium for (and "on") its terms. No stream of consciousness. An accumulation of cognizance maybe. Stuff caught in the branches as the Liffey passes (Gaelic for Life). Language dense and inscrutable. A sequence of feints at meaning only to leave a morass of mal-meanings in their wake. Metaphors heaped in discursive piles like wrong turns taken. Being displaced by oblique symbols. Some semblance of human nobility in the face of material bathos nonetheless. But I am now some days drive from Unity (Mass.). Words emanating out of all parts of my head like thorns. Each new insertion inducing another teleological disjuncture. Time being such a poor chassis for Being. And all just to squeeze out a few puny sentences. Often, I feel like it's never going to transpire. But I have lived with my text for many seasons (many stark seasons) and I come and go as I please into its Hieratic modes or out of them. They are a trench along which words pass brimming like water: froth along the muddy banks = rhapsody; slow seepage over Ophelia's dress is evidence of the Sublime; a receding water-level indicates Meditation. Eventually, FORM looms out of the far-too-distant screen causing mild flutters of surprise until the SLAP of my daughter's body along the hall reminds me of life's true hierarchy. Insects spending their brief existence, as Virag whispers in Circe, stranded on shore watching a dragonfly hover and dart over the surface of a still pool, a rippling pond. I abandon the screen to pick her up in my arms, press my mouth against her soft hair and provide the comfort of some pre-linguistic murmur. She stops crying when her fingers become distracted by the pointed tip of my left ear. Her tidal sobs ebb. We re-form. I'm glad MY LIFE has finally reached stalemate. Fatherhood is my ticket back to normalcy. For a start, it rusht me through moral coma. It also satisfies my attraction to personal oblivion; which I used to expend on drugs. Even someone as steadfast in his craft as James Joyce tried to emphasise the value of paternity; in his case, to Samuel Beckett. To no avail. But I suspect that Beckett consciously set his entire life at a tangent to Joyce. Their crosstown accents; crosstown arts. More bravura Joyce; more genuine ingenuity Beckett. Finding a way around the Joycean impasse took all his consummate skill and detachment. Hence his concept of a 'retrogressive tendency' in *Proust*. It enabled him to go back to their common ancestor, Walter Pater, thereby reinstating one of Joyce's unspoken influences as his own point of departure. This is what Harold Bloom would call a Scene of Instruction. I'd like to put my own interest in Victorian Aesthetics in the same category. But such vanities of scale in this analogy. I have been toiling on the period when Romanticism finally shook its shiny taile loose on the marble path and scuttled into the Swinburnean pubis (pewbiz?). After that, you can watch it unravel in the tinny green dusk of Wilde's London. It was the first faithless utterance post-Darwin. Modernism's dam. I love those nineteenth century novels of which I can no longer partake. I miss their antinomian rage. The contemporary novel has withdrawn from any sustained experiment with form, occasionally diverting itself with occult fantasy. This is the strategy of most Magic Realism [INSERT QUALIFICATION: TEXT OF A FAT BLOKE IN A PICKLE SHOP WHO EXPLODES]. But who am I to condemn Peter Carey? I, too, am about to manufacture a fiction behind which to shield my leering skull (I am quite bald now) and with little of his cheerful talent for caricature. The first thing you notice about *Ulysses* is its unbalanced structure. It bears no resemblance to a conventional novel. It comprises only three chapters of completely different proportions. It sucks in the reader with an apparently simple short first chapter before ostensible form melts, spreads and warps. It becomes organised by unstated, shuffled segments of Homer and structuring devices like newspaper headlines, catechisms, dashes, exaggerated spacing and separation bars. This is an extraordinary act <u>against</u> readerly habits. Only with the intervention of interpreters like Bugden and Gilbert could its meaning be ultimately disclosed. Joyce's campaign of hiring hermeneutical seers intensified with *Finnegans Wake [F(W)ake]*. It became like a PR campaign to rescue his last work. Sam Coleman's prosecution speech in 1933 remains the most incisive analysis of *Ulysses*. The Assistant DA in the Southern District of New York was forced to read *Ulysses* for the obscenity trial. He concluded that its style was new and startling; it offered a new system of presenting people to themselves; it was both scientific and poetic; it represented an encyclopaedia, thorough and classified, of the very substance of 2 beings, both physical and psychological, both external and internal; and even the remotest characters are 'limned' with unmistakable distinctness upon its canvas. James Joyce effectively healed the nineteenth century breach between poetics and matter in *Ulysses*. It is Modernist

High Style in a demotic setting. The basic urban scene is imbued with complex Classical referents which increase its potency and induce additional layers of meaning about Dublin. Like the *Odyssey*, *Ulysses* is a text about a world ruled by conflict and arbitrary death. It relies on appropriation of Homer's meta-narrative to achieve an architectonic power that a confined, quotidian structure could not otherwise sustain. But Joyce is wilful in his use of Homer. The *Odyssey* is selectively employed. Loose or tangential associations are promoted. Characterisation is fluid and relative to Joyce's immediate needs. For example, Molly acts as Calypso to Bloom's Odysseus when she is first introduced only to be re-cast as Nausicaa in recollections about her youth, Circe with Boylan and Penelope by the end of the novel. Such shifting characterisation has already been justified by Stephen in his discourse on *Hamlet* when he talks of how the artist must "weave and unweave his image." It is a distinctly Shelleyan form of literary relativity. Joyce ignores things that don't serve his purpose. He doesn't need to ape Homer. There is no Cicones episode in *Ulysses*, even though it was the first major narrative event after Odysseus left Troy, preceding Lotus-Eaters in Book 9. Joyce took notes for this proposed episode from Berard's *Les Pheniciens et l'Odyssie* (see Buffalo Notebook, VIIIA.5). The Cicones were allies of Troy. Odysseus surprises Ismara, kills the men and takes the women as slaves. Later, reinforcements attack the Achaeans, slaughtering so many troops that Odysseus is forced to flee. It would have been difficult to slot this episode into the start of Bloom's adventures in *Ulysses*. Its leitmotifs of retribution, violence and rape run counter to Joyce's humanist themes, which are embodied in Bloom from the start of Chapter Two. It would have misrepresented Bloom at the outset. *Ulysses* is complex yet it can also be stripped down to its component parts quite easily. It always inverts expectations. Its Classical title signals the likelihood of sweeping narrative action over an epic period. However, it is a largely psychological, centripetal quest set on a single day. It becomes an anti-quest like Browning's "Childe Roland." The narrative can be likened to a TOP set in motion that never really comes to rest. It is gripped with the frenetic daily patterns that constitute modern life. This energy dwindles into nocturnal lethargy as the main characters embark on a long inconclusive walk towards Bloom's home. In this way, the text capitulates to halt. Thus, *Ulysses* follows the *Odyssey* but it is also its inverse. Where the *Odyssey* is concise in its language and packed with events, *Ulysses* is all elaboration and insignificant proceedings. It starts conventionally but ends inexplicably. Its classical template is never fully exposed. Form is thus present but broken, covert and scattered, only to be pulled together at critical junctures. Mallarme's Chance seems constantly in play. Yet the whole show is rigged by Joyce. The movement of the cavalcade of the Earl of Dudley across Dublin (251–4) in "Wandering Rocks" is a fine example of Joyce's practice of fusing incongruous and apparently arbitrary narrative events and characters to create new meaning and cast new light on actions in the novel to date. This creates formal density. Yet *Ulysses* actually offers a very plain plot. In essence, it traces the movements of two individuals, Stephen Dedalus and Leopold Bloom, around Dublin through a cycle of twenty hours. It builds towards their intersection, reaches no apparent apex during their engagement and seems set to end after their separation. But this doesn't happen. Ultimately, it yields to the terminal monologue of Bloom's wife. Like "The Sensitive Plant," *Ulysses* continuously resists teleological closure. The notion of disrupted journeys is as essential to *Ulysses* as it was to its Homeric model. Stephen's activities achieve no genuine conclusion by the end of the novel. He simply exits into the night (624). Most critics leave him hanging. Some argue that he has established a new connection with Bloom as a surrogate father. He can now develop as a man and artist. Others believe that Joyce creates a platform for Stephen to efface his own father through negative comparison with Bloom. I believe it is most likely that Stephen would find Bloom to be a slightly pompous and pretentious steward like Malvolio and the strongest signs are that he is returning to the home of his biological father to go to bed. Such a decision would be in keeping with Joyce's own fidelity to his father. He always remained fiercely loyal to John Joyce. Joyce presents the climactic engagement between Bloom and Stephen as a sequence of three hundred and nine questions and answers. This device achieves profound emotional detachment between the subjects. After Stephen's departure, Bloom reverts to habit by replaying customary fantasies and anxieties. He prepares his candle, burns the prospectus for Agendath Netaim (628), partially undresses while ironically contemplating a statue of Narcissus (631), compiles his daily budget (631–2), dreams of farm life and gentrification including an assessment of his financial means (634–41), analyses objects in a drawer (641–4), remembers his father (645), contemplates death/escape (647–50), goes to the bathroom to complete his ablutions (651), gets into bed upside-down (652), lists Molly's lovers as always jealously (652–5) and gives a summary of his conversation with his wife (658). At this point, Molly Bloom is finally introduced as a character (659–704). Here, Joyce drives the final nail into another literary convention: that of character development by sustained presence over the course of the novel. Molly does not 'appear' in *Ulysses* prior to this episode. Instead, she is fully MISDRAWN by the time she finally speaks. She has been distorted by a stream of slurs and innuendo by men. Elsewhere, Joyce employs precisely the opposite tactic. He revises initial characterisation with new information that compromises positive opinions, such as with Tom Rochford or even Mulligan. Characters names are misheard or changed. Nicknames come into play (insert TMAC character list). *Ulysses* represents the apex of Modernism. It updates Walter Pater's dense prose with radical attacks on style and form. There are numerous experiments with language including the thirty-plus styles used successively in the Oxen episode and the intentional clustering of rhetorical tools in Aeolus where Joyce employs up to sixty devices including metonymy, diaresis and palindrome. Oscar Wilde was a master of form across all types of text (novel, play, ballad, essay, oratory). Joyce was a master of forms within one text. *Telemachus* re-assesses *Ulysses* from the POV of the son. This is also a master metaphor for the relationship of Australia to England. Joyce's references to Homer are reworked and extended. In *PAYM*, Joyce aimed to 'forge in the smithy of my soul the uncreated conscience of my race.' Dublin in 1904 is re-applied to Sydney in 1984 which is also like Trieste in 1914 – a melting pot of rusted-on locals, transients and migrants all hustling for life. It is *Ulysses* post-scriptum. *Ulysses* was the end of fiction as we know it. Fitzgerlad off erred to jam pout a win doe for Joy[ce]. Djuna Barnes said she would never right another line. She went onto write 5 works of fiction including *Nightwood*. Hemingway was one of the first prose writers to work out that it was best to ignore *Ulysses*, reverting to simple tales of wartime service that Joyce could never threaten. Arnold Bennett said "the code has been smashed to bits." E. Pound used *Ulysses* as a stick to start the Cantos. Eliot recognised it as a completely new mode of representation – what he called 'mythic method.' He could never convince V. Woolf of its merits, although the book infested her psyche thereafter (see C6). Eliot wondered how Joyce could ever write again after Penelope. He was right. Nobody could escape its clutches. Everyone tried. I am the first writer to try to wriggle free by making a centripetal movement back TOWARDS Joyce. Fiction, literary analysis, biography and autobiography blur in TMAC. Time gets shifted in a way Joyce didn't envision. Characterization is distorted. It apes different literary forms as well as styles from Joyce. So where do you begin such a story? A story of lust, hatred and betrayal. A story of romance, redemption and the Soul. You can't just call down the Goddess of Song anymore. She went to the grave with Dionysus. Since then, we're all trying to manufacture a new opening gambit. To confect a new Martello Tower. Make an unmatched pronouncement. Update the uneasy awakening of Josef K. Dawn has always been a popular trigger. *Faust* begins in a laboratory at night. Or is that *Frankenstein*? Gothic onset either way. Flaubert always favoured schoolyard reminiscences. Pater chose the pagan child. Sal Paradise was sick at his aunt's house after getting divorced. Chronicles of what Milton termed "man's first disobedience" abound. Modern movies compete in gimmicky gore. Has anyone started down a hole? Yes, Novalis and Zola. Other stories begin in garrets. You must come down, moving through hostile arenas to exit (the staircase beside the residence of Raskolnikov's landlady, for instance) and even then you're only on the street! Perhaps there's a dining-room full of lodgers beside the front door as in *Pere Goriot*. In Australia, they'd be stuck out the back of a pub: a scientist, the … the … 'poet,' some seasonal workers, a prune-faced gambler. A big-nosed country barmaid enters. She balances a column of inverted schooner glasses in each grip. It is the tropics and only ceiling fans stand between us and disorder. Robert Browning always commenced his poems with a disclaimer. *Sordello* starts with, "who will, may hear Sordello's story told," as if Browning didn't give a damn about the presence of a reader. This was a wise precaution given Browning's trademark opacity (self-joke). In the next line, he immediately robbed his text of authority by adding a second codicil: "who *believes me* shall behold / The man" (my italics). This virtually conceded that the reader's credulity may wane as the Poet doggedly pursued Sordello's fortunes to closure as if a luminous trail of lime was draining from his anus. Yet at least Browning settled on a genre. I have never been sure which form to employ. The novel has been the preferred mode of literary expression for the last two centuries. Its comfortable paths are inlaid in our minds like deep-set stepping stones. But *Kunstlerroman* or *Roman à clef*? Austere nineteenth century Realism or experimental Modernist chronicle? Maybe an assemblage of literary modes suggesting a postmodern approach that denies itself the solace of good forms? A fable would certainly be apt for my enterprise as it announces itself as a symbolic fabrication from the outset. Allegory also has merit. I have always been attracted to characters with names like Pilgrim, Empty and Vile. They suit my simplistic ethical standpoint. But this period of my life lacks the capacity to slip into any easy form. There is no comforting resolution as in Comedy. There is no sense of self-righteous certainty as with Satire. It doesn't possess the relentless drive of Tragedy (what the Greeks called 'goat song'). It is neither Ibsenesque, Beckettian, Fovist or Ionescoid. It is melodrama by design, but mummery rather. Maybe I should turn to poetical drama. It was considered the quintessential medium for extended metaphysical posturing prior to the 19th century. You know the score: "Vision of the seer, craft of the maker / That beginneth in light and endeth in wisdom. / To Be, not mean. / Sanctifying language. / And I believe in Romantic and Classical tendencies, / The four emplotments / And in metaphor the barstead offspring of imagination, / Give us this day our daily rhetorical, aesthetic and mnemonic purposes, / The hegemony of style over matter / And lead us not into doggerel." Sometimes, I would like to get right up into the reader's face as in Epic. At other times, I would be rather be concealed by the mask of characterisation as in Drama. On still other occasions, it would be better to conceal the audience from my muse in the manner of Lyric so that I could inscribe the truth without censorship. Am I going to make a confession then? Not really. Though perhaps Tom Hallem's absolution is my sublimated goal. James Joyce powered *Ulysses* on progression through successive forms. This repeated the pattern of Stephen Dedalus' evolution in *A Portrait of the Artist as a Young Man*: lyrical pre-occupation with self during infancy; adolescent awareness leading to epic negotiation of social constructs; and dramatic detachment in maturity. These stages roughly corresponded to the three qualities of Beauty defined by Thomas Aquinas: *integritas*, *consonantia* & *claritas*. These were symbols of wholeness, harmony and radiance. Sun beating down on our backsides on greaseproof beaches. Bright orb inducing orbit. Hyperion's realm. Fat flocks abundant. Succulent spitted flesh. The nemesis of Odysseus' crew in the consumption of. Triggering the threat by Zeus to shine a light on the dead (this was the first Naturalistic impulse). His thunderbolt followed. Six-headed Scylla and pitiless Charybdis. Odysseus drifting for nine days on a plank. INSERT ANALOGUE. I was in limbo, resting on a couch, my service days behind me, resisting only unconsciousness, which would yet demand me, struggle as I might, until I gave way to the light reveries of a doze, as you do on a bed on route, underfed and scanning poesy. This is a state that triggers the Muse. I pluckt a black felt-tip pen from my bedside table and hastily scrawled some shorthand notes. But why go on with all this wishy-washy diplomacy? One of the flaws of Australian Literature since the death of Patrick White has been the absence of real malice. They say a cat always lands on its feet. So does a man wearing cement shoes. Henry James invented the term "reflector" to describe the specially-selected centres of his narrative universes. You were that kind of THING for me. You embody different characters like one of Hugo's mythical types which concentrate a whole family DNA into a single human being. I will need to deploy many requisite models to depict our experience: Telemachus, whose father was a physical absence; Hamlet, who tortured himself with doubt; Faust who felt the same self-contained drive towards knowledge; Shelley who was reckless in youth; Paris that was indolent; Rimbaud who outgrew ART; Coleridge who was crippled by drug abuse. Then there are the brothers: Cain and Abel, Romulus and Remus, Shem and Shaun, Jim and Stan. Us. Perhaps your life is a Modernist parable. As with Gold Cup Day 1904, it is possible to isolate a single day when you set off on a definitive course towards closure. At that turning point, you took the first unwitting steps from being Stephen Dedalus to becoming ... who ... Leopold Bloom? No. It is only with the imposition of direct narrative power that an observer could register definitive change in your prospects from the events of Melbourne Cup Day, 1984. To move beyond this snapshot to the Odyssean struggle, and complete the truncated representation of Stephen Dedalus and his Homeric model, Telemachus, that is my burden; in both its popular senses as an oppressive duty and un-sung meaning. This *Tessera* must negotiate both these characters to reach closure. It must also navigate James Joyce (see Table 1).

Telemachus is not a prominent figure in Classical literature. He excited no interest in the ancient corpus after assisting his father, who is known as the "Last of the Heroes,"

Table 1. Major literary correspondences

Odyssey	*Ulysses*	James Joyce – young	James Joyce – old	*Hamlet*	*Telemachus*
Telemachus	Stephen Dedalus (*Rudi Bloom*)	James Joyce	Samuel Beckett	Hamlet Jnr	Tom Hallem
Athena	Leopold Bloom (*feminized*)	Nora Barnacle	Harriet Weaver	NIL – problem	Elizabeth Archer
Penelope	Molly Bloom	Mary Joyce	Nora Joyce	Gertrude	Penelope Hallem
Suitors	Hugh Boylan	Various	Michael Bodkin	Claudius	Les Hallem
Odysseus	Leopold Bloom	John Joyce	James Joyce	Hamlet Snr	Don Cane, Leer
Nestor	Deasy	George Moore	WB Yeats	Polonius	Westacott
Menelaus	Kevin Egan	Ezra Pound	Eugene Jolas	NIL – a second mentor missed	Hensley
Nausicaa	Millie Bloom, Gerty	Lucia Joyce	Lucia Joyce	Ophelia	Ana Lafei Papese
Peisistratus	N/A	Harriet Weaver	Ezra Pound	Horatio	Francine Hackett
Pan	Mulligan	Stanislaus Joyce	George Joyce	R'crantz & G.	Billy Capri

to reclaim his realm. His name means 'fighter afar' in Greek, which is something of a misnomer given that his only combat took place in his homeland; although Robert Graves argues that it should be interpreted in symbolical terms as "decisive battle." His life in the aftermath of Odysseus' reinstatement on Ithaca attracted only cursory interest. An unnamed source in the *Dictys Cretensis* stated that *Ulysses* was warned by an oracle that Telemachus would murder him and therefore banished his son to Cephallenia (vi.14). No details are provided about his life in exile. *Telegonia*, a sixth century BC epic cycle by Eugammon, recorded his marriage to Circe. She seems an unlikely partner for Telemachus even in the implausible world of the Gods. Some ancient scholars argued that he actually married Circe's daughter, Cassiphone, who bore him a son, Latinus, the kind king who offered Aeneas a new home in Latium. Elsewhere, he is said to have accidentally killed Circe and fled to Italy, where he founded Clusium in Etruria. By contrast, there are many accounts of Odysseus after the term of the *Odyssey*. We know from the *Odyssey* that his journey did not finish after the slaughter at the palace. He was required to restart his quest to propitiate Poseidon by finding a land where people had never seen the sea. Pseudo-Apollodorus wrote that Odysseus journeyed to Thesprotia, a country of Epirus, a kind of Menindee, watered by the rivers Acheron and Cocytus, although he could have gone on forever like Leichhardt or Burke and Wills, which Homer called the 'streams of hell,' where he married Callidice and reigned peacefully over the locals. Pseudo-Apollodorus recounts how Odysseus was indicted by the families of the slain suitors, tried by Neoptolemus, who is sometimes called Pyrrhus for his golden locks, and condemned to exile at Thoas in Aetolia where he re-married and lived to an old age. Elsewhere, he is said to have found Penelope unfaithful and sent her away or even killed her. Pausanias quotes the poem, "Thesprotis," as his source for the claim that Penelope was driven into exile. One ancient commentator says that Odysseus returned to Ithaca to find that Penelope had borne a son, Poliporthes, in his absence. Both Pindar and Herodotus report that she gave birth to Pan by the god Hermes during Odysseus' absence. Hermes is also the father of Autolycus, the grandfather of Odysseus. He bestowed the talent for cunning on Odysseus in his role as the God of lying and thieves. It means his wife's son is his own great-uncle. This breaking-down of blood genealogy is a key to *Telemachus*. In another variation, Servius wrote in the fourth century BC that Pan was born of ALL the suitors, as testified by his name which means "all" in Greek. The sight of Pan amongst the household gods was alleged to have disturbed Odysseus so much that he fled Ithaca. One of the most intriguing references to Telemachus concerns his role in the death of his father. Pseudo-Apollodorus relates the story of Odysseus' son with Circe, Telegonus, travelling to Ithaca to introduce himself to his father. Shipwrecked on the coast, he plundered a local village. Odysseus and Telemachus were called out to defend their subjects. In the ensuing struggle, Telegonus killed his father without realising his identity (as per the Oedipus trope). This was the subject of a tragedy by Sophocles of which only fragments remain. According to Hyginus, Telegonus returned the corpse to Aeaea for burial. Telemachus and Penelope accompanied him. Athene decreed that Telegonus should marry Penelope. They had a son, Italus, who gave his name to Italy; meaning that both the language and country of the Romans are named for the grandsons of Odysseus. This is ironic given the Roman distaste for the wily Greek. Hyginus' goes on to depict the union of Telemachus with Circe meaning that both half-brothers wed their step-mothers. Telemachus is rarely cited in Western literature. Saint Telemachus helped end the gladiatorial games in Rome by his example of non-violent protest. This makes him a worthy precursor to the mild pacifist Leopold Bloom. The Archbishop of Cambrai wrote *The Adventures of Telemachus, Son of Ulysses* in the eighteenth century as an instructional manual for young gentlemen. Alfred Lord Tennyson depicted him in the poem, "Ulysses." Assuming the voice of Odysseus, Tennyson portrayed Telemachus as a super-bureaucrat who would "make mild the rugged people" with "slow prudence" and "soft degrees" (ll.36-7). This representation justified Odysseus' decision in the poem to renew his expeditions. It is also an allegory of British Colonialism as it evolved into its administrative phase. *The Odyssey, A Modern Sequel* by Nikos Kazantzakas, author of *Zorba the Greek*, describes Telemachus in similar terms as a mild-mannered conciliator who is disgusted by his father. Odysseus arranges his son's nuptials with Nausicaa in Book II before departing on new adventures. Michael Kohlmeier released a novel, *Telemach*, in German in 1995. Wikipedia calls it a "casually told antique myth." There is no English translation. A Google search for the author registers hits for John Kohlmeier, a professor of accounting and information systems, and Ryan Kohlmeier, a minor league baseball pitcher in the USA. The top search results for "Telemachus" yield statistics for the journeyman South African cricketer, Roger Telemachus. This is apt because Telemachus incarnates the first change trundler, the dispensable co-star, living in perpetual reaction to events as a conduit or accomplice to the main narrative, making cameo appearances yet never able to gain entry, force events or enact closure. He must remain forever hanging, but not like Prometheus, no, rather fixed in place like the serving girls he once slaughtered so crudely, without prospect of termination like Shelley's Sensitive Plant, positioned beyond the margins & thus ALWAYS OUTSIDE THE PRINTABLE AREA. The eclipse of Telemachus will be only too familiar to contemporary viewers. Celebrity offspring are invariably trawled out of obscurity for a moment of warped magnification in Warhol's fame machine. It constitutes a rite of mis-passage in which they are finally purged from collective awareness. The son is consubstantial with the father, Joyce wrote. In the context of the *Odyssey*, it can be claimed that the son must repeat the journey of the **father**. He must break the paternal impasse or turn from life forever. *Eperon* or *Clinamen*. Stephen Dedalus tries to sidestep this choice in *Ulysses* by arguing that Shakespeare is both young and old Hamlet. This enables him to shed both his physical and creative fathers and become his own progenitor. Telemachus never gets this opportunity. He is shunted in-and-out of his father's story by Homer. He dominates the beginning of the *Odyssey* as a residual symbol of Odysseus' collapsed influence on Ithaca. His subsequent mini-Odyssey to Sparta mimics the paternal voyage in miniature. It is suspended at the end of Book IV as the action shifts decisively to his father. When Telemachus is finally reintroduced in Book XV, it is as his father's accomplice. Likewise, Stephen Dedalus only appears selectively in *Ulysses*. He is the central figure in the short opening chapter, which corresponds to the "Telemachiad," before ceding this place to Leopold Bloom. After that, he is only reprised in the novel when Bloom comes into contact with him. He never initiates union. Even his famous discourse on Shakespeare's genealogy in "Scylla and Charybdis" is presented like a chance occurrence generated by Bloom's random entrance into the National Library to avoid Blazes Boylan. In the next episode, "Wandering Rocks," he is an incidental character. He is excluded from "Sirens," "Cyclops" and "Nausicaa" before being reunited with Bloom in "Oxen of the Sun" for the final drive to closure. This subordinate position is not challenged until Stephen exits *Ulysses* in "Eumaeus" by making a decisive act of separation when he refuses shelter at Eccles Street. John Byrne lived on Eccles Street. It was where Joyce received reassurance about Cosgrove's claims about sexual congress with Nora in 1909. He stayed the night at Byrne's house and woke up purged of angst. He never forgot his debt to this address. During their bookend appearances, the reader is told something of Telemachus and Stephen Dedalus before the concentrated period of the masterpiece. Telemachus is twenty years old at the beginning of the *Odyssey*. His father embarked for Troy when he was two. His mother has been beset by one hundred and eight suitors ("*Proci*") from neighbouring cities and islands for the past three years in a parallel to the siege of Troy (interestingly, an uncanny emblem breaks both blockades: the wooden horse containing Odysseus at Troy and Odysseus disguised as a beggar at Ithaca). The suitors are consuming Telemachus' inheritance. His grandfather, Laertes, has retired to the other side of the island. Thus, Telemachus has no male role model. I grew up in similar circumstances. He is confused and restless. He oscillates between compliance and wildness. He is an uneven risk-taker. His quest to Pylos and Sparta is critical in providing meaning for him. At the very moment when Odysseus has been driven into extrinsic space – outside Time – Telemachus leaves the parameters of his known universe to enter the Iliadic arena. It is a calculated risk to force resolution. It represents Telemachus sharing a comparable experience to his father for the first time; creating a narrative parallel in which both father and son are working actively (if unknowingly) towards reunion. This centripetal force sucks them both back to Ithaca. Yet Telemachus is more than just the minor strand in a metonymy. His relationship with his father is synecdochal. He overcomes significant hurdles in his own right/rite. Where Odysseus was trained by his father, Laertes, in the Hellenic concept of manhood, Telemachus has been forced to skill himself. Where Odysseus was an experienced man at the time of his departure from Ithaca, Telemachus is really just a lad. Where Odysseus has fixed destinations to drive him, first to Troy then back to Ithaca, Telemachus is leaving home for the first time with no tangible goal. He is alone. It is bravery against the void. This may be the first Romantic quest. It has important implications for events back on Ithaca. It breaks the continuity of submission to the suitors and takes pressure off Penelope at a critical juncture. The suitors become distracted plotting his demise. Further, it enables Telemachus to assume responsibility for his own future and establish his own identity; a feat which is validated when he receives direct assistance from Pallas Athene, his father's muse. His voyage also serves ancillary narrative purposes. He shares in a full family experience with Nestor, sharpening his sense of lack and difference. He gains invaluable first-hand information about his father, where previously he had only heard vague whorls. Any lingering doubt about his own paternity is dispelled when Menelaus and Helen immediately cite similarities in his appearance and bearing to Odysseus. Finally, Telemachus learns about the recent revenge of Orestes for the murder of his father, Agamemnon. This acts as both a barb and a spur bolstering him to play an active role in Odysseus' vengeance against the suitors. Likewise, James Joyce separated the narrative depiction of his young hero into distinct and separate compartments across two texts. *Ulysses* updates the fortunes of Stephen Dedalus after *A Portrait of the Artist as a Young Man*. His growth in the earlier novel was traced from an infant experiencing each of its senses for the first time through successive engagements with philosophy, sex, religion and art. It was an episodic quest for aesthetic empowerment. Methodical progression through different belief systems projected Stephen towards self-reliance in the manner of Telemachus, although to quite different ends. Stephen abandoned Dublin and his family for Paris at the end of the novel in the same type of bold gesture as Telemachus departing Ithaca. Absorption in the physical world was gradually replaced by Existentialism; a movement reflected in formal terms by the shift to diary transcriptions by Joyce. This enclosure inside the character's consciousness provided the template for the famed internal monologue of *Ulysses*. Each chapter in *A Portrait of the Artist as a Young Man* follows a pattern of ennui, despair, urgent quest, discovery and ecstatic climax which is succeeded by 'Fall' at the beginning of the next chapter. The same method is repeated at the start of *Ulysses*, establishing correspondences with *A Portrait of the Artist as a Young Man* as well as enabling Joyce to alter the meaning of the earlier novel in retrospect. In particular, he revises the optimistic conclusion of *A Portrait of the Artist as a Young Man*. Stephen Dedalus is confronting total dispossession at the start of *Ulysses*. It opens with him back in Dublin having failed to achieve artistic or personal consummation in Paris. He is a failed prodigal returning to a divided family in reduced circumstances. His only dubious progress has been to advance from university student to part-time teacher at a private academy. The death of his mother dominates the first chapter. He has left the family home after a dispute with his father and sought refuge in an abandoned coastal fortress at the southern tip of Dublin. This is a physical manifestation of his desire for sanctuary as well as a symbol of Ireland's subjugation to the British Empire. He is effectively besieged inside the Martello Tower at Sandy Bay. He is mocked by his ostensible friend, the faux-Hellenist Buck Mulligan, and vexed by the Gaelist, Haines, who represents the worst type of Colonial patronizing. He is even being evicted from this place by stealth as symbolised by Mulligan's request for his key. He faces the start of the day with no destination.

Tom Hallem was surrounded by decline like Stephen Dedalus. Raised in a rent family like Telemachus. Then fixed in amber like a bug at a point of climax. There's lots of apocryphal history about that period. It swirls around the facts in bitter gusts. There is reluctance to speak about it even to this day. Many people would like to silence me, just as Odysseus held fast the mouth of Anticlus inside the Wooden Horse. But I cannot accept severance or avoidance. Not for me the Lethean ointment. My purpose hitherto has been to transcend the blockages to transmit beautiful idealisms in the name of Art. My strategy now is to let those blockages speak. *Gittò voce di fuori e disse*, as Dante said. INSERT TRANSLATION (SEE K. INK): "Say something. Express thyself/yourself" (repeat) then scream (~7 seconds). The writer opened WORDPRESS to update his blog. I love the thought of the void that sits just beyond this screen, he typed. Major Tom must have felt the same emotion sometimes, at least at the start. He took up a pencil. Show space with webcam, he wrote. Make sure lantern in C1 is always mounted above your head online. Exhibit art works (*Untitled 1–10*) on the backdrop. Include notebook fragments in a dropdown menu. Also, deleted scenes (e.g. Eggsmother). This creates a loop with the website, which was developed some time after TMAC was finished, of course. It proposes the digital format as a new type of literary form like Beckett considering his English translations as new products. I believe that everything I do is ORIGINAL like Henri Rousseau or some Naïve painter. INSERT BRAND SLOGAN: "The text is fixed but everything on this website is provisional."

You don't have to read TMAC like a normal book. Just click FIND on the FREE PDF. Search MCCOMB. It appears eight times in the navigation column, usually in conjunction with the phrase, "Tom Hallem." Discuss. I have stopped wanting to put more things INTO the text and started to want to load them ONTO the website. Install VR headset. Treat yourself as if you were a legend like JJ, GS or Proust. Make the webhost like the writer but NOT ME. Like another character. Add more protagonists like Proust. Click Close. Because it would be better at this moment if we turned backwards in time; backwards in time, which is ironic, because it is only by going forward again, beyond this point at which we are now stationed, that we will reach the close. Joyce too cast back. TIME. It was invented by Swiss watch-makers. Proust is most famous for his dissection of. It meant the same thing as HONOUR in Ancient Greek. A man gained time through the merit of his actions during life. And honour thus bestowed was not forgotten in death. It literally held oblivion at bay. It is impossible to put Tom Hallem's life in perspective in this manner. He is gone, but not peacefully. There was no neat conclusion as per Tragedy. Even his autopsy was inconclusive. This lack of definitive closure somehow illegitimates my anger. It can never be properly discharged. This makes it much like Love. He even invades my weak visionary realm at night, exacerbating the lack of each waking hour, until I start with a gasp in the cold tranquillity of dawn. I am tired and I want this all to stop. "Whatever happened to your cousin," someone asked recently as if they were speaking about the co-star of some Seventies TV series. "He's dead," I replied; surprised at my phlegmatic tone. I couldn't think of anything else to say after that because I was so busy chasing him. I wandered into the garden. High up in space, a 747 was arching across the sky. You could just make out its metal wing-tips pulsing from the last sunrays as it corrected its flight path towards Asia. It left a trail of white vapour in its wake; shredding the bruised vault. The cool evening came thick and fast. Dew kissed the wended grass. Its deep heart bounced. Insects drowned in insistent dreams. The nightingale's chant was choked by a lizard's brace. Only a single mosquito still ebbed and flowed like ocean tide in my ears. In the P(a)lace of Symbol, all we are left with at the end are borrowed voices and provisional modes. Spring married the sky once. And the sky was penetrated by the moon. Don Cane parked his hired car outside his ex-wife's gate. Odysseus had finally reached shore. He dozed. A feeble child cradled night's apparently endless hold. His son rose uphill. He passed the orphanage. He turned off the footpath and went inside his step-father's house. A screen opened as it closed. I wish I was mist. Then I could slip back to earth like some cast-off feather. And be laid over Space. To slowly extinguish the dwindling lamp. And be slowly extinguished myself by dawn.

2.
Telemachus & Athene

FIRST VOICE

Walespurgis night. Bloomsday eve. Tis now the hour when graveyards scream and fog breathes calumny over the unhumaned highways. Pass along the rat-smoothed ramparts. Act 1, Scene 1. A sparse recording studio in London. Low lighting. The profile of a small round man hunched on a smaller rounder stooltop. A greasy mop of black tangled hair tick-tocks with the rhythm of his mandible language as his flushed pugnose flues cigarette smoke against the articulated mesh of a steel microphone. One finger wags once at the grey-suited technicians in the effects booth. The sound engineer places a phonographic needle onto the spinning disc. A distant Town Hall clock strikes once. Flushing carstream. Brakes. Tyreskid. An idling engine lulls. Pallas Athena binds her sandals and drops. Two shapes pushing an overladen trolley pixelate across the audio-stage.

ANNOUNCER

Tonight, we present *Ulysses* as a radio play.

BURTON

Onec upna tiem, anna vary gud tiem twas, to start at the starting: it is a sprung, moonless night along the blistered commercial thoroughfare of New Town, satellite suburb of the great Olympic metropolis, Sydney, celestialless snagblack on sable asphalt, gleamering from rainsmirch, omni-cement, and the blind factory squats dun, dung, dumb, dingle-dingle as its blank panes shudder from jacent truckpass then still. The glaucomal nightshades of the flat-faced terraces are all drawn. Nerve sashes pluck at the edges of my strained eyeballs. A faux Jesuit enters his home through a cracked kitchen casement and crawls across the uncleared bench. His mendicant suitor approaches the barred hour. Oedipal darkness masses a haze of hot termites around a neon sign branding the moniker Salona's Talking Tables on the ever-warm urban airspace. Hush now! The public servants, flight attendants, yappy Jack Russell's and widower landlords, gaunt seamstresses wreathed in moth-eaten finery from England, their oversized cats, the latex barmen from the Imperial Hotel, are all sleeping all dreaming. It is five hours until incoming planes will overfly the ruddy, tiled roofs jolting them sentient. Bust the surface and let their slumbering lives stream. The Vietnamese shopkeeper, vacant-faced by daylight behind her refrigerated counter, chortles in the belly of atavistic dreams in her fast, globular language ... ebullient. She spends all day serving sticky sweets to school children and all night poisoning Americans in her ruined hamlet. Her newborn baby whimpers in its cane cot transporting her back to that sinking burning stinking churning seasick rust-bucket bobbing on the Timor Sea. She escapes into the schoolyard naked as fleshly formed dough and ascends over the Camphor-ribbed canopy lowly. A sodden slab of warm beer slumps like some Pisan relique on the edge of an abandoned barbeque area. One perspiring stubby is slowly shat. It cracks dully on the pavement. Effervescent ale is released into bat-weighed atmos. A solitary figure, leaning on whorled elbows on a concrete bench, his riveted face ludden in calloused palms, lurches left. Two coins flop out of his pocket. Lizzie's profile in dirt. The Spinner takes the Kip. Time called. At last, the Boxer speaks.

MEILLON

A cluster of youths loiter against the bonnet of a Torana Sunbird.

BURTON

Flamed orange body, black hood and chrome wings of the Beast.

MEILLON

A shot is fired. [*Insert FX*]

BURTON

The shattered telephone booth spreads its glass guts.

MEILLON

Diamond-scud.

BURTON

Gaze upon this glittering tableau. Open your eyes and SEE. Only YOU can detect sudden unsequent spray diving full forty feet off the roof of Beta House to stain their polyester garments, making bronze flesh quiver in nocturnal draught. Only YOUR mind's skin with their skin weeps. And only YOU can hear the blithe birdlike cries of the Gods' spilling from the void like the crumble of fizzy cola.

VOICES FROM ABOVE

Faugh a ballagh!

MEILLON

They raise their heads full-vertical.

SOPHOS

What can you see?

DICK

Nothing.

ANDY

[*Smelling his shirt*] They pissed on me. Give me your snotrag. [*Sophos passes a piece of fine Irish linen to his friend*]

DICK

Incoming!

[*FX: A crushed can deflects off the pavement*]

BURTON

More liquid tallows the mane of Achaemenides Papadopoulos, apprentice car detailer, of Homer Street Earlwood.

SOPHOS

[*Emerging*] It's only beer this time. Let's go.

MEILLON

He extracts a wad of keys from his thigh.

BURTON

No! grunts Dikaiosynē Polites.

DICK

[*With quiet hot panting, he extols*] Philotimo!

SOPHOS

But we know not the enemy's scale.

ANDY

It's not how many that counts!

SOPHOS

The door is bolted.

ANDY

Kick it in!

VOICES FROM ABOVE

Come up, come up, oh proud Achaeans! [*Falsetto*] Molon labe!

GREEKS

[*Charging the battlement*] Alale Alala! Alala Alea!

MEILLON

The fresh sole of a brown zippered boot is applied to the ageless ingress beyond which lies a comb of abandoned offices once abuzz with Bakelite telephones, manual typewriters, carbon paper, blotting pads and barrels of luminous ink. Crawford's ghost cuts a swathe between the presses. Mister Bloom proceeds to the verge of his office.

DICK

I can't make it budge.

ANDY

Let me try. [*FX: He throws his shoulder against the door repeatedly*] It's no good.

DICK

[*To Sophos*] Get the Jemmy.

BURTON

Theodoris Dragonis, fishmonger's son, of Ninth Avenue Campsie retreats to his car, flips open the boot and disappears inside its deep maw, emerging with a crowbar and a frayed beach towel hardened and discoloured by grease.

MEILLON

Sword and shield of Achilles!

BURTON

Dikaiosynē accepts the swab. Andreia the blade. The factory door receives its deep impress. Shiny screw-threads appear like diaphanous locks.

ANDY

I can't wait! Stand back!

[*FX: He takes a pistol from his pocket and fires it into the lock. It blasts open*]

MEILLON

Cut to the fractured roof.

BURTON

Like the firmament pass within.

MEILLON

Move unseen like spectral air.

BURTON

A SHOUT IN THE STREET!

RHINO

[*Peeping over rampart*] Shit. They've got a gun.

FISH PUMP

[*Perched on the ledge giggling. Legs dangling*] It doesn't matter. The staircase is barricaded. They can't get up here.

RHINO

But they can reach the Mezzanine.

TOE CUTTER

So?

RHINO

Tom Hallem's down there.

FISH PUMP

[*Snidely*] His dealer can take care of him.

[*FX: Toe Cutter zips his pants. The men laugh. Rhino rushes towards the staircase.*]

BURTON

Within the obscure interior, the too-long unlithe body of Tom Hallem crumples awkwardly under sweat-shiny bed sheets to ease the chronic back ailment which has delivered him up to the surface of sleep. He becomes conscious of place and conscious of dreaming of:

TOM HALLEM

Father!

MEILLON

Idealised image of the sire.

BURTON

Hyperion's curls tallith Jove's forehead.

MEILLON

A never-seen father's face reconstructed in a cracked shaving mirror.

BURTON

Dream of a dream then.

MEILLON

Reflection's mean.

BURTON

Hamlet the son witnessing the ghost of Hamlet the father as a young man as himself. Bloom seeing SD on the way to Dignam's funeral. Old Joyce observing young Joyce. Caliban's rage at his own image. I my own father.

MEILLON

Bring down the Joycean motherlode!!!

BURTON

Hamlet re-fathered. Stephen Dedalus de-fathered. Freudly slant. Amor matris. Artist, creator of Wordworld ...

MEILLON

[*Assuming Mulligan' dressing gown*] *Liliata rutilantium / Turma circumdet / Iubilantium te virginum.*

BURTON

Gloria Patri.

MEILLON

Major Donald John Cane balances his camouflaged trunk in the open hatch of a Bushranger helicopter as it strains to rise from the paddy field into consumptive tropical night. Its flashing underbelly withdraws from earth unsteadily.

BURTON

Hovering.

MEILLON

Ma Rung, Phuc Tuy, 1966.

BURTON

Daniel Boone extraction. Compass in a tailspin. Magnetic deposits. Rotor blade swirl. Ill-symmetry. He beckons his son.

MEILLON

Ftt-ftt-ftt-ftt-ftt-ftt-ftt ...

BURTON

Bluddy address bubbles forth from his speakeasy lips.

MEILLON

[*Ejaculatory*] "Poison down me earhole, lad!" he says.

BURTON

All the while old Uncle Cuck and Mother Grogan were going at it like a couple of goats.

MEILLON

The son must revenge the murder of his father.

BURTON

Orestes the avenger. Stephen the dissembler. Hamlet the sieve.

MEILLON

Nobbled Telemachus.

BURTON

Give over that pagan crap. Enough of Arius and Sabellius also. *Introibo ad altare Dei*. God the father, Christ the son. Respectable receptacle bog-ignorant Mary Immaculate. Dove-fucked as Leda was swanned.

MEILLON

Impalpable sheen of her piety.

BURTON

Stephen Dedalus' mother. Her peach-platinum Faith. Now phlegm-hued.

MEILLON

Andreia finally breaks breaks the seal of Athena's temple. The sack of Troy begins.

[*FX: Door frame splinters*]

BURTON

[*Ejaculating*] Ftt–ftt–fit–fitt–fatt–fa–FATHER!

MEILLON

Tom Hallem stirs. His eyelids part. The whitewashed ceiling announces his unwanted entrance into the awakened realm. He shakes off the uncanonised bones of his father. A digital clock brands the darkness with four red numerals: One–two–five–five. Heavy footsteps shake the temporary walls of his makeshift quarters.

BURTON

Dim figures enter the vault. Martello violated. Ajax inside. Pyrrhus has gone hunting. Invasive humours. Closed damp beating wombal black. Only YOUR eyelight can reveal the dried-out paps of the printing presses, the scarred benches and dormant clocks once punched to pulp by fitters in gun metal jackets and clickers in black croupier caps. Only YOU can see the intruders map this scripted space. Piles of electrical cabling brood in Medusa-traps. A grasping hand reaches out for some crutch to sustain its body vertical. The town hall clock strikes. A single long bell. The first hour of the Sixth of November, Nineteen Eighty-Four has passed.

DICK

Stay close.

SOPHOS

Where's the staircase?

ANDY

I can't see.

DICK

Got a lighter?

SOPHOS

I got matches. [*He strikes*]

BURTON

Spark. Illumination. Fire's small dividend glows against discoloured walls. Its vesta in the uplifted hand softens as if palms had slowly covered tiring eyes. Fading to char. Mould dyed air closes around them. Darkness darker for light's brief intervention.

ANDY

Strike another match.

DICK

[*Groinking*] I can't breathe.

SOPHOS

I'm down to the last one.

DICK

Burn the box.

[*FX: Sophos lights the matchbox. A small fire takes grip. Dick rolls newspaper into a torch and holds it above the pyre. It ignites freely. Shift FX. A shopping trolley proceeds along a damp cave. The man stops*]

BLOT

Light the lamp!

MOTHER BLOT

Not yet, Father.

BLOT

But that's my cue.

MOTHER BLOT

It's a literary allusion.

BLOT

You mean 'magic'?

MOTHER BLOT

Yes. But weak. Help me back into my mound. And put on your boater.

BLOT

But my name isn't Willie.

MOTHER BLOT

[*Optimistically*] Let me dream!

DICK

Here's some old books. We can torch them.

BLOT

[*Excitedly*] Burn the sordid ones first! They're more ... 'incendiary.'

SOPHOS

[*Collecting a wastepaper basket*] Stick them in here.

MEILLON

Sparks hiss. Flames fly. Blot dances a little jig. His fingertips glide through the bronze air.

ANDY

We should burn the whole place down.

MEILLON

The censer flares on the concrete floor. They feed it savagely. Cult classics cleft for fuel. Greer gutted. Castenada consumed for coarse kindling and coked. Irigaray also. Smiling Mildling rent. Morehouse doused. Heaving ink. Weightless prose. The metal crucible disgorges pliant smoke. Burnt dust crackles. Ink bubbles release thick fumes. The belly of the dark tower is subtly enlightened. Roland gazes within. No howlet. No bat.

SOPHOS

[*Excited*] A path!

BURTON

He ascends the staircase.

SOPHOS

[*Pushing against nailed-down boards*] It's blocked.

MEILLON

They lapse on the steps ... Priam's inner sanctum ... as yet unbreached.

BURTON

Paris leaves his lover, slips on a grey nightshirt, picks up a cracked wooden broom handle and walks across the vacated space to his kitchen. Human movement ebbs and rushes beneath. He places an aluminium cooking pot on his head and makes his way to the ledge. Sterile promontory. No movement is apparent in the concrete bays below. Yet foreign voices are close.

ANDY

There must be another way.

SOPHOS

Go find it yourself. I've had enough. I want to go home.

BURTON

They descend to the stage.

MEILLON

Wild eyes roam.

SOPHOS

Look!

DICK

At what?

SOPHOS

[*Pointing upwards*] There!

BURTON

Aloft an apparition beetles upon manifest space.

MEILLON

His headpiece glistens dully in streetlight.

SOPHOS

[*Whispering*] What is it?

ANDY

[*Yelling*] Hey you!

MEILLON

No answer.

BURTON

Gone!

[*FX: Tom Hallem withdraws. Sirens heard in the distance.*]

SOPHOS

[*Pulling at Andy*] Let's split.

ANDY

Wait up. I'm tangled in wire.

[*FX: They seek to unravel Achaemenides desperately.*]

MEILLON

Copcrow barks: noman noman noman no ... noman noman noman no ...

BURTON

[*FX: Exit*] The crew abandon their comrade to his fate. Recessant footfalls resound through the now-still void. Squelch of polyphemus bags under hoof. Exeunt.

MEILLON

The pavement snaps. Cardoors crack. An engine stutters. Two men huddle inside deep lamb's wool seat covers. The Sunbird's belly rumbles. Wheels skid. It is launched down the dunny cart lanes around the railyards and working-class terraces of Macdonaldtown suddenly.

BURTON

Hearken! A hole!

MEILLON

They break-out west like Aeneas. A paddy-wagon idles at the kerb on Georgina Street.

BURTON

In the so-still, toneless aftermath, only Poseidon's rage remains.

MEILLON

Lester Byron rises pulling a loose bed sheet over his naked shoulders and ambles over the wide hayloft. His bladder is full. He flicks a light switch. The bulb is broken. He is a stranger to this place. He rubs his eyes and strays across the floor. Sudden drafts shoot him beneath. He drops. A police siren is strangled emitting a low mechanical quiver. Revolving blue and red spotlights shimmy up cracked panes and wash liver brick walls. Powerful torches illumine its cavity. Byron lies prone at the base of the abandoned elevator shaft. Tom Hallem withdraws to his keep. A bedside lamp is ignited. Two figures shuffle together on a mattress then turn away from each other. Flat words. Indecipherable. Light quenched. They doze. Time passes. Thunder afar rolls into the rumble of jet planes. Cockcrow.

NARRATOR

The naked molescaped torso of Elizabeth Archer probed blindly into the sunlit doorway, her head bent and swaddled within a saturated towel as she scrubbed oily residue from her hair. Framed for a moment in this space, her body appeared as a series of marble blocks sculpted and stacked into being. Her hot skin glittered with sweat and soft down. Dark tendrils shuddered perceptibly, releasing tiny sprays of water around her feet. A purl contemplated gravity's drive from the underside of her breast. It swelled – massing weight – like a diver contemplating the drop into Sandymount baths. At last, it was released down her kyte, where it sheltered on a reef of scarred skin across the centre of her abdomen, swelling until the Caesar rim was breached, and it shook off attachment to her body altogether, crashing to the floor. Elizabeth bristled at its course. The flesh on her thick biceps contracted into tiny braille. She set her heavy thighs apart and stamped on the bare boards. The dim mezzanine shook. Blasted motes produced brittle sparks. Eyeblight. Gloam. Elizabeth covered her gleaming eyes with Tom's cloth. The fabric was musty and close. She sucked humid air into her mouth. Close steaming vapours like Vathy, 1968. Ex-colonial residence at the port. Papered-over remnants of Empire peeled back by relentless heat. What Byron died for. Drinking Thessaloniki beer in a bar under a crumbling apartment block. Shack facades punctured by decay. Glimpse inna. A makeshift brown room. Gaea passed the open door in black mourning to serve some British officers. A single yellow light was tacked against the high ceiling. Ticktock. A fan sliced the atmos *omni-omni-om*. Leon withdrew his cock too late. The last web of semen spattered her gut. Her body rocked like a dark scarred sea. Green bile.

Stephen's Apostacy. Leon's steps receded down the hall. Rise up like a spout in bed to smoke. Petals were rusting on the mantelpiece. Mesh-window wire twisted from failed escapes. Beyond, a sombre compound was rimmed with weak lanterns. Broken wooden pegs broke underfoot on rendered stones. Jump cut. The English fall landscape slowly emerging out of dawn's drain. Nets on pallid sun. Standing over two lopsided gas jets preparing Dayglo slop in a sunken Earl's Court bedsit sick of morning sickness. Pregnant belly sticking through ill-shapen goatskin vest. Worse than a circus freak in Swinging London. We named the baby, Chaim. It means 'life' in Hebrew. John and Mary Joyce had 10 children, four of whom died. Paps leaking useless colostrum. Raw trench along twisted back exacerbated by grey profile against starched hospital linen. Soft against stiff. Ericthon had nine children. I, none. Metagenesis. Elizabeth's arms began to toil in merciless rotation, stretching curls and loose filaments until her fingers were stained with orange dye. Her aura dimmed as a stray cloud sliced the late spring sunshine. Helios. Bloom saw it too. She smiled as usual – and as naturally as usual – as if it preceded any decision about whether she was happy. Her eyes became pellucid in this setting like the triumph of some subtle lapidary. Tom Hallem let his gaze ripple towards a tattoo of a small hawk above her hip. The morning mass of native birdsong came sudden and clear in all its fullness. He wound his oversized bulk within a mound of worn day cushions. His kneecaps poked through the front of a frayed dressing gown. Suddenly, his head lolled sending slick black hair sliding off his face. He exhaled loudly. Elizabeth charted the course of a scar between his eyebrows until it turned at a right angle across his brow. Track marks punctured his forearms daintily like the product of filigree tools. She tied the towel around her chest tightly and examined his averted face.

"Look at me," she demanded softly.

"That's what sent Tiresias blind," he replied yielding then allowing her body to blur again by projecting his sight onto distant roller-doors in the bays below. He peered deeper into the low chancel where abandoned presses were corralled behind a rusty cyclone wire wall beneath heavy beams in shadows shorn of light. Beyond, tiny workstations folded into a neat quire. He could just make out the varnished panels of the manager's office. Solemnly, Elizabeth lay a discoloured palm on his forehead. Her calloused fingerprints provoked recognition. She stroked his cheek, charting his tapered jaw, equine in length, hued like oak, then ran the pad of an index finger down his nose until it reached his lips, which she parted slightly to reveal worn teeth. Hallem's eyes met those of his benefactor. She spoke with steadfast spirit.

"What time was all that ruckus?" she asked.

"One o'clock," he responded. "I heard the town hall chime. It was lucky they didn't find the light switch."

"They would have been in for a shock," she said. "You looked quite fearless."

"Ever vigilant," he deprecated.

"My protector," she replied.

They let the irony of these remarks stay unregistered.

"You had a nightmare," she said.

"I never remember dreams."

"You dreamt about your father. I heard you call his name."

"I'm glad I forgot then."

Elizabeth ignored him. She abandoned the towel, positioned her dress on the floor, placed her body inside it and lifted it over her shoulders. Zip me up, she said. Tom obliged. Servile Mulligan as to Haines. She fastened gilt sandals over her feet.

"What are you thinking," she asked finally.

"Why?"

"I want to know."

"Nothing much," he said.

"Crap. I know that expression," she replied.

"You tell me what I'm thinking then," he answered.

"You were wondering why I came back last night. You might even suspect I've used you. And you're pissed off at being evicted."

"All good theories."

"Well I came back because I've missed you. You were there. And I couldn't help myself."

"That's sweet. But what about my workspace? That's the key issue."

"My hands are tied in that regard. I've got to sell the factory. If things keep going downhill, I'll have to shut the gallery as well. And that would affect you far more than losing cheap studio space."

"I could always find another dealer."

"Don't threaten me Tom," she laughed. "Nobody would touch you if I put the word out."

"Charming," he replied. "Would you like tea?"

"Yes, please."

"I don't have milk."

"Black then."

"Sugar?"

"No."

He pulled himself from the sofa, went to the sideboard and collected an electric jug from a vacated shelf. He shook it. There was barely enough water. But there was. Just enough. The kettle hummed to life. He collected two mugs and a handful of teabags from the top of a box of kitchen ornaments.

"They printed all the radical writers of the Sixties down there," said Elizabeth glancing over the ledge into the print works.

"Now I know why I've always felt so uncomfortable up here," he replied.

"I thought you liked that stuff," she asked quizzically.

"I like the rent."

Present tense. A fleabite. Dog with a bone. Link dead presses explicitly to Joyce. Ben Huebsch published DH Lawrence and James Joyce alongside unabashedly communist books like *Mother Earth* and *The Masses*, which advocated greater sexual freedom. Note the difficulties of getting *Ulysses* published. Great art and shit are almost impossible to get done. Miss Weaver sacked 4 printers in 2 years when *The Egoist* printed *PAYM*. She wouldn't let anyone change a single word. Most printers would not touch Joyce's work whether it was France, Britain or America. Harriet Weaver visited Virginia Woolf and begged her to publish *Ulysses* using her handpress. Woolf was relieved to decline on the basis that it would take two years to set. Leon Woolf's hands shook too violently by that stage to participate in print setting. She hated *Ulysses*. Woolf allowed visitors to read excerpts from the novel, which Weaver had left in good faith. The critic Desmond MacCarthy mocked the beginning of Chapter II whilst reciting it in her drawing room. Katherine Mansfield loathed the work as well. Fall 1921 (Birmingham, 215). Darantiere's printers assembled *Ulysses* one letter at a time. JJ's insertions forced them to reset the entire text continuously. They started to leave blank spaces to reduce their workload. In June 1921, they began to send galleys, which contained eight pages per sheet with wide margins for corrections. Joyce filled them with arrows and inserts. Every addition forced the printers to shunt sentences, lines and pages into the future. Joyce requested multiple copies of each galley and started to revise and extend them simultaneously. When Darantiere started to send the page proofs, Joyce continued to make substantial insertions of new content and amendments. He went through as many as four galleys and five page proofs for every page of *Ulysses*. In August 1921, JJ began revising ten episodes simultaneously. He inserted "Agenbit of inwit" at this late stage. He wrote at least 33% of *Ulysses* on galleys and proofs including half of Penelope. He was still writing all the way to ink publication. In this regard, Joyce predicated the malleability of text using contemporary technology. My plan is to keep coming back to TELEMACHUS until I die. Only then will it become fixed in place like a bug in a display case, sealed in digital form against the atmosphere to slow its decay. To RECHAOS, Joyce's DECHAOS. That is my ambition. Joyce used structuring devices to organise the chaos of thousands of insertions into *Ulysses*. His ordering tools included the famous Linati schema/schedule as well as adherence to superstition, urban myths, legends, WHAT ELSE and numerology. This fragment of text is currently domiciled in a file called TMAC INSERTS awaiting insertion into Draft Two. All new inserts arising from Birmingham begin life as pencil annotations then proceed to typed dot points catalogued individually before final cut/paste under a sub-heading, "Chapter Allocation," for insertion into specific chapters. "WHAT ELSE" = events like opening an umbrella inside, placing a man's hat on a bed, the number thirteen and passing nuns on the street (BAD); or black cats and Greeks (GOOD). Nausicaa was banned because it was the 13th episode, according to Joyce. The numerals of the year, 1921, added up to thirteen. Editorial updates to *Ulysses* cost Sylvia Beach 4,000 francs. Elizabeth Archer ran long fingers into Tom Hallem's hair and jerked his head upright.

"You and your funny ways," she said. "Just like the great god Pan."

His parentage was clouded. Some scholars say he was sired by Jupiter and Calisto. Others by Hermes and Penelope while Odysseus was away. Stephen Dedalus knows his father. He's there all the time in Dublin. He could easily find him if he wanted.

"I know who my father is. I just don't know if he's dead."

Hawk-like. Fabulous artificer. I in a labyrinth of his (un)making. By his death constituted. Icarus at least had. At last from his father took flight. He was a despot and a murderer, said Doctor Pentecost nodding. Talos was his own nephew. Abraham all set up on an altar. Famous filicides. Agave ripped the head off her son. Heracles was sent insane for mass murder. Medea. Oedipus pinned by the ankles on a hillside. Inadvertent deaths. Oedipus and Telegonus. Cuchulain killed Connla. Bad families. Atreus killed the children of his twin brother for seducing his wife. Served them up to him for dinner. Thyestes conceived Aegisthus with his own daughter. I'm relatively benign in comparison, thought Don Cane dozing in economy class.

"Does your mother ever talk about him?"

"No. Our people aren't into oral history."

"You could always ask his old friends."

"Rissole warriors? Give me a break."

Elizabeth Archer pressed Tom Hallem into the sofa and stood over him.

"Did you know that the god Pan was also associated with lust."

The kettle was boiling. This is a hackneyed symbol these days, although it was still salacious when first employed by writers like Ibsen and Joyce. It clicked off. Steam sweated on a Bakelite lid. Elizabeth leaned into the cushions with each knee. Her skirt rose. Naked beneath. Unkempt. She ran palms up his arms. Her mouth shot warm breath against his ear. He shivered.

"He was beast-like, you know, with the legs and ears of a GOAT."

She bit his lobe hard. He giggled. Involuntary.

"I want you back inside," she said.

"I'm pretty sore," he responded.

"I'll be quick. Are you hard enough?"

"Yes."

She lowered herself. Put a ducat in my clack-dish. Overload the key metaphor. She locked her elbows straight and commenced grinding. He presst his palms into her biceps feeling sinew and bone (Mulligan's arm: Cranly's arm). Perfunctory union. When he complained of some difficulty with orgasm, she gusted upright off his chest and thrust a hand between them. He came in a primal burst. She will leave now, he thought. Elizabeth coughed into his cheek. This spasm ejected him. Some sperm flowed. She tried to grasp it.

"Lend me your hankie," she said urgently.

He retrieved it from the pocket of his dressing gown.

She swabbed her vagina then hacked again.

"Look," she said holding out the rag tenderly.

Emerald from tripemine. Agenslag of Inspiss. Snotgreen. Sham/rock. Joyce's emblem for Ireland. Heir to Wilde's Yellow Book by Pater's Golden Book out of Huysmans. Gold Cup Day favourite. Symbol of jaundice, adultery, jealousy, degradation, death. Smell of the charnel-house. Begat beget begotten begone. Absent Odysseus. His unguided boy no template had. I too son w/out father. Australia also. New Hell(as) in bush. England's Edmund. He placed his hand into her hand and stroked cracked pads almost mournfully.

"The green and the gold," pronounced Tom Hallem.

Mucid wattle. Under Southern Cross we stand. Spissfields. He twisted.

"Think of it as a memento," she said rising.

A flag to wave on the Queen's Birthday. Our home. Girt by semen.

"Is this the end?" asked Tom Hallem.

"We'll see," replied Elizabeth.

"I guess I don't have much say in the matter."

"You need a shave before tonight," she said ignoring him. "And where's my tea?"

"I'll get it presently," he replied.

Hallem rose and collected the kettle. Most of the water had evaporated. He started the long walk downstairs to the wash room. Take down the milkjug Kinch, Mulligan loqt. Batonpass. Udderpress. Grasp. Prospero's serf. Each corner of every step raised tight dust-nests. JJ scribbled notes and phrases on scraps that he left around the apartment. The famed Stream of Consciousness was pieced together by stealth. Joyce continuously updated and expanded the novel, slotting new material into the existing manuscript. *Ulysses* was an act of granular composition like sandstone. INSERT INTO YELLOWBLOCK SECTION (C8). ALSO, BACK IN C1 (arduous process of revision). He wrote Nausicaa in small purple notebooks bound with string. Harvesting inserts from various note sheets. Joyce revised this episode to make it obscener after censorship was imposed. Celebrity drove him to greater risks. There were 894 insertions from note sheets into Nausicaa. Joyce was a compulsive list maker. He categorised fragments under headings and themes. Joyce crossed out entries into his notebooks as they were inserted into *Ulysses*. He used different coloured crayons for insertions. Everything was orchestrated. Stream of consciousness happened BEFORE THE TEXT. Its reconstruction in the text was a simulacrum. The soles of Tom Hallem's unshod feet ached from the brush of seagrass matting. Freshly hatched fleas hopped onto exposed skin. The walls of a small landing enclosed him. He scraped open a heavy fire door, slid through the aperture and followed the staircase to the back door. Dim closet. He took a key off a hidden cup hook and inserted it into a padlock. It submitted. He unbuttoned the bolt and entered. There was a long bench along one side of the wash room, opposite some open toilet cubicles. Rust-stained porcelain. England's thrones. He reached the last slot. It contained a single shower rose connected to an instant hot water system by a piece of hose. He was allowed irregular use under sufferance. Hallem filled the jug and shuffled back. Enter Old Milklady, distaff stuffed inside her girdle. Bunch of keys on her waist. Perhaps a goddess in disguise at the Martello Tower – Joyce's symbol of All Ireland under Imperial yoke. Both SD and TH have none by the end of the chapter. Pince-nez perched on her beak. Always toiling at a boiling copper. Bermondsey merchants sinking pitchforks innem. Press down (insert curdles). What about my lot, she moans hoarsely pricking some Pearlie Charles Prescott. Jiggle jangle. Never satisfied. Restless like worm in sun. Crying poorhouse. Full of bile. Green stuff. Wads. Pity the poor bloke crung under her rod, salving day-wages, a slave seated on a production line, sweaty brow. The son of Kevin Egan, named Patrice in Gallic homage to Ireland's patron saint, another overshadowed heir, was the only Irishman that Stephen encountered in kinship-penury in Paris drinking milk, not liquor, in what amounted to a symbolistic beverage choice. Artistic destitution became a standard plot device in the nineteenth century as the new mercantile middle-class produced by industrialisation spawned a genuine authorial caste that wilfully sampled the drop from bourgeois comfort to garret-life. The largely external depiction of poverty in Realism and Naturalism paved the way for Modernism's deeper curiosity about the ironic interplay between a debased setting, a depleted body and the human spirit, especially after WWI in the work of writers like Hamsun, Kafka, Hesse, Orwell and Miller. Joyce barely supported his family giving English lessons in Switzerland and Austria-Hungary (later Italy). By contrast, Goethe never worked a day in his life. Shelley neither. Sometimes he sponged off Byron. Flaubert had a stipend. Proust lived off his mum. Aristotle was a billionaire. Joyce had rich supporters. Robert McAlmon gave him $150 per month. Pound and Yeats secured institutional grants like £75 from the Royal Literary Fund, £52 from the Society of Authors and £100 from the Civil List. New York sponsors donated a thousand dollars. Edith McCormack gave him 1,000 Swiss francs per month for a year. Weaver gave him £200 (equivalent of his annual salary). Quinn wanted to print and sell Ulysses for $10 with Joyce receiving royalties of $2 per copy. This is known as the $3,000 plan. JJ rejected it, bargaining for $3.50 instead. In 1916, Miss Weaver sent Joyce £50. In Feb 19, she gave him a £5,000 war bond, yielding £250 interest annually. It is ironic that JJ gained sustenance from war loans. In Aug 20, she bestowed another £2,000. JJ now earned £350/year from these capital contributions. It would have been enough for a frugal man like Bloom. But Joyce remained like SD, squandering money on luxuries. He put all his good intentions into Leopold Bloom. He was the hero that Joyce needed for himself. In 1923, Weaver have him another capital gift of £12,000, bringing her total endowment to £20,500 (£1 million income in today's currency). Interest was £850 per year after taxes (more than £40,000 today). Joyce still squandered money like a guilty Saracen. He began to eke at the principal. The Depression only made him worse. A cool breeze from Botany Bay carried the scent of Kingsford-Smith Airport and Port Botany. Elizabeth's thick mane fell into unfaltering shoulders. Perfect collarbones harboured shade. He drew back her tresses but she took them from him briskly, twisting them into a single coil which she secured with a gold band and wound into a tight bun skewered by hairpins. They sat on stools at either end of the picnic table with tea.

"I wish it hadn't turned out like this," he said.

"It doesn't matter," she replied. "Look, I've got to go soon. Let's try to end with some style. I've brought you a nice gift. One of Leon's suits. It doesn't fit him anymore. Also, a pair of shoes."

"He's lost a lot of weight lately."

"He's obsessed with running. It's his latest fad. Come out to the car."

"Are you going to watch the Cup later?"

"No time. I've got the Christmas show to prepare. What about you?"

"I've got to get everything back home."

"I don't like you going back there."

"I haven't got a choice. I might catch up with Billy later. It'll be my last chance before he goes to England."

"It will be good when he's gone," replied Elizabeth. "You need to focus on work." Orestes. Carping. Let her speak her flame out. A burnt ember. Almost char. Joyce used rejection as a goad to expand the scope of his latest work. Grant Richard's letter about *Dubliners* stimulated the epic scheme for *Ulysses*. *Dubliners* was completed in 1905 but not published for 9 years. It was rejected by Grant Richards, John Long, Elkin Mathews, Alston Rivers, Edward Arnold, William Heinemann and Hutchison & Company. *PAYM* was rejected by 13 publishers in total including Richards, Secker, Jenkins, Duckworth, Cape and Werner Laurie. When pressed for comment or rationale, publishers always abandoned their platitudes and unloaded invective on Joyce's work.

"It's only been a few months," Tom Hallem whined lamely.

"Matt Supplejack has produced enough new work for two solo exhibitions in the same period."

"Well, Read's not producing."

"You're not Read. He's got a back catalogue going back twenty years."

She poked a polished fingernail against his chest.

"You're a blessing really," she said suddenly. "Now get dressed. I'm running late."

Tom Hallem recovered last night's clothes from the floor.

"Hurry up," she urged.

Power/Art. A crude dyad. Have Jester will brush. Medici-grip on your throat. Draw a happy portrait of the Duke's youngest inbred son. Olympus squashing a bug. Cilia on larvae. Stephen Dedalus said the cracked looking glass of a servant was a symbol of Irish art. Joyce's stream-of-consciousness style hops abruptly along prosenchymatic paths, remaking words into quips against prevailing themes. Australian Art. A fart in suds. Imperfect ana/grams. See Chapter Ten for explanation. Miles Arthur O'Hallam O'Hamlet Bung. Tod Hallam. His story is to blame. Punnets punts punt puns. The boys are playing hockey in the fields. Stephen Dedalus watches. It is a symbol of coming war. 1921. I-land treatied rather unfairly. Blame the Anglo-Nomans. Crete an Irish Fle(e/a) State. Flower's correspondence. An old ham/letter. Flounder founder flow foul (A fish, origin, the Liffey, Mulligan). Send foodmail. Bloom reading the knewspaper frying flresh kid knees. Polyphemus rampant in a school hall. Make a fresh hamolette. Les Hallem opened the fridge. He looked at the available contents and decided to make bacon and eggs again. Link to start of Chapter II of Ulysses. Add toast (two square white pieces). Make instant coffee. Boil water. No sugar. He picked out two rashers and ran a kinch around the edge of their guts. Tom Hallem his steal ate. This is a junky image. Willy loaded the canula. Artistic runes. Maze devices. The write stuff. Icarus merchandising clues. Da Vinci's robots. He stuck graffiti in Dymo on a mirror with his own LH. Send Sforza your updated CV. Most illustrated Lord, I offer a free thirty-day trial of patented contraptions. Tom Hallem dressed. His black trousers felt moist and loose. Bright Argyle socks shone in the gloom. He slippt on a pair of boots with large silver buckles. Elizabeth Archer padded down the steps daintily, went out the back door and walked down Soudan Lane. A car alarm beat back. His distorted reflection came into focus on a side window. Its smooth arc elongated and expanded his torso so that he looked as a Titan might, albeit with an under proportioned head. Usurper of Kronos. Gaea's tool. The child swallower. The son must repeat the journey of the father. Kill or be killed. Et or be et. He watched Elizabeth Archer fumble through her bag. She extracted an oversized bunch of keys. The brake lights flashed. She gestured towards the boot. It popped. He gathered a dry-cleaning bag hung over the back seat.

"Don't forget the shoes," she said.

He collected a pair of black brogues.

"They look too small."

"Women squash into tiny shoes all the time," she said getting into the driver's seat.

He approached the passenger door. The window dropped.

"Wear the whole costume tonight," she added.

"If it all fits."

"Stop complaining. It will fit. Oh, I almost forgot. Can you leave a key?"

"What?"

"Your key. I need if for the agent."

"Where's yours?"

"I left it at home."

"Can't you get it?"

"I'd have to drive home and back."

"But I need it myself."

"You're moving out. Look, just leave it on the ledge above the back door when you're done. I'll tell him where to find it."

"Alright."

She picked an envelope off the dashboard.

"This is for Matt. Will you see him today?"

"Maybe."

"I need to get this letter to him before tonight."

"I could try to see Ana."

"Good. Give it to her then."

"What is it?"

She pressed the envelope into his grip without answer. ALP's letter to Shem. Entrusted to Shaun. His brother. A postie. Never got there. Chucked in a midden heap. Biddy the Hen's toy. Exhumation at a later date too late. Tom Hallem became Elizabeth's messenger by this act in TMAC, even to the extent of mobilising third parties on her behalf. She couldn't lose either way now. Deasy puts Stephen in the same position later in Chapter One.

"I also need ten cents for the phone."

He took a silver coin from his pocket and placed it in her palm. Link to Mulligan soliciting pin money from Stephen Dedalus. The window closed. Money rules the world of *Ulysses*. Joyce follows its meagre trail all the way from Garrett Deasy's purse to Circe four hundred pages later, where Bloom salvages the remnants of Stephen's salary from profligacy. You will find that people are always lying and doing corrupt things for money in this work. It begs a basic question – can love survive the failure of trust and faith. The car pulled from the kerb. Tom Hallem hung his new garments off a grill and wedged the shoes into some bars. He felt for more change in his pocket and walked around the corner. The panels of the telephone booth had been shattered last night. Glass was scattered across the pavement. He gently impressed his weight on the fragments and lifted the receiver. Link to Marion's installation in Chapter Ten. He inserted a coin. It stuck hard in the slot. He pushed it harder. Chewing gum oozed out. He dialled his mother anyway. A political poster wrapped around a telegraph pole read: **US BASES OUT!** Go the start of C4. A linocut mushroom cloud exploded over Pine Gap, which bulged like a cluster of blisters on the Outback. Silent domes. As if the desert had been blasted into a vast intrusive lens. Foucault's carceral. Crackt looking glass, Part B. Les' voice clanged. The connection cut immediately. Damn, exclaimed Tom Hallem dropping the receiver. He tried to extract his coin but failed. There was another public telephone at the entrance to the service station. He walked across Georgina Street, passing between a fleet of empty taxis. An advertisement for the Neo-Barrere truss caught his eye. "No hard pads no springs," it announced like some Duchamp parody. With testimonial from a ruptured gentleman, proclaims the Nymph in Circe. Useful hints to the married. What passes for art these days. Armory > Duchamp > John Quinn, collector and lawyer> JJ. That was the connection order. Both artists shared famous scandals in New York. They lived a few blocks apart in Paris throughout the 1920s. They were probably on nodding terms, if JJ's eyesight allowed. Man Ray took a series of portraits of the Irish novelist including the definitive profile of Joyce in a felt overcoat buttoned up to the neck and apparently spawning a halo. He was a close friend of Duchamp. But there is no record of any exchange, such as the famous verbal curling contest between Proust and Joyce at the Majestic Hotel in 1922. The closest thing to evidence is contained in Mary Reynold's biography, where she speaks of holding open-house at 14 Rue Halle and lists visitors including both JJ & MD (her erstwhile lover). Reynolds was also close to Beckett and Giorgio Joyce. Joyce disliked Duchamp's treatment of women. He cast Duchamp as Professor Ciondolone in *F(W)ake*, according to William Anastasi, then bound them together into the twins Burrus and Caseous (Shem/Shaun). Quinn was their MILK (money). We know that Joyce was a gadfly. In Zurich, he was exposed to Dada, whose linguistic performances hastened his belief in literary experimentation. Duchamp peaked early thanks to superior opportunism. Joyce had to wait until middle-age. That also reflects the nature of their crafts. Painting is a fast hit-job. Prose is too slow. Both D&J realised that ART must make a complete break. They exalted ordinary stuff. There was no way OUTWARDS after they finished. Everything became centripetal and self-reflexive. Some tried to go backwards. Beckett sought to define a retrogressive tendency in *Proust*. Others returned to eternal themes. INSERT LIST OF ACCEPTILE SUBJEX: birth, love, war, religious scenes, history, mourning, death of a knight, my mother's body. Kiefer is the only modern painter to tick off this entire inventory of topics. Bloom's laundry list. Redemption comes through form. Style fades against mass. Make an amalgam out of Greek legends, French theory, Joyce's life and the Nighttown episode. A pub full of mates like the Inferno. See C7. Apparently arbitrary constructs arise. Link to *Happy Days*. Marcuse's Cosmos of Hope. INSERT ON LABOUR. Artisanal qualities are evident in all great works of art. Cite Duchamp's *Mona Lisa*. It is two simple swipes of ink across a cheap print from the Louvre gift shop yet betrays deep theoretical thinking. Like Athena, Duchamp seemed to arrive fully-formed. Picasso's foil. Scylla and Charybdis. Each reworked traditions of gigantism in art. *The Large Glass*. Last gasp of novelty via brushwork. Stupid as a painter. Set alongside *Guernica* in history. Duchamp 1 (Joyce), Picasso 1 (Stein) at the end of extra time. *Large Glass* 4, *FWake* 1. MD defeated JJ in a round-robin tournament. Checkmate by Legal Trap. Joyce didn't have the patience or eyesight for games. Art was deregulated by J&D but to what end? To hate your own vehicle of expression, they both concluded thus. JJ with *F(W)ake*. MD: *Etant Donnes*. The public telephone stood by the entrance to the shop next to a huge wire basket of plastic soccer balls. The shopkeeper was hectoring her husband, who left. Tom Hallem rang home. Les answered. Your mother left half an hour ago, he said. CUT. Tom went into the shop and selected a bottle of warm grapefruit juice from some out-of-date fruit juice drinks on the counter. Elizabeth Archer stopped at a phone booth on Abercrombie Street. She dialled. Ring tone. Click. Connection.

"It's me," she said.

"How are you?" asked a gentle tone. Note inversion of symbol between Tom/Elizabeth.

"Sore," she replied.

The voice laughed.

"Let's just hope his count's good."

"Yes, I don't want to go through that again."

"Where are you?"

"Newtown. Will I see you before work?"

"I've got surgery at nine."

"You should stop that."

"I know. I'm taking every precaution. I've stopped taking new bookings. I'll just finish my current round."

"I'll see you tonight. There's dinner afterwards. I picked that French place. If the agent calls, tell him I won't make it back. I left a key for him on the ledge over the back door."

The shopkeeper bent low. Tom's eyes rested on her crown. Shrewd hag. The end of Leon's career was the real reason they were selling Beta House. She turned her body upwards and askew. One roving blind eye hit Tom. Cold milk shot into steaming tea. Dense hard passageways. Iritis brought on acute glaucoma that reduced Joyce to blindness in effect. Blood seeped into intraocular fluid and mixed with dead cells and pus, all of which floated inside his eye. Viscous fluid was congealing into a solid membrane covering his pupil. The pressure of the swollen iris was agonising. Joyce collapsed on city streets in a grotesque parody of his drunken dance routine. He underwent eye surgery without general anaesthetic precipitating a nervous breakdown. He was prescribed drugs which caused hallucinations. Insert into Cyclops episode. One of the explanations for SD's interrogation of the sense of vision at the start of episode three is that he had broken his spectacles the previous day, allowing Joyce to pass his own affliction onto his young character. The other pupil slid slowly to the outer rim of her skull-socket as if locked in mechanical orbit. Metaphor of Joyce's metaphor of an allegory. Mother and milk-bearer. Both milk-bearers in truth. Silk of the kine. Wandering crone. To patriots, beautiful Clathene. Lower form of an immortal. Heine's cow. Oh Io, you image sweet! Sightless as Oedipus on the arm of pale Antigone. The local realtor entered. The shopkeeper spoke.

"Ugly dawn this morning, Mister Monaro," she said.

"It'll be summer soon enough," replied the businessman.

"Summer is too humid."

"You should get down the coast."

"I'm too busy."

"Try Kiama."

"It's too far. Just a pint?"

Seven mornings half litre tuppence is seven twos. Buy in bulk. Hide the stash under yer bed. The cash register sounded. Missus Brennan inserted a one dollar note under a spring and extracted the correct change. She is the projection of Joyce's old milkwoman. The realtor shuffled aside.

"What do you want?" she demanded.

"The drink please," replied Tom Hallem holding up a jar.

"Forty-five," she replied roughly. "It's on special."

He transferred a handful of coins into her palm. She counted them into respective compartments.

"Weight's right," she concluded.

She closed the register sharply.

"Melbourne Cup today," she said to the businessman. "Three minutes that stops the nation."

"Biggest day of the year," he answered inanely.

"Have you put on a bet?" asked Missus Brennan.

"Not yet. Got a tip?"

"Bounty Hawk is favourite. But I fancy Foxseal."

Odd name, thought Tom Hallem. She handed the form guide to her companion. He scanned the list of starters. Race Five – 2.40 PM – 3200 m – Apprentices cannot claim – $525,000. Hussar's Command, Rose and Thistle, British, Colonial Flag, Mapperley Heights, Black Knight, Lancelotto, Admiral Blair. Miscellany of empirical states. I AM AN ENGLISHMAN, stated Haines in reply to the old woman's query about whether he came from the West. What's in an accent? What's in a name? JJ pronounced his work OOLISSAYS. The M.Cup race-field will be used as a structuring device for Chapter Five. Tom leaned against the outside wall sipping.

"Can I use your phone?" asked the businessman.

"Of course. Come behind the counter."

"I've got to ring Mrs Archer. She's selling the warehouse."

"I didn't know that," replied Missus Brennan.

"It's a forced sale."

"That'll learn 'em," determined Dot Brennan gleefully.

He waited for a connection.

"Hello, is that Doctor Archer? It's Lou Monaro from Monaro Real Estate. Is your wife at home? Oh, I see. Look, we've got an appointment today but we haven't firmed up a time. I was thinking of 12 o'clock. Oh, OK. Great. Of course. I understand entirely. Very important. I'll let myself in. Thank you."

Suddenly, she noticed Tom Hallem.

"You waiting for something else?" she snapped.

"Gum," he said moving back towards the counter groggily. "I wanted some gum."

He took a packet off a tall stand.

"You should be careful mate," interposed Monaro. "It looks like you're just loitering around here until this good lady turns her back so you can get your hands in the till."

"Oh, let him be Lou," interjected Missus Brennan. "He's just a stray. On your way ... or I'll call my husband out of the pit."

Tom Hallem withdrew. A crucified fruit bat billowed from some power lines in the morning breeze. He collected his new possessions. The old lock was almost falling off. He forced the key. The iron rail brushed his palm. It left powdered rust. He shuddered. A track no one turns to climb. Grim odour. A scraping sound above. He gazed up the stairwell. Two men were hauling an old refrigerator out of the building. They stopped on the last landing.

"Looks like hard work," Hallem noted.

"They made stuff to last back then," one of the men replied grinning.

They pressed against the heavy base. It teetered awkwardly. The door sprang open. A metal tray shot down the steps, landing at Hallem's feet. He collected it, jammed it back into the void and pressed the door shut.

"Got a strap?"

"Nope."

"I'll hold it."

Hallem laid down the suit and shoes. He rose and wrapped his arms around the refrigerator, leaning into its bulk. Cool cream paint coated his cheek. Its weight was slowly delivered against his face. He studied the chrome door handle. Belated images burst and tapered. Refused memories. Follow their thread. Dilate to pass. Contracting behind. No way back. Pulled down Stygian veins. When the author says "go," I do go. Eventually, there is a slip then limbo. "Have you seen Pepe?" his mother asked. No, I replied. The women withdrew into the back lot. I followed. They moved towards a cold box pitched in the earth like some fast-fallen rocket. Pepe's mother cracked the door. They quickened their gait. I glimpsed his lithe form. Head at rest. Apparent peace. His mother lifted up the dead body. The black base scraped the landing. Lay it down. Let go.

"Thanks," said Slope.

"Are you leaving?" asked Tom.

"No point fighting the Man," shrugged Non.

"That's how I feel," replied Tom.

"We've gone over to the Glebe squats. Tenant's Union is occupying a lot of empty terraces. We got a big place on Mitchell Street. You should sign up. There's a meeting at the Community Hall tomorrow."

"I'll try to get there."

Tom turned from Non and Slope. He collected Leon's castoffs and went upstairs. The gum was rich, sweet and false. He ripped away the cling-wrap and assumed the jacket. It felt thick. Tattered mourning clothes. Only need an ashplant to complete the set. Trail its ferrule in muck. I want this chapter to have the same economy as Joyce. He began to dismantle the bed. Odysseus' secret post. A thick olive trunk inlaid with precious gems and strung with crimson ox hide. See Chapter 10. He lifted a thin checked blanket and sheets and stuffed them into a garbage bag then rolled the mattress, an uneven off-cut of foam, into a bundle and secured it with elastic straps. The base comprised two house doors laid side by side. He leaned them upright against the wall. This exposed his bed base made of stolen milk crates. He turned one over and began filling it with books. Thames and Hudson monographs. *The Crisis in Modern Art*. *Australian Scapegoat*. Two large-format books: Kirchener and Kiefer. Gifts from Elizabeth. He opened a metal chocolate box and picked out his father's service medal. That unfaced man had come silently last night, a crumbling phantom, teetering over Tom's bed in a dream, his body generating gunpowder-grit and sandalwood-laced steam. He opened a parched mouth to speak. His breath stank of liquor. Stalactite gums. Words stumbled out of his mouth like insane fables. Tom's gaze contracted until it fixed on the mundane buckle of his headmaster's belt. A brass barb pierced fraying leather. Underneath, he bulged. Don Cane hobbled along the parapet. I followed, thought Tom. It was at this point last night that external hubbub had forced him awake. The reader can work out why he withheld the content and fact of remembering his dream from his lover. A buzzer cut him short. He looked out the casement. Sweet silence. His mother pressed again. Armoured incantation quired. She gazed upwards. A look of recognition. No smile. He negotiated the stairs briskly and opened the door.

"Mum," he sounded softly.

"Tom," she shot back.

Cooler than Elizabeth. They rose.

"It's been a while since you bathed," she noted.

Not washing is a symbol of incipient self-loathing in the characterisation of Stephen Dedalus. A phobia to contrast Mulligan's relish of brine. Odysseus as a beggar refused a bath for tactical reasons. All Sydney is washed by Southerlies like Joyce's gulf stream. Ballad by Henry Lawson. Glorious Buster. The observatory flies a flag when it hits JB. One-hour warning. Red light on GPO. His mother started fossicking through a box of coloured pencils. She collected a worn Lakeland stub.

"If you dig deep enough, you'll find yourself as a twelve-year-old child," she said.

"Actually, I was going to pop back to school later this morning and check out some of my early drawings of the chapel. Can I borrow the car?"

"That's a nice thought. Perhaps you'll see Mister Westacott. You owe him so much for your fine education. Not that he'd understand what you've done with it. Give me something to carry."

"Take the lamp. I'll take the mattress."

They loaded the station wagon. Silent consensus. Like mother like. After they finished, Tom Hallem went back alone and loitered surveying the dark mezzanine. His withdrawal from this space had made little difference. He pulled the door shut behind him and placed his key on the ledge.

"What are you doing? You're not going to leave your key up there?" asked his mother.

"Yes."

"But it's not safe."

"Elizabeth needs it."

"She should have her own keys. You hang onto that one. It's yours."

"OK," he said taking it back into his palm.

His mother turned away. She resumed the driver's seat. He popped it back and got in the passenger's seat. She turned on the engine and reached for the radio.

"I'm running late," she said.

"Sorry."

"It doesn't matter. Turn on the news."

He obeyed. Female announcer. Bounty Hawk was favourite for the Melbourne Cup. "Won't win," his mother interjected. Sydney cleans up after the flood but more rain predicted, continued the news bulletin. NOTE CHOICE OF WEATHER. TMAC is set on a wet day to cut against stereotypes of the Australian climate (desert > heat > drought > surf). This is also a deliberate literary decision. Joyce was terrified of thunderstorms. His list of fears also included ocean, heights, horses and machinery. He hated dogs. Each of these things play their role in *Ulysses*: ocean = Mulligan; heights = Nelson's column; horses = funeral and cavalcade; machinery = various do-hickeys like Tom Rochford's machine. Rain got in the paper stock last night. Mr Besley rang. Insurance assessor is coming at ten. Strikes at hospitals across New South Wales. They ought to call in the Army. Good morning Sydney. It's nine o'clock.

"Are you having a flutter," she asked over the top of the broadcast.

"No."

"I'll get you a ticket in the sweepstakes at work."

She increased the volume. Most interest centred on the controversial scratching of last year's winner, Kiwi. Alec Bannon reports. To other news. The Royal Commission into British Nuclear Testing has heard evidence that radioactive clouds scattered plutonium across the Maralinga ranges in the 1950s. Churchill's payback. Emu Field. A black mist approached the shanties. Turn your back, cover your face, see the bones in your own fingers. Evidence has been given that British scientists continued testing Strontium Ninety levels in the Australian food chain until 1978. Nation of lab rats. Stolen infant femurs. Good trade in bones. The British Museum smuggled one dried head and one hundred and twenty-four skulls from South Australia. Ngarrindjeri exports. Penelope Hallem switched stations. A Kensington family had been rescued from their home. Cars floated down suburban streets. Power was cut in the east. Accidents blocked all major roads. At Randwick, more than one metre of floodwater had surged into homes and gardens. Staff at the Royal South Sydney Hospital were forced to sandbag entrances. Eighty-one millimetres of rain fell in the six hours to 3 pm yesterday. More rain is forecast with heavy falls near the coast. Penelope punched a channel button. A walk-out in two large Sydney social security offices yesterday disrupted payments to thousands of handicapped people and pensioners. You try, she said angrily. Her son complied. He found some music. They turned onto down Canterbury Road. Take my love to a foreign shore. She shut down the radio with a poke of her index finger.

"Why did you turn it off?" he asked.

"I never liked that song," she answered.

The Perspex pane caught low morning sunshine as it smashed through welling storm clouds, momentarily causing sparktrails across its scratched surface. Don Cane's eyes opened languidly over the passengers as the airplane dropped. Each person had twisted to various angles to examine the gulf below. His ear burned against the headrest. He stiffened. A slender pillow slipped from his nape. He lifted his rump until the seatbelt pressed against the firm arc of his abdomen. Who had secured him thus? Pinchgut. Fort Denison. The last Martello Tower. Where *Ulysses* begins with Mulligan shaving in a parody of Catholic mass overlooking Dublin Bay. Sydney Opera House tipped onto Bennelong's Point. A venue for the making of O'Dowd's version of Australia. One giant shotgun of a wedding cake. Mulligan invited Kinch to join Haines in a national crusade. The use of a sonnet form was integral to O'Dowd's contention that a new Classical culture in Australia was possible. The sun shot a fast line. Deep and dissolving verticals of down. Delos of a coming Sun-God's race. Its ossein arcs winked. New Hellas in Blush. It had been a concrete ribcage gridded with cranes like a wired-up jaw when he departed. Time moved by little fidget wheels since then, as Slessor put it. Millennial Eden now lurking 'neath your face.

Donald Cane tugged a mustard blanket to his throat. Cloth of gold. Drowsy pallor. Eyes fickle. Close.

"I was knitting you a new pullover," said Penelope Hallem. "It looked nice in skeins. But it just wasn't right. I've had to unpick it. So, I'm knitting some scarves instead. Quite Bohemian. You can have one when I'm done."

Mother's craft. Hot around my neck. A remote endeavor. Strangling vines. Arachne. Wire gossamer. Blunt needles clicking in spun rhythm. Overhanging terraces. Let everything pixelate. Looming jet. Still distant. Hardly a murmur yet. But felt. The plane locked onto its approach. Don Cane accommodated the unrestful landscape below. His homeland. At last. Strangely thus. Yet still uncanny. Like reversing contact lenses. Viscid memory. Sticky. Honeycombal. Accept change in all formats. People also. He smiled ruefully. They'll be unrecognizable as folk. I also. Ghosts crossing paths in Hades. The son does not recognize father. The mother does not acknowledge the son. Don Cane lifted his gaze to the haze that bistered Port Botany. Face through flyscreen. Rugged outskirts of Ithaca. Odysseus must have been appalled by the decline in his estate. The captain's voice offered salutations. Ground temperature fourteen degrees. Heavy storms forecast. Over silver tracks, silver trains crossed. Stanmore Reservoir. Too much soda water and cheap McIver Scotch. Carbonated bubbles blasting through water. ACKACK. Now we're low enough it all goes down pretty fast. Sight the target. Steady. Hold. SWOOSH. Arc through oily plumes. DMZ. Modernist blossoms. Tom Hallem registered the brutalist water tank blooming aloft a steep bank. I need to go as soon as I get home. Home, he pondered. A plane howled over them unseen. VOIR! Rain began massing on the screen. His mother started the wipers. The wings droppt over a jumble of cottages, roads, warehouses and rail yards. Discoloured wagons slid over timber sleepers on pulverised blue metal base. Suddenly, motion was half-withheld. The plane drifted across the brown surface of Alexandra Canal. Downer. Downer. Doze. Distant resistance. Dip. Stern raised high. The greasy tarmac made the big bird skid towards halt like a boat scraping sideways over liquified sand and shore water.

"I won't have time to help you unpack," said Penelope. "We'll empty your things on the footpath. You can take them inside yourself. Have you got a house key?"

"No."

"Les'll let you in."

The plane taxied towards the terminal. The passengers around Donald Cane rose, leaving him utterly alone at the heart of the hull. Squirming brood. A young Filipina with a flat pious face stretched towards the locker above him. The latch lifted with a clack. Hand luggage rained down on him. Gifts for her family. Cheap perfume in a sealed bag. Martha

Clifford asking after Molly's favourite fragrance. Epistolary sex. Letters full of innuendo. Bloom's impotence is patent nonetheless. Soft toys. A carved Sungka board. Pinoy Lego. Coconut leaf.

"Paumanhin," she blurted in Tagalog before adding so sorry in English with a wide nervous smile. They were the first words she'd uttered to her neighbor all flight.

"Yun bay un?" Don replied quickly.

"Marunong ba kayong Filipino, poq?" she asked incredulously.

"A little," he answered.

Don scooped some objects into his palms.

"Iyan ba ang tip ko?" he asked smiling.

Toe in water. Step on a line. Claymore tit. Tripwire. She hastily collected her belongings. Light laughing convent girl like Gerty McDowell. Her unbearable scent of roses. A decoy. Bouquet that soon sours. Molly's jessamine. Open wounds. Almonds. Emma Bovary burning Turkish pastilles that she bought in an Algerian shop. Italian migrants. Molly in Gibraltar as a girl. Abyssinian hawkers. A barbary ape ate a whole family once. Joyce always accompanies references to Gibraltar with smells. Don covered his trousers with a ponderous camera lens. Jollibee collectibles wedged in his lap. Face down face up. *Girl Turning in a Lake* by Rossetti. Inflatable pool bed in Boracay. Juice dripped from the fried breakfast hanging onto Les Hallem's mouth. Enfleurage. Huey raising cattle off a paddy. Raining fresh dung clumps. Phan bo. Solvent extraction. Homebake. Somatic pleasures. Coleridge had some. Olfactory sensations. Proust a master of. Printing-ink scratched into the walls of Beta House. Burnt books. Diesel grit. Steaming pie gravy. Margarine warehouse in Marrickville. Broken biscuits in bags. Stench of soft Madeleines. Originally, it was drafted by Proust as ... toast. Slants on involuntary memory. Stink bug whorls. Old pads stuck against a bin. Smell of life done. It hung in the atmosphere even after they had purged the palace walls with formaldehyde. Potted herrings gone off. The hitter ripped filters off some cigarettes and jammed them up his nose. Rotting bodies all summer. Sow chloride of lime on their treacle at least it redistributes flies. Gas masks worn on Sari Bair ridge. Steam distillation. You can't see smell. Mustard clouds massing in no man's land. Don't run. It penetrates the skin faster. Don't drop. It's thicker in the mud down below. Just stand upright near the lip of the trench and pause until it passes. That which diffuses itself all through the body, permeates. Source of life. Why Molly likes Opoponax. Sweet myrrh. Strawberry and cream bathwater. Desdemona's hankie was a subtle shade of thyme. Joyce's instructions to Nora: "buy some whorish drawers and be sure you sprinkle the legs of them with some nice sent (sic) and also discolour them just a little behind." Nora still retained the air of a working-class woman dressed in faux finery as they gained status and wealth whereas her husband always looked like a middle-class gentleman regardless of their fortunes. The girl reached above Don Cane to retrieve a last item. Taut tissue of ocean purple fabric. Metal underwiring of her brassiere. Retracting form. Somewhat like Richie. Not the face. Visayan. Cebu City maybe. He was lucky to get off that Angeles incident. Paid off the Pulis. In episode thirteen, Bloom is depicted masturbating in front of Gerty McDowell. This is the extreme point of Joyce's rendering of his wrong sexuality. Don Cane with careful hand recomposed his wet shirt. Boar taint. You know its present when women go crazy for ham. Put it on hot bread. Bread, the staff of life. Earn some. Palatable odour. A trail of breadcrumbs is dispensed throughout *Ulysses*, left by the author to alleviate our wanderings. Clues are laid in teacakes, Banbury buns, rolls and the daily bread invoked in the Paternoster. Bloom's favourite advertising slogan: O tell me where is thy fancy bread? At Demeter bakery, it is said. Derwent Street squats. No running water like the spry Liffey. Ana had not washed her body for days. Joyce became a maestro of perfumery in order to write the Nausicaa episode. He was known as LE NEZ in Trieste. Havelock Ellis spent many hours in the natural science section of the British Museum researching the sexology of odour. I picked the wrong week to stop sniffing glue, thought Willy. With animals, oil is naturally secreted into a pouch or pod then chemically extracted. Musk is squeezed out of cysts near the buck's arse. Bear bile extraction is more advanced in China. Their four great inventions were gunpowder, the compass, paper and the printing press. One end of a rubber pipe is surgically attached to the gall bladder. The other is connected to a fluid bag inside a box. A metal jacket tightly holds the mechanism in place under the abdomen. It is emptied every fortnight. The animal is fed a blend of sedatives and whey protein. Haut-goût. Water buffaloes hate the smell of humans. Once, I had to knock one down with a burst from Woofer's gun. Dope leaf stewing in butter-bricks in Non's kitchen. Killers must bury their prey. The grave too short. I smashed my machete. Sound of shattered bones. Tom's dead stalks poking out of an untucked sheet in Prahran. Place a mirror over his mouth. Small mist on the surface represents the Signified. Not present (1999). Bloom's obsession with the smell of his own toes. Contorted on the floor like a crumpled foetus. Inhale the odour of the quick. Lacerated fragments. Metaphor for deleted text. Bloom's reveries. Receding chambers of Babel. Momentary insights into dim core LOST. A pyre of spent cartridges. Use PE to boil water. Kumander Bucay. Ilaga cannibals eating Father Favalli's brain. Consumption of a human heart protects against bladestrike. The Boxers became bulletproof after meditating for one hundred days. Incense bells. Dropping grains onto hot coals. Sparks of campher. Burn three sticks together. Trinity. Me Tom Billy. Raise your arms. Cross the river. Keep your rifle dry. Poisoned water. Reciting spells and incantations as they strolled into battle. Killed where they fell. Enfiladed. Sugarloaf salient at Fromelles. Our introduction to France. Haig's gift. Kept on giving. Corpses piled against the exterior walls of the British Legation. Five thousand dead in one night. Onwards came Chinese volunteers until they overwhelmed the American's fortified positions. Stalin's ladder. Wading over flesh piles.

"Was your hometown hit by Typhoon Agnes?" asked Don Cane.

"No. I come from Ilocos. But I live in Manila."

No accent. Child of privilege. Marcos' birthplace. Probably sending her to safety in Australia. I could have done that for Richie. Menelaus' dilemma. He gave Hermione to Orestes then he had to take her back. An Indian gift. Re-packaged for Neoptolemus like a fake Chinese phone. Telemachus visited Sparta and took part in her original nuptials, shortly before she was sent off to Achilles' son. He threw Astyanax off the city walls then took his victim's mother as a concubine to Epirus where she bore him Molossus. Perverse love triangles. Agamemnon taking Cassandra back to Mycenae. Penelope and Helen. Richie's husband. Elizabeth and Leon. My sons. Shanghai Dog's refusal. Chinese emperors not allowed to cum. Andromache kept Hermione barren with spells. Elizabeth Archer paused at the entrance. A cramp flicked her gut. Orestes wasted Aegisthus and Clytemnestra then bumped off Neoptolemus to retrieve Hermione. Pag ibig ko sa iyo. Bloom reaches the same point by stealth. It's different for a mature man. There are no more epiphanies. He decides to hang onto marriage by cold calculation. Molly also. Billy had Xiao Fang but wanted Judy. Or his wife. Unrequited love. Infatuations. Beatrice and Dante. Hephaestus. Nora. Francesca da Rimini. Wife of a brave cripple. Clifford Chatterley. Got his nuts shot off in the War. Nicholas hiding in the bathtub. Swirling in perpetuity in the second round of Hell. No narrative power in a good marriage. Tolstoy's dictum. Philemon and Baucis. Blot and Mother Blot. Revenge never satiates. Abraham got a hot poker. Les Hallem propped. Lame men are often well-endowed. Picasso's Minotaur. Gold bikinis shimmering on a bar top on Broadway. Topless barmaids 12–2! See Chapter Five. Also, the fish bowl in C6. Alisoun is built like a weasel. Lovely Lingerie Ladies. The gods are always fucking all the time it's just fever. Hard wanks down a Camperdown Beat. Pater's Marius. Sleaze Ball toilets slippery with condoms. Bareback madness. Everything changed with the Pill. Now it's changing back with AIDS. Bring syphilis to your honeymoon like Churchill's father. He went crazy at the Treasury bench. Crimes of passion. *Boogie Nights*. See Aphrodite. Athena's rape. Breaches of faith. Countess Ellen. A staple of 19th century fiction. Someone has to pay. Invariably female. Poison by convention. Emma Bovary. A knife or later a gun is considered a symbol of ignobility. Anna Karenina threw herself under a train. Emblem of Modernity. Keep your c-belt locked. Princess in a tower. Sulky Mellors. Constance Chatterley updated Elizabeth Archer for twentieth century tastes.

Bernini's mattress. Sleeping Hermaphrodite. Tralala. Guinevere taking sanctuary in a convent. Mistaken identity. Filipino ladyboys. Turn yourself into a bull. Go down Makati. Protean. They wrap their organs flat in a jock strap. Salome strangling John. Maids hanged in the compound. Marry your brother's wife like Henry Tudor. Impregnate her cousin. Envy. Lust. Greed. Human nature. Bloom could seduce a woman and feel OK for a few minutes. More weight given to an anonymous escort's orgasm. Try not to bring yourself too close to Molly when you get home. Smell of another female. Chew gum. Monogamy is just a social construct. INTEGRATE WITH NATURAL DISASTERS. They reopened Manila airport yesterday after the monsoon. Agnes lost power over the Philippines, picked up again in the South China Sea and battered Vietnam. Don Cane began to shed his load. His camera dropped. The girl trapped it by pressing her knee against his thigh. Touch. It behaves like battery ends. You either stick or else you're repulsed. He pressed. She withdrew. A steward intervened.

"Is everything alright, sir?"

"I need a little help."

"Let me assist you."

She laid his possessions on a vacated seat. His neighbour exited. A crush of passengers passed. He repeated her name tag aloud. Miss Theresa.

"Are you on a break now?"

"Yes. I've got three days in Sydney."

"Where are you staying?"

"The Hilton Hotel."

"Where's that?"

"George Street."

"The place they blew up?"

"What?"

"They put a bomb in a street bin."

"Who did?"

"That's anybody's guess, Miss Theresa."

ASIO bin-switch. CHOGM. Path of bliss straight down George Street in a municipal garbage truck. What Ananda Marga means. CSIRO bomb-makers. Republicans finally blew-up Nelson's column in 1966. Fiftieth anniversary gift. It left a jagged stump like Nelson's arm. An irony. Two grenades hurled into San Pedro Cathedral at the end of Easter Mass in Davao City. New People's Army. PKP splinter group backed by China. I was sent out to finish the job with Nick Rowe when Marcos got distracted by the Moro. How I got to Manila. Three bombs in rush hour. South Leinster Street 1974. Colm Toibin felt the last one in the reading rooms of the National Library nearby. A thud then silence then sirens then pall. Late Friday afternoon. Stay up all night listening to radio reports. The bombs ran east–west down busy streets towards rail stations. Thirty-three dead plus a full-term foetus. Doesn't count if still in the womb. Richie. Spina Bifida babies. See Chapters 4 & 7. Use Navigation Tool. Chaim. Six days it was left exposed and raw. The Army finally demolished the granite stub to the acclamation of a swelling crowd. Humid February 1978. On the previous run, the cops blocked us from emptying the bins even though they were overflowing onto the footpath, claimed driver Bill Ebb. Council workers Carter and Favell were killed immediately. Constable Birmistriw died next day. Blew out the plate glass windows in the arcade. Marble Bar downstairs unscathed.

"It's a five-star hotel," said the stewardess.

"You can have your bomb palace. I'm going up to Kings Cross where it's safe."

"Is Sydney your hometown?"

"Yes."

"You don't seem to know it very well. How long since you left?"

"Twenty years."

"Where have you been?"

"Lots of places."

"How long have you lived in Manila?"

"Walo taong."

"I heard your Tagalog before. It's cute. What is your line of business?"

"Import–export."

"I see," she grinned. "But not barong."

"No. Light manufacturing. The Philippines have been good to me."

"You mean the Americans."

"I mean the Philippines," he said with emphasis.

"Then you mean President Marcos and his cronies," she said laughing openly. They started to stuff his belongings into a bag.

"I can see you're passionate about your country."

"I hate Marcos."

"Do you also want to get rid of the Bases?"

"Of course."

"Despite the economic arguments?"

"What about the moral ones?"

"The Philippines is a complex country. Just ejecting Joe and Macoy might not make as much difference as you hope."

"I know your argument. And I know what you're going to say next. Ramos. Aquino. They are all part of the same gang. But we have the Church. And the people. And we are ... pikon."

"It might take a long time."

"You've got to start."

"There could be more risk than you bargained for."

"You're a clever man, Mr Cane. You are one of those foreigners who advocate limited change. There are many people with vested interests who want to slow the pace of reform. But the people are in a hurry. And so am I. I must get back to my job. Your baggage can be collected from the carousel at arrivals. Goodbye and thank you for flying Philippine Airlines."

"Thank you," answered Don Cane as she moved out of earshot down the cabin.

The car pulled into the kerb outside a weatherboard house with brown trim and a brown roof. Tom Hallem's mother hurried to the hatch and began plucking articles from the carefully composed mass. She dumped them on the footpath randomly then began passing boxes to her son. When the car was empty, she kissed him brusquely. Her attention was caught by a thread of charcoal on his cheek. She licked her index finger to lift it from his skin. The chill of her saliva lingered long after the aroma of Spanish soap had blown away. She departed. Tom Hallem walked up the concrete path alone. Rotten porch flakes gave way to his boot. He opened the heavy screen door and turned the doorbell. The front door opened.

"Gooday," said Les Hallem squinting. "Come in."

"Got to get my stuff off the footpath."

"I'll help."

Don Cane flicked the last drips of urine against a long silver urinal and straightened himself in front of a mirror. He swabbed at his forehead with still-soapy palms and ran the residue through his hair. He stiffened his stomach. Hard under burnished hide. This suit will do the job, he thought. Shower and a clean shirt. Do the funeral. Move on. The decline of Marcos was inevitable since Aquino's murder. It was time to go. Lots of vets went Bush, mainly up the North Coast. He proceeded to baggage claim. A blank conveyor belt ground its mechanical path. He maneuvered an empty trolley alongside the carousel and waited for his suitcase. Les Hallem came down the path to collect a crate of books from his stepson. He turned. Tom noted his uncomfortable gait. He followed.

"Let me take that," said Tom. "It's awkward."

"Thanks. I'm stuffed."

They stared at each other. Stay silent. Show nothing. Go.

"I'll get the rest," said Tom.

"OK. Yer know where to go," replied Les.

Tom Hallem strode down the hall. Deep carpet resisted the withdrawal of each footfall. He placed the crate before his room and proceeded to the bathroom. Orange wallpaper burst forth. He slammed the door. An old brass handle tinkled. He fumbled with his trousers. Go fwd turn squat. The plastic seat sucked his cheeks. At this stage, I still want to work by allusion to Joyce not just direct statement about his manner of representation. He washed in the heavy basin gazing all the time at his face. Silver foil corroded in the corners of the mirror. The reflective membrane was yielding to transparency. Tom felt stubble that he saw. Diaphonous locks. This image is analyzed at the start of Chapter Three. Ineluctable modality of the visible. Vision was unique, according to Aristotle. Form and substance were distinct. A metaphor for writing as well. Stephen feels them in stark opposition. Signature of all things. Boehme's theory of opposites. Joyce was already anticipating Saussure (see Chapter Six). Stephen is assailed by the external rush of things into the tempest of his own internal monologue. He is obsessed by his chosen mode of acting in the death scene of his mother. It is both deeply felt and deeply affected like he is watching himself in a fit on a screen. Who chose this face for me, asks Stephen Dedalus. He can always see its tracing in Simon Dedalus. There's no ambiguity to the task. My own birth certificate is blank against the category titled FATHER. I bear a stranger's name. Another alias. Malory's Arthur. Candide. Edmund in Lear. A device often used by Austen. Popular in Victorian fiction also. See Hugo, Dickens (x 4), Thackeray, Collins (multiple), Tolstoy, Gaskell, Hawthorne, Eliot, Hardy (x 4–6). Usually, it disclosed hypocrisy in villains. Pansy was the daughter of Gisborne and Madame Merle. Helen Schlegel. Paternal mal-constructs were a feature of Classical drama. Names as imperfect anagrams. Hamlet Hallam Hallem I am. Fluid naming. Use of letters instead of names. Puns on characters from other books. Direct appropriations. Affected (nick) names. HCE goes by 190 naming variants and allusions in FWAKE. Filipinos ascribe them to babies at birth. Fretful Bard. Mulligan called him KINCH. He knew him back as BUCK. His ascribed name, Malachi, was a strange amalgam like Dedalus. Hebrew for messenger. Name assumed by the Bishop of Armagh in the twelfth century. Joyce is mixing names arbitrarily without regard for Naturalism to get across his basic point – that these guys are fake cross-currents just like the author himself using Homer as a freeform template. No stepping forward to applause. He left the bathroom on ageing linoleum tiles. Les had just finished cooking bacon rashers and fried eggs. The pan was still steaming in the sink. Blobs of grease wafted across the surface water. He picked up a tall glass out of the white dishwashing rack. Jet of cold tap. Bubbles frothed thru'n'ebbed. He drank.

And continued into the sunroom where Les was hunched over his breakfast reading the local newspaper.

"Smells good," Tom said.

"It's the fat," Les replied with relish as he lifted a neat pile to his mouth.

Juice dripped into the napkin on his lap. He lifted it to his face and scaped some more liquid from the corners of his lips. Skin colour mashed banana. Eight schooner night last night. MRKGNAO! Les kicked a skinny cat mewing under his feet across the textured linoleum. HESSE, it said loudly. She came to rest against Tom's leg. He reached down without comment and began stroking its spine. It walked along his fingertips leaving streaks of pale fur across his trousers. Les threw a strip of rind on the ground. It held it down with a paw and dragged at the fat with worn-out fangs.

"Did you know my father," asked Tom Hallem.

"Nah. I was stationed down in Duc My. He was deployed at Dong Ha near the DMZ. But I knew of him," said Les grinning bitterly.

He speared a charred remnant with his fork, skewered some crust and wiped yolk over its dry carapace. His head dipped suddenly. Shadows cast across the room dimmed his hungry mouth. Cartilage crunched dully. Polyphemus chewing bones. Hallem averted his gaze towards a mug of tea. The cream had risen to the surface as it cooled and now circulated in streamers on its lamella.

"What did you hear?"

"Blokes like him are always surrounded by rumours. People said he was operating for the Yanks across the border into Laos. That's where he got killed. Near Dak Seang. But some say he never died. There's a story he went to the States. Another one that he's been working out of the Triangle. I also know a bloke who claims he runs a bar in Phuket."

He drained the mug and cracked its metal base against the table decisively. The telephone rang. Tom collected the receiver.

"Hullo," he asked. "Sorry she's at work. Can I take a message? Alright."

Quick cut. He replaced the handset.

"Who was it?" asked Les.

"Dick he said," then added, "do you know him?"

"Local businessman."

"What does he want with mum?"

"Your mother's still a fine-looking woman," smirked Les Hallem.

Tom tried not to register emotion. Classical queens make multiple marriages until well advanced in age. More like ententes. Even treaties. Put Penelope with her nephew Telegonus. Telemachus with Circe. Roman crones. Gertrude shifting. Strategic unions.

Chaucer's knight. What women most want in the world. Keep asking that question. CONTROL. Governe as me lest. Bedroom abdication. Cheseth youreself. Uncle Barry. Mum married Les in the school chapel.

"I'm going to unpack," he said finally.

He passed into the living room. An eclipsed celebrity was advertising diet powder on the television. Spoonblasted. Brown undertow. Oar in mud. He stroked another cat bundled in a grey armchair. It turned its head to press his fingers into its ear. He reached beneath its chin. A knob of cartilage rattled. He cut transmission. The image died into a single point of white light that dissipated in the grey screen like a fading coal. Ghost stars slippage. He went into his bedroom. There was a knock. Phone, yelled Les. Who is it? Your cousin. Tom went back to the lounge room. Les handed him the receiver and withdrew to the kitchen loitering just out of sight. I got a suitcase of your books from the studio. I was going to drop it over to your folk's place. I'll leave it down the side. I don't think anyone would steal a copy of *Return to the Chateau*. Yes, you told me it was the sequel. See you at Woolley. I know. One PM. He killed the call stone dead. To write Penelope, Joyce needed a briefcase from Trieste that contained letters from Nora in 1909. She had already burned his stuff. This correspondence remains some of the hardest core erotica in human history. I do not intend to list its contents. It has no place in this text. Nothing could be gained by its recitation. It would only reduce this work to sordid disclosure. Sex in this work is calibrated for maximum impact. Birmingham describes the look of the letters beginning with a large, red express stamp affixed sideways in the top RH corner on each envelope, holding thick twice-folded pages filled on both sides in Nora's neat handwriting with frequent misspellings and without punctuation. This was the style Joyce used. It was class transfer of literacy. Write the dirty words BIG, he instructed Nora. Insert to explain use of capitalizations. Tom Hallem dialed a new number immediately. I'd like to speak to Ana Lafei please, he asked. Ta. He waited. Hi, mate. Can you pick me up on your way back to town? Great. What time? OK. I'll be waiting at the bus stop. See you when your worms are straighter. Interpret her name. Ana Anna note palindromes Le fey an ironic link Ana Lafei Plurabelle ALP/HA HOUSE Lafayette anannal publishing. Meanings in *Ulysses* are coy thrills, concluded Kevin Birmingham. Invert this tactic. Remove all suspense. Make the future movements of the plot quite clear. But at the same time, disorder JJ's ordering strategies. Scatter them through the text. Cloud drift uncovered the sun. Don Cane tightened his gaze. Cling to day. Mist still coated the landscape. A place rendered blank. Retake. Go back. Conflate. Step onto shore. Here for Choc's funeral – out of the blue – exit Richie – nullified babies – fuck Manila – safe haven – keep the oxygen flowing – backwards - Saigon – Special Forces – Cambodia –

working the Highlands - Katu, Bru, Rhade, Mngong, Gar – the whole Conflict – a place to get lost in – Malaya was the best training ground on Earth – always wanted to be a soldier – too young for Korea – missed the Pacific War – recruited in Campsie's paddocks – hunting Mother's lean drunken body in bleached bed sheets – spraying the clothes line with machine gun static. I never saw her dead dogsbody. In exile. Why did she come back? Ask myself that question. I will visit her grave after I see off Choc. Fox on a mound. Pain that was no longer love crackled in his ribs untamed like a wild panther. The trolley stuttered in a gutter. His toilet bag popped onto the footpath. He rubbed uncomfortably at his jacket. Postcards from Glendora. Jean Wheaton's letter. Poor Choc. Damaged lives. Richie's miscarriages. Too much. She left with my driver. Now she was a mother at last. No hard feelings. I got too much fly spray on my skin in the jungle. Our baby was born with multiple congenital abnormalities: left talipes (club foot); bilateral dislocated hips; spastic quadriplegia; bilateral hypoplasia of both optic nerves resulting in total blindness; abnormal contractions of the fingers both hands. Poor scrap. Squirming in life. Merciful release really. My sons in Sydney. Young men now. How to approach? Or if. Inevitable questions. I was in hiding. Serving time. Staying out of the line of fire. Acts of avoidance. Maybe they're old enough to understand. Tom Hallem replaced the receiver and returned to the kitchen. Les withdrew onto a soft purple stool. He pawed the sugar bowl. What held Mrs Dedalus' bile. Mulligan's razor.

"I'm going to get the car off mum."

"Where are you going?"

"Campsie. Look, I don't have a key. Can you let me back in?"

"I'm going down the club later."

"I'll be back before 12."

"OK. Look, tomorrow is pension day. Could you spot me ten bucks?"

"It will come as coins and small notes."

"All hard currency. I'll put it back in the top drawer of your bedside table tomorrow night."

Tom took a clump of coins wrapped in a five dollar note from a bowl. He handed the wad to Les without comment. It was pulled from his fingertips gently.

"Ta."

Les Hallem lifted himself and walked towards the front bedroom. Skinny sunken hulk. Claudius the freeloader. Gertrude's stud. Now look at him. He leaned in the doorway. To my mother's room, he goes. A crack of light between door and frame. Telemachus overhearing Penelope and Odysseus in bed. Les Hallem removed his nightshirt. He bent and took a frayed singlet from the top drawer. He turned in profile. Shattered hind all exposed. Tom Hallem gaped. Swollen lips of flesh had been pulled together into thick folds and sewn hastily. Hemingway was wounded when a bomb exploded in the trenches in Italy. Over 200 pieces of shrapnel penetrated his right leg and foot. Link to Oedipus, Byron et al. He dropped his strides to display the rice-paper legacy of the wound to Miss Beach. Link to Les Hallem's hind. Mother's bed vacant and unmade behind him. Tamed like Miltown. Link to Lowell. Him and me both. I will not sleep here tonight. That is a pivotal line in *Ulysses* at the end of episode one. It is followed by the real clanger: "Home also I cannot go." Joyce muddles syntax to get the lost concept fixed to the fore of the sentence. Les knew that he was being observed. He covered his torso modestly. Tom Hallem entered the room.

"Sorry, I couldn't help myself.

"Sure," replied Les Hallem mildly.

"I'll go now."

"You may as well help me on with a shirt. It's usually your mother's job."

Tom lifted the sleeve over his step-father's broken wing. This is a corrupted allusion to Daedalus. Les shuffled it down his arm and secured the cuff. He spoke into the corner.

"Have a good day, young Tom. I'll leave the key under your mother's geraniums."

Tom Hallem hedged. Stephen Dedalus would insert some caustic bon mots at this moment: (a) the cracked looking-glass one; (b) whole nation washed by the gulf stream; (c) smart double negatives.

"Is ten bucks enough?" asked Tom.

"I'll double it on the pokies then stop."

Les Hallem did not turn around. Don Cane raised his arm. A taxi pulled into the rank. Thunder resounded. Clouds banging heads. Destination, asked the driver. A thick white scar ran from the base of his nose to his jawline. Skinny neck. Thick black plumage. Cheap sunglasses. Crest Hotel Kings Cross, Don said. Roger that, replied the driver tapping the accelerator blithely. A cool breeze rushed across Botany Bay. A mound of empty containers was piled down the north end of the runway. A seven-o-seven dropped into view suddenly. Don followed its path. It slid braking hard. His eyes returned to the road surface.

"Do you mind if I put on some music," asked the driver.

"Go right ahead," replied Don.

He punched a cassette into the stereo and whipped up the volume accelerating down Airport Drive. Songs of a type Don had never experienced.

"Do I detect a trace of Blarney?" he asked the driver.

"I been here since I was a boy."

"Where were you raised?"

"Campsie. Do you know it?"

Don sharpened. Give him to ARVN. Stick him in a cage. Send him to Con Son. They'll do the dirty work. Wired-up to a jeep battery. False interrogation. Is my wife alright do you know her does she forgive me how would you know what about her cousin did she love me her husband he was my mate how's he doing my sons you must know them they're both about your age never seen them myself but look at me now can you see a family resemblance. Mutilated corpses. Cut off the testes stickem in his gob send a snapshot home. Odysseus was a happy man before the whole show started. He had to be goaded to enlist. Forget about honour. Pledges are rum. He just couldn't kill his son. Made peripatetic by war, he was always on the road home after that. Diverted by fate all the time. It was always so easy. Maybe he never really wanted a homecoming. Vets never got one. Maybe he lost sight of its consequences during the long arc of survival. A wish of willpower rather than logic. It soon became apparent that veterans would never be able to acclimatise back home.

"Sure. How the Berries?"

"Where've you been mate?" the driver chuckled. "They're called Bulldogs now. Just won the Giltinan Shield. Second time in five years actually."

"Amazing. We were crap when I left. St George had won seven premierships straight."

"They got to eleven. We stopped them in Sixty-Seven. Kandos Ryan was coach. But we lost to Souths in the grand final. Where have you been all this time, man?"

"Asia."

"Cool. My name is Stephen."

"I'm Eric."

Don Cane shook his head. Relief of Odysseus when he heard the local dialect. Penelope yielding to my persistence beside Cook's River. Helen fixed him with great green eyes. Fat cabbage awful hot. Dixieland recordings. He released his last scruples. One-eyed cat peeping at a fish store. Jam-jelly rolls. Oh Daddy. Penelope sick in the outhouse on split knees. Molly in labor at Holles Street. The death of Rudy, their second child, adds poignancy to Bloom's visit to the maternity hospital in episode 14. End of sex. Molly doesn't have coitus for ten years until later that day. Leon came out definitively when Chaim died. You with your fooling / see what you're doing. He waited for the dim light in Helen's bedroom to douse. The back door opened a crack. His signal. Don pushed Bloom's old Tabby out of the way with his boot. Joyce nudging aside Homer. Persistent circuits. Doubling-back. He slunk along the wall like a skink. You'll curse the day when you were untrue to me. He turned into the screen filling it quickly with. Finger flicking safety catch. Helen felt then observed Don Cane lapping her back in the dressing table mirror. Separated sense triggers. Link back to Aristotle. She shifted to display her body. Dash your boat against Scylla. Penelope singing "Japanese Sandman" in bed rubbing castor oil on her half-term gut. Listen to your mother from within, Telemachus. Your father was the one creeping out in the dew like that lullaby's eponymous character. An old second-hand man trading karma. You'll never see him again. Made his wife a cast-off. Turned your aunt into used merchandise. Sold at a steep discount to Barry Capri. He'll bury the old day, sell you new stuff. Trace repetition of the word STUFF in this chapter. No version of the future was feasible in Sydney after that. Odysseus abandoned the plough, leaving random furrows in the field and went with Palamedes. Stephen Dedalus left for work. Mulligan demanded his last coins. Our hero threw them into his erstwhile friend's soft silk chemise alongside his iron house key. Sink into the earth lowly, Joyce wrote. My thinking wasn't mature when I started this chapter, fifteen years ago. I have so much to update as I loop back. This is the real Pyrrhic victory. References to Asculum by Joyce connect Asculum to Ireland, Pyrrhus to Britain. Episode one is too short. It must be the most read and re-read part of *Ulysses*. Lots of readers get stuck on Joyce's juvenilia. He was still working out his ultimate mode when he started. I don't think he could be bothered revising those early scenes after finishing the rest of the novel. There just wasn't any need, especially after he really got rolling in Proteus. He could have commenced *Ulysses* with "Ineluctable modality of the visible." It would have been a great start. He challenged readers to grind past his mawkish pastiche of teenage angst on the outskirts of Dublin to get to Bloom in the CBD. Many people find the opening passages about Stephen Dedalus an unsatisfying gambit. The scenes and images in Chapter One often seem like an arbitrary assemblage, a sequence of clever notebook entries connected by a governing Anglo-Irish trope. *Ulysses* is a form that became much greater than its parts by the end. Joyce's audacity with Modernist high style means many critics gloss over its flaws. Don Cane carried a plastic-coated code of conduct throughout the conflict. It could be pulled out anytime and shown. In those days, I just took what I needed from Joyce and left the rest unascribed. Stream of consciousness just kind of starts around this point in *Ulysses*. Its introspection drives the rest of the text. I add all kinds of tangents. My intent in this chapter is to show Telemachus with Athena. Joyce diverged with Homer on this point. He kept SD isolated. I did the same thing using physical contact. Tom Hallem is manipulated and used by his mentor. I finally reached sanctuary at the end of the first draft. I should have stayed there where it was safe. Scourge of leaving Ogygia. Go back to Circe, find a new Calypso, get blown off course again, never get too close (to close). Now I'm bogged back in text that I don't even recognize. This first part has become the last draft. The endpoint of an interminable siege. Don Cane never stopped wandering at any point. Never really went home. Does Penelope miss me? Helen long to kiss me? He had no stomach for this kind of reflection. Covert reunions. Invincible lies. They were more his kind of job. Meet you down the pub, said Mulligan. The Ship. Half twelve. He knows I'll have a whole month's pay in my pocket by then. Ritual parasites litter *Ulysses*. Joyce presents this type of behaviour as emblematic of Dublin, particularly the upper classes. Stephen's profligacy can be contrasted with both his father's selfishness and the sensible parsimony of Leopold Bloom.

"As a matter of fact, I grew up on Ninth Avenue. You one of John's boys?"

"That's us. He owns this very coffin."

"I remember your birth. Paddington Women's Hospital. How old are you? Twenty-four?"

"Good guesswork. Where did you live, Eric?"

"Back up First Avenue. Next to the shop."

"Near Mrs Horne?"

"I was mates with her son Bobby."

"He died in the War."

"Bobby?"

"Yea. Down the tunnels near Saigon. Very early on. I was probably six."

"I was long gone by then. Did you know the McFadden's?"

"Of course. My brother trained at their gym."

"What about their daughter, Helen?"

"Mrs Capri? Yes, I went to school with her son Billy."

"Hardcourt?"

"Yep."

"Did you also know Tom Cane?"

"No."

"They were cousins, I think."

"Maybe you mean Tommy Hallem. He went off to Burwood with his mum."

"Moved up a notch?"

"More than a notch. His father got killed in a car crash. Mother got a big insurance pay-out. Re-married a bloke name of Hallem. Son took his name."

"Interesting," answered Don Cane. He dozed in the dry cabin as it clattered up O'Riordan Street like four black stallions yoked together and whip-stroked towards the palled city, its stern lifted and dropped, swishing great waves of rain-ash in its wake, unswerving, faster than any falcon, sweeping all troubles from his mind. Tom Hallem stood on the threshold. Another cloud passed. The rain baulked. Cold air rushed his cheek. Time to head out. Contained journey. He had no idea why he was going. Circuit inside puny circuit. Inspirals. Passive capacitor. Twin terminals. Lapwing. Go looking for clues about your father. But not too hard. Look what happened to Hamlet. I still don't know if he found much in the way of evidence, let alone truth. All theory. Rumblings of a ghost. Reading body language. Mousetrap. An act of entrapment. It would never hold up in a court of law. A sequence of corpses in his wake. Open out their wallets on the ground, looking for any kind of clue. Be careful of snares. Their little caps can take your finger off; prick out an eye. A photograph with a place-name often pinpointed the victim's unit. The Telemachiad appears like a minor journey, especially when you consider the extent of Odysseus' travels. But the reader isn't aware of this comparison at the start of the *Odyssey*. Telemachus is introduced as the central character. Nothing is known of his father yet. He is beset by suitors. Every man in the palace is an enemy. His mother appears quite callous. This is really a protective tactic. But he isn't aware of her logic. He feels utterly alone. This can all be related to *Ulysses* and this work. He steals off in a boat for Pylos and Sparta. It's like Stephen Dedalus quitting Dublin at the end of *PAYM*. Rotten boards sprang under Tom's soles as he released his body down the path. Metonymy of a quest. Joyce inverts the plot resolution of his previous novel at the start of *Ulysses*. What was all closed off in *PAYM* is dredged back up and revised. Joyce represents the gap between the two works as a reductive Telemachiad set against the prospect of his *New Odyssey* (which is really about the possibility in life of a 'second go'). Telemachus gained first-hand knowledge on his journey. In contrast, Stephen Dedalus endured a subsistence existence in Paris until he was forced to return home by news of dying mother. He is back in Dublin working a dead-end teaching job now. It makes a mockery of his academic pretensions. His family's station has declined still further. His slight art products are brushed. He is endured under sufferance. Mocked by Mulligan. Court jester to Haines. In penury. Embittered of Self. A genius in search of context. All faux Aestheticism. Like petulant Achilles sulking in his tent. Posturing along the Strand. Uninquiring. Closed. Or rather immobilised by the pinball dialectic that remains unresolved in his head. Fixed in place but like Achaean strategy. Agamemnon was as bad as Haig. Put Troy under siege and just wait. He can't assume Pelian armour like Odysseus after Achilles was slain. He needs to find a different methodology to write Ireland's epic. He got something out of Bloom. We never find out what it is, although we know that Stephen Dedalus left the stage in 1904 and came back with a puff of smoke as James Joyce in 1922. Mulligan hugs him. Greeker than the Greeks. Phihellenism. Recant liberation. Got to find Molly. Metaphor for Ireland. A mother and her butcher. Uncle Cuck and Old Dick Stone. Fucking Colombanus. Walk down Weldon Street. Drowning.

Climb to the prow. Tom regathered a well-trodden route along Ethel Street. It was lined with grand mansions built for the middle-class flight from plague in the early part of the twentieth century. He passed onto Burwood Road. Single Gentleman's Dormitory. Keyless apostolic cells. Shared bathroom. Own kitchenette. Furnished. St Paul's Church. Now there was a wanderer. Wrote half the New Testament lying on the road. Five lines of plot and ten pages of notes on the *Apocrypha*. Joyce hot-housed his narrative inside a pinball machine. Such centripetal force met its end-point in Beckett's mounds and bombed-out warehouses. *Sola Fide*. Artist's creed. Site of Don Bradman's wedding. My father's namesake. Joyce shifts gears from lyric to heroic trope. Stephen's debasement benefits the narrator. Elevate yourself by reduction against. Daemon rivals. Joyce observed his own creation with total detachment. Steady decline. Retail fringe. Golden Fleece service station. Spartan Milk Bar. Barry's Sports and Hobbies. All allusions. Red Dragon restaurant. Draw a grid. Insert various kinds of Irish art – song, riddle, legends, Yeatspeak, epigrams. Connect the dots. Tom surveyed the straight road. No other course was open. Avenging son? No score to even. Stupid Hamlet? At least he had a ghost. Park the Orestes trope out back. Get the car. Mother no Clytemnestra. Les hardly Aegisthus. My flip. A secret sharer. So secret, he doesn't even detect. Jim and Marlow. Fly low. Under the radar. To the drop zone. Dust-off tracers. Outlines of scepters on ramparts in spit. Of a substitute father. Of false fathers. Of a father unknown. And/or belated. Of character(s) sketched out of models from Homer and Joyce. Ill-symmetry. Telemachus morphing. Tom Hallem stepped over the threshold of his mother's work place. Billy Capri stirred milk into his tea. Lester Hallem dead-locked the front door and slugged the street. Ft-ftt-fit-fitt-PHT. He perambulated asymmetrically as he rose. Stephen Dedalus yielded the future. A father by any other name. Middleman. His realised text. Agenbuyer. A compound. The Latin text of Mulligan's mock mass is repeated now, looping back to the start, enclosing the text, dribbling to silence at close as Stephen recedes down Sandycove Avenue. As noted earlier in this chapter, Stephen reaches two vital conclusions now: (a) no to Martello ever again; and (b) no to back home. He will countermand the second decision by inference in approximately fifteen hours. Likewise, Tom Hallem has exited Beta House but will end up back at his step-father's house tomorrow morning. The chapter ends with the rich, beckoning cadence of a seal inheriting Mulligan's sharp squawk. Stephen acknowledges it in one of the earliest samples of the rich bestiary employed in *Ulysses*. Joyce concludes Chapter I with the word, 'usurper,' out on its own as an orphan. It is the only time Joyce uses this word in the whole novel. In this instance, we can replace the active noun with the passive past participle, enabling us to recede into ONEC, as uttered in bitter undertones by the victims of such disinheritance, say, Edgar in

King Lear while he shivered, naked, in half-real, half-mad tempest, or soiled Hamlet groaning in anguish as he finally contemplated the totalness of his uncle's piracy, this is what Joyce did to fiction, what Eliot felt, not just a word that Stephen used about Mulligan, it's about Ireland as well, about Britain, about Haines, Australia, what we did to the locals, also about the Roman title chosen for the novel, it's what I want to do to Joyce, write about him while in fact I am writing LIKE Proust, shifting between personas like Proteus, flattening the board and fragmenting representation like Stein (see Cubism), aping her technical persona, natural sentences exist in arithmetic she said, wandering away from Saussure like Melanchtha Herbert, coming back at Joyce from a subaltern posture, also shunting TMAC from the conventional narrative in this chapter towards its final form, I no longer need the received form of *Ulysses*, I can create my own plot, my own mythemes, also take his tropes and snap them, make R. Burton or J. Meillon lean into the ribbon microphone and churn each syllable of that last, fateful word: "usurped" (Cym. "trawsgip", Ir. "forghabhaim").

3.
Proteus

In the stink of morning, along straight Campsie streets, the garbage truck can flatter itself saying: I AM ANONYMOUS. Astride it, feeders sustain this myth by barking in unison at the driver. They don't shout words – there are never comprehensible words – but chants from another era when First Avenue lay unguttered and grey Holdens sat on gravel and mud. Tom Hallem dragged a school case towards the car. Its crumpled silver studs scraped the concrete. A dog whined. Passing fishvan. Rainwash. His mother's beige stockings were spattered with slurry. She swore and unlocked the driver's door of the Chrysler Valiant. His shoes, already soggy with dew and grass clippings, slipped into the passenger seat apace. She settled on the red vinyl seat. He was still panting after racing his cousin to the kerb. He looked out at Billy. Who waved. Kidsgrin. I raised a bright face. Joyce sends Stephen back to school in Nestor. This time as teacher. He explores Stephen's relationship to the father/son dyad through interaction with the school principal, Garrett Deasy. Everyone is defined by this relationship in Homer. Patrilineage determines status, social relations, divine attitude, and identity. For Telemachus, everything depends on finding Odysseus. Same as Stephen and Tom. I see Telemachus as a totally passive figure until the climax of the slaughter of the suitors in the palace when all his repressed anger at rejection and lack is unleashed. The garbage men peered down on my mother's finely hosed thighs as they stretched against the black pedals. She looked up suddenly. Beaks turned as suddenly in denial. Our Last Heroes. Kokoda Chocs. There was a battle, sir. At Tarentum. Forgot the date. Maybe 1965. America's high watermark. England's Empthroes. Joyce cites Asculum at the start of a chain of images and symbols that clearly relate to the Great War and the Pyrrhic nature of victory. Billy's salutations pierced the safety glass. Penelope grimaced. Don's bastard. Barrel chest busting out of a grey turtle-neck sweater. Mordred in chain mail. Shiftless lineage. Sometimes he was Arthur's nephew. To other scribes, a foster son. The true King via Lot, according to John of Fordun. Guinevere's SUB. A false monarch. Locked in fatal grip with his father at Camlann. He became whatever type of trope suited the writer. Unlike Stephen Dedalus, Telemachus is not certain of his paternity at the start of his voyage. My mother says I am his son, he states, but I do not know for sure. This situation equates with Tom Hallem. Penelope crunched the gearstick and rolled the car workwards. History is the theme of Nestor. It is the subject of Stephen's class. It was also the art of the episode, according to Gilbert's schema. Stephen's sense of history is deeply personal. That is why he terms it a NIGHTMARE which needs to be awakened from. This is also the title of Lawrence's chapter on the Great War in *Kangaroo*. The technique of the episode, "catechism (personal)," suggests that interrogation is mainly directed at himself. Stephen has many questions but few answers. This is in keeping with his identification with Hamlet. Tom Hallem crosst Cook's River and accelerated through the Byron Street intersection, triggering passage with local government's engagement with the Canon when this suburban grid was formed. Burns, Dryden, Browning and Shakespeare Streets passed in quick succession. Shelley Avenue was one block west, star-crossed by Tennyson Lane. Such a conjunction would have dismayed Frank Leavis. He clenched a wordworn face. RAMC plaster across his right bicep. *Sanitaire Anglais*. Hauling buckets of cocoa along the roof of an ambulance train with a pocketful of Milton. Grand cortege of youth and glory, Chris Brennan would have called such stripwork laconically from the front bar of the Mansions Hotel. Australia's own Mangan. Another self-styled Romantic wreck. Stephen Dedalus gone old. Shelley's "fading coal" in flesh. References to *Hellas* abound in Proteus. Also Blake's notion that vision is the full representation of what really exists. Tom Hallem envisaged a street map as he drove. Back along the concreted riverbank, Adam Lindsay and Gordon Streets had been laid down in sequence. A touch of comic flair, smirked Tom, from some Antipodean Homais. A car backfired. Pigeonflight through fruit trees. Pomological units, added the Apothacery. Powderflash. Tea-tree scrub. Sound of a shot. Space and time flashed together. Physics of a starter's pistol. *Nacheinander*. Poor b(ast)ard knocked his head with a barrel-organ down Brighton Park. *Adiaphane*. Bloody bubble and froth sprang from his unhinged lips. He lay as dead men only lie. *De Te*. Close his eyes, Shem. Put pennies upon. If you can put your fingers through, it's a skull; if not, a head. *Diaphane*. Tom Hallem reached the Beamish Street intersection and turned into Eighth Avenue. Canon to nullity. Crossing Styx. Erasing memory. Blessed void. A canopy of Bangalow palms enclosed his mother's vehicle. He crossed Fourth, Third and Second Avenues in turn. Mao wanted to replace all names with numbers. Tomb-sweeping Algebra. Anonymous. Tree-urned. In common usage, Protean means very variable, highly adaptable and easily or continually changing. A medical definition used the following example: "the ways in which AIDS may present are numerous, and thus, protean" (https://www.medicinenet.com). This entry notes that it is not to be confused with the word protein. Proteus was the shepherd of Poseidon's sea creatures. He possessed the gift of prophecy like Daniel. But he hated imparting his insights to humans. He continuously changed shape to thwart their attentions. The only way to obtain his divinations was to approach him by stealth as he rested and restrain him while he changed shape until he ran out of energy and forfeited. Then he would tell you everything he knew. Like Proteus, Ana Lafei is left thrashing on the ground in C10. According to Homer, the home of Proteus was Pharos off the coast of the Nile Delta. Menelaus relates the story of capturing Proteus to Telemachus in Book Four of the Odyssey. He wanted to find out which gods he had offended at Troy and how to pacify them so he could return to Sparta. Proteus' daughter betrayed her father. When Proteus went to sleep amongst his colony of seals, Menelaus and three companions disguised in seal skins grabbed him and held him fast as he transmuted successively into the forms of a bearded lion, a snake, a panther, a monstrous bear, running water and a towering tree. This is a secondary source for Haines' dream of shooting a black panther in Proteus. It is also a metaphor for his feelings towards Stephen Dedalus, who he wants to kill for being such a smartarse. He becomes a panthersahib enrolling Mulligan as his pointer (a polysemous word-choice and image that covers servant, dog, informant, pen and even phallus). But its real bedrock is simply Joyce's actual experience of Samuel Chenevix Trench. This is all peculiarly British: a dream, use of a gun, exotic beasts, terror, intellectual insecurity, subordinate targets, excusable victims. Proteus also informed Menelaus that Agamemnon had been murdered, Ajax the Lesser killed, and that Odysseus was stranded on Ogygia. Telemachus takes this as hard evidence that his father is alive. The car abutted the junction with First Avenue. Tom wheeled across the face of some liver brick bungalows past an idling garbage truck and steered into a vacant space opposite Billy's house. He killed the engine. Pursuit of articles forfeited. There are four scenes in Nestor: Stephen testing his class on Pyrrhus and Milton's "Lycidas"; tutoring the student Sargent on algebra during a hockey match; meeting Deasy to collect his wages; and finally being pursued by Deasy out of the school grounds with an anti-Semitic joke. The stretched suburban landscape drew Tom Hallem to a distant row of Camphor Laurel trees monstering the public-school grounds. They rocked a little in the morning breeze. Stiff-scented leaves wafted over the fence. No grass survived below. Just dust or mud. Penelope Cane contracted her gaze so that it rested on some Greek laborers arriving at the building site over the road. "All those sandwiches to make," she thought, struggling with a tray of wax-paper loaves. Her baby's whelping broke the back of her quiescence. She went inside hastily, where it was always dark, to the stroller wedged between the curved display case containing trays of lollies spread across sheets of greaseproof paper and the makeshift shelves which held tins of baked beans and unsweetened pineapple pieces, paper bags of plain flour and jars of Riverina jam. Les Hallem closed the front door. He steadied himself against the white-washed woodwork as he took each step towards the gate. He wore a veteran's ribbon on his pummeled chest. The corresponding scenes in this chapter are: Tom Hallem going back to Campsie where he experiences an intense reverie of childhood; Don Cane attending Choc's funeral at Botany Cemetery; Tom meeting Bent and Westacott at his old school; and Tom visiting Missus Hensley at the aged care hospice before Ana collects him on the Hume Highway. All these scenes are informed and distorted by personal interpretations of shared history as in Joyce. Penelope calmed the child. Odysseus still overshadows Telemachus at this stage of the *Odyssey*. He is just too eminent even as a lack. She went back outside to start hauling in crates of milk bottles that had been left perched uneasily on the footpath to sweat at the approaching day. Thick cream was collecting under beaten silver caps. Milk is an ironic emblem throughout the early stages of *Ulysses* until it is replaced by liquor as the day goes on. The crates screeched through track-marks in the textured linoleum tiles that chronicled the trail of Penelope's days; jangling all the way to the refrigerator. It shut with a thud releasing a sharp gasp in its wake. She returned to the threshold. Eggs next. Weak cardboard lattices. Get your palms underneath. Rise. A tiara presented on a soft velvet pillow. Some Faberge glob. Twelve-twelves is one-forty-four. Itemise what's broke. A cement mixer arrived. Drum-churning floss. Ferris wheel. Tide-swell. Cycles. Stop at the apex and bob in tide-swells in a little wooden tub. You can see the city's cunt quite clearly from this panorama under Bradfield's hem. Ghost train. Iron gates. Creaking hinges. Accelerator grades. Steeds of Mananaan. Roller-coaster joyrides. Catch the Wild Mouse (see HELEN). Luna Park betrothal lying on the lawn behind Kirribilli pylons against the harbour-fast wind. Coathanger logic above. I drew Donny into my sleeveless white blouse under the wing of a triangulated collar his heart went mad YEAH I said YES I will YEAH the text closed Joyce moved on to fame and *F(W)ake* but life continued through TIME for us. Is it only four years now since? At least Molly Bloom got the best part of a decade before it all went wrong after Rudy. Her husband was probably steadfast up to that point then he went poledark. Penelope ran her finger along the edge of a corroded metal sign advertising Vincent's Powders. Genuine Pink. Pour another sleeve. Moly. Smell of kerosene burners. Whirl of a milkshake baton. She dragged the last crate to the threshold. This is a symbol of reduced circumstances like Mary Dedalus AKA Joyce. Helen McFadden passed below. Morgause deferring. Clean gold band on her ring finger. Almost ready to drop. Haines' pistol shot. Probably happened the first time they copulated, mused Penelope. Long as Don was. Presst open her fresh cervix. Nogooddonnoh. Fresh eggs pack of six per shilling. All a matter of misfortune. Stephen Dedalus is too young to feel life's randomness yet. It is left to Bloom to give experience its thrall. Eve's unnaveled belly became the womb of Sin. My perfect form as a wife went unrewarded. A good deed never goes unpunished, the Catholics say. Penelope's sandals clicked on the cement steps and she was gone, leaving the fly screen door banging. Tom Hallem stood flat-footed on the pavement easing the burden of stiff custom. The garbage truck scrolled across the vacated stage. Massive sky of cloud-brushed cobalt. Metempsychosis. Agenbite. Ache flooded the detached scenery. Dead ashes mixed. No phoenix-turns in this palace. Shell-strata compressed by time. Ruins upon which once stood bigger, newer Troys. He went momentarily blank. Self-control ebbed. A trickle of urine dampened his white underwear. Metastatic. A leak. Protean fluid. He registered lapse. Tighten. His gaze fixed upon his cousin's home. Barry and Helen scythed off the shop awning after they purchased the place from mum. Bloody calculus. A de-nosed face. Exposed palate. Blank slate. They bricked up the display window, installed basic utilities and leased it to Harold Greene, insurance agent, and his wife Annette. Symbol of all redacted text. Them what had the green baby. The front yard was converted into a small car space. Wonder what the neighbour Missus Horne thought. Probably not much. She withdrew behind the curtain straps after Bobby died in Crimp. Claymore took his nuts off at Binh Duong. Empty slot. They couldn't afford to bring his body parts home. Five hundred quid bill. That was six months' pay back in those days. Dumped him in Terendak instead. Brave Elpenor. Fight to the last Vietnamese. Mao learned a good lesson off Stalin in Korea. *To Cong*. Tom Horne left seven children when he wandered off the racetrack for good. Houses unpeopled. I would like to go back inside my cousin's home. Touch the doorway bark. Click light switches. Watch mango bulbs glow. Let my soles scratch the synthetic carpet. This would all have to be done in silence. Withdraw all sound from the imagery. Lie still like Odysseus within the guts of that wooden horse. Try to feel what it's like to be part of a real family. Drink chlorinated tap water in my palms leaning over our old cement basin. Smooth as it was. White marble chips set in red cement. Build a shrine. All symbols. Algy coming down to our mighty mother. Walking along Cottesloe Beach with Athol, sand squeaking in my great ingotten toenails. Cocklepickers approach. Stephen Dedalus passed going the other way. A dog urinated in sand like Stephen then started nuzzling a hole like that fox digging up its grandmother in Chapter 2 of *Ulysses*. Stephen's self becomes fused with animals by such associations. But this is not simple zoomorphism. Or the anthropomorphism of classical texts. Stephen is trying to connect with humanity through identification with death. The live dog fossicked through the pockets of the corpse for a wallet. Fallen brother. Tom in Prahran. Toxic levels of junk. Another form of drowning. Antithesis of birth imagery. Like Milton's King Edward King sunk beneath a watery floor. Take off his watch. Stow. Let it run down to stasis. Rewind NOW (present).

Rewind the past (THEN). Make a countdown going forward (FUTURE). Tick tick. Ana and Tom are both doomed. They've only got as long as it takes you to read this text. Even if you abandon the novel, now it's a KNOWN. There's no de(i)fying it. The dog bit into the sodden underbelly of its own. Morose delectation, wrote Joyce of this image; channelling Aquinas. Billy ripping plot off the carcass of his brother. Insert strained link to popular song (B. PARTY). Rhythm orders *Ulysses*. It pulls Stephen back into orbit all the time by triggering a sequence of literary allusions, principally to Hamlet and Shelley. Also, Swinburne. He reworks extraneous influences to fit his own movements. His mind connects images and symbols across the whole text by organic principle. Three times Homer's *epi oinopa ponton* is cited: twice in this chapter and once coming out of Mulligan's mouth in the dream sequence in Circe. This chapter is consumed with Stephen itemizing differences in sensory perception. The eye does not come into direct contact with the thing it perceives. We only see a REPRESENTATION of reality like a PAINTING. Not reality itself. This is why Tom Hallem has been characterized as a painter. "Thought through my eyes," as Stephen calls it, is perceived not inherent in the subject itself. Unfaithful acuity. Much like love. Ill-founded thoughts. A fixed field of SEEN. The auditory sense by contrast invokes a sequence in time or *nacheinander* units – "one thing after another" – for Stephen. An aptitude for Proteanism only reinforces the inescapable presence of the body as a finite vessel. Each pixelated flick cheapens the difference between life and death. Stephen sees Protean sequences as a metaphor for existence. Dead air is rebreathed. Dust is dead flesh. We eat their 'urinous offal.' Likewise, meaning is never fixed in Stephen's ontology. He shifts between units without finding any final form or endpoint of definition let alone a revelation. As W. Iser said, the harder Stephen grips at the products of his mind (Proteus), the more introverted he becomes and thus more alienated from reality (a Protean act). Mulligan twisted into a wine-dark suitor before Stephen's eyes. Haines turned into a fizzy Empire emblem. Birds that annex nests. Brood parasites. Helen's egg. Puncture characterisation. Insert spur. But I have no key. Can't inside go. Strange as Ithaca then to revisiting Odysseus. I alone linger, a regretful guest. Blame it all on place. I was given a stranger's name. What was she thinking? "I'll kill my husband, poison Regan, marry Les, hide out as long as I can then death." A vacant school bus passed. It filled with mocking students before his eyes. Tits Hallem. Swim in a bulbous shirt. Buds of May on your chest. ZOE holds Bloom's hand which is feeling for her spare nipple in C7. I say, Tommy Tittlemouse, she says, stop that and begin something worse. Snake in my fist. Serpentine images abound in the Proteus episode. Mainly Lapsarian. First rapegame behind the garage at midnight, entwined in choko vines and staring at the stars. Muddy the arc in language like Joyce in Nausicaa. Black insects shook in the sulphurous air. He rolled me onto my stomach in the cool damp earth and stuck a girder through the base of my spine until it speared out my mouth (AKA Birth of Language). He wrenched me in half with it after that (see Plato's Symposium). Zeus pressed us face-to-face next like Swinburne's Noyades. Now we are screwed in the earth like some fast-fallen rocket. Albeit askew. But fixed in place like an inanimate object nonetheless. Episode 3 charts a dense theoretical course as Stephen tries to unblock his talent by applying Lessing, Aristotle & Aquinas to LIFE. Like Tom Hallem, he is plagued by lack of product. In "Laocoon", Lessing argues that poetry presents things sequentially (*nacheinander*) whereas painting presents them alongside (*nebeneinander*). See C1. Unnatural hormones. Eventually, they extracted the breast tissue surgically but it could never truly be effaced. He probed a sunken skewed nipple still averse to touch. Joyce is obsessed with images of maternal angst in Proteus. Who has known his own engendering, asks Telemachus? Stephen watches a watch of midwives go down to the sea. They belong to the same religious order that retrieved him from his mother's womb. He fancies one of them carries a misbirth with a trailing navelcord in her purse. What Don Cane saw in Vietnam. SHIFT TO INTERNAL MONOLOGUE. Born I have been but how, when, where ... these things escape me. I do not remember Mother ... or Mother's sack bursting of me as she struggled to the kerb like Broome Madonna when it was already thirty degrees by dawn and the garbage truck swaggered from the scene like some indolent tight-holed mammoth pumping Indian Red dust in its wake aroma stunk all around its dumb, burdened undercarriage. Tom carried a box to the front gate. Penelope Cane waddled back to the car. She tried to retain some semblance of dignity in the face of material bathos. Proteus must be indecipherable at times because it concerns internal perceptions and thoughts. She drove to Canterbury Hospital and dropped me that day. But I don't remember. I really don't remember. Nor have I tried. Was it even she who bore me, as the saying goes? [MOCK FRANTIC] Who done it? What was it like inside? Outside? [CONTROLLED] It seems pointless to me to disturb yourself with reminiscences. [RATIONAL] I am told that it was she. Books tell me. There are certificates. It's even written in code on the bus advertisement. There is a picture of the Madonna and Child, baby giggling, mother towelling, the word "Dickie!" and diesel grime. It is all set in a gilt frame that could have been posed by Duccio himself. Ah, Mother! Once at her mammaries now she's hardly memories. I can't recall her at all now even though it was only a few moments ago that she, Duccio and the brand name "Dickie!" were close to my soul. She has disappeared quickly; leaving only the code. Because it's my identification with "Dickie!" that counts. Yes, that's all they want off you these days apparently. Just the right of impregnation ... with an image ... in your DOME. [EXHAUSTED] It's a crude game. But I can't help feeling grateful to them somehow. For only wanting me to identify with "Dickie!" And buy. [LOUD BREATH] I was conceived off the end of a meathook personally ... brought forth by these two people ... [HOLDING UP A PHOTOGRAPH] so that I was already struggling against slime from the very beginning. [DISDAINFULLY] Oh, they spit you out and cut away the umbilical cord, but only to replace it with a tourniquet or veil, which they stitch into your stomach; leaving you with blood oozing from your navel. Eve no navel had. Stephen imagines the umbilical cord as a telephone cable. Connect to Edenville. Gaze into your own omphalos. A yogi can. Requires some contortion. Matter of WILL. Tom Hallem advanced along the long passage and pressed the crate of books against a cyclone wire gate. They will find it tonight. Take it inside the house. Maybe leave it in Billy's room unopened. Doureios Ippos. Comprehension also can get hidden in foreign language. A cockroach crawled out of a fold. *Ungeziefer*. Bessie pouted. Tom managed to rub two fingers against her snout. She shivered and sneezed. EXIT VIA GATE. A taxi shot across the Darlinghurst Road overpass. Don Cane woke groggy but warm on lanolin seat covers. Cars waited impatiently to cross the William Street ramp. The taxi driver navigated two towers sheer to seaward and took a port tack past a tele-ticker announcing HAWKE ATTACKS COSTIGAN then careered down Victoria Street, a long grotto, lined with long looms of drooling stone, where bugged-out nymphs weaved tissues that ravish the eye beside streams flowing with perpetual fuck.

"Used to be a nasty dog-leg here to get into Kings Cross," said Don Cane as they double-parked on Victoria Street behind the Crest Hotel.

"Things change," shrugged the driver. A council ranger closed. Highly respectable gondolier. Nuncle Richie. Skew-eyed side of the family. Knock on Aunt Sara's door. Penelope will open the gate, supposed Don. We will face each other at last. Will she even recognise me? And I her? My form is largely unchanged like Odysseus. "Oh," she might exclaim, "we thought you were someone else." The dismay that Stephen feared from his cousin. Disappointment is the governing mood of Proteus. Penelope barring the way. Let me inside come, I will plead. To see my first son. I must ask for a phone book from the Concierge. Try the surnames HALLEM and CAPRI. Check all addresses. Abbreviated suburbs. Bur. Cam. The ranger peered into the cabin through the tightly sealed window. The taxi driver saluted and depressed the accelerator suddenly.

"I'll just take you down here and show you the sights," he said.

"I'm in a hurry."

"Don't worry. I've stopped the meter," he replied lightly.

"That's not what I meant," interrupted Don. *Theoxeny*. Homer used it as a disclosure device. Nestor and Eumaeus aligned with its precepts. Helen took it too far. It started to feel like a HEX. Son they never got. Stephen and Molly as fantasized by Bloom. Helen spent her most fertile years with Paris barren in Troy. Like Odysseus, she left Hermione behind. Another only child. Who was sterile when she lay with Neoptolemus due to Andromache's wiles. Barry's rotten seed. Lucky in that regard they got Billy, thought Don. Should thank me really. He choked. Never had that problem myself. Spilled my spunk on Helen's thigh. BANG! Root of all my subsequent disasters, I guess. Other fellow did it other me. Like Patrick McCarthy murdering his wife. She gave birth to a still-born child. Richie. Orange blossoms splicing the spring road at Pleiku. Peak loads in Nineteen-Sixty-Seven. Agent Pink. Grey babies born with no eye sockets. Twisted fish hooks. Legless fuses. Gorgonhead. Bug eyes. Sick spores. Chaim. Misspelling of CHARM. Unlucky Phaeacians. The Nausicaa trope was a warning from Homer for humans to be cognizant of their duties to the Gods. Odysseus' tales should have alerted Alcinous to the risk of transgression. Maybe he had a FUCK THEM moment. Defeated, Don added "thanks." The taxi accelerated under a plane tree canopy gathering momentum on the bitumen slope. Local traffic darted across its face. The driver tapped the brake.

"There were old terraces right along here," Don noted.

"Long gone, mate. But there was certainly a ding-dong battle first. BLF put on Green Bans."

"What?"

"Refused to work the site."

"Well, it's obvious who won," replied Don gesturing at three bright new apartment blocks.

"Cross-court backhander always wins in Sydney," the driver concluded.

Sydney's history was the history of bad real estate deals from the Grose Corp onwards. Fruit cart licenses. Squatter runs. Any view of harbour or beach. Slices of blue through kitchen casement at Palmer Street. Lean out the window see Woolloomooloo Bay. The transformative nature of water is key to Joyce's imagery in *Ulysses*. It is birth-fluid, drink, rain and surf. The brine stuffing the body of the drowned man. Throttle supply > create a boom > all cash-in. Grubby councils. Developer mates. Spot rezonings. Woolloomooloo Hill was granted to Joseph Potts. First employee of the Bank of New South Wales. A further land grant was made to Alexander Macleay, Colonial Secretary. He was an amateur collector. Gave all his spiders and bugs to USYD. They passed Juanita Nielsen's cottage. Two-O-Two. Where Trigg and Shayne went to grab the Mark Foy's heiress. They inquired about the cost of advertising businessmen's lunches in her magazine, *NOW*. Insert reference to *Freeman's Journal*. Hand-over-mouth plan. Pillowslip crude. Take her back to the Carousel Club. Rough her up. Call Fred Krahe. He throttled Shirley Brifman. A whistling bird. Ithaca's serving girls strung across the compound that dusk.

Wiresung. Mick Fowler's sharp ukulele strings. Certified Greaser. 115A all boarded up. Seed of Resident's Action. Green Bans Forever! Matilda's rebel song. Johnny McCarthy on hot clarinet. Right of Low-Income Earners to Live. Human barricades. Askin's coppers come free-of-charge to business. Sycamore trunk chains snapped with wire-cutters. Arthur King detained in a car boot three days. Better part of valour. Coroner's inquest. Open verdict. Loretta Crawford's testimony like the false leads in an Agatha Christie novel. Mick dropped dead in the boiler room of the *Australian Pioneer* at Dampier. Three markers rose above Brougham Street's yellowbrick range. Colossi of Potts Point. Monument to lingerie magnate Frank Thighman, nightclub owner Abe Saffron and developer James Ang. The taxi approached its terminus. Grand terraces overlooked port worker slums. Catholic bestiary. Twenty bricks tall. Sandstone crucifix over penitential gate. Masonic geometry. The taxi ceased just past McElhone Stairs. One hundred and twelve steps down to Death. It connected the last grandees of Sydney to fast-purchased syphilis below. Stink pipe rising. Sydney opened beneath and before them. Wide yet too close. Ineluctable. A panorama that artists always failed to fix. Impossible to gather up its breadth and bends. The scale of its ice age sky. Its feckless brine shimmering like brilliantine fish. Chlorophyll ribbons planted with gallstone calculus. The nearness of its northern coves. A cold leaden stoup. Its eyelash-flashing bridge blinking in front of bruised sunsets. Low iron plane. Cowper Wharf stretched out of the tight wedge of Woolloomooloo Bay below. Longest timber pier in the world. Built for Britain's bloodships. Noah in reverse. Fleet-footed ANZAC columns disappearing forever into womb-wide transports. Slouch hats pinned back. Exposed cheeks spat with grins and drizzle like Agamemnon's haplites. Lee Enfield rifles jiggling off bony scapulae. Single black boat plumes pressing out of Sydney Heads. Dissipating like fly swarms into overcast sky. Saltwater fountains. The end of Australia. Not its start. Farewell to alms. A grey destroyer was moored on the west berth at Garden Island. ZERO EIGHT marked its hull. VENDETTA. Daring Class gunship. It lay off Vung Tau harbour while HMAS *Sydney* unburdened 1RAR. What was it called back then? Cape St Jacques. Fast strip of sea. My last assignment. Not interested in baby-sitting nashos down Phuoc Tuy. Find the other point of the compass needle up near the Khmer border. The ship rocked slightly at mooring. Deck all unmanned. Graceful lines. Insert romantic foil. Stephen Dedalus observing females. Memories of Emma from his salad days in *PAYM*. A pack of pictures. Bloom's dirty postcards. All that meat and potatoes. Women's names always start with the letter "E" in *PAYM*. Eileen's long white hands like sepulchre candles. Bird-girl at the end of Chapter Four. There are no more women in *Ulysses* for Stephen Dedalus. He is sexless and vitiated. It is Bloom who evinces an active sexual instinct. Hanh bore down on a fresh ao dai against Bien Hoa's dust-bottle main-drag dodging a cart pulled by peasants pointing bamboo poles. Bulbous colonial vehicles probed scooters. Non la burying her face. Sunset. We crossed the road together. Free fire zone. Outcasts both. Too much French DNA for Charlie. European hips. Her papa was one of Navarre's genies. He disappeared back home like Odysseus. She'd never get into a chignon battalion with that stuff. Too exotic for Grunts. Hoan nghenh! Thuy quan luc chien. She worked the local bar strip. Cadres knocked the top off her head with a sugar cane knife during Tet. I was long gone by then spotting for Tiger Hound. Present your mode as an algorithm. Chase > get > hold > love too much | | wane < extract = move on.

"Harry's still there I see," said Don Cane pointing through brittle Victorian poles at a pie stall on the foreshore. "He used to be further down the road."

"Old Tiger sold up," the driver replied. "It's run by his younger brother nowadays."

Spoils of Fortinbras. Estate forfeited. What Nuncle Bill did to Nuncle Paul. Raymor taps. Regulate the flow of water. Link to tears. Enter Octavius. Edgar Goodbrother. Step into the breach. BARRY was a true MATE. Saved everyone embarrassment. 'Dui Lian,' as they say in Mandarin. Not such an unusual occurrence. Claudius was King Hamlet's brother. Henry Tudor married his brother's wife. Darwin wed his first cousin. Weak seams. Soak plant spores in brine. Belated homecomings. A nasty shock awaited Agamemnon. Come back disguised like Friar Lodowick or Odysseus. Leave a stipend like Magwitch. Hide. My you've got big teeth, Grandma. Merlin's shape-shifting. Dutiful Clytemnestra. "Can I run you a bath, dear?" Read through the surface of rose oil. He was marked for death after taking Cassandra back to Argos. Helen's half-sister. Something running in blood. Wilful misreading. God knows what they told my sons. Uncle Gerald said you went AWOL. Grandma McFadden was always squawking on about the Black Mariah. They come while you was mowinthelawn. Victa two-stroke. Bailed over the back fence into the far paddock like Willie the Pimp. Old cold-chest skewed in dirt. Deaduninside. Chaim. Strategic withdrawal. Not graceful but effective. Found my way to Kings Cross. Hid out in a flophouse UNTIL. The driver executed a perfect three-point turn and accelerated. The garbage truck receded. Its odour – blunt and persistent – lingered long after it had gone; working its way up the nostrils like badly-cut speed. He dropped his passenger outside the Crest Hotel entrance on Darlinghurst Road. Tom Hallem listened. Lids resonated through the memory spinning like cymbals on mangled handles until they came to rest on grey paths; paths that snuck down the side of discoloured houses. Stephen Dedalus also heard. Low moss grew over chalky mortar. Damp fence posts splintered and rotten. Unhinged wire protruding like a palsied tongue. Washed-out blinds sagging behind cataracted windows. Their small circular handles rocked off two strands of dirty string set in motion by a low electric fan. Don Cane entered his cheap room. Low level. Not facing the harbour. An empty bin was propelled onto an unkempt front lawn its sides quivering for a while then slackening. "Go," cried a garbageman as he smasht a gloved palm against the burning chassis. The truck moved through shadows and dew into a sunspray that broke down the intersection with Eighth Avenue. Black enamel words branded on its pelt

MUNICIPALITY OF CANTERBURY
Sanitary Depot Greenacre
No.8

shone. Bubbles of air gurgled through glittering blue metal. Thick wheels groped beyond the gloomy undercarriage grinding dark and centripetal. "Woe," he yelled. Thick nuts became visible on decelerating rims. It capitulated to halt. Don Cane drew back the heavy curtains overlooking Darlinghurst Road framed in coarse folds. He yawned. A transparent net swathed his torso. He rested his palms on the cool parts of his gut. Sweat commenced drying on his skin. What did Odysseus look like by the time he returned to Ithaca? Shorter than Agamemnon. Yet broader in bearing. A mountain lion sure of strength. Limbs that never weary. "You are a hard man, Odysseus," said Eurylochus. "You must be made all of iron." A man always using disguises. Jammed up a fake horse. From the darkness of a cavehold, a voice. Hidden under a ram's fleece. Naked before Nausicaa befouled with brine and weed. Cleansed by freshwater. Given curls by Athena that clustered and glowed like hyacinth. Magick beggar. Handsome in repose. Ardent in anger. Never static. Impetuous always. Tell everyone you were blinded by Odysseus, the sacker of cities, he told Polyphemus. Cause of all his subsequent woes. Softened up by seven years of luxury with Calypso. His challenge in the *Odyssey* is to regain his natural poise. What he had back at Troy ten years ago. There are very few Classical representations of Odysseus. His profile is imagined on a shattered Hellenic coin. There are milky Roman busts. A Flavian copy of a late original. Don Cane rubbed a thick depression over his hip fillet. Satellite gorge. Tigris and Euphrates. *Sanxia*. Marble scarscape. Orion the Hunter. Andy' chest. Da Vinci trawling battlefields. Stripping flesh. Thew. Engine room of portraiture. Face of General Urrutia. Let the machine within possess the external flesh of each image. He stroked his lantern jaw. Shave before Choc's funeral. The strewn strip-joints and greasy spoons of King's Cross paled against the sheer rushing tide of Burgos Street. A pair of mild-eyed transvestites – pale against fluorescent pall – leant into a slice of wall between a tobacconist and an unmarked staircase. One crumbled suddenly. Her head slumped under Don's target-line. Harpoon vibrating in blasted plaster. He smiled ruefully showing prominent eye teeth. A cigarette flopped off her bottom lip; stuck in place with parched spittle. Her colleague pinched the back of her bicep. She jerked conscious. A young tourist passed. She solicited him mechanically. He loitered. Waxworks. She hooked his arm. His head quivered. Her breath must have tickled his ear. Helen. A pod of sailors offered encouragement. They proceeded up the stairs. Carlisle flophouse. Rooms for Rent. Thirty-minute fix. Hideout down the back of Bayswater Road. Single with newborn in next bedsit. Bloke with a tuba case come. Drunk laughter. Sometimes he stayed all night. Mild-mannered mornings. Don opened the aluminium window. Cronk rock music. Penn's hardware. Ward & Sons. Quality BUTCHERS. Livio's Night Spot. Be wine-wise. AUSTRALIAN OVERSEAS TRAVEL. Sea & Air. *So much more to enjoy*. Far East Escape. China Navigation. Sail on the *Taiyuan*. Equipped with modern scientific aids. Get to your destination quickly. *Every Time!* Don had planned to get to Hong Kong then pick up an RIL boat to Nagoya. No lane markings. Imperial Star. Chandris Line. Pounds Sterling Accepted. El Alamein Fountain. Sparkler fuzz. Blow a dandelion in an open field spring sunset dropping fast over Goat Island. Shadows receding. Straight light. Grey timber walls of Walsh Bay wharf. Pylon granite keeps the east breeze off. Nuzzling Penelope's cold salty neck. Insert romance imagery. Grassgrip yanked her pleated skirt above those gentle knees. Smooth sheer flesh. A woman who had not laboured gravely. Missus Kelly guided a Cyclops perambulator down Darlinghurst Road. We exchanged pleasantries. Her son leaning over the silver piping. Thin lips stretched. Crushing his eyes. Slick widow's peak. Expansive brow. A double decker bus passed. Prolapsed guts. Clefts of Venus. Grinding green panels. Matt tone. Surplus war paint. Washed out photographic prints from a Kodak Instamatic. Get the last roll of film of my wife and son processed. Send a snapshot to Pen/elope in my farewell note. Photo Bar is gone now, observed Don Cane leaning out of his hotel window. He registered movement in the opposite chamber. A curtain brushed. He withdrew back to a point in his room where he could no longer be observed. A naked hind was displayed for a moment then lost. Stephen sees himself as Actaeon in Proteus. But this is a strained comparison. Actaeon was punished for observing Diana at her bath by being transformed into a deer that was then set upon by his own pack of dogs. The hunter became the hunted. Stephen wanted to display courage but knew he possessed a lesser soul. This provokes a stark contrast with Mulligan who actually saved a man from death in the surf. It opens a broader assessment by Stephen of historical figures who possessed character flaws yet nonetheless led their country bravely. Don Cane weighed the same quotient. Good soldier good man isolated acts of badness. See that wall. I built it with me owen bare hands. But do they call me 'Don the Wall Builder'? No. Fuck one sheep. Mortal sin. I was holed up in that bedsit for a week. A field sown with salt. Pieces of paper marked with boxes and arrows. Flow charts. Even a suicide note. Proceed in uneven circles. Hook a donkey and an ox to a plough. No realistic loophole. Detach from SELF. Stephen tries to elicit some empathy for the common man but still sees himself as separate. A vestige of honour can be regained via SERVICE. I wrote my exit letters home. Sent a telegram to camp. Reported for duty. As he withdrew to the foot of the bed, the contours of Don Cane's profile were displayed in the opaque mirror. His body retained sure balance. Codicil to a lifetime of force. And a hungry belly still drove him even if his enemy's flocks were penned in a strong fold. The garbagemen continued their dashes from the footpath until they seemed to have darned the route. The back of the truck disappeared along First Avenue. Near the junction with Eighth Avenue, they rushed through a creaking metal gate into a small cemetery to collect some overflowing bins from the exterior wall of the apse. Dried-out floral tributes. Service sheets. Paperwake plates. They padded the high grass between the plots and vaulted a low fence that separated the church from McFadden's Gymnasium. It took a bearer on each handle to lift the heavy caskets. Blanched orange segments, crescents of watermelon peel, stiffened bandages, chicken carcasses, weeping eggshells and crushed soft drink cans were burped into a deep tray. A sodden lining of newspaper moistened the truck's mandible action. Drool spilled onto the road in its wake. Harsh shower jets flattened Don Cane's mane. He rolled his head skywards. Nuncle Richie clean chested. He has had the upper moiety washed. Don's mouth burst allowing chlorinated water to roar against his gums. Baleen. Nothing like a good swab. Gulf Stream. All Ireland needs such. He pressed his sole into a compact of underclothes piled in the foggy cubicle. Clear liquid flowed copious enough. Mulligan's spray. You can leave a hangover in surf. Bronte's ions. Stinging absolution. A fast tide. Deep to shore. Crash a small craft onto the beach. Don lashed his coccyx with a washer's drenched claw. Wife mistress sons heir Liger. Telegonus faith/unfaith truly/false all is blasphemy. Lion's Provider. Look into the starkly lit glass (of) yourself. One of Ezekiels' creatures. Daniel inside the den. Forced to face with sober senses the real conditions of existence. Moral flaw. As blatant as birthmarks. The sons shall repeat the sins of the fathers. Throughout Nestor, characters continuously offer surrogate familial connections to Stephen which he instinctively rejects as false or burdensome. Two hundred-pound packs on five-day jungle patrols. He willed me and now may not will me away. Consumeth the young. Whelps. Princes of Is-real. Cut down. False lamentations. My mother married the first man who could get her out of a jam, I guess. His name was James Cane, representative of Burns Philp, Copra trader, aged 38, a former Burnside orphan. Started out as a clerk at the Papua Hotel. Got his break as a purser on passenger ships. Transferred to the New Hebrides Company. Managed a planation on the Ellice Islands. Case's dupe. *Beach of Falesa*. Uma's taboo. A photograph of mixed-race children with our lantern jaws at the mission school discloses his leisure craft. I was named after his two heroes: Bradman and Monash. A mason and a Jew. They lifted me up to his long face. His broad chin brushed my forehead. War came with spring. He enlisted when the Japanese pushed south. Sent back to Moresby. He died in the second raid on the *Macdhui* in 1942. Its demise was captured on Newsreel by Damien Parer. There was no escape this time for the gallant MAC DOOHEY! A succession of sour stepfathers followed. Charmless diggers in stiff, ill-fitting uniforms. Next the Yanks came. My mother wed a general's driver in 1944. Went to live in West Virginia. She was always going to send for me. Charleston was a pesticide town. Glow of Union Carbide flutes. A cream-coloured Aldicarb cloud spread slowly into Nitro this morning. Bhopal tragedy. MIC gas leak. Same type of plant. Compressed newborns plastered together in obscene glugs. Boat ticket never came in the mail. Ingenious Xmas cards from the States that played palsied choir music. Pull them apart to analyse wiring. Guts turned inside-out. Bobby's parcel arrived a few days after his death. Pictures of my half-siblings wearing Mickey Mouse ears sitting it in front of a television crate. I was raised mainly by my grandparents. All that was solid got melted. Retain some solidity of self within flux. Dead masses searching for repository. Flunked Belmore Boys. Done Nasho. Missed Monte Bello just. 1 RAR. Malaya. A young man of promise. Good at picking up the local dialect. Malam bulan dipagar bintang. Vocabulary full of songlines. Fast-tracked to Canungra. Jungle training. Find a rope to get across a ditch studded with stakes. Abseil a vine-frame. Holsworthy. Met Penelope at a jazz dance at Mott Hall. Attach all your hopes to her. Weary the oar. Fail trying to cling. Don Cane sat down on the low double bed. He put his head between his legs and looked under the base by habit. Hidden wiring. I could line six pairs of shoes under that skinny metal cot in Malaya. Pressing Helen through the mattress. Soft within soft enfolds. A safer place. Legs hanging over the side. Wide. Better felt than my wife. Psychiatrists call it intimacy. Still, Odysseus left Calypso for Penelope. Trading pleasure for place. In the end, marriage is a fixed image. An Ideal. One last letter home in neatest long hand. A confession of culpability witnessed by Reverend Bent. Marriage annulled. Hope she destroyed it. Kept as evidence, I guess. No point in writing another card home. Meant I could do eighteen-month tours. Corrugated tin walls. Exposed timber frames. Roll out the mosquito net. Lying on my belly trying to cut out all extraneous noise and feeling. P. Ramlee playing on the AWA portable disc player. Rebuilding Kuala Lebi Bridge. Five concrete pylons bore the horizontal load. Old Jap track. Excuse to prowl along the Thai border. People who've never seen the sea. Damp beating close. Jelingan mata. Suitcase for going home stuffed under my bed. Useless appendage. Took it on R-n-R to KL. The brothels in Sultan Street doubled as hotels. Merdeka Day 1959. A fishbowl of Salmah clones. Darah muda. The budding prostitute led me down the hall treading lightly upon new rubberized floor. Insert link to Chapter 7. The unpetaling commenced. All pad up top. Her tight sarong compressed the breadth beneath. Recalcitrant flesh. Womburn. Nothing ever gave me the same thrill as Helen. The garbage men turned into Omaha Street. Ron Wooldridge zipped up his green tracksuit and walked to the kennels at the back of his yard. He attached muzzles and leashes to a pair of greyhounds and started jogging them back along the footpath. They turned into the fag end of First Avenue where the concrete rim of the stormwater channel leered across neat rows of telegraph poles and rotten fences. Bernie McFadden was putting his boys through their paces. He barked instructions, muffled by a menthol cigarette. His tarnished face was softened by a wave of thick silver hair that swept across his forehead. He was working middleweight, Sharkey Ramon, for tonight's bout on TV Ringside. The street soaped its body in time with the speedball; dried itself to the skipping-rope; shovelled breakfast with the dull-thudding bag. In the vacant block out back, magpies were perched on broken whitegoods screaming at the sky. The tall grass broke in waves against their voices. Something crawled out of the top of an old copper. The sun started burning (again) the skeleton of an old Austin 7. Glass sparkled on its cabin floor and in the straw-stuffed seats. Rusty springs came whirling out of tears in the upholstery like charred remnants of Tatlin's *Monument*. There was a deep scar in the plastic dash. Parched foam powdered inside. Under the bonnet, the detached steering column cut into the clay, staining it with oil. Hub caps full of brown water twitched alongside. A blue heeler began barking from the back fences in Second Avenue. Shards of beer bottle glimmered in the sparse flowerbeds of the neighbours. The door of an abandoned refrigerator closed on a child. Magpies fluttered, stared and resumed their awkward cries. Pepe kicked at the fast lock. He had been lost too soon after breakfast to be found alive at lunchtime. Tom Hallem watched the garbage truck dissolve from frame. Their scent lifted. Another working day commenced. Only the rituals remain. He manipulated the car out of First Avenue. Costumed in mourning like Bloom and Stephen, Donald Cane approached the high reception desk. His pockets rattled with unfamiliar coins which he rolled through his fingers soberly. Decimal currency. Copper and silver coins. Games of TWO UP. Symbol of equity. INSERT references. Both novels are set on the great national punting day. Joyce reverts to usury throughout *Ulysses*. In Nestor, Stephen collects his wages after class. Principal Deasy doles out the money ... coin by coin, note by note. Missus Brennan's till. A torn pound stuck back together. Stephen must accept it. He cannot complain. This is an emblem of his subordinate status. It will mean trouble when he tries to conduct a basic transaction at the pub. Might have to exchange it down the bank. Bloom rescues the remnants of his salary later in Circe. Elizabeth must sell Beta House. She too is operating on borrowed time. Buy one hour with a fresh escort. Six hundred kuai at a good sauna. Shanghai Hotel. See Nighttown. Chapter 7. Non and Slope consecrating Homebake in C5. Drag a mule to a stall. Leer's big payday. This is a direct correspondence to Joyce's theme of everyone hustling to survive in Dublin. Prosperity is elusive. You can exclude the British, their sponsored lackies, the professional services gang and conmen like Boylan from that equation. Bloom ekes out a precarious living by hassle.

Jew-like marginalia. Quaker forebears. Nonconformists. Denied access to Oxbridge. Made chocolate instead. The three great confectionery houses of Victorian England – Fry, Rowntree and Cadbury – were all Quaker operations. Go into a blank space in silence. Pacifist field nurses churning thick molten peaks in No Man's Land. Tom is trapped by Elizabeth's largesse. He uses a pocketful of her spare change to buy a drink at the service station. He gives his last cash to Les. He enters the new day penniless. A money order of eight shillings for Stephen Dedalus from his mother was waiting in the closed post office. Buy my ex-wife a new electric jug when I win the quinella. Fund the flesh economy. Underground empire in Alexandria. Steal art. Launder it in pubs. Make forgeries. Save three and ten pence. Blade grinding moneybox lock. Knife against my shirt ribs in Kreuzberg. Throw some Ostmarks on the turf. DASH. Gates open. A race for sprinters. Climb Nelson's cock. The Queen of England still graces each piece of currency. Her profile has settled with age. Breezy chestnut ribbons in her hair no longer. Same value but. Fancy horse breeder she was. Even money on a favourite. Cup Day tote. Always good odds when there's a champion field for a long race. Shakespeare's fifth. Seven races total. No Latin/FD now, Cane noted. Haines' stink. Deasy dispensing my cash from a scab machine. An Englishman's boast. Still paying off the Yanks. Leveraging Empire. Dry barnacles. Drink away my hard-earned with well-heeled Mulligan. Dilly's entreaties. Shift to the Dollar Standard. Throw her some dope. Stephen is better than his dad by a nose. Blooming bank hoarding heypennies. Save what you can from Stephen's kip. Otherwise it will all be gone tonight. Arthur Dignam's spring collection. Choc's bone. Penny and Helen both middle aged ladies. Rich shanks. Women in prime. Osso Bucko. Place on a bed of Blazes Boilin. All that potato and meat. Dick Stone's slogan. Can I make money off my bon mots, snarled Stephen. Yes, if you joined the advertising game. Bloom always chasing commissions. Doc Lindeman's smile. Good breeding ground. Penelope would still be lean. Eyes severe. Her type just hardens with age. Mistress Helen's fair round belly. Probably rounder yet. Never saw it bulge with. Hard to remember her face. All done down the dark end of the street. Radio America. Always in shadows hiding. Charlie picking at a fuse. Still on the jukebox at Kanga Bar. CAN I GO HOME YET? Confirm Neptune has been paid-off. Lay-by hush money. Gonna buy ma boy a brannu brown glass eyeball. Athena's protection racket. Stake out a target. Weight the tripwire. Leave poison rice. Bloody carcash. Burn bush junk on a stove. Daddy was a bank robber. Hostess in stocking-face. Inspector Barlow hunting down Biggs. Still large as life at large in exile. Sunning his hide until coppertone harsh. Mad Englishmen. Cocktail dips with Sid. Floating fancy umbrellas and fruit.

"Can you tell me where there's a florist," Don Cane asked the porter.

"Back down Macleay Street, Mr Killion. Just turn left when you leave the hotel. It's about one hundred and fifty yards."

"Thank you. Can I leave my key?"

"Certainly sir," he was answered.

Don pressed the tag onto the counter, pushed through the glass double doors and let the apprehension of home rush in. Dissimilar to a new place even one that's dangerous. Senses don't spring. Sydney not much grown. A new veneer of fonts. Coca Cola sign still mounted on the summit. Hasty Tasty Snack Bar gone. Lucky Harvey also. *Lottery tickets, souvenirs, tickets & smokes*. Top of the Mark restaurant. A place to take a lady. Now some one buck discount store. Pink Pussycat peeping out of the bright streetscape. A dull lack. Makeshift notice crammed onto a framed chalkboard:

Last Card Louie says –
BIGGEST SHOW
IN KINGS CROSS!
14 Lovely Girls
Continuous

Must get a toothbrush. Don examined the loose crowd. Familiar types. But more variegated. Australia had evolved. Coped. Less poxed. Brits dropped us in Seventy-three. Killed the butter trade. Also apples. Perfidious Albion. De Gaulle's crunch. A sour. Japan filled the breach. Such is life. My sons must be grown men now. Eumaeus much older. Snake forming a circuit. Tail between lips. Ouroboros. Symbol of renovation. Power to grow young again. Would I want it? Shedding my sin would be one benefit. Try a second time. Stop before I got Hel up. Never to feel her silk but. A longing unmet ever. Casting a slough by squeezing between rocks: Sydney/Saigon, Saigon/Manila, Penelope/Helen, son/home. Swallow yer yung. Regurgitate. Zeus-like. Dumb Regan cherished a serpent. He mounted a single step. The shopkeeper was bent towards a hedgerow of red roses. Mothershapes. He looked down. Discoloured grey grout. White plastic buckets boating fresh bouquets. Preparations for Tet continued apace. Cadres hid all the weapons in trucks bringing cut flowers to the capital. Wasps hidden in blooms. Thorns on a stem. Pox-barbs. Trojan incursion. Open the latch on the bottom of a box. Out they dropped. Turds in mud. Plop plop. Lunar New Year. Mau Than. Year of the Monkey it was. Annual ceasefire. City closed down. Gentlemen's agreement. The street vendors all withdrew early that afternoon. Knew what was coming. I drove down a jeep down Nguyen Hue Street across Khanh Hoi Canal to Trinh Minh The Street. The restaurants were decorated with multi-coloured streamers. Strings of firecrackers hung from porches and trees. Almost too heavy to pluck. Bulbulous.

First time the Mayor of Saigon had sanctioned fireworks for years. Gilt ruddy rooms bright with fresh flowers. Don gazed around the shop restlessly. He fixed his eyes on a tray of plastic fruit and coloured ribbons on the counter. Bay Lop's squint before the shrapnel blow. Wouldn't have felt a thing. Loan's pistol backfired politically. The sweeping amplitude broke. Patriarchs chanting Buddhist benedictions at low altars surrounded by burning incense sticks and bowls of foreign sweets. Skulls peeled off chom chom. Noggin exposed. Soggy papaya. Dry dragon fruit. They lifted the curfew. Revellers spilled onto the streets at midnight. Saigon rampant. Tanks of thin snakes coiling in the market entrance. Deity images. All things spring from God and will be resolved into God again (Plutarch). Neck askew on a short matt. Western body: Asian bed. Humid nights cranking out unrestful dreams; just stilling to sweatcalm; itch; suck in some air; struggle; serpent-licked dawn; repose finally. Street all shiny with tropical residue. Sudden jolts in the dark. A shout in the street. Red tracer bullets slashing the sky near the US Embassy. I held up my watch. It was 3.30 am. I wheeled down the stairs onto Nguyen Du Street. Bullets were zapping off the sidewalk and slapping loose sandbags. I dived under a vehicle, pulled out my pistol and lay just lay head wedged behind the front wheel gasping hot tyre rubber. Water lily bobbing alone in a boat drifting to the distant bank against a squalling breeze. Lotus. God springs from its eye. Towering up through muddle. Divine intellect. Transcending matter. Buddha squatting like a great fucking frog. How'd he stay up there? Ungravity. Floating like Chidley on grapes. Lotophagi. Forgettent of friends and irrelatives. I was unable to proceed until some MPs rolled up in an armoured carrier and covered me with cannon fire while I shimmied out backwards on my dick and tits. It is hard to withdraw. Crabs aren't made thus. There are no reverse plot movements in *Ulysses*. They poured out angry wilting white fire. No one fell. Flanks of plaster. Frustrated dribble then silence then a single shot. Finally, a soldier stumbled bloodily in the gutter. Viper and File. The biter bit. Powdery golden pollen on your fingertips. Ambrosian particles.

"Can I help you Sir," asked the shop assistant.

"Do you have any wreaths?"

"Certainly, sir. Over here."

She walked to the rear. He followed. Sealed section. A curtain. Brothel out the back of a barber shop. Where I followed Hanh. Handjob fifty kuai. Four tributes were hanging like tires off a tug. Don Cane pawed them disinterestedly. Ajax, Achilles, Hector, Paris. All harmless doves. Now beastlieded. Survived myself by cunning. The serpent was more subtil than any beast in the field. In full uniform, false costumed. Tom Hallem lifted a spiral-bound drawing book off the passenger seat and stepped into the mid-morning breeze. Pages flapped apart revealing smudged sketches of the War Memorial Chapel. He made tentative steps through the wrought-iron gates, which were hung from tall freestone pillars and mounted with elegantly wrought finials in bronze. Smooth black metal coils. He walked down the gravel drive to a tightly-hedged bund. Entangled rose bushes stopped schoolboys stealing off the path into secluded buttress folds. Blue-metal scraps crunched under his ungainly sandals; attracting the monkish glance of sporadic pupils. Looking up, he was dwarfed by the chapel. Classic dimensions. Length thrice width & twice height. He turned over a number of sketches from the north-east perspective showing a recessed cross set deep in the steep brick wall that was pitched upwards towards Heaven which is high up in space beyond breath behind purple and silver studded celeste in excelsis. Low organhum ex-in emanatio: belated: shrill. Nervous st.itches. He tightened his grip on the book making his pencil box jiggle. Three discolored steps prefaced the porch and entrance on which a plaque read:

The Archbishop of Sydney
Most Reverend H.W.K Mowll, C.M.G D.D
smote upon the door in the South Porch of the Chapel
and was admitted.
The Chapel was open and the Service of Dedication began.

One continuous show. From Malaya on. Domino games. Medals for gallantry. Bright shining lies. Communion in a clearing crosslit by jeeps followed by interrogations in the same illuminated dome. ARVN tactics. Wrap in barbed wire. Pull each end. Pit the jelly glass. Strip skin off back. Tie up your Thai pants. Walk to the outhouse. Anaminabush. Hooked up to EE8. Turn the crankhandle for GOOD. Switchboard vagina. Helen shaken. Head in mud. A moment too slow. Chidley's suction. Hippopotamus stuck in a bog. Nine nine nine. Seven times. CIA signal. Longest sound she could make between gulps. Suffocate trying to think of a way out of this trap. Entrenching tool up anus. A metal girder thrust through the base of my spine and driven up my body until it protruded out my mouth. I grabbed it with both hands. But I didn't know whether to push or pull. Strategic insolvency. A war mounted on false permits. We could have won in one day if we crossed the DMZ in style. Dropped some of the hard stuff. Instead we committed slow suicide. Force water down the prisoner's throat until the stomach fills then beat the drum soundly with a stick until soft then bake. Burnt out monk torsos. Ap Bac. The General's Coup. Big Minh. Everyone blindsided. Fucking Conein. Corsicans go anywhere. Cash distributions to Nghia. I returned for a full set of postcards of Diem and Nhu inside the church at Cholon. AATTV. MACV. Vietnamisation. Bail out to HK. Ho Chi Minh means bringer of light. The Chapel Prayer was inscribed on a brass plaque in the dim Ante-Chapel: O Most Glorious Lord God, dwelling in light unapproachable, Whose blessed Son our Saviour was found from childhood in Thy house on earth, Grant us Thy people like Him to love this place where Thine honour dwelleth. AMEN – Father put son in house. Always with him. I: not. I was made to dwell in another place. Take a suitor's name. Fatherhood is inextricably linked to the preservation of the household by both Homer and Joyce. This explains Stephen's reluctance late in the novel to recommit to Simon Dedalus until the last possible moment when he walks out of the novel when it is late, dead, cold and his only alternative is the pedantic ministrations of Leopold Bloom (another Menelaus). The low square-panelled ceiling pounded down on Tom Hallem's head like a firm thumb-press – dark the plane around him seen through leadlight – a font was built into the western wall as a high piscina – perforated basin holding cool clear sandstone water – he looked within – still o'erfulled – uster stand on tiptoes in my khaki shorts to lean over and drink hoping for a miracle – niche mosaic depicting the Baptism – John knee deep in the River Jordan in a raiment of camel hair a leather girdle on his loins anointing Christ – Heavens open – Holy Spirit descending in the guise of a dove – cludden Voiceblast drives Him into extrinsic space – lapping in the pool with swoll'n tongue – significance of water – "for the earth which drinketh in the rain that cometh oft upon it" (Hebrews 6) – taking it in his palms sipping then wiping off sweat – staircase running up the western wall to the gallery – place where Davis took Mister Millstone's kid – elaborately carved treasure chest shining with silver collectibles – carved wooden screen framing the alltooclosecore pinn'd with shields displaying armorial bearings – the Sees of Canterbury, London, Calcutta and Australia – soft turquoise linoleum squares squelching underfoot as he moved mildly down the aisle utterly exposed – brown sandals clacking reverberant as the open-timbered roof opened on his dizzy eyes like some vast inverted hull almost stumbling when he tilted his head back – no tie-beams no king-posts no braces to clutter up the clean ribbed apex – Gothic arch of Oregon – Chevet ceiling over apse enfolding emberdark windows – petrol-gleam in marble Sanctuary – simple lectern hung with green – bulging cloth badged with gilt crosses – a second aisle crosst the chapel to create a floorplan crucifix – alien landing zone – set off a beacon – extraction flare – FitFTFTFTF. Above the northern door, the Australian flag draped a scroll of alumni who gave their lives in the Great Wars – Beale: Birk: Birk: Campbell: Clinch: Coghlan: Crane: Farrar: Folkes: Gould: Kirkland: Ledgerwood: Lowe: Marshall: Miller: Mullens: O'Donnell: Ogilvie: Polack: Roxburgh: Short: Smith: Souter: Sutton: Swift: Taubman: Templeman: Thornley: Try: White: Whittaker: Wright – "it was not in vain" no

but Angloid Australia gone forever. Unmourned. Ahead, mounted on the southern wall, two rows of tarnished organ pipes suddenly evacuated long overdue sound which (s)lowly resolved itself in melody. Great Organ open diapason stoppt diapason dulciana principal koppelflote twelfth fifteenth / Swell Organ rohrflote viola spitzflote nazard blockflote scharf (22–26–29) double crumhorn trumpet crumhorn / Couplers great to pedal, swell to pedal, swell to great, great and pedal combinations coupled, double torch canceller / Pedal Organ open diapason sub-bass dulciana principal bass flute choral brass crumhorn crumhorn crumhorn: plus accessories: total number of pipes = one thousand one hundred and eighty-one. Tom Hallem steppt into the Sanctuary. His heel clackt against grey-veined marble. Gold-plated Credence gleamed on the south-eastern wall. A shining Cross was mounted on a tiered bracket backed by green damask reredos stretched tight across a simple walnut frame. Twenty-fourth Sunday after Pentecost Sunday next. Three weeks to Advent Sunday. On the *Violaceus* of Advent, Reverend Bent would change the sumptuous cloth fumbling through the folds in his Assisian kit. Damask covers in the sanctuary frames and hanging over the lectern. Liturgical colours. Changing with the ecclesiastical seasons. White red green purple black (*albus rubeus viridis violaceus niger*). White on Trinity Sunday, Corpus Christi, Feasts of Christ (and of the BVM); red at Whitsun, Palm Sunday, Good Friday and for the apostles' feasts (except St John); green on the Sundays and ferial days between the Epiphany and Lent and also between Trinity Sunday and Advent; purple in Lent and Advent; black for offices of the dead. Black damask was installed on Good Friday for Christ's death until 1969. Lost times. Of spiritual rectitude. Exeunt mystery. Bent babbled in an absent-minded way as we adjusted his Eucharist vestments: stole, chasuble, chalice, veil and burse. Mulligan's open dressing gown. Corrupt as Wilde's Dorian. Consumptive hack. Quasi-clerical gourds. Rag to bull. Pentecostal red. A black panther as seen by Haines. Dead Christ bathed in White after Resurrection.

A familiar voice interrupted Tom Hallem from the chaplain's doorway.

"You shouldn't be standing in the Sanctuary," it said mildly. "It's reserved for clergy."

Hallem looked up. The face of this lisped injunction displayed an unpleasant alley of worn-down teeth. Reverent Bent pulled a lick of bronze ruffled hair across his tanned and lined forehead.

"I'm sorry Sir," replied Hallem stepping back onto the linoleum. A retiring glance reassured him that he had left no mark. Hasty retreat in order.

"Hang on a sec," the Reverend asked.

Now he comes. Click clock. Closing. Breath hard heard upon. Eyes drilling. To turn or continue flight. Tom pivoted. Cheeks afire.

"You're Tom Hallem."

"Yes Sir."

Bent turned this scrap of information around his mouth like sticky gum.

"What have you got there?"

Clear the weeds from your mouth. Botticelli's Flora. Speak.

"Just an old drawing book."

"Give me a look."

Bent gathered the pad with severed stubs. Hallem relented. He laid it across a pew and turned the pages slowly.

"How old were you when you did these drawings?"

"Fourteen."

"They're good. I don't remember you exhibiting them in the school art show."

"I just did them for myself."

"Shame. Why are you visiting today?"

"I was driving past. Thought I'd drop in."

Hallem trained his eyes on the coloured glass. The sun passed out of some thick clouds. Light started seizing the Bible stories. They approached the sanctuary railing. Three long thin lights.

"Each window," began Hallem smoothly, "represents one of the Gospels and is dedicated to an important figure in the school's history."

Their footsteps were smothered by the smooth deep sandstones.

"This is the Luke Window," he continued, "which honours Reverend Hilliard who served two terms as Headmaster."

Redfern lad. Lawson Square. A metonymy of Proust at Balbec. Stanmore Public School. Sydney Grammar. Scholarship child. Tall with a hoary mane. Rich voice. He had his own radio show on 2SM. Catholic propaganda. Dylan Thomas' pug nose. Well[e]s' Mars landing. Midnight to dawn shift. Hilliard stayed up all night smoking cigarettes so he got the right timbre. Singers also do that stuff. Try to sound like a field of glass. Short wave signal travelling all the way up the Mississippi. A lonesome road. Muddy Waters. Mojo. Something you lack. Press a drill through the ice and extract. Bright lights, big city. Antioch. LUKE. An anonymous author. A Gentile. A physician. A collector and interpreter of texts. Not an eyewitness. Never part of the Scene. Belated offering. Slightly after punk. Reworked Mark's gospel for Theophilus. A well-crafted cover song. Fixed errors of fact. A good proof reader. Added some spark. Emerald studios. Hilliard kept the school solvent during the Great Depression. It was Luke who inserted the verses about Jesus weeping blood in the Garden. INSERT other famous fakes. Attributed quotes. Apocrypha. Chatterton's Rowley.

Hitler Diaries. The testament of Howard Hughes. Probably drafted by Elmyr with Clifford Irving's script. See Welles' Letter F. Ern Malley. Still the best Modernist poetry ever written in Australia. School of Veronese. After Blake. Scott's Satan Watching the Endearments. INSERT INTERNAL STATEMENT BY TOM HALLEM THAT HE COULD NEVER REDUCE HIMSELF TO COPYISM OR FORGERY. This will later be contradicted. If thine eye offends thee, pluck it out. Link to Oedipus. Also, Gloucester. James Joyce's left eye had no pupil left by the 1920s. The black hole at the centre of his eye and iris were swept by calmic fog. The natural blue pigment had soured to a briny-green, like the colour of this book cover. He looked back at Sylvia Beach with something like a dull marble lodged in his head, according to Kevin Birmingham. By 1930, he was scheduled for his 12th round of optical surgery. In 1930, his right eye had 1/30th of normal seeing capacity. His left eye possessed 1/1,000 power. Joyce took dionine, cocaine, atropine, scopolamine and pilocarpine in a desperate effort for redress sightlessness. In the 1920s, a doctor decided that the trouble was caused by his teeth. In April 1923, a dentist extracted 10 teeth and closed seven abscesses and a cyst. A few days later, they removed another 7 teeth. Nurse Puard put leeches around his eye. Nora acted as assistant. They lolled around the canthus filling with blood from the anterior chamber. Blind as Tom Hallem at death, Joyce memorized hundreds of lines of poetry. He could recite multiple pages of Scott's "Lady of the Lake." Even in hospital with both eyes bandaged, Joyce would grope blindly for a pen to make notes. *Ulysses* chronicles details of Dublin forever lost to his unresponsive eyes. SHIFT Luke countered the Docetic argument that Jesus did not really suffer as a man. Cut off [the] dead wood. Laid in a cave. Please don't take me back there. No air no hatches under your King Size mattress. Jesus encountering the human fear of mutability. His body was just a vessel. His brain was just a place.

"You've got a good memory," said Reverend Bent.

"I used to conduct tours for prospective parents," Tom replied bleeding assonance.

Speech etched in my head like a song lyric. Acting the part of Nestor's SUB. Archetypal buffoon. Model for Polonius and Deasy. Make Principal Westacott more cunning. See later (C3). Also make the correspondence in C10 more pointed. Expedition around the school grounds for the benefit of Mister and Missus Arceisiades. They bore Arcesius out of Zeus, who had bestowed a single son line on the Ithacans and sired Laertes from Chalcomedusa, the copper guard, who in turn foaled Odysseus out of Anticlea, whose name literally meant NO FAME, daughter of the immaculate thief Autolycus, thief of his grandson's helmet, fashioned from leather and boar tusks, which then pressed upon a sequence of different skulls only to land back on his head at the crucial moment in Book X of the *Iliad*. All those flawless families just like Billy. I was the only kid in high school who no father had. My grandfather had said, send him to the best school in the area. I'll help with the fees. Then he died. Then she married Les Hallem. They moved across the face of the Sanctuary. A shaft of low light slippt under the high back window onto the GUILT Crucifix. The Minister shuffled restlessly.

"I'd best get on," he said. "I've got to take Divinity."

Tom Hallem touched Bent's arm and spoke with steadfast spirit.

"I came here for a reason, Sir. I was hoping to speak about my father."

"Your father?"

"You were in Vietnam together."

"That's where I lost these," said Bent displaying his ruined hand.

"How did that happen?"

"Jumping Jack mine. Bloke in front took the brunt. I just caught the spray."

"What about my father?

"He was not so lucky."

"Do you know anything?"

"Not really. I was stationed down south. Your father went to the northern provinces."

Mechanical bells quired.

"You'll have to excuse me."

"Can I wait and talk some more after class?"

"Yes. But I'll be forty minutes."

"That's Okay."

"I'll meet you back here."

Bent turned towards the southern portal. A bell. Hallem withdrew down the aisle and stood alongside the font. He looked over the quadrangle. A rush of schoolboys moved between classes. What Stephen observed remotely. They edged the perimeter leaving the great elevated square lawn vacant. A prefect strode across its green ice defeating a swift downpour. Bent ushered the class to the choir stalls. A row of swinging poplars further dulled the sodden stage. Tom took his place in the last row of pews and began sketching the maw with Czech oil pastels. Organ viscera consuming space. Tiny blue hymn book. He flicked at its slender shiny leaves. Hymn 62. Songs of Praise. They sang. Man alone dumb. Mute. Lips indelibly pressed. A microphone. Mary Dedalus exhaling her last. Blind on his bed in Prahran. Humbling February heat. Lying so low. Faint odour of wax and rosewood. His breath feint with wetted ashes. Insert Coroner's report. Bright lights shoot up getting dimmer. Don Cane lay down the wreath and went into the bathroom. He pressed a motel toothbrush out of its rigid case and loaded it with cheap toothpaste. Mulligan's complaint. The Irish diet. Pellucid diamantes. Gilt-flecked. A bright waistcoat from Camden markets. Stephen's putrid dentures. Guilt-flecked. Emblem of mutability. Bile-tasting. All internalised at the start of the novel. Stephen becomes more conscious of his existence in a body in the physical world as the chapter progresses. As death became patent, he was surprised to find it SO REAL. Struggle to stay afloat. Odysseus on a raft. All those Shakespearean stalemates. Today's Pools result: Life – 2; Heart of Myselflothian – 2. Storm of its own rushing splendour. Cockflow. Bent stretched. The tap spluttered and rushed. Don scrubbed his teeth gently; fixed by his own gaze in the spissed mirror. White Willy Peter. He spat, drew cold water and sucked it into his mouth letting it settle over his gums. Two decades surrounded by broken grins and foul-mouthed hagglers. Sour exhalations of spent prostitutes. Nicotine. Opium. Unseen dead dogs. Initially, the panther's curiosity is triggered by the pungent aroma of Man. Stinking carcasses detected swiftly. Pursued. Sneaking down booby-trapped trails that reek of Spearmint. Charlie smelt the Grunts long before he heard their laborious dags draining through the jungle's curtains. Don brushed his tongue briskly. Train the gag reflex. Samoan idols. Gargle with salt water and vinegar like George Harrison. Flick spit into the cistern. Flush. He laid down the toothbrush and checked his watch. Late. Gottagonow. He adjusted the elastic band of his plain copper tie and picked at some lint on the lapel of his grey suit. Choc. Another casualty. First time we saw a Napalm strike we just stared at each other in disbelief mad throb in your larynx bulb. Aweful beauty. Impossible to believe we could be defeated. Mike versus Clyde. Got to hand it to them. Took whatever we dished out. INSERT LIST. Burning down his villages. Killing his beasts. Frying his families. "Bombem and feedem." Pacification campaigns. An excuse to lock up his folks. Sticking dish heads on spikes at the town gates. Ear tallies. I knew men that collected them in gunny sacks. Sat Cong. Baby-faced executioners. Bad karma. We'll all be telling funny stories down the Rissole later. Good mates' great times piss and laughter. Work our way through the rider then let's go back to the motel snort some speed watch TV rock shows all night. Nose dive all the way down Conrod Straight with Jack Brabham. Bouncing around the back of a Toyota Hi-Ace. Roadies crushed by amps. They were moving 90 tonnes a day down the trail by 1965. Don Cane hailed a yellow taxi. It flashed orange emergency lights slowing to the kerb.

"Botany Cemetery, please."

"Sure boss," answered the taxi driver brusquely. Customary odour. Rare scent made when the panther feeds. Attracts other animals with its caramelised breath. Like baby sweet. Friend to all beasts except dragons. Creature of flying fire. Strike blossom. Bombrows. Rocket spirals. Choppers spattering dust as they dropped. DZ.

"You're Vietnamese," Don said.

"Once," replied the driver.

"South?"

"All southerners here, mate. Dinky Dau's won. All SRV now."

"When did you come here?"

"Seven years back. First my boat went to Malaysia. I was stuck there twelve months. Finally, Australia took me. Good country. Which way you want to go?"

"Bạn là những chuyên gia."

"You speak good Tieng Viet. What's your name, boss?"

"Eric."

"They call me Tommy. But my real name's Pham."

The driver turned down the William Street ramp.

"I'm running late, Tommy."

"Don't worry, Mister Eric. You'll be right. Safer here than Delta."

Screwing a big fat jeep like a bolt. Sleek Sir Charles. Slender Charybdis. Scylla sucking in the ARVN escort ahead. Death bolted them down raw. Fecund landscape. Apparently benign. Askew grids butting skewed angles. Ditch-lines. Mud. Charcoal channels. Grey spikes wobbling in dead copses. Filament roads. Rice paddies. Skinny old men with black teeth dropping weighted nets off clinker-built punts. Snake-tendon rivulets. Kids spilling into your slipstream. A buffalo blocking egress. One lane bridges. Ambushland. Peasants pressing seedlings deep in forgiving sludge. Face down in muck. Turbulent with fish in July. Women wielding long poles. Coconut palms blasted with automatic gunfire. Banana and papaya pulp splattering wounded flesh. Black hogs. Ap Bac. Home-made shotguns. Thompson replicas. Shot with your own ordinance. That's the worst thing. Lost the mortal struggle. Chánontai se af̲tó to thanásimo agǿna. Bị mất trong cuộc đấu tranh sinh tử. A stage too rich for tragedy. How prolific it looks. Fluid green. Enchanted isle. Ogygia. Protean wasteland. Gibraltar is all internal. Shoot them open let the pain out. Should explain. Don't bother. Only betrays weakness. Inscrutable Pham. In Manila, they'll drive into a pole to knock you out and rumble your wallet. From a place and time where corruption was the only constant. Nothing else makes sense. Peace. Impassible. Go on. Stuck in a weary worthless dream. Himself the Ghost of his own Father. Blast the canopy. Dead man dangling in vines. Enchanted stem laden with gourds. Crucified flares. Panther storing its prey out of reach. Blood going drip drip drip onto my Boonie. Red on jungle green. Tom Hallem stood at the end of the hymn. The boys departed in a rush of loose clothing and bags. He approached the altar.

"The Headmaster did two tours of Vietnam," said Reverent Bent. "You should talk to him. He might know something. I've got to take a boy up to see him. I'll take you to his office."

They passed into a recessed sandstone porch alongside a small courtyard ringed with buttresses. A deep pond was set in its heart. Kidney shaped. Stone seats. A thin jet pushed high then flopped into the water in unsequenced blobs. Cool place in summer under the mullioned windows of the eastern wall.

"Moody," sounded Bent sternly.

A thin blonde boy turned from a dark corner and stepped forward.

"Sir?" he asked.

"Come on."

Bent gesticulated with his crumpled hand for the boy to lead. Patrol scout. Field of glass.

"Where, sir?"

"Headmaster."

"Oh sir, please."

"You should have thought about that before you disgraced yourself ... AGAIN, boy."

He gestured. Moody marched obediently. Shocked into obeisance. His palm will remain stable even as the cane cracks. Hallem felt thus impotent. Merely an observer. Why plead his case. Sargent is seeking a father figure in Stephen but he can only think of *amor matris*. Something soft in his features. Warm Antinous. What would one act of forbearance achieve anyway? Spare a single insurgent. Probably pick the prettiest prisoner. Wave her off. She'll just come back tomorrow and murder your mate. Hadrian's proxy. The mini-Odyssey of Telemachus aligns the son with the father but also shows their vast gap in experience. Joyce places Stephen in a triad between Deasy and Sargent in NESTOR. Past-it metonymy. Younger mnemony. Still raw enough to eat.

"His father's an old boy," explained the Chaplain. "I let the Headmaster deal with him."

They strode along a shaded portico within which Moody's top was sunned and shaded, sunned again and shaded once more. Its Flavian radiance was reinforced with each new beam floating off the Yellowblock columns. Long grey socks covered his lean copper calves. Smooth folds behind his knees rippled. Platinum nylon downed his thighs. Citron-stroked. Show him the Golden Book. Touch him like you touched the others. A sodden yard opened. The Headmaster's Office was located almost like a wormhole in the far eastern corner. They entered the tight foyer. Typewriter clatch. Pause. Mrs Calvin looked up from a low seat behind a high counter.

"Wait here," said the Chaplain.

Moody slouched against the wall.

"Not like that. Turn and face the corner."

He pointed. Moody assumed his pose.

"And stand at Attention," added Bent. Vexed. Moody's body tensed.

"Good morning, Mrs Calvin. I'd like to see the Headmaster, please."

"I'll just check if he's free, Reverend."

She depressed the intercom. [BUZZ] Familiar eructation: "yes"?

"Chaplain, Headmaster."

"Send him in."

"Tell him I've got Tom Hallem," added Bent.

"He's got Tom Hallem, sir."

"Oh alright. Has my next appointment arrived?"

"Not yet."

"Good. When they arrive, say I'll just be a few minutes. Send Tom in."

"Come on," said Bent to Hallem lightly.

Mrs Calvin looked up from her console and smiled. Bent leaned against the schoolboy's ear in passing and hissed: "you wait here, Moody." They negotiated the corridor to the Headmaster's anteroom. Weatherboard walls. Jerry-built. Organic almost. Daedalian. Pen for the Minotaur. Insert Caliban. Cunning Minos imprisoned both father and son. Wings of wax and feathers. Sunshaved Icarus sunclose. Door ajarred. Wide dark studded couch. Picking nervously picking in the leather craters for crumbs. Await. Finally, the Headmaster's door opened definitively. A shoe-tip came first shining like well-attended armour. A crisp white cuff followed. Then he appeared fully. Coatless eminence. Trademark starched collar buttoned onto a striped blue shirt. Recognition induced a thin-lipped smirk. His hollow cheeks stretched. Lines everdeeper everstarker around clenched eyesockets. Fissures.

"Tom," the Headmaster stated heartily outstretching his hand. Wooden tiller. Grab me, it urged. Tempest motion. A 'shake' literally. Never get it out of your grip. Soggy batter. Not until you confront the gaze.

"Mister Westacott."

"What brings you back to The School?"

"He's come to talk about his father," interjected Reverend Bent.

"Right," replied Westacott without surprise.

He buffeted them both aboard.

"I'd better keep moving Headmaster," added the Chaplain.

"Very well, Lloyd."

"Moody's waiting."

"What is it this time?"

"Spoonerisms, sir. He ruined choir practice."

"What will we do with him," chuckled the Headmaster. "Utterly unlike his father."

He turned to Hallem.

"His father is based at Butterworth. Expat posting. Ruined the lad. Spent his primary school years at one of those 'sinternational hools'."

He presst Hallem deeper into his office.

"Thank you, Reverend," he said by way of dismissal.

"Goodbye, Tom," said Bent.

"Thank you, sir," replied Tom Hallem.

Bent withdrew. The door closed. Warm inna.

"Tea?" asked the Headmaster.

"Yes, please."

The Headmaster walked to a high sideboard, flicked the powerpoint switch on the wall and fiddled with an ancient lead. The kettle commenced gurgling.

"What are you doing these days?"

"I'm an artist."

"Really. Do you live in a garret?" enquired Westacott dramatically. Vowels pressing through leather cheekflaps.

"No. I've just moved back to my mother's house actually."

"Marvellous woman. Great supporter of the School. How is she?"

"She's fine."

"And Mister Hallem."

"He's struggling."

"Shame. A brave man. Is your mother still singing?"

"Yes."

"Such a rich voice. I always found her gospel recitals quite ... uplifting."

The kettle called. Blind tuning fork. Tap of a cane. *Nebelwerther*. Westacott extinguished its whistle fussily. Dare to ask him of. Hubris to challenge. Flayed Marsyas. Sound of an inverted flute. Steam rose silent in aftermath. Westacott started humming a tune. Hey youse inners ear my call. Satan is waiting. Region of his brimstone. Get your soul bleached. A mouthful of cream. Plea bargain.

"Milk or sugar?"

"Neither thanks."

"Admirable. But I can't resist," said Westacott greedily as he ladled two heaps of refined sugar into a cream-coloured tin cup bearing the school crest.

"I got 'hooked' in the army," he continued conspiratorially. "A hot mug of tea always reminds me of the old times. Do you like these cups?"

"Not really," replied Hallem inhaling the broth.

"Well they wouldn't satisfy an aesthete such as yourself. But they're an excellent fund-raising vessel ... so to speak."

Westacott laughed and stirred his beverage with a silver teaspoon that also bore the school trademark. It clanked against the tin lining. Glamorous green enamel. Shitmetal frame. Marketing strategy. Paint the breakthrough image. Win a prize preferably Archibald. Eat with Collector regularly. Articles in the popular press. Presence in group shows. B2B. More exhibitions in Melbourne. Produce small works. Sales targets. A more decorative style. Drugs sex Sydney fecund lime SELL. A different type of moral decay to Garrett Deasy. Fast moving coins. Poker-machine. Herd the lemons into sheds. Buy more intel. Meet Kill Ratio. Bloom's tabulations. Thrift. Five thousand-dollar bounties for any Ma Rung **dead or alive**. Did you get a full pension? Alcinous' gifts. Each man should add a cauldron to the pile. Also slaves. To be funded in this fiscal year with a special tax on helots. Call it a LEVY. Penelope's dowry by default. Ithaca was not a grand city like Corinth or Sparta. A crate of gold bars discovered under a flap down the arse end of Chu Chi tunnels. Call in the Spooks. Stuff it in a body bag. Drag it up the guts. Use proceeds to fund covert operations. Stalin was a bank robber. Mao a drug baron. Poppy fields in Yunnan. Rice sales to East Berlin. Get hard currency. Spend it all on war machines. Overtake Britain in steel production. Ironic misread. Empirical decay. A row of straw boaters hung off old hooks in the sports rooms. Disparities of scale in the experiences of Telemachus and Odysseus are closed by Joyce in his characterisations of Stephen and Bloom. Losing your mother. Virag's suicide. The death of a child. Life eventually claws you into its keep. Loops of remorse.

"It's all commerce these days. You can't deny Mammon. My predecessor was a great educator. But those were different times. That was all before the Oil Shock. When I was appointed, I cleared his office of every piece of school memorabilia... except that bird."

He gestured at a stuffed hummingbird fixed in mid-song upon a Bakelite stand adorning the walnut credenza. Rotten in light. Faults in its desiccated pelt. Stitches exposed. Some cochineal wadding disgorged. Hold in his guts. Call in a Huey. No hope for Bobby but. Westacott adjusted its tonsured head.

"I just couldn't bear to part with it," he added distractedly.

The intercom buzzed. He disengaged.

"Excuse me," said the Headmaster moving to his desk. He turned on the lamp to better see. Tom Hallem held up his mug and studied the worn triangular logo. Godhead. Stick a flamin' eye on it. Aleph Yod Nun. Sound of air through a cylinder. Sirenfart. A moth suddenly dropped onto the grubby serrated rim of his mug and toppled into the warm brew. Helicopter dropping through field glasses too far to hear. He felt no inclination to remove it or complain. It sank quickly. He blew over the surface to cool and churn the water. Looking for snakes. Defoliated jungle. Poisoned water. Outbreak of Guardia at Camp. Westacott hacked and chipped at each syllable. Yes he remembered the memorial service for Sergeant Wheaton. Hallem began to search for the body of that sunken insect with his spoon; flakes of which now floated on this sea like so much jetsam. He never discovered it. Yet drank all the same. Westacott sat down in a deep studded armchair facing him.

"Where would you like to start?"

"I want to ask about my father's disappearance."

"Why?"

"I'm not convinced he's dead."

"Why would one presume otherwise," asked Westacott.

"Some of his mates think he's still alive."

"Then why hasn't he contacted you?"

"I don't know."

"It seems strange that he would just abandon his family."

"Yes."

"It's been a very long time."

"Yes. Almost 20 years."

"His wife has re-married. You've taken her husband's surname. Wouldn't you rather believe he was dead than that he just ... rejected you?"

"There might be a good reason."

"Quite," said Westacott smartly. "Then let logic be our guide. What have you heard precisely?"

"He's running a bar in Manila."

Westacott scoffed openly.

"Lots of ex-servicemen run bars in South-East Asia. That doesn't sound like the man I knew. Do you have any physical evidence?"

"No."

"Confirmed sightings?"

"No."

"No photographs?"

"None."

"Letters? Local news clippings?"

"Nothing."

"So it's all scuttlebutt," concluded Westacott. "Now let's examine the other side of the equation. Your father is classified MIA. Correct?"

"Yes."

"Paperwork's in good order, I presume."

"Yes."

"You were granted access to the official report?"

"Yes."

"What was the conclusion?"

"He disappeared during a hot extraction west of Pleiku in 1968. His body was never recovered."

Westacott composed his face. Thirty-year rule still extant. Don Cane went into the mountains. Spent time with AATTV. Dragon Mountain. Helped secure Camp Enari. 2-1CAV. Late 66. Base for cross-border operations. Re-assigned by MACV-SOG. Daniel Boone Squad. Salem House. Grubby little jobs. God knows what he did after 1971. Last known date in Australian records. Aristotle de-defined. Motion of matter through space. Cochrane's memory. Surfaced in the Philippines recently. Tell Oswald.

"Were there witness statements?" asked Westacott.

"Yes."

"Did they itemise the sequence of events?"

"Yes. My father volunteered for a night mission. The location has been censored from the report. It must still be classified. He rappelled out of a helicopter. There was heavy ground fire. Extraction was attempted. But he lost his grip."

Tom Hallem held tight his cooling mug. My father as a falling bird like Icarus. Wrong symbolic alignment in Jung's archetype. He should be the groundedone. I should memolten be. Stephen Dedalus was given a debased father's name by Joyce. Emblem of its intrinsic connectivity as a symbol in his BEING. Shorne of the letter 'A'. Like taking out a piece of ribcage (see Adam). Stephen wears Daedalus' evil in his nomenclature. He must be reminded of its meaning every time that he inscribes his signature on paper every time he reads. Killer of Perdix his nephew. Cousin to Icarus. Billy Capri mine. My father made Perdix fall from the Acropolis. Relate myth back to Billy. How could Donald John Cane kill him. Ironic correspondence to the death of his own son. Me.

"Was there any subsequent search?"

"There was a two-day search including foot patrols."

"Did they have the flight path?"

"Yes."

"But they found no sign of him."

"None."

"Were his possessions returned to your mother?"

"Yes."

"Have you examined them?"

"Not really."

"You might go back and analyse them. Ask yourself some key questions. Is there anything which might shed some insight into his state of mind? A diary that suddenly changes subject matter. Or stops shortly before his death. Unsent letters home. Unusual mementos. That kind of stuff."

"What are you getting at?"

"Let's be candid, Tom. Try to work out if there was anything in his papers that might indicate your father was mentally unbalanced. Or look for the presence of another woman. That was a pretty typical story for our chaps."

Sketches of Elizabeth entering my day book. First her unengaged face. Straight down the gun barrel. Blue-eyed redhead. A rare coin. Naked at last. Forearm over her face. Bloodbath spread across Portugese sheets in her window-walled bedroom. Late afternoon. Her husband was extracting the wisdom teeth of a government minister as we fucked. Sunset fresh across Kettle Bay. Her body papercut white. Gaping metal brace. First the mouth pellucid then the gap swollen slowly with blood. Shove a pipe down. Suck out all seepage. Hearts pumping as we unload. Plug the cavity with wadding. His absence. If he is still alive. Freckles marring flesh. Bitter truth. Leon Archer pulled back the light bedding. Watercolours of menstrual blood strafed with hard semen. Thy will bed one. He balanced her infidelity against his. Underground cubicles in Oxford Street pubs. Green Park cruising. Just sux. No penetration. Twenty bucks. Motel rooms on Crown Street. Borromean knots. Held prone. Entered suddenly. Feel his gust. Hook him deeper. His micture. A foal lifting itself upright in placenta. Burrow loam. Deception. Henry Flower Esq. Don't ever disclose the facts under any circumstances. Twenty-four hours bound under lights. No sleep for three days. RnR musk in Hong Kong. Normalised solace. I left my wife with Julia still in a cradle. Candy pulled out of your grip at the camp gates. Yakuza sex tours. Widows of local officials. Beating up Khmer cadres. Desperate games. Tours of twelve months so you couldn't bring your family over. Long distance phone calls. False correspondence. OUTGOING outweighs INCOMING. A couple of Kodak instamatic prints trump language. Burn them all when you get back home.

"It sounds like an open and shut case to be honest," concluded Westacott suddenly. "Why should all this evidence be disputed?"

"I was told his death was a cover-up."

"You've been listening to too much ABC propaganda," scoffed the Headmaster.

"I believe it."

"Then nothing will change your mind, Tom. It's like Faith. Do you believe in the Lord?" he asked changing subjects quickly.

"Every human society has gods," replied the young man.

The Headmaster gazed at the shimmering blue and mustard diamonds bound together in the tall window frame. All soothing lines and angles. Emerald-saint-merge. The last morning rays were slicing across his face; drifting down his body; evanescent. He met them lovingly raising his prominent chin. One day the sun itself will explode. Thence a great manifest. JEHOVAH! A letter from Patmos had been placed on top of his mail. Greek Stamps. Hercules and Geryon. Easier to get at his cattle than home. Remove them with a sponge. Place them in his albums. Got the whole world trapped. Each continent its own volumes. Europe already bulging. Also Australia. Africa lags. A good illustration of national development. Images form history. Dates and locations. Time to drive to Botany Cemetery. Westacott rose and paced to his desk. He adjusted some papers.

"The Vietnam Conflict is full of rumours, myths and lies. People think that Tet was a decisive defeat. In fact, it was a military victory. They think we were winning the war up to that point. Actually, we were losing. They believe we were floundering after Nineteen-Sixty-Eight. Well, the truth is that we were winning the war under Abrams. South Vietnam would still be alive if we had stayed the course."

Tom Hallem listened mechanically like Stephen Dedalus. Do not contradict the false father figure. Show Protean dissembling. Listen to Deasy's dissertation on foot and mouth. He was a fringe dweller. Not respected in Dublin. Unionist Tory. Mouthpiece of Archbishop Sloane. Dindshenchas. Shield with three spittoons. Stephen is seeking TRUTH with his calculations in Proteus. He wants to discover the same kind of FACT that enabled Menelaus to beat Proteus and get home. But his intense entropic is always moving towards a state of increased fragmentation. There is an endless piling of references, allusions and associations as the chapter unfolds. No single idea gains primacy. Each sequence only ends and gets reset when he encounters some REAL THING – a dog, people or a boat. His dense, confused thought-processes contrast with the clean, simple lines of each lyric and song he cites. Likewise, his feet – representing the BODY – continue to motor in solid "proud rhythm" unregardingly. A desperate edge enters his tone.

"Is there anyone else I could talk to?" Tom Hallem asked the headmaster.

"Not in Australia. Your father changed paymasters. He went off with the Yanks up north. Our boys were all stationed down in Phuoc Tuy."

The Headmaster sighed.

"Look, I know it's hard to accept but, on the balance of probability, your father was killed in action. It was an honourable conclusion to a good life. That explanation is certainly more plausible than a man of his stature abandoning his family for this long."

Tom Hallem bent to shield his face with a purple cloak.

"Do you really believe that?"

"I do."

"But you just said that the whole war was riddled with misinformation."

The Headmaster spoke with passion.

"Leave history alone, Tom. It's not something to rake."

Hallem watched the light abate on the mock Tudor facade. Shakespeare in lime. Aweary like Mariana. A VISION. Just as soon be delirious. Clouds pass undoing redoing. Chance formations. Mallarme meets Vico. Given sentience by need. *Qualia*. Call Time 'history' if you like. Infinite atoms some colliding become instants of fact. Lean-eyed bewares. Unslept. Flux. Options lost. In art you can always change the plot. Cordelia can get married to Edgar like they did in Restoration Theatre. Not in real life. A spray of shots. Any can hit. Any miss. Did my father take one shot to the body or was it a spray or was it just the drop through space which killed him. A pick-up game of touch football was starting on the edge of the Main Oval. Unpredictable bounce. Down dead-ends stopped or ends left hanging. Thus, the olive-shaped ball of English renown. Gan lan qiu. Stephen hearing hockey shouts. Public-school sports yielded Haig's battle tactics. Still medieval in format. Advance with VIM. Spirit will carry the day. Cavalry charges. What Joyce called time shocked rebounds. Jousts (bayonets), slush (trenches), the uproar of battles (Creeping barrage), frozen deathspew of the slain (see No Man's Land). Dead dog on a beach. Vikings landing on the shores of Ireland. Grind through German gunners. Bloodbeaked prows. Rushing out to slaughter a pod of whales. Stephen's antecedents hacking into green blubber. Metaphor for human slaughter across the wages. A shout of spearspikes baited with Charlie's guts. Great War heroes beastly dead. Trojan wallpiles. Climb up to the brim of the mug. The whistle sounds. Over the Top! A cymbal. Some drums. Blunt survival contests. Insert Malthus. Darwin was his biologist. Bad seeds. King Hamlet was one. Lear's repudiation of his offspring. Locked out in the mire in a storm in a hut. Get naked. Back home is schemers turf. Here I disclaim all paternal care. A misunderstood writ. John Joyce's drunken threats. "I'll leave you all where Jesus left them!" Roll a rock back. Straw boater blowing across poppy fields. Gallipoli, Fromelles, Tobruk, Crete, Singapore. Major > Minor. Anxiety of illegitimacy. My father took a QANTAS flight to Singapore then a plane to Saigon. Photocopies of his itinerary are held in army records. RnR on a few occasions in Taiwan and Hong Kong. Never Manila. MIA. The jungle consumes. Erases. Vines weft. Deluge. Wash away all evidence. The cistern contains. Blood overflows. Splits in the canopy where Icarus fell. Four o'clock tempest each day. Drying to dust in the parched season. Hallem rested his forearms on his thighs and looked straight at the floor. It must have just been deodorized. Sanitised stench. He surveyed his surrounds quickly. Everything was arrayed symmetrically from a series of illustrations on the back wall depicting the Life of St John to the delicate arrangement of cut sherry glasses around a crystal decanter of Scotch. Defensive perimeter.

"You'll have to excuse me. I've got to attend a funeral this afternoon. An old comrade of your father, actually. Sergeant Albert Wheaton. Career soldier. Served three tours of Vietnam."

They rose together.

"I remember Mr Wheaton," said Tom. "He came and saw my mother once. He gave me a photograph he took of my father. It had Quang Nai written on the back. How did he die?"

"A lot of things killed him."

The Headmaster's palm cupped the young man's shoulder.

"Survival is sometimes a Pyrrhic victory," he added bitterly.

They walked from his office. Westacott paused to admonish Moody and waved him off. He told Missus Calvin that he would return to teach *Othello* to Year Twelve after the funeral. The bells announced recess. Triple alarm. Hasty footsteps pursued Tom Hallem. He stopped at a small garden overlooking the Main Oval and leant against a Doric post. A high bank ringed with soggy eucalypts dropped to the arc of a four hundred yard running track. Some senior boys were removing their shoes and socks. They rolled up their trousers. Never I. Last chosen. To be an artist but by accident. His cock in my brush hand. Class room gone sideways. Schwitter's *Merz*. Only a bad harvest can save us. The Headmaster passed rattling a bulb of keys.

"I won't offer you spiritual counsel Tom," Westacott said self-deprecatingly. "But I can give you a lift into town if you like."

Boat ride to Sparta. Bonds betwixt. Shake. Trawl for memories of Belvedere College. A conga line of boys in white athletics singlets. ANZAC embarkation. Finger wharf. HMAS *Sydney*. Big knees cruel tongues sharp skinny shins like blades. Pigeonribs thrusting heraldic chest-plates. Hector doing eight laps of Troy. Mortar dropping in the shot-pit. Cobra javelins unstitching sand. No point in hardening. Rather end up as pulp.

"No thanks. I've got my mother's car," replied Hallem.

"Must dash then. I have to deliver the eulogy. I like to break a lance with you. Goodbye Tom Hallem," exclaimed Principal Westacott.

Tom watched his master's withdrawal around the Main Oval. Through time and space receding. Cosmos to vision apparent. Stephen as passive eyewitness. Nearing tide, a rusty shoe. Synchronic existence SEEN. Temporal diachronic events HEARD. Time as the dimension of audible perception. Boots that crush wrack and shells. Striding. Thru. A cacophony a thud then silence in logical succession. Everything in the text relates to language. Even the dumb sand on the beach is a script about tide. Sound carries sense like in Milton (see A. Burgess). INSERT CHARACTER LINKS: listen to music (Dave); view a painting (Tom Hallem); read a book (Billy). Proust's tripod of Vinteuil, Elstor and Bergotte. Music was preeminent in that era due to Wagner. It was the same after PUNK for about 10 years. Equate sensory experiences to plot: a biographical undertow is like music; surface narrative equals paint; the book is the ultimate end of all expression (see Mallarme). Joyce navigating Scylla & Charybdis as sound and sight motifs. Listening to the sucking swirl of the bitter whirlpool. Observing the many-headed monster once all once. Alex Pope's "Essay on Man." Time is a moment. Our point a space. Man as perfect as he ought. Fathers either/or. Equivocal honour. Proteus is the first stream-of-consciousness episode in *Ulysses*. Stephen's thoughtlines are consistently interrupted by the intrusion of popular songs, nursery rhymes and light poetry. Random events draw him back. He turns them into literary references and it makes reality dissipate. This causes him to lose direction literally and figuratively. He evidences disinhibition at times. At one point, he finds himself marching to internal music involuntarily. This causes him to miss the turnoff for Aunt Sara's house. Proposed visits become chance non-events. It is often difficult to interpret Joyce's intentions and meaning in Proteus due to the dense nature of Stephen's esoteric bluster. The reader is still not sure if Joyce is channelling his own theories through Stephen or deriding the meditations of his neophyte hero. Possibly both. Also deriding himself maybe. Joyce oscillated between hubris and self-deprecation but never self-hate. Stephen is dissatisfied with any fixed meaning. He is thus the first poststructuralist character. Joyce turns to other languages when English does not possess suitable terminology. Untranslatable terms and arbitrary interjections are used side by side. He creates NEW WORDS. Concepts are confirmed by erecting a WEFT across multiple languages, achieving meaning through analogue and entelechy rather than strict definition (see C6 Derrida). He would take this tactic to its ENTH degree in FWAKE. Stephen displays a capacity for cynical change to meet the prejudices of his audience in Nestor. Tom Hallem is the same kind of character. Bill Capri is not. Joyce got his whole theoretical shebang out of the way at the start of *Ulysses*. This left him free to pursue intense stylistic experiments over the membrane of a simple, mainly-appropriated plot. This kind of art is a war of attrition. Stephen cannot attain Gnosis in Proteus. He is too unformed as yet to configure a cosmic system. Squeeze fresh-tasting architectonics out of the tube. Inverse of an egg. The body of the work is turned inside out. Diastolic sprawl. Greek dromaios. To abandon. The flow of intellectual correspondences must be made as quickly as possible. There is no time for grammatical niceties. Lists will suffice. The beauty of speed. Marinetti said Time and Space died yesterday. The motor car is more gorgeous than "Victory at Samathrace." Lyotard revived pace bowling. Apollonian & Dionysian dialectics. Surdity & Utterance locked in perpetual flux (see C6). Stephen Dedalus channels Aristotle with his notion that the ear provides pure engagement with reality unlike the eye. Like a weathervane twirling in a cyclone, he goes speak, stifle, move, stop. Dromology & Stasis. Walking down the street shooting into the crowd. God is a surrealist act, according to Breton. Pistol shot in a steel chamber. The strange life of with Arthur Cravan. Dada gratuities. Systolic clamps clasp. Derrida's eperon. That which 'presents' itself to view. Animated eyes peering from the hollow sockets of an antique portrait. Poe-eyes. Comic almost. The school horn announced next class. Imperfect heroes are made blind by the Gods as a prelude to punishment. Oedipus. Tiresias. Paris. Cupid's victims. HOMER HIMSELF. Joyce as well. His sightless piano tuner tap tap tapping his cane. Joyce named him Pen/rose. It combined Stephen's literary weapon with an allusion to Bloom's nomenclature. Also, a sex pun. Swinburne's nameless heroine in "Les Noyades" is a lyrical exemplar of Joyce's struggle with the senses in Proteus. See Chapter 6 (Virilio). During the Terror, an aristocratic lady is blind-folded during her trial. She can hear (but not see) the sentence of the revolutionary court and the accompanying laughter of the crowd; perceive the sound of the switch in the instant before she experiences its taste physically (this moment is repeated without any loss of intensity across its sharp repeats); record the smell then the feel of the rough body of the labourer against whom she is bound back-to-back like Plato's first humans; listen to his close whispers; experience the moment in space between the Loire and its swirling waters; sink to her death as their bodies combined with the mass of water drag her down inexorably. Stephen Dedalus imagined himself also being hauled down drunk into the sea with the drowning man by Poseidon. A blast of dispute suddenly swamped the football field. Bang! All words fell to the ground. Mutilated language expiring in a heap. One word left known to all humankind. What is it? Asked Stephen. A password. A cry. Rosebud. Mehr licht. Goethe. Insert LSD 100 micrograms IM. Refill Tom's canula. Joyce examines notions of eternity and mortality throughout Chapter One. The ultimate utterance for Stephen Dedalus is "Mother!" The paternal figure shifts from the status of a God to a bloated corpse in Proteus yielding by decay the raw matter of new life (i.e. THE SON). This is man's sperm. Stephen debases the paternal corpus with his acts of urination and nose-picking. He is obsessed with the changing face of reality. He wants to hold down the image so it cannot transform itself into another sickening emotion but he is constantly cruelled by the limitations of his own apprehension. His idea of reading "signatures" prefaces Structuralism although he finds it restrictive not freedom-making. They send him down metonymic spirals of thought. See signification systems of Saussure and Levi-Strauss (C6). Joyce gives the reader a psychological template of Stephen Dedalus in Proteus which is used in later chapters in manifest forms. The taxi spiraled down Anzac Parade towards Nine Ways. It deviated onto Bunnerong Road bisecting Housing Commission estates. A sequence of nondescript small shopping centres lined the roadway. Occasional street life. Bogged.

One pub suburbs. Matraville Hotel. Chalkboard read "Counter Lunches – STILL ONLY $1." Roast dinner. Local dainty. Trotters in Aspic. Hungarian delicacy. Pork Katsu. Favoured by the Japanese. Pig's Head. Christmas dish of Saxons. Skulls mounted on stakes at hamlet gates like Atalanta's suitors. Famous tavern frequented by Shakespeare. Destroyed in the Great Fire 1666. Source: Master Farryner's Bakehouse, Pudding Lane, Thames Street. Scapegoats like Princep. From Tower to Temple and Thames to Smithfield. Four hundred and sixty acres of London incinerated. Sparse sandy ground near the Botany peninsula. All ravished. Calydonian boar. Artemis' payback. Lumpy heathland separated the last houses from Brotherson Dock. Massed cranes maneuvered stiffly above; distant; simply.

"Muggy," said Pham.

"Yep," Don replied in a pig's whisper. "But not as bad as Saigon."

This type of weather would have suited Choc. Dirty with ticks like North Queensland. He came downhill from Charters Towers to enlist. Sank a dozen ponies behind the lace skirt out the front of Buchanan's Hotel. NCO in Malaya. 1ATF. Gaunt dry flaking clay. Shifting sand and blowflies. Low heath line. Can't build a bluddy boghouse. Always slips into shit puddles. Patrolling the fence north of Long Hai. Install a lattice of Jumping Jacks. Graham's folly. Sir Charles: what a fox he was. His helots jemmied those mines out of the dirt at night with shit metal spoons and re-interred them right under our patrol routes. Five hundred grams of TNT in a tin jam-jar. Surging like a startled brown snake. Rip off yer nuts guts arsehole n thighs. Kill everyone in a fifty-yard radius. Lloyd Bent's fingers were resting on Bobby Horne's shoulder when someone stepped on the fuse. POP. He heard the word "shit." Then got slapped with Horney. Sappers' all gone flying. So fast too slow. Stare at the sun on your unburst back. Eyes sharp with dust. Hand holes spewing blood and bone stalks. Shreds of gore hung from Bobby's thigh. Dickless he was. Eardrum screeching. Guts flopping through torn fatigues under a withered flak jacket. Protean horror. Sticky Saigon River clay. Hold it all together. Bent, Choc and Don Cane made a cast over him. Impotent as ghosts. Nothing to disclose. Terminal partition. Ana shaking off her m. coil down the Lake. Lost her footing on the final step. Laid her body down. No trapdoor. [SING] I can tell you precisely how this story's going to end (FOR ME). Caved veins pumped full of junk. A paramedic laying on vinyl pads. Shaken awake by black-out. Speck of light in darkness. A candle blown. Blink for a second, they dissolve. Aftershade of thirty VC sitting at a bench. Small arms fire like taps inside a fridge. You are the hole. Fill all openings with wax. NCR machine clattering'n'churning under a single strip lamp. Click click click: clacketty clacketty clack. Click click click: clacketty clacketty clack. Stuck in the car outside the Meadow Lea margarine factory in Mascot *tralalaladdy*. Lock the doors, keep the windows up and don't open them for nobody. Iron flaps shut tight. Eighteen-inch apertures. Masks for tunnels. Send the Rats down first.

Smokem out. Slow low Dioxin mist. Fire-hosing jungle. A tonsured face. Legless orphans rushing to class on calloused knees spread like foot soles. Passages turning at one-hundred-and-twenty-degree angles. Games along the footpath. A brainless bulb screaming while congee is forced into its tiny mouth. Brain surgery with industrial drills. Litters of Catholic kids in grubby frocks and corduroy pants in Campsie. No pullovers in winter. Soft exposed thighs. Gooseflesh. The Dedalus sisters in C5 are a strong plot device disclosing the abandonment of the father and the impotence of the son. Sixty students per classroom. Take turns sitting down on well-thrashed buttocks. Stew Green squatting on a nail. Punji traps down vertical shafts. Neighbour's kelpie snapping. Blinds drawn. Rooms without sunshine. Smooth flat river stones spread over black plastic sheets. Flyscreen nailed over the window frame. Sunset curfews. Red smoke grenades. Never play down that side of the house. Missus Horne's calamity. Robert towering over me in his thick new uniform and spats. Swinging off the ironwork on the front gate until it scraped a brown arc in the cement path. Five-ton fortified truck convoys free-railing along deep dry-ruts. Route 19. Ma Deuces. Name of Lil Sure Shot. Browning meat choppers. Crumbled paving. They kept everything imaginable down those underground passageways. Three hundred-yard hospital wards lined with mattress rolls. Theatres draped with parachute silk. Outhouses stuffed with broken shop fittings. Standing on a Shelley's soft drink crate at my father's workbench filling clear plastic containers with bugs. Cotton wool beds entangling their legs. Lowered fifteen feet from the surface straight onto the operating board. Lift with fat-paddle tweezers. Medivac out of a hot DZ in a light Huey. Scrape thirty centimeters per day with a small hoe. Compressed like a foetus in three-be-two feet slits. Problems when stinkbugs crawl off the slab. Make them lie still like Isaac. After you pass, they creep through null grasslands to the safety of the jungle. Punch a matrix of airholes in dirt. The red smoke that we pumped into the tunnel complex perforated the prairie grass all over the battlefield. Perforations facing east to catch dawn light. Turn towards the prevailing wind to fumigate. Keep your eyes on them. Climbers. Shake them back into place. Fed on leaf scraps. Balls of coagulated rice in their cotton pockets. Convenient how they flip onto their backs when they're dead. Different gravity of corpses. Chidley at Troy. Dead soldiers float. Shells mounted on cardboard trays. Skewered with dressing pins. Not going anywhere. Cracked carapace. The hard soil at the root of bamboo trees can withstand the weight of a tank. Flies left to dry on the windowsill. Slotted into an old shoe box. Encased and displayed like Pater's anonymous narrator in "A Prince of Court Painters." Compartmentalised. Units of feeling. Military Road opened onto a bountiless sandstone plateau. Rugged Ithaca. A land of unrelenting harshness to the eye. Exposed to Poseidon's rage continuously. Hapless Scherians. The rocky ground collapsed suddenly – horribly – off a crumpled cliff overhanging the gouged-out ampitheatre of Bunnerong Power Station. Botany Cemetery spread like a massive lens under a sheer grey sky. The car park was overflowing. Don Cane paid Pham, stepped onto the sodden sand-blown path and walked alone up a steep driveway fringed with ornamental shrubs. The crematorium was painted cream and laced with art deco embellishments. Flames and columns of smoke unraveled on false friezes. Methodical puffs were released from a concealed chimney. Flesh-fuel. The rich aroma of roses hung like spring cat-spray. Fragrant charnel routes. Transplanted palm trees bounded a field of modest headstones; punctuated by the occasional angel chiseled and smoothed into prayer. Stone crypts for the Catholic clergy had been set on a mound overlooking Yarra Bay. Vista to Above. Closer to the Boss. Dumping ground beneath. Port and factory workers. Keep an eternal eye on those cunts. Hotbed of sedition. Street signs directed visitors to sections reserved for each denomination – Protestant C: Catholic AA: Orthodox A: Catholic 6: Catholic 20. Neatness of suburban lawns. Kept distinct by mounds of grave gravel and sand. Don Cane entered the chapel and slotted into the best shot arc. Odysseus standing near the door at the suitors' feast. Don't want to steal Choc's limelight. Briney light presst through pitted vestry glass. Submerged sensing. Family gathered along the front railing. Solid bodies importuned into ill brown suits. Comrades had borne the coffin into the chapel. They lined the aisle. Straight rows of service medals rested on puffed guts. Familiar profiles bloated with age. Jean Wheaton's shiny black bob still obvious. Silver veins. She turned to kiss the nullified forehead of Choc's mother. Tape recorder churning out ambient muzak. Colonel Cornwall read Psalm Twenty-three. BBC English with a hint of American drawl. There at the Fall of Saigon it was reputed. Thieu's Tiresias. "He maketh me down to lie," Cornwall intoned. Incoming. A cry made a pale father lift back the plastic flap of a McLaren stroller to reveal his squirming newborn. "Quiet waters by." Face down in murk. Shriveled face gripped by agony. Spine exposed. "E'en though I walk." In columns. Patrols. Hold position. "Death's dark veil" fluttering across all of us. "Yet will I fear no ill." But I do. Did. Always have. "And thy rod" was brought down on a line of Nashos punctured by JJs. "For thou art with me." Whimpering for love. The baby's shrieks intensified. Its father rose and reversed the pram out of the chapel. Carrier gone backwards. Not made for retreat. NV rocketrain. A female attendant in a pleated uniform opened a set of Kauri doors. Sudden lightshaft. Alone indefinitely. Turning from the glare to embrace the solace of steady words. Plastic wheels gently stuttering down stone stairs. The spike that falls unequally on good and bad. All those credulous young killers shunted around that hate-filled landscape filled with dizzy loathing. Dragging nogs to shell holes and kicking dirt all over them just in case. Let off a volley if the dust moves. One of those Gooks took so many shots to the belly that we pulled him in half trying to drag him towards the pit. Quartered Patricides. Draft horse on each limb. See

Foucault's dichotomy at the start of *D+P*. It took one Digger on each leg and arm to get the pieces into the quarry. We dropped the top half on the bottom half / so many dead that we're running out of space / pile them in deeper graves even unto the third or fourth generation / stack them vertical / compulsory pyres. "The sins of the father shall be visited unto the sons." All that retribution down the backend. Yes yes of course the whole fucking game is based on the bad apple. My own father: a scrapper out of his depth. I also. Absence makes the heart flounder. If our son had survived, it would have all been different Richie. How could a merciful God punish us like that? The death of Annie was the last straw for Darwin. William Shelley. Strangled by his mother's monster. Sons I sired but never fathered. A family plot listing the whole game show. "Goodness and mercy all my life ..." INSERT DISCLAIMER "... Shall surely follow." Io's gadfly. "And in God's house forever." Redoubts. Motel shots. False sanctuaries. "My dwelling place shall be." A flooded hole in the glug. Rossetti dug up his wife's grave to get back lost manuscripts. Swinburne with a shovel composing a hendecasyllabic. The funeral service terminated suddenly. Swift benediction. Glazed faces like some shining portrait gallery. Humanity's greatness before Death. Bravery of sheep in a slaughter-line. Greater than God. Confronting mutability. The earth grows thicker, our graves deeper each day. Sappho's logic. The Gods too would die if death was a good thing. Choc was flat inside his wooden nag atop the shoulders of Sgt Barry Evans, Ray Farrar DSC, Lieutenant Don Schofield and Messrs Beath, Deverill and Stone. Suspend operations as they approach my dugout. Eyes straight. Mechanical pace. Nobody looks sideways. Out on patrol along the Long Hai fence. They can feel me. Wait for gut instinct to kick. Only landmines defied human senses. A footstep in the wrong place. You could never predict where history will fall. Major Ian Westacott GSM (V Clasp) at the tail. Vampyre in clay. Let them pass. Escape. Visit my mother's grave. Not possible to return. Adrift forever.

"Major Cane."

A palm was laid on his shoulder. A soul felt and heard but not yet seen. There is no tactile component to Proteus. Stephen Dedalus experiences no human touch.

"Colonel Cornwall," replied Don Cane turning.

A second figure emerged from the undergrowth.

"Brigadier actually," that man said.

"Retired," added Cornwall deprecatingly.

"So Thieu finally promoted you," replied Don.

Last gasp braid. Solicited prize. Never get that far in our army. Too much time spent in Spooks. Worried his way into the palace. Help build the South's defence strategy. Pull back to Saigon. Hope world opinion turns. Give the Gods time to mass against Achilles. Ford might launch bombers. Catch the NVA in open fields. But Thieu preferred to hear oracles by that point. Stretch-out chicken guts on a parquetry floor. No stomach for another fight. France 1940. Just get out safe. Like Chang. Take the gold into exile. Leave the dan toc to Charlie.

"Do you remember Major Oswald?"

"Yes. You attended jungle training school."

"Good memory. But I guess you've had plenty of time to reflect. Where have you been?"

"Manila."

"Sound choice," said Cornwall. "A regime that is well-disposed to the West. Close to the main theatre. I've got some business in the Philippines. We should talk."

"I'm only here for a few days."

"Catching up with family?" asked Oswald smartly.

"Haven't made up my mind yet."

"Your wife has done a good job," said Cornwall. "She sent your son to school with Ian Westacott."

"How did she afford that?"

"Scholarship, I think."

Last organ chords. God in three persons. Counter-melody. Descant Satan. Milton's hero. Smooth-sided shape. Me and two women. Two sons. Richie and her husband. Me. Our child. Holding it tightly in your grip. Trying to will it back life. Let go now. Triangle caving into its core. Ousia.

"Lloyd Bent is the school pastor," added Oswald.

"How's he going?"

"Still a few cards short of a full hand," added Cornwall. A well-seasoned joke.

"Not him," replied Don. "I meant my son."

"He's turned into a fine young man."

Stephen Dedalus as seen by others. Something wrong in the genes and chromosomes. A drunk like his dad. Squandered his education. Just crawled back from Paris, taille between kneecaps. Saw off his mother. She was no Penelope. Hangs with a smart crowd. Still got tabs on himself as poet. The character of Stephen is a semi-parody of Peisistratus by Joyce. Hard to make space for Telemachus within any narrative citing his father's exploits. Sheer weight of actual performance.

"What's your line of business in Manila?" asked Oswald.

"Import-export."

"Are you close to any Opposition figures?"

"You mean the Ramos faction."

"Yes, them. Marcos is spent. Soon we'll have to deal with a new government."

"Nothing much will change."

"Clarke will be shut."

"A gesture to the masses."

"Who do you know?" pressed Oswald.

"Tuason gang."

"Ex Squires Bingham crowd?"

"Right. I'm mates with Bolo. I also know the guys from Floro Corp."

"We could use a good man in Manila. We represent a number of substantial family offices. Our clients are looking to repatriate their assets. Quietly ... and fast."

"Your work is common knowledge around Makati, Chas. I was mates with Ludwig Rocka. He was the conduit for IDPC. When he died, Elizabeth lost cover. Marcos sacked her last year. Now they all want OUT."

"Her son has a bright future."

"Ramos will have to go after him. He's got no choice. Young Mick ran Gintong Alay for his uncle. They'll just follow the money. But Ramos won't do anything that is irreversible."

"Like Roxas."

"Precisely."

"Are you interested?"

"I'm always open to offers."

"There's also snake runs," said Oswald.

Cane shrugged.

"Yes. It's not always ... conventional trade," added Cornwall.

"What kind of stuff?"

"Mainly small ordinance."

"Good old M16," said Don Cane mainly to himself.

"A2."

"I've tried it a few times."

"Central Luzon?" asked Oswald.

"Hunting trips," replied Cane curtly. He leered. Flushing out NPA jungle bases outside Manila with Nick Rowe. Mao tactics. Control the countryside like Sir Charles. My first mission in Vietnam. Organise the Ilaga. New Montagnards. Folk Catholics. Put some shit back on the Moro. Machetes marking victims with a Cross. Flesh amulets. Seen that stuff back in the Hills. Maybe nineteen-sixty-four. Two platoons concertinaed in scrub. Quick click. Friendly fire. An instant's meaning. Fragging parties. Kill a buffalo charging. They hate human turps. Spring on Damansky Island. Soviet Behemoth. First Andropov. Now Chernenko. Sick men all. Red China. Hard to get a fix on Deng. He suckered Carter. They've always got a long game. Make proletariat from scratch. Game of statistics. Kill Ratio. Lure the US army to Henan. Insert Soviet pops. Mao's boast. I can take three hundred million casualties and still come out on top, he told Khrushchev. Sheer weight of numbers. Invasion of Vietnam. Teach a lesson to Hanoi. Re-adapted the notion of Pyrrhic victory. It took twenty days to capture Lang Son. PLA got a bloody nose. But it showed the world that China would expend its troops without scruples to meet strategic goals. Rerunning the tactics of Korea. Human walls. Vietnam as fulcrum. No shift on Kampuchea. New Soviet reticence since Kabul. Ogarkov's back. Downsizing the Red Army. Expend an ox. First military parade since 1959. Reel of bottled museum pieces. Irish expatriates Stephen knew in Paris. There is always a political undertow to *Ulysses*. Stephen on Kevin Egan. He worked in a Renault factory. Served by a waiter called Thanh. Visit Versailles. Stand outside in the cold. Wilson passed Nguyen Ai Quoc in a limousine as he entered the palace. Scrape away frost from his limousine window. See a spasmodic face. History's missed moments. Later, he became known as Chen Vang, a Chinese merchant. Then Ly Thuy. Finally, Ho Chi Minh. Name-shifting Proteus. Joyce also malleable with such. A landslide victory is forecast for President Reagan in today's US election, said the radio. Despite all the hype of the Reagan Doctrine, the Contras still need funding, replied Cornwall. We can't get money off Capitol Hill. Sell whatever you got. Mulligan: nine pounds, three pairs of socks, a suit inter alia. Lend Lease bill to Britain was four billion pounds. Lao Tigers. Griffith dope shuttles. Siphon off Iranian bucks. Met Colonel North once in Saigon. Son Thang testimony. Stephen pities the loveless, landless patriots in Paris that he sees floating between taverns and a night time brothel. The model for Kevin Egan was Joseph Casey. He tried to recruit Joyce in Paris. Like Stephen, Joyce used the notion of artistic detachment as an excuse for withdrawal. But he was truly pusillanimous. Only when his writing was suppressed did he summon courage.

"Well, what do you say?" asked Cornwall.

"Like I said, let's talk."

"Where are you staying?"

"You know where," replied Don Cane smiling. "Pick a time that suits."

"Twenty-one hundred tonight."

"Alright. But just you, Chas. Ground floor bar. Table on the street. Nothing personal, Ossie. I know you'll be nearby."

"Done. Now you really must excuse us. I must have a quiet word with Choc's widow."

Tom Hallem commenced his run through the back streets of Ashfield. He proceeded beside Pratten Park, crossed Milton Street and wound his way to the back of Western

Suburbs Hospital. At the Weldon Street intersection, he sat the car on its handbrake and waited for the final descent. Costumed in a cuckold's suit and Victor work boots. My version of Stephen's Latin hat and ashplant. An Irish exile in Paris. Australian expatriates in London. Sewage froth on a bank. See Deleuze and Guattari (C4). Cynical emissaries. They colonised our outsider status. Last straw. They just don't GET the basic disjuncture: from DOWN here everything UP THERE looks part of IN. Extrinsicspace.exe. Odysseus returned as a beggar. Becoming Minor. Dog retaking its pole. Kill the priest for praying against my return. Stooping to conquer. Home game. Telemachus lost. Collateral damage. Beasts expel their offspring from a cave. Clear the temple. No place for an heir. Hamlet-like incongruous. Go naked into night like Job. All part of manhood. Son must repeat the journey of the father. Unfortunate Oedipus. Look what Paris dragged home. Some other man's purse. Priam's moan-you-moaners. Eteocles' intransigence. All that shit over Polynices' corpse. I'd have left it rotting at the bus stop. Fighting brothers. Cane and Abel. Joseph and Esau. Bill and Paul. Stanislaus Joyce. Functional foil. Tom extinguished the engine, opened the car door, grabbed his satchel and stepped into the unprepossessing rain working the keys to his fingertips. He pressed them through the letterbox slot. A hand reaching into a pale sickroom. His mother's house. Life gone out of the masque. Stephen's visit to Nuncle Richie. A flatbed figurine. Winter gleam fighting reticulated branches. Sunshades of lacework across borer-tapped floorboards. Jigsaw of an unkempt face. Propped-up in bed in unbuttoned rags menthol compress coagulating on his chest. Floating in and out of morphine mirrors. Time of least discomfort, they say. Leon Daniel smacked down hard by the Sisters of Charity. Swimming like Bobby Goldsmith. Morphine suppository blooming in Tom's guts like a Morton bay fig canopy. Tree of Hope hospice. Cabrini Private. Blanched hair sprouting out the top of a worn singlet. What did they do to your chest? A long line spluttered with stiches. Silver bristles sprayed his face. Tumor well dug in. Sewer veins main-lining all the way down his lymph system. Uncle Paul's eyes opened. He laid aside the hack-towel and pulled his body up the iron bedhead. The smell of his soil split the room. Softness of flannel on scarred midriff. I don't want any last-minute fixes, he said to his wife. No priests. Nothing. He turned a savaged eye on his nephew. A teardrop cyst covered Leon's face. Carmine gone grey. CMV. T Cell count exhausted. And I don't want your uncle anywhere near my coffin, he said to Tom Hallem veering close to his face. Whistlewords. Sweet hard drops. You look just like your fucking dad, he added unhappily. Bloodline conveyed. Can't wash it off. Heart transplant doesn't change your brain. Something stuck in yer head. A birth certificate. My father's name is missing. Perpetual transfusions no difference make. Shem in his ink battleship. Bic Martello. Joyce told the Clongowes gentry that his uncles were millionaire tap merchants. Houses of decay: his, mine, all. Get me some morphine, asked Uncle Paul. Equivalent of Richie's whusky. A potion denied three times before being drawn. His wife demurred. Go fuck yourself then, he scolded. Richie is shown to be a cruel man by Joyce. Tom Hallem opened the gate, walked up the path and sought refuge on the balcony of his mother's home until the thunderstorm abated. A sudden gust lifted threads of rain-spray from her camellia trees as he mounted the step. Wind out of a bag. No point knocking. Les not home. Turn away. Go. Some mourners gathered on the driveway. Don Cane strode across the chapel courtyard. Tribal electricity. He straightened. Birnam Wood to Dunsinane. "Is that Don Cane," asked Barry Evans jabbing Brian Deverill in the ribs. He swallowed. Buddha choking on dried boar's flesh. Symbol of esoteric knowledge. Third avatar of Vishnu. Wild as an uncastrated pig. Deverill murmured. Yes, thought Don Cane. Atalanta's prey. Who would be Meleager? Fated to destroy his own family like Heracles. Or Althaea who threw the fatal stick. A mother killing her own child. Medea also. Partial to sacrilege, she was. Suckled by a she-bear. Motherless child. Sometimes I feel like one, sang the blind man. Orphaned. I must visit her grave, thought Don. Go now. Go. "Let's take up a collection for Choc's kids," said Ray Farrar. Brian Deverill extracted his wallet and pledged five bold Redbacks. "Or else two Pineapples per head," he said. "All in," added Evans. "I'm banker." Money flowed into his palms. He stuffed notes in his pockets and began a list of benefactors on the back of a funeral program. Don Cane passed within earshot.

"I'd like to make a contribution," said Don Cane.

"It's a ton," replied Farrar.

"Put me down."

"Name?"

"Eric Killion," replied Don Cane slowly. He extracted a wad of different currencies from his wallet and carefully extracted two mint fifty-dollar Australian notes from a clump of pesetas and greenbacks.

"Thanks mate," said Evans.

"How'd you know Choc," asked Brian Deverill slyly.

"We were mates up north."

"You never served then," asked Ray Farrar.

"Number never came up."

"A lot of blokes just volunteered," said Brian Deverill.

"Wasn't my form," replied Don Cane engaging Deverill's eyes directly. His body pressed forward slightly. Odysseus never took a backwards step. A mate grasped Brian's shoulder.

"Thanks for the pledge," concluded Barry Evans. "But you ought to show a bit of respect. There's blokes here put their lives on the line for this country. Including Choc."

Don Cane nodded and proceeded without. Down a set of blonde brick steps. Bald crown displayed. A damp mop. He pulled at his belt to hold the underside of his belly in place. His body assumes different shapes at different times to different folks. Note the arbitrary nature of character descriptions. Stories of war service. Noxious tales. Apocrypha. Been every place. Done every battle. Keep up the Show. Misinformation. Spook-static. A realistic figurine. All morning the low-pressure system hovering off Sydney's coastline wasted periodic spray against the city's crust. Varnish gone dull. Cold lava. Umbrellaless, Tom Hallem waited for a break in the downpour and began to climb. His body was shielded by a big mimosa clump that scattered the footpath with a lode of seeds and supple flowers. Some continuity of shelter then. Lilypad jumps. He moved past darkened Federation houses. Splintered strips of faded joinery offset their prim geometry. A ragged cat slipped between the bars of a metal gate and placed herself in his path. Mkgnao! Mkgnao! He bent to stroke her coat and felt each succeeding vertebra as she withdrew along his palm. She passed back. Mkgnao! Mkgnao! He stooped to her chin with his index finger and felt her throat rattle. She followed him for a few yards and paused groggily. The back entrance of Kent Convalescent Home rose on thick foundations overlooking the full carpark. Happy Valley. Five metres up to the deck. Imperial Citadel at Hue. Outer crust. Noman's Land. Fifty-metre fire zone. Barbed wire inner fence. Zigzag trenches. Rock embankments secure my domain. Rise out of the sea. Go up the beach face. Trojans skulking behind their vaunted parapets. German officers had arrived just in time to direct the Turkish defences. Under new management. Enter Apollo. War, horrid war, approaches your borders. Helen o'er smooth walls reclined. Share some intel with Priam. Paris swept off the field. Go to his bedroom. Unscrupulous Venus. Settle into a siege. Ucalegon leaning against a dugout basking in the sun. Sharing a smoke with Louis in the ANZAC trench. Telling a joke. Play you again next Saturday at Bolton's Ridge. PJ Harvey's lyrics channel Les Carlyon's prose. Death was everywhere, they said. Priam means GUTS. Layout of Troy. It all started with infrastructure. Ripping off Poseidon. Bad dope. Walls made of stakes. Crystal labyrinths. Yon devoted. Troy's proud walls must lie levelled. Wrap in fire. Troy overlooked the plains of Scamander. Khe Sanh squatted in a drain. Stick Grunts out in the jungle and the NVA will come. Outposts in the hills. Mountaintop beauty. Tracer slicing nocturne. Low organhum. AK47. Unique pop. Once tried, never forgot. Infiltrating our trenches. Hand to hand wrestle. A grenade threw me against the side of the ditch. Both legs shredded. Calling out "Choc!" He dragged me back to CHQ. Wet bandages covered my shame. KSCZ. The Greeks built a defensive barrier around their port along the coast after the death of Achilles. See Books 12–13. Paris' random shot. An anguished mother hurled a tile down on Pyrrhus from a rooftop which crushed his skull. Joyce would have seen exquisite justice in that image. Life's aimless ill-purposes. A back-kick, Stephen calls it. Nightmare's consume our end. Each person reduced to a sequence of events good, bland and useless. Lost the protection of the Mediterranean fleet. Vung Tau. Every type of work ship chained together. Loose wire perimeter. A couple of dozy guards. Evacuation point IF THE SHIT EVER. 75 it did. The fishing trawlers were overwhelmed by refugees. Stuck in the tide like Odysseus. IN/OUT/LULL. Forced back to shore. Re-education camps. Tom Hallem closed quickly on the familiar form of Bob Hensley. His long, crooked back was set on a deliberate path. Our packs o'er-pressed us. The heat toppled our bodies forward. Hills twice as steep up Kosciuszko's side. He visited his wife each day. Tom arrived at his shoulder. The old man turned stiffly.

"Tom," he said peering through thick bifocals. A karst face. "You gave me a shock. How are yer, lad?"

He stuck out a cattleman's hand. Its crust had been sucked dry by Snowy sunglare. Callous pelt. Hallem shifted his satchel to the other shoulder and offered his own palm. Enfolded. His thumb hung on the webbing between the old man's thumb and index finger.

"Fine, thank you. How's Mrs Hensley?"

The old man exposed enormous dentures and withdrew his hand gently.

"She's alright," he said in a broad accent; its power fractured by age. "She doesn't remember much." He grimaced. "No, that's not fair. She's ... inconsistent. Will you pop in?"

Tom Hallem glanced at the Incabloc numerals on the pearly watch face. Timepiece: gift from his mother. He kept it on his wrist unto death. Let it tick on after he lay tickless in Prahran. He was killing time until he met Ana. This passage mimics Stephen Dedalus wandering Sandymount Strand while he waits ninety minutes to meet Mulligan.

"I'd love to," he replied.

They walked into the car park together.

"Have you noticed the cranes?" asked Mr Hensley.

Shadow-grids traversed their upturned heads. Heavy chains jangled on descent scraping along a truck tray.

"Hard to avoid," replied Hallem grinning. Mr Hensley chuckled. Workers hastily wound chain around steel rods and secured a shackle. A shrill whistle rose. Canary hardhats gleamed in the wavering air. In the *Odyssey*, Nestor is Telemachus' first stop. He is a well-respected ancient who counselled the Greeks wisely during the siege of Troy. But he cannot explain Odysseus' disappearance or whereabouts. Telemachus must proceed to Sparta.

"They want to buy my place. But I'm not ready to sell yet."

"They must have offered good money."

"Not interested. Not while my wife is here."

He gestured. Tom Hallem smiled. They ambled onwards. Talk held in abeyance. They climbed the concrete staircase. Mr Hensley steadied himself by gripping the iron rail. He was rising slowly enough for Tom Hallem to count each step. Twelve in total. INSERT NUMEROLOGICAL MEANING (NOTE JJ FIXATION). Take the cattle to high country each spring. Where the fledgling Murrumbidgee cuts across Blue Waterholes. Mount Analogue. Up where Oedipus was saved. Cattle left free to roam and forage. Government put a stop to all that in nineteen-fifty-five. Confiscated our stock. Mustered the stragglers. Forced relocations. Flood Adaminaby. In autumn, the cattle used to find their own way back to the plains. Water rolling from mountain springs with a soft inland murmur. Death gurgle of Jounama Creek into a stagnant pond. Ex Tumut River. They sank the Franklin homestead. One kilometre south from the dam-side road. They stepped onto the porch. Distant sound of cheap cutlery scraping against thick crockery. A long window revealed a row of kitchen-hands in lemon uniforms. Steam escaped in a stifling gust when the industrial dishwasher was opened. Searing plates stacked in piles on stainless steel benches. Mister Hensley ushered Tom down a corridor. Stephen proceeds along the beach cracking shells under his boots. He closes his eyes. He hears. A volunteer was bashing out a honky-tonk version of "Bill Bailey" in the recreation room. Bouncy bass hand. Eye slits so narrow they could hardly receive light. Just enough to perceive the keyboard's wide horizon. Knew it by touch. Tom recalled the lyrics: chores undertaken gladly for presence returned BREATH Free bed and board also BREATH Guilt acknowledged PAUSE Fine-toothed comb his sole possession. Rhetorical request for remembrance of happy past events. Speed into morass. A confession. Low down dirty guilt etcetera. Finally, the drawn-out imprecation of the title. Clever syntactical modification. End on the word HOME. Tom Hallem pondered the repatriation of such a man. Depend on the bloke really. Maybe a quiet sort of chap. Odysseus in rags. Penelope's guile. Neither needed to apologise. Was Helen repentant? Unlikely. Menelaus was a shrunken figure by the end of the *Iliad*. He could never get his hands on Paris. His brother ran the show. Directed him to kill Adrestus. Execute a POW. Low act. Not even a foetus in its mother's belly was to be spared. Agamemnon was always a ruthless bastard. Slaughtered his own daughter for God's sake. But was he too cocky or too trusting when he went back to Mycenae? Fatal error. The brittle applause of the small crowd flagged. Be careful banging those joints. Shake yer dentures. Running a scrubbing brush over your soul. Time cancelled by music. All art aspires to its condition. Penelope stroking my hair while the broken notes of "Japanese Sandman" crept in a whisper. Embers. Shelley's coal gone cold. The old man reached the front door.

"This way," he indicated.

A clerk opened the heavy plot register. There were three results for the surname "CANE." Waterfalls of seconds. Hourglass pending. Sandspit o'er'n'o'er. Dunked in time.

Weighted drag down. His mother's grave was located in Anglican 5C section. The clerk marked a pamphlet with a pencil cross and sent him out. He turned from the heavy sandstone gates and plotted his course through the grounds. Cook the navigator. Palm trees lining the route. If only I had a donkey. Pass Catholic 29D. Turn right. At the arse end of the cemetery, a market gardener was tilling his field. Rows of Rau Muong, Vietnamese mint and shallots had been cut into the slope at odd angles above a deep gully full-frothing with blackberry weed. Conical hat. Flannelette shirt open. Scarecrow staked in dirt. Don studied the headstones. A plaster bust mounted on a black marble block. Verse from some Matt Munro song. "No one could explain / Just why this sorrow came ... our way / But til we meet again / Remember the promise we always made." Odysseus to Penelope. A duet. Wedding vows. Dear John letters. Sorry Pete, I've become a feminist. Dearest Arthur, I don't approve of this war. Babe I can't wait any longer. Met a yank. Gone to a monastery. A stormwater basin was set like a pillbox inside mounds of construction waste like one of Westacott's dioramas. Garbage dumps of Manila. Flow of blood from the palace. Gravity. Across the perimeter path, a single grave was marked with a homemade cross decorated with rusty stubby caps. It was bound together with fishing line threading lead weights. He read its inscription:

ERIC KILLION
9 May 1935 – 18 Apr 1961
"Simple man, simple dream"

Cane looked up at banks of broken roof tiles crushed in asphalt scabs. Killed in a training exercise at Canungra. Missed the send-off. Off on psych training with Pete Young. Three iron cranes of Brotherson Dock bowed and rose. Distant skyscape. Concrete-blocks of the breakwater. Midweek sailing race. A tanker moved past Bare Island. Curling sand dunes. I also missed my mother's funeral. Not much of a show I bet. He wiped sweat from his cheek as he approached her grave. Blistered plaster letters were peeling off the sea-worn, colourless sandstone face:

IN MEMORY OF
Florence Miller Cane
Née Kelly
Died 1 February 1982
Aged 70

Bare facts. Some names she used. Some jettisoned. Everybody called her Rita. After Hayworth. Ironing board curls in dyed red hair. Weary old blues. He sketched a eulogy. A woman he hadn't seen for the last twenty years of her life. Why did she come back to Australia? Criminal always returns to the scene, Bloom thought. Lyndall made it all the way back to Emmy's farm. Died trying to give birth. Careless Love. Penelope Hallem's numb contralto underwrote the lyric. Wrecked the life of many a poor girl. He surveyed the concrete retaining wall. Mosaic of tiny white tiles. The aunt thinks you killed your mother, Mulligan tells Stephen. But I can't be held responsible, thought Don. Insert list of dead mothers. Rachel died giving birth to Benjamin. Anticlea killed herself on a false report of Ulysses' death. See also Aegeus. Dickens killed them off in childbirth. Mary Dedalus succumbed to cancer. Mary Joyce died 13 August 1903, aged forty-four. Less than a year before *Ulysses* is set. Her son broke many a true vow. It shipwrecked her wrecked husband. Church of the Three Patrons at Rathgar brought the wrong man into her life. Ten births three misbirths eleven mortgages pawned furniture. Indigent Children. Absconding fathers. Why I sing this song of hate. Sell the piano. Black sail of Perseus billowing off Piraeus. Careless sons. Careworn sires. Flying through my head like wine. Or a stray bullet. You've filled my heart with lead. Wearing its copper jacket. Now I'm walking, talking to myself like Stephen Dedalus. Orpheus turned back to check on Eurydice. I twisted on the track straight after Bobby Horne shuffled off that Jumping Jack. His eyes held my gaze for a moment as the rest of his body exploded. Don Cane turned from the blank slab that had erased the shape of his mother. Distant Kurnell blurred by rainspray. Steel pipes pressing skywards. Cook's sails sped between these tight heads and turned port for shelter. Owners said: you're all dead, all ghosts. A petroleum plant on the opposite headland was pummelled out of view. Long pipeline jetty. Tanker docking. Skinny blue flame rising into grey air blazing to oily vapour, glutinous smoke. Basted skyscreen. Speciosa locis. Fly-blown, wind-battered, exposed, inbred backwater. Anywhere else in the world they would have built a shrine. Not Australia. Instead, you got the broken façade of the E-Z Breeze Café. Palsied "For Lease" sign posted in its painted-out window. GO COLA. Have a go, yer cunts. Product of Australian Convenience Foods, Beverage Drive, Taren Point. Exporting nutritious snack foods to Asia. Sid Fogg Coaches. We Move the Shire. Pipe King for all your PVC needs. A strip that reeked Australia. Couldn't have built a better monument if they'd mounted Paul Hogan on a point post. Drowned, starved, parched, murdered in foreign wars murdering poisoning killing the locals back home. Occupied ground. Forced cultivation. Trial and error. Cross the Goyder Line. Never able to impose ourselves on a map. A light vestige. Jet planes breached the low cloud cover dragging streamers towards the bay. Don Cane shifted across the plot to his father's memorial:

TOM WILLIAM CANE 1893–1942
Beloved husband of Florence
Father of Donald John
"A just upright man"

Job 12:4. Inadvertent pun. Drunk wobbles of Simon Dedalus smoothed by a sympathetic wall. Barely erect beast. His son used the same method in Nighttown. Like father like son. Cradled in my father's arms in the backyard. A single frangipani yielded crisp broken limbs. Slab of green concrete. Hose it down on hot days. Watch steam rise. Shelley's down/up imagery. Don Cane pulled some weeds out of the cracks in the cracked slab. Involuntary buzz in his palate. HE MET A SIGH CLOSEST. Compartments in man. Impossible thresholds. INSERT Professor Edkin's system of self-classification.[1] Classical literature depicted humanity in all its fullness and flips. Pathos of blighted Heracles. Daedalus shoving his nephew off a truck. Paris and Helen as dolls in Venus' playroom. Irrational envy, insecurities, misunderstandings, random events all unleashed terrible disasters upon the Ancients. Only the symmetrical symbolism of their tropes held chaos at bay. Unmoral tales brimming with ectoplasm. Farce short-circuiting pathos. Australian mindset. Got to laugh or you'd wane. Pessimism of the intellect. Optimism of the will. Nation founded on misprision. Defeat has the same value as victory. Gallipoli. Reactionary coups like '75. Equalisation policy. An atmosphere of failure and crude irony surrounds our national leaders. Curtin expiring on the brink. Chifley pointing the army at his trade union mates. Mad Doc Evatt unravelling along the Bench. Jack Lang kneecapped. Puerile Scullin. Lyons pandering to Niemeyer. Judas Bruce betrayed by Judas Hughes. Mercurial Iago. Withered as the Kaiser leaking racist paranoia at Versailles. Treachery can't be easily stuffed back into the box. A black body politic. Senile Deakin like bemused Lear. Bankrupt Parkes. Deluded Wentworth. Mistreated Macquarie. Disgraced Bligh. Embittered Phillip. Don Cane yawned. No more shapes. A massive ship was being piloted through the heads of Botany Bay moving apace towards Brotherson Dock. All-sort containers rose from its maw. Tom turned towards footfalls. The wide deck was shielded from Liverpool Road by a dark camellia hedge. Sound of cicadas and traffic. Mister Hensley dragged a metal chair along the

---

1. Suburban Father with 5 realistic action phrases!
1. "That's a good idea! We'll do it next time."
2. "Let's go shopping instead!"
3. "Don't worry about me, I'm OK."
4. "I'm not criticizing you BUT ..."
5. "Have you cleaned your room yet?"

balcony to his wife's side. An unstoppered metal leg scraped the terracotta tiles; momentarily enlivening the crowd. Calm restored by silence. Doze again. Crawling through the mob like Coriolanus. Unlock the gate. Stephen comes to regret his Dandy's disdain for common people in Proteus. Human husks were scattered in chairs and walking-frames around Tom Hallem. His fingers stroked his wife's transparent hair.

"Is that you, Dad?"

"It's me, dear. Bob."

"Oh, you again."

"How are you?"

"I'm worried."

She turned in her chair and planted keen eyes on their pokered faces.

"I'm very worried about the Race Week Ball. The School of Arts is too small. Do you think there's enough cover if it rains? I've prayed for fine weather. I've prayed for that a number of times. And I've prayed for you as well. Just because I was praying. Hello Sophie dear. How's school? Still having trouble with history?"

Bob turned to Tom and spoke frankly.

"She thinks you're her late niece."

Mistaken identity. Gender flips. Death by friendly fire. Prison-switches. Ghosts reborn. Stock tropes. Death of Sydney Carton. Gallows hubris. Far, far better thing etcetera. Accidental beheadings in Shakespeare. Usually caused by administrative malfunctions. Sew a new flower onto the same old dress. Harmon's sailor as depicted by the author of *The Curved Plough*. Prisons where escape was impossible like Siberia (Ivan Denisovitch), French Guinea (Papillon) or New South Wales (various convicts). Build one long rabbit-proof fence. Helen identifying Telemachus by gait. Odysseus and Eurycleia. Cyrano's nose. Hapless genetics. Sitting in a kitchen full of strangers in Wolverhampton everyone talking through their adenoids. Kris Richards walked straight up to me in the crowd at Birmingham Bus Station. You must be Uncle Eric's son, she said. Eric the father and Eric the husband. My mother's dissembling. Unrequited Trinities. Parnell went under several aliases including Fox and Stewart to cover his turns with Katharine O'Shea, which bore fruit in the form of three children (see EUMAEUS). Twins hiring twins who were separated at birth. Sebastian and Viola. Henry the Fifth disguised as a yeoman. Tartuffe's mask. Looks a lot like Charles Darnay. Fake piety. Go back to the circus in Nebraska. Switcheroo. Swap exile with Hermann Stoeffer. Take on the guise of Eugène L. Your nickname is Napoleon. Gogol's bureaucrat. Wilde's Jack posing as Earnest discovers what his name actually is. Eliza Doolittle > Darwin's bet > Empire linguistics. Henry Lawson in London. Lionel Logie teaching ANZACS how to speak through holes. Our Protean tongue. Dominioned literature. Stooping to Conquer. STRINE. A barmaid grinds out the term, tie'm pleas jennermen. The old woman continued.

"It's my first go on the organising committee. I would hate to fluff it. The spring race meeting is the highlight of the social calendar in both Tumut and Adelong."

"I'm sure it will be a great success dear."

"What would you know? Have you put the posters up at Quong's yet? We should be getting them out to folk as far as Moorang and Glen Marsh. And then there's the advertisement in the Star to be placed. Ask that Jewish tyke fella: Broeom. Bookings are very slow this year, Missus Halliday tells me."

Mrs Hensley took Tom Hallem's hand.

"How's your brother?" she asked suddenly.

"Who?"

"The slut's son," she replied.

Her husband told her SHUSH.

"Here's your tea, Mrs Hensley," said an attendant arriving suddenly in a sky-blue work dress with a tray of beverages.

"Is the sun bothering you?" her husband asked.

"No," she replied blithely. "It looks like it's doing a good job. Leave it where it is."

Hallem drank. Sunshine burnished his eyes. Steeples of electricity raced from the perimeter through haze. His hangover shed its trippy detachment. A formation of geese passed across the porch. Mrs Hensley withdrew her hand. It left his palm aloft. Gingerly, he rolled his fingers into a fist and put it in his lap. She reached into a bag and withdrew a stained quince cardigan.

"I hope you're not coming down with a cold. It's a funny spring. Here. Take this. It will keep you safe."

She pressed the garment on him. Soft Mohair. She grinned. Not her own teeth. An orderly advanced into their midst behind a sparkling new wheelchair. The watch pinned to the front of her uniform read eleven forty-five.

"Time for your sponge-down, May."

"Thank you, Sister."

"I'll see you afterwards, dear."

Mrs Hensley turned to Hallem.

"You can return it next time."

The orderly linked hands around the old woman and lifted her into the wheelchair. Mrs Hensley waved brightly. Tom Hallem pulled the cardigan into his lap and rose. The old man chewed at some imaginary pulp. A truck was braking in increments on the Enfield bends. Eerie abeyance.

"I've got this letter for you," said Bob at last.

"Who is it from?"

"Mate of a mate from the Rissole. Don't tell Les I gave it to you. Read it on the bus."

He passed Tom Hallem a small envelope with typed face. Don Cane recognised a figure moving through the car park. Young face. Unbright. Bowed. Hold hard. Every one of the three thousand five hundred oaks that make up my hull groaned. Image of his late father.

"You must be Choc's son," said Don Cane.

"Yes. I'm Greg Wheaton."

"I'm Eric," he replied offering his hand.

"How did you know my father?"

"We were mates."

"You're not a soldier?"

"No. I gather you don't get on with the Vet crowd."

"How did you work that out?" he replied sardonically.

"You weren't ... mingling."

"I lost touch."

"Even with your mother?"

"She was loyal to Dad."

"He was a good man when I knew him. What was he like as a father?"

"He was a drinker. I left home as soon as I could."

"What did you do?"

"Got some work anti-fouling yachts down the CYC. Learned some joinery and electricals. Now I know my way right round a boat."

"Do you sail?"

"Yes. I'm going on the Sydney–Hobart for the first-time next month."

A most treacherous strip. Gone on the rising tide to face Van Diemen's Land. No land, no harbour, all about us black water, above pure sky. Crossing Bass Strait. A shallow ledge. Roaring under the continent's sterile gut. Elijah, a skiff, a crumpled throwaway, bobbing east. King Island listing to starboard. Piercing Scylla's pinnacles. Pinhole-stretch. Needlehead through flesh. Saline spray. Stay above fifty degrees south. Flanks of ships and trawlers smashed by southerlies each night. Antarctic currents. Whirlpool off Eden. Chill summer surf. Numb fingerprints. Cold undertow. Wayfarer still holds the record for the slowest race time. Eleven days. Blown awry like Odysseus. The Mediterranean represented Homer's entire cosmos. The known world emanated around it. Dawn emerged over its wine-dark meniscus. It hauled sunset down as well. And scrolled the constellations. The geography of Odysseus' voyage is hotly disputed by scholars. Some say that its western extremity was south of Tarragona in the Hades episode. Others maintain Ogygia, Calypso's island, was further south of Gibraltar off Morocco. The Lestrygonians episode has been sited anywhere from Sardinia to Telepylos on the African coast. There is general agreement that Lotus-Eaters was set on Djerba Island off Tunisia. With moderate seas the bulk of the fleet enjoyed hard working down to Green Cape. The breeze then freed up to give fast reaching conditions across Bass Strait and a fast run down the Tasmanian coast. A headland, a ship, a sail upon billows. Farewell Queenstown harbour full of Italian ships. I'm tired of all them rocks in the sea, he said. Salt junk all the time. Captain Cat. Ahab. Don Cane admired the young man. He was set in Athena's mold. Versatile. No privilege. A labourer. A technician. Master of mechanical arts. An artist of sorts. All the skills of Man chiselled into a fine frame. Give him a garland. Could be an astronaut. Put him in the jungle: he would thrive. Drop him onto a plank in the ocean: he would get to shore safely. Everyman's offspring. Not-Everyson.

"I gather you didn't make peace with your father. Or he with you?"

"No. He just dropped dead one day at work."

Dark and vicious place he got. By fate mandated. Not natural disposition. Call it chance. Perforations in a sound vessel will cause it to sink. The Gods are never just. His service cost him dearly.

"Do you live in Sydney?" asked Greg Wheaton.

"No. I live up north. This is the first time I've been here in years."

"Where are you staying?"

"Kings Cross."

"I'm going that way. Let me give you a ride."

They proceeded to the car park. A four-eighty bus to Railway Square ground through a progression of gear changes as it negotiated the s-bends of the Hume Highway. The driver turned the large horizontal wheel into a sharp curve just after Burwood Road. Sun hit a bright silver badge shimmering on his blue shirt-pocket. In the rear mirror, he could see the receding art deco facade of the Golden Sheaf Hotel. Footsteps clomped down the black boards of the grimy aisle. Talkback flared from a small transistor radio swinging off a strap on the window handle next to him. Time for a Traffic Update, said the announcer. Let's cross to Chris Burns in the Budget Rent-a-Car helicopter. What's it like out there, mate? A voice emerged over close chopper blades. Dust-off. Well Gary, there's been a four-car pile-up on Parramatta Road near Leichhardt. Congestion all the way back to Strathfield. As a result, there's a ten-minute delay getting into the city. The Australian Bureau of Meteor–CHEEP!–ology rates pollution in the low range. Another wet aft CHEEP! will be followed by an unsettled evening. Winds in excess of forty kilometres per hour are forecast. City top of nineteen degrees, Liverpool twenty-one. And a wet track for the Cup in Melbourne, Gary CHEEP! Mudlark's delight. I'm Chris Burns for Budget Flat Rate. Twenty-five dollars-a-day including mileage. Thanks, Mate. Coming up to midday on this stormy Sydney spring afternoon. Time for another Solid Gold Classic. Horse with No Name on Sydney's W-ROCKS FM: INSERT LYRICS Tom Hallem reached the roadside and looked west. On the wide exterior bend of the Appian Way, a Kingswood station wagon swept towards the bus stop and halted suddenly. Tom Hallem advanced from the kerb. Another man's suit. Exposed. His hair waved. He tensed as the transverse face of Ana Lafei Papese reached across the cabin and cracked the passenger side door open. INSERT CHARACTER DESCRIPTION. Papese (TO SING, PLURAL). Also, the word for dolphin. Note irony that she dies in a puddle at the end of the novel. Must be imbued with elements of ALP (beautiful plural). Also, M le F. Link to Arthurian legend. She is taking Tom on his final journey back to Avalon.

"Wara wara," said Tom Hallem grasping the frame.

"What?" she asked.

"It means 'fuck off' in Dharug."

"Wara wara then, you idiot. Get in."

A bus horn blared. Ana pushed her guitar onto the back seat crushing some dried flowers. Tom Hallem dived into the vehicle. In Paris, Kevin Egan told Stephen tales of wild escapes and outlandish disguises as a lure. Another false father figure using him. How different to Bloom then? INSERT COMPARISON TABLE. Why should Stephen think of Eccles Street as his father's palace? His REAL version of the battle with the suitors would have involved confronting standover men trying to evict his family from his father's latest house next day. Link to Father Conmee's arrears. His landlord was Reverend Love, an Anglican cleric from Sallins who appears in sub-episode 8 of Wandering Rocks. This is another narrative remark by Joyce on the relative power structures of Ireland. It suggests the compulsory tithes imposed on Catholic farmers to support the protestant church. Molly Maguire groups went looking for him (see Cyclops). In Dublin, they were called Peep O'Day Boys. Link to Battle of Union Street, Newtown, 1931. Ana manoeuvred the gearstick upwards promptly and jerked the Beast to life. She represents a type of independent female character unknown in Joyce. His women are dead, pregnant, post-natal, chained to a pram, stuck in kitchens, working draught taps, waitressing, selling their bodies for survival-cash, delivering milk or begging for pennies as waifs. Even Molly Bloom never gets out of the house. Her only leverage is adultery. This representation was undoubtedly true-to-life of Dublin in 1904. However, Joyce never attempted to invest any female character with the power and authority of Classical female goddesses, in particular Athena. This was a missed opportunity. Contemporary authors like Henry James, Oliver

Schreiner and later Hemingway and D H Lawrence all depicted the struggle of modern women in a patriarchal society. The depiction of females in *Ulysses* will be analysed further in Chapter Six.

"Who taught you that shit anyway?" asked Ana Lafei.

"I found it in a book. I want to put some Aboriginal words on a new painting."

"Well I don't speak fancy-pants Sydney tongue. I'm a Meanjin girl. Grew up in Serviceton. I speak Turrbal. That's my mum's language."

"Where's that?"

"Brisbane. You know. Fringe dwellers. From housing estates. They call the place INALA these days."

"What does Inala mean?"

"How should I know? They probably made it up. Sounds boong enough. Be careful of the stereo," she said. "I spent all weekend installing the speakers."

Hallem lifted his workboots off some wires taped together into a colourful bouquet. He looked at Ana's profile peacefully. Her thick hair was pulled back with a bright red hairband, displaying the full arch of her soft face. A single strand had escaped and was brushing her cheek. She stroked it back over her ear absent-mindedly. When she turned to speak, her deep brown eyes and wide brow glowed at Tom.

"This is a nice surprise. Haven't seen you for a while. Want some beer?"

She lifted a brown paper bag between her legs and handed it to him.

"Thanks," he replied taking a short slug from the silver bullet.

"I've also got chips," she said brightly pointing at a butcher's paper parcel wedged between the dashboard and windscreen.

"They should be hot," she continued. "Open them. I'll have some too."

Hallem pulled the package onto his lap. Its warmth suffused his bowels like morphine. He ripped off the sticky-tape and spread the newspaper releasing steam throughout the compartment. Babe in swaddling. Ruddy jowls.

"Don't forget Empty," Ana said gesturing at a cattle dog sulking on the back seat. "She's pregnant, poor bitch. Look at her tits."

Ana raised her sight line in the rear-vision mirror.

"Been waiting in the car all morning, haven't you girl?"

Tom Hallem pressed a handful of chips in his palm letting warm oil seep through his fingers then reached over the car seat towards the dog. It took them from his palm gently in its muzzle. He then fed a crisp fry into Ana's mouth.

"Delicious," she giggled.

"What've you been up to?" he asked.

"Went to see Whores Manure last night. Ended up at the Taxi Club. Matt went home at his self-designated curfew time. I kicked-on to Farquhar's flat. Scored some speed. Kept me going 'til dawn so I went straight to work from there. What about you?"

"I stayed with Elizabeth."

Ana ignored this comment. The car settled at the Brighton Street lights. Place where ALG blew his lights out. Go back to the start of C3. Tom looked past her to the hospital entrance held-up by Doric columns inside square cream piers.

"Push in that tape," she said finally. The car moved. Tom inserted the cassette and browsed the track list on the front of the scratched plastic box. PURE WARS, it read. Side 1 Stooges – Loose, Feedtime – Fastbuck, Scratch Acid – Crazy Dan, Velvet Underground – Can't Stand it, Butthole Surfers – Cowboy Bob, Sonic Youth – Death Valley 69, Salamander Jim – Black Star, Wurm – Dead, Birthday Party – Sonny's Burning, Black Flag – I've Heard it Before, Husker Du – 8 Miles High, Minutemen – Bob Dylan Wrote Propaganda Songs.

The opening chords of Crazy Dan registered through stop-start static.

"Already bung," Tom Hallem said.

"That's a Yarrbal word. And it isn't bung. Just keep your foot off the wires."

She leaned down and shunted a coil of wires bound by electrical tape into invisibility.

"Great tape," he said. "How's Chullora?"

"What can I say? I'm sorting mail. The course takes 33 days – fully-paid – then I get work through the Christmas rush. Nights and weekends. Lots of overtime. I should have enough cash to go Bush for a few months."

"Where do you want to go?"

"I want to drive into the desert. Want to come?"

"That'd be great."

"What are you doing out here anyway?"

"Moving my stuff."

"So, she's selling Beta House."

Tom nodded. Ana scooped up some chips. Goodbye to Ithaca. Farewell Troy. Brick blockhouse guarding the north end of King Street. Squat like lozenge. Stretch of watchtowers. The last Martello was Fort Denison (see C5). Commanded a fire arc across the length of Dublin Bay to the Poolbeg stacks. Siege of Valletta. Ogygia. See Brueghel's painting. Gozo. Visit the Azure Window. Caravaggio was sent there by the Colonna. Knights' gave him sanctuary. Clark Air Base. Warrior monks. Study of Saint Jerome translating the Bible into Latin. Homosexual guilt-trips. Terrors of hell down catacombs. Chu Chi. Ana face-up on the Lake. *Horror ubique animos, simul ipsa silentia terrent*. Napoleon's double-cross. Beheading of John. Ends justify means. Salome's dance steps. Broadway Hotel. Lingerie

Ladies. Tuesday lunchtime. Foxseal. Calypso's entreaties. A sad case. Odysseus rejected immortality. Matter of a mere vampire bite.

"I'm going to see Matt. Want to come?"

"Can't. My cousin's giving a paper at uni. And I need to see Willy."

"Scoring?"

"Yep."

"I wouldn't mind a blast."

"What about Matt? He hates it when you're using."

"Don't worry about him," she stated with a leer.

Calypso as visited by Hermes. Insert list of complaints. I saved him when he was alone. Inspired his art. He'll be nothing alone. I have no ship to give him. He needs a prop. I can only counsel Ulysses on how to reach his own land unscathed. What is he seeking anyway? To reclaim the past. A safe harbour. See Joyce and Sylvia Beach. Someone with good networks. A patron. Not a Muse. Not Bonnard's wife. Or Manet's Olympia. Victorine. Dali's Gala. Or Lizzie Siddal. Get with the INC.ROWD. Duchamp and Peggy Guggenheim in Venice. Chipping frescoes off the wall at Pompeii. Twelve days with Samuel Beckett on a velvet chaise longue. Pollock's sponsor. Funded by the CIA. Insert terms and conditions into the papers. Separate politely for the sake of the children. Nausithous and Nausinous. Maybe Latinus as well. Prepare a magnanimous farewell speech: "listen unhappy man no need to stay here I will let you go so take up your tools and make a vessel that will carry you home I will not stand in your path just GO." Still Odysseus hedges in the *Odyssey*. He doesn't believe in Calypso's good faith. What does this say about his attitude? Or is it just plausible human unease given the Gods' capricious natures? He demands a pledge. Calypso gives it. There is a feast in her cave. She compares Penelope with a goddess unfavourably. That was a tactic which backfired. It only makes Odysseus reaffirm his commitment to get home. They fuck. Dawn comes. She provides the means. He builds a boat. The wind rises. EXIT.

"I'll try scoring for both of us," Tom said. "But there's been a drought."

Ana went quiet. Hallem gazed out the window. Light industry clustered along the highway after Croydon. He looked across the cabin. Ana's belly. A safe p(a)lace. Thick legs set in tights. Open buttons on her blouse. Look away. It used to be so wonderful to wake up on her couch in the morning and get up and smoke too many cigarettes together and drink too much coffee and love her so much without remit. Reference Patyegarang (see C4). Matt got Ana like that. Putuwá. Elizabeth calling Tom back to her bed yesterday. Same score. He fingered a carmine pastel butt. It melted on his finger pads. Don't ever let on to Ana. Like Stephen Dedalus remain obscure. See *Twelfth Night*. A cluster fuck of cross-currents. Mainstay of popular fiction. Orsino loves Olivia who loves Cesario/Viola who loves Orsino. Mary's love for Toby. Ophelia's feelings for Hamlet that may or may not be returned. See also Lysander who loves Helena who loves Demetrius who loves Hermia. Resolve with fairy dust. There's no such balm in *Wuthering Heights*. Maybe Tom felt more like Werther. Cloud shadow drifted across the chicanes prefacing Ashfield shopping centre. Hallem absorbed fleeting symbols: a sandwich board on the church footpath advertising the fact that ELIJAH IS COMING; portholes of Andrews Funeral Parlour; Monaro Realty; Ashfield Quality Butchery ("*Meet the meat / all the family eat*"); Glencastle Wines; a garland of throttled salamis in the window of the Europa delicatessen; staccato steel castanets of Psaltis' Barber Shop. Hercules Street dipped towards the railway station recess. Ashfield Hotel Ray's Florist Dom Polski Club Vibrations Zagarella Tailors Spicer's Family Surgery Ken Carlton Chemist Golden Dragon. Demountable classrooms of Ashfield Boys High School hidden behind a thick cyclone wire fence. Office of Paul Whelan MP, Member for Ashfield. Ashfield School of Arts (1912). Nick Scali furniture. Ampol Service Station. Faded face of the Western Suburbs Rugby League Club. Magpie crest. Railway bridge. A last cluster of vacant shops. Wayfarer Motel. Orange apartment blocks. Tom started doodling with a biro. Ana jacked up the volume and gripped the steering wheel tight. They caught the traffic lights and hung hard right. Starboard tack. Parramatta Road dropped in a long arc towards Petersham hollow. They passed under a rail bridge. Ana accelerated into the steep ascent towards Taverner's Hill. Caryards, street-signs, signals, wires, the innominate face of the Petersham Inn, abandoned shopfronts, Trevillino Electricals, Mad Barry's building supplies spewing fake marble vanity units along the footpath. Art deco frescoes of the Miller's Brewery. Fort Street High School. Prestige Caryard. Ristorantes, bonboneries, tobacconists, cafes & barbers around the entrance to Norton Street. Red & green loaves when Italy won the World Cup. Living with Dee, Anna and Mark at Renwick Street. We survived the great marijuana shortage of '81 on hash cookies, spotting and goons of Lindeman's Moselle. Saturday afternoon walk to Sonia's Leichhardt Hotel see Jimmy Jessup's Bopcats. Find that Big Uranium Rock. Black gold. Texas Tea. Beverley Hillbillies. Maralinga. Money money money.

"Want to see Nick Cave tonight?" asked Ana at last. "We're first support. I can put you on the door."

"I don't know," he whined. "I got Elizabeth's exhibition at seven then there's a function for patrons. That won't end until at least ten o'clock. Probably later. So I don't think I can make it."

"Look, the Bad Seeds come on at ten-thirty. I'll wait out the front. If you're not there when I hear Tracy Pew's first bass note, I'll just pick some random off the street."

"Sure. Thanks. I'll get out at Johnson Street please, driver."

The car ploughed around the corner and stopped in front of a grim take-away.

Exit Peisistratus. He supplied Telemachus' first real fellowship. How did he explain Telemachus' refusal to his father? We'll never know. He disappeared from Classical literature for good after that. Another footnote. Real history commenced like a crank handle. "This is for your husband," Tom Hallem said slotting Elizabeth's envelope between Ana's legs. Across both faces, he had drawn a sequence of small skeleton-puppets floating through space with their fingers linked like parachutists. Stephen starts Proteus wanting to paint everything black but he is slowly charged with colour during the episode. He deploys a typical Victorian palette of gold, yellow and green. They are each cited nine times. There is golden sun and sand, gold teeth, lemon streets and yellow mouths engorging *flan breton*. As with Wilde and Pater, yellow has a pestilential edge. Custard is perceived as pus. Queen Victoria is represented with rotting yellow teeth; an image immediately reworked in French so that she becomes an old ogress with "dent jaunes." Wilde's solvent green is cited in the fairy fang of absinthe, the Irish sea, whalemeat and the drowned man's body in its jade grave. Ultimately, the colours merge into the "greengoldenly lagoons" of rising tide. Stephen writes a scrap of verse on the back of Deasy's letter. Its form has never been disclosed but it is likely to have reflected his internal monologue in Proteus tempered by the intellectual pretensions and limitations of age. Will of a creator not yet the means. Fame ineluctable. Missus Horne wrote two letters to her son in Vietnam twice per day. A telegram from his father called Stephen home from France to his dying mother. It commenced with the misspelt word, "Nother." Suggests 'another.' Also 'not/her.' Even 'no other.' They all resonate with a sense of VOID. This error is seen as more than an emblem of his father's haste. Of carelessness. Maybe pain. Make your own choice. This incident happened in REAL LIFE and was thus an instance of reality being aligned with Joyce's technical praxis. Critics generally pile onto Simon Dedalus with disdain wherever possible. *Ulysses* is more complex. The author was famously loyal to his father. Simon Dedalus appears in 7 episodes in *Ulysses*. He is presented in extreme forms from abusing his daughter on the street to singing magnificently at the Ormond Hotel. He is introduced in a carriage proceeding to Dignam's funeral. Bloom points out Stephen, calling him "your son and heir." He quietly curses Mulligan's influence then his creditor, Reuben J. Dodd. He makes clever, sardonic comments. Bloom calls him a "noisy selfwilled man" at first. Later, he notes that Simon is "full of his son."

"See yer when yer worms are straighter," said Tom Hallem getting out of Ana's car.

"Don't forget my taste," she shot back.

Unturning, Tom Hallem descended the stark slope of Parramatta Road shimmering with lowly glare that illuminated a line of disposal stores, second-hand furniture emporiums and cheap carpet retailers. Sun-shafts projected his elongated steps along the concrete & glass channel, fading by increment, like hand-wound picture frames, tick tick, cars creeping westward, past and beyond him, a movement that is associated with sunset and death, the direction Odysseus sailed post Ithaca to appease Poseidon, whereas Tom now continued east, backwards towards dawn, the place where the moon rises as a heavy pastille over Bondi Beach. I ... pressing against carmetal tide. Elizabeth has possession of my home. I now none. No key. I will not sleep there tonight. Nor in the house of Les Hallem. Nor Ana's couch either. I could just wander off the page tonight like Stephen Dedalus and let the end of the novel overtake me. Away now each footfall suspended in light like pulling out of a warm wet bath, my soul, to chance the tide of "Elsinore's tempting flood." It fixed Ophelia. A four-person inflatable dinghy flapped off a piece of plastic twine. Enamel mugs, silver billies, gas cylinders, kerosene lamps, cookers, cool-boxes, tents and air mattresses cluttered the doorway like Aladdin's cave CUT itchy forearms, I scratch CUT an annihilated cat was exposed in the gutter outside the Annandale Hotel. Bloody furclumps. My gaze will not shift from its astray upward gaze. Ana on the Lake. Why do they bare teeth at death? Animal reflex, Bloom guessed. Human faces are more compressed. My mother took out her dentures to die. Slumped in her great brown armchair in front of a television she had long since lost the ability to tune. Head lolled back. A crevice in her face in repose. I touched her silver hair. No wake-up. Kate's dead, I said with breath-pangs when I got back upstairs. We placed her on the floor for the paramedics. Then we picked her back up at each end and lay her straight along the bed to wait for the coroner. Silvan weight. Look close. A headless mannequin modelled a lime linen overcoat behind op shop glass like some bottled museum piece. Look down. Drown. Glassy brine off Esperance. I alone saw John. My brother did not want to be rescued. I dropped a lifebuoy. Bade him: TAKE. Ana flipped manically. Last vital sign. Un coche ensable. Joyce citing Veuillot on Gautier's prose. Terence Maloon called my paintings: bad ... mud. Stephen fears drowning, losing his verses and losing his teeth in that order. I: exposure as a fraud, obesity and speed-stained teeth. Two of Mister Monaro's assistants started to wrench open the large roller door in the delivery bay. Slow shift. Low light started within. One of them crawled on his belly into the warehouse. He could be heard pulling a chain. Bibulous hunchback. Ring the bell. Church greeting. Raise the ramparts! Ding dong ding. Clacker Clayker clack. Try up then try down then try up then try down again. JAMMED MECHANISM. Incremental movements. Up a click then NOTHING. The roller stuck fast about four foot above the earth. The labourer jerked the chain emphatically. This sudden pressure caused it to dilate until it burst out of its iron runner; warping inner. Hernial bust. Neither up nor down anymore. Fixed in place. Monaro cowered. He walked to the side door and entered Beta House. Ham actor. My key in his grip. A theatre shorn of darkness. Unadorned space. No longer a set. No drama possible. "We'll need to secure the premises before C-O-B," lowed Monaro gesturing at the breach. "Call Brian Deverill," he added. "Say we need him right now." Stop up a gap. Paper over egress.

Equivalent of Stephen Dedalus letting Ireland's past unfold below Poolbeg Road, planted on a rock over sedge and oarweeds. Link to Australian history. "Galleys of the Lochlanns" (Danevikings) || First Fleet. Malachi wearing the gold collar || Federation. Frozen Liffey (1338) || drought fuel. A school of turlehide whales stranded in hot noon. Whales in the bay-folds of North Harbour. Great famines. Blighted potatoes. Baited flour. Smallpox scars. Lash marks. Indigenous misprision. Private sector provision of services for the Second Fleet. See Reverend Johnson's testimony. Wretched, naked, filthy, dirty, louse-marred, utterly unable to stand, creep, crawl or even stir a hand for food they staggered to shore to die. Fruits of Empire. Twenty thousand dead in coffinships. Push them back towards Sydney Heads. Start a Quarantine Station. Tiki carvings. Spanish Flu. Monstrous fauna. Natural disasters. Prospero in Port Jackson. Foucault's carceral. Ever-receding sites of exclusion. Right enough the harbours only no ships ever called. Bigge's pattern book principles. Morris paper peeling off daub and wattle walls. Beaten dirt floors beneath woven hearthrugs. Civilisation was absent, this was an island and, therefore, unreal, as Auden said. Tom Hallem stood pale and bayed-about like Actaeon waiting for a break in the midday traffic. A couple came towards him with a bowed dog. It rotored methodically sniffing a succession of markers. Search for lost relatives. Old comrades. Some new sensation. Jack Russell cross. Bad bloodline. Its owners trailed obediently. Joyce's Egyptians. They arrived in Sydney fifty thousand years before Homer. Eora land. Twenty-eight nations. Cadigal tongue. They lived by the coast and fed from the sea like Ancients. The women gathered oysters in the shallow rocks when the tide waned. Hooks of brittle turban shell. Pounded-bark fibre lines. They speared the catch with prongs of sharpened bone. Inferior tools handled with superior dexterity. Setting bushfires to flush out prey. Get the spirits smoking. Enter Regina. All poisoned, infected or slain. The breeze blew the woman's light red skirt – already uplifted still higher. White cotton knickers stuffed into folds of slack fat. She soused from a brown bag. Hallem baulked. "Gonownasty," she yelled at the dog. No time for niceties. Cross broken lane markers. Tom's earshot registered a different dour voice in his wake. "Out of that you mongrel," the man said. He took precarious refuge on the median strip before steering himself into a tight gap between an accelerating taxi and a decelerating bus. Stephen Dedalus' kenoma. Safe. He turned back curiously. Faithless Orpheus. All goes to dust. The dog was apprehending the cat. Another kind of domesticated beast. But no brother. Its glassy eyes held the dog in thrall. Blade of Pyrrhus pausing over Priam's prone form twixt purpose and fulfilment. Gap between thought and expression. A lifetime. We find words only for what is already dead in our hearts, said Nietzsche. Why speak then? Bootless inquisition. Crush soles into wrack and shells. Cuts. Hamlet, Laertes, Fortinbras: all sons trying to avenge their fathers. Orestes a model. Sudden acts annihilate phony intervals. The dog struck at last, burrowing its teeth into slick fur so that it was able wrench open the guts. It shook the corpse maddeningly. Its skull collided with the concrete path repeatedly and lolled. Mrkgnao! Hallem looked AWAY. Afraid of chickens it was once. Who cares now for foibles? Ghostly faces dissembled at the bus stop in crucible shadows. "Gaarrout ya farker," cried the master trying to slap the dog's hind. But he was too bent and the canine too cunning. It laid a careful paw on the broken hind and tore rapid meat out all tasty guts. Leave the proud head staring away from this blasphemy on its form. No longer sensitive. Cue Berkeley. Hallem ripped his gaze. Traffic smashed daylight into spectral cullets. Its radiance was embedded in his brain flicker flicker fluck. Deformed shapes pixelated as if trapped beneath water's choppy lens. Man and beast struggling over scraps. Scene for ALL AGES. A crowd gathered to watch this replay of their own dismal origins. Interlopers in a primal tableau. Inscrutable faces. Old young male female ghost-thief student worker gods. Tom Hallem was adorned for display in Leo's cast-off suit. A mendicant (no key but!). Rank cloak of heroes and exiles. Become Minor. Like Edgar or Vincentio gone to earth. Odysseus scouring every part of the palace. Count them. Gaze through vagabond holes. Odysseus was a great list-maker like Joyce. But he only kept one column in the ledger for **REVENGE**. None but Telemachus could plead for small mercy. Would I have the credibility to influence my father thus? Who knows. I make him in dreams. I have not laid eyes upon him. He woke me last night same as always or almost. A descending beast. Haines' panther. Illusory landing zone like Hallem's shaved hallway. LZ dust off. Field of fire. Strip harlots. THUD! A human jumped out of the open hatch. Suddenfilade. The helicopter reared then hovered unevenly then sped off. The rappel mound upon its steel floor unravelling after. Faster as it lifted. A stretched cord. HE watched his father's body dragged through jungle lashings. Sharp sounds all over. FTT FTT FTT. Rise. Pop through the canopy. Out! In silence, I watched him released into atmos. Galling Icarus fled. *Cogito*. Cite secondary sources. His ghost told me. Leopold Bloom peeping through the keyhole at Boylan's clenched buttocks driving down his bride bed. Odysseus' trick chamber. I have no place to sleep tonight, thought Stephen. Put it out of your mind go drinking with yer false mates something should come up you expect. Penelope 's doorframe received the impress of her lover's forged head. Molly slippery asunder. Shiny screwthreads. The soft sides of fists banging on white panels. I awoke. Ceiling above. Digital clock branding time. Female weight against me. Confused. Touch her body. It is Elizabeth. Tom Hallem slipped through the brown pub doors and went to a public phone next to the saloon machines. Coin-in-slot. Ringing. Soundlessness indicates an answerer. Speak with conviction compellingly.

"Hi. It's Tom," he said. "I want to drop by."

"Not now," came the stern reply.

"I'm just around the corner."

"Bad timing."

"Later then."

"Not here."

"Where? I'm going to the campus."

"That's OK."

"Woolley Building. Two PM. Can you bring something for Ana?"

"Nope. Just you."

"What do you mean?"

"Would you rather go without?"

"No. I'll take whatever I can get. Where else can I score?"

"Try Leer. He's working the Bard. Look, it's twenty this time."

"For one cap?"

"It's good stuff. I'm sourcing off some new guys. But you need to be careful. Cut hard."

"Cool. Remember: Two PM."

"Yea. And you remember: no credit."

Signalcut. Silence. Tom Hallem replaced the receiver, tested his bladder and moved towards the toilet. Mustard tiles softened fluorescent glare. Clean cubicle still to be soiled this day. Dawn @ Augeas' stables. Not so great downstream but. He manipulated his penis through fabric folds. Each aperture par-opened to allow passage. Uncircumcised dog. Delighted when it fitted into Esther Osvalt's shoe. *Delectatio Morosa*. Joyce's lyrical piss (55). Hard to work out what's really happening. Fox-phoney as Swinburne's mandible medieval prose. Cunning Odysseus. Side-stepping censors. Make the text clear and steady as a brass stream. Phonetic render. Innovative in its time. Seesoo hrss rsseeisss, ooos. Releasse thy rill of gylderne metal! Pissfield. Porcelain bound. Stuff about cunts, wombs, priests and vampyres follows. Women set naked in his kindome. Flaming swords. Succubi folded over a dreaming body. Fetid lava. Not to mention the menstrual moon leaking blood like Saint Ophelia (*oinopa ponton*). Mounted on a bejewelled dagger. Seaside fauna fanning out underwater like dank petticoats. Millais' subject matter. She was fearful of the stream's light meter. For it dragged her down, inexorably, to a dark God, to drown with no air above in totality. Without sky, sun or flood. And without vanity. Follow Joyce down the pithead. *Introit* > Requiem Mass > dead mother > moth fluttering against her womb > inside > assorted beddings > bluddy mens > creative acts > an orgasm > conception > birth > death > Nature > earth's mother > humanity's tomb > starspray > space > immutable. BISHOP BERKELEY. Ireland's philosopher. A Cheat's Guide follows.

1. All knowledge is a mental activity.
2. Mind is the active principle of experience.
3. Man perceives nothing but ideas (sensations).
4. Things exist only in so far as they can be perceived. A thing cannot exist in its own right independently of a mind.
5. Abstract ideas do not exist.
6. Ideas are passive. They are assimilated by an incorporeal substance: the soul.
7. The soul (spirit) is active and can perceive ideas and cause or influence them (Will).
8. Knowledge of the soul is attained by way of a reflective process. This is termed 'notion.'
9. Berkeley recognised multiple spiritual substances and the existence of the infinite mind, God.
10. He is claimed as a founder of Objective Immaterisalism.
11. The real universe is solely phenomenal and nonmaterial in nature.
12. The essence of reality consists in its being perceived by personal spiritual beings who function as agents of perception.
13. Matter is a fiction, a non-existent entity.
14. The physical universe does not exist independently but only exists in so far as it is perceived in the mind of its agents.
15. Two kinds of things then: those which actively sense, perceive and experience; and those which are passively sensed, perceived and experienced.
16. A stone only exists because I can sense it.
17. God makes things potentially perceptible. For example, the dark side of the moon.
18. Books don't jump off the desk into my consciousness. They are perceived as a sensation of seeing.
19. Natural laws are God's habits.
20. When we think of the universe existing before finite minds who could experience it, we assume an Omnipresent Mind observing the universe.
21. Everything in the world is contained in your head.
22. Existence is a projector. Ignore external exigencies. Turn within. A stone sensed.
23. Natural laws are God's habits.

Compare each statement in the list above to *Ulysses* and TMAC. Insert as a graph or table. Hallem left the bathroom. The end of the Telemachiad is nigh. Bloom is rising. Soon we will escape the suffocating void of Stephen's existence in Chapter I. Get outside yerself, opined

Principal Deasy. Fresh air'll do you good. Grow up like Hamlet via self-statements of predicament (see The Quaker Librarian). Sprout soliloquies. It all seems better once spoke. Internal monologue is the same kind of revelation when it is placed on the page. It makes the writer what Hegel called a 'free artist.' Not that Stephen Dedalus arrives at any place in the Telemachiad. At the end of Chapter 1, Joyce leaves him suspended on the shore gaping at a three masted boat wearing another man's clothes. In prosaic thrall like Shelley's Sensitive Plant. Another dumb lack in Elysium. By contrast, Homer completed the Telemachiad with the steadying disclosure that Odysseus was alive. Joyce just reruns key terms and symbols then turns for lyrical effect to the moon. Swinburne's mother. Handmaid of the Lord. Angelus prayer. Butt of peasant limericks. Update its currency for a belated epoch. Diana's blob all pale and weary like one of Pater's milky hims. Companionless as Hamlet, Alastor and all those Samuel Beckett characters. Can't one of them find a mate? Stephen's monumented snot. It's a symbol of the physical asserting itself over melancholy. Krapp collected the large black dial in his fingertips and turned it – CLACK – depressing the red RECORD button simultaneously [steady drone]. There is a legend that everything wasted on earth is stored on the MOON. It must be a vast warehouse. I need storage space like Les' garage. Events keep expanding inside time like fresh Guinnesshead. To reclaim infinity is the poet's job, said Joyce. I am stuck on a loop. It's a kind of infinitude. I keep all my old papers in shoe boxes under the house. Gradually, I have been transcribing this material onto a computer. There is no pattern to this task. I'll open a box at random and stare at its contents, objectified there in a lump, not knowing where to start, then pick up the package for a single year, unbind the pink legal string and commence. They built the Great Wall of China in disconnected stages thus. Another mound. More pinpricks. I am pierced in a thousand places. Light comes through. Ideas begin to droop through my fingers like runny egg. Some adherence nonetheless. Time passes. Dust covers them. It is very dry now. I take my place in the plot. If life was a human head, I was being pumped like a blood clot to the brain from the farthest place. Also sailing against history and Empire. That feels good on my skin. A white taxi cut across Tom's path as he set off towards the Shakespeare Hotel. A semi-trailer ground to a halt at the traffic lights. First challenge of the Quest trope. WALK. He proceeded across the road, turned into Australia Street and headed uphill along the verge of Camperdown Park. Joyce finished C1 on 16 June 1915. It was the 11th anniversary of his first assignation with Nora Barnacle when she gave him a handjob at Ringsend where the River Liffey emptied into the under-used docks at Dublin Bay. She smelt of balsam and rose from scented handkerchiefs. What is it dear, she asked grinning when he moaned when she tightened her grip around his cock. O sweety, she wrote. All your little whip I saw. Dirty girl. Made me do love sticky. He went inside the toilets under the grandstand. A man was loitering in an open cubicle. Their eyes met. Both nodded. The clock strikes

NOON at end of this chapter. GAY SLANG. When the cad with the pipe asks Earwicker for the time in *F(W)ake*, he answers 12 noon. Denotes twin erections touching. See Genet. Also, Gide and Proust. Tom and Willy. The hour of Stephen's Paris reverie. Also, that time when Menelaus was told to seek Proteus in a cave. Mallarme passed. He was undeniably a handsome man. Juxtapose heightened imagery with a base sex transaction. See C7. Also, Proust's narrator in Volume Two. Joyce is trying to link Stephen's nascent poetics to the keystones of production for a great poem (by Joyce) even if he can only grasp association by raw visual correspondences with female beauty as yet. "PM of Mister Faun" became a symbol of artistic intransigence. Rejected twice by publishers like Joyce. Took a decade to perfect. Or rather to find an audience that had evolved into the suck of its serpentile melody. The first variegated poetics. All headings, ellipses, italics and indents. A sign of the explosion in Modernism to come. Joyce in comparison deployed relatively modest graphic renders throughout *Ulysses*. The first work that put poetry back in music. A key element for Joyce. Debussy's fake spurts announced entrance into an awakened realm. Ireland's airs and pub-tenners. Note Pater's dictum.

"What's the time?" asked the man.

"Twelve o'clock," answered Tom Hallem. Neither looked for a watch. "It's ten for a handjob."

"How much for suck?" replied the man.

"Twenty," said Tom.

"And sex?"

"I don't fuck."

"Come on then," the man said.

He extracted a twenty-dollar bill from his pocket. It was folded like a flute. Ex-speedline. Tom went inside first, undid his trousers, pulled them down to his ankles and sat on the toilet seat. The client closed the heavy door behind Marius and made fast the lock. He took a snort of amyl from an umber jar then offered it to Tom. It kicked his head back. The client opened his jeans. Tom pulled them down to his shins. A heavy key chain rattled on the left side of his belt. Tom took the cock in his hand. He made it hard enough for his mouth. Swineherd's hovel. Mattress on milk crates. Copy of *Cupid and Psyche* open on the floor. Buttoning down corduroy breeches. Physical transaction. Dumb animals in a pen. A wave of calm swept over him. Tom Hallam stood and grabbed both cocks in his grip. Achilles and Patroclus. Dirty louvres let in a humid breeze. Cars rowing below. Such a nice tail on thee. Hallem pressed his forehead into Flavian's soft shoulder. Young Pausanias. Real soft sloping. Remains of a chop. He looked across the valley. Hardening. Alexander's fist. A row of worker's terraces sinking towards the Liffey. Theoclymenus' prophecy. Joyce guiding my pen. Stephen's grandiose ambitions. The tallest structure in Dublin is Donnybrook Tower. A mast for Radio Eire. Elizabeth predicts I will hang in the Paris Biennale one day. Edmond nodded sagely. Soul full of decayed ambitions. The man was panting hard. My lips on his neck and ear. Little Pentacostal flames. Stale breath. Londonderry Air. Hallem squeezed the scrotum. Bulb of clay. A workingman's respiration. Dry mouth. Sperm shot across the deck. The man went down on his knees automatically. He took Hallem's cock in his mouth. Tom placed both hands upon that fair hair. Gloves of Absolution. Lift me up. Two temporal pillars. Homer + Joyce. A leper came forward. Soft auburn curls. Stroke those wiry locks. No different to a woman. A finger swam up my anus. He worked me harder. But Hallem could not. No snowdrops on snow. The man flicked Hallem's cock with his index finger angrily. This sharp pang made Tom suddenly aware – and wary – of the limits of this carnal cell. He tied off his trousers. Joyce also. Insert Gerty text. LB post orgasm. "Bloom recomposed his wet shirt," wrote the author. Transient connection. Disembodied voice.

"Is that it?" asked the man.

"What did you expect?" asked Tom.

"A little more affection," he replied with a weak grin.

The oval was hosting a schoolboy cricket game. Tom turned nervously at the sharp crack of a new ball propelled off willow. It spat off the cyclone wire fence in front of him. A boy retrieved it from the gutter. Once I was. He passed the Dairy Bell ice cream factory and scampered across Salisbury Road. Approaching the top of the ridge, he cut across the park behind Saint Stephens Church. Parched yellow grass gave way to a children's playground. Hazy northside skyline so heavy. Buildings diffuse. He sought the shade of the cemetery wall where huge trees canopied rotting gravestones. Two old men were propped against the wall passing a brown bottle. Gloucester and Kent. Gogo and Didi. Old ANZACs. Wading ashore. A flock of pigeons paraded in front of them picking at a plastic bread bag. Greg Wheaton crossed Gilligan's Island at Taylor Square. A derelict clasped at a piece of rope holding up his trousers while he skulled freely. Crazy Edgar. Dyssguised. Hallem cut through the supermarket car park. Church Street traffic lights changed. Cars were flooding around the corner only to be wrecked on King Street gridlock. Hallem tapped the bonnet of a Ford Falcon as he crossed the road and held his breath as he passed the fish shop on the corner. It was cool and wet under the wide awning. He glanced into *El Bahsa Sweets*. Stainless steel trays of bird's nests and baklava glistened under bright fluorescent beams. Sweet rose water poured from fine-stemmed spouts. Abundance of Sparta. Such a contrast to what Telemachus had endured at home. A row of newspaper placards announced bingo numbers. He surveyed the wide double doors of the Shakespeare Hotel. They had been wedged open by the publican so that the strong breeze from Botany Bay could be received fully. A frosted crest proclaimed the hotel's name. Some locals were leaning on a bench at the street window ignoring pedestrians. Half-spent schooner glasses sat frothless from inattention. Dizzy rattle of a race call within. First race at Flemington just run. Bar mirror allbright. Distant waterspray. Shallow pool reflecting its signifier in the glassy sky. A LooP. Hallem walked straight up to two men on high bar stools directly under the television set.

"Seen Leer?"

"Too early," said one man without diverting his gaze from a broadsheet.

"Do you know where he is?"

"Try the TAB."

Hallem paused to honour pub etiquette.

"What's the news of the world," he asked.

"Reagan landslide," replied Grassy Noel. "Hawkie's caving. Floods. Oh ... and Sophia Loren's in Australia."

He stretched the page aloft.

"She's still in fair nick for an old bird," said his mate approvingly.

"They built them to last back in my day."

They returned to their betting guides. Fair Helen of swan-cum made. Forty years old when Telemachus visited Sparta. Always a stolen vessel her whole life. Perpetual trophy. Theseus' wager. A game of Two-Up between thieves. Die rolled in a marble vault. Paris' prize. An impulse purchase. She was only a ghost, according to Stesichorus. Telemachus arrived in Sparta just as Hermione was leaving port. Their paths passed. But did not cross. Another only child. Her wedding was more like a funeral. Her daughter's exit freed Helen of her last moral constraints. She hijacked Telemachus from her husband. Bloom fantasises about Molly sirening Stephen Dedalus in this manner. Learning Spanish together. Duets in Italian. He would have happily observed them engaged in coitus. Even partaken in a supporting role if so instructed. Getting Stephen to sleep on the couch was the first step in his nefarious plan. Menelaus also wanted to detain Telemachus. He had no son. There was a conspiracy of needs between the connubial pair on Sparta. And Telemachus was so easily delayed. His first experience of real families took place in the Telemachiad. Indeed, Menelaus acted as a kind of medium by extolling his father's virtues. His elaborate hospitality provided a strong contrast with the suitors trashing Telemachus' modest home on Ithaca. Helen's drugs gave him wings sedating grief. She told such marvellous stories. Yet she was always somewhat sinister like Circe with his father. Time stalled. Telemachus was pulled towards her reef. She claimed to have recognised Odysseus when he went spying in Troy. This was a reductive metaphor for the later episode in the *Odyssey* when Penelope recognises Odysseus disguised as a beggar in the palace. Helen insinuates that she is cleverer than Odysseus. Nobody else in Classical literature would make such a claim. It was her Arachne moment. It severed any hopes no matter how many acts of manipulation she tried. LIST PROTEAN ACTS IN C3:

Joyce re-Homer; TMAC re-Joyce/Homer; garbage (churning of); narrative continuity; narrative POV; memory (Tom, Don); A. L. Gordon poet, Pepe, Ana, Tom (life > death); childbirth (mother, child); Sydney (as seen by Don Pane); identity (Don as 'Eric' Kill/lion); relationships (eg. Ana/Matt); sport; Australia (Europeans, war, migration); historiography; light; truth; and the mind (Missus Hensley and Bishop Berkeley). Likewise, some things never change. Proteanism needs stasis to react against. For example, base business is a constant as represented by Cornwall and Willy. So is war (Classical, WW1, WW2, Malaya, Vietnam). Also corruption; lies and disingenuousness; a higher idealism debased by realpolitik (Westacott, Cornwall, Don); the church; and death (Bobby Horne, Chaim, Juanita Nielsen, Albert Wheaton, Don Cane's parents, his child with Richie). Motion is the narrative constant as in the Telemachiad. Don and Tom are always traversing the page.

"Do you want us to mention you're looking for him," asked Grassy Noel.

"Don't bother," answered Hallem rere regardant.

No. Don't alert him. Might flee. Like father. I thirst. Check yer watch. No time. Get along. Tuesday is always the longest day. Bleachtaste. Two notes coiled in my pocket. Mouth full of brine. Joyce's masculinised ocean. Hold my father's head under paddy water until he expires. Kill Proteus. Make him a ghost. All fluid. Down with the topsail! We split, we split! Seadeath? Not to drown. Jettison Asenahana's craft. Float on wood. Make your way through the straits. Artful Prospero. His carceral storms. Calculated shipwreck. Tidesmaw buffeting my body towards shore rocks inevitably. False refuge. An uncharted isle. Bitter dealers directing pawns on a board. Look up. On a poster, a white-washed ship sailed across the frame of the Student Union travel agency. Sail Away from Cares Today! Find silence in exile. Odysseus' twelve black ships all proud vermilion. Joyce's proud three master. This image at the end of Chapter One allows the reader to sail from Stephen's internal monologue on a tranquil tide. It is another Trinity symbol. A tripartite novel. Three chapters. Three characters: Stephen, Molly and Bloom. The oven for making the poet is mind, body and soul. Ploughing upstream. Smoke-rack veers to seaward. Sinbad the sailor. Joyce is recalling a favourite child's tale from *1,001 Nights* with this citation. It was another great story-cycle powered by apparent coincidence. Neither Joyce nor Homer allowed such cycles to rest. Go past Gibraltar. Never come back. Telemachus. In a small vessel. A smaller ask. Rotten carcass of a butt with no rig nor tackle, no sail nor mast, the very rats instinctively having quit it. Yet mine nonetheless. Unarrived as Stephen Dedalus or Tom Hallem on the chosen day. But all days make their end. Move towards disjuncture. It is marked in publication with blank paper at the fag. A new page comes in *Ulysses* monumented with twin bars: **II**. The second mast. Homer & Joyce. Add a third. At this point, they both shift decisively from the son towards the father. Tack hard against. Stay with the son. Joyce's text is lodged in a middling man's wits. Roadmaps given out and taken back. You leave Ithaca SSE. Round the Peloponnese. Pass north of Crete. Troy is due east. To return home, reverse the journey. But you will need to find new currents. It takes time. West equals Empire. I am but mad NNW. That's eleven o'clock for mariners. Time please gentlemen. If you were installed in an empty white room, how would you express yourself? Write words on the wall with your own defecant. Hawk eating a dove. Call Theoclymenus to interpret this omen. You will be king and your father is alive, he said. Joyce ate Homer. Snake consuming its tail. Joyce's Telemachiad is a self-contained story. As a Metaportrait, it would have done Pater proud. What we call a 'sketch' in Australian literature. How to end it but. Invoke Beckett. Tom Hallem slunk around the side of a rock. Clock ticking down to the big race. He gazed in a pawn shop window. Scratched watches and rings mounted on display. Dumping ground for stolen *xenia*. Junkies whorde. Rob your own parents' grave for pin money. Get to campus. Willy is coming (repeat with exclamations): Elijah. Don Cane slammed the car door shut and waved Greg Wheaton on his way. He entered the hotel. The son stayed on stage. Aweighting.

4.
Scylla & Charybdis

"the whoreson must be acknowledg'd."

– *King Lear* (Act I, Scene i, Line 24)

William Capri BA (1H, UM) departed the public bus at the weatherboard shelter on Parramatta Road and loitered beneath its dark awning, although it provided only partial protection from the sudden storm breaking around him, until enough time had passed to judge whether it would dissipate or he should accept saturation and press into its tight eye. A student in a wet business shirt rushed within its corrugated eaves. He shivered. Tom's a cold. This wretch apathetically surveyed the discoloured mustard walls overlaid by blocks of yellow *Resistance* posters advertising **FREE LECTURE Ronald Reagan & the Capitalist Conspiracy**. Juxtapose political activism with the esoteric content of Billy's paper. A campus life would never satisfy him. The Scylla episode (number 9) takes place at 2 pm in the director's office of the National Library of Ireland. It corresponds to Book XII of the *Odyssey*. Scylla is pronounced with a silent C (think 'Silla') while Charybdis has a hard C (as in Caribbean). This episode represents a kind of Troy in which Stephen is trying to act like a Trojan Horse. Those present are Richard Irvine Best, John Eglinton (William K. Magee), A. E. (George Russell), Lyster (the Quaker librarian), and, later, Leopold Bloom, who has sought refuge from Hugh Boylan on his procession to Molly, as well as, lastly, Malachi Mulligan (O. St. John Gogarty). This makes six heads in total, like Homer's Scylla. Both creatures' express power through their mouths. Scylla yaps like Stephen Dedalus. Dublin's Charybdis swirls with mystic Platonism. Stephen is bored shitless with their platitudes about Shakespeare. He longs to radicalise discussion (link to Billy's paper). This episode contains Joyce's AGON with Shakespeare through Stephen's exposition of his Hamlet theory. It is the intellectual core of *Ulysses*. The Linati Scheme designates the organ as brain, the technique as dialectic and the art as literature in this episode. Stephen connects biography directly to art product, deploying Aristotle's concept of Experience with freewheeling abandon. It's a virtuoso piss-take. For let there be no doubt – the entire rationale for Stephen's discourse in Scylla is to force biographical correspondences with the life of James Joyce to be considered in any critical analysis of *Ulysses*. Joyce introduced a new (outer) layer to fiction with this device. An online contributor has called it a *mise en abyme*. But it is much more than just a reductive sequence of the same image. Joyce places himself (1) around the Homeric template (2) then drills into Shakespeare both older and younger (4b, 4a) through Stephen Dedalus (3) until he reaches *Hamlet* at the core (5). This tactic was crazy-brave impudence TBH because, at the time of writing, Joyce's literary eminence did not possess the full weight of *Ulysses*. His reputation rested only on *Dubliners*, *PAYM* and a handful of short lyrics. On this date, Billy Capri had published two book reviews in *Southerly*. His first meta-portrait, "Of Virgilia Without Sound," had been rejected by a new journal. He had drafted but not produced his radio-play, *In Black Box*. Joyce wrote, "New Year's Eve, 1918 | End of First Part of Ulysses," on the last page of the fair copy version of what he called the 'Hamlet chapter' to Ezra Pound. It marked his entry into the home straight. This race over 3,200 metres had probably begun in November 1912 when Joyce presented lectures on *Hamlet* at Università Popolare in Trieste. Shakespeare, *Hamlet*, Stephen and the whole fucking crew become marionettes in Joyce's crude revenge masque against Dublin. Joyce is settling ancient scores in this episode. Stephen Dedalus stands his intellectual ground on repeated occasions in Scylla – including attacks on his lack of literary achievement – in his only dominant performance in *Ulysses*. Resistance = Means x Will was Clausewitz's equation. Success need not bear any relation to truth or ethics. It is simply a matter of having a platform and sustaining utterance. Stephen Dedalus is vehement at making-it-up-as-he-goes-along in this episode. William Capri will perform the same act later in this chapter in Question Time. Stephen says that the middle plays were dark because Shakespeare's life was bad but he lightened-up in his last works after the birth of his grand-daughter and reconciliation with his wife. There is no historical record to support this conjecture. He also makes a number of fake claims: that the death of Shakespeare's mother inspired the demise of Volumnia in *Coriolanus*; that Hamlet, the black prince, is Hamnet Shakespeare; that Hamnet's death was depicted in the death of young Arthur in *King John* jumping from a prison wall (was it an escape attempt or suicide?); that the female characters in *The Tempest*, *Pericles* and *Winter's Tale* were all well-known local strumpets; and, lastly, that the identities of Cleopatra, Cressida and Venus can all be 'guessed.' Stephen's audacity was essential in Scylla so that Joyce could swallow Shakespeare and position himself as the culmination of the Canon; although he never deployed hubris without the counterweight of self-deprecation (see C11). In the rest of the novel, Stephen Dedalus is shiftless, dissembling, petulant, trying to break out of traps mainly of his own making … even a figure of fun. He does not really believe his own theory but it is clearly well-rehearsed. Mulligan and Haines have already tried to elicit it in Chapter One. Stephen probably knows its fatal flaws better than anyone so he seeks to dazzle the audience with a stream of bold throwaways. There is credence to Mulligan's jibe that SD proves by algebra that Hamlet's grandson is Shakespeare's grandfather and that he himself is the ghost of his own father. This is the type of perverted logic on display as Stephen negotiates false passage quickly in S][C. I too have no interest in consistent reasoning. Just speed. Jam *Lear* into *Hamlet*. Drop a stitch by shifting to the evolution of Australian literature. Own your own history. A bastard offspring. Link to the high watermark of British Imperialism no matter how otiose it seems today. Jump forward to French theory. Make arbitrary connections. Pile dead references across a prosenchymatic field until you overwhelm the defenders. Create great puns and bad puns with no filter. Invent your own terminology. Invert when cornered. Push it all onto characterisation. Revert in the end to Homer. But don't mention Joyce. That too is a tactic. Make sure that YOUR OWN SELF inflects each spiral. Suffocate the text with the lamina of your own persona. Joyce was the first writer to put a whole apparatus around his text through the work of third parties like Gilbert, Gifford et al. I don't possess that kind of network. I have to do it myself. Devise several selves then. At least get that one up on Joyce. He solely used Stephen Dedalus. Grit interpolated Billy's strained eye-workings. An old man sitting on a bench said mildly, "I should give you my coat." Shiny neatsleather. The student demurred. Too little taken care of. Still it was some refuge from oh yea the wind and the rain until Billy's clothes had achieved the requisite dampness to compel motion. Another bus past meantime. Sinkapacing. Hugo was a master of writing about breeze. See Zhuangzi's pipings. Nanguo Ziqi's great clod. K'un with wings. Shelley's fast chariots. Also Aeolus episode [C10]. Those that weave the wind end up in the void, concludes Stephen Dedalus pretentiously in Scylla. Loom imagery is constant in both Homer and Joyce. Jesus' dark sayings are perpetually "re-loomed" (see Nestor). Penelope works at her machine all day and unpicks her product each night manually. This makes it much like the rush and ebb of hermeneutics. Proust tried to achieve this nullifying effect by flipping his character's opinions incessantly (link to Proteus). He inserted their axioms into a mechanical sequence of set-piece inversions as artificial as possible. This was what Wilde later called 'our first duty.' It placed authority-within-text-itself into doubt and left only the splendours of style (see C6). Flip everything in the air then. Represent temperate Sydney in tempest. Manufacture some logic. For example, to align weather with plot as an arch symbol.

In Dante's *Inferno*, the second circle of hell punishes carnalism with an incessant gale that pounds the spirits of the dead sex addict. Billy Capri tries to bust out of this confine in Chapter Four. Use navigation tool to search for the word "TEMPEST" in TMAC. Examine its usage. Also, examine the representation of sex. Write a comparative analysis. James Joyce was a scholar of Dante. Consider this link in *Ulysses* as well, in particular during the Aeolus episode. Gifford notes that Irish tradition connects weaving with prophecy. He cites Isaiah as Stephen's source. But Stephen Dedalus is a HATER. A passive punishment like a 'void' would not satiate him. He would rather reap a wild whirlwind like Hosea. A lean-jawed passenger wiped steam from the window and peered forth.

"Now there's a great friend of yours," purred Dougie the Animal jerking back the stiff Perspex screen to make a gash through which to expectorate. He spat. A fishing-line of slag blow'd back along the pane. Angler in Styx.

"Who," responded Weasel Bob Akers urbanely.

"Tom Hallem's faithful Achates."

"The Goatrider?"

"Yes. Yung Mulebludd."

"He's in with a lowdown crowd to be sure," Bob blurted.

They sniggered; green-teeth glinting in the try-hard glare.

"He's off to flog his pigs at a pretty market," added Petra Debravich leaking ice cream through starched Lutheran lips. Gleaming cur-cream whirl.

The bus reached the junction of Derwent and Arundel Streets. At the traffic lights, it halted. A slow black low black hearse crossed its path grimly. Petra shivered. Berlin crows on a grave. Coffin framed in portholes. Odysseus' ship. A motley retinue of private vehicles, out of how deep a life, sprung in its wake, rising up the mound to the Great Hall. Link to Hades episode. Allude to Dignam funeral. The bus wheels jolted. Aloft the footbridge, Billy Capri turned from the four silver chimney stacks of Fielders' Bakery to the flat landscape west. Heel of my past. Future a cleft hoof. Snoutruffle. Dogs dig. Rats burrow. Proceed. Campus entry. A canvas theatre banner advertised *Beach Blanket Tempest*. "High energy rock spectacular," it proclaimed. The stage doors had been flung open revealing ropes and scaffolds. Ribcage of a Cyclops' cave. Extended by Popular Demand. Thence proceeding on tour to Goneril's castle. Billy hurried towards the high columns of the National Australia Bank branch on Science Road. He turned right. Downhill slope. A stone satyr drooled cool water plopplelopplepIop into a deep semi-circular tub. Black juice. An assemblage of temporary buildings hid the walls of the compound. Organic shanties. Woolley Building spread over a low plain. All liver brick and sandstone. Repository of the Canon. Pyred atop Dickensian labs. Department of Crop Sciences. He descended the last steep staircase. Upwards crosspath rose the Jesuitical bob of Maryanne Dever. She raised an officious gaze. Neanderthal jawstick. Milton Mons. Toothwort. No salutations. My direct competition for the Government grants that suspend us both in working poverty. Gods doling out largesse.

A boot floating in broth. Better served tepid. Got to keep on her right side. Pass. He crossed the driveway. A moat. Divert sacred waters. Insert reference to A. Guillerme. Slow Burnham Wood. Goinna. Up a jerry-built marine board ramp. He entered the administration office and greeted the secretary. A pigeonhole unit was mounted on his left. His gaze dropped towards O's slot to ascertain if it had been emptied. Yes. Go forward then with confidence. He negotiated the plain wide corridors, unlatched the sagging lock-handle on his office door and entered its tall cramped space. Another desk was crammed into the back corner. It showed no sign of recent occupation. Julia must still be ensconced in her lover's library of first editions in the Southern Highlands, he thought. He leaned on an armchair to rise, reach and release the stiff iron hinge of a cast iron window. It swung freely until it contacted a tin ventilation shaft then rattled insistently in time with air conditioning turbines below. He depressed the **PLAY** button on his cassette recorder. Instantly, he was consumed by the chorus of "Mutiny in Heaven." He checked an alarm clock on the whitewashed sill. His parents were due to arrive in ten minutes. Enough time for tea. He inserted a fraying female cable into a ceramic kettle. The element shuddered to life. He picked up an infuser, pressed the handle wires and a gauze ball sprang open. He plunged it into a jar of small leaf tea. It closed. He brushed aside some motes and dropped it into a red enamel mug. His symposium paper sat in front of him on the desk in a fresh manila folder. He surveyed the pile of loose sheets within. Priceless pages. Sweat of my brow. Boiling water pried open the thin kettle lips. He flicked hastily. A knave who came into the world before he was sent for. Last chance to speak. John's detached head went yadda x3. He rehearsed his opening sentences then partook of the brew's bitter smack. Time to put myself into the play, he reasoned. Stephen places Shakespeare in the same kind of setting at the same hour of day in the same month as *Ulysses*. He is thus imprisoned inside James Joyce. Stephen tries to lure his audience into compliance by painting a pungent waterside scene. The Liffey becomes the Thames. It is all about creating local colour and composition of place. Stephen shifts to the present tense to bring his portrait to life. It is a scene redolent of Hogarth like "Gin Lane." He builds a sense of veracity with incidental imagery. We become accomplices. Shakespeare is strolling to work. Sackerson the bear growls from a pit alongside the playhouse. Navvies who sailed with Drake chew dry sausages. He passes the Swanmews unassumingly. It was built across the Thames in Paris Gardens by Francis Langley in 1594. Scholars are split as to whether the Chamberlain's Men ever played there. It could only have happened in the summer of 1596 before Shakespeare's troupe found a permanent home. But *Hamlet* was not written until 1599. Joyce has thus coded Stephen's discourse with yet another flaw. Today's play begins. A bass voice sounds. It is Shakespeare himself playing the role of the ghost of King Hamlet. Burbage is his son. INSERT SD QUOTE. "To a son he speaks (ie. Don/Simon/Shakespeare.), the son of his soul (Richie's dead baby), whose mangulated form symbolizes his own guilthroes, the prince, young Hamlet (Stephen/Tom) and to the son of his body, Hamnet Shakespeare, (Rudy + see above) who has died in Stratford (Manila) that his namesake may live for ever (James Joyce, Billy Capri, Shanghai Dog et cetera)." Hamlet has now become both younger Shakespeare and dead Hamnet. He is both Stephen Dedalus and Rudy Bloom. These are words that Tom Hallem had never heard uttered by his father. Don Cane had spoken them only to himself. Exit EDGAR. Billy rose from his chair and stepped into the student rush. O emerged from her office.

"Are you ready?" she asked touching his forearm.

"Sure," he replied wavering.

"You'll be fine," she said scraping at his sleeve. "Just watch out for the rips—"

"And shallows."

He laughed as he spoke. Scylla is a rock (Aristotle). Charybdis: a whirlpool (Plato). Stephen goes closer to [A] like Odysseus. He rejects the neo-Platonic realm of forms and essences. Rather, art must be material, quotidian and autobiographical. In allocating characters, Stephen casts Shakespeare as King Hamlet with his dead son, Hamnet, as Hamlet and Anne Hathaway as Gertrude. This system can be transferred to the Bloom family. However, it is not fixed. Stephen also recasts Hamlet as young Shakespeare. This is aligned with biographical critics who contend that Shakespeare made a mistake in his marriage and bailed out as fast as possible. "Bosh!" exclaimed Stephen Dedalus in reply. He goes on to make the famous declaration that "a man of genius makes no mistakes. His errors are volitional and are the portals of discovery." Stephen has reached a height of youthful pretension at this point. This is a deeply ironic statement if transferred to James Joyce. It certainly would have made Nora Barnacle spit on the floor of their rented apartment at 29 Universitatstrasse, Zurich where Joyce composed Scylla; maybe even throw a pot at his head. It bounces off the wall. He is drunk again. She loses their third baby on the first floor of the Via S. Caterina, Trieste. This is the wellspring for Bloom's agony over Rudy. Joyce became infatuated in late 1918 with a young woman named Marthe Fleischmann. He finds out where she lives as the mistress of an engineer named Hiltpold (Poldy?). He writes an ardent letter in long hand on perfumed paper signing his name by using the Greek form of the letter *e*. He advises her that he is the same age as Dante when he began to write of Beatrice and Shakespeare when he fell for the Dark Lady. So began a secret correspondence in which Marthe Fleischmann acted as the prototype for Martha Clifford. Bloom always uses the Greek character for *epsilon* when he writes as Henry Flower. The motif of the experienced woman and young lover can only remain consistent with Stephen's characterisation of *Hamlet* if Gertrude/Anne fucks Shakespeare/Hamlet: a direct usage of the Oedipal myth. Joyce was familiar with Freud's theories by 1918.

In Chapter 10, we will examine his contempt for Psychoanalysis as well as his tense relationship with the amenable Carl Jung. Stephen Dedalus is partaking in wish-fulfilment on behalf of James Joyce in this structure by alluding to his own attempts to cultivate Maud Gomme in Paris in 1904. Add Yeats to induce a false trinity. This fantasy is later reprised in *Ulysses* when Bloom imagines Stephen and Molly together. It is explored in this work in the relationship between Elizabeth Archer and Tom Hallem. But in fact, it is inherent in any romantic condition involving gods and humans. Joyce makes nothing more of this trope in *Ulysses*. His women are always subjugated to men, except Molly.

"There's a lot riding on this paper. It's my last chance to get something published before I go overseas."

"You don't need to prove anything. You're the one going to Oxford. They've just got second class B.A.'s and cheap tenure."

"I've got to come back someday," Billy replied. Still unaccomplished like Stephen Dedalus. A poet without product. Bard-un. Incapable of writing in the manner of Mangan, McCreedy or Jabber Davies. Anne Hathaway's other fuck. Fatal love triangle at Court with a lesser stag. Swimming against a rip. Bitterness of a fresh-minted barstead. Over-baked tweakings and feints. Aborted ladlings. Award-winning book about an aspiring novelist in five parts set across three continents. He dropped off the map altogether in 1992. He didn't reappear for almost thirty years. Gibraltar is just a diminishing lump of rock looking back. Convex sea line ahead. No shore-heading. He had been excluded from Laby Weffy's End of Semester party in Greenwich. Mildling, so rumour has it, is gathering a sheaf of our younger critics (not I amongst) for publication. McCreedy will scribe the national epic. There is consensus in the Faculty. It will be shot by Baz Luhrmann in Thailand. Starring Russell Crowe as Dorrigo Evans. With Cate Blanchett as Theodora Goodman. Michael Caton in the supporting role of Old Don. Stephen Dedalus is not part of Russell's coterie of young poets nor invited to Moore's function at night. Mulligan, however, is included. Already a spearsman. Model schoolboy. Bring Haines. He's decent for a British chap. An expert on Gaelix. O's big face parted in a broad blind smile. Gap-tooth Kathleen a stone you couldn't budge. Capacious mouth. Soft vibrations in her risen cheeks. A thick mask of foundation. He held her gaze with difficulty.

"Just don't get sucked into their personal clashes," she continued. "They've been holed up here since the Leavis wars."

Leavis refused to separate art from life, or the technical from the moral. In this regard, he was aligned with Stephen Dedalus' Hamlet theory. Leavis initially admired *Ulysses*. Later, he called it a "dead end." His feeling of sublimity before Joyce's radical rendering of the Humanist voice dissolved in his fixation on the squalid content of *Ulysses*. Joyce's characters seemed thoroughly satisfied with indulging their impulses towards masturbation, voyeurism, adultery, blasphemy, drunkenness, prostitution, gambling and sado-masochism. Leavis believed that form must with moral purpose be shot to achieve eminence. Likewise, form must AIM HIGH in technique to amass sufficient integrity to impose ethical verdicts. Morality was defined in personal terms by Leavis. His work was perforated with value-judgments. It all started with *Rasselas*. Lawrence, Conrad, James, Eliot and Austen were classified as serious moralists. Not Hardy or Dickens. This left him utterly exposed to Post-Structuralism. I cannot pass judgment on Tom, Willy, Ana, Elizabeth or Shanghai Dog. Chart a middle course then like S][C. Professor Ilks commanded the heights above the staircase. Goldstein's camp was barricaded at the rear of the building on the ground floor. Find secret sewer-bars on the down side of castle-keep which can be cut away with hacksaws. We can then proceed with Prince Caspian to the tower in the student's common room. A fine prospect. Westmoreland inverted the precepts of Sun Tzu. He wanted to draw the NVA into a cage fight using Khe Sanh and Dak To as bait just like the Frogs at Ding Bing Foo, as Johnson called it. But this time he wanted to hit them with nukes. Bold stratagem or battle scam. Depends on the result. Napoleon always did the unexpected. Summon the gods Bacchus and Silenus. Bring the woods to life. MacArthur at the Yalu. Clyde liked to get up real close so you had to call down artillery on yourself. The enemy rushed in successive waves until they overwhelmed the shallow fire trenches. LIFE was not just a word in the wagons behind the poppy fields where Leavis lost his LIGHT. In essence, S&C is a CONCEIT. The Telemachiad is a kid's Odyssey. Stephen's exchange in the library is obscure. It had no formal status. There was not much of an audience. Even Russell is a minor figure. There was no record kept. It was a non-event in literary terms. Billy lifted a stream of straight bronze hair that covered O's ear exposing a shell of serrated cartilage that resembled Proust's petite madeleine.

"Don't," she protested quietly.

"I'm sorry," he said laying down the smooth strand. He could not express his true feelings. That he was owned by her body's ferrules. Made/lines. Obsessed like Swann or Marcel. This is a mood induced by sudden absence in Proust. He examined the claret skirt that stretched across her raised belly. Gut of an athlete. Black stockings wrapped her firm legs. Vale of her cunt.

"You wore the same outfit last Thursday," he said.

"It's my lucky charm," she said. "What else do you recall?"

Lir's loneliest daughter.

"The taxi ride to your place. Making love for the first time. How it overpowered my fear that your boyfriend would come home."

"He could've arrived at any moment."

"What do you remember?"

"How you folded my clothes and put them on the edge of the bed while I was in the bathroom," she said.

Her ragged mascara gleamed. She held a finger to her mouth. Polyhymnia. A grunted laugh. Jericho teeth. Kiss her. Not. Al might come. A gadfly. Spies everywhere. I and O. Molly and Boylan in deceit. Our alchemy. He had acted without theory in her bed, letting facets guide him, his impulse to serve, to delay release, to continue giving her orgasms until he was so bent and hard that he could no longer cum then speaking instant truths unalloyed by taste then dumb then making provisional passage along a raw uncharted channel. Goethe on Hamlet. Be not that hesitating soul. Hamlet the disassembler bequeathed cruelty. Violence by remiss. A hopeless mismatch. She no mother had. Inadequate Polonius. An axiomatic parent. Fondling a baby-bird in his guttered palms, Barry Capri climbed the unsteady garden ladder to restore the nest. Menelaus was thus. Odysseus with Calypso. Joyce tried to atone for his self-possession to Lucia; albeit belatedly. Antigone cleaved to Oedipus. She died for truth. Hamlet compares unfavourably with Prince Haimon. Another remnant fixated on family honour. Posh/lost.

"I've got to go," Billy said. "Bob and Helen are waiting outside. Will you come to the pub later on?"

"I'm teaching until five."

"We're meeting at the Shakespeare."

"You know I don't like that place."

"I'm just tagging along for a couple of rounds," he shrugged.

She touched his cheek with dry lips. Their rejection was not hers. No secret adepts.

"I'll think about it," she said.

Keneng was how Zhu Di put it much later on. Turn away mechanically. Chart a middle course. Crack open the gap between Plato and Aristotle. Stick Art up the Spiritual. Abhor the vegetable world. Don't treat with shadows. No magicians neither. Neither Hieratic nor Demotic speak. Accept disenfranchisement. Don't present a blueprint. They'll only wipe their wasted theories on it. Mock the national epic you long to create. Retain all technical insets despite every atom of awareness telling you to edit or even delete. That risk is your only edge. Stephen Dedalus predicts how James Joyce will spring full blown from William Shakespeare. Writers are solo performers. Never really part a gang. No creed like painters, who work in pods. Attach yourself to a crowd then by proximity. Too late to change disposition Conradically, as Nabokov said. JJ = Mister W. H. There is no father's name on my birth certificate. No paternal line acknowledged. Stephen says that "Paternity may be a legal fiction." Telemachus also wears this doubt. Billy Capri has it confirmed in this Chapter. Stephen Dedalus asks a rhetorical question, "If the father who has not a son be not a father can the son who has not a father be a son?" This is directly relevant to Telemachus as well as the author's personal experience. It is NOT relevant to Stephen Dedalus or James Joyce. Joyce de-coupled from all ancestry to free himself to become the son and father of the Canon. It's like the myth that Penelope fucked all the suitors then gave birth to Pan. *Ulysses* is a host story. Barry and Helen Capri clustered with their son in the car park as Tom Hallem emerged from the bunker beneath Badham Library. Low talk. He observed them enviously. Father, mother, child. Humanity's template. Blessed Trinity. Odysseus, Penelope and Telemachus standing outside the palace at dawn. Two decades of separation immediately erased in the easy smell and body lilts of DNA. Rosey-faced maids were still swinging off wire bloody and bloated. Barry Capri stamped on a cigarette butt and placed his hand on his son's shoulder. TOUCH. My lack of. That airport scene in Chapter One. Odysseus sending Telemachus to bed. Les' wound. A big dull scar. Billy Capri departed suddenly. A soul unfit for great action. His parents watched the recusant figure. Close enough now to see their expressions. Barry chased after his son suddenly. Some last paternal insight into human existence to transmit, no doubt. His wife turned towards my careful footfalls and engaged my face modestly.

"Here's me," I said mock-gaily.

"Hullo Tom," replied Helen flatly. "You look just like your father sometimes."

She touched my lank hair slick with California Poppy. *Putuwá*.

"But he always wore short back and sides because of the Army. And he wasn't tall like you. You get height off our side. Off your mother."

An ivory sports car rolled towards them. They parted to allow passage. Tom on port side. Helen starboard. Its back wheel slipped in a pothole. It lunged right. Some muddy water spattered Helen's ankles. Scylla was loved by Glaucis who was loved by Circe in turn. Bad triad. She was transformed by monster potion in her bath. Grew six long necks with heads all wearing pale green eyes. A pregnant outcast. Gone up to Kings Cross to hide. Bolted men down raw. Helen observed it passively. I took a stiff handkerchief from my coat pocket and passed it to her. Leon's used leftover. She dabbed at the muck. Barry returned. Bloodshot looks never clear nor bright. Grim as Poseidon. A God of the pre-Hellenic world. Darkly. Throwback to a dead age.

"I saw Bob Hensley this morning," said Tom expectantly.

"Long time since I've seen him," replied Barry. "How's his wife?"

"Okay. I visited the Home."

"It's not such a bad place, I believe."

"He couldn't keep her any longer at home," added Helen.

"She seems bright enough," said Tom. "A bit confused. Mistook me for her niece."

"You should cut your hair," Barry sniggered.

"And someone she called the slut's son," Tom Hallem added tightening his gaze. Ghost-of-a-meaning. Barry Capri shrugged. A trained horse hoofing dust. Helen kept her countenance. Scylla is a rock to break against. Swirling Charybdis down. Flooding past. Never dormant nor flat. Pain, primal pain, was still raw, felt, like Stephen's all-consuming guilt at betraying his mother, that terminal theft, that can never be redeemed, a mortal blasphemy. Tom Hallem grew impatient. Hold it up. Deasy's letter. Blurt.

"Bob gave me this letter. It says my father is still alive."

"Vets are full of shit," scoffed Barry.

"Stop it," interrupted Helen grasping his forearm. "That's good news, Tom. If it's true."

An absent father never wounded me daily. Not a sharp rock. Who gave me this fucked-up name? He shook off her palm. What really happened?

"I bet you've known all along," said Tom Hallem suddenly. Barry Capri bobbed his head at the pavement like Stephen Dedalus looking down at his cane. His wife released her nephew.

"I'm going to tell Billy," said Tom.

"Maybe you should leave him alone right now," Helen said. "This is a big moment for him. He needs to concentrate."

"Rubbish. He'll be glad to know about my father."

"Go on then," urged Helen Capri.

The liver brick alleys of the English Department unfolded beneath vaulted ceilings like some faux Augustan maze breaking at right angles into a common area with four doorways. Crucifix floor plan. Faceless pine doors displayed white name tags. I padded over the synthetic grey carpet that suppressed the speed and sound drag of my boots. I could hear Billy's voice nasal and deep down the plasterboard lane. A woman's words also. Maybe one of his students. Wait until she goes. Hold hard. Tom Hallem withdrew towards the noticeboards. A blind spot. Students racing. Bide. He scanned the course lists fussily. **Early Australian Prose**. Rust in wheat. Drought of a dry season. Poor soil + dry seed = stunted yield. Mother England blackened her breast. Australia also son w/out father. Suddenly, Billy Capri walked straight up to him. Enter the agenbuyer.

"Thinking of coming to school?" he asked.

"No way. You're right to get out of this dump."

"Australia?"

"Yeah," he drawled. "Have you got a moment?"

"I start in five minutes."

"It's important."

Billy Capri gestured to his cousin to follow. They returned to his open office. Billy sat and turned in his desk chair looking upwards. Tom Hallem leaned against the doorway. Smell of water in a rusted tank. Through high windows, windows higher still were visible across the interior courtyard. Grid on grid.

"You look buggered. I've got some sandwiches. Are you hungry?"

I chucked a bundle of plastic wrap at my cousin. He caught it in his gut. Salted lamb. Hecatombs from Helen. Telemachus observing Athene's prayer to Poseidon. Odysseus' enemy. He loved Polyphemus. Pain of any child scalds. Tom Hallem took a bite from the soft bread then placed it on the bookshelf. "Fastbuck" stuttered to life. I poured water into a mug. Wine in a gold cup. Wind hissed in the pipes. List! List! O list! Panacea.

"I've got something to tell you," I said.

"I've got something to tell *you*," replied Billy with added emphasis.

"Mine's big," I said seriously.

"Mine's bigger," he exclaimed. "Shall we toss?"

Coat of arms UP. Lizzie's face in dirt. ODDS.

"Off you go then."

"OK," I said pausing my lungs. "Helen just told me that Barry's not my real father."

"What?"

"He's not my biological father."

"Bloody hell."

"Wait. There's more. Don Cane is my real father. That makes us brothers."

"But we were only born four months apart," said Tom.

"He was having an affair with mum while your mother was pregnant."

"Wow. You've got to hand it to the old man," Tom Hallem snorted. "But I can't imagine Helen ..."

My voice trailed. At that point I had to chuckle myself. Involuntarily. Like drooling. See Appendix A. A clown juggling two balls. Prologue to the swelling act. Pluralise. His other wife. Myrto. Brothers but not quite. Like Luke and Leia. Truth like Astyanax hidden in my father's tomb. Thrown off the walls by my mother's pimp. Take a horse ride to Sparta. Bonding on the plains. Telemachus must have been struck by the difference between his own life and that of Peisistratus. Now Billy's reduced to my level. Lower even. Barstead's are beneath sons. Edgar and Edmund. Got to snigger or weep. Protean like Shakespeare. Various versions of Life. He died dead drunk. Shylock was based on his own self, said Stephen. Falstaff was another. Myriadminded. Coleridge's phrase. His family experience was not important. The theme of the usurping and adulterous brother is the most persistent theme in Shakespeare's work. He laughs to free his mind from bondage. My mother like Andromache. Also Penelope. *L'mmense majeste de vos douleurs de veuve*. Me most like Molossus. Sticky bronze. No direct Classical analogue. Our father left, the women stayed, we looked hard at each other. To hold Tom would normally be good. To feel his top-heavy chest against my forehead. Rest there in situ. But not at this moment. Lyster returns. Two of Shakespeare's villains bear his own brother's names. Brother motives in Irish myth.

"Why did they tell you now?"

"They wanted to tell me before I left Sydney," Billy almost sobbed.

"That doesn't make sense. Why not tell you tonight after your paper?"

"It doesn't matter. What was your news?"

"Well ... my father – I mean, our father – is still alive."

"What?"

"I got this letter off Bob Hensley. He's been living in Asia."

Tom held out the letter. I took it. My head whirled. Mulligan presenting Stephen with a telegram. Mumma's wire. Read later. Joyce will often split events in *Ulysses* with long stream-of-consciousness passages. It's designed to show how fast the human mind goes (32 ft/sec). Promethean flames. Burn our evidence. Doomed to walk a stage like Old Melmoth. Starring Lester as John. Hamlet Senior knows the manner of his own death. How? Only Shakespeare could tell him. Stephen thus argues he must be part of Shakespeare himself. Life + art =. Cut all suspense. This is not a murder mystery. Kevin Birmingham waits until page 289 to reveal his controversial claim that Joyce was going blind due to syphilis. Virginia Woolf said that *Richard Feverel* is cracked with the fissures of a writer in twenty minds at once. Precursor of New Method. Sir Austin's SYSTEM. When his wife ran off with a poet, he resolved to educate the boy at home. Parallels with the author. Master George he done had or/deal. Fell for a farmer's niece. Peacock's sister. Secret marriage. Don and Helen writhing. Catfish flippin' in a dinghy cradle. A good joke: two lovers struck by lightning. The bride died and the bridegroom went insane. Evil Lord Mountfalcon. Set-up with a courtesan in London. Escape. Exile in Paris. Hung out with Kevin Egan. Addled vet pumping barely-legal girls with cheap cocktails by a kidney-shaped pool in Angeles City. Eighteen holes in golf cart with driver. Blowjob on Par Five. Degree from Beijing Golf University. Mister Brando he nothin hotel Boss. Gone up Pagsanjan. I was offered a role as body-double by Coppola, said Don. Kurtz or Willard? Discuss protean physiology in TMAC. Meredith was the life-model for Wallis' famous picture of Chatterton. Mary Anne Meredith eloped with the painter. Already pregnant with his bastard. Another fatherless child. My uncle's dying wish was burn it. Link to Dorian Gray. Also, Joyce's portrait of his father. Chatterton took a hot shot in Holborn. Fatal duel. Lucy dies (1859). Then his wife (1862). Ana's lifeless gaze directed at a street grill in C10. Pseudonym: Rowley. More false naming. You make good use of your strange enough name, said John Eglinton. Saltpeter turned on his head. *Nacheinander*. A good bang-up. Bard-un. Anti-Shakespeare. Puns on various Wills. Aristotle. Stephen recalls his exit to Paris. Boat from Newhaven to Dieppe, steerage class. Later, he came back wings-between-his-legs to his mother's last spit. Icarus' risks. Fathers take them all the time with children. Lapwing you are. Lapwing be. A father is a necessary evil, concludes Stephen. Stephen says nothing much links a father and a son except an "instant of blind rut." Truth of my genesis, thought Billy. Tom was made in a marital bed anchored by an olive branch. I was mistaken. Misled. Ill-conceived. An accident. Splitting asunder the family. Penelope and Helen. First cousins. Neighbours. Tutankhamen married his half-sister. They shared the same father. Their mothers were first cousins. Don Cane = John Shakespeare. Simon Dedalus' sperm. Les Hallem. Barry Capri. All false father figures. Are you better off without a father? Fatherhood contains a certain shame, says Stephen; but this is really the angst of the mature James Joyce contemplating his daughter's collapse. The son's growth is his father's decline. A mother's love may be the only true thing in life, thinks Stephen. He was summoned from Paris to his mother's deathbed. My mother passed away in front of the television. Knitting in her lap. Kit-kat wrappers stuffed down the side of her brown armchair along with coins and tissues. She was making another elongated scarf. Her mind could no longer handle the complexity of weaving sleeves. Her last day was a happy one. It was sunny. She played in the garden with the puppy. She boasted about how the cat had moved into her flat. She went looking for Xavier when I called home at lunchtime. That evening, she climbed the ten steps after I got home from work to chat. This was unusual because the stairs were hard work these days. We touched for the last time. A kiss on a cheek now sagging. I went downstairs to check on her after dinner. I had seen her dozing like that countless times and moved silently off. Not wanting her to wake. But lately I had started to dwell. Her breathing had become so shallow. This time she wasn't breathing anymore. She had passed away quietly. Without fuss. Just as she would have wanted. My mother lived her last day as she lived every day – independent, determined, useful and kind. There were her special qualities. She wasn't a gusher. The ambulance came. Then the police. Then the coroner's van. Then she was gone. Stephen Dedalus remembers being calmed by a doctor who did not know him. I also. Comforted by strangers on a late-night job so kind. We all have mothers. My real Elizabeth. Walpole's forgeries. Even the darkest life must have a bright side. Richard killed in a duel with Hardaker. Chatterton re-created his lost father in the mythical figure of his patron Canynge. Lucy loses her mind. Dead Ana. Shelley's dead children then dead himself. His body washed up on the shore of Sandymount just under the tower. Tom Hallem released me suddenly.

"Wait," he said. "It's all starting to make sense. There's a bloody good reason why they told you today. HE'S BACK! He's here in Sydney. And they think he could arrive at any moment."

Elijah is coming. He is almost here. A stone rolled away. Footprints on the beach. Scour the crowd for a vagrant with clear blue eyes. Camouflaged killer. Look for the glint off his gun sight. Bright arrowheads. Billy Capri leant against the edge of his desk and tubbed his face in his palms.

"Why don't you just cancel the talk?" asked Tom.

"I can't cancel. Not now. Don't say anything to mum and dad. We'll talk afterwards. I need to get ready. Please go."

I stuffed some sandwich in my mouth as Billy pressed me into the corridor and closed the door. A pure noble nature but no hero. A shrub in the shade of a great oak. My tea had cooled on the edge of the desk. I sat down, drank and let my head slump over the back of the chair gazing at the high ceiling. Air gathered behind my nose. Blood-weighted eyes. They do ceilings best in China. Tian Tan is like the roof of Alibaba's cave. Restaurants with tiered ceilings displacing direct light. But that was a long time hence. I collected my papers and left the office. I walked upstairs. A small crowd was filling the seminar room. I surveyed the yellowing course lists behind their glass shields as I waited for my supervisor to arrive. **Australian Literature 501 Core (Weffy)**. You could swallow that whole course list on a wet weekend: convict novels, bush ballads, Anglophile fiction, bucolic sketches, Romantic throwbacks, poetic hawks, Catholic reactionaries, token Beatniks, two plays. The first documents produced in Australia related to the administration of the penal settlement. Wafer-thin autobiographical novels by emancipated convicts followed. The miracle of *Natural Life*. Giant amongst turnips. Boldrewood and Kingsley wrote Imperialism's wired idylls. Australia as Anglican earth full of proud squatters and fiends. No blacks. Ethical certitude. One lecture was devoted to interesting offcuts like Ada Cambridge and Rosa Praed. He shifted gaze. **Henry Lawson 505 (Mildling)**. Conrad and Kafka filtered through the Australian landscape. Anxiety, futile subsistence, hostile bush, filth, unstable shelters, isolation (the arena of madness, alcoholism and crime), extrinsic space, rationalised cruelty, fatalism. Daily setbacks as mini-tragedies (spilled milk, for instance). Rituals that preserved some sense of civilisation in grotesque adversity. Mundane objects assuming the significance of religious icons. Fleece. Homage to common practicality undercutting abstract discourse. Egalitarian speakeasy. A masculine cosmos. Ironic, gentle and macabre in turn. Stress the 'unlikeness' of place; not its uniqueness. Accumulate the Steelman stories and you've got a picaresque novel.

Reduced plot. Episodic scope. A type of modesty really. Perfect for television. Blank refusal to accept the void. Refuge in humour. Is that such a bad thing? Biographical snarls. Mode of emplotment: Tragedy. Scribbly martyrs. A national misology. Should have been born a girl. His mother invented Liquid Paper. A Child in the Dark lying alongside his drunk dad. Eddie Twyborn. Go now to Gulgong. Go directly to Gulgong on Archiblad's commission. The son sunk on the grand Australian Bush. Alcoholism (the wet nurse), poverty (my tutor), destitution (as home). An aloner. Concept of mateship: another delusion. Not metaphor but mate(r)phor. "Pursuing Literature in Australia." Text of a broken man. Cracked spirit of an old servant. Cowered. *Bulletin* frotht up his legend. The foetal plant of organal wiriting in Stroya. Anew natal. Latan wena. Love of the ornate and allusive undercut by constant play of low images. Lawson's dry comic rhetoric spawned Furphy. Fulfilment and knell. Tempah democritic. Bias: offensively Faustralian. Havelock Ellis was Olive Schreiner's Id. INSERT CHIDLEY. Heterogeneity is the real hallmark of the *Bulletin*. It regularly published experimental overseas writers like Mallarme and Zola. Openness of an unformed culture. Ungathered momentum since. Marginalised works and minor writers. Frances Webb said that Art ought to spring out of you like Minerva or a new head which is "glued to the ear, and in it nothing but rage ... a transformer in which sound is tuned" and when you turn the knob all the way clockwise you get *Hamlet*. A little lower on the dial is Pope. McAuley and Hope muttered that "Brennan was solid second division" as they lifted the Maenad cup. And drank with thin lips clenched. How to measure epochs? Channel Leavis. Great works. Hired narratives. Short format. Quixotic even. Exhausted. A sudden pang. "Love's ember" blown. Bitter breath. My father like Hamlet's ghost. Professor Milo Mildling dropped his corduroy strides before the oval mirror and slid the thick steel ring over his penis; fitting the neat leather strap around his scrotum and securing it with a press stud. His testicles were thrust against the sack articulating a field of silver follicles. Nuts of Knowledge. He admired his tanned midriff. Age seemed to be separating the skin from the muscles. But still in good nick. He hardened somewhat under the watchful eyes of Jack Kerouac. Beautiful mug shot almost five foot nine in his Merchant mariner skin. Stick my cock through his fat French lips. Mulligan asks Best who is the male figure in Shakespeare's sonnets. Anonymous. A lack of identity insinuated in code. Ghost man. Popular theory that it was William Herbert, Lord of Pembroke. WILLY THE PIMP. AKA Marius the Hardrake. Pater's Epicurean. Flavian's love. Joyce's joke on Eglinton who asks Mulligan if he is speaking of an Englishman's love for his lord. Mulligan insinuates twice that Bloom has homosexual tendencies. He also tells Stephen that he saw Bloom in the library lobby looking under the skirts of a marble statue of Aphrodite. Ironic preface to Bloom's later voyeurism of Gerty McDowell. Mildling adjusted his garments, left his office and sauntered down the hall passing Room S304. Modern American Poetry @ 2 pm. I'll force feed them

John Ashbery. But first another damn colloquium. This time they'll nail Goldstein's bum-fluff for sport. Set an ambush. Lure him in. Sink Telemachus in the straits. His mother will never find out. She will finally be forced to give herself to one of us suitors. Down the curved staircase, along the corridor, betwixt colleagues milling around the entrance, strode the evergreen Don. Turn cryptically, thought Mildling as he approached the lecture theatre. There stands the sacrifice with his master. Of bestial appearance. Light bearded. Kid-like. A lover of sprouts and highlands. Dowden on pederasty. Mulligan warns Stephen of Bloom's homosexuality. Evidence of his tin ear. Yet what man is not susceptible. Bernini's hermaphrodite. They all lived so highly back then! An appreciation of Beauty leads them astray. Mildling watched Capri and his supervisor enter the theatre. I could fuck a boy like that, he mused. Pigskin condoms. Shuffle accident-prone limbs over my desk. Stroke his bruises with a feather. He passed into the room, barely nodding. Grey-eyed, chiselled Associate Professor Able Goldstein shuffled above the audience rubbing his palms together and intermittently stretching a beige cardigan over the plain Cadbury belt of his crisply creased slacks. He sought a Quietist's escape in the landscape beyond the Tudor panels, hoping for a scrap of continuing revelation, trying to hear its music, until Milo Mildling plopped his rump in the gap smirking. It had been thus since 1974. Goldstein had been 'invited' to chair the colloquium series after an ill-tempered staff meeting at which his lack of publications was noted. Dignitaries flopped into their respective places for programmed worship: a square-backed Georgian chair with elaborate woodpecker motifs for Emeritus Professor Dame Nellie Krafter AC DBE (centre); a comfortable armchair in Modernist High Style for the late Laby Weffy (left); and an old bit of stool for Ilks (right). Although technically an informal occasion, ritual was everything in this place. They positioned their caudices above manifold fulcra and lowered with dignity their autocratic eminences upon. Urbane, to comfort them, Goldstein purred apologias and qualificatios then commenced a light-hearted introduction scripted on the back of a large bronze envelope.

"Today's seminar," he began, "is intriguingly titled, *From the Without of a Dominioned Literature*, by William Capri. As most of you will all be aware, William is about to leave for Oxford."

He paused. Barry and Helen had not yet arrived. Joyce starts Scylla with the Quaker librarian admiring Goethe. My family were Bourneville Quakers as well. My mother's ethical wellspring. Succouring the Dragonis family next door. First wogs in Campsie. Greeks in exile. *Xenia*.

"For those of you who are new to this series—"

"You mean that poor bastard in the corner," interjected Angus McCreedy gesturing at Tom Hallem. Obligatory smile from Professor Barbour. Perjured lips. Last of her line.

Joyce showcases Mulligan's need for display in Scylla. A buffoon. Lear's clown. Juxtapose his insipid ballad with the high intellectual aspirations of Stephen. All surface and eyeliner. Sight gags. Antics. Physical humour. Cry Eureka. Grab a pen and start phantom-scribbling notes. Mock Stephen out of hate. *A Honeymoon in the Hand*. Base materialism. Goldstein resumed. "It is designed to give our postgraduates the chance to present papers outside their core subject areas to the faculty for friendly deliberation. In particular, it is an opportunity to test new ideas and offer fresh perspectives on comparative literature." He paused, grinned and added smartly: "So sharpen your steak knives, ladies and gentlemen! Over to you, Mister Capri." Canned laughter. Sew eye stood up end lookt out and refelt sutch surgecal discust like I was gunna leak beeswax watt wif myma's revaluations of re-sent tiems and my now-is brother revelated like Euclid Crow at the are's end of the rhume but then unctuous phrases broke from my lips nun the less not with standing. "Thank you, Professor Goldstein," I utt tho' I was thinking about ma and ma/pa or new pa and ole pa or whatever I should call him now maybe SUB or 'Uncle Cuck.' A fly on a window got squashed. Buzzbuzz. I contemplated my speech as it lay on the lectern before the reader. Long theoretical asides are not new. They are actually an ancient tactic (Plato, Sterne, Pater inter alia). And all that stuff I felt and thought and just recounted was all stuffed inside a flash then the whole damn thing got put at grunt's length for the duroblation. No epic crank-start *in medias res* for the reader. Mulligan's boots were misshaping Stephen's feet. Leon's coat cut into Tom Hallem's underarms when he leaned against a seat-back. The following paper is the equivalent of Stephen's diatribe on Shakespeare at the National Library. It, too, seeks to remake the apex of literature (WS > England > Majority) into a prophet for a minor figure boldly assuming the mantle of Christ (SD > Minority > Australia > me). Like Horace throwing off his shield at Philippi, abandoning Brutus to grasp amnesty from Octavian and assume the mantle of fey 'blame poet,' mangling appropriated Greek meters from Alcaeus thereafter into Latinate arrangements of puce elegance and concision, blowing molten artifice like glass with barely suppressed tones of autobiography, I pedalled a gutful of spokes.

> At the beginning of their chapter "What is a Minor Literature?" in *Kafka: Toward a Minor Literature*, Gilles Deleuze and Felix Guattari offer the proposition that: "a minor literature doesn't come from a minor language; it is rather that which a minority constructs within a major language." Setting aside value-judgments over what constitutes a minor or major language – because Deleuze and Guattari are not really discriminating between the prestige possessed by various languages here but, rather, constructing an internal hierarchy for any language – this formulation is

predicated on subaltern enclosure 'within' a master language and excludes the possibility of perpetual rejection and exile to ever receding sites of exclusion – spreading, for example, from London to Sydney then Hellhole, Port Arthur, Moreton Bay and Fremantle – that act as exit-points into Extrinsic Space. In short, Deleuze and Guattari's conception of the relationship between majority and minority has an implosive spatial projection that excludes the Colonial experience and what I will call 'Dominioned Literature.'

In this paper, I will formulate some basic precepts for Dominioned Literature as it stands outside Majority, forgotten and never-faced, gazing back at a past that may not even exist, but that may be seen as an idealised inversion of its LACK, wearing a demeanour of impossible deference in a place of utter remoteness.

For this is the essential posture of all Dominioned Literature – to be positioned beyond the margins & therefore OUTSIDE THE PRINTABLE AREA.

Deleuze and Guattari fundamentally misjudge the experience of Dominioned minority because of their status as privileged creatures of the Within: creations of the most conceited intellectual system in human history.

Dominioned Literature does not possess the skills or finesse to differentiate between the blocs and factions that compose any major literature. It can only perceive the Canon as a totality against which it registers its own negation. Such a consciousness cannot comprehend the national, spatial, linguistic and temporal distinctions between figures as diverse as Kafka, Joyce, Dostoyevsky and Flaubert – let alone historic icons like Homer, Shakespeare and Goethe. They are all collapsed inside a sheer culture-machine that produces a homogenising wall of sound.

So how do Deleuze and Guattari construct minor literature in the first place?

To reveal the meaning of various marginal literatures, Deleuze and Guattari advocate "setting up a minor practice of major language from WITHIN" (*my emphasis*). For them, a Minor Literature is a synecdoche of the superordinate language, intervolved within it and possessing the capacity to become insurgent discourse. When it exercises this function, it becomes what they call a "literary machine." Its subsequent capacity for subversion is valorised, for example, by the work of Kafka as a Czech Jew writing in Prague German. Such Minor Literature then becomes a revolutionary force by enacting a "deterritorialization of language"; a procedure which necessitates linguistic movement to poles of either "exhilaration and overdetermination" or "dryness and sobriety." Joyce (like the Prague School) and Beckett (like Kafka) are held to be representative of these antipodal usages. According to Deleuze and Guattari, these Irish writers are located "within the genial conditions of a minor literature" as if Imperial Dublin was some kind of Gaelic Arcadia. Here, encased in a dialectic and thus intervolved forever, they are able to partake of the "glory of this sort of minor literature to be the revolutionary force for all literature."

This effusion over the insurgency of Minor Literature becomes the harbinger of paradox. Deleuze and Guattari state that "there is nothing that is major or revolutionary EXCEPT THE MINOR" (*my emphasis*). This stance is supplemented by a call to arms. They urge readers to "hate all languages of masters." Predictably, this subversive pose offers seditious elements within the enclave of Major Literature – such as Deleuze and Guattari themselves – the freedom to indulge their pretensions to outsider status, rebellion and sub-alternity. They finally detach any residue of literal political and economic submissiveness from "minor" and designate it as the rebel "within the heart" of all literature (18). This enables them to bemoan their own privileged status: "even he who has the misfortune of being born in the country of a great literature must write in its language." This elicits an outburst of degraded set of similes. ALL who "must" write are like a "Jew" or an "Ouzbekian" or dogs or vermin. All writing (and now the discourse is indubitably directed at those who are not subject to perpetual thrall) must therefore fabricate its own subjugation. It must make its own mimesis of retardation. It must affect its own Pidgin. It must profess its indigence. And it must move into the Without of its own desert.

The recommendation of a subaltern pose becomes the predicate for a strategy of usurpation by Deleuze and Guattari. The credentials for such a strategy are established by contrast with the grandiose intentions of a plethora of failed literati (and I quote):

> How many styles or genres or literary movements, even very small ones, have only one single dream: to assume a major function in language, to offer themselves as a sort of state language, an official language (for example, psychoanalysis today, which would like to be a master of the signifier, of metaphor, of wordplay). Create the opposite dream: know how to create a becoming minor. (27)

Against these thwarted fantasies of power, the injunction to "create the opposite dream" is an affectation of subaltern status to achieve expropriation. Writing like an obsequious clerk. A disguised tyrant. Is an artifice of humility analogous to Uriah Heep. Or a "becoming minor" that ultimately re-consolidates power like the concealment of Duke Vincentio or the return of Odysseus as a beggar. It is no longer a question of subaltern insurgency. The term "minor" becomes a metonymical appropriation from above: a *becoming* minor. It poses as Minor only so that it can exploit what Homi Bhabha calls "the *menace* of mimicry." The literary machine of Major Literature thus becomes closed by an internecine struggle that internally generates power.

This shameless colonisation of the concept of Minor Literature, so that the text speaks from a position of privilege at the privileged above the level of subaltern utterance, valorises the tactical advantage of "seeming" deficient and evokes the perpetual arrogance of the European Colonial enterprise. No place, no perception is to be denied it. It must be allowed to permeate all regions like the Blob. It can withhold all status yet nothing can be withheld from it. It is prepared to appropriate anything in the name of self interest. It will barter with beads. It will inhabit you. Yet its gaze is always backward and Within; always reverting to a home that it can still and one day will inhabit. But it will only return there on its own terms. And it will discard you again to the Without when it becomes convenient.

The perfect closure of the Within in a self perpetuating literary machine codes the Without with lack and disallows the concept of extrinsic space. Everything in exile becomes – like Ovid or Machiavelli – in constant expectation of a Prospero-like reprise. Deleuze and Guattari's centripetal compulsion replicates the structure of their literary machine: every part is integrated into a perpetual sequence within limits that are itself. Thus, it appears completely self sufficient from Without. An inviolable entity. There is no slippage. No leakage. Nothing can intrude. Despite every failure, even the "how many" failed literati are still enclosed in Major Literature like a protective cocoon (or an "antenatal tomb" as Shelley paradoxically terms it in "The Sensitive Plant"). They exist within the flux between Major and Minor in a perpetual antimetabole where they retain delusions of promotion undispelled. Thus, whether it is the "one single dream" of the "how many" or the "opposite dream: a becoming minor," there is a common oneiric faculty directed at Power.

But what of the individuals who gaze back from an Extrinsic Space which is so severe, so dislocated from its source in terms of both Time and Space, that they cannot clearly distinguish the Within or its hierarchy so that even Kafka appears to be just another privileged figure located within the master discourse?

What is their dream but the nostalgic reverie of the Without for lost unity ... itself an act of revision that completely effaces the truth of its servile position?

-This is the consciousness and condition of **Dominioned Literature**.

In 1867, "Dominion" status was first granted to the Canadian colonies when they united as a self governing unit of the British Empire. In 1907, it was utilised again to define New Zealand. All relations were henceforth handled by a Dominions Office. They were no longer the direct responsibility of the British government. They had been displaced into the labyrinths of the bureaucracy. Their needs were now to be handled by notaries. To turn to Kierkegaard's metaphor of rejection, the mother (country) had blackened her breast against them. Yet this action merely formalised the stance of the Within towards its detritus.

In Australia, the added association with convict settlement exacerbated disjuncture with Great Britain and hastened a desperate search for status.

As a result of this urgency, the colonial condition in Australia essentially became one of rushed misreading and mistroping throughout the initial phase of self-representation. The output was a desperate 'hit or miss' strategy. This occurred both because of nostalgic errors about its actual (historic) status as well as delusions about its future role in Empire. To their minds, colonisers were acting out a pioneer trope in Australia for which they would receive reward in due course. They had created outposts which replicated their perception of the Within; thus, imposing a received and transferred conception of how power operates onto a new landscape. We only have to look at how Governor Philip first mapped out space in Sydney to observe that sensibility. The difference was that the architectural emblems of power – the surveillance positions and walls of the convict settlement – held Nature OUT in New South Wales – rather than enclosing prisoners WITHIN. This perception of how power should operate was magnified and distorted until it appeared somewhat like Kafka's Harrow in *The Penal Colony*. It became a form of self-flagellation. Reintegration into English society was not considered relevant because no one believed that a cord had been severed for Colonists (as opposed to Convicts and Emancipists). Like Malayan rubber, the Imperial bond was supposed to stretch to the farthest corners of Empire and rebound all the way HOME (Empire as membrane). This was a gross error of judgment. For the circumstances of the Colonist once sited in Australia did not accurately fulfil the tenets of any extant trope of the Within. The Dominioned condition was totally without precedent. There was no mechanism for re-integration and no will to create one in London. Biblical precedents are the best means of illustrating this inability to 'trope' satisfactorily in Australian conditions. For example, the story of Joseph in Genesis could never be completed in Australia because the Within could never be segmented or transported to extrinsic space let alone placed in any posture of lack or need. The self-conscious adoption of the trope of the Prodigal Son by Dominioned Literature further illustrates the futility of this effort. Richard Mahony as a character and Henry Lawson as a human represent prime examples of Australian misprisions of this trope. Christina Stead's characters Teresa Hawkins in *For Love Alone* and Baruch Mendelsohn in *7 Poor Men of Sydney* are futile and fatal variants of this trope respectively. These characters were certainly able to relocate physically to England but they could never insert themselves WITHIN its hierarchy. Their outsider status became obvious as soon as they opened their mouths. There was a fundamental difference of VOICE. The best symbol of Dominioned Literature attempting to break back into Majority is found in Charles Dicken's Abel Magwitch. He must act as a fugitive in England who invests his wealth in a surrogate inside the machine. He resembles Odysseus who, after his long voyage home through the known world, returns to Ithaca only to see it used by the Gods as a slingshot to ricochet him into extrinsic space – in the other direction beyond Gibraltar – on a quest for something totally unlike him: people had never seen the sea.

This place is or was Australia.

We are "stranded far from home," as the Saints put it, and we are not able to conceive, let alone get back inside the Within to mount, what the Birthday Party called, a "Mutiny in Heaven."

In fact, the best correspondence to the Dominioned condition is the Post-Lapsarian trope. It applies equally to convicts and to colonists. But everybody proceeded on the basis of ignorance of such a proscription. It was never defined for good reason by Empire. It was only in a moment of existential crisis for Australia that the person at the centre of that power – Winston Churchill – crystallised its existence in his deviosuness against John Curtin's commitment to get Australian troops home rather than squander them in a futile defence of Empire Burma. Withdrawal of deference represented a fundamental de-dominionisation – or maybe de-minionisation – against which the Mother Country baulked.

Eventually, Australian literature transcended its Dominioned status by fusing Shelley's Alastor trope with its ANTIPODEAN: the prosaic fixity in dystopia of the Sensitive Plant. This apparently oxymoronic Master Metaphor overlaid the Within. It induced some of the most powerful writing in English from the 1880s by enforcing acceptance of permanent relocation to extrinsic space and thus effacing all angst about it. Indeed, it even legitimised nostalgia. It was a trope attached to fatal movement, true, but its air of Existential abandonment was well suited to an Australian ontology giving it a direct lineage to Beckett and post-war French theory. In this chronology, Adam/Eve became Currency Lad/Currency Lass became Warrigal Alf/Nosey Alf became Theodora Goodman and David Malouf's Ovid. Of course, the fatal consequences of motion for women is a key trope in literature. But that discussion is for another day ... a later chapter (see C9). In this sequence, there comes to each character a moment of fundamental self-realisation in which they assume the Romantic trope of the isolated individual dissolving in a false moment of prospective union with an unattainable Ideal and die. Other examples of this *askesis* include Voss and Laura Trevelyn in *Voss*, Eddie Twyborn in *The Twyborn Affair* (among many examples in White) and in Eve Langley's *The Peapickers*.

But it would be imprecise to represent this outcome as the product of any coordinated drive to national self-expression in Australia. It has been a patchy and uneven progression with many retreats and revisions as well as failures of nerve which continue even unto today. We have not yet created our own semantics. It is not clear thus far how it will be done. But we will never do it with conventional narrative. We will never do it with depictions of place. The Great Australian Novel cannot be defined by location. It must be a technical performance at the same level of accomplishment as arch-canonical texts. It must disrupt historic continuity. It must induce a fundamental BREAK.

The condition for this 'upshot' is already in place.

It will be based on what Harold Bloom called *clinamen*: a wilful misreading of received tropes.

For the literary machine of Australian Literature is founded on a flawed and incomplete simulacrum of the Major Literature from which it originated; something like the patchy, distorting Modernism of the Ducal art collection in Walter Pater's *Duke Carl of Rosenmond*. Its product cannot be considered a skeleton of any extant machine. This would imply that a complementary basic framework exists. Not so. In fact, it is a completely misshapen abomination whose lack of utility should really discount its signification as a 'machine.' It cannot conceive of itself warranting any naming that is not derogatory. The heroic rhetoric of Deleuze and Guattari cannot be branded on its hide. It remains in its own mind 'minion' literature. Yet even the use of this word MINION implies that it is still enclosed within the sphere of Major Literature like a slave or pet. It does not even attain this status: of being locked away every night in some dank *ergastula*. For it is always driven out of the enframing. Yet even in this formulation, there is still the promise of instructions to which it can offer acquiescence: stuff that it will be ordered to DO, Minion. The task it will be ordered to fulfil is to continue its own perpetual removal from the site of the master language. The indigenous peoples which it pursues and annihilates are, in fact, a metonymy of its own metonymical position. It is cast out of Heidegger's En-framed space like

Queen Mab and forced into acts of continuous self-abnegation. It is, thus, truly Dominioned Literature: one perpetuated by the repetition of the acts of its expulsions, which are the furthest point in the past repeated so often that they inhabit the present and fix the future.

It is to the extrinsic space of the Without that this paper has travelled. To a place where a 'true' (as in both genuine and loyal) Dominioned Literature was first heaped. It is not unlike Milton's undeterred Innumerable (*Paradise Lost* 1.338) in that it was content – as in both 'substance' and 'satisfaction – in such an "abject posture" (*Paradise Lost* 1.322). This loyal refuse of Major Literature was unaware that it had been expelled from the Within forever despite common heritage and regardless of its certainty that it had maintained itself faithfully as a loyal outpost of the Within by perpetuating its institutions and ethics. For it was originally of the Within but it was the Within set in motion. Such satellites stay in orbit after their usefulness is exhausted. They are then allowed to drift in space. They are the inverse of Icarus. A capacity for subversion was inconceivable to Dominioned Literature. It never altered its posture of deference. It was not a literature of subversion – but of imitation. It was not a "revolutionary force" in Deleuze and Guattari's terms but a totem held in prosaic thrall. It was like something suddenly detached from its Signified awaiting new classification to be imposed upon it. It did not have the resources to define itself. It knew only of itself as a metonymy. In a variation of Saussure's famous analogy, it was a pawn which had been removed from the board. Even today, its discourse is trapped between Major Literature and the subversive Australian indigenous voice of dispossession.

So rather than quibble over what constitutes the term, Minor Literature, so that it appears that we are begging yet again for re-inclusion, it would perhaps be better to abandon Deleuze and Guattari altogether, along with the entire Within and its vast literary machine, which we know of only through lack, so that it always appears more vast and thrilling, and detach ourselves from majority once and for all.

Let us grant to Deleuze and Guattari anything intervolved within Major Literature. And, accepting all this as given (for the Major Literature only dispenses largesse and nothing can be taken from it), let us at last seek to establish the characteristics of the literary machine of the Without of Dominioned Literature. To advance this distinction, let us use Deleuze and Guattari from this moment as a Thesis from which to extract Antithesis. Let them become the means of our exclusion from the discourse on Major/ Minor Literature. This enables us to use them as they would wish, as a truly revolutionary force, by characterising their literary machine as the antipodal element to the Without.

Deleuze and Guattari summarise Minor Literature in the following way:

> "... the three characteristics of minor literature are the deterritorialization of language, the connection of the individual to a political immediacy, and the collective assemblage of enunciation" (18).

Against these features, let it only be known that a true Minor Literature could never conceive of enacting a de-territorialising language; is never "political"; never takes on collective value. It is mimetic, craven, cannibalistic, alien to both itself and its fellow beings. Its energy is consumed in producing memoranda and internecine purges. It is known only by the definition granted to it by Major Literature. If its impersonation is flawed, this is an accident. It will do everything in its power to correct such an aberration when it is brought to notice. If it produces anything deemed of value, it will be met with surprise and offered to the master gladly. Ideally, it will be deemed in such a manner that it makes the Master feel that it was HIS idea all along. In terms of Wilde's *Salome*, it is not the Tetrarch nor Salome nor Iokanann but Narobod. It is 'O.' It appeals to Major Literature as if to an arbiter. Yet it gladly accepts punishment as its due. It also accepts that its prayers (as if to a God) will be ignored or perverted. It cannot entertain the prospect of usurpation. Sir Robert Menzies is its Prometheus. Any association with insurgency could only be the product of arrogation by dissidents from Major Literature. Thus, it resembles the working class mobs in *Coriolanus*: driven into the streets but utterly without destination; easily mollified by aristocratic platitudes; easily perplexed (as if hypnotised) by big words and smart paradoxes; almost honoured to become the butt of insult (this, at least, acknowledges its existence); ultimately expelled back into servile oblivion when no longer necessary.

Deleuze and Guattari would approve of this dense political metaphor for Minor Literature because they consider that "its cramped space forces each individual intrigue to connect immediately to politics." However, their notion of cramped space is at the nexus of language: WITHIN Node. In the extrinsic space of Dominioned Literature there is a surfeit of latitude. Out here, nobody ever makes contact. It would be good to use this vacant space for innovation. Yet how can invention be spurred? For all that Dominioned Literature craves is to graft the precepts of Major Literature onto its self in a blasphemy of cosmetic surgery. Its subsequent abominations are twice damned. Spurned by the culture that spawned them, they lay their already feeble mimesis over the aberrant landscape like a waterproof picnic blanket. Eventually, this nostalgic construct of Major Literature must be abandoned as a site that can never be replicated. It will only produce a grotesque perversion of the Original; in other words, Frankenstein's monster. This analogy is actually more apt because the monster is named after its maker, Doctor Frankenstein. But that is not understood at the start. It is the core ambition of every Dominioned Literature to be pulped into Major Literature. Therefore, its first tactic is simulation. It is a form of adoration. Dominioned Literature thus constructs its own perversion of a literary machine: its own canon from which it excludes its own discordant elements. What could be more pathetic than these texts that are proscribed even from the Without of a Dominioned Literature and residing in the meta-extrinsic space of the "never" (x2) or "never-never" where Barcroft Boake's "dead men lie." This DOUBLE-NEVER is a landscape beyond the mis-replica of its literary machine – it is the arena of taboo upon taboo ... or of a tattoo effacing another tattoo to create an illegible image like Kafka's harrow. In fact, the proscribed texts of Minor Literature such as the *Confessions of William James Chidley* are the true Utopian texts of the Without. Only neglected or proscribed utterance from Within could offer any kind of analogy to this truly transcendent offspring of Dominioned Literature (as of Sin's incestuous offspring by Death in *Paradise Lost*). Certainly not the icons of Major Literature. To those places, there is no light. Only the minor works of major writers could act as its tropes. As well as those works of "thwarted literary groups" that Deleuze and Guattari dump on their drive to hegemony. To plot our route through this marginalised Minor Literature, we must make our way through the backwaters and proscribed regions of the Canon. The consequent heap resembles a mound in the desert (what Olive Schreiner would call a "kopje") that conceals a rich shallow grave.

What does Dominioned Literature appear like in comparison with what Deleuze and Guattari call a "literary machine"?

It would bear some resemblance to its model. It may be a Spartan sort of replica, true. A shambles of the true machine. In conceptualizations of size, the relationship of the words Minor and Major suggest that it would be diminutive in comparison to the original. This is improbable. In the vast expanse of exile, with only the exaggerations of a dimming memory to guide us (for example, adults appear huge in our memories), it is more likely to overestimate the scale of its model. So, it would be huge. In addition, some individual components are likely to assume *uber*-significance and their proportions will then distort the machine. This could result in the head being enormous, the torso well tapered and the legs quite withered so that it topples over on bound feet. Alternatively, the replica could be extraordinarily well grounded with a severely under developed head. This, surely, is the best analogy as Oedipus means "swollen foot" in

Greek. Yet it could avoid scale together. That is possible. But, either way, it will end up as bloated as one of those primitive computers that use billions of punch cards to answer a simple equation. As a dubious signification of a true machine, it is certain that the Dominioned Machine would be built out of gathered materials like stone, twine and wood. The complex alloys and plastics which construct a true literary machine are unavailable in its barren environment. It can only rely on scavenging and over-priced imports (i.e. expendable discards of Major Literature). Academic appointments in Australia are a good example of this practice.

But even if it is not a grotesque parody of a machine at rest, even if it bears an extremely close resemblance to the model, even if it is a masterpiece of ornamentation (and the shells of a Minor Literature often outstrip their icons in ostentation), closer examination with it will always reveal that it is UTTERLY UNFUNCTIONAL. For the Dominioned machine is a travesty of utility. Its pieces are fitted together without method. If it possesses some relevant parts, there is no understanding of how they can be combined to make a working machine (although the chances are still good that obsolete components were purchased). And even if a plan of the machine was supplied, it would be held upside down by the frauds posing as engineers. But even if they read the manual carefully, its instructions would be indecipherable.

Thus, like the Trojan Horse, a true Dominioned Literature is a grotesque parody of its signified. In other words, it is a signifier of a signifier not a *trompe l'oeil* representation. If you placed this abomination at the fortress door of Major Literature, it would be shunted into a stagnant moat outside the city walls with its brave volunteers trapped inside like the tunnellers of Hill 60.

But let's assume for one moment it was wheeled inside the compound and allowed to rest overnight. Allow this concession: having this hollow semblance of meaning enclosed within the territory of master language. The result would be that its comic figures dropped out of the trap door and surrendered in the hope of being kept on as slaves.

Yet I could discard this entire formulation by asking one question: who would want to be part of any literary machine given the appalling record of Major Literature for suppression and censorship?

Better no machine, better no majority, better no text than merely to reimpose the brutal solution of tyrants. Better to move around extrinsic space with no map, in circles, governed by the need for sustenance and shade.

This is a truly Australian version of experience channelling Romantic and Modernist symbols.

It provides one version of the process of Becoming in Australia.

Capri stood silent as if in a courtyard. He looked at Bob and Helen in the back row jamming Tom Hallem into a corner then directed his gaze at the ceiling where wide iron shades like medieval girdles housed eight unlit bulbs in frosted fittings. His family. Shambles of a machine. To become Edmund or not. That's the ask. The bastard sits beneath the fatherless son in hereditary order.

"Thank you, William," quired Goldstein. "That was quite ..." he paused to search for the right word then added keenly, "fantastic." The crowd calmed. "Questions?" he asked with firm self-satisfaction.

Associate Professor Godfrey Smalls suckt AUDIBLY on the stale shavings in his pipe, exhaled and borrowed the hiatus politely.

"Thank you for your paper, Mister Capri. Of course, your theory should really be read and contemplated. It is far too dense for an audience to consume readily even with your plethora of helpful examples."

Insert on speech/writing gap (see C6). Plato privileged rhetoric. It was the verbalisation of living and dying as instants. Writing was just fixity of locution for time. It represented a kind of confinement (or enframing) of sublime utterance. SHIFT TO ARCHI-ECRITURE: Derrida conceived a pre-conditioning structure in language that dictated to expression before/of/by both tongue and hand. Words wild in form and thought to electrocute his deniers. Rendered by Joyce as words. A transcript that creates an impression of verbal spontaneity through a dense process of refinement. A purple smokescreen of Goofey Grape churning out of a LIVE LZ as the helicopters cancel out sound so communication is reduced to the movement of fingers. That is the basic template of this chapter.

"Nonetheless," continued Smalls, "I would note, as an initial observation, that you have collapsed the distinction between literature and biography. This is what Joyce did to Shakespeare. Remember the Scylla episode? There is no separation of man from text. This brings us back to Leavis. There is intellectual inconsistency present."

"Wimsatt would call it Affective Fallacy," said Ilks coldly.

Eglinton ridiculed Stephen's theory. Search for six brave medicals to take dictation. Russell kicking a corpse. Make it seven monkeys with typewriters. Twelve men with resolution could free all Ireland. Insert data analysis. It only takes three per cent of a population to instigate revolution. Cut off their ears make a necklace give it to Yeats. Shakespeare was a middle-aged man when he wrote *Hamlet*. Thus, he identified principally with Hamlet's father. He had reached Jacques' fifth or sixth stage of manhood. Joyce was forty when he published *Ulysses*. Maybe he had reached stage four. A stranger full of strange oaths like Odysseus. Jealous in honour and quick in quarrel. Blowing his "bubble reputation." Joyce knew that *Ulysses* was going to be GREAT. The feedback on each episode he published in *Little Review* confirmed it. Even notoriety was therefore welcome. Sales booster in the States. Pulp the machine. A different type of churn for Irish butter. *Ulysses* as contraband. Pirate copies were kept under the canvas hood on a book cart by the Liffey on top of Sinn Fein bombs. It was banned in Australia until 1967. Leopold Bloom perused a thick volume looking for dry yellowed pages. Huang se dianying. Classical Roman name. Might have scenes of debauchery. The vendor pulled a wad of pirate DVDs from a milk crate. Shanghai Dog flicked through them. What would Zhu Di like to watch tonight? She enjoyed Japanese movies. Sorrows of Satan. Sweets of Sin. Tokyo Hot. Re-write *Paradise Lost* from the loser's POV. Shelley's real hero. Bloom pays a pretty penny for books to excite Molly so she finally takes Boylan to bed. The ghost in *Hamlet* is preoccupied with infidelity. Les shuffled from a fruit machine to the bar; enough coin in hand for a middy of New. Penelope was going to meet Dick Stone in the Westside Motor Inn. Who am I to condemn her for getting what I can't give. The Blooms have not had sexual relations since Rudy's death. Doctor Daniel does not want to transmit HIV. Stephen Dedalus would have rejected *Ulysses* because he never wrote it. It would have meant one extra clawhold in the Canon to climb. Sirmounting Shakespeare. Stay closer to Scylla like Circe said. Elizabeth's advice to Tom Hallem. Paint some bold landscapes. Get a portrait in the Archibald. Forego the Ideal. Try the revelation of a living wage for a change. Signs of destiny. A star rose in the sky when Shakespeare was eight years old. Some people in England thought it was the Second Coming. The audience looked satisfied with this omen of the Bard's arrival. Lyster nodded. Stephen didn't tell them that it faded. Later, he pisses with Bloom underneath said stars. I can't shake off the black dog of my internal discourse as this novel proceeds, he thought. The freewheeling intellectual spirit of the Proteus episode is gone by the end of Scylla. Stephen gets drunk.

"Precisely," affirmed Smalls bowing his silver quiff towards the Dean.

Ilks gave unction. Capri watched him quash the rheum. His hairline exposed two bright smooth lobes. Piercing pale eyeballs hidden behind heavy spectacles.

"I'm concerned about the way you undermine notions of literary excellence," began Professor Krafter. "Your theory prevents any judgment about what constitutes good or bad art. Your elevation of Chidley is the most obvious example."

"Yes. There is something *Fin de Siecle* about the whole sorry saga," added Mildling helpfully.

"Madman as seer," mocked Smalls.

"I thought we got past that chestnut with *Solid Mandala*," replied Mildling squeezing his trousers.

"Quite," added Krafter.

"Chidley," interrupted Professor Milkmaid decisively, "was what Harold Bloom would call a great reader in an age of great readers."

Capri held fast. The old lecturer continued testily.

"His *Confessions* displayed a genuine stylist struggling gamely with radical subject matter. He tells it as he sees it. Like Thoreau or Emerson, there are no taboos. No apostasy. He doesn't displace his material into second-rate characterisation. It's not easy to write coherently and honestly about sex. Think Petronius. Think Catullus. Think Sade. All vilified. Of his nearest contemporaries, think Freud. Think Havelock Ellis. They presented their interest in this subject as ... pure science."

"But what about literary merit?" inquired Krafter less lofty.

"Look how Chidley went about his task," replied Milkmaid. "There's your proof. He deliberately chose an epistolary form because it is the best means of confession. He employed a personal Quest narrative. He crafted an effective chronological structure. And he is no more fragmentary than Montaigne or Rousseau."

"So," responded Krafter, "does it mean we can't judge a rich period in Australian literature like the 1890s against a weaker time like the 1930s?"

"With respect Professor," interjected Associate Professor Judith Barbour, "I think there is a strong sense of periodicity in Mister Capri's work."

She turned towards me. An attendant came to the portal to inform Lyster that a gentleman wanted to see files of the *Kilkenny People*. He left. An intense undergraduate couple followed him. This surprised Billy.

"In fact, Mister Capri employs a triumphant metaphor for the development of Australian literature although he seems ambivalent about its rate of progress. He quite obviously divides the local canon into periods of fertility and barrenness. In the end, it becomes a kind of extended metaphorical joke."

"We've bottomed out now I hope," added Mildling smiling.

"Well we've just about recovered from your pastiche of Sixties sub-culture, if that's what you mean," replied Goldstein smartly. Inserting Kinch's blade.

"Milo gave good party. You've got to grant him that," said A/P Donald Tuck before exclaiming: "Australian literature has never been stronger, I believe!"

Capri swallowed bared teeth. Cut with incisors. Think fast unaloud. Retreat like Xenophon, who perfected the art of rear-guard fighting. Surreal affectations on a bed of stale Dickens with pale Borgesian sauce. Junkies with A-List looks churning out underdone novellas for future film rights. Professor Pan's fourth novel is dedicated to his third undergraduate wife. Gritty romances set in coastal caravan parks in winter. An ex-advertising executive and his favorite prostitute find love beneath the annexes. Masturbating Nazi brats. Expatriate fantasies about convent grrrls. Rich fat chick meets smart lean chick. One likes Bartok; the other Bach. Stephen lies blacked out in Camden Hall in a pond of his own vomit. The young women lift their plaid skirts to step over him. Our heroine starts menstruating on the threshold of a dormitory window in San Sebastian before a full moon. Ample arms suddenly press her head into forgiving flesh. Nervy pleasure centres are exposed to desperate digitation beneath a bust of Mary Immaculate. They wake next morning as bells summon the peasants to Mass. Cue Nick Cave album. One moment it's 1938. Next 1990. The narrator is seated on a low stool in a café in Barceloneta researching the life of a female journalist who died in the Civil War. Everybody's making vague eye contact. She's just finished a free-form poem in a large black notebook about a bowl of mussels that evoke the odour, appearance and texture of love. She dips fresh *churros* through the frothy face of a *café con leche*. Sleazy old men are sipping brandy. She imagines them marching towards the border in driving sleet fleeing the advance of Franco's army.

"I'd like to change tack," continued A/P Barbour. "In relation to minor literature, are you saying a minor poem like Shelley's 'Hellas' is more valuable to the Dominioned writer than a major work about a rebellious outsider like *Prometheus Unbound*?"

Capri winced. Eglinton asks Stephen if believes his own theory. Stephen's answer is negative. You don't get paid if you don't, he is told. That would rule out almost every deal I've ever worked on, thought Shanghai Dog. Voltaire made money to indulge his interest in writing. Baudelaire calculated that he earned one franc and seventy centimes per day across his career. You can publish the lot for a guinea, added Stephen. He would trade anything for fame.

"No," replied Capri. "What I'm saying is that an apparently minor poem like 'The Sensitive Plant' was intended by Shelley to be seen as <u>equivalent</u> in stature to *Prometheus Unbound*. To him, a lyric was as powerful as an epic. The small was equal to the large. This was a moral position. He wanted them to be read in tandem. They acted as foils. This was telegraphed in how he presented these two poems in publication. 'The Sensitive Plant' is placed directly after *Prometheus Unbound* in the 1820 volume. It reverses the progress from torture to utopia in the Prometheus epic and reduces affairs from an immortal to a mortal and mutable scale. Action is decreased from High Mimetic to Low Mimetic. The static fable with its basic quatrains, simple rhyme scheme and cliched iambic meter acts as the antithesis of the extravagant Promethean saga with its dazzling array of forms and characters and sweeping shifts of place."

"That's all well and good," interposed Doctor Deirdre Sackerson, larding the air with bile from her honey-bear mouth. "But I'd like to interrogate your so-called critical method. Or, rather, lack thereof."

She exhaled audibly.

"There is no core to your thinking, Mister Capri. You never keep your eye steadily on a single text. You seem unable to deny yourself the opportunity of throwing in likenesses to other works and historical minutiae."

"So?" asked Capri genuinely perplexed.

"Your endless references and asides accumulate to the point of overload and obfuscation. The bird's eye view is unrelieved, your detailed readings forever accumulating and the texts under discussion endlessly proliferating. Repeatedly I was forced to ask myself during your paper: what is the argument here? Where does this lead us? Is it just unprocessed list-making?"

"Glosynge is a glorious thing," added Milkmaid opening his arms. Capri stood silent. The audience hummed. Sackerson removed her wireless bifocals. She frizzled phonetic lips. I do have a method, he thought. No time now to explain. One day I will write its definitive product. Start with both Blooms. Proust's vase of. Chains of misreading. Hieratic code. The irony of one generation converted into the synecdoche of the next. Troping on previous tropes (See Appendix C). A field of interlocked volumes. Leaves resting inside spines. Leaves of paper stock. Reading that makes prosenchymatic path-mosaics which curve and rise until it becomes a transparent bubble that encloses the author. Heidegger's sphere. What Proust said. Un livre interieur. Virginia Woolf said that life was a clear envelope surrounding us. This was a statement of prolepsis about the final action of her body in the Ouse. See Proust's Marcel in the Guermantes library. Go past Chapter 10. Goethe's *urpflanze* as the basic structure in Nature. A concept later updated by John Ruskin. Define *Einfluss*. To infuse with secret power. Also, the flowing from the stars of ethereal fluid. Sperm splashed Chidley's tunic. O'Dowd's *Australia*. New Hellas in Bush. An anomaly. Last sea-thing up-dredged. Sydney is an Odyssean place. Brennan's Homerics. Haines was interested in the *Lovesongs of Connacht*. It epitomised his anthropological engagement with Ireland. Hyde ended up King of All Eire. *An Craoibhín Aoibhinn*. He was famous for filling out his census form in Gaelic. Took the presidential oath in Roscommon. A dead dialect. There were three hundred languages when the English arrived at Port Jackson. Twenty now extant. They died in battle cries. Chewing on poisoned dough. In smallpox whispers. Against mission school canes. As stolen children learned to communicate whitely. Protean acts. Pretend to be a wog. Dharuk is called the Sydney language. Vocabularies were collected by Collins and Dawes off Arabanoo and Bennelong. Patyegarang was only fifteen when Dawes got at her. *Nyímuŋ candle Mister D*, she said. Put out the light. *Putuwá*. Come back to bed. They held each other. Stephen's theory: where there is reconciliation, there must first have been sundering. Note relevance to the Bloom marriage. To the Hallems. Also, the Archers. Barry and Helen left the lecture theatre meekly. Tom Hallem leaned back in a chair. A palm cupped his sneering cheek. We looked at each other. Brothers. Mulligan's lie that Synge wanted to murder Stephen for urinating on his doorstep. Elizabeth caught me crapping in Capon's pool. Why did she come back last night? Anne Hathaway died before she was born, according to Eglinton. Black people burned the Waratah to resurrect spirits. Chaim. Do a big painting for Elizabeth. O'Keeffe close-ups in flames. Bosschaert. Russell on love songs. Real poetic power comes from the peasants, he said. MAO was a kulak. As Stephen to A. E. so I to Elizabeth re-debt. Stephen's defence: I IS NOW ANOTHER. Molecular reconstitution of debt. Metaphor for Vico. Eglinton says their marriage was a mistake. Like Penelope and our father. Willy is due. Hallem checked his watch. Shakespeare's silence about his wife has perplexed critics. Blows too low is the consensus. O's mendacity. Shakespeare left Anne his second-best bed. The one she now shares with Les Hallem. Joyce gets Stephen to compose a Modernist poem about his dormitory condition during the latter stages of the literary discourse in Scylla as he loses interest and reverts to silence.

Theylefthimoutthere
Alonenobed
Secondbested
Lefthimthey
Bestnobed
Secabed
Onnobed.

This poem reminds the reader that Stephen is fundamentally an Artist and that he is thinking in the newest poetic mode. Its imagery of beds reflects Stephen's current predicament. He has nowhere to go after surrendering the keys to the Martello Tower to Mulligan. He has also been 'put outside the house' by the Dublin literati: both in publishing and physical form. The olive-bough bed built by Odysseus with its secret trick was a key symbol in Homer of legitimacy. Joyce inverts it to stress Stephen's severance from Dublin. Billy Capri too felt the utter aloneness of defeat. Second-best like Anne's bed. Note that the questions largely did not confront his core thesis. Tom Hallem was abruptly consumed with the events of the last twenty-four hours. Elizabeth's return. Removalist. Billy's place. Westacott. The suck. Some cash. Ana's score. The message from Bob Hensley. Deasy's letter. Russell will get it printed alongside Synge. An acerbic contrast by Joyce. Stephen is promoting an idiot's message. INSERT ON BILLY'S REALISATION OF NO FUTURE ON CAMPUS. But he has no alternate option as yet.

"I think that's a topic for continued discussion at the pub," said Goldstein awkwardly to close proceedings. "We've run out of time today."

"I still don't think we resolved the question of whether Shakespeare is Hamlet or Hamlet's father or neither or both," moaned Mildling.

Eliot's complaint. Main problem is not Hamlet but the play. The character is not fully formed. It is an artistic failure. Stolen Kyd. Not really concerned about his father's murder. In truth, Hamlet was distressed by his mother's involvement. Loss of face. Goethe made Hamlet into Wilhelm Meister. Coleridge did the same. Form is the thing. Objective Correlative. Write a chain of symbols that connect. Show don't describe feelings. Write, "Billy scratched his forearm vigorously tearing skinny white twigs in thin sun-burnt flesh." This will exemplify stress to the reader. He twists and turns. He advances and retracts. Nothing like Bradley's tough Hamlet. Art must reveal ideas and essences. From how deep a life must art spring, asks Russell rhetorically. I spent the last 30 years working in government and the private sector across continents to gather enough authority to write this book. It has been composed in bursts and ebbs using a method much like Nabokov's file cards. It was a life led in the same city as my former colleagues and peers but our paths never crossed. I moved like a sceptre across Sydney. *Hamlet* is a ghost story. I faded into impalpability through absence and changing fashions, as Stephen Dedalus said. Like Odysseus, I was king of a minor kingdom: MY MIND. No/man of genius. No volition in my errors. Just average mistakes. Amoral snubs. Ancient slights to be avenged. There were no portals. I was that absentminded beggar shuffling amongst the sandstone cloisters in the main quadrangle as the rain fell on Browning's grasping jacaranda weed. The Man in the Brown Macintosh passed. Discovery came in patches. It glowed and ebbed. Insert Mulligan's clap. Applause is a bucket. The audience began to rise.

"Isn't Stephen Dedalus every character in Shakespeare," replied A/P Tuck.

"He must also be Master W. H. then," added Mildling.

"And thus Patroclus," affirmed Smalls.

"Yes. And Achilles *au dessus de* Patroclus," replied Mildling.

"What about Coriolanus?" asked Tuck.

"Coriolanus was the first Byronic hero," added Milkmaid.

"He is martial Hamlet."

"They had to kill him to shut him up," Smalls interpolated.

"He was the first Spasmodic poet," replied Mildling.

"I prefer the term 'Hyper-Romantic'," said Milkmaid.

"That term would suit Mister Capri's writing admirably," stated Professor Ilks coolly aloft. "I believe he has achieved a carefully-calculated Euphuism. There is merit in such an approach."

Professor Ilks bowed slightly and strode languidly from the room.

"That was quite a show," Goldstein said slapping Billy on the back.

"Thanks. Now let's get out of here," replied Billy smiling but shook.

The supervisor chaperoned his student towards the exit.

"Will you write up a condensed version for *Southerly?*" asked Laby Weffy as the group passed into the corridor.

"Is there a dollar in't?" asked Billy.

"Two thousand words max ... including footnotes and bibliography."

"A most ludic paper, Mister Capri" groaned A/P Tuck scrubbing his neatly trimmed mane. "Though my colleagues think you're as mad as a cut Blake. I'd love to peruse it more closely. Could you furnish a copy?"

"Only if he wants to see it recycled in your Saturday arts column as your own work," laughed O.

"Very amusing," said Tuck insincerely. "But seriously. Give me a loan. I could just take that copy."

He pointed hungrily at the folder in Billy's grip.

"Take it," said Billy.

He passed the folder. My sole transcription. The last key.

"Consider it a down-payment on his referee's report for your first Australia Council application," sneered Mildling.

"It's a bit like fagging," added Liddle wistfully.

"There's a proud tradition in English literature of dealing with a source by effacement," said Blind Basil Kiernan who had inserted a dry pipe into his wet mouth.

"Joyce never attributed his sources," broke in Barbour.

"A skill he learnt off Walter Pater," agreed Milkmaid.

"Like a dog burying a bone," O postulated.

"Ironically, Pater suffered most from this approach," added Capri. "Nobody knows of him today. But his disciples are considered the greatest writers of our century."

"Just as Pater subsumed Ruskin so Pater, in turn, was subsumed by Wilde," said Mildling making a cross of benediction. "*Obscurum per obscurius*."

"Dorian's Yellow Book is a corruption of Pater's Golden One."

"Lord Henry Wootton is Flavian full-formed," added O.

"Grown to proud manhood," smirked Mildling.

"Wilde's texts are all set-pieces," said Tuck.

"Aristocratic music hall comedy," scoffed Mildling jealously.

"Yet they all approach Paterian perfection of form," stated Judith Barbour decisively. "His trademark was the seamless execution of familiar forms. There isn't one he didn't master: ballads, farces, fairy-tales, plays, horror stories, even the mystery novel."

"But there is always a mechanical spirit to his texts," concluded Liddle anaemically.

"There is far less dilation in Wilde than Pater," she replied.

"Pater was utterly self-reflexive," agreed Milkmaid. "In all his works, he speaks by historical metaphor of the self-absorption of late nineteenth century art. Remember his famous statement in *Marius* that even the work of genius must be largely critical. He identifies the rationale for this analytical drive in the exhaustion of matter. All that remained for Art was perfection of style and form. This drive – Pater would call it 'centripetal force' – is the very basis of Post-Modernism. It is the portal to a new Theocratic Age. On that point I must go and teach Pope."

"Will we see you at the Bard?" asked Kiernan exhaling stale breath. Milkmaid waved his hand ambiguously. Circe offering cheese meal honey wine. Stand beyond the pack. I am tired of my own voice, the voice of Esau. My kingdom for a drink, thought Stephen. The desert wilderness of Paris, Texas. Pasolini's Oedipus. Die like Kafka unread. Erase all self-vestige. Pin the baby's feet together around a stake and expose it naked on a hillside. Burn the corpus. Gone. Over. Capri stood in the corridor with O.

"Et tu Sadosanct," inquired the voice of Tom Hallem slapping his cousin on the shoulder blade.

Capri turned.

"You've given me a great idea," his brother continued. "I'm going to build one of your 'book machines' for my next exhibition."

"Every backyard shed in this great nation is a laboratory," cut in O wryly. A nation is just the same people living in the same place, said Stephen Dedalus. Joyce rejected all concepts of nationhood. Except maybe Ireland which was an island. Imperialism was the cause of the Great War (source: Wikipedia). They walked towards the entrance. Names of all my bosses on painted plaques on their doors. My cardboard name-tag has just been removed from Room 341. A new neophyte will scribe at my desk. No memorial lozenge.

"You'll have to excuse me," said Tom acknowledging a slight figure following them down the corridor. Spittle sprayed Billy's cheek. Exit Tom Hallem. O took Billy's hand.

"I've got to run a two-hour seminar now," she said.

"Will I see you at the pub later on?" he asked.

"If you like," she replied coldly. Then withdrew. Billy hesitated. The moment is now. Hamlet standing on the dock. Sliver pieces. Mulligan and Dedalus in the National Library. Joyce at Trieste Station. No Burberry coat. The brothers were never close again, wrote Ellmann. Miscarried exits. Inadvertent stays. Hold onto the brink. Hedge. She has moved out of range. I may not see her again before I leave Sydney. She does not know about my paternity. Daughter of Caer. Swanderbound. I have given her my apartment. A kind of safe house. Face Helen and Barry alone then but not yet. It's all about the manner of Becoming. A hero is just an actor in shock. Move concussed like an ethics puppet. Hamlet always vacillated. Couldn't strike like an animal. Except at Polonius in error. For all his faults, a genuine father. Like Barry. If the father who has a son be not a father, can the son who has not a father be a son? Hamlet's crime mimics that of Claudius. Oedipal shocks. Laertes versus Hamlet. Orestes versus Telemachus. Models of mien. I need to reconnect with my parents somehow, thought Billy. One real: one false: one abstract. CAN I EVEN SPEAK? My face is set in aspic. Go out of the vaulted cell into what Joyce calls "shattering daylight." Billy watched O receding. A slight silhouette of a man had lashed himself to the wall with Tom. Goldstein entered his office. Stephen stands on Kildare Street mulling over the impact of his Shakespeare theory. Bloom passes. Mulligan greets him. Bloom's cameo appearances in Scylla establish his suitability as a replacement father figure for Stephen. In this schematic, Bloom is aligned with Shakespeare by an unfaithful wife and dead son (Hamnet/Rudy). As Shakespeare wrote his wife into his work, so Bloom considered composing a story based on Molly at the end of Episode Four. The young men follow Bloom. Stephen sees two plumes of smoke. They bring to mind the end of *Cymbeline*. Gods in Council. Crookedsmokeclimbs of Fielder's bread stacks. END. I lifted headphones out of me earhoalz. Cut PJ Harvey off mid-verse. Why am I so obsessed with BACK THEN? Anyone can write that story. Only I will write canon. Text genes and chromosomes. Correl. Pater'n'all DNA. It is so late that it has become very early but I can't sleep. Sounds real and recalled assail me. Poor Wat. A single car headlight flashing at tangents against Roman Blinds then gone. A propeller plane descending towards the third runway. It is forty-five minutes until the curfew is lifted. Ambulance sirens recede along Canterbury Road. Empty passenger trains career to the city fringes to thread back in the morning peak. My father's slippers sanding the grim linoleum floor of the ammonial hospital corridor. Orderlies propping him up under each soft, thick bicep. He fell. More luscious bruises. More rainbow-mica pelt. They laid him on a trolley and inserted him headlong through the MRI machine then huddled behind the lead screen watching his brain through a Perspex visor. Press the big red knob. Wait. All this process when we all know the facts about the end game. They take him back to his room. He has-been laid there for days. They prop him upright in bed to jam morsels at his mouth. Mush scabs stain his cheap night shirt. A straw of cold coffee purls on his gut. He will be dead soon I hope. INSERT VARIOUS DISEASES. Life is calling out a last dice throw. A faded coal gone stone-cold black. All the done and all the undone things are equally out of reach now. Before the last stroke, I asked him if he was content with his life he answered YES but he should have said NO. All the time left is boring. His voice started clawing out a Will. I told him forget it. There was no house. No money. That was all lies. I'm the only one left. He'd used up and discarded everyone else. Tom was dead. Penelope and Helen would not see him. I look on my role as a form of charity. He smiled meanly. Glibly. With disdain. Even with barely any ammunition left in his cellophane body he can still try to wound me. I stayed with him half an hour. I processed all this stuff long ago. Now it's just subject matter because of parallels to Joyce. He's on a triple dose of diazepam. Endep for pain. He gave the morphine button a solid pump and soon became comatose. Like Simon Dedalus after closing time forces him home. I'd never seen him asleep. I am now about the same age as when I first met him in 1984. I observe some of my own features fall out of his sunk screen. Scylla and Charybdis is a very brief segment in the *Odyssey* after Sirens and before Oxen of the Sun. In *Ulysses*, these episodes are nine, eleven and fourteen respectively in Chapter Two. Here, they are Chapters Four and Six with Sirens as a sub-episode in Chapter Ten (when Tom meets Frances). The bulk of Homer's depiction covers the advice of Circe. The actual travails of passage amount to only twenty lines. Six of Odysseus' crew are consumed by Scylla. He calls this sight "the most pitiful of all" things that he had seen on the sea. That's quite a conclusion given the weight of his maritime adventures. I lay down and dozed fitfully on a camp bed in his room. I woke in foetal thrall in grey light. Shift to present tense. My routine in Chisel is mundane. I traipse to the staff room to shave. I wash my face in cold water. For a moment, reality is suspended. But it is only a temporary respite. I gaze into the filthy mirror. Through trails of dried spittle, my father's gormless features stare back. Stephen and Bloom in Circe's brothel observe a statue of William Shakespeare with rigid facial paralysis crowned by the reflection of a hat-rack made of reindeer antlers. Link to fluid stand whose potions sustain my father's life. Cuckold horns. Les wears them. Leon also. Wallis' painting. Ben Jonson holding up the Bard's death mask. Gerard Johnson chipping at his monument. Bad sculptures have been placed in strategic hamlets across Europe to commemorate Joyce. Plonked around the corner from the GPO on North Earl Street. This is virtually the only place in Dublin without any geographical connection to Joyce. Richirishironyinsitu. He lived in twenty different homes. Limbs akimbo in a bed of Swiss shrubs: a man who never bothered much with nature. Shuffling over the Ponte Rosso. Poking out of a retail wall in Szombathely. Bloom is the Hungarian connection. Peeping out of a massive bronze greatcoat in Moscow. Facing his former university at Newman House, animated by furtive, wavering lips. Not to forget the various plaques and seats. He was born at 41 Brighton Square. He died in Zurich. "Does nobody understand," were reputedly his final words. Thus, a question to end. Set against a statement of self-regard at the start when Stephen Dedalus said: HERE IS ME in *PAYM*. You can take a tour of sites that filled the interim in Dublin, Paris, Trieste and Zurich. It's like Wandering Rocks. When I returned, my father's eyes were stuck. I peeled them back. Bloodshot rafts. Scylla ends with Mulligan bullying Stephen about a telegram. He assumes the role of rejected friend. This is actually Stephen's rightful part. As with all minor literatures, he is allowed no personal status. Willy = Haines. A drug dealer and a dealer in prestige. Moneyed classes. False transactions. Stephen encounters the madman Farrell as he passes through the reading room. He is a symbol of what Stephen could become. The endpoint of a fixation on words. You can write the same book forever and never finish. You get caught in a loop in the editing void. It's a kind of delaying tactic. I can never publish this work. In the last lines of S][C, Stephen's forthright speech collapses into a sequence of questions, word fragments, scraps of poetry, transcriptions of Mulligan's babble, reprises and recriminations about his Shakespeare theory, disconnected images linked by ellipses and punctuation gaps making spaces on the page like Mallarme's A DICE THROWN. Joyce employs incremental repetition to give reactive depth to thoughts and scenes as Stephen is exposed to them: Aengus, lubber, murmur/mummer. To efface precursors = to efface the father. Minor/major literature = son/father (Telemachus | Odysseus). Hamlet Snr/Jnr = real/ideal manhood. The son vacillates because he cannot live up to his own image of his father. Shift from lecture theatre to my father's death throes (see also C6). Kill him off in text. He died at 11 am today, just after I finished this passage, IN REAL LIFE. It goes on valueless and flat. Stephen Dedalus is trapped in extrinsic space after the end of Scylla until Joyce resurrects him in Oxen of the Sun in pursuit of another false father figure. This is a long span in terms of reading time – maybe 160 pages. This is about 20% of the novel. The average reader will spend 16 hours and 58 minutes reading the 783 pages of *Ulysses* at 250 WPM, according to Readinglength.com. But it is a short period in Joyce's narrative chronology (approximately 7 hours). Yet, no matter how much time elapses, no matter how often it is re-explained, how many excuses are made, and how much adult experience I bring to the situation, I can never forgive my father's actions. Juxtapose detached critical oratory with highly personal writing (invert Plato, Derrida et al). He was a bad man like Simon Dedalus or John Joyce. Inadvertently, I sent a text message to a colleague as I left for the long drive to the dementia ward, which read, "Feather dead." This was a chance correspondence with the misspelled telegram from Stephen's father, announcing "NOTHER DEAD." He was laid out on the floor on a blue gymnasium matt. The son must subvert the journey of the father. It all becomes clear to Stephen Dedalus after his mother dies. She was a human shield FLIP His father is exposed. In the beginning, I was only able to grasp at him (sucking tentacles). I feared collateral damage from his DNA (Exodus 20:5, Numbers 14:18). Sometimes, I idealised him. He became Odysseus, Hamlet Senior or Leopold Bloom. I blamed myself. Eventually, I placed myself in contradistinction to him. He became Don Cane. Richie's dead son with him was Hamnet. Also, Chaim. In materialist terms, he was my half-brother, Robert Richards, who succumbed to spina bifida on the operating table in 1958 at the age of three. I am

Telegonus to his Telemachus. Tom Hallem is Hamlet DEAD. I am not just Billy Capri. We are all wired to Homer. And all refer to *Ulysses*. Stephen's conclusion at the end of Scylla is that we deploy various guises in life but always meet up with ourselves FLIP Immediately after coining the famous proverb, "Je est un autre," in a letter to Georges Izambard from Charleville on 13 May 1871, Arthur Rimbaud added, "tant pis pour le bois qui se trouve violon." This can be translated as "it is that much worse for the wood that finds it is a violin." This apparent afterthought acts a master metaphor for Dominioned Literature SHIFT By the end of Chapter 4, it is clear he's worked out a plan, given it the right structure and now he's self-consciously trying to execute a truly innovative novel – and he knows it – just like JJ and Proust, but, unlike them, he's beset by performance anxiety about the correct rendition of every successive unit of expression (it's a curse), and whether it will all fold together, how to sound like a violin, and the virtues of discarding "good form," which you suck like a thumb, and he doesn't know, can never know, if he will get the reader on board or even if there will ever be a reader. In summary, Billy Capri walks to the physical (and symbolic) HOLD of the English faculty in this chapter. He reviews course lists fixed behind glass in locked noticeboards and effectively rejects this compartmentalised canon. Next, he renders his own theory before an expert audience. It is coolly received. He is being prepared for departure by the author. Tom Hallem also starts the process of disconnecting from Sydney at this point. He begins to observe his body FROM WITHOUT like the subject of some grim Cartesian self-experiment. This split is a pre-condition for some types of hard drug addiction.Likewise, Mulligan and Stephen separate decisively at the end of S&C in *Ulysses*. Stephen is irrevocably cut loose from literary Dublin. Billy Capri leaves *Telemachus* as an active agent ~~although he comes back in part as Shanghai Dog~~. INSERT PROLEPSIS: Billy dropped into the pub, O didn't come, he felt disaffected, his brother dishonoured him, he went back to his apartment, packed some final items, got a lift home off Barry and left Sydney.

5.
Wandering Rocks

"The society emerging from this unpromising beginning was callous, hypocritical, legalistic, but good at making the most of anything, whether native grasslands or human weakness. It was self-reliant, enterprising, with a kind of cocky confidence partly Irish, partly native-born, masculine and energetic."

– Beverley Kingston, *A History of New South Wales* (35)

1. BLACK KNIGHT (2 PM)

If one enters an office in a skyscraper, turning the gaze from the internationally renowned harbour of Sydney, Australia (Cadigal/Eora) to a glass door and travels across open-plan space, somehow made maze by carpet-coated partitions, to the reception area, the traveller must undergo scrutiny from a busy bespectacled woman settled on a low chair before a typewriter. One might be forgiven for thinking that removal from this station would leave a bas-relief behind her on the wall. The front of the desk at which she sits is surmounted by a solid and ungainly, almost overbalanced, plank of Swedish lumber. Atop it, trays are brimming with files and correspondence. Her left shoulder is surmounted by a black plastic emblem depicting the profile of Byerley Turk, the first British sire, captured at the Battle of Buda in 1686, long and high set of neck with high carriage of tail, whose progeny included the mare that founded Thoroughbred Family 1 as well as the famed "Dam of the Two True Blues," taproot of Thoroughbred Family 3, according to Weatherby's *General Stud Book*, positioned above the appellation of the apparently prosperous financial services organisation, the Welles Investment Group ("WIG"). She is watching us without generosity; for we are without status for her. You sign for your cheque. This is a new indignity imposed by the CFO and apparently approved by your brother. She closes the book and opens the intercom. Les Hallem closes the front gate. Ana Lafei scores a plumb parking spot opposite Artspace. She walks down Governor Bourke Street. A hire car emerges from St Peters Lane. She baulks. It was Bourke who created the domestic conditions in New South Wales that rendered transportation impractical. Currency Lads and Lasses, the first generation of British offspring were called. Their existence was thus defined in juxtaposition with Sterling. Non-legal tender. A gold sovereign set against mere paper. Inferior in value in perpetuity. Sydney was an economic bubble-bath nonetheless. This was Charles Darwin's lament. Everyone is hell-bent on wealth, he wrote. Mere sensualists. Why, an ex-convict could return to England with £100,000 in notes! This represented a failure of punishment. Commissioner Bigge had been appalled. Yet New South Wales was still a penal colony that compared favourably to Spanish settlements in South America and thus engendered pride in an Englishman. The "Wandering Rocks" episode dramatises the spiritual sterility and moral cannibalism of Dublin under occupation. Ireland's position as indentured servant of both the Roman Catholic Church and Imperial England is framed in the first and last sub-episodes by Father Conmee and the Earl of Dudley respectively. Both characters epitomize the tactics used by their caste for Joyce. The former moves through the local population eliciting information and smoothing the surface of a traumatised society. The latter races through the crowd in a sealed carriage showing no interest in the local people or their welfare. These extremes are used by Joyce to establish the conditions for the emergence of the Holy Trinity of: Bloom as Elijah (Humanism), Stephen as Artist (Joyce himself) and Molly as Earth Mother (see three-master at the end of Ulysses, C1). Together, they will redeem all Ireland. Ana passed across a porthole in the recessed wall of Aston Hall. Their letterbox was empty. Matt must have gone to his studio already. She unlocked the door. Darwin's mysterious agency. Strong extirpating the weak. Cruel but unavoidable. Turning from the sceptical glare of the receptionist, wrote Bardun, her voice rising richly to greet an established client on the switchboard, while lesser mortals are left at the mercy of recorded muzak, we await the elevator. Its wires cried. A seagull shrieked angrily. Les picked up a piece of gravel and shot it sidearm towards the bird. Joyce kept a pocketful of stones to fling at stray dogs. It flapped part-airwards angrily. Three quarks for Muster Mark! It landed, ran then bounced. Ana entered a first-floor apartment, discarding her uniform as she walked. A coin dropped onto the damp tessellated tiles. ALP was the sound it made. Puakaeafe. INSERT WHITE GAZE. Fairy Princess Moe. Admiring eyes. Gaugin's wicked art. Don't you remember Black Alice. Mix European & Aboriginal experience in this episode. Also, English and Australian history. Plus expose yourself against Joyce. Naked, Ana entered the bathroom.

She went to the pedestal basin. *Te Nave Nave Fenua* composed in a shaving cabinet mirror. Bust of Truganini by Benjamin Law. She dipped both hands into the flesh-coloured rinse limply. Our unsteady eyes are engaged by a press cutting mounted in a fine tortoiseshell frame of rising business identity, Ambrose S. Welles, known colloquially as Stan, being presented by the Premier of New South Wales, the Hon J.J. Cahill, to Her Majesty Queen Elizabeth the Second during her maiden visit to Australia in 1954, the first by an English monarch, part of the House of Windsor's benighted lap of honour to apply belated unction to a fast-unravelling empire. The bright monarch gloves his hand lightly. Cocoons of spittle grip the corners of his mouth. Shower steam fog. She lifted each leg into a cornsilk bath. Pomaded waves shone darkly. His buck teeth caw with delight. His son measured himself against his father in the bleary reflection of the mount. I am not so tall, he thought, though of more robust stock. Incisors withdrawn by expensive dental procedures. Straight sorrel hair. A water spirit like my mother. Phar Lap was also a plain horse. A great big lump. But the more races it won, the more majestic it became in the media. The telephone rang. Joyce's style occasionally disappoints the hieratic reader in this episode, especially when he relies on the one-trick pony of stream-of-consciousness internal monologue. In general, he depends on past-tense "said" when composing dialogue between characters. "Replied," in comparison, is only used 14 times (whereas it is employed 117 times in this work). "Asked" is equivalent across both novels. Coincidentally, it is employed 193 times in both *Ulysses* and the current draft (as at 04/09/2018). By contrast, the post-modern technique of signposting correspondences with "INSERT" is wholly absent from Joyce. He selected this word on only ten occasions and always for purely functional purposes. Here, it is utilised more than 240 times.

"Reverse charges call from London, sir," the receptionist announced into her headset microphone. Old Albion. Always up for a free feed of lamb and damp(en)er.

"Tell them I'll call back later," crackled the immaterial voice of Edmund Hamley lowly. CUT.

Tommy Townsend planted a seed in secret. Cast-offs sent seven months hence. Cenotaph of dead species. Call Arthur Philip in Spain. Mix omens with auguries. Bastards bearing their father's coat of arms altered with cadency. Gin-busting gangs. Shoot a blackfella take his woman back to camp everyone rapes her then we kill her with an axe. Whorehouse rabbit cages. Fig of tobacco leaf. Truck-stop grog-swaps at Moree. Eureka race riots. Irish revolts 1846. Lambing Flat. Buckland River. White Australia. Haigh's trench cattle. There was no Imperial Preference in 1930. Just Niemeyer's cold facts. Pay back your war debts or else we'll send Jardine. Or here's a deal. You stop Rommel: we'll fuck you over in Greece. Do not pass Rangoon, do not collect 200 Spitfires. Changi's sagging stalks. They planted a seven-star cross on Maralinga. Black mist over Anangu country. Death march like Sandakan. *Puya* entered their bodies. Tumour-clouds floating as far south as Ceduna. Femurs harvested by British Intelligence. Dead Robert. Richie's baby. Chaim. A long bell.

"What's next in my diary?" his brother asked.

The stainless-steel gates slid apart. Edgar Welles farewelled the receptionist, mumbling salutations. Her head pivoted on its uncomfortable socket and stretched sideways to follow his departure. He contemplated the bare compartment.

"Your next appointment is Colonel Cornwall," she continued. "The US folder is in your tray. I thought you could watch the race in the boardroom. It starts at two-forty. The executive team will assemble at two-fifteen. Beverages and snacks have already been purchased."

She cupped the mouthpiece. Ana brushed gleaming teeth. She rubbed her armpit with a wet cloth. He had a crisp cheque in his pocket. Maybe it could still be cashed if he hurried to the bank. Fetch provisions from South America. Telemachus leaving port. A virgin helpmate ocean. Ana passed rag through cleft. Athena sitting in the stern. Peter Cook in the saddle. Barrier twelve. Ana stroked her breach. Get three wide. Go fwd come back draw a diagram mix characters. Need a Gantt chart. Would extend even Joyce. Don't just stitch places together. Ana moved her fingers testily. Become clairvoyant like Tiresias. Insert Shanghai Dog. Like Telemachus, reach all the way back. Evidence from Nestor. First detective story. Fingers punching a worn-down keypad. Surftide suck'n'spit. Rush away thus returning. Ana rested her forehead on glazed tiles. Lead footprints on sodden sand. Yielding flooding effaced. Leon's first sarcoma. A death sentence. FINAL RESULTS STILL PENDING. Seven nuclear tests. Elizabeth Archer picked up a medical notice: "Your next appointment at the Albion Street Centre is with [handwritten] *Dr Julian Gold* [next line] on [next line] *Tuesday, 6 October, 4.30 pm.*" Elizabeth crumpled the sheet and threw it in the bin. The Tank Stream bore a Throwaway down its sandstone vein. Blood verdict. Ana Lafei severed the gush. Now the adventurer must cross the crevice between floor and elevator, beneath which drops black and ineffable space. She drew back the curtain. SEE ABOVE. These are all mutability symbols. Occasionally, a coin spills out of your pocket, drips into this slot and descends towards Earth; reminding you of a pebble plummeting silently down a bottomless well in some childhood fairy-tale. Perhaps the crack itself is the stimulant for fears of anarchic descent: all too explicable when they grip you. Edgar Welles passed over the threshold. Mast in a hollow mast-box. Twisted hide ropes. Stretch tackle. The wind bellied out. The keel lapped loudly. Sail. You turn to the board, press the ground floor button and wait. Ana Lafei slunk against the wall, flushed eye sockets out. She observed her own fingers moving manically in the mirror through a chink in the stiff shower curtain. Bathsheba at bath. Jags in the scrub over the fence watched Penelope Hallem unbutton her blouse. A heavy white brassiere. Both wings moved to her back thrusting her chest forward as she detached its intricate wires. Bloom handling his cock watching Gerty. Klute documenting Bree's tricks. Pakula's Paranoia Trilogy. It is disconcerting inside the cabin to be confronted by your misshapen reflection (link to Ana above). To turn to the lighted keys across walls draped with coarsely stitched padding. To look at the ceiling (as if for God) to avoid the glances of familiar strangers. You are never alone in here yet somehow you are always turning nervously, alien to both yourself and your fellow-beings. The doors close. Space tightens like a damp cathedral baptistery, all too close, until you want to press your cheek into the thickly stitched swabs, as if into a loving shoulder for the last time (link back to Tom Hallem in Chapter One), not to be salved but rather smothered and ultimately denied Life. For just a moment you recall the name 'Desdemona' although who she is – and her context – completely escapes you. Edgar Welles was the successor of all those defenestrated heirs shut out of their birthright by paternal angst since Adam and Kronos first crawled out of the muck demanding obeisance all-the-time modelling inappropriate behaviour. His father had not covered well-bred mares. He was poor at stud. Only got one-in-three mares in foal. Low sperm count. First me. Then Edmund out of Shagga Maher. The dark and vicious place where thee he got cost him eyes. A metaphor is turned into a physical infliction by Shakespeare in the blinding of Gloucester. My mother and I writhed along the dunny cart lanes of Sydney with miscellaneous bags after we left. A series of bedsits in Kings Cross, Marrickville and Kirribilli followed. Poor plots. Regional racetracks. Weak fields. She died at the start of a Dickens novel like Mary Wollstonecraft. A common chambermaid swept from a burning room. Dad sent us both to boarding school. Godwin's Utility. Either save the valet, my father, and thus our line, or else rescue Fenelon, who could ameliorate all of mankind. Put aside such niceties. Call in Larry Conrod from Perth. Raise some capital. Launch a hostile takeover. Take back the family business. Conceal madness with mildness. Wear a patient's face. The outsider will race in blinkers like bung Gloucester. Dark bay. Molos. From that outstanding racehorse and useful sire, Donatello, out of One Thousand Guineas runner-up, Aurora. Daughter of Hyperion who sired Helios, Selene and Eos. Ranked amongst the best stayers in history. Fifty kilos in the saddle. Quiet as stone. Adrift Sargasso. Proceed. You are travelling through the floors. Encased in the elevator and proceeding through its workings. Listening to its intestines as they rave at you. Following its shifts through stasis and decline. Observing its patrons entering and departing. Some parrot its noises in the rumblings of their own bodies. Others remain silent staring at the doors. Some drop single storeys. Most will fall until even at the street. Everybody's off to the pub to watch the Cup. There are many umbrae. Most have signalled their intentions by leaving their briefcases under their desks. This will simplify the trip home along Sydney's over-burdened rail system half-drunk and holding onto a bladder full of piss hoping their wives will surprise them at the kiss'n'ride. Otherwise, they'll be forced to queue in the dark in a leaky shelter for a Bosnjak bus. They fiddle with frayed umbrella straps > note the apparent impossibility of competent dry-cleaning > recall a recent holiday (did they say it was on the Gold Coast or near a golf course) > grind their teeth recounting the flaws of incompetent support staff > speculate about the length and depth of the current recession blame Keating praise him scarify Lynch regret the fall of Whitlam and/or Fraser cursing our apocalyptic rainfall (what kind of spring is this, anyway) until at last slotted into their conversation like an afterthought although in reality haunting every waking moment (like sin) emerges the prospect of retrenchment in the current corporate downsizing. The cost of attrition can be discerned in their dislocated faces. They glance sideways, heads tilted at an unusual angle, cheeks vaguely swollen by harsh fluorescent lights that gouge out each imperfection. They chew on Quick-Eze until it burns like some long-forgotten teat. In this Purgatory, they await punishment in a daze. The car doors part. They jig forth. You watch their hinds gallop around the bend. Lastly, an elegant lady. A jogger waits impatiently to rise. The security guard offers short blandishments. The lift doors compressed shut methodically. None will remain with you for the last descent. Invisible from the place in which you are standing but lying just beyond the marble foyer is the bustle and excitement of the modern city. Workers mimic busy streams of ants, cars stutter like beetles, buildings burst like beacons blocking out the day. Fresh thunderstorms press perspiring air down skyscraper wind-tunnels. Sydney is busy tearing itself down to reassert its ego out of sandstone wells. Centrepoint revolves high in space on Phoenix wings. You can drink coffee by the mountains. Beaches stroke its eastern flank. Concave Pacific bending against a teal horizon. Olympic metropolis. Dublin is the main character in "Wandering Rocks." Joyce creates a tone of postpartum stress in the population as 3 pm arrives. The daily grind has started to slow inexorably. Activity is frenetic yet unproductive. Symbols of decline surround all characters. Sydney displayed the debility of High Modernism. Trapped between a dead economy and one yet powerless to be born. What Keating was fixing. A one-dollar note floated down the gutter. Edmund means Wealth Protector. For all this discursion, *Ulysses* is still charter-driven in Episode Ten. The progress of different characters can be plotted across time in each sub-episode. CREATE SPREADSHEET. The Right Reverent Arthur Kemp picked up the soggy bill, rubbed it on his coat sleeve, deposited it into his cassock and brushed a cable of lank hair over his exposed skull, displaying two black hands on his pearl wristwatchface. The longer leaner aspired to reach One. The smaller thicker dropped beneath Two. A red second hand ticked out each allotted instant. He crossed the road at an illegal angle. A busker's tin whistle whined some patriotic aery. Aengus' heart still pulsed for antipodes / Despite comparables like New York, Paris and London / Far and wide roaming made no difference / he stilled call Australia HOME. A security guard wagged his finger at Pan pressing him to keep on the get-go. They exchanged fond whispered words, heads flicking from side-to-side like sprinklers, before the musician hustled past the scaffolding girdling Mark Foy's building and crossed Liverpool Street. At the centre of the novel, Joyce's central characters recede as if to suggest that the world can no longer yield heroes. The episode's technique is "Mechanic." The hand of the author is continuously displayed in the arbitrary criss-crossing and forced interpenetration of passages: in both its senses as 'course' and 'discourse.' Reverend Kemp (Father Conmee) proceeded along the footpath towards the anxious gait of Missus Janet Howe (Mrs Sheehy), wife of the Deputy Opposition Leader. She lowered her bowed head still lower. The Minister called her name. She confected a tight grin.

"How are you, Mrs. Howe?"

"I'm in good spirits thank you, Reverend," she stated fanatically. "The children are well. Richard starts primary school next year. Then I will have more time to help John in the electorate office. He's stuck in Canberra most of the time."

The Minister delivered correspondence on the benefits of a consumption tax from a recently retired constituent. Professor McNab got down on beige knees and shone a flashlight through a grate in the car park wall. The security guards strained to observe his latest discovery. The illumined letter "G" was extinguished. Edgar Welles hung in limbo watching the lightless screen. The counterweight stretched at the top of its ascent. He neared the bulwark. The slow-down switch clicked. Finally, all motion ceased. The "B" of Basement shone. Edgar Welles collected his white sports bag. The doors of the elevator spread like oars and he moved across a stark concrete floor. Its echoes were so sharp that the space seemed overhanging. The ceiling bulged under the weight of sprinklers and light fittings. Wide pliant air-conditioning pipes had been swaddled in foil. The stark cubed columns possessed nothing of colour. They were pitted with the fossils of tiny air bubbles from the moment of construction. Sailor Time from Space. Only the luminous paint gridding the car spaces warmed and directed Edgar. Sequenced numerals propelled his path. Their shape and colour cut the very eye which struck them. The executive car park had emptied steadily all afternoon. SHIFT TO DIRECT PERSONAL PRONOUN. By the time your leather-sole shoes crackle across the bald surface only a handful of vehicles remain. You move towards a car with personalised numberplates. A car alarm light beats back from the cockpit. Its red pulse blasts off the chrome gearstick (Pisa). Lamp-throb-over-heart in dim reflection. In the gap between each beat, your head is noted by the window. You select a car key, press it into the lock, and turn it so brutally that we must really fear for its shape on extraction. The indicator lights begin bleating. You wrench open the door. Howling commences. Systolic/diastolic. Clamp/release. You slip sideways into the driver's seat. The dashboard is covered with instruments which have been perfectly positioned by computer program to resemble a children's toy. You defuse the alarm. You check the glove box. There is a log book, a service book, a street directory and a small hand-compass trapped in the corner by a screwdriver on a bed of dust and copper coins. You extract the directory, lay it on the passenger's seat and open the back flap. A foil is secreted in glossy magazine paper inside the sticky thick cover. Crumbly white powder quivers. It cracks with each compact movement of your body; slowly gathering in the folds. You take a small blade from the moulded plastic tray behind the gearstick, dice the powder, separate it into two mounds and stretch them along lines. This scene has barely any parallels to the *Odyssey*. You collect a five-buck note from your wallet, roll it into a tight purple straw and place an index finger over your left nostril. Inhale. Suck mucus. Change hands. Re-inhale. Your head it simply swirls. Lovely seaside boys. Accelerate machinery. Joyce's love of speed. He lent Boccioni's book to Bugden. Your technique is so methodical that there is almost no scorching. When it is all done, you lean back into the bucket seat and stare through the windscreen at the blank wall right on top of the bonnet. You perceive a security guard approaching as his image cuts across the rear-view mirror pane. Palazzeschi. He comes to your aide. Trouser belt before pane. Forearm on roof. He has bent. His bald dome glistens like polished stone. Nestor. You shunt the street directory onto the floor. Return upright. He leers. Millennial Eden lurks beneath his face. You turn the handle to allow ingress. Humid air. He thrusts his beak through the available casement.

"Look at this flyer, Master Edgar" he said, pressing a brochure into my soft hand.

HARD COCKS, it read. Elijah is coming. New Hellas. Demesne for mammon to infest. He assumed an expression of wonderment. TOP ADULT EMPORIUM!

"It was lying on the ground," continued the guard, "right underneath your car door."

"Must have blown there," replied Edgar nonchalantly. "Windy down here. What horse you on?"

"England and Scotland," quipped the guard. "Each way."

"You'll blow your dough," I replied.

Mouth weeping spit. Young man seeks mature Dom. Well-compact dimensions. My pricksong plays. Bona constrictor. Pox of antics. Duellists. Let him recoil in disgust. Zip it off. Would he beat me? I mean punch my face in anger not love.

Keith Carpenter looked at his wrist watch suddenly.

"Must dash. Almost time for the Cup."

He withdrew into the shadow of a concrete column. Edgar Welles smiled. Wandering Rocks is directed out of the page. The reader must navigate its scattered dividend, forever keeping in mind the story to date, whilst being drawn down an 'unambitious underwood' of local journeys that dwindle towards stark dead ends, as if mis-guided by Robert Browning, in order to reach the other side of the page, unwaned, and stand Hieratic. Joyce needles the text with recurrent images, characters and themes like sew-many Ariadne. But he also shreds narratorial authenticity with what Clive Hart called lies of omission, mal-connections and deliberated gaps. The technique of the episode is 'labyrinth.' Yet even Joyce is ultimately driven to formal closure. He must start, cross and finish the episode directing every journey across mapped space. This is no anti-closure Romantic trope. It is a finely tuned schema. You could set your watch by it. Everything is clockwork. Father John Conmee opens the episode. He is an affable imbecile whose attitude is symptomatic of the veneer of civility exercised by the Roman Catholic Church. Joyce repeats his name and title fifty-seven times in this short sub-episode. He is a weak reader of life with a reductive mind that misrepresents people and activities in his haste to pin unthinking slogans UP/on a grateful populace. He is a cultivated CON artist. Voyeurism, materialism, envy and repressed sexuality are his most prominent traits. This is a familiar group of vices in Victorian fiction. Swinburne's *Faustine* got Ruskin "all hot, like pies with the devil's fingers innem." Chidley wore sweat at a washer-woman with her skirt up standing over a bubbling copper. Pale Nausicaa in a stream. Let us F**k, ejaculated the Superior in *Autobiography of a Flea*. Amen, chanted Father Ambrose. Good luck Mister Edgar, said Keith Carpenter in echoes departing. A servingman proud in heart and mind. Who gives anything for poor Tom. Vaults. Underground. The pipes. These things remember me. My name is still such and such and thus I am thy son. He does not begrudge status to his brother. It is Edmund who possesses all volition in *King Lear*. Edgar speaks on less than one hundred occasions. Many times, it's just single lines. He uses the phrase, "foul fiend," on eight occasions. He weeps in pity for another old man's plight. He is stoic towards his own. At the end, he turns a knife in his brother's guts saying "let's exchange charity." His trouser pocket contained a $50 TAB ticket on Black Knight. Third in the Dalgety last Saturday coming home. Five-year-old gelding. Right age; correct birthplace; requisite number of nuts. A technical decision. A five-year-old had won 13/28 Cups since 1955. New Zealand bred horses had been successful 19 times in the last 28 races. Lighter bags would help it over 3,200 metres. Flat wide Flemington track. Not hard like Royal Randwick. Up the rise and over the hump. The car bumped on metal plates at the Hunter Street exit. Good preparation. Raced every ten days since August. The engine purred. He moved off. Never back top weight. Get some rush in Newtown maybe trawl the stalls at the bath house on Albermarle Street. Place a sign on the noticeboard. Bottom seeks Top. Thirty years old. Tanned. Muscular. Likes Bears. Meet opposite Camperdown Grandstand. Ten pm weeknights. You press down the accelerator pedal. Rise up like a spout. Tom Bass urinal. QANTAS House's double curtain wave. Old tram tracks shining through worn asphalt. The passport office queue stretches onto the forecourt in jaundiced light. Idle in front of pedestrians at Macquarie Street. A bronze of oxidised characters is marooned on the median strip in the Cahill Expressway. Cut off from the State Library. Abiding metaphor for Australian culture. Betwixt high columns, scholars and shelter-seekers alike stride or stagger. Plane trees give way to State Parliament set back from the track like a Colonial homestead. First legislature. 1856. Bob Askin helped all his developer mates to the trough. Sydney Rum Hospital built by the Blaxcell family for a franchise on rum. Piked fences. Statue of Albert the Good. Orb protruding from his well-garnished groin. He invented birth-stirrups. Queen Victoria flat on her back cunt aloft under stinking gas lamps. Pass the Convict Barracks. Stop. More traffic lights. Gaze left. A rigid gold arm covered the hour-hand utterly. L Macquarie Esq Governor 1817. Take the swerves past St Mary's Cathedral. Spireless sandstone block. Hyena anem. Sauce of all distaste. Squat gargoyles. Its quire marks time. Two-fifteen. Rough palms. Wiggling my buttocks on the warm leather seat. Strap off his trousers long and unwound. As you came fwd, palm-thrust-on-nape. Go down, old Hannah. Rise you no more. In the gloomy presbytery, his arthritic talons manipulated my nut. Hard-on rising deep behind the shaft under my arse-flap. Sticky, he lifted its web in gloating fingers. Sick stomach-lust. Power of first orgasm. Still craved. I cannot detach myself from it. Need sordid places. Shame. My family name begins with the letter HAITCH. He raised a black cassock. Systolic spasm. Revelated depths. High cum fountain. Tartan kerchief swipe. Remove the evidence into his uniform hastily. Quiet instruction. NEED IT HERE. NOW. DESPITE. Unobserved in College Street. Milky stained-glass light. Frrip Kleenex from box. Shuffle the zipper on your pin-striped trousers over the rises and falls in your lap. SPRUNG! Well, hullo there. Left hand on steering wheel. Right hand upon. Cresting hardness. Stroke the badly stitched underside with your index finger freewheeling down Elizabeth Street. Red arrow. Two-twenty on Central Station clock. Broken alabaster face. Recent hail damage. Turn out of Eddy Avenue. Rise slowly. Wait. Put on the lock. Those dirty first rapes still dry out my gums. Need to suck be sucked swallow ammonia. Trapped at the clogged entrance to Broadway. Pause. Some air out of my balloon. Repair your clothes don't be stupid. Pass Kent Brewery left. Fairfax buildings all gone grey. Broadway Hotel opposite Saint Barnabas. Competing chalkboards. The eight faces of Grace Bros registered eight different times. A metaphor for the use of time in this chapter. Accelerate alongside campus. Under the footbridge. Cute student seeking shelter in bus shelter hard right. So wet you can see his plate. No place to turn to offer a ride. Edgar Welles proceeded down Parramatta Road. At Australia Street, he ceased in front of a high terrace. The French doors of an upstairs bedroom flapped. A young woman in a loose singlet moved into open space rolling a dirty white bed sheet. Her breasts spread in crescent arcs. Worn cotton. Cheap hospital detergent. Rows of bunks along the dormitory wall. Thin fabric partitions separated the junior boys. Silently, late, on heated summer nights, the house monitor would come and rouse him, placing a gentle hand over his mouth, inner arm wound around his hips, turning him flat on his belly. Final weight. Relax, he said. A few pumps. Orgasm released. Cum and a little blood on extraction. Silent parting. Tissue-paper remnants attached to his deflated head. Alone again in my cubicle as the empty goods trains clattered along the freight line past Mungo's flour mill. Harbinger of grinding sleep. Peroxide Girl looked straight at the car. No recognition in turquoise eyes. Edgar surveyed the compartment. His guts churned. Temples roiling. He left the vehicle. He walked through a playground. Grandstand hatch. There was a single entrance under the west staircase. He advanced to the far cubicle. Leave the gate slightly ajar. He sat on the toilet lid. His cock snapped. After some time, he heard muddled footsteps. Light pressure applied to the flap. A gentle breeze settled upon the thin page of his breviary. Stand in awe. Valiantly, I wait. *Pax multa diligentius legem tuam*. Psalm 119. Hebrew letter S(H)IN. Second last condom. Kiss the Mazzuzah. Shabbai. Yeshua. Shalom. Number 300. Letter "T" (Gk). A Cross. He takes my covenant and presses it towards his robes. Screwing my wig. Will he bruise my plump willing cheek? Pulse racing.

---

2. CHAGEMAR

FX: A single lamp set on a wide desk illuminates a male figure front of stage. He is wearing a navy pin stripe suit, which accentuates his robust casing. His fingers are poised against an intercom switch. An enormous industrial clock is suspended above him centre stage. It ticks loudly. The time is One Forty-five. A mechanical pulley raises a palette of Sodium Hydroxide drums from a concrete loading bay. Human silhouettes feed vats. A storm is raging. Hail peppers the corrugated iron roof. A chorus of characters enters stage left prefacing a regal cavalcade. They begin the strophe. Exeunt. He tosses back a fringe of sandy hair and depresses the intercom. Epode.

EDMUND HAMLEY

I want to begin speaking now and never finish and I will continue without pause if you will allow me. It would be good for us to talk quite frankly ... or, at least, it would be good for ME to talk and YOU to listen. I have been talking long before this moment when you finally joined me. And I am the kind of man who is delighted to continue; delighted, at last, to have means of mass communication at my disposal. [*Strokes intercom. Primitive feedback*] But enough *ploce*. If I'd known about these devices at the beginning then all the many explanations which I've dredged up ... in times of panic ... out of necessity ... with some vain hope of being just once in my lifetime comprehensible ... would have all been unnecessary ... as would all the complicated cross currents which, ultimately, failed to reconcile my manifold untruths ... until, at last, like Ibsen's Gregers, I became trapped in a procedural impasse. And always at the worst moment. And always in the midst of the harsh audience. [*Sighs*] That's the "play." [*He drinks wine*] My words have never been allowed to rest on their relative merits as well crafted prose or vivid scenes from the Imagination. No. They had to be summoned to an Ideal. And that was a mathem-oracle ... mathem-oratical ... anathem oral ... moral impossibility! [*Wipes brow*] Because you could hardly call anything I've ever said "cast iron evidence." My natural impulses fall under the classification of tactics. I feel somewhat fortunate to have held Shakespeare as well as his spastic sons like Ibsen, Ionesco and Beckett at bay for a few scenes while nature takes sport. [*Reflective gaze*] Yet it hardly seems worth it sometimes. I am empty as blind Gloucester's sockets. Saggy as Corny Kellaher's soggy left eye. The epic savagery of Classical drama has been rendered absurd by progress. Sometimes when it's dark and cold, futile movement-and-speech reveal the essential stupidity of the human condition. I call that artwork, "Storm on Polders." [*INSERT ARBITRARY ACTION TO ALLOW TEXTUAL SHIFT*] I've often asked myself after yet another synopsis so implausible that it astounded even me: "Why, Sir? Why go on with all this holy-poley ... diplomacy?" But this sort of feeble speculation soon gives way to renewed cunning. For example: "If they've fallen for such patent garbage, then why not concoct still more outrageous fraud?" I'm that kind of chap. I'll ejaculate without difficulty what I've extorted from the flames. And I'm likely to go on sprouting whatever it is that I've just plucked out of ether ... like ... like ... ZEUS! [*He turns sideways and spits phlegm into a stainless-steel spittoon then examines it.*] Ha! Horrible green phlegm. But still OF me. And for that reason, precious. [*Picking up a microphone*] Ladies and gentlemen, my name is, and I am, Edmund Jollymount Hamley, Vice President of the Welles Investment Group, whom the great God, Bacchus, granted the secret to cultivation of the vine. His life-story was the atomic seed of Greek drama. Sadly, like a penis, its rise dominated its form. But that story is immaterial to this one. In other words, it can't help me out of the jam that I am currently inhabiting ... right here ... right now ... and therefore I have no desire to recount it. Instead, I'll reconstruct some other tale from my retinue of japes. Get them out of my thigh, as it were. For the sake of posterity. Or just to get my version onto the public record first. [*Garrulous*] What does it matter so long as I speak? For I love talking. Like Coriolanus, I love to hear the sound of my own voice. The oral field is where my intellectual content is processed by live streaming. And I have never been without it ... never stilled it ... never allowed it to be stilled ... even when masking tape was applied and Sirens assailed me and the cymbals of the Corybantes clanged in my ear in a vain attempt at plugging my audition. I have talked, I talk, I will talk, I continue, and I will not cease or perish. If you leave the pit, I will be waiting for your return. And I will be all the more insistent for your absence. For so much has happened in the interim! So much for ME to tell you! And YOU to hear! [*Menacingly*] But are you really 'listening'? Are you really out there, mummy? [*Despair*] I have long feared it would come to this. No, that's not correct ... never feared ... well, only for my survival ... that's a whoreson's right ... but rather I have expected it would come to this: YOUR questions and incredulity; MY excuses. I'm sorry it's come to this, believe me. I had hoped, when you realised what you'd let yourself in for, that you'd quietly evacuate the stage. But that's not possible. I can see that now. Very well. [*FX: Turning to desk. Depresses intercom*] Miss Gallagher!

MISS GALLAGHER

[*Officiously*] Yes, Mister Welles.

EDMUND

Is Edgar outside?

MISS GALLAGHER

Yes.

EDMUND

[*Aside. Exasperated*] What does he want?

MISS GALLAGHER

His weekly allowance.

EDMUND

Ah. His twelve-guinea prize. Hold him.

MISS GALLAGHER

Yes, sir.

EDMUND

Are you physically restraining him?

MISS GALLAGHER

Yes.

EDMUND

Is he also bound by Nature's law as well?

MISS GALLAGHER

Truly.

EDMUND

What?

MISS GALLAGHER

Relatively, I mean.

EDMUND

Good. What time is it?

MISS GALLAGHER

One fifty.

EDMUND

Send him in. [*Footsteps increase in volume along hall. The door begins to open*] No! Wait! [*Racing to the door. Slamming it shut. Returning to intercom*] Hold him there. I want to prolong this moment. Don't let him enter my world prematurely. [*Alarm goes off. Intercom*] MISS GALLAGHER!

MISS GALLAGHER

Yes, Master Bill.

EDMUND

Don't call me that name. Is Edgar still present?

MISS GALLAGHER

Still.

EDMUND

Do you mean that he is static? Or that he remains a material presence? Or both?

MISS GALLAGHER

Present.

EDMUND

Plus stationary?

MISS GALLAGHER

Inert.

EDMUND

And denying struggle?

MISS GALLAGHER

Yes.

EDMUND

A true Gloucester. His placement?

MISS GALLAGHER

He's seated on the stool.

EDMUND

Has he been tightened?

MISS GALLAGHER

Like a tap.

EDMUND

So no dripping?

MISS GALLAGHER

None.

EDMUND

Good. And no creaking when you revolve the seat?

MISS GALLAGHER

I don't know yet. I was waiting for your order.

EDMUND

Turn him, girl. Turn him! [*Listening over intercom*] Good. Is he being rotated clockwise or counter-clockwise?

MISS GALLAGHER

Clockwise.

EDMUND

And no sign of mucus?

MISS GALLAGHER

None.

EDMUND

What time is it?

MISS GALLAGHER

One fifty-one.

EDMUND

Then send him in. [*Pause. Footsteps. Door opens*] No, wait!

He rushes to the door, shunts it shut and deadlocks it with a key that has been hanging from a heavy chain off his belt. He moves to the rear of the office. Over the next 60 seconds, he pushes and drags a heavy metal filing cabinet towards the door. Sporadic improvised phrases by the actor, including the following precepts:

1. *The final format of my execution is still subject to arbitration.*
2. *Heads of Agreement have been signed to the effect that I will finish second, in a field of two.*
3. *A documentary is to be broadcast, articulating my personal philosophy.*
4. *Codicil: did I really use the term, "philosophy"? Substitute another word (insert various options).*
5. *My heirs have been injected with The Blue Dye under the aegis of 'oral history'.*

[*He returns to his desk*] Keep him out there just a few more moments, Miss Gallagher. Just in case. [*Quizzically*] Are you sure it's even him?

MISS GALLAGHER

Yes.

EDMUND

Does he bear the mark?

MISS GALLAGHER

What?

EDMUND

The special symbol.

MISS GALLAGHER

He doth.

EDMUND

With cadency?

MISS GALLAGHER

That's only for bastards, sir.

EDMUND

[*Wistful*] I know. [*Opening his business shirt to display a heraldic tattoo across his gut*] Mine is spectacles. [*Intercom*] Can he answer the secret question?

MISS GALLAGHER

He already has.

EDMUND

What did he say?

MISS GALLAGHER

'Metempsychosis.'

EDMUND

[*Expectantly*] And?

MISS GALLAGHER

He said it was the happiest day of his life.

EDMUND

More turpitude. Outline the plot.

MISS GALLAGHER

He had a sequence of false father figures. He followed a precept. He seduced two sisters. Their children were abominations. He married his father's mistress. Their daughter is his sister. A man is jailed for a crime he did not commit. A period of apparent domestic calm follows. There is a dramatic revelation. The harvest fails. He goes off to war. Insert various fatal women and female martyrs. A long time passes. It all ends in tragedy. There is justice in the last Act.

EDMUND

[*Exasperated*] That's out of order! In sequence please.

MISS GALLAGHER

Alright. Martello, the dead dog, Dignam's funeral, Shakespeare, statues with arseholes, Gerty, the brothel, pissing, Head to Toe.

EDMUND

What of my own soul?

MISS GALLAGHER

It's still bung.

EDMUND

Then fix it. Maybe you can graft it onto something symbolic. Does he still retain our father's portrait?

MISS GALLAGHER

Yes. It's an heirloom.

EDMUND

Speaking of which, when did he last see Gloucester?

[*FX: Background whispering.*]

MISS GALLAGHER

He said last night.

EDMUND

Did they part on good terms?

MISS GALLAGHER

[*Laughter*] Are you serious?

EDMUND

[*Also laughing. Slapping his thigh*] No. Was he given any signs?

MISS GALLAGHER

[*Irritated*] YES!

EDMUND

Then the trap is set. What time is it?

MISS GALLAGHER

One fifty-three.

EDMUND

Have you examined him?

MISS GALLAGHER

No. And I won't.

EDMUND

So what proof have you got that it's really him?

MISS GALLAGHER

[*Comically*] I don't got nothing, boss.

EDMUND

Are you angry?

MISS GALLAGHER

[*Exasperated*] Of course.

EDMUND

Good. What time is it?

MISS GALLAGHER

It's still one fifty-four.

EDMUND

[*Decisively*] How time flies. No need to send him in. Just get him to sign the paperwork. Give him the cheque. Let him go. Then bring me the documentation. [*Walking to front of stage. Musing*] Ah, Edgar. Dear simple Edgar. Edgar the wastrel. Edgar the heir apparent. Edgar ... I-must-have-your-land-and-birth-rite-Edgar. [*Calmer*] Naked in tempest. Feigning the fool. Absolutely committed to depicting the uncompromising truth of average lives in his hometown as they pass before those steel-blue eyes. Closing his lashes at sundown and spreading his petals at dawn. Nourished by the Tank Stream! [*Sensual. Emphatic*] I spent the best years of the worst part of my life hating that person! [*Shrugs*] But he's really not such a bad chap. Quite the actor! I enjoyed the scene where he and our father provided the template for all of Samuel Beckett's plays. He should get royalties! But he had to go the same way as all the others. It was something to do with my stature. And era. It was a time when tyranny against the aged was afoot! It's enough to make my grandfather harden somewhat in his grave. [*Picking up a family portrait from his desk. Grinning*] We're those kinds of chaps! [*To door*] Perhaps I'd better remove these impediments. [*Scraping cabinet from door to create a thin aperture. Buzzer sounds. He rushes to his desk*] Are you still out there, Miss Gallagher?

MISS GALLAGHER

Yes. Reverse charges call from London, sir.

EDMUND

[*Collecting a bust of Churchill from his desk. Stroking it. Smirking*] Ah! Old Albion. Always up for a free feed of lamb. In return, they just dished up Niemeyer's cold hard gruel. We deserved it! But how the worm has turned. [*Intercom*] Tell them to fuck off, Miss Gallagher.

MISS GALLAGHER

Right. I'll tell them to call back later.

EDMUND

Great. Who is my next appointment?

MISS GALLAGHER

Your step-mother.

EDMUND

Don't call her that. Call her Daisy. And then?

MISS GALLAGHER

You're seeing Mister Cornwall. The folder is in your tray.

EDMUND

And what of libations?

MISS GALLAGHER

The Cup starts at two-forty. The executive team will arrive in the board room at two-fifteen. Catering has been arranged. Your father rang from Chinatown to say he might be late. He has a meeting with the Minister.

EDMUND

Fine. Send Daisy in. [*Door starts to open*] No, wait! [*He rushes to the door and presses his body mass against the cabinet. There is resistance. It begins to close. Finally, it shuts. Returning to intercom*] Has she killed the wild duck yet?

MISS GALLAGHER

Yes.

EDMUND

You're not taking her word for it, I hope.

MISS GALLAGHER

No. She's got the carcass.

EDMUND

Good. Tell her to leave it on your desk. And send her in. [*He removes the filing cabinet and stands at the entrance. Enter Daisy. He follows her to the desk and pulls out a chair. Ingratiating*] There's my girl! [*Bowing*] Sit down, Miss Daisy. [*She sits*] Such a long wait! Such a heavy weight! Let me look at you. Bonny Sweet Robin, what happened?

DAISY

I told you before.

EDMUND

[*Distracted*] But I love to hear it! Tell me again!

DAISY

You shot motion pictures of the event.

EDMUND

[*Panicking*] What will it cost to 'disappear' them?

DAISY

[*Perplexed*] What?

EDMUND

[*Winking*] To get my hands on the negatives. [*Holds out a fistful of battered notes*] Take some hush money, Gertrude. Get out! Take my keys. Go!

DAISY

[*Checks her watch*] But it's too late now. I'll never get a bet on.

EDMUND

Is that all you care about? [*Recoils*] This country! This unbelievable place! But that's typical of me. Always looking on Ibsen's oeuvre as a master metaphor for my personal woes. Always assuming that you've painted the castle in the worst possible shade of puce when it's really only a horrible sort of magenta. *Ipsa omniparente natura*. Forgive me, mother. [*Intercom*] Forgive me, Miss Gallagher! [*Cuts. Rises. Returns to intercom*] Also ask Regan for forgiveness.

MISS GALLAGHER

She's not here anymore.

EDMUND

Look her up in the book!

MISS GALLAGHER

[*Sound of pages being shuffled*] There's no Grogan's listed in Sands Directory.

EDMUND

Have you checked her married name?

MISS GALLAGHER

[*Pretentious*] It's too common.

EDMUND

Fair enough. Cross her out and insert 'Cordelia' on my will. And hurry. We don't want another war with France. And get Edgar back here at once.

MISS GALLAGHER

But he's gone.

EDMUND

Run and fetch him. I need to hear that story again about our father. The one with the runny eyes. And the cliff. He really played the old barstead for a fool that time. [*Wistful*] I could almost love him. [*Reaching window*] But that's not possible. We're locked in mortal struggle. I have already beaten him twice in this year's Spring Campaign. Apprentice Darren Gauci in the saddle. But today is the race that really counts! *Deformis formositas al formosa deformitas*. We're dramatic foils: Edgar inhabiting a formal narrative in prose; me living out a freewheeling absurdist farce. Not inexplicably evil like Iago. More like Angelo with his deformed head. I mean, 'deed.' [*Picking up a framed picture of Gonerill and Regan from his desk*] Yet Edmund was also beloved! [*A document slides under the door. He collects it and opens it to the last page. Macabre laughter*] Fool! Now I have his imprint! I shall forge a bogus contract and disclose it to father. He shall be disinherited. I will become the legitimate heir. [*Noticing Gertrude is still present*] Tell me exactly what happened, mother. Tell me where it hurts. Trust me. I'm a doctor. Here. Drink this.

FX: She drinks from a steaming beaker. Trumpets peal. His retinue enters. A jogger crosses the stage. Lou Monaro enters and waits centre stage. He checks his watch. He clicks his tongue. Brian Deverill arrives in a panel van. The Vietnamese shopkeeper stands idly behind her shop counter. She is expecting her lover. Barry said he would come over straight after he dropped his wife at the shop. The Tank Stream dribbles down a tormented drain towards its sluice at Circular Quay. Wet swollen motes of Banbury cake float upon. Elijah riding down Anna Liffey. Edmund forces a stamp onto a large red ink pad and presses it against Daisy's forehead. She falls to the ground dead. Enter a Gentleman with a bloody knife. The protagonists are married in a parody of the conventions of courtly love. More paperwork. Various messengers. Comings/goings. A tangled node. The climax of King Lear *is like the terminus of Wandering Rocks. Insert man carrying young woman's corpse from the stage. Curtains close. Juxtapose the brothers in sub-episodes One and Two as loser and winner respectively. The reader should have noted by association with Black Knight (Edgar) and Chagemar (Edmund) respectively that their current situation will be reversed at the end of the Melbourne Cup. Applause.*

—

3. MAPPERLEY HEIGHTS

A dishdirty busker tripped on the thick lip of an iron fire hydrant, forged by J. Burrows, outside the Market Street entrance of David Jones. His dilatory frame rattled inside an oversized coat. He braced himself against a black marble panel between two display windows and swore. Cloudy fingerprints striped the glass. He checked the inside pocket of his checkered coat for a TAB stub. Two oversized mannequins looked down pointy plaster noses at his unmade pate. He raised defunct eyeballs on their cleavage. A greyness occurred in the unlit recess of his lips. Peroxide Girl drew shut the blind. She stepped into a short white summer dress and lifted it over her shoulders. A hand-written card which read Unfurnished Room for Rent fell off a ledge of the boarding house. Molly Bloom, invisible from Eccles Street, physically appears for the first time in the novel in sub-episode three of W.Rocks as an anonymous arm throwing alms to a crippled sailor. This body part is used as a metonymy by Joyce as well as suggesting the missing portions of Venus de Milo. Her coin goes awry. An urchin retrieves it and deposits it in his cap. Leon Daniel sprang across Elizabeth Street like famous Jorricks, the Iron Gelding. Named after Surtees' grocer. A writer ranked with Dickens by William Morris. Keith Carpenter, perceiving a silhouette fossicking under the dashboard, walked briskly towards his master's car. Hurriedly, he extracted a heavy Maglite torch from its holster. Daisy Tonner-Kelly walked straight across the road to the pub. The Tank Stream shimmered under Hamilton Street sluiced by blistered stormwater. Vessel lens. She entered the saloon bar. Here's to all the steeds that ran / and all the ones I rode, she toasted. Young Healy bestrode the grand bay. Henry VII came off a horse. Lester lay comatose where he landed in the vacant shaft. Ophelia fell in the water. Ambrose E. Welles fretted over a carnation in his lapel. Eighteen carat watch-chain. He nearly bumbled into a beggar. Poor chap. A valet in a red equerry jacket and top hat held the door ajar. A slate podium exploded in sliced bright reflections. The busker laid a rectangular piece of emerald rag on the footpath in a recess before the department store window. He placed a battered blue cricket cap on its lip with sixteen sucking stones to hold it in place and plucked a tin whistle from his crumpled white shirt. His rippling black hair gleamed with grease, sweat and rain. Silver threads spotted his beard. He moistened thin lips and probed his mouth with the cool tip until it rested on his forgiving tongue. Soft incantation. Missus Maree Swain, perched on the gutter, nudged her son, Tug, for change. *Ma bouchal.* He dug into loose second-hand jeans. She took a slender silver coin from his open palm and turned from the traffic lights to propel it onto the jade cloth. Green flag of freedom. Come fill up my cup, come fill up my can. Her late husband brung back a chunk of that stuff from Singapore when he'd done sailoring. Intricate stone lizard curling and rearing on the mantelpiece long after they'd dumped his legless carcass in mud. Too many smokes on the spree got his veins clogged. A dbrop of the crathur. Inked by the harrow in Old Rangoon. Jumped a steam packet to Nantucket. It was a dang and stormy night. One carpet bag and one harpoon his provenance. He entered the St Outer Inn looking for lodgings. A greasy cook with a sore-eyed look was making bad hash cakes by the slush-lamp. "Maria's Lament" churned out of an old barrel-organ. A callow mewt in smack-fits wetted the straw. German Eva heard the thump above. She looked at Francine whose gaze remained fixed on the television set as she lit a fresh cigarette. *Days of Our Lives* continued after the break. Edmund Hamley left the office. Jittery stallion in the mounting yard. Just 12 or 14 moonsores lag. No paternal stamp or birth rite. A blank certificate. Light the lamp! Maree compelled her gaze onto the flashing red WALK symbol. To race. Or not to race. To wait? Or to advance on one's destiny and bearing forward make it real? This is not fucking *Hamlet*, exclaimed the author. She lapsed. The clock at the tunnel entrance to St James Station was surrounded by orange and blue neon advertising Chateau Tanunda four-star brandy. It slid towards Two-Thirty-One. "Anshewealderwheelbarroe," ummed Maree to the merry tin whistle melody projecting herself down them manky lanes of various apertures in restless manual labour. John Dengate gulped. Listeners presume that Miss Malone is engaged on some jolly Southside procession with all the pretty Milly Bloom's, Lame Gerty's and Martha Cuntworthies of Dublin, but it is a tragic song. She is fading from death fever as she passes through the city's shattered shell. A ghost poisoned at a billabong. Grey forms wheeling. Plover song. Insert scenery from a Sean O'Casey play. Joyce mainly deals with the lower middle class in *Ulysses*. Low sandstone prospect of Hyde Park shat with figbulbs. Moneygrub sipped his claret. Two plump private schoolgirls, candy sticks protruding from flushed orange lips, halted at the back of a parade ring of pedestrians. They turned towards the skinny pisspot and sucked. He lowered his eyes onto the pinchgut belt holding up his stained crotch. Not enough takings for another dab. A runner in synthetic shorts streaked through the crowd ruffling damask. A flaky gelding. I've run Centennial Park ten thousand times. Jocks knew how to steer. He trod on my kingdom. Send him on his way, chum. It doesn't keep me square but I need every swy and zac this evening. A hand tossed thick copper coins at my bowl. They dull-jangled and exploded across the track. Velocity of History. The schoolgirls chased them into forbidding columns of legs. Straight shiny flesh covered in transparent down. They laid the retrieved coins carefully in his cap. Jesus wept! John Dengate had made the wet uphill walk from Central Terminus on the wrong side of Sydney's rail girdle past Sharpie's neon hole-in-one along Wentworth Avenue to the arse-end of Mark Foy's bankrupt titan all glazed orange stripes like Twelve July in Belfast available types of female finery inscribed in black brocade get Laces > Gloves > Corsets > Silks > Millinery > Mourning Gloves an obituary by Warren Fahey said John was a failed punter in that all punters ultimately fail he has backed number fifteen today for a WIN NO PLACE never take no middy measures he preferred the full schooner shout like his hero Henry Lawson the son of bare-legged Kate a country lass give him paper and pen he'll travel any place Bush his first teaching job was out of Menindee reciting Banjo Paterson to peach-pickers blowing the *Apricot Express* through Riverina orchards his father worked as a sheet metal worker at the Eveleigh Railyards dressed in an oversized smock he dominated the union picnic singing boss in a cane bottomed chair drugged with summer cicadas song / drunk with freedom horses that raced all day he loved ALL sports never got a car license Jimmy Carruthers fought Toweel and Gault at Sydney Stadium 30-foot tapeworm unscrambling his guts outside the Communist Bank on the prow of Foveaux and Queen Elizabeth Streets Silent Bill McConnell his trainer click click he took over Bells Hotel at Woolloomooloo Bay where he made a stand for the waterside workers against Corrigan's scabs and thugs we won't go down the union's strong I drank there sometimes myself but not a FANMAIL type fuck Menzies Askin L.B.J. and all the mindless mob that Big Business likes robbing our Ashes defeat last summer left him run out at the non-striker's end he loved Australia tin whistle in hand strolling through Saint James like the Pied Piper serenading the bare-bellied ewes at lunchtime then taking his tips to the front bar of the Friend in Hand pint of Guinness in his grip or some Jacaranda Juice he preferred guitar but his whistle worked better in Sydney's bustling streets beautiful old Irish tunes and bush ballads or the words of "Faces in the Street" set to a traditional air he was a bridge between Australia and its Irish past sometimes we win, sometimes we lose the Battle of Castle Hill England home and beauty growled the one-legged sailor citing 'Death of Nelson' many have sung along to the 'Song of the Sheet Metal Worker' his last lyrics attacked Murdoch's phone-tapping Duke Tritton of Five Dock once told John if the audience can't understand the eighth word of the sixteenth verse then you've buggered the song fat chance for Joyce the Penman then Ballad of Les Darcy poison ate his massive frame like Big Ben Pies and Coopers Sparkling Ale like Phar Lap in the Irish corner of Eveleigh railyards with Mannix and Bold Bill from Erskineville who got warned off the yard in 1917 Joe Cahill was one of the greatest Labor men he died at his desk on Macquarie Street they played "Freedom on the Wallaby" and "Waltzing Matilda" at my funeral I took The Lidcombe Train last stop Rookwood a Republican the Answer's Ireland his songs and stories about his uncles in My Name's Eric captured Australian life just after the Wars you've not heard the last of O'Meally, Jin and their battler mates they go on disobeying FRASER LYNCH ANTHONY AND ALL THEIR MEDIOCRE SCUM we'll pillage your banks and rob your stores blue asbestos breeze of Wittenoom blasting crocodiles through the miners' lungs we'll keep the mine open each link is stamped with dead men's names sons of toil arising to welcome the bright morn braving the anger of the purse-proud mocking Moneygrubs we won't surrender we won't give in we'll never bend the knee no matter how far nor wide tin whistle straining to regather the proud days of the Moratorium movement playing real folk music at Green Ban pickets down Victoria Street near the home of Smacka Fitzgibbon blast those developers Welles, Theeman and Saffron cronies of Sangster I bet I'll never cut cane for those bastards wasted all my hard-earned kip on his nag Sir Tristram out of Claudine won the big Australian Plate piled with Susso from Fraser's coup a Dark Eureka night the squatter's keep gone silent in old pioneering days down south with Snake, Razorback Warrigal, Toad and Brown we'll kill the tyrants one by one and shoot the floggers down. He dropped amongst the green traffic light mass counting up his coins, cherishing most those coppers retrieved by thoughtful schoolgirls.

—

4. ROSE & THISTLE (2.15 PM)

Brian Deverill left Lou Monaro in no doubt. None. He had cut out on a mate's wake at South's Juniors to fix the roller door on that warehouse in Newtown as a personal favour to Lou and he would get it done by COB but he was going to knock off at two-thirty go down the Shakespeare to watch the Cup then come back at 3.30 pm to repair the second track. Greg Wheaton pumped the hand flush on the toilet. It suckt and exhaled sharply. He had a buck Each Way on Rose and Thistle at sixty to one. Colonel Cornwall took a spreadsheet from the safe. It was labelled New Business Development. The first column was titled: Deals. Row One: Farm, Riverina. Next: Stud, Hunter Valley. Followed by Nickel Mine, North Queensland in Row Three. The next column was headed EV. The last two columns contained Fees. He turned the page. Ian Westacott marched down a bright alley towards the School Quadrangle. A boy was drinking from a bubbler on the north wall. Creamy sunstruck tiles. The Headmaster stopped to inquire. Mister Doyle had given him permission, sir. A friendly lad. Not good at sums. Mister Doyle said he needed private tuition. An extra hour on Tuesday and Thursday at 7 am. Cash OUT column. Codes. It was almost time for the two-twenty bell. Westacott wanted to ensure that the School moved smoothly. The students were not to be distracted by horse racing. He took up a concealed position on the east side of the Quadrangle underneath the Poplars. Missus Brennan hated the thirty minutes before the Cup. The shop was always empty. Not a single soul for a quick chat. No action at the bowsers. She never even sold a pack of gum. Her husband was hiding under a car in the oil bay with his transistor radio tuned to Johnny Tapp. He had his bets on. All tuned by a head algorithm. You couldn't stop him. Why try? Perhaps Mister Monaro was not wrong. Maybe it was not time to continue. *Keneng*. Shanghai Dog watched Xiao Fang move to the bathroom. Her hind flicked lazily. The horses were parading in the Mounting Yard. Skelton on R&T in royal blue with red stars, yellow sleeves, grey armbands and a blue and red quartered cap. We could pass on our clients to Barry Capri. He's a gentleman. He might even take on the mechanic. Daisy ordered a glass of Hock. She liked a horse with a classic physique. Sculpted sprinters. Not stayers. Edmund Hamley had been raced too young. Before his bones set. Same as Tom Hallem. Too alert. I prefer a relaxed one. And I worry about a horse that's sweating. Ed Welles welcomed the executives on behalf of his father who was unavoidably detained. The reception girl was acting as waitress. She carried a tray of cold Crown Lagers around the room. Jean Wheaton and Eleni Loukopoulou annexed an empty table near the doorway of the Crest Hotel. Gary Hampton sent an urgent signal from Electrical Stores (Naval), Zetland. Capacitors for HMAS *Hobart*. He hummed a popular love song as he leaned against the heavy iron filing cabinet. INSERT CLUE. The singer was the registered proprietor of a desolate organ of blood circulation. "The Thrissil and the Rois" is a poem composed by William Dunbar to mark the wedding of King James IV of Scotland to Princess Margaret Tudor of England in August 1503. It was a time of false hope, and all delighted. The poem utilises the popular medieval device of a dream vision. Elizabeth and Leon standing under the canopy in Newtown Synagogue. Don and Penelope, Penelope and Les, Don and Richie, Shanghai Dog and O. A wedding photograph of Helen and Barry stood solid by the shop phone. S. Spams encountered Jackie as she left Broadway. Come back thou lost one. Shanghai Dog waited for Xiao Fang to dress. He needed time. *Nor hald non udir flour in sic denty*. Fresche Rose. Goad her to the barrier. Text message from his wife. Their son had been struck in the face with a ten-pin. He was in hospital. Plastic surgery would be required. She needed details of their global insurance policy. It had lapsed last month. Call later. He must serve Doctor Gu tonight. Maree squeezed her eyes. Poem 43: "The Headache." Her son patted her shoulder jerkily. Ed Welles was distracted, seeking the time on Grace Bros towers. His car veered onto the road markings. Clunk. A horn sounded. I'll take that big one, Ambrose E. Welles said. Professor Milkmaid recited a line of Pope. Than say not MAN'S IMPERFECT. Katey and Boody Dedalus surveyed remnant keepsakes and books for something to sell. Their mother's LAST KISS. The School Sergeant roused the boys from the west side of the Quadrangle. Mister Westacott strode across the elevated turf to join him. The class bell cut. No soft incantation. Tin whistle steill dertis. John Dengate packed his swag and proceeded down Elizabeth Street towards the NSW Rugby League Club. I'll grab a schooner of Reschs, he thought. Watch the Cup. There'll be a decent crowd from Wentworth and Selbourne at the main bar. Simon Dedalus launched into song at the Ormond Hotel. Lost Mary. Yes, I am lost for she is gone. Weeping still for dear Martha. Why do the other characters still respect him in *Ulysses*? He has maintained a veneer of respectability. It is only his family who see the sharp sad drunk. Don't deceive your free will, sang Jon Anderson. A man buys honour with good deeds and mirth. Opportunity cost of capital. His quotient had not yet expired. Farquhar sat bolt upright in the front seat of an unmarked Holden Kingswood on Wilson Street, Chippendale alongside the railyard fence. His face was set. His eyes unseen behind broad sunglasses. He laid a hand-drawn map on the dash. "You just got to turn right then go straight," he said to the driver pointing ahead wanting to clip him on the side of the head for good measure. He checked his watch and told the driver: TEN. He was timing his run to coincide with the horses coming down the straight. Maximum shock. Same as Tet. Quick run down Shepherd Street. Allocate two minutes for the Cleveland Street lights. Idle outside the Native Rose. Two-thirty-nine on the dot. GO. I'll take the Parramatta Road entrance. Gravy's got the west door. One sweep across the bar. Grab the Gear. Bolt out the fire door onto Grafton Lane. Getaway car waiting. Go back to the Iron Duke. Divide the junk. Pay out the wheelman. Buy Deb a decent feed. She's whippet-thin since James was born. Don Cane rested. Sleeping as I lay. Reliving Episode 9. Faithless Richie. Our dead son. Bound to an altar of my preparation. I have been an unfaithful husband. Multiple wives. Two living sons. Keep them all separated. Man and Ideals. Stephen sails closer to Scylla. Shakespeare's life loops and pools in Charybdis. The Tank Stream crossed Crane Place under the NSW Rugby Club and entered low lying swamp. Plato was a soldier's philosopher. Beat your enemy's head with a rock. Ambrose E. Welles entered the foyer of David Jones. Two strippers were dancing on a makeshift stage. That's a nice giggle. There, boxed in the corner stall, sat Young McCann, whose fault it was not really, being poorly raised, I mean what kind of father, it's not a trade like plumbing, next to him was a small cunt, blond and tanned, hairdo like a bluddy Shire slut going down Caringbah Inn, expatriate orphan, mule for hire, then Costello, that deadhead drongo what crawled out of the muck and at his side squat Madden, all blisfull soune of cherarchy, showing off his collection of teratological slides by J.P. Witkin. Gravy kicked open the door and went straight over the top of the bar. Farquhar blocked the Broadway exit. Get under the table like a BLUDDY GREAT CRUMB. Insert map of Dublin. Insert picture of hand-drawn GANTT CHART of the movement of characters in Wandering Rocks. Insert chart of "times and places" (Hart, 215). Overlay with map of Odysseus' travels from Troy to Ithaca. Check for correspondences. Insert traffic flow model of the 1984 Cup. The Wandering Rocks episode occurs from 2.55 to 4.00 pm. It contains 19 sub-episodes that all commence between 2.55 pm and 3.26 pm. It involves over 30 characters with leading, secondary or minimal status in the rest of the novel. There are numerous cross-currents throughout the episode. An exhaustive analysis is not possible. We will focus on the main characters and events. The opening and closing scenes of Father Conmee and the vice-regal cavalcade are the longest sections. Wandering Rocks is not sequential. Each sub-episode commences at a time dictated by its own internal needs. They are WANDERING in their own right. The vice-regal cavalcade retrospectively links most sub-episodes from 9 to 19. It is referred to directly and obliquely. It starts when the gates open at 3.39 pm. Plot intersection with characters in other sub-episodes does not adhere to a strict temporal sequence. The first four sub-episodes occur in North Dublin. They are relatively self-contained. Sub-episode 5 depicts Hugh Boylan in South Dublin moving north from Thornton's shop. A gift-pack of perfume acts as a substitute for his basket of fruit in this chapter. He has not yet crossed the Liffey. Welles is still at Town Hall. He is far from Molly in Eccles Street. Elizabeth Archer has already arrived at the Menzies Hotel. We hear the only internal thoughts uttered by words Boylan in *Ulysses*: "a young pullet." Sub-episode 6 finds Stephen Dedalus and Almidano Artifoni (note pun) discussing the former's future from 3.22 to 3.24 pm. They separate. Stephen reappears in sub-episode 13 at 3.30 pm outside Russell's the watchmaker. There is a general discourse on time. At 3.35 pm, he meets his sister Dilly who has just encountered her father at 3.22 pm at the start of sub-episode 11 (see below). There is a telling contrast in the sensitivity exhibited by father and son. But it is all care no substance. Joyce reinforces Stephen's material privileges over his sister. He has attended university, lived in Paris and has salary in his pocket while she scrounges enough money to feed their family and buy a French-language primer. He is notably absent from home on an existential crisis throughout *Ulysses*. This is the end of Stephen's involvement in Wandering Rocks. Sub-episode 7 comprises Miss Dunne answering a telephone call from Boylan at 3.11 pm (see Welles as). Ned Lambert is conducting a tour of St Mary's Abbey in sub-episode 8 for a visitor later identified by his card to be the Reverend Hugh C. Love. He is Conmee's landlord. He is trying to evict his tenant. Tom Rochford demonstrates his music hall machine in sub-episode 9. This appears to be an inconsequential piece of narrative but it acts as a symbol of Joyce's technique in Wandering Rocks. Sub-episode 10 covers Bloom's exit from the Merchant's Arms at 3.08 pm. He walks to the book cart by the Liffey at 3.17 pm. He is next found at Wellington Quay at 3.40 pm. He crosses Essex Bridge at 3.45 pm and enters Daly's shop. He leaves at 3.49 pm, meets Stephen's uncle, Richie Goulding, an attorney who specialises in corporate rescues, and they proceed to the Ormond Hotel. CHECK! Sub-episode 11 starts at 3.22 pm with Simon Dedalus encountering Dilly for four minutes. He walks on to meet Cowley and Dollard within 120 seconds at the start of sub-episode 14. They proceed to the Ormond Hotel, arriving at 3.43 pm. During this trip, he observes the cavalcade at 3.37 pm. Sub-episodes 12, 15 and 17 are largely ornamental with the crossing of multiple minor characters. Sub-episodes 13 and 14 have already been discussed (see above). Mulligan and Haines discuss Stephen's mental condition at a restaurant in sub-episode 16. Mulligan makes a joke that Stephen will write something in 10 years. Haines comments as an aside that this might be prophetic. It is a self-reference by Joyce to the composition of *Ulysses*, which began approximately 10 years after the events of 16 June 1904 and was completed in 1921. Sub-episode 18 takes up the case of Master Dignam dawdling along Wickham Street with sausages. The principal event is his observation of Boylan with a red flower in his mouth listening to a singing drunk. His recollections of his father on his deathbed and his current state of mourning are relevant to the death of Stephen's mother. Young Dignam exhibits the detached recollection of an immature boy. Stephen Dedalus showed similar detachment in front of his mother only to be later tormented by regret. Sub-episode 19 chronicles the west–east course of the cavalcade passing many of the intersecting, adjacent events of previous sub-episodes. Joyce lists thirty-four characters in total, including the man in the brown mackintosh and all five letters of the HELYS sandwich board. Various persons and items with no other role in *Ulysses* are cited, including Mrs Paget, Miss de Courcy, Mr Ward and Lt Colonel H.G. Hesseltine (inside the gubernatorial carriage); an elderly female (outside the office of Reuben J. Dodd, solicitor); a tongue of liquid sewage at Wood Quay wall (Joyce passed up the opportunity for an anti-Imperial symbol by naming it Wellington Quay, which is where the event actually occurred); a poster of Marie Kendall (soubrette); a hoarding of Mister Eugene Stratton; assembled guests at a restaurant; and a chessboard being evaluated by John Howard Parnell (thus he is NOT a direct observer of the scene although his pose is highly symbolic). Of note is the fact that the avowed nationalist, Simon Dedalus, bows and offers his hat to His Excellency. The main characters are introspective when they appear in "Wandering Rocks." Blazes Boylan is moving inexorably north. Bloom reaches the outward goal of his journey by purchasing *Sweets of Sin* while Stephen confronts his guilt over his mother as external events harry him. We learn more about Bloom as he is observed at the book cart by Lenehan and McCoy in sub-episode 9. McCoy notes his ability to cut a good deal by buying a valuable book cheaply. This is evidence of his prowess in commercial negotiations (or "sales" as McCoy calls it). The subject of his purchase, astronomy, becomes relevant later in *Ulysses* when he is urinating alongside Stephen in the Ithaca episode. Stars also serve as a symbol for Shakespeare as a child. Billy Capri was conceived under the stars. The narrative of sub-episode four shows three of the Dedalus sisters back at home after a failed attempt by Maggy to sell Stephen's books to McGuinness.

She is washing shirts in a bubbling vessel on the range. Alongside, a pot of peasoup from the Sisters of Charity is boiling. Dilly has gone to meet their father (see above). The lacquey's bell intrudes on the text. Barang! This alludes to section 11. At this exact moment in the plot, their father is cursing them outside the auction room. Boody makes a blasphemous aside. Maggy chastises her. They eat. Joyce ends the scene with an image of the throwaway making its way down the Liffey under Loopline railway bridge along George's Quay. It's a symbol of resurrection. But the tide is going out. Soon the abysmal floor of Joyce's Anna Livia Plurabelle will be exposed.

—

5. FOXSEAL (2.15 PM)

The assistant in the black stretch skirt sorted lipstick testers into slots in the Perspex display stand. She tidied fingerprints off the nebuliser triggers with a crimson cloth. A brief spray fell in a weak arc. She wiped the top of the glass case leaving an evanescent streak. Beneath, bottles of French perfume nestled in silk boxes. She disappeared under the counter. A customer approached. He waited at the vacant register silently. A hawk hanging. Old fox amongst chicks. The sales assistant was surprised to see him when she arose.

"Do you sell gift packs," asked the man.

"Yes sir," she answered turning to the top shelf and pointing.

"I'll take that big one," he said pointing also.

"Yes sir," she replied lifting down a heavy pack.

"Do you provide a courier service?"

A dark figure streaked across the department store gates. It is Bloom en route to the bookcart. Boylan is buying items that will satisfy Molly physically: fruit, wine and perfume. Bloom is seeking to find a gift that will satisfy her at a psychological level. Boylan is aiming to seduce Molly. He will do the rest of the job himself. Bloom is focused on the imaginative side of her sexual gratification.

"Yes."

"Then take down this address. I would like to send the package to Miss Elizabeth Archer, care of – the next bit is complicated so make sure you get it right – E.A. Squared – that's the mathematical sign ... not the word – Gallery, 13 Hargraves Street, Paddington."

She transcribed the address into the order book.

"Would you like to fill out a gift card?"

"Yes please."

She handed him a biro and a white card bearing a lilac bouquet. Yours forever SH, he wrote hastily. Her dry lips pouted. Enormous mouth. Jaws of life. Io. Tethered to a tree. A tender, blemished cheek wearing the gadfly's blush. She lowered her head over the gift pack and tied it shut with scarlet ribbon. Straw bobs he always liked. SH. His little joke about silent tristes. SHSHSHSH.

"It's for my sister," he added unnecessarily.

"She'll be delighted. It's a beautiful presentation."

"Can I try this perfume as well?" he asked.

"Of course."

She grabbed a paper tab, sprayed some sampler and passed it to him. He held it to his nose.

"Oh, that's nice," he said. "I'll take it too."

"Shall I put it with the parcel?"

"No. I'll take it with me now."

"Would you like it gift-wrapped?"

"Yes please."

Ambrose E. Welles watched the girl's movements. A wenche thikke and wel ygrowen she was. Fat lips. She unfolded pink wafer embroidered with white dahlias. Swaddle the babe and slice it down the line. Turn the edge. Firm taping. Lovers can see to their amorous rites. Only when the door had been locked did Fiona let go. Slip a ribbon under. Cross stitch on top. Turnover. Make a bow. He had known Elizabeth forever. Like Victor and Nina, they came together with mechanical assurance. He knew exactly how to tread lightly. Strip, said Tomas. Just leave the bowler hat. One of the most famous images in modern cinema. Lie Tereza down like a plank. Buttokes brode, and brestes rounde and hye. Fat heavy garters. Set the shores a little wider, as Henry Miller put it. Flower of the valleys. Kissed under the Moorish wall. Eyen greye as glas locked on mine. Kamus nose. Stew'd in love with Dog Mellors. There had been no sex scenes for three hundred years before Lawrence and Miller. Acquire their glued-up novels in seedy premises like Gould's in Castlereagh Street. It all changed when I met Elizabeth. Reciting *Tropic of Cancer* on a pension bed in Greece, sunset breeze blowing back plain curtains. Almost horizontal flow. The sea gone crimson sometimes like fire. Fig trees in the Alameda gardens. Come, civil night. She relit her candle from his. Gertrude sucking off Claudius. First, I put my arms around him yes and drew him down so close he could feel my breasts all lumpy yes his heart was going mad on my thigh. Last time at Fialta. Nina symbolised the motherland for

Nabokov. So different to London women. They reconnected in Sydney last year. Living in the rank sweat of an enseamed bed. Strange love, grown bold.

"You can never get the smell off," he said tweaking his nose.

"Pardon?"

"The smell," he repeated sniffing his fingers. He smiled horse canines. They resembled her father's undernourished mouth. Output of a wartime diet in England. Seaside evacuation to Wales. Black hairs sprouting from his ears and nose. She collated the cost on the cash register. Welles extracted some bills from his wallet and placed them on the counter. She lowered the package before him. He glanced at her unbodiced breasts drooping inside a silk shirt. She didn't flinch at Boylan's gaze so he held fast. In *Ulysses*, he extracts a red carnation from a vase and places it between his teeth. He is already half-planning his next conquest. This scene is different in intent. It describes an ageing lothario who must play the odds these days. Seduction has become a game of ratios. There is no Athene to temporarily conceal his turpitude. He will employ any means necessary. Cash is a bait. He is still confident in his technical skills once he has got them back to his place. She offered a mound of change for his palms.

"Can I leave a tip?"

"It's against company policy."

"What about a 'hot tip' then?" he asked flirtatiously.

"I don't have time to go to the TAB," she said. A retort of deep symbolism for Daisy. But I've got Foxseal in the sweep, she added. Where do they get these silly names? Stan Welles blurted. She shrugged. A pawprint, she guessed. Why don't you call me some time, he added pressing a business card onto the counter. We can have afternoon tea, he added. Or cocktails, he concluded gaily. She read his name. And then as a bank business. Be noncommittal. Keneng.

"I'll think about it," she said.

"That's something. What's your name?"

"Gabby," she lied.

"It's says Vanessa there," he replied pointing at her tag.

"That's my birth name. All my friends call me Gabby."

"I'll be seeing you soon I trust ... Gabby," concluded Welles, biting on each consonant. He turned away. She watched his long retreat over the marble floor. Blazes Boylan claims his gift is for an invalid. Perhaps this is ironic. Molly is certainly bed-ridden. She tore the card in half and shoved the pieces in the bin. A customer stood at the counter somewhat impatient. Welles departed by the Elizabeth Street exit. Foxseal. An odd name. Hasty dance step with a marine mammal. Linguistic amalgam of unlikes. Seal: to block up and make impervious. No passage. No breath beneath. Against fox. A smart scavenger. Highly motivated. Great in an open field. Also, a burrow builder. Parnell's pseudonym. Riddle of Stephen Dedalus. Fox burying its grandmother under a holly bush. Suffocating earth. Metaphor for the past, self, mother. Virgil's tomb. Inscrutable symbol. See C7, FN 5 for the solution. A newspaper placard caught his attention. KIWI SCRATCHED, it said. The vertical spatial projection of Classical literature is always UP. That's where Olympus stands. Romanticism inverted such. Shelley's vapours are always going updowndownup. Rooster barracking as some church bells bonged. Cunning Odysseus stuck in a cave. Polyphemus capped their exit with a massive rock. Foxsealed. At least until Foxysseus poked out his tongue. Curl into the underbelly of a ram clinging for dear life as it shot out of the barrel. Exit stage right. Foxeyed Bloom, Celtic heir of the shrewd one, was bestowed with this favoured animal metaphor by Joyce. Also, Shakespeare, who Joyce tagged Christfox. The Wolverhamptine Ba-ba-bard of Stratfox-on-Avon. Bloom equals Shakespeare. A father figure. What Tom Hallem had in abundance (falsely). Hamlet's spiritualised sire. Stephen as son. Saw himself as a wily one. Dodging Simon's paternity. That's easier if you've got a tangible father, thought Telemachus. Luxury of detachment. Avoid capture for as long as foxible. Sometimes I feel like a fatherless son. There is a legend that Sisyphus enjoyed Anticlea's favours so she was already pregnant with Odysseus when she married Laertes. Bob the breach-filler so to speak, cuck-cuck. Hamlet myself then: bitter stepson of Claudius. Regicide. Cain to his Abel. Shaun to his Shem. Joyce's brother Stanislaus was a potent commentator but never a competitor. Edgar and Edmund. Bifurcated seed. Forked tongue in the mouth of Medusa. Nothing straight in Denmark. All is subterfuge. Riddle me this. My mother's cousin is my father's wife. My brother was my cousin. My father is not my father. Intersown/scattered genealogy. Seal/fox. Compulsive craving for unity and closure. Always a misadventure. Joyce the father. I the son. To be so Minor is TO BE. Defer. Joyce annexed Shakespeare by reconstructing the Bard's life to suit his own personal and aesthetic agenda. I will become Joyce's father through a text about HIS SON. Homer inside Joyce around Shakespeare inside me. *Absurdio inflatus*. Russian dolls. Build a bigger one. Gigantism of Modernist Art. Guernica. *Ulysses*. Strategy of most minor literature: make a bloated replica of the TRUE machine. Self-deprecation of Joyce's triumphant SELF. Metonymy of the Irish national epic in Australia. Sacrifice readability to form. Use the style of Joyce. Also, substance. Wine and wafer. *Uselessys*. Why go on? Go on. GO. Welles left the department store and walked towards Parliament swiftly.

—

6. AFFINITY (2.30–3 PM)

"Jackie," exclaimed Starpunk closing quickly on a sculpted blonde leaving Grace Bros. He wriggled his feet inside glittering blue socks within worn cowboy boots. She was wearing a tight red polka dot dress. Pat Hyland in the saddle. She carted a black bass guitar case.

"Stuart," she responded averting her gaze to a billboard above the cast-iron fence of St Barnabas' church. A signboard read: Don't Punt on Eternity – Back Jesus! Stephen Dedalus bumps into Almidano Artifoni in this sub-episode. He has been transplanted to Dublin from the Berlitz school in Trieste where Joyce taught and pulled backwards in time. They converse in basic Italian. This is a gesture by Joyce rather than a narrative imperative. There is no corresponding scene in Homer. He has a relevant comic name, which no doubt tickled Joyce's fancy. Artifoni tells Stephen that he could make a career from singing. I guess the only thing it does is help build the narrative theme around Stephen's vocal potential. He asks him to reflect on this opportunity. Like father, like son. I guess the only thing it does is help build the narrative theme around Stephen's vocal potential. He asks him to reflect on this opportunity. He asks him to reflect on this opportunity. Music is the connection between these sub-episodes.

"Are you here to see Holly and The Nut?" he asked.

"What?"

"The Lingerie Ladies," he said pointing at a chalkboard outside the Broadway Hotel. Sacrifizio incruento. Make sure Holly and the Nut are named as Lydia Douce and Mina Kennedy at least once. Maybe while they are dancing on top of the bar to BP. Underneath, it read Cup Day Show 1–2 pm.

"That's them."

"I didn't know anything about it," responded Jackie.

They reached the traffic lights looking south across Parramatta Road. A man was holding up a broadsheet newspaper. Last year's champion had been scratched with a suspect foreleg.

"Come along. It'll be fun."

"No thanks. I think it sucks. They're just junkies stripping for cash."

"It's just a performance," he replied.

"Dealing has fucked with your head. You should get out."

"I want to. But I can't. I got to detach myself from Chubby carefully."

"Disappear."

"There's nowhere to hide. He was part of the Paltos syndicate. He's got contacts all over Asia and the Middle East."

"Go to Europe."

"The States is the plan. The Buttholes live in Texas. But for that I need serious wedge. That's why I got to keep working. It's chicken and egg."

Green WALK sign. They crossed Parramatta Road. A tour bus idled. Sydney–Katoomba announced a sign on the driver's sunshade. A tourist in the front row of seats raised a heavy camera. The punks sneered theatrically. Groveller raised a middle finger. F-flash. The tourist smiled. Her husband waved. Jackie and Stuart waved back. There's my bus, said Jackie racing towards the bus stop. The guitar case hammered her leg. Wait, replied Stinkbug face full of feeling. She flew through the doors. Fine Kiwi stayer. Fifth to Bounty Hawk in the McKinnon Stakes (2000 m). Winner of the Caulfield Cup (2400 m). Some members of a school cadet band disembarked. The doors closed. The bus commenced grinding uphill loudly. Tempe Depot was imperfectly scrolled on the side indicator board. Spams watched it pass trying to find Jackie's face inside the cabin through filthy panes. A black BMW cut off the bus causing it to break suddenly. Tired hydraulic grunt. Horn blast. The car straightened back down Parramatta Road. The driver shook his head and accelerated harder into the steep incline leading to City Road. Spams turned to the pub. Two men were pressed against thick glass. One had clear vision between two dark curtains. He was relaying information. The other leaned against his back. Spams approached. Black leather jackets. Both secondhand. One blank. The other bore a CRASS logo.

"The Nut's stripping," said Toe Cutter to Fish Pump gleefully.

"What can you see?" Fish Pump asked.

"Her gear's off. She's well-oiled."

Bersabe at bath wesshe her body. Gerty McDowell pressed into bold cardinal sequins. Holly twirled. Dumbshow Nausicaa grinding on a pole. Enter Starpunk.

"Hi Stew," said Fish Pump in an unsurprised tone.

"Are you going inside?" asked Starpunk.

"We feel a bit reluctant," replied Toe Cutter extracting his gaze.

"Far out," replied Starpunk. "I don't know what's got into everyone lately. Come on."

"Yea. Let's go inside," said Fish Pump. Spams opened the door. "We Are All Prostitutes" by The Pop Group relayed their entrance. Stuart patted Fish Pump on the back. They smiled. Toe Cutter split to the bar. Everyone has their price, sang Mark Stewart. Puker was propped on a high bar stool leaning against a flat middy. We're the ones to blame. A lean knight with sharpened eyes sunk in a reptile's face. Black mane falling upon a bright blue dinner jacket. Brindle. Blood of some Abyssinian hawker. Far West genes. A silver piercing shone in his nostril.

"This is a pretty masque," said Spams to Puker.

Fish Pump had taken a seat next to the stage peering straight up Holly's grind. The Nut bounced towards a drunk businessman beckoning. He stuffed Lawson's face under a tight elastic strap. She leered carmine lipstick. Doll-baby blonde. Her ample bosom hung low. Crassus made the universal sign. She held out an open palm. Five full fingers with tongue. He extracted a Pineapple from his damp shirt-front pocket and crunched it into a torch. Doc Florey was gazing sideways sheepishly as if mildly discomfited at his predicament. The Nut abandoned her mount. It bounced off stage into Nature's sticky underworld. She grabbed the note then the hand that offered it. Varinia come to my cell. They disappeared.

"Will you endure such insults," asked Spams.

"I was rather enjoying the prospect," replied Puker lugubriously.

"It does add a certain piquancy to life," added Toe Cutter joining them. Puker took a mouthful of beer. O'ervolumed. A tad of froth slipped from his mouth.

"What bounty?" inquired Starpunk.

"That's commercial in confidence. But I can confirm it's a lucrative trade."

"So, cash plus tips plus free use of backstage for tricks."

"Backstage is a bedsheet around the fire stairs really. How goes the life of a humble mule?"

"I'm late paying Chubby."

"That'll make for bold adventure," replied Puker gaily.

"It'll be okay. I've got a plan."

"That's fixed then. Come on," he said draining his glass. "We're late for rehearsal."

They rose to exit. Puker waved at his girlfriend. Holly opened her legs and thrust. Puker raised a fist and grunted. Fish Pump whooped as Holly's foot hovered inches from his tongue. 'We Had Love' smashed to life. She kicked hard. His head flicked back. Blood advanced into the margins of his teeth. He jeered. A car pulled up in Grafton Lane. Exit Puker and Fish Pump. Two men walked to the boot decisively. They each extracted a polyarmour cricket bat. Farquhar slammed the boot. The musicians turned into Knox Street. Vivien turned off the tape recorder. Overdose thanked him for the interview and asked when the next edition of *Vibes* would be released. The boy shrugged. They both thanked his father Bruce for milk shakes. The rest of the members of *Gag of Corom* arrived.

---

7. ROCKY RULLAH (2.15 PM)

Ms. Dunne hid her copy of *Dolly* magazine in the top drawer of her desk under a retractable stationery compartment and returned to typing. Madonna or Cyndi Lauper, it asked. She applied the date to a piece of stationery bearing the Welles Investment Group letterhead. Flashback to Hely's sandwich-men. Who will win the New Wave Diva Battle? She stared at a poster of Marie Kendall. Two advertising firms are competing for trade on Dublin's streets in *Ulysses*. Special Issue. She doodled and daydreamed. The telephone rang. It was Mister Boylan ringing from the fruit shop. She told him that Lenehan had just called. He'll meet you in the Ormond Hotel at four o'clock. Yes, she'll ring someone else after five. She hung up and examined the newspaper. Melbourne Cup Lift-Out. Rocky Rullah. Yes, Lear divided his kingdom causing mayhem. Rocky Thumb out of Butterscotch. He had three daughters. A gelding. Xi Jinping has got two former emperors still alive at court. Cerise with grey sleeves. Capable stayer with two victories over 2500 m. Better off with a sweepstakes ticket. Ms. Dunne turned to the foyer with an infant's innocent smile. Ms. Iris Gallagher glared back. She was settled on a low chair before a self-correcting typewriter with her head mostly hidden. A tall beehive vibrated as she attacked the keyboard. Occasionally, she peered over the top of the counter like a soldier peeping over the lip of a front-line trench. Marie Brennan waited for customers at her support post. Maree Bung hustled her son down the St James station tunnel. Ms. Dunne returned to a spreadsheet of ABN registered businesses controlled by WIG. It incorporated 303 Imports, Aquatique Pools and Spas, Australian Direct Investment Group (A-DIG), BCCI Australia, Brown-Gouge Dry Cleaners, Budget Rent-a-Car, Castle Bank and Trust (Asia), Green Beret Healthcare, Lok-Blok Construction Technology and Pastika Investments Ltd. She screwed up her nose as if partaking of an unpleasant odour. A call. "Yes, Mister Welles," she said. "You're stuck in Episode 12. I understand. About to enter Town Hall Arcade. The room at the Menzies Hotel will be ready at Four. Yes, I've booked the Beach Boys suite. I'll make sure that Miss A. gets the message. Thank you, sir. Goodbye." Ms. Dunne examined the dormant handset. A one-legged sailor jerked into Eccles Street. Retrieve a coin from my dresser. Peroxide Girl opened the front door. Her boyfriend entered. He went straight to the kitchen cabinet and collected his Gear, which was kept in a tin labelled "Oxford Set of Mathematical Instruments." The bed sheet had a bloody nose. Candy stripped it off the mattress and cursed. She picked fragments of bleached hair off the pillow. Jackie wrenched the Grace Bros door inwards. She held it open with her back twirling her guitar case through the thin egress. Francine passed Eva another cigarette. The television advertisements ended. The serial recommenced. "Pamela, how do you get your money for drugs," asked Doc Evans. Willy left his girlfriend. He had an appointment with Old Tom Hallem. She went to the kitchenette to retrieve cleaning products from underneath the sink. She must scrub the mattress of menses. Hired bedding. See Elizabeth (C10). The switchboard illumined. A call on the private line. Ms. Gallagher's voice rose richly. Ms.Dunne looked at the wall clock: 2.25 pm.

"Hullo, Mister Welles. Successful meeting, sir? Alright. I'll tell Master Edmund. When will you arrive? I took the liberty of purchasing a ticket for you in the office sweepstakes. You got Rocky Rullah. Yes, I know it's a roughie. But you never know. That's the wonder of the Cup. Don't mention it. Yes, sir. I'll get onto it right away. By the way, Mrs. Archer called. No message. Have a good afternoon, sir."

Abrupt disconnection.

Ms. Dunne started to decipher Ms. Gallagher's shorthand notes. She clicked at the typewriter. Mr. Cesar Tuason, President, ARMSCOR, Marikina City, Manila 1800, Philippines. Dear Sir, I am writing in regard to recent disruption in deliveries of M1911A1 hand guns. Holly's dressing room was a blue plastic tarpaulin hung in front of the fire door. A folding picnic table displayed her wares. She bent over crackt laminate. It bit her soft white thighs. Master Lenulus pressed her cheek flat with a firm palm. Her speedrush was gone. All the showbiz adrenalin. Lousy twenty-buck strip job on the dead side of the city. He fiddled with his trousers to get his great fat cock onto the stage. Box opener with a carved wooden grip. He thrust into her cheeks. She was greasy from oil and sweat. It went in fast. He grumbled about Tarzan's Grip. She succumbed. Breathslown. A hater. Best zone-out. She was glad not to look at his face. Penelope at her loom never observed her interrogators. All the suitors wore the same mask. Scrawled frantic smiles. It is a wise child that knows its own father. Edmund Welles held a bottle of Crown Lager tight. Holly ground her teeth to exorcise speed shudders. Air close'n'bad like a drifter's swag. Edgar awaited the sacrament. *Et non est illis scandalum*. Had to beat it hard. No cumshot. Hardness ebbing. He retracted. The condom slimed off. *Fundant labia mea*. I ought to get my money back, he muttered madly. Odysseus pumped the bat. Gravy had reached the hall. Peroxide Girl looked off her balcony at Willy's back tightening along Australia Street. Helen gazing down off the ramparts at Troy. PAM: (Restlessly) "I don't have a home, Doc." Helen Capri waited for the passenger's side door to be opened from within. A short old woman in black behind the baklava watched a student enter the unassuming doorway of her son's Lebanese sweet shop. "But where do you sleep, Pammy," asked Doc Evans. "On the streets," she replied. Francine stretched upright in the sofa. She held her elbow upon which a hand raised a cigarette. This short scene discloses the date of the novel. It also contains the only appearance of Boylan's secretary. Compare and contrast her condition with that of the strippers. Her life is a sad minuet played out of tune, out of time. The tone of this short passage is redolent of *Dubliners*. She is like Shelley's Sensitive Plant rooted inside Browning's dystopia. Yes, I am stuck like that, thought Ms. Dunne too.

---

8. LANCELOTTO (2.10–2.30 PM)

Les Hallem was watching the horses travel. Watching the lemons drop. Pulling his lucky arm. Sensing the movement of shrapnel through his body; movement of drugs through his head. Under Loopline bridge, shooting the rapids where water chafed around stone bridge piers. Minefield threading Phuoc Tuoy. A horizontal severance to traverse. Gouge apertures. Suicide peasants digging up Claymore's with jam tins. Rebury them on the track. Exhumed corpses re-interred. A real game of Battleships. Hair trigger. Wait for the blow. The Jumping Jack heaves. Vertical uplift. Dirt and bodybits sail eastward past hulls and anchorchains. Sparkles of Corporal Horne wet the most sensitive nerves of my face. Saltspray off harbour. Manly ferrychop. Suspect some of my own stuff is missing. Frisk frantically. Bore's lance in my side. But I'm NOT dead. Lloyd Bent massaged his stumps with retained fingers. Ian Westacott shaking hands with General Westmoreland. You Aussies got to get more kills, said Westy. Same gripe as Macarthur. I sent a firm directive for more aggressive patrolling from my desk at Saigon. Light fire seduced us. Suckered into foothills above Long Hai. WHOOSH. A trap. Get up. Fast. Rise. Find sanctuary on eggshells. Hopping from rock to rock like fucking frogs. Not to touch the earth it's a fuckblast. Run run run out of the clearing. Hop into the gaps between big boulders. Bayonets probing dry dirt. Descend. Grovel. Collect human scraps. Kevin Coles got caught in the wrong place in a napalm drop. Carcass spluttering flames in No Man's Land. Not much difference from the immolated monk that started this whole fuckup. Lucky Les Hallem got blown above the blast cloud. Sheep threw a thresher. Mostly intact. Bloke should buy a lottery ticket. He picked up a wet drink coaster advertising Dick Stone Meats. The medic was lowered into Charybdis from an Iroquois. Keep highest height. Don't want the downdraft setting off more mines. Mortar fire stun. Doctor Lippett swung off a strap. Applebee beat back forty NLF with borrowed armor. Les Hallem got up for a piss and leaned his stool against the poker machine on two legs. Siege Perilous. Nine mates lost in one blue. Jewels tossed out a casement. Zero kills on the other side of the ledger. Bad odds. Desk jockeys at HQ sent the platoon back out next morning like it was a game. Ulysses S. Crossin walked towards his boss across the car park. Mister Carpenter was talking to a scrawny bloke sucking a pipe. A third gentleman was circling. The odour of Erinmore Flake enticed the young man to close-up the triangle.

"Could I have some light please," asked the Professor.

"Whatchoo look infer?" asked the young guard flaring his torch.

"Tank Stream," explained the Building Services Manager.

"Whah?" queried Crossin.

"It's the creek that fed Sydney with drinking water," replied Keith Carpenter sternly. "That's why they started the settlement right here and not Botany Bay."

"I'm writing a book called *Underground Sydney*," opined Professor McNab composing a false title instantly. Actually, he was writing a history of urban water systems. But that had no cachet. Fast-flowing streams. Mill wheels turning. Trap for defence. Build deep moats. Scrape saltpeter off the subterranean walls of the castle for gunpowder. Start another plot. The NVA invaded both sides of the Pearl River. Like many cities, Sydney's past has been iced by progress. In Wandering Rocks, the ancient council chamber of Saint Mary's Abbey is all boarded up with seedbags. Joyce creates an emblem of Irish dislocation from the condition of its neglected legacies. We will examine Joyce's use of water imagery in Chapter Nine. McNab placed an ear against the thick concrete sleeve. Blood leaking lungs. Diastolic rush. A lament imbued the dim pub backroom. Holly tightened her gaze. Pinhole light. Wet business shirt flap. Pants tying his ankles. WHOMP. He dropped off. Crawl like a slug. They used cockroaches like canaries down Sydney's phone tunnels. His hair a blood mat. Does Private Richardson still heave? She observed a man swinging a bat into her customer's hind and fled.

"Why would anyone be interested in that stuff?" pondered the young guard bluntly.

"This is the most historic site in Sydney," enthused the Building Services Manager.

"I don't get it. Greek culture goes all the way back to Styx. This is just a puddle."

"Quite so," replied the Professor smiling.

Mister Carpenter grabbed the young guard's arm and mouthed some words.

"Stop, Keith. Your young colleague's quite right. There are grander waterways than this. Paris has the Seine. London grew along the fast-flowing Thames. Berlin was well-positioned on a bend in the River Spree. But this was all they could find around Sydney. Just a dribble."

Why is it called Tank Stream?

"It was nameless at first. There was a drought in 1790. The stream dried up. Governor Philip ordered three tanks to be cut into the adjacent sandstone to act as wells. Hence its name. The Tank Stream was abandoned as a source of water supply in 1826 but it remained an open drain. It was progressively capped until the job was finished in 1878. Incredibly, it was still used for sewerage until 1939 when a new pumping station was built to stop overflow reaching Circular Quay and creating noxious conditions around Wharf Eight."

"On the other side of this wall is the end," added J.J. O'Molloy patting the car park.

"Back that way," said McNab pointing with his pipe towards King Street, "it gets too narrow to pass."

Where is its origin?

Its source is marshland on the west side of Hyde Park near Park Street. Sydney is a steep town. The catchment started at Brickfield Hill in the south and continued in a vale between York Street and Macquarie Street. Sacred lochflows. Maid of Astolat shining a shield with her strawberry handkerchief. Glimmer in gloom. Dusk at four-thirty. She knows the story of every scraping. Ian Westacott admired his clean service revolver. A barge draped in black carries her casket down river to a lonely grave. A concrete diversion channel was installed when they built Australia Square in the nineteen sixties, said McNab. After that point, it turns into swamp. The cistern contains. The fountain overflows. Dry dirty canula. Les chopped off the dribble. Spent drops spreading through his underwear. He wandered back to his lucky machine cadging smokes. Rooting around the dump for scraps outside a fortified hamlet. Cashing his pension cheque at the bar. Simon Dedalus dropped a coin into his daughter's palm. She scoffed at him. He is all fault who hath no fault at all. The barmaid tapped a middy of New. The bar manager was distracted by the horses parading in the mounting yard. She waved away his money and winked. Number 19 passed across the screen. Jockey in orange with purple sleeves and a black cap. Ron Quinton. Six successive Sydney premierships since 1979. Four Golden Slippers, 3 AJC Oaks, 2 Doncasters, an Epsom and a WS Cox Plate. But no Melbourne Cup.

"There is another tunnel in this vicinity built in the 1890s to link the GPO with the Royal Telephone Exchange. It extends up Broadway all the way to Newtown. You can still walk—"

"Excuse me for a moment Professor," interrupted Carpenter striding from their orbit abruptly.

Ulysses S. Crossin, Professor McNab and J.J. O'Molloy followed his withdrawal towards an apparently vacant car. Elizabeth Archer stumbled off an escalator in a low-cut lime dress carrying a large black cardboard cylinder. Her boots clomped on the steel landing. She gathered herself, scratched beneath a heavy zipper cutting her calf and preceded onto the waxed floor of David Jones tea room. Move languidly if you can. The Francis sisters. Ugly Carol. Plain Kay. Skinny Liz. Their father spent every pay day at Randwick racecourse until he got home drunk and broke. A rented flat in Kingsford. Three girls sharing a bedroom. Small pair head to toe on the bottom shelf. Kay up top. Charity soup from Our Lady of the Rosary. Spotted pears from Castellorizo's fruit shop. Broken bags of biscuits. The tea room seemed distant – impossibly distant – across the meltwater surface of Ladies Fashions. Elizabeth proceeded across the ice age of shop assistant glares.

"What did you get for those prints," asked Lady Peasoup looking up from a deep wide wicker chair.

"Not much," replied Elizabeth Archer slumping.

"Even the Miro?"

"There's no market in Australia."

"Quite. Ruined by Ken Doll. What will you do?"

"It's okay. I've got a plan."

Lady Peasoup removed a fresh packet of Peter Stuyvesant cigarettes from her Chanel Classic Flap Bag and ripped away the cellophane wrap.

"Woodbine?"

"I can't smoke. I'm meeting Stan."

"So that's your 'plan'," replied Lady Peasoup derisively tossing the box onto the coffee table. "Not very original."

"He's my white knight."

"Knight!" her friend exclaimed. "Well he's certainly *moyen age*. Bordering on *ancienne regime*."

"Don't poke fun. He's good on the job. And modest in his needs. Which is most fortunate. I'm sore all over today."

Elizabeth Archer cradled her abdomen. Triton lapped the Quay.

"Why?"

"I spent last night with Tom Hallem."

"Oh God, it's the tragic tale of Menelaus, Helen and love-sick Paris all over again."

"Don't mock."

"I thought you'd moved on."

"I want a baby," replied Elizabeth blandly.

"What?" exclaimed Lady Peasoup.

"I can't have children with Leon."

"Of course not. What prompted your ... change of heart?"

"I realized I'll have no one left when Leon's gone."

She spoke awkwardly wiping a single tear from her eye with her friend's used serviette. A scrap of wool. Burnt thigh. Erichthonius. Put it all in a small box. Troubles borne of earth. DO NOT OPEN. Lady Peasoup couldn't help prizing it apart.

"What do you know of his family," she asked spitting soggy cracker sparks across the glass table. "They could have all kinds of flaws."

Half baby half snake. Chaim. Spine medallion. Wet and unfloored. Sump hole. Touch his underformed back. Go down a tunnel. All inside-out. Shoot a man through a loose singlet. Blow his guts out. Roll over the corpse. Check for documents. Insert autobiographical note on spina bifida.

"His mother is in sales. She has a husband on an invalid pension. They live in Burwood."

"Promisingly bland," mocked Lady Peasoup. "What about his father's bloodlines?"

"His father was a soldier. He died in Vietnam."

"Any hereditary diseases?"

"No. Leon got into the Medibank records. There's no mental illness. No birth defects. No cancer."

"So, Leon is 'in' on the deal?"

"It was his idea actually. And the best part of the whole scheme is that Tom will know nothing about the baby until it's done."

"How will you pull that off?"

"All will be revealed tonight," smiled Elizabeth conspiratorially.

Outdo Joyce in drama. Write a ripping yarn. Holly scooped up her backpack and palmed the fire rail. The latch dropped. Light steeped the alley. Sisters throwing themselves off high places. She jumped to the lane. Another body followed almost immediately. The Nut crumpled against the liver brick wall of the Humanist Society. Herse and Aglaurus. Farquhar stood there shaking his head. He was a father himself. Agamemnon's staff hung by his side.

"Go that way," said Farquhar to the girls gesturing to the western stand with his bat. "Piss off!"

Eva turned up the volume on the television set. Pamela, how do you get your money for drugs, asked Doc Evans. Let's just drop it Doc, okay? she replied. DOC: But I want to help you. PAM: Don't you understand, Doc? Tom Hallem released the Mexican belt from his bicep. Leon Daniel turned towards an acquaintance as he jogged on the spot at the traffic lights. Nil recognition. He shrank. Risk of mixed fluids. Farquhar and Gravy reached the laneway. Farquhar signaled the driver. He had McCann's stash in his massive grip. Billy Capri walked across the pedestrian crossing at Carillon Avenue. Why bastard? Wherefore base? The Vietnamese shop keeper realised too late that the young man who ordered a tin of pineapple off the high shelf had burgled the cash drawer when she'd turned. She chased him down Eton Street. He vanished left or right. Down to the velodrome or over Salisbury Road who knows. She trudged back to the shop. A handful of lobsters had taken flight. She would have to find a way of replacing the cash before her husband got home from the markets. Les Hallem lost his last ten-cent coin down the slot of his lucky machine and proceeded to the lounge to watch the Cup. He'd put his last two-buck note on Lancelotto each way because he liked the pun. He preferred to bet on machines. They were less engaging than flesh and blood. Dick Stone delivered a frozen meat platter to Besley's Stationery as a sweepstakes prize. A folded note was hidden inside the invoice. Time and place proposed.

Holly and the Nut struggled out of Grafton Lane. A chopper lifted the remnants of Applebee's platoon off the LZ. In a tone of quiet desperation, Pam looked Doc Evans straight in the eye and said, why don't you just do the world a favour and let me die. The shopkeeper telephoned an anonymous number. Bobby would bail her out. Les Hallem steadied his drinking hand. Arthur's love for Guinevere. Tennyson's exemplar of an unfaithful wife. Lancelot rejecting Elaine. Degraded icon. Their child was perfect but. Leon Daniel rolled against the wet humid grass like a wolfhound. Ana Lafei was drowning. Her face pressed the towel. Flat on her belly under her husband's palm his workbench legs held taut by fallen overalls. A comma of gleaming hair fell over Boylan's handsome face. After he withdrew, she rolled onto her back and brought herself to orgasm blank pupils staring into an access hole in the ceiling that disappeared into a void of webs and cracked rooftiles.

---

9. PASS THE BATON (GOES BACK TO 2 PM)

Persian Jones reached the Mitchell Street squats after dodging the Filth down the arse-end of Toxteth Estate. His pockets were stuffed with analgesics procured at the Ross Street Family Pharmacy using a forged prescription off a stolen prescription pad. He had Petra and Dougie the Animal in tow. Weasel Bob had gone off to collect his wrap from Barry McCann Jnr down the Broadway Pub. Ambrose E. Welles ascended Pitt Street from the ruined wedding cake of the Universal Provider. Farquhar met Gravy out the back of the Iron Duke Hotel. He passed him a cricket bat. Gravy produced a controlled shot pulling John Snow to leg. "Nicely weighted," he smiled. Six lunchtime schooners exhaled from his gums. Steak-laces tortured his canines. He picked at them with a soft fingernail incessantly. Someone cracked the reinforced front door.

"You missed *Vikings*," an unbodied female voice disclosed granting entry.

Persian Jones shrugged. A scraggy arm harrowed with scabs hung a burning cigarette like a censer as he passed. *Days of Our Lives* projected seriatim plotlines unremittingly. Farquhar tossed Gravy a warm KB from the boot. Francine closed the door and resumed her seat. Adbreak. Wayne went straight upstairs. His body ascended out of frame. The stairs creaked underfoot despite a cushion of thick bone carpet pomaded with wear. Tony Curtis and Kirk Douglas star as Eric and Einar in this tale of star-crossed brothers. The King of Northumbria has been killed in a Viking raid. His wife is raped by the Viking warlord, Ragnar, played by Ernest Borgnine. She becomes pregnant with his child. The bastard is sent to Italy to hide him while events unfold. Gravy let trapped lager fly. Welles gazed at a shop face uncomprehendingly. Eric takes out one of his brother's eyes with a pet falcon. Farquhar eyeballed the wheelman. "Just do what you're told," he advised. "Don't think, just drive like I said and you'll be home safe tonight." Tom Rochford disclosed the top disk of his machine. The Nut inserted a cassette into the sound system. Rewind to start. Unsettle the temporal plate of this chapter. A baton relayed backwards by a backwards travelling runner. Beckett to Joyce to Pater to Shelley. Starter's pistol smoke seen. Then sound. Crockery rises off a milk bar floor re-assembling. Time spelled backwards. Hieratic utterance. Reflection of a signifier in a still POOL. Gnawn Narcissus. Odin reverses the tide. Eric rises. Tom Hallem was a giver not a user, reflected Shanghai Dog. I was not one of his best friends but he was mine. He showed me fidelity. I just couldn't reciprocate. But you can't expect equivalence from people. They just save what they can. Nut pressed PLAY and rushed to Holly's side. Puker wupped. Fishpump friezed. Dougie got up. He twisted the volume knob hard on the big TV. Close-up of DOC EVANS. I've been reading about it in the papers but I never believed it. These kids are actually LIVING ON THE STREETS! Oliver replied. Yes, Doc. Runaways like Pammy. They got no place to go. So, they drift. They beg and steal. They hide ... from the law ... from their folks ... but mostly from themselves. HAND'S UP WHO WANTS TO DIE! smashed the shallow bar. Holly and the Nut raised their arms. Stan Welles made bold signage across a moat. A false quest founded on a false premise. Edgar as Tom Bedlam. A decoy. Gravy's job was to distract McCann while Farquhar forced his way through the ruck. Holly displayed an unshaven pit. The Nut followed. Peroxide by tarnished bronze. "Are the plates off," asked Farquhar. The driver nodded. Some locals leaning on the bar looked up then re-studied their flat schooners. One glanced at a bright wall clock. Two pm struck on one of Grace Bros various timepieces. Frayed denim jacket sleeves taped a poster against the glass lens. White frog upon clover green background gaping. The Lingerie Ladies assisted each other onstage. A scarlet stiletto heel slipped through the brown milk crate frame causing Nut to slump. Read scraped a pencil arc across a sheet of Kohzo paper. I shudder to think how she survived, Doc said. Mick Harvey's drum pattern kick-started the song. FRENCHS TUESDAY 10 PM. Just remember. Sydney is my town, counselled Farquhar. I got the green light. And I don't tolerate weak cunts. If there is a fuck-up, I will find you and I **WILL** kill you. Nick Cave grunts. The Nut grinded. Fishnets diastolic systolic diastolic clamp. Tautslacktaut. Traverse the parapet. Two hills right. Turn when you reach the weeping silver taps. Count SIX. A tall scalped mountain. The gang got into the car. Stan Welles disengaged. He climbed harder faster older past the Lismore Hotel. Skinny relic like him. First floor bar quite intimate. A nice place to take a much younger lady. Bloody devil-horns shimmied on the strippers' flips. The bone Kingswood rolled into McEvoy Street. Scarlet-sequined bikini briefs rose. Precious clear flesh twixt groin'n'garterbelt. Sweats of Sin. Read scored his wife's wide buttocks. It hardened the drawstrings somewhat on his white linen pants. Cuthbert's reddening face disclosed his struggle. Francine wriggled in the sofa. Her patterned black tights clamped her crotch. Elizabeth Archer's warm milky gut received his impress. Zakinthos. A Greek island near Ithaca. Classical parts litter the fields since the big earthquake. Did Hellenic sculptures possess anuses, asked Bloom. This spurred his visit to the National Library on Kildare Street where Stephen Dedalus was rending his Shakespeare theory. Young McCann focused his attention on the strippers high up on the bar. Cuthbert and Jiles blocked his gaze. OLIVER: You know a lot of these kids are forced into prostitution, Doc. I'm afraid that's probably what Pammie's been doing. CUT TO DOC'S FACE IN SHOCK. INSERT CAVE: (Sudden. Forcefully. Down.) Have you heard how Sonny's burning? Rowland S. Howard's o'erspeeding all-but-falling guitar slid untrammeled raking the speakers' dock. Like some bright erotic star that Bloom and Stephen piss under. Holly's breasts went spilling at the crowd. Gravy leaned across the back seat languidly. Arms all akimbo. Guffawing. She rose as the guitar ceased. Welles crossed Central Street. Farquhar sat bolt upright. The Nut thrust her hips jipp-jangling. Guitar ferris-wheel. Down again she plumbed. FLAME ON! They rotated face to face to arse/arse to tight tits slapping. FLAME ON! Cane pushed the par-open door. Non and Slope were baking in the front bedroom. Beakers and pipettes arranged haphazardly upon a bench made of an old door. Ana Lafei's forearms spread across the greasy workbench. A raft's wings sea-born. Held fixed in place. Her heavy cheek had been turned against coarse Laminex. She was wistful at the forest-fall odour of Rowney oils. Empty cartons of coffee milk, crumpled crisp packets, bog, clay and rubble, chocolate wrappers, sand, crumpled cans and discarded hypodermic wraps were corralled into the stark black corner of the lab. Read felt tremors. Holly centered her speed-hit to accelerate her movements. Circular Quay souvenir stalls leaked Japanese tourists under Read's smashed window casement. Stan Welles stared into a battered garbage bin on Bathurst Street while he waited for traffic to pass. Read drew a great black bird. An Ibis picked at scraps with Giacometti beak. Apollyon's bosom. A roaring ambulance gained traction surfing carspread. HEY HEY HEY HEY HEY. A single syringe had been speared into the rotten woodwork at a heroic angle like Tatlin's Monument. Holly bucked. The Nut extended her tongue. Jiles bumped against Fishpump. Matt's pressure. Manhole entered Glamour Bar in Shanghai. Marked labels on a neat row of brown chemical bottles read: CHLOROFORM, PYRIDINE, HCL. Slope was mixing bronze solution at a vacuum flask. Alligator wine. Shanghai jingjiu. They prepared the glass separator. Supplejack rose on canvas pumps to spear the slughorn home. A bit of stubbed ground. Ana was not really his type, as Swann mused. This made it hard to get the job done. Heat was generated by an ordinary twin burner camping stove. Read let the black ink drag his brush. Non swirled the mixture. Garniture of curly gold. Mad brewage. Slope added the magic solution drip-by-drip. Persian approached. Non greeted him with a warm smile. Slope did not look up. Nor Read. Ana neither. Barry McCann stared at Cuthbert. Jiles at Nut. Farquhar seemed mesmerized by the dashboard. Gravy let his gaze rest on the padded ceiling. Elizabeth Archer contemplated a fresh flute. PH must be 7–8, Slope explained collecting a strip of paper with junk-hardened prints. Ambrose E. Welles passed the summit of Brickfield Hill. Mere ugly heights and heaps. Peace in the cabin. Matt got up the plateau grey plain all round. Gravy gripped his bat handle. Cuthbert his crotch. One stiff blind horse.

"Got a package for you," stated Persian Jones.

He displayed his wares. Jiles slammed some silver crunch on the bar and poked two lean fingers at the barmaid. Fishpump hung off his shoulder yelling. Weasel Bob cranked the volume.

"Got a taste for a mate?" asked Persian.

"Always one for you," answered Non.

"Can you take care of Read as well?"

"No problem," said Slope.

Read was a top customer. Bought big bags of flake. Always paid top dollar. Persian Jones shook his gypsy mop. He needed cash upfront or drawings to sell. Igraine. Foot on a dead man's cheek. Farquhar wanted to get his paws on McCann's stash. He'd been short since bribing Harding to get off bashing that bouncer at City RSL. Plus that was his half pound they planted on Kelleher. Also it was his hash they took off Bazley's slut. Still it kept him tight with Burke and Gilligan. Welles reached the Criterion Hotel. Main bar half-empty forty minutes from race time. He turned onto Park Street facing the big hotels on William Street. A base afternoon opened over Hyde Park. Warm in the damp and rotten seed. Ray waited to cross. There was an interval of ten seconds between Rogerson's shots. Lanfranchi lay face down dead in the gutter in front of an unmarked police car. Read only had to knock up a few drawings to keep everyone flush with dope. Francine could always hit up her father for cash. It was a great deal for Ong. A denim-clad arm removed a twelve-inch copy of the Stooges' "Gimme Danger" from a plastic sheath stuck to the window. Rogerson was wearing a bone cardigan for the execution. Some scratches. He carried loose papers in his left hand. The gun was no longer hanging in his right palm. Cover signed by Ron Asheton! INSERT BROWNING. He had replaced it into his holster by the time the journalists arrived. Ray needed to keep the parties to the transaction separated. Those bastards would cut him out in a heartbeat. Farquhar shook. Blotches rankling. They'll load you up soon as the press crackton. One mistimed shot and you're gone. A howler or a bat. A slither of glass from smashed spectacles lodged in the Prime Minister's eye. The apple of which was bruised by drugs. Like a penniless drunk, he staggered from the pitch begging for a draught of earlier happier sights. Blind as enflared Oedipus. Don Cane beheld Richie full-term on the Baywalk leaning against a palm truck in the cooler dusk breeze her bare feet ceremented in turf. A father's agony. Ray calculated Elizabeth's equity requirements. He slipped some dried ink sketches into a satchel. Take them to Liz. Get some dosh. Leverage. The stuff of business. Stick a branch down a manhole. Say: hang onto my hand. Acts of a God. Raglan's twenty-two traits. Historic arraignments. Oedipus 22, Jesus 19. Burke had been sucking out my cash since Seventy-Six. Fixed up that poor cunt Dolly Dunn right royally. They gave him a fucking medal for that. Supplejack withdrew. *O le amio fa'apua'a.* Gift her to Urien Gore, influential art critic. Ray fingered his lapel listlessly. Holly fixed Cuthbert as he advanced to the bar. What turns is on; what turns is done. She disclosed all her assets. The lad stood to attention, as Tom Rochford said. Boylan with impatience, so to speak. What's in a name? A column of disks rising. BVI structure. Transfer funds into a Hang Seng account under surname NUGES. Welles entered the department store. Plods at the ATO would never be able to trace my gossamer. He spent the next 10 minutes flirting with the sales assistant. See sub-episode six. Correspondences to H. Boylan.

"How does it work?" asked Persian.

"It's quite an elaborate procedure," replied Slope. "You extract codeine, convert it into morphine then turn it into heroin hydrochloride."

"Hot Cherry!" sang Non. Add moly. How come it taste so good? Slope contributed harmonies. Link to Stephen Dedalus: fine voice. Lickwid red, added Non. Jamaicanally. Holly shimmied towards Cuthbert. The wheelman reached Waterloo Towers. Redfern Oval was weed-rutted, bankrupt and blown dry with Botany Bay salt. Mere earth desperate and done with. The Kingswood loitered alongside an abandoned concrete hulk sewn against Souths Leagues Club. Gangrenous limb. Ruined landscape. Leon Daniel removed new runners from a shoe box. Matt dried off his cock. Holly banged the bar. Ample curves of air. Bloom's into a demon flower, sang Cave. Note double-meaning. Nut settled a boa. The Filth had brokered a truce down Chippo. The Dodger wised up Domican. Took out Lanfranchi. All was sweet until Fluckingferalgohannery got into the loamlight. Now fire fire was all consuming. Nut scoured the bar. Stuck in the stalls. A game filly. Light load. Pass The Baton went 5, 6 and zero in its last three starts. Certainly knows its way to the finish line but. Twelve wins in 62 starts. Under-rated stayer. Ana as Albertine. What you covet is unattainable. Once got, it feels soft. Ophelia. M hearing his mother laughing at the table downstairs. Orpheus turning to check that Eurydice has followed. Lack of trust.

A myth of inconstancy and disobedience. He lost his head. In the end the Gods literally detached it like a boombox.

"Good set up," said Persian admiringly.

"This fit-out cost two thousand bucks," announced Non. Slope eyeballed him punitively.

"Where did you get that kind of dosh?" asked Persian incredulously.

"Barry McCann," confessed Slope.

Non started cracking Persian's tabs into a flat metal bowl. Pling plingk clingkp. Shelling peas. Moist skin. Hard nut. Joyce's liked making such phoneticisms. Molloy counting sorting stones. Shylock at his purse. Deasy's coin dispenser. Rain on corrugated tin. Bowl of beer nuts. Ray felt the front of his teeth with a burnt, frangible tongue.

"You're going to shaft McCann in the end, I presume."

"Well he's screwing us," answered Slope deftly.

"Spoken like a true junky," laughed Persian back.

Nut slashed the fag air with a fake cowboy whip. Evaporated dust drifted down-nelly mapping the surface of a schooner of Reschs beer. Slope explained how he just walked straight into the chemistry labs at Madsen to steal equipment. Long laminate corridor. Past the POWER collection. Should nick some artworks. Read could fence them. Farquhar prevaricated. To drop or not to drop Young McCann. What a piece of work. Value of a contract. Not worth the paper they're written on these days. Someday I think I'll cut him down. Farquhar yawned. Don't overload the job with process. "Deal-making is a lost art," mused Stan Welles composing a flow chart in his head. Non paused. The blend was giving off evil heat. Francine lit another smoke.

"They're not mixing right," said Non, waving smoke. Flame on! Slope strode to the palsied bench.

"What base did you use?"

"That," giggled Non.

"You've got no fucking idea John," replied Slope. He turned off the tap. "Forget it. I'll fix it up later." He opened his kit. Want a shot, he asked. Sure, replied Persian. They paused at an abrupt sound beneath them. What was that, asked Slope. Non rushed to the window. He drew back a chink of checked blanket. A figure withdrew across Mitchell Street. Holly was disclosed. Bloom at the bookstall observed without. Peroxide Girl watched a young man move restlessly from his car towards Camperdown Park. Turquoise eyes. Unjudging. He inspected parked cars closely. Saliva filled Edgar Welles's mouth. Earth. Bloodtaste. Broadway Pub. Barry McCann Junior sprawled amidst bejeweled glass. Show over. Lester touched cognisance briefly. Alive. Head uncased. No gaze. Dry blood made pipes of hair. My form. Still intact. Some kind of membrane. This unlit place like birth.

"Who is she," asked Persian?

"Francine."

"Is she a Freak?"

"Nah," replied Slope. "Slummer from Perth."

"And there goes her shadow," laughed Non.

"Ali can certainly spot a mark," added Slope. Welles ascended King Street towards USYD law school. Cheap Brutalist slabs. Sandstone lozenges of dead counsel. Associate Professor Leroy Certoma emerged from a hidden portico swinging a brown briefcase. He crossed Phillip Street before the Supreme Court building. Stan passed. They gazed right at Saint James Church together. He was the first apostle to be martyred. I guess they related to him back in 1824. One observes its spire every time a ten-dollar note is perused. First sight of Sydney from sea. Ships set compass by it. Converted courthouse. One of Bigge's skewers. Greenway's Georgian lines without transepts or chancel were later slathered with Victorian sprawl. Marsden consecrated the corner. Shine, for thy light has come. Gold streams over tarnished Yellowblock. Bloom and Stephen micturating under starshoot, as Joyce puts it in Ithaca. Helen McFadden on her back behind the shed. Ana looked up. Forward charge. Leon Daniel changed out of white scrubs. Blanched lustre. Isaiah 60. Government nearly knocked it down for railways. High church station box. All stations back to ancient liturgy. Sydney loves a dirty deal. Build a new apse on platform sneakers. Gleaming eagle lectern inflamed by the testament of John Evangelist. In the crypt, they give Eucharist to children. Statues of Victoria and Albert in Queen Square separated forever by traffic. Convict Barracks straight ahead. Golden arms read 2.30 pm. They knocked the spires off St Mary's Cathedral in 1914 to deter Zeppelins. Get down Macquarie Street. Greg's bringing his Slavonic mate. Good block of dirt at Randwick. Lobby the Minister. GFR bonus for party donations. Stan Welles scanned the decrepit wooden balcony of the Mint. Originally part of the Rum Hospital. Paid with piss. Monopoly on rum. Bastards still went bankrupt. Could only happen in Sydney. Gravy skulled fast from a Bundy flask. Spirit burnt his lips. Barry McCann Junior sipped at a middy glass refreshed by Weasel Bob from a fresh jug. At the top of Martin Place, Greg Devlin beckoned wildly. Anonymously, Molly Bloom inserted a card in the windowsash of 7 Eccles Street which read: Unfurnished Apartments. This image augurs Lenehan's recollection of a carriage ride after a function at Glencree reformatory where he was able to rub against her cleavage persistently. This type of external description of Molly recurs throughout *Ulysses* coding the reader's impressions before she is finally introduced in her own right in the last chapter. Every jolt the bloody car gave I had her bumping up against me, Lenehan says. LINK TO OTHER VEHICLES. This coarse tale negatively influences our opinion of Lenehan – erstwhile hero of the manhole rescue. Holly arrived at Cuthbert bearing palms. Lashings of stuff on the bar: port wine and slops and curacao. Ample justice done. Brown bags all round. Nut whispered a sum in Jiles' ear. Hell's delights! exclaimed Lenehan. He shook negatively. No discount she implied. No bartering. She turned away definitively. He followed.

"How's the bub," asked Non.

"Screamer," replied Persian.

"Clean?"

"No. The shaking does my head in."

He demonstrated his son's natal tremors.

"My kid was the same," said Slope working the fix. "It'll pass."

Slope extended a bare olive branch. Persian swabbed. Raspberry soda bubbling in a Pyrex beaker. Slope sprayed. They sat on the bare floor. *Xenia*. Persian wound back his sleeve wearily. You're truly bugged, Non joked. They all grinned. Some junkies just get harder and tougher with age. Cuthbert extracted Holly's warm wet milky globes. Molly has a fine pair, God bless her. Farquhar checked his holster. Stan Welles grabbed his cheque book. Ana jammed toilet paper down her briefs. Slope sucked and backtracked pumping the handle. Clean withdrawal. Touch of an artist as. He passed the bloody needle to Non. A fair plump arm light-pelted. He tied-off. Work less expert. Matt Supplejack examined his canvas of a great big flower lurid pink on a magenta frieze. Symbol of Ana. Too wild. Her band. The wrong one for his career as well.

"Pass me the stick," said Persian Jones.

"Gunnit," encouraged Non losing face volume until he crumpled graceless and folded into the floor. His head lolled. Persian fitted. Clanmuck. Bruise by gold. Carmine. He mined the needle. Growing weary, he dozed like Alastor; fingers reaching through darkness towards a lost but once accustomed shape. The corridor emptied. Goldstein shifted his penetrating gaze. Billy watched his brother RETREAT. "Willy," exclaimed Tom Hallem pock-sweaty and blind over the modular music of a small bedside fan. Don Cane sleeping as I lay. His fingertips played the dull strings of his son's spine through soggy linen. Monster or whirlpool. Man and Ideal. Stephen sailed closer to Scylla, it is said. Towards Aristotle. Persian Jones slid into Non's lap. And lay. The Nut sneered. McCoy's face cut him down. Lenehan backtracked. Ana Lafei gazed at the pressed iron ceiling. What star is that, Poldy?

—

10. FOUNTAINCOURT (2 PM)

Bloom at bookstall. Centre of the novel.

The audience was finally liberated into the corridor outside Marion Flynn's office. They gathered in awkward dags along the cream gyprock walls, blocking transit. Holly entered the milk bar in haste. The Nut followed. Motes of beer glass scorched her filling flesh. The shopkeeper was watching the races on a portable television mounted on top of a refrigerator. His wife asked, "What horse you on?" He ignored her. She poked him with tongs. A plate flipped over the baine marie crashing to the floor. "Fountaincourt," he yelled. She shook her head. What kind of nag is that, she said? He picked up a tea towel and went to the counter. Vivien took a sodden swimming towel from his school bag. Chlorinated stench. He passed it to Puker who wiped blood off Nut's arm. His father graced a handkerchief to Holly. She mopped an enamour'd ear. Overdose thanked Vivien.

"They trashed the pub," exclaimed Holly.

"Who?" asked Spams.

"Some crazies with bats."

"Did they get McCann?" asked Stuart anxiously. Nobody knew the answer. Sirens wrapt ether. Sweet silence prinkt. Brennan's clock tower bells. Sound dislimning as it arrived outside the pub. The shopkeeper brought out a garbage bin for their bloodied swabs. The group left. They stood awkwardly on City Road. We better move on, said Fishpump. Vivien had begun sobbing softly. Spams nodded. His father touched his dome. They began trudging towards Beta House. Flight to Fuckithurts. Find a deep cave. Hide. Perfunctory conversation. Noticeboards announced out-of-date units on Victorian Literature. Tennyson abutted Pater. Crooked blotched print. Not to yield. Grey sandshoes shuffled apart. Oscar Wilde's sequence of flawlessly executed set-pieces. Style bends matter. Kingsley on Shelley. Organic Form. Classical fusion. Eliot stuck on a raft. Coleridge's Aristotle. The burgeoning plantation. Rousseau's ruined bed. My fair face. Quasimodoid. Sweet grass. A slashed face. Calico wrenched apart the cambric folds of Missy's dress. Them are two good ones, the bookseller said. LINK BACK TO LENEHAN. She held his smooth black chest at bay with spread palms. Molly kept them in her drawers. Ease of access. His nostrils arched themselves for prey. Stan Welles shook hands with Bob Raspudic. The buck gently burst her maidenhead. Bloom followed. Awkward disclosures of Maria Monk. Blood made moist the mustee's thrusts. A steady stream of students was returning to class after lunch. Backpacks hung over their boney shoulders like pelts. Academics held court. Calico left Miss Missy burning and murmuring with pride. An imperceptible smile played on her lips. Judith Bourbon turned to Mildling calmly. Aristotle's Masterpiece. Pirate edition. 1903. Ana forced its ruined pages apart. PLATE 1 depicts a poisoned quadroon infant. Ana studied its weeping spine. Justine. A flaccid hand matted with tiny perforations. Bloom's conflict with Freud. His ideal woman hunts a wolf and despoils its fur. Quest for a third party called "the Greek." His father cancelled the triumph of oral woman. Tripartite system: mother composed of soft molecules; father represents primal nature; daughter an incestuous accomplice. Marion Flynn rose from the invoices piled symmetrically on the left-hand side of her wide desk, traversed an enormous carpeted office and approached the par-open door. Her mantis-face peeped out. Some would say admonishingly. She closed it gently and placed an ear against its light barrier.

"That paper had relentless ... speed," Judith Barbour said probing.

"It was very well-crafted," nodded Mildling with emphasis. "But it would not stand up to a dispassionate eye."

"Where are we going now?" asked Tuck.

"The Bard," replied Blind Basil Kiernan.

Sinbad Sailors exposed prominent eye teeth. Gossamer Beynon caught his reflection in the noticeboard. A Sick Woman's Looking Glass. Still boyish. Cusped maybe. But fair game nonetheless. I might join you for a pint, exclaimed Mildling. Kiernan patted the pipe in the interior pocket of his stained white jacket. Able Goldstein observed them from his alien camp. Ivan Illydicker returned to his proofs of the Badgery tome. Agent flogging a dead horse. Dostoyevsky's nag. Meaningless plot entrails. Dame Nellie Krafter refrigerated Goldstein with steeleyed discourse. The University is suffering recession, she whispered choking on her buttoned frill-neck pinafore. We need to cut staff levels. Goldstein shuffled tired flat feet. The weight of his body bore down. It needs a strong hand, he grimaced. Around your throat dear, beamed Mr Pugh's compliant face. Farquhar ignited the driver. Stan Welles crossed Macquarie Street. Penelope Hallem put down the telephone and left her desk. She had received a last-minute invitation from a major interstate supplier to a function in the city tonight. Helen Capri withdrew down the corridor gamely. Goldstein observed Billy's parents depart. Most different stock. He wanted to beat Phoebe to the plane. Raise the drawbridge on his office down the arse-end of the department like a belltower. He couldn't leave the Professor's audience but. Be Emerson's adhesive self so to speak. Not much room to manoeuvre. But who wants much? Dog: leash; cat: box; chicken: coop; pig: pen. Enough passing trade crosses my threshold. The Liffey is comfortable for vending most seasons. I have a canvas rain cover for my wares in the event of inclemency. Palsied condom writhing on the floor behind Mildling's filing cabinet. Goon's torn-off finger. PLATE 2. Finger in a jar. Bloom retrieved a folded sex trade advertisement now scented with lemon fragrance from his side pocket. Young woman, well-appointed, seeks sensitive gentleman of means. Mail to: Ms. Flowers, c/- The

Clinic, Holles Street Hospital. Get them. Use them. Grow bored. Hard to shake them at first. Agenbyte of Indicker. Only a fool would jeopardise his wife's dowry. Miltonic sham? Hardly. Chosen pathways. Twisting with each twisted answer. Pentagonal gnosis. Abel as Jacob wrestling Elohim. I thus Esau. My brother's foil. A sequence of meaningless symbols before my stubbornly uninterpreting gaze.

"Willie," expostulated Tom Hallem.

Goldstein turned to admire the new entrant. Pint-sized stayer. Sixty kilos in bags. Tight saddlecloth. Black boots unshined. Worn down by pacements. Tentative movements. Pulled up lame recently. Hit the glands with his stick. Tender baubs.

"Where's the bathroom," asked Willy.

"Over there," replied Billy Capri pointing at an unmarked door.

"Is there another one," queried the Pimp.

"What?"

"Another one," he repeated tensely.

"He means a more private one," added Tom Hallem helpfully.

Goldstein was puzzled. Foibles of evacuation? No. "An expedition." To find a blank vein. Ana discarded used tissue paper into the cistern. She took an ice cream bucket, filled it with water from the basin and used it for flush. Molested remnants floated in the tank. Penelope Hallem wriggled as she hit the damp toilet seat. A storeman slid boxes across the warehouse floor. Packers filled orders.

"Right on top," said Billy pointing skywards.

"Let's go," said Willy to Tom ignoring Billy.

"OK," replied Tom Hallem. "I'll see you down the pub," he said to his brother.

"Don't you want me to wait?" asked Billy.

"No. I'll catch you later. Say goodbye to your folks."

The broad high hunched frame of Tom Hallem and the small straighter form of Willy the Pimp receded down the corridor. O passed them heading back from the front office. She greeted Billy with touch. Emma entering a cage. Ana Lafei adjusted her clothing. A sad unattached orgasm tied her eyes. Penelope Hallem wrapped the boundary of a coarse diaphragm with gel. The third edition of *Aristotle's Masterpiece* remained available until the twentieth century because no clinical sex manual was yet available. Havelock Ellis was the first self-proclaimed Sexologist. He started to gather qualitative evidence; largely through correspondence. Freud, by contrast, relied on Classical references and case studies. Billy frowned. Chidley's corrugation. Muffled footfalls passed above him. Wreck on an ocean floor. Swaying with engine wash. Involuntary. Ana Lafei gave way on the shore of the Lake. A surface lit too high above. Willy and Tom approached the undignified portal. Lacan's toilet stalls. Tom Hallem turned a loose brass handle and pressed the heavy fire door. They passed into an antechamber. Coastclear. Soft natural light bathed them. Six silver spouts at the urinal burst forth simultaneously. Water fanned the scratched silver tray then bubbled down an encrusted grate. The citrus odour of chemical blocks was released. Willy followed Tom into a cubicle. Twins sharing a womb. Corded. Invective against Asians and Gays had been gouged into the paintwork with a pen knife. Thick ink defaced these defiles. Vonnegut's graffiti from *Deadeye Dick*. Do-be do-be do. Socrates and Sartre. Algren subbed. He called De Beauvoir his filter. She used their open relationship as content for the *Second Sex*. To articulate her OTHER. Cancel out words like 'unhappiness.' Think rather if it FELT aligned with theory. Penelope Hallem manipulated the contraceptive over her cervix. Lawrence adjusted his nib. Connie's SEX-NEED was great but it was just that. Strong fucking in a hut. She longed for a better connection than cramped-up Mellors. Penelope let her core lapse. Michaelis crying. I need Les. I suppose if the love-business went, said Lady Bennerley, then something else would take its place. "Morphia, perhaps," she concluded.

"Have you got a clean stick," asked Tom.

"All prepared," replied his dealer. "I'll hit you up. I know you're squeamish. Sit down."

"Got something for Ana?"

"Like I said, I got nothing to spare at the moment. Try Leer."

"Okay," replied Tom Hallem as he removed his coat and placed it on a hook. Willy took a syringe from his leather jacket. Kinch-blade. "Here. Taste," he said putting a fingerprint against Tom's tongue. He shuddered so bitter was its taste. Tom wrenched the belt from his midriff. It slapped his stomach as it unravelled. He looked to the wall. Willy examined the tip before even afternoon light. Tom rolled-up his left shirtsleeve. Will tapped twice. He removed the plastic cap. A tiny head almost invisibly shone. He rotated it so that it gleamed ... beat ... gleamed. A short spurt jerked forth. He placed the hypodermic between his teeth and wound the belt around Tom's bicep until a vein bulged in the maw of his soft elbow. Willy hit Tom suckt then shot. Bludd wandered through the chamber then gushed back. Opiate surge. Willy released the syringe to pick at his face. It hung from Tom Hallem's arm like a broken wing. Tom leaned back into the toilet lid. It creaked under his weight. His last sensation was taste still thick on his tongue. His head lolled depressing the flush button. A surge of water rushed beneath. His bowels relaxed. Small urine. No immediate feeling then warmth then null: no epiphany. Judith Barbour passed Mousy Roche in the corridor. No words exchanged. Somebody turned up a radio in an office with an open door. The jockeys have come to attention for 1984's Melbourne Cup. And they're racing. STUCK INTO THE MIDDLE OF THE TEXT LIKE A KEY. In a hole. Or contained inside a display case. As if of some museum piece squinting through the squalid pane while a servant cleans the transparent surface from the outside. Televisual then. For now, we see through a glass darkly. Corinthians I, Chapter 13. Insert meta/portrait based on "A Prince of Court Painters." Update Pater's imaginary portraits with full disclosure of his – and my – subject matter and form. Break the fourth wall. These descriptions from behind the meniscus are blurred by mucus; which still covers the lens. For they would always spit on it. Though it was hardly personal. Like Bloom, you will always be the butt of inadvertent insults. Not that they could discern you there in a position of impossible contrition. Still, it cut. More spittle. And a short whimper followed each clang as your heart murmured. Watteau's bloody slag slid down the steel rim. God knows what you were doing in that box how you got there under whose authority it hardly matters. You never dreamed of moving from your station. And your compliance went on without acknowledgement. How could it be otherwise? You will never be the subject of conversation. Romance is never wasted on you. Gasps you do elicit but of shock not rapture. Both observer and observed. Pater's heroes are always deployed in a Bildungsroman from which they can only be released by death. Note his typical means of textual closure: CAPITULATION TO HALT AT A MOMENT OF VAIN PROSPECT. But James Joyce couldn't kill off Stephen Dedalus, any more than he could kill himself, otherwise *Ulysses* was never going to be written in the post-partum real-life after the novel ends when Stephen Dedalus is converted into James Joyce by the author (link to Proteus). Thus, Stephen Dedalus just leaves the text quietly near the end of Ithaca. He is suspended out of time and place like Pater's anonymous female narrator. Silence consigns her to oblivion. O attended but did not speak. Penelope Hallem stood. The diaphragm gave a thick feeling. Outside noise. She listened at a keyhole. The discourse was male. Billy swayed. Penelope opened the cubicle door. A storeman in a khaki uniform smiled. He handed over a meat tray. Ana stood by her husband with grace. He silenced her with the sheer scale of his ominous essence (Sub. portmanteau word like omninisescience). The periods without words continued to tumble out of her. They were the large part. Of these, there can be no record. Pater infers them by lack. She inspired no visual representation. Voyeurism, our highest honour at Themme, this visual, no not her. Of her, then, only our over-sights, only her non-fragments. And even in these, she can only be reconstructed from her own reflex jerkings at a Self somewhere perhaps maybe there amongst them: YOU'RE A RUMOR! Yet there must have been occasions (surely) on which, having exhausted all possibilities, you became the Subject; though when this may have been ... no, it's impossible to tell. Maybe some time in the middle, not at the end but merely as an aside, not a last resort (no, not even allowed that solace: of being the last port left standing) but just "because" it could be. We can imagine you neutral of significance like that. We gaze but either side of the image only, you exist. Likewise, Wandering Rocks, which is really the ground zero of *Ulysses*, also acts as a hiatus in the narrative's course. As noted, it contains nineteen intersecting scenes of quotidian life in Dublin. Chapter 5 corresponds to that number, but only by chance. There happened to be 19 runners in the 1984 Melbourne Cup. *Ulysses* is a procedure-driven event. It is divided into eighteen episodes, each vested with a particular colour, art, organ and location. THIS EPITOMISES MODERNIST GOOD FORM. Link arbitrary numerology in this work with the deep-set, highly symbolic numerology propagated by the mystic Joyce. C1 & C11 bookend the hermeneutics of TMAC. C6 is the core. C5 is the centre of the plot. C6 was originally conceived as eleven episodes sequencing French theoreticians in the spirit of Joyce, using the composition of a cricket team as the governing cipher. This was an ironic Australian numerological gesture. In the end, it has seventeen episodes (including Joyce). This was just how it turned out. Although it does correspond to the composition of an Australian Football team, this was entirely accidental. W.Rocks was the epicentre of *Ulysses*. Sub-episode 10 represents the limit of the outward journey of Joyce's Ordinary Odysseus (sub. ordinysseus). Leopold Bloom is disclosed scouring the shelves of a riverside stall for soft-centred pornography. He is a religious gadfly intrigued by clerical miscreance. The profane and the apparently profound are juxtaposed. This is a trap for the reader. Joyce cites Aristotle's *Masterpiece* but it isn't the same Aristotle as the *Poetics*. Rather, he is referring to a popular pseudo-medical compendium from the seventeenth century. Bloom also fingers the apocryphal tales of *Maria Monk*. This is the tale of a woman raped in a Montreal nunnery. Roman Catholic blasphemy was lapped-up by crack-lipped Anglicans in the Victorian era. See also *Autobiography of a Flea*. Chapter Eight. For the purposes of this section let it only be known that: (1) it is the story of louse secreted in the *mons veneris* of a voluptuous virgin named Bella; (2) She is surprised by a priest during her first act of sexual intercourse and coerced into a clerical orgy; and (3) It ends in a parody of absolution with the following exchange: "'Let us F**k,' ejaculated the Superior. 'Amen,' chanted Father Ambrose" in retort. Penelope Hallem collected the company car keys from the front desk. Her rump moved stiffly. She would attend the reception at the Marble Bar at Five pm then meet Dick at the motel on the way home. Religious confession becomes the butt of ironic interplay in Victorian literature. Its main protagonist was the poet Swinburne. He perceived the artistic freedom that could be attained from expanding into the void left by the withdrawal of Faith (post-Darwin). His poetry offered no pretence to philosophical systemising. Rather, it just demolished social mores employing an array of styles and forms that showcased his virtuosity. Buck Mulligan represents the softened shell of this attack with his provincial quasi-Hellenism. Time alone brought Tom Hallem back. Not Will. My world as? He turned towards the melamine partition. Pale grey moccasins peeped out of sunken grey trousers in the next cubicle. Pockets and seams peeled across the tiles like guts. It was not Willy. He was gone. Tom waited. A strangled gasp. Trousers hoisted. Zipper closed. Flush. The adjacent cubicle opened. A hand basin released fast water. Receding doors ground to a halt with pneumatic certainty. Silence. Tom Hallem staunched the weak bloodflow with a flap of moist toilet paper and wound down the sleeves of his shirt. Willy had discarded the syringe on the floor. Tom Hallem unscrewed the top of the cistern, lifted the porcelain lid and dropped it in. He replaced the cover. Go out. Telemachus leaving Ithaca. Billy Capri made his way across the west end of campus. Don Cane in Kings Cross then/now. Ana Lafei left Matt's studio. Penelope Hallem walked to the car. Tom on a causeway. A student came to loggerheads with him at the egress.

"Can you tell me the time," asked Tom gently.

"Ten past three."

"Shit. I missed the Cup. Who won?" he asked.

---

11. FORWARD CHARGE

Leon Daniel moved stiffly through his surgery in new runners negotiating the ergonomic stool, instrument trolley and x-ray partition before crashing through a thick fire door. It creaked. He shunted himself onto the landing and fled downstairs pursued from above and below by his own echo. Sound of shofar from a pit. Rabbi Caro's *Shulhan Arukh*. Radius of piety. Chaim. Losing balance on the stark descent, he skied on suspensionless buttocks turning his body sideways as he smashed into the bottom of the sharp stairwell. He rose wearily and swore. Exodus 21:33. If an ass falls therein the beast is forfeited. He wrenched open the fire-door and emerged onto the street, merging with the polished stone and whitewashed scaffolding surrounding Currency House. Wet air pinned his singlet against black hair spouting from his chest. High thigh muscles stretched and constrained. Systolic clasp. Aerobic trigger. Future a death sentence. Past stillborn. He COMPRESSED Hunter Street. A postman bearing a heavy leather sack checked his trace. Greg Devlin and Joe Raspudic ascended the stairs out of the Emperor's Choice. The floor rumbled from a Kings Cross train. *Nebeneinander*. Raspudic looked left as they pitched into the traffic on King Street opposite MLC. An embroidery of swollen lightbulbs (bronze by gold) announced the New Theatre Royal. Seidler certainly copped a pasting on that job. Lesson to everyone. Drop the old stuff fast, preferably at night, with no warning, aided by a squad of wallopers, or at least get the fucking fuckade off, that's a smart tactic, before the bluddy B.L.F. slaps on a green ban and it's off to the Land and Environment Court for a master class in sanctimony from Diamond Jim McLelland. Wind whirred up from the Heads. More raincludd. *Adiaphane*. Pause of pedestrian signal. Leon jogged on the spot at the Elizabeth Street crossroads. Forward Charge has drawn barrier three. A bus advertising Mansours' curtains passed. Curved QANTAS fascia. A queue of passport applicants unravelled out of the Commonwealth Office Block. Remote uriney glaze of oil-encrusted lanterns gave an unwarranted luster to a tray of Big Ben pies and sausage rolls (link back to e.3). Gonnerill and Cornbeef. Sauce-softened scabrous pastry like dry sarcomas. **Mystery Disease!** Wire news placards outside the Wentworth Hotel scattered hateful clay. **AIDS kills three in Sydney!** Chaim stretched out sideways on the slab like a skinned rabbit, his torn and bulging cleft exposed. Reverend Nile MLC has petitioned for the closure of gay saunas. **He's got a map!** His agents are everywhere. Loitering in Ionic columns with notebooks. Soliciting confessions. Willy waited behind a telegraph pole to cross Parramatta Road. **Marilyn Monroe Sex Addict!** Best blowjob in Hellas. Icon of my straighter days. A tampered copy of *PIX* magazine in the bottom drawer of my school desk. Clandestine visit to a brothel in Darlinghurst with Mewling and Lawrigan. Lear's hundred knights. Elizabeth's body pressing down on my cock like alloy. *Nacheinander*. Marriage. **Hawke wants AIDS Summit.** Defensive ploys. Trace references to HAWKE. Twenty-five in all. They construct a political thesis. There is also a personal side. This nexus indicates the intimate scale of Australian society. Joe Raspudic clutched his long red ledger. A depositary. **TRUTH. Secret book busts scam wide open!** Ambrose E. Welles straightened his jacket and fluffed his lapel. T.J. Smith MBE is Sydney's top trainer. A passenger train burst through the underground tunnel at St. James and screeched towards halt. Willy passed between sandstone gates. Fourth to Chagemar in the Dalgety last Saturday. Must get back to the office straight after we meet Doug Truck. Small matter of presenting a carboy of *eau de cologne* first. Special gift. For a fine boned lady. Daughter I never traduced. Cordelia. Throw Dilly a few coppers. Cheap discharge. The jury returned its verdict this morning. Get a glass of milk & a bun. AIDS Risk in Kinky Sex, says expert. Monkey virus. Stand straight up for the love of Lord Jesus you'll get curvature of the spine, said Mister Dedalus. He was allegedly a member of a coterie of prominent businessmen in Adelaide known as The Family. Dilly has just left the bookstall after seeing her brother when she confronts her father in the street. Stephen's internal monologue revealed guilt about his sisters' circumstances. This differs from his father who is only observed externally issuing self-pitying invective. The race is not yet run for the son, suggests Joyce. There is still hope. Repeat the journey. Transcend paternal weakness. Conduct Navigation Search on 'transcend.' Trace its trail through this work. The girls lifted themselves on-stage. Mister Dedalus impersonated an ape for the denizens of Bachelor's Walk. The star's sodden body, wrapped in a royal blue flannel robe, trailed the swimming pool edge, past camera dolly by floodlit night, her blonde locks hopelessly mangled, sprung arc of her back exposed, reciting her husband's flat patois, routed off stage. Exeunt Ophelia. A cut snake. Trailing melody. Hazel pressed PLAY. **AIDS spreading like wildfire! UK Sun.** Von Einem sentenced to life imprisonment. A postman left the Attorney-General's building bowing under the weight of his thick leather satchel. Read and unread notes, fake and true, are dispatched and withheld, delivered or aborted, recited aloud and consumed in silence throughout *King Lear*. It's all about language like *Coriolanus*. Wrong word selection > false interpretation > gross flattery > lies > coercion to utterance > marriage vows. A bold convenience. No dowry was thence forthcoming. Her father's permission: a cursory wave out the fly screen door. Clack. *Modus vivendi*. A block of passport-sized photographs wafted to the pavement. Leon stooped. We left Circular Quay on the *Flavia*. Record number of Sydney premierships. But not a Melbourne Cup specialist. He returned the images. Telemachus in a t-shirt. Cast off from port. Long tin whistle blown. "I Still Call Australia Home" trailed after the arse-end of a black BMW. Brake lights emberhot thru muck. It paused behind a taxi turning right into Phillip Street. Rainspat. Far hard drops. Infected bloodflow. Crowds escaping the ticket barrier at St. James Station slowed Stan's progress. Thrilling jerks. Genius with sprinters. But he has only won two Melbourne Cups. Twenty-six years apart. Age when I manufactured my whoreson. A capable type who has always showed great staying potential. Cannot be forgotten. Gravy barred the Shepherd Street exit. Leon passed unadorned office-backs. Pipes and entrails. Look under her skirt. Saddleback limbs. Holly shook. Nut ground. Ran-gong out of Always Rushing. Miss Crowdy had drawn Forward Charge in the sweep. The orthodontist in Suite 704 got the favourite. A dice rolled in a marble vault. Fool's puzzle. The auctioneer's bell ... *barang!* An unplated car sat idling in Grafton Lane. Les shuffled a blob of TAB tickets in his pocket. Willy's kit was stuffed down the back of tight black Lee jeans. The new extension to the State Library beamed warm diffused light. Leon dashed across Macquarie Street entering the canopy of a dark drooping ficus. Birthday Party kicked into life. Ana spread bare-faced on the bier. Statue of Matthew Flinders on a plinth. Holly rode high up in space. Farquhar prowled the pub windows. Willy entered Woolley Building. Flinders' cat, Trim, Uncle Toby's manservant, is commemorated, mid-step, one paw aloof, his head turned towards the viewer's gaze, on a keep on the dirty window ledge aft of Mitchell Library. Another endless Menippean scat. Greg Devlin checked his watch opposite U-SYD law school. Ten minutes to showtime. Farquhar nodded. Gravy leered. Joe Raspudic checked holding costs in his head. The clock is a money-counter. Toc. Proscriptive debt instrument. A bus advertising Mansour's curtains passed. Fishpump gaped. It was all colour, all movement, all sound. Billy Capri extracted himself from the audience seeing slow Tom Hallem. The vast uterine subscape of the city suckt up Ambrose E. Welles. Daylight ground slowly into lanes unshading his gaunt lumpy face. Town Hall clock chimed the hour. He stepped off the kerb at Bathurst Street and walked towards his own silhouette in plate glass doors. A fine cut, he thought, admiring his uniform in a long reflective screen. Hong Kong tailors are still good value even with the dollar in free-fall since Keating's float. Pin stripes flapped his longbow legs. Link back to Holly and Cuthbert. The Nut tucked Jiles' crumpled note beneath black fishnet. Gonerill's letter in Edmund's keep. It's been a pleasure to put a face to the voice at last, said Ambrose E. Welles. Willy caught Tom's eye. Stan passed the contract over the desk to Mister Ong. Their gazes met. Miss Dunne responded to the switchboard light. Yes, it's heritage-listed. But you've seen the engineer's report. It's unsafe for refurbishment. Farquhar and Gravy entered the public bar. A bat swept the black Formica bench raising beer and blast. Mister Dedalus drew himself upright and tugged at his moustache. Ray reached the intersection of Park and Elizabeth Streets. A government bus passed advertising Mansour's Curtains. I've struck a deal with the Premier, he said. If HKG will refurbish the Queen Victoria Building, the government will let you drop Hordern. Open slather on land use. Universal Provider, I am. Yes, I know that demolition is banned under the current zoning. Holly rushed towards the fire exit. Anna crumpled wet soft objects with her palm-press as she landed face down on the bench. Abducted childboy. We can get the application called-in by the Minister as a State Significant Project. Willy exchanged magazine origami with Tom. He's a mate. I organised the branch stack that got him preselected for Peats. Ray gazed skywards. That's a really sensitive piece of façade preservation, he thought. You'd hardly even notice that forty-floor skyscraper jammed out the back of such fine masonry. Girder shoved down yer throat. I particularly like the Colonial wrought iron trim masking bare carpark cavities. A Chinese woman bustled downhill. They all look like lads, Welles determined. Slower in ageing. Like good plimsolls. A soggy runner struggled across the slippery footpath dappled with cracked paving stones. Kent has gone into exile. A ragman sprayed invective at his back. Tomsacold. Leon Daniel slipped behind the edifice overseen by Governor Richard Bourke. A bitter gall, charged by its flight over ice and ocean, struck his fallen cheek. He hurried across Mitchell's stone face. Massed Corinthian pillars prefaced the thick studded copper doors of the State Library. A statue of Shakespeare had been left marooned on a traffic island like Prospero. Metaphor for the arts in Australia really. Pinchgut exiles. Far Eastern Distributors. Tragic stars gazed from the Bard's girdle. Legal minefield. Refer the bond to pale Portia. Exploit a technicality in the head lease. Gentle rain. Leon negotiated the junction at Hospital Road and threw himself into direct communion with the common, chronon-hoton-thologos! Click claek. Nut bit the gutter. Go down on raw knees holding seasick onto the steel cistern. He spread his torso on rotten earth. Ana was pressed. All flaxen his pole. A kidnapped lad. Muddy Domain. Clinging. His corpse had been discovered wrapped in grey office carpet at an airstrip, held fast by a military belt with a chainmail dog collar around its neck and a beer bottle shoved up his anus. I did the act of darkness with him. Greg Devlin and Les Raspudic paced Macquarie Street. World Square will be a world class development, Mister Ong. It will position Sydney South for renewal. Property values are forecast to increase by 100 per cent in the next 5 years. Black with Sugarine please. There will be three towers. Total of 150 levels. Each tower will be themed. The retail plate will be spread across the whole site on four levels. It will contain food halls; cinemas; supermarkets; light electrical products; fashion. Quality brands. Established names. Welles counted them firmly on outstretched fingers: Sportsgirl, Country Road, Dick Smith. TAPtap. There is ingress from four major thoroughfares: George Street, Pitt Street, Liverpool Street and Goulburn. Five levels of underground car parking. He held up four fingers and twirled a double-jointed thumb. Nice gimmick. A tidy little earner in its own right, he concluded. Mister Ong grunted almost inaudibly. Face done. Balding pate. Greg Devlin chucked silver confetti in the pig pond. Leon Daniel sprinted along the gutter behind Modernist exhaust stacks in the Domain. Darkness falling permmaturely. He straddled a wooden jogging aid. I've secured a government agency as anchor tenant. Spoke to the Premier himself. Very enthusiastic. It will enable him to dispose of a surplus building in Bligh Street. Contra deal. We can get TNT to re-route the new monorail. Direct link with your new casino. High rollers just one stop from a six-star Hong Kong Gardens International Hotel. Construction can start next year. Private sector project. State will provide seed funding ... tax incentives ... guaranteed base return on investment during the ramp-up phase. They'll use compulsory acquisition powers to consolidate the land envelope. Fifty-year BOOT. Leon thrust himself back to earth against flattened palms. Sink through the surface. Unused railway tunnels beneath. They say a lake has formed in the tunnels which is inhabited by monsters. Sediment has gathered on the shore. A beach. Leon crawled towards its dim waters. Threshold of a still dark pool. Raise yourself up! Twenty repeat sets. Grit clogged his harshly clipped nails. Scrub hard back at surgery. But what if I've infected someone already. Shudd. Forget house calls to cloisters. The security guard at Currency House turned up the volume on his portable TV. Victorian Health officials have contacted 40 hemophiliacs who were given blood products believed to be contaminated with AIDS. He pulled his body vertical like the first ape. Gravy bound along Grafton Lane. Farquhar waddled. Outpace anonymous corpses. Ulcerated mouth. Little can be done. Some Benzocaine gel. Rest. Ong gave assent. Mister Welles smiled. A secured deposit on the site in ESCROW is next. Great lawn unfolding down a snot-gem slope. Glowering skyscrapers. Garden Island crane perched like a brittle beak. Specks of Kings Cross. Other lives let them drift. Leon dragged the dark side of Art Gallery Road. Robbie Burns leaning on a ploughshare. Arse-end of St Mary. Where the Pigeon fuckt. A mess of traceries, spikes and gables. Yellowblock ramparts of Hyde Park Barracks. Macquarie's berth. Steeple of St James Church dulled into dusty bister by time-shed stains. Leon spat on the flagstones. Fizzy bubbles pressed flat. Hyde Park foreground. Deep uneasy stillness. Sydney's first race course. He entered its lungs. A labyrinth. Apollo's veil. Vapors of the Archibald Fountain sprinkled Japanese tourists. Spraying gloam. Burrow like a mole in a clearing. Ana shrank. Jets saturated the bronze sculptures. Matt Supplejack released his wife. The Minotaur's struggle against Theseus shone like greasy pages of pornography. Stan Welles walked boldly towards the department store entrance. CHECK TIME. Helen Capri left Woolley Building. A storm inundated the ground quickly. Raindrops from a corroded gutter touched her face. The Honorable Douglas Truck MLA, Minister for Housing, gazed from his office over the Domain. The Minotaur was held hard by a horn at arm's length – beyond the range of its vane – its head bowed and turned so that its hide was utterly exposed to Theseus' blade. Pasiphae's brood. The severe sword of its conqueror, hidden from the victim behind his mighty back, glistened from blasts of turtle spittle. Edgar Welles took the barman's heavy load through a torn aperture. A Nikon camera clicked. The switchboard glowed. Truck turned to admire his office artworks. Call on Mister Welles' private line. Ms. Dunne looked at the wall clock. Japanese honeymooners strolled towards the transept. Ms. Gallagher passed a note. Tell Master Edmund that his father is running late. He may not make it to drinks. Ms. Dunne rose. She entered the boardroom. Edmund Welles was telling a joke. So what do you call Leprechaun farts? He asked. Don Cane weighed the change in his pocket. Greenarse gas emissions, Edmund exclaimed. His underlings laughed. Leon wheeled the fountain. Apollo pointed back down Macquarie Street. He approached the straight. Diana brandishing a spent bow. Helen Capri passed Mephistopheles fountain. Water was dribbling steady into a deep sandstone trough. Put a lid on it and you've got Ophelia's coffin. Her husband looked in vain for distraction in the tall bank columns. Elizabeth Archer drained her glass. Her palms were damp from condensation. Diana's hounds cowered. Sleek reptiles. Hephaestus hunched at his forge. Pan's pipes slung across his slender abdomen. Athena's gold. Hooves stable in froth. Matt Supplejack's cock dripping lowly. Leon wiped his sobbing brow. Sweat drained his shorts. Willy picked at a scab. Bloodribbed. Eleni bit into a Maraschino cherry. Lady Peasoup turned her beak at the prospect of copulation. Ana slumped pale like the moon does mid-morning. She observed paint-splattered boots. Pollock's drips. Her mouth jerked. Leer rolled up tonsured oils, placed them under his armpit and set a fire. A bagwoman spoke to Leon with a dismembered face. The shop assistant's protruding jaw chewed pasturagely. Oh Io, you image sweet! She grinned. Agat. Leon made mute signs of rejection. Go. Tiny lights strung through the park canopy. He turned into Hyde Park stretch. Wind-tunnels poured between skyscrapers with mechanically cranked clouds o'erpitching. Pedestrians slid between vehicles deftly. Willy made his way into Woolley deftly. Barry Capri held his wife's hand when she slipped in a muddy puddle going aboard Victoria Park. Taxi drivers pumped accelerators irrhythmically. A courier van twisted behind a stationary bus. Two cars screeched halt. I passed. A helicopter julienned the sky. More traffic lights. Newspaper stands. Giant clock enfolded in neon advertising Chateau Tanunda. Entrance to St James. A pounding Hades. Footsteps flap like heavy wings down long tiled corridors. A busker lisped into a tin whistle. Fair Hibernian metropolis. Sweet Molly is introduced at this stage of *Ulysses*. A gay sweet chirruping is heard. England Home and Beauty. A generous arm tossing a substantial coin. Leon Daniel passed a busker. Sound now pursued him. Also, deductions of conscience. Blood, AIDS, circulation, body, decay. A handful of coppers sped into a begging bowl too fast, breaching its wide brim. Bronze rolling on shiny rims along a footpath. Paltry commonweal. A public schoolgirl helped retrieve them. Ineluctable. She laid them on the plate. Poor woman casting mites. Christ's calculating eye. No Rich Men in Heaven, read a placard held by a lunatic outside Parliament. Greg Jones grinned. "I Still Call Australia Home" was forced out of Apollo's reed with aery spag. Window displays in David Jones promoted the Magic of Christmas. Cures AIDS. It will need a large cheque written in a false name for a fake bank account. King Street lights gone green. TAB leaking white and green bouquets. Cornwall did a fee-split in his brain. Everyone's getting greedy for a cut in these darkening days in Manila. Saigon all over. Sashed girls in clover bikinis handed out betting cards. Fat lady revving up her vocal cords. Leon Daniel returned to Chifley Square redux. Passport office > QANTAS building. He ground to a halt at the end of Hunter Street and leaned against a large concrete ballast. Whitewash smeared his forearm. He dropped his head. Tobacco roam. A security guard was smoking in the doorway. He held the door of David Jones open for Ambrose E. Welles to pass. Joe Raspudic shoved gum at Greg Jones' face. Willy the Pimp chewed on a SCARED lip. Elizabeth Archer refreshed bright lipstick in the Ladies Room. She looked out the cast-iron casement on Level Two. A jogger was crossing Prince Albert Road in jerks. She checked her watch. Two-Forty PM. Leon Daniel nodded as he walked towards the elevator. Descending numbers. A guard approached. The doors parted. A young woman left the stall. She negotiated the marble foyer on slender stiletto heels uneasily. An anonymous businessman remained in the open elevator. He looked straight at Leon. The doors closed. Leon started. Perhaps a face from a cruise lounge. Don't confess. Hide until everything is tidied then escape in death. The elevator descended to the Basement. "I seen that girlie arrive two hours back," commented the guard drily. Leon grunted. Message without words. Sometimes it needs reinforcement to get out the meaning. Sometimes not. Go to a booth willingly. Touch a cheek first. Bring together two mouths. "She's been up to see Goanner," the guard added.

—

12. SECURED DEPOSIT (2.30 PM)

Greg Devlin, Raymond Welles and Joe Raspudic slipped through the half-hooked iron gates of the NSW Parliament. A black BMW passed. Greg nodded at the security guard. He adjusted large rectangular spectacles. Perfume warmed Ray's wrist. A small gin. Dennis Breen, grown disillusioned from waiting for an interview with Attorney-General Landa, paced Macquarie Street holding a bag of law books and a sagging placard which read: "NUGAN R.I.P. OFF." Wran's young chum. Easy to get a meeting if you're Berhad. Or going to build Neville's aquarium down Darling freight yards. Got to make something out of that motorway Stonehenge. Looks like the end of *Space Odyssey*. Irish non-Jew like Bloom. Father born in Belfast. Mother a Pole. Kept those Margies locked-up. Stuff Mary Gaudron's legalese. Keep the heat off ASIO. Pays off in the long run. Don't want to end up like Murph. They'll drop you dead on a tennis court from some poison-umbrella spray. Couldn't shield Buckets but. Best we can do is cover his legal costs. Put up the Cabinet-in-Confidence shield. They crossed the forecourt and climbed the damp stairs towards the Legislative Assembly.

"It was just a tin shed," said Devlin, "when the Government bought it at a receiver's auction."

"CIA killed Frank Nugan," yelled Breen.

"How long back?" asked Raspudic.

"After the gold rush," replied Devlin. "Late 1850s."

Raspudic nodded sagely. "Abeles is part of the deal," Breen stammered. "Hawkie's ... *mayt*," he crowed. Give a council inspector a clip to turn a blind eye on compliance. Regular cyclops. He squinted at Stan Welles's suit shimmering in winecludd. I should wear threads like that, he thought. Gives you gravity. A plastic bag floated onto the fence. Greg Devlin paused at the top of the stairs beneath the timber colonnade to catch his breath. He tucked his shirt over a fruitful gut.

"They finished a big build-out last year. You should've been in on that one, Joe."

"And Bernie Houghton," rasped Breen.

"Oh, fuck off, Pete," yelled Devlin lovingly. Come on, he continued to his companions. I'll show you around. They crossed the threshold. Plush carmine carpet softened their blows. A portrait of Slippery Charles Cowper gazed at eye level. Dark foyer high arches. Sustained mechanical bells quired. What's in the bag, asked Devlin. Perfume, replied Ray. For my wife. Devlin leered and turned towards reception. Raspudic and Welles followed him. It's her birthday, he added needlessly. Raspudic nodded. Dimmed lamps. Once gas now globes. Gilt finials upon plain square pillars with ornate stenciled patterns. Chiaroscuro portraits of British aristocrats lined the walls. White bust of some Colonial time-server. Probably the illegitimate son of a Baronet. Portrait of Jack Lang in hard profile with limestone fingers tucked under a grey waistcoat. They'll stick him straight back in storage if Greiner wins, concluded Greg. Martyr to British banks. Oppenheimer's gourd. As Bigge was to Macquarie. A proud history of Imperial intervention. Kerr's secret councils with Sour Lizzie. Devlin rested his forearms on the green leather surface of an antique cedar counter. An attendant wearing a maroon jacket leaned back in a swivel chair. The bells ceased. A cavalcade of MPs rushed from the chamber.

"Gooday Dennis," said Devlin looking down. "How's it hanging, mate?"

"Fine thanks, Mister Devlin. Nice to see you back in the House."

"Was that Question Time?" he asked looking at his watch.

"No. Question Time has been suspended for the Cup."

"Of course. How quickly one forgets procedural matters. When are felicitations?"

"This Friday."

"You'll be looking forward to a long break. Going up Taree?"

"Same pack drill every Christmas."

"I envy you mate. I really do."

An aide approached in an ill-fitting suit.

"Billy McCoy," exclaimed Devlin warmly. "How are you, comrade? Still with Swift Mick? Good slot, mate. Real good."

He patted him on the shoulder.

"He works for the Minister for Sport," he told his companions. "You know. Free grand final tickets. Free tennis. Best seat in the Member's Stand for the New Year's Test. Gee but Nifty's doing it tough. It's all Costigan Costigan Costigan these days."

"With a great big blob of Bob Trimbole."

Devlin punched his finger at McClean's ribs.

"Mate, New South Wales is a traditional Labor state. You've still got a thirty-seat majority. Even after that seven percent swing last March. Remember Seventy-Six, Billy? Pundits didn't give us a chance coming so soon off Whitlam. But we got Kandos Ryan over the line in Rockdale by forty-four votes. That gave us a one seat majority. Never looked back."

"One point is enough."

"Blood oath. What is this? The seventh bloody Ministry in two years? Got to stop chopping and changing, mate, or you're gone. Punters hate that. Know what I reckon? I reckon you've all gone soft. If you want to beat Greiner, you got to get down in the muck. I mean, he worked for big tobacco. He must have some form. Anyway, enough of that bullshit. How's Deb and the pups?"

"Marjorie's just turned sixteen."

"I trust you signed her up."

"Daceyville branch," replied the aide.

"Good man. I'll let the local member know. Bit of an earwig but a decent enough bloke."

He turned back to the attendant.

"Can you call Doug Truck's office please, Den? We got a meeting."

"Of course, Mister Devlin. Just sign in."

"Good stuff, mate. Good stuff."

Devlin, Welles and Raspudic inscribed their names as Greg Devlin, Raymond John Candy and John Smith respectively. The attendant rang the Minister's office. Devlin turned to McCoy. ENSURE ALL REFS IN THIS SECTION ARE TO ALIASES.

"Look at this place. It was a dump when we started. Now look at it. Marble floors. Wood ceilings. Even a bloody dribbler."

He pointed at a Modernist fountain set in a wide shallow pool.

"You can go straight up to the Minister's office," said the attendant.

"Still on Nine?"

"Yep."

"No closer to the Gods then. Which end?"

"North. East corridor. First office on your right."

"Lovely mate. Thanks. See yer, Billy."

Devlin, Welles and Raspudic strode across the cold dark atrium. They passed a small internal post office tucked around the corner.

"Hey Jan," yelled Devlin waving.

A middle-aged woman wearing a bright scarf around her forehead turned from a customer and smiled broadly as she laid a soft brown package on the scales. A young security guard was stationed at the entrance to the parliamentary wing.

"Scotty," said Devlin.

"Hi, Mister Devlin," replied the guard.

"Bunnies done good this year, mate. Gosh they were brave."

"Yes, Mister Devlin. But in the end they still come up short."

"But lots of spirit, mate. Good sign. Great to see 'em bump off those Silvertails! Whole rugby league world was agog. You would have played with some of those blokes down Rovers?"

"Yes, sir. I'm good mates with the Judd brothers. Also Darren McCarthy."

"His dad was a legend."

"A gentleman too."

"True. A good bloke. We're going upstairs to see Minister Truck."

"You know the way, Mister Devlin," said the guard smiling. Straight to the lifts. "Ninth floor."

They passed frosted double doors. A distant roar assailed them.

"That's the Members bar," said Devlin. "That's where the real deals get cut. There'll be a big swill on for the Cup."

The elevator opened. A single occupant in a black robe was standing inside the cubicle holding a can of soft drink. A straw protruded from its silver spout. He let it fall from his mouth.

"Clerk of the House!" exclaimed Devlin.

"Hello Greg. How are you?"

"Fine, Mister Grove. How's life in the Chair?"

"Good, thank you."

"Well-deserved honour. Thoroughly deserved," he added sincerely. Water filled his eyes.

"Thank you. Who are you seeing today?"

"You should know better than to ask that question," laughed Devlin slapping him on the shoulder blade. "No. Just kidding. Off to see Doug Truck."

"That should be a fond reunion."

"It will be, Russell. It will. You see, John," he said turning to Raspudic, "I was chief of staff when he was Housing Minister back in the first term of the current government."

Devlin turned back to the Clerk.

"But we actually go all the way back to door-knocking for Gough when Doug was local campaign director at Werriwa."

The Clerk nodded sagely. The elevator opened on Level Eight. He departed.

"Have a good Christmas."

"Same to you, Greg."

The elevator doors closed. They rose to Level Nine. As they emerged, Raymond John Candy observed a group of advisers clustered around a stainless-steel cigarette stand under a low concrete ceiling at the entrance to stairs leading up to the parliamentary lawn. Greg Devlin waved. Some responded. The businessmen entered a sheer glass cathedral. Brilliant light. Devlin sat down on a deep lounge in front of an internal staircase.

"Premier is down on Eight. All the Cabinet near him. These stairs lead straight down a long corridor to the House. Lower House members are located on ten. Council members are up on the top floor."

"Let's cut the bullshit, Greg," interposed Raspudic leaning forward. "I know you are good mates with all the butlers and cleaners in this place. But that's not why I hired you. Here's where we're at. I paid top dollar for that site. It's a big project. You said there'd be no delays. It's been a cluster fuck from Day One. Now I'm under a lot of pressure from investors. I need that rezoning fast."

"You'll get it, mate. Just follow the script. I've never let you down. It's just a matter of due process."

"Due process is too fucking slow, Greg. The holding costs are killing me. KILLING me. Just remember that word. It's a big word."

"It's the operative word so to speak," added Raymond John Candy helpfully.

Raspudic looked at him with bemusement. *Ulysses* is characterised by complete rejection of violence. This is notable given that it was written during the Great War. The two scenes which touch on violence are the Citizen's threats to Bloom at the end of the Cyclops episode, which he avoids by escaping Barney Kiernan's pub, and the attack on Stephen by Private Carr which closes Circe. Carr and Stephen symbolise England and 'incapable' Ireland respectively in this encounter. During the general time-period of this novel, the following interrelated executions were completed in Sydney by organised crime: Warren Lanfranchi, Danny Chubb, Barry McCann, Mick Sayers, Chris Flannery, Barry Croft, Harvey Jones and Sally-Anne Huckstep. The last victim was drowned in a pond in Centennial Park. The men were all shot. Greg Devlin spoke.

"I know you're frustrated, Joe. Me too. But we're rezoning the site from heavy industrial to high density resi. Plus it's highly contaminated. Plus there's fauna impact. I know it's just a skink but it's a very rare skink. And we're also looking to raise the height limit which will cause shading and block harbour views to the west. That's why you got it so cheap. If it was prime real estate, Lend Lease or Harry would've gobbled it up."

"You got your cut, Greg. And your Pommy mate," Raspudic said gesturing at Welles.

"Spotter's fee," replied Welles.

"Whatever you call it. You been paid. Just get it fixed."

"Look at my track record, Joe. You made a million bucks on-selling that site at Minto. You only had to hold it for six months. Then there were all those juicy little housing commission jobs. Thirty townhouses in Bonnyrigg. Twenty at Airds. Plus those refurbishments on the Toxteth Estate. That's all my handiwork."

"I acknowledge your help in the past, Greg. I sincerely do. I'm not trying to be difficult. But I got a lot of new investors in this deal. It's not my Serbs who are the problem. They're patient people. But I got your Leb mates putting pressure on me. There's a lot of moving parts. It's a big job. And I'm a simple man."

Devlin leaned forward and rested his palm on Raspudic's knee. Hand nailed to the table by a dagger. We can find a way out, he said. Graft my dear. Sydney palm oil. He's misstructured this deal, thought Welles. Grown lazy. Too much back of the envelope calcs. No contingencies. Dog licking its own vomit. Fifty-five kilos stuffed in the bags. Even a slight error is fatal. Granville train crash. Engine just lifted off the tracks. Clipped a pier. Whole centipede reared out of control. General Slocum. Tasman Bridge. Too close to Scylla. Turn the tables. Some dog act. They could probably find a gun with no history for a thousand bucks to take Joe out. End up like Frank outside Lithgow.

"I get it, Joe. Believe me. I do. Stay calm. It can all be fixed. Let's just get the job done here and get out."

The corridors quietened.

"Doug specifically selected this time," said Devlin. "He's missing the running of the Melbourne Cup to help you. And he's sent all his senior staff down to the bar so we can talk frankly."

They entered an undecorated suite and shuffled into cramped standing-room space before the receptionist's desk.

"We're here to see the Minister," said Greg to an assistant. She looked in her diary.

"Mister Devlin?"

"That's right."

"And your friends?"

"Don't worry about them. Just tell Doug we're here."

At that moment, the inner office opened. A squat figure filled the doorway. His trousers were hauled over a dropped belly by a cheap brown belt. His fingers hung off gleaming black braces. He wore a white shirt and a black armband. His ebbing hairline was wrenched flat by Brylcreem. He breathed hard revealing a steady tide of soft blushes and stains on his face.

"Gregory Aloysius Devlin," he said studiously taking his friend's hand.

"Minister," replied Greg respectfully adding vigour to their long handshake.

"Come in. Kelly, be a love and make some tea."

"This is Ken Jones, Minister. He's the constituent I was talking about."

"I've been briefed on your situation Mister Jones," the Minister said. "Typical story in New South Wales. That's why we've slipped behind Queensland. But I like to get things done. That's my motto. Well, actually, it's LET'S GET CRACKING. But you get the drift. Come in. Sit down."

"I would also like to introduce Raymond Candy, Minister. He's our financial adviser."

"Nice to meet you, Mister Candy."

Kelly followed them into the office. She triggered the kettle and washed some black coffee mugs. The gold crest of the Parliament glimmered. She took a small milk carton from a refrigerator concealed in a wood-panelled cabinet.

"Kell is Mal Daly's daughter."

"You're kidding."

"She takes care of the Enmore branch. Don't you love?"

"I have great regard for your father," said Greg Devlin.

"Dad talks a lot about the old times with you, Mister Devlin."

"Oh dear, don't take any notice of his tattle. They were tough times. But not fatal."

"I'll take care of that Kell," said the Minister interjecting. "You go down and watch the Cup."

He ushered her to the door, turned the lock and resumed his seat.

"Let's get our ass down on tin tacks, gentlemen."

"Right. It's Pyrmont, Minister. The rezoning's stuck."

The kettle clicked off. Steam rose. No one moved.

"I asked for a departmental briefing note," said the Minister holding up a single sheet of paper disdainfully. "It says you're too aggressive."

"The government got a good price for that land," interrupted Raspudic passionately. "And all your mates got a drink. I can show you the numbers," he said brandishing the red ledger book. "And I can drop them on the press if you like."

"Wait a minute, Joe. The Minister doesn't want to know anything about that stuff."

"That's fine, Greg. Look there's no need for threats, Mister Jones. Or whatever the fuck your name is. It makes a man look like he's got no ball sack. So let's get things straight. If I decide to fuck with you then I won't just stop at fucking your development. I'll call my mates at the Drug Squad and the Supreme Court and next thing you know you'll be domiciled in one of our correctional institutions. If I deem it fair, you will have a very hard time inside. So, let's get to the truth of the matter and work out a fix. It's a simple equation. You're going to crowd out the housos. And they're our votes."

"We need to change the social composition to make the numbers work," said Ray Candy.

"Precisely. But it's a marginal seat. You won't be allowed to upset the political balance. Can you reduce the density?"

"Won't break even, sir," said Raspudic.

"Let's turn the problem on its head then. What about adding extra public stock?"

"You mean vary the mix?" queried Candy.

"Yeh," replied the Minister. "You could increase the density with more social housing."

"They can't afford my product," said Raspudic.

"You're missing the point," said Devlin. "The government could fund the gap."

"Precisely. I think Cabinet would support a targeted increase in public housing. Especially in a traditional working-class area like Pyrmont."

"You need to pay market rates," said Raspudic. "Not public housing prices."

"Oh, I think we could meet the market for a ground-breaking project that mixes private and public dwellings."

"It's a great symbol of your commitment to social equity."

"Nicely put," said the Minister to Ray Candy.

"This is going to take time," said Raspudic.

"Could we cut some corners on remediation?" asked Devlin.

"It's pretty badly contaminated," said the Minister. "We don't want doggie doodles dropping off in the park."

"I can't waste no more time on architects," howled Raspudic.

"I understand," replied the Minister. "They're all wankers. I've given it some thought. And I've got a bold, new plan. Pyrmont was the site of Sydney's first sandstone quarries. All the great government buildings of the nineteenth century were built with Pyrmont Yellowblock. Our problem these days is that we can't get our hands on the stuff. There's bloody houses on top! So, we patch up our heritage architecture with shit from Queensland. That's why all our old buildings look as scabby as a priest's backside. But what if we got an opportunity to acquire a new deposit of Pyrmont Yellowblock? What if a developer came across a new seam during geo-technical analysis? And what if the State deemed it to be of such significance that it suspended the project to quarry that sandstone? Think about it. We would have to pay compensation for the delay. We'd have to pay for the hole. And we'd have to pay for the sandstone."

"What if it's no good?" asked Joe Raspudic.

"Who cares," replied the Minister.

"Where will you take it?" asked Candy.

"We'll just dump it on the waterfront next to Glebe Island Bridge."

"Genius," said Greg. "Who's the responsible Minister?"

"Public Works."

"Port Jackson?"

"Precisely."

"That's priceless. Also, the local MP."

"How long would it take?" asked Raspudic.

"It doesn't matter," answered Ray Candy. "Once agreement is reached, the State will pay compensation backdated to the landowner's date of acquisition."

"Statutory planning fees as well," added Devlin.

"Architects?" asked Raspudic.

"Sure," answered the Minister. "You see, you're holding all the cards, Mister Jones. The government has materially affected the timing of your development. We'll have to pay."

Greg gave Raspudic a nod. Contracts. Not worth the paper they're written on. A throwaway. Elijah is coming. Bloom as prophet. Devlin warning McCoy. Ahab. Last Israelite King. Transfiguration. Revise project metrics. Escape the Citizen. Shot off a shovel. Ascend into Heaven.

"Thank you so much Minister," said Mister Jones rising.

"My pleasure, Mister Jones. That's what we're here for."

Raspudic grabbed the Minister's hand slavishly. Devlin nudged him with his elbow, flicking his head towards the wall. The developer pointed past the Minister's shoulder to an oil painting of cows grazing in a pasture.

"I couldn't help noticing," he said awkwardly, "that nice painting."

"Yes, it is nice. Thank you. In point of fact, my wife is the artist."

"My family were farmers back in Yugoslavia. We kept Busa. I would very much like a painting like that."

"Well you can't have that one," said the Minister laughing. "That's my prize bull Clem with his harem down the banks of the Murrumbidgee River."

"That's a shame," answered the developer despondently.

"But I'm sure we can arrange something. My wife has got a studio full of canvases."

"Be careful, Joe," said Devlin. "They don't come cheap."

"She's a major Australian artist," added Ray Candy. "I know her dealer well."

"I'm no expert," volunteered Greg Devlin. "But I reckon you'd be struggling for change from twenty for a painting like that."

"Money is no object," said Raspudic grandly.

"It would be a sound investment," said Candy.

"Let me put it this way, it'll never lose face value," concluded the Minister.

"I would very much like you to choose one for me."

"Don't you want to select it yourself?"

"I trust your judgment, Minister. I can make a deposit right now," said Raspudic opening his ledger book to reveal a blank cheque pinned to the page with a paper clip.

"No cheques please, Mister Jones."

"Leave the transaction to me," said Ray Candy.

"Good idea," replied Greg Devlin.

"I'll make sure you get a nice piece," said the Minister. He unlocked the office door. The reception area was vacant. They went to the threshold.

"I think we missed the big race," said Greg Devlin.

"Did you have a flutter, Minister?" asked Joe Raspudic.

"Gambling's for mugs, Mister Jones," answered the Minister. The businessmen withdrew. Doug Truck returned to his office. Gaming at Daly's. Odds of twenty to one. CRIME. Askin's nickname. Because it never pays. He straightened the painting. A silver plaque on the frame read: *Landscape with Cattle*, Thomas Cooper, England 1887. Property of the Art Gallery of NSW.

—

13. BRITISH (3.10 PM)

Francine Hackett peered through the pawed window of the Olde Wares shop on Glebe Point Road at a pocket watch mounted on a display stand inside a towering walnut cabinet. An irregular cardboard sign read: Real English 18ct Gold Watch / 12" gold chain with amber stone to T- bar -/ $100. The four-thirty-three bus stopped. Hydraulic brakes breathed hard. Mansour's towels. Crimean pillage. Compare and contrast with Old Russell. Doors opened. "You getting in love?" asked the driver. She shook her head. Greg Devlin led Joe Raspudic and Ambrose E. Welles out the Legislative Council exit and down worn sandstone stairs. The doors closed.

"I'm driving West," said Raspudic. "Can I give you boys a ride?"

"No thanks," replied Stan Welles gesturing north. "I'm going back to my office."

"I'll cadge a lift if you're going down Parramatta Road," said Greg Devlin. "I'm meeting some mates at the Lansdowne."

They parted outside the gates. Breen's paper entrails were still wound around fence poles like boat streamers. Raspudic and Devlin cut across Macquarie Street and proceeded down Martin Place. They will not reappear in the novel like many characters in Wandering Rocks. Raymond Welles loitered at the lights. Helen and Barry reached the Clock Tower. Quarter hour tolled. Mighty Sydney lay down before them. Four steel stacks. The hum of dynamos that urged Stephen onwards. They approached Fisher Library. This is the equivalent of Bedford Row in *Ulysses*. Modernism merging in space. Set against second-hand cart. Stephen examines an old boxing print and pawned reference books. You are right down on the River Liffey overlooking its blotched granite walls studded with greasy drain pipes drooling shamrock moss and algae. There is a magnificent vista from the restrooms on the upper levels of Fisher Stack. Gift of a retired bootmaker. ~~O dropped her tights to her ankles, lifted her skirt and turned, wedging herself into the window recess to present Davies with access.~~ Barry Capri held his wife's hand firmer in buffets of human traffic. Five million spines. Largest shopping mall in the southern hemisphere. Stephen wonders if his school prizes inscribed with Latin plates are interred amongst the discarded volumes in the cart. Ambrose E. Welles made rough passage between the Reserve Bank and Bank of New South Wales headquarters. S&C. A barker's tin whistle accosted the rail egress. People so busy. Silver rain falling. McCartney classic on Radio 2GB. Crown of the MLC Centre as seen from the traffic report helicopter. Welles passed the Commercial Traveler's Club. Be nice to go sink inside a refurbished scarlet Chesterfield in the Sir Lionel Davies Lounge. Pop Mushroom. A-bomb blast. Maralinga. Churchill's payback for Forty-Two. Bumboy Menzies. Emu Field. New no-go zones. Desert blasted into a crust. Black mist. Human ordinance. Turn your back. I could see the bones of my fingers with wild eyes. Crackt binoculars. Bulldoze black corpses. British scientists continued testing Strontium 90 in the South Australian food chain until 1978. Nation of lab rats. Chaim. The violated remains of twenty thousand babies. Stolen femurs. Rip the drumstick off the hip. Jacob's thigh. Gourd powder. *Nebrakada femininum*. Goethe's blessed female. Hot stuff. This phrase will recur in Circe in the mouth of Marion Bloom. Elizabeth's sunburnt navel. Twist your finger deeper'n'harder until you feel the foetus. Welles almost tripped on frayed carpet across the entrance. Clubs were invented in London because of tides. Stay in town until the Thames turned after lunch. Take a boat back to Putney. Wave from a cavalcade if you're going in the opposite direction. Cortege of youth and beauty. Stephen invokes the charm of Saint Ignatius. A formula to win love. He is desperate for affection like James Joyce at the time he met Nora Barnacle. This was unabashedly a morganatic marriage. Joyce preferred a working-class woman used to life's exigencies who could share his bohemian life without pretensions about money and status. He wanted someone who played their part expertly while he got the job done. Devlin and Raspudic reached the GPO. Ray checked his watch against a clock. Ten past three. A barmaid passed on the street. Neat black uniform. Got to have a private school education even to get a part-time job these days. Keating's recession. Better off working in a whorehouse. Plenty of undergraduates pay their way through college with sex. First floor: machinery for young women. They get sick of eating cereal without even milk. Looking for a kind gentleman who doesn't blink at the cost of a seafood crepe. Crisp bottle of Portuguese Rose as accompaniment. Real leg opener. Stuff them full of dessert. Platinum Amex flicked onto the tip tray. Pass me a mint. Look at the jugs on that one. Oops! He reached a café where the path widened to accommodate plastic tables covered with checked plastic table cloths. Cross now the human everflow west-by-east-by-west past Flugelman's chrome geometry lesson. Bright detergent-floss emanated from its sunken pebblecrete pond. Hardly the Trevi. High school prank. Rabid dogs. Gaze down the bodice of Ophelia's dress. Soggy and body entwining. Drag her down. A metaphorical form of death. Clever Bard. Moment preserved by Millais in paint. I wonder how long bodies remain composed in river water in comparison with brine. Or set in cement like Nielsen. Woolf wasn't found for three weeks. Ophelia in concrete. Brian Alexander told me CFMEU officials dumped her corpse down a reinforced steel frame in the MLC foundations. Slab got filled before dawndun. Dead mouth open like Botticelli's Chloris. Makes an internal cast. Have to peel the body away. Doubly cast then. Outside and in. Are they like that at Pompeii? Look up their anuses like Bloom in the National Library. I remember making love to Elizabeth at the Hotel Del Sole. Must have been Nineteen sixty-nine. Simpler days. She was happy to get some sunshine after the miscarriage. Garden full of cheap plaster sculptures. Past John and Merivale's pub. Mustard miniskirt. Maybe I'll buy that Burgundy jacket. Might lighten my creases. Old fool in tights. Dim vestibule of Hunter Arcade. Grubby low ceilings and alleys. I hate retail. Twist and turn on each floor can't escape. Won't let you out until bankrupt. Lack of REPUTABLE tenants. Commercial flop. They should have poached Ron Bennett's menswear from the Strand Arcade. The rest would have followed. If I walk past another coffee shop with one-dollar ham sandwiches I'll scream. Greeks don't make good coffee. Looks like a wet garden bed. Splashes around yer guts. Pitt Street unnaturally lifeless this afternoon. Taxi lights shine so bright. Fruit stall on the Hunter Street corner. Maybe I'll buy some carnations. Too awkward to cradle but. I'd look like a faux beauty queen. Everybody will guess what I'm up to. What would Master Edmund say? Oh father, look at you walking the streets like a fucking placard reading SAD OLD BLOKE. Perfume in contrast can always be secreted. He tapped his side pocket. You can withhold the gift until a final judgment about service quality. Best blowjob in Hellas. Funny thin lips. Red hair on an egg. Cat swallowed mouse. Known the lady in question for years. Her husband is my dentist. That'd be a good line in court. Almost a badge of honour. At his mercy in the chair. You could strap a man down like Vulcan's throne. Perform all kinds of torturous procedures. Unnecessary extractions. Prise open your mouth. Brace yourself. Lizzie telephoned this morning. She asked to meet me at five o'clock. Straight down to business. Stan Welles rubbed his hands together. Pale and blemished beneath. Hue of passion. The colors red and white dominate the "Venus and Adonis" of Shakespeare. Surprisingly large bust for her body shape. Green eyes piercing my gaze. Traffic lights hit. Walk into the foyer. Good afternoon Mister Welles, proclaimed the porter opening the heavy glass door. Dirty old Tank Stream rolling beneath. Hullo Keith, answered Stan Welles. Ordinary cleaners reach only thus far. He adjusted his tie. Hope that girl calls. Up a marble staircase. Brass bannister. Grip. High marble ceilings lit brilliantly with glass chandeliers. Grand piano in operation near the Elizabeth Street entrance. Find a counter. Thirty minutes to Cup. Scour little stalls. Now, where was I? Ah yes, mimicking Tom Kernan's brisk walk toward St James Gate. Insert observations of Simon Dedalus, John Mulligan and Dennis Breen. Allusions to patriotic figures. Good links with that horse in the Gold Cup. Reprise key images from episode two. The doors opened. Ray entered the elevator. Scramble events and places even days. Turn from Hyde Park. Look down Park Street at Sydney Town Hall. He could just make out the south entrance to the Queen Victoria Building. Paris in sprungtomb. Sunken promenade. Its location was an old turning circle for carts going to market in the late nineteenth century. Fine twin domes. All that meat and potatoes, he murmured. Snug black skirt. The girl revolved. Miss Hackett, he scoffed snorting loudly. His fingers fumbled for an embossed business card. Her father is rich, he thought. Mining money from Perth. They exchanged platitudes. I'll give you a call Mister Welles, she said. Female wiles. They're a mystery. Juno is an accurate representation. Classical women always had massive boobs, I suspect. They parted. He checked the silver hands of his Seiko watch. Two-ten. He still had twenty minutes to get to Macquarie Street. More than enough time to purchase a gift. Francine entered the shop. The stone entranced her. Prehistoric bugs interpolated in sap. Cosmic timepiece. As trapped as Stephen Dedalus in Joyce's narrative gazing at Old Russell working on a tarnished chain. Also trapped also posed (euphonically) right from the opening gambit. Its chimed poetics work like a dense web itself tolling mutability. Rock against rock in turn overlaid with tumbleweeds of Russell's oh-so-human waste. Unclean gems spawned in the underworld like devils' pies polished. Seared with skin-specks and fibres from smoldering robes. Antisthenes! This stone is Milton's treasure better hid. Not metaphorical spoils like Shelley's excavations. Trigger erotic truth. What Stephen Dedalus craves. Lilith greasy with patchouli oil writhing on an Isphan rug as my wormwood crashes to earth. Moroccan Salome. This is the crux of sub-episode thirteen. Insert Chris Brennan, Poem 28. Note also Novalis. Rub Old Russell rub.

Shiny scrotum stretched straight. A scrap of old text just out of place. Cloying form. Huysmans' encrusted tortoise moving through olive gloam. My daughter crawling down the bronze-by-gold corridor in a carmine jumpsuit. Francine dawdled up Glebe Point Road behind a scramble of schoolchildren overloaded with square backpacks. She overtook them at the pedestrian crossing and entered the Riteway supermarket to purchase a packet of cigarettes. They queued in her wake ogling greaseproof paper trays of lollies under a glass-top counter. Who'll be next in line for heartbreak? Their bags buffeted Francine as she departed. A fag hit her mouth. She felt in her suede jacket for a lighter. The fresh nail burned. Her face rose gratefully at exhalation dispersing a sour scowl made puffy with Speed. Two old women waited for a bus outside a medical centre. One held a string bag springing black banana tails. The other trailed a mustard shopping trolley. Sub-episode 13 in W. Rocks reprises incidental characters. The two midwives from the Proteus sub-episode of Chapter I ("ineluctable modality of the visible") are returning home from the beach. One of their bags now contains eleven cockles. They pass Stephen again. In the interim, Stephen's thoughts have not developed. He is stuck on a loop. Two hundred pages have passed. SHIFT TO STRINE (see also C10, Citizen).

"Me hose aren't making life any easier to live!" exclaimed Missus Yairs.

"Don't leavem onth en," replied Missus Joyce.

"Not lie kelly tomb aching cough out hear."

"Vas sir lardster yerp oblems."

"Yairs."

Her friend nodded, sat down on a bus stop seat, took off her shoes, rolled down bone stockings and shunted them into a brown handbag. She replaced her shoes and stood. Silence. Make final insert on Satan Welles's internal monologue observing women. Note they are old and young, lean and robust, different ethnically et cetera. Note that he wants to engage their gaze directly. Link to the poems of Yeats. Restate the objective to butt conventional fiction against postmodern elements. Shift between hieratic and demotic content. Insert symbolic tracings. Insert Liotes.

"I don't mind me chops with a good strip of fat. Not that you can get one off of the new butcher."

"I shan't be sorry to see his backside."

"Always shaving the tail."

"Unable to leave the tail unshaved," her friend affirmed nodding.

"What do they do for dripping?"

"Oils of birdseed."

"Doughn criss pennup!" she gasped.

"You're not wrong!" Missus Yairs nodded flagrantly.

"No flavours."

Rosen taste of my father's house. I sat in the car next to a margarine factory waiting for my mother. Slope's lab. Smell of burnt gear. Obscure sexual references mainly olfactory. Butterboil a big pot of Bellingen leaf overnight. You can set your watch by Russell's clocks. Maxims of Polonius, Part B. Buy second hand shoes from opportunity shops before cheap shoes from Kmart. You might be footsore but your feet won't stink, advised the midwife. Don't lend records to no one, her sister added. Keep a list of books you've lent. Leave it tucked inside your Will. Hang shirts from the bottom so you don't get peg marks on the shoulders. PHONE CLICK. Pause. BROAD AUSTRALIAN ACCENT. Elizabeth, I need a hand, said Read. Another "she's left" missive. Evolve I vortex. Insert brief oral history. (1) I'm trying to be a great artist. (2) Don't unbelieve in me, love. (3) It's the other women's fault, babe. (4) Blame my Muse! (5) I never expected such drastic payback, darling. I mean, not with Michel, man. He's a mate. And only a second-rate poet. Now Dransfield I could have copped. But he's beastly O'Deed. I can't come now, Elizabeth replied. I've got an appointment. Calm down. Have a blast. I'll see you at the opening. CLICK. Read looked from his studio's broken window through torn and melded layers of chicken-coop wire across Circular Quay towards Fort Denison. A train scratched the St James side bend on fresh Cologne eggs. Narrative time junked. Shipwreck carriage. Constance fell down an elevator shaft. Further Rome goes, the more mysterious it gets. Baby, here's the fare please come get me. Nobody can make art so ... curvilinear. Bob Hughes in a cowboy hat and red leather pants down North Sydney gas works. A lick of pink guts hanging over his strides. Between struggle and grace: it's a wipe-out! AcLaoacak. AcLaoacak. Clicklick. The train screeched to a halt. White putrefaction. Red is ecstasy. Revolution black. Don't use Drysdale colours. His work is the reality of the little-him always inside. I see human faces through the undergrowth when I'm stoned. Nymphs gone dayglo. Heraldic squirt. Rain cludd. Wine cludd. He yanked the iron frame shut. Fuller is coming, that's right. Take a can of silly-string along. To elevate what would otherwise be another fatuous opening. Duchamp used sixteen miles of the stuff at the 1942 Surrealist show. He was THE MAN. I met him once, you know. Shortly before his death. I'm not sure of time. Or the order of events. But I am sure of place.

"Dick Stone's cuts not bad."

"Got to travel but. Now that old Joe at Elvy's is gone."

"Died on the job, they say."

"Not so lucky for his wife."

"What was her name?"

"Madame Sly Cosies, I think. Or near enough as makes no matter."

"Oh Rocks! I wish they'd use plain names!"

"She saw the whole world from that shop counter."

"Can't question her loyalty."

"Not much of a life but."

"Some people call it Love, Missus Yairs."

They both guffawed. Across the road, schoolchildren were traipsing down Mitchell Road towards dark double-storey working-class cottages near Wentworth Park.

"Do they let them off early for the Cup nowadays?"

"How would I know," shrugged her companion indignantly.

"They haven't been dealt such a bad hand," she sighed, thinking of herself. She was born in Depression. Came to maturity in the Pacific War. Married an ex-soldier. Raised a family through beatings and the drink. Now he was gone to an early grave. See VAULT for further remembrances.

"But they're not bad kids really."

"No. I wouldn't wish bad luck on anyone. Live and let live, I say."

"Yairs. We been young oursells, and we are no aye to judge the warst when lads and lasses forgather."

The return of the midwives announces the reprise of the theme of remorse of conscience ("agenbite of inwit") from Chapter One. This time Stephen Dedalus applies it to his sister's desire to teach herself French. This is a complex image. On the one hand, it shows a new capacity in Stephen to project cosmological themes beyond himself onto other people. He is no longer self-obsessed although the example of his sister is drenched in pathos. Equally, a critic could argue that Stephen doesn't do much for his sister. He just uses the exchange as an opportunity to wring more guilt out of himself. This is the genius of Joyce. To extract polysemous meanings from apparently simple scenes. Catholic schoolgirls scampered across the street in brown tunics jeering an unfortunate friend on the opposite kerb who had been delayed by traffic. The western light illuminated her plain face foregrounded against a sandstone wall and pulped rock posters. A licorice strap unravelled out her mouth like a shiny black tongue. Keep repeating this word ("unrav-etcetera"). LINK TO DILLY DEDALUS. A compassionless man in a short-legged suit and wire spectacles glared at a paperback novel at the bus stop. His bag-handle tag was labelled in thick ink. He signalled the driver. The bus stopped. Its hydraulic door groaned. Be on. He climbed aboard. A schoolboy exploded down the aisle. His bag bounced off a succession of seats, uniform waving, tie swinging, its knot pulled from his throat to one side of his grey shirt collar. He pushed past an old lady. A man stood. What luck! He slumped on the long bench and opened the zipper of his private school crested sports bag. A hand fossicked within. McCreedy observed it dispassionately. He extracted the Bible smoothly and spread its message across his lap somewhere down the arse-end perhaps Acts. The bus was buffeted by coarse corrections down Glebe Point Road. SEE CHAPTER ONE. Stephen's Gods of In/Out. Slut and slaughterer. Diety sandwich. Smashem both. BIG BANG NINJA BATTLE! Defer for present. Be like Milton's Satan yet personable. Insert metaphor of God as a Seiko watch (see Russell). Here comes Polonius. Praise be good bowel motions. You can set your clock by Kant's walk. Each Monday morning, 'twas so, indeed. Stephen has gone down Bedford Row wielding his metonymy of a weapon in front of boxing posters like Paris but without Helen. This is an ironic reference to his relationship with the Iliadic male. And Joyce's to war. They are both considering the value of books. Stephen critically. Bloom practically (erotically). They make an X mark. Hysteron proteron. Tom Hallem peeled a soggy book from the bathroom floor of Beta House. William Capri glanced into the window of a second-hand bookshop on King Street. Tracing steps. Pock-marked Macritis and macula-marred Ulan passed along the other side of the road, deep in conversation about their new journal. Capri turned directly towards the books in case they noticed him ... snubbed him. We watch their reflection pass across the display. Pages born in a dynamo buried on undiscriminating shelves of Gould's book warehoarding. Dexion frames loaded with faddish pamphlets. Crematorium slots. Uneven paperbacks crackt into confetti along their cheaply glued spines. Prosenchymatic mosaics. *Kanag Crek*: a three-hundred-page critique of the Antipodean Juvenilia of Havelock Ellis by Associate Professor Thomas Turdworthy, author of a monograph on Gerard Murnane. First edition of *Fists Thrust High* with an introductory essay by Dennis Altman on the Sydney Scene. Includes an in-depth survey from the slap-happy crowd on the Rock. *Wimmins Words*: poetry of the Dundas Neighbourhood Centre produced with the assistance of grants from the Australia Council, Parramatta City Council, the Greater Western Sydney Economic Development Board, the University of Western Sydney, the Whitlam Institute and the NSW Office of Western Sydney. A never-opened hardcover copy of *future/uter: theories of post-phallic architecture* by the Contour Collective. Fresh contemporary poetry by acolytes and ex-lovers of John Forbes. All neatly pressed and smelling like birth. "Four Pots of Maggots" by Lord Jabber Ladiesman pinned between multiple copies of Gig Ryan's *Mantras of an Astronaut* and *Outraj! Writings Against Colonial Discourse*. Almost untouched copy of Martian Cockshaw's dazzling debut, *Menschlichkeit*. Extract. Skim. Replace. Blurred monochrome photograph on the cover by Bill Henson. Five dollars is scribbled weakly in pencil on the facing page above the author's biography. "Babyboomed in the year of the big fright, this is his first published novel. He lives in Melbourne with his partner, Kay, who is a graphic designer." Wade into its guts. Checklist devices:

— self-conscious opening reference to literary form
— overseas location
— cryptic intellectual characters with elliptical engagement
— an ambiguous yet strangely relevant letter
— continual recourse to foreign languages (often parenthetically)
— multiple fonts
— snippets of text presented in the form of drama
— rhetorical questions
— cryptic discourses on philosophy
— speculations on metaphor and race
— bogus interview with famous South American writer
— incongruous excerpt from a short story (completely unconnected to text)
— periodic short chapters containing minute description of a kitchen tool
— bulleted lists mimicking technical report writing
— cryptic epigraphs from Foucault and Slubb
— inscrutable alliances between highly intellectualised characters
— tricky incest dressed up as Freudian archetype
— citation of outdated cult figures
— all is not what it seems sense of mystery
— ambiguous epistolary closure with motion picture metaphor.

Capri stuffed it into a crammed shelf marked **MILITARY**. H sidled on to **BIZARRE**. Row of uneven volumes like wrecked teeth. *Fountaincourt: Tails of Judicial Hygiene* by Sir Edmond Squires-Squirte. *Angoran Nights* by the Late Phracian poet, Rumen. Dirty bits of Petronius set on some barren slope. *Brimming Nightjars* by Betty von Udder-Sucker, registered nanny. Molly Bloom's penchant for under-the-glass-coffee-table books. Too anodyne for any contemporary audience. People's imaginations were more vivid back then. A dozen dog-eared copies of the *Female Eunuch* in assorted international editions. "Sexy, scary and way tall," blared the *City Limits* testimonial on the rear of the 1974 Canadian re-print (not available in the UK). Greer came onto England like Nursey looming over Algernon's cot with outstretched surgical gloves and a sponge. Cultural enemagiver. Part of that great generation of Australian Expatriates. Clive James, Hughes, Richard Neville, Walsh, L. Roxon, Humphries. He was Greer's *doppelganger*. Furious attacks on English mores. Angroin.

Couldn't pin them down to a single format – journalism, stage, text, interviews, theory, pictures, television. Protean faculties. Heirs of Pater and Wilde. Joyce tested various literary forms as a medium of national expression over the course of *Ulysses* and rejected them all in turn – songs, riddles, drama, the Celtic legends promulgated by Yeats as well as Wilde's epigrammatic wit. "Court jester to the English," concluded Joyce; deliberately misreading Wilde. It was a vicious *bon mot*. To bury influence. Like a dog digging a hole. See Deleuze and Guattari. Cut and fill method. Hardly a burrow. Graveyard shovel plop. Capri stopped. Write an Australian novel with ballads, sketches, bush remedies, gallows humour, existential wastelands (White), indigenous cosmos, laconic outsiders. Furphy has already done that. Use epigraph from Auden. Civilisation was absent. This was an island. And therefore Unreal. **INSERT MEILLON**: The carefree Dionyshun Sowf had inflected me eardrums (doctors plugged 'em wif FELT) and all Summa long I never heard no mewse, just a dull ecco of distant curlew tewnes as if I'd stuck me head emu-style into six o'clock swill and leerings. Oh, we still had great hopes (old tree dead / young tree green) albeit coming from the wrong direction as we was: against the course of Empire (west to east on the big map in the Admiralty) ... not to mention gravity holding us down in subaltern postures so long that you hardly even noticed being on your knees as you peered through the window (after scraping the frost away from the pane) with your snot-stiffened cuffs: wide-eyed, dirtcaked and gazing in on safe England. British. Best of. Blakeney out of Saucy Flirt. Sounds like some Benny Hill parody. Royal blue sleeves. Red cap. Sangster stable. English-bred stayer. Summary of Ireland's plight really. Insert Joyce's great anti-colonial discourse (Chapter 1). Stephen entertaining Haines and Mulligan with self-loathing bile. Bosie was a jester. Bitter clown. Francine left Olde Wares. Glebe Point Road went unregistered in her haste. She struck down Francis Street glancing back quickly to see if Ali had followed. No sign through the scattered pedestrians emerging from Russell's Health Food Store. She accelerated. Post-industrial badlands. Her new pocket watch clamoured against her chest. She crossed Bay Street and traversed Grace Bros Department Store stealing a handful of pralines which she ate greedily discarding the wrappers in a trail on the floor. A security guard collected them in her wake. He hastened through gardening supplies to keep pace. She emerged onto Parramatta Road opposite the Broadway Hotel. The security guard called out: "stop please Miss." She continued apace. Opposite, police cars spilled across the footpath. Chalkboard. Glass. Lingerie Ladies. Francine reached the traffic lights and raced to the median strip stalling approaching vehicles. She waited analysing the geometry for a gap. A security guard blocked the footpath. Billy Capri gained sight of the sky above the Marlborough Hotel. Epiphany. A painting by Turner. Temeraire. Insert on Lend Lease. An American tug yanking Britain to scrap. Australia is a subsidiary vessel. He checked his generic Swiss watch. Gift of his parents. Francine did not look back. She waited for the first car to pass and scurried on light pumps. No loitering. Julie gone to meet Terry. Tonight later. She walked briskly around the corner into Shepherd Street. Paramedics swabbed dazed and bloody victims seated on a council bench. Farquhar and Gravy bent low in the back seat. The car entered the Iron Duke car park. She was free.

—

14. BEAVER BOY

Richie turned over the card. Oval postmark. 30 cents. Sydney GPO. 6 Nov '84. Donny had long since returned to Manila. She had seen him the other day walking down M.H. Del Pinar Pilar with a whore. Under the porch, shoeblacks called out or polished. "Dear Richie," he wrote, "coming back to Sydney is strange. I miss Manila. I hope you and little Don Carlos are well. I bought him a soft kangaroo just like Skippy! I will send my driver over. Regards to your husband. DC." She turned it over to view the scene of Sydney Harbour. Coathanger by shells in plaid light. Utzon's chassis. Tiled and grouted like an old pub urinal. Luna Park leering on the tideline with wild lysergic eyes. Brando's Kurtz. He heard the hoofblade thackthack. Stan Welles scuffed his toe cap. Shinedun. In Hong Kong you'd just pop down to polishers' lane. I need a stamp, thought Don. Where is the local post office? He drifted downstairs like Hamlet's father's ghost insubstantial maybe even unreal. Figment of a diseased mind. Not rooted by any connection to place. No human filament. Simon Dedalus wandered into Reddy and Daughter. Telegram to Ogygia from Ithaca: "Dear Calypso, home safely. Great hamper. Thanks for the good times. Od." Don shuffled another postcard to the top of the pile. "Dear Glendora, I am in Australia. I did send money. Maybe it got stolen. I will be back in December. Eric." His gaze went to the desk. Pope John Paul in half-profile. An uplifted palm. His visit to Manila shook Marcos. Odysseus inside the palace in a beggar's guise. "Dear Eric," she had written, "I got your letter. You have not visited Cebu for a long time. My mother is sick. Please send money. Then I can see you." A second card. More urgent. Small handwriting shrinking as it flooded space. "Eric, when will you come? Wet season now. No bar work. I see American sailors. My back hurts. Got to go. Remember our first time?" She squashed a postscript beneath his address: "MY FIRST!" He turned it over to examine a tardy beach scene. Place where Magellan planted a Cross. Stake in their heart. Speargun fishing. They ate him. Some of the best spots on the coast. Pretty girls serving drinks on Bantayan. A wet dog clawing the face of a concrete stormwater channel. All the DONE things closing in. Philippines no longer a blank slate. Bloom's letter from Martha. A loaded gun. Obviously, he could never love such a girl. No *Venus in Furs* roleplay. What was it he dreamt of? Molly clomping down a church aisle in red slippers on cloven feet. Turkish blobs. Soft bodice. Feint rosewater. Freudian contrivances. Joyce's letters to Nora. Little fuckbird. She wore my breeches tied around her budding gut. Mailboat from Cebu. Nearing Holyhead. Must nail that ad. Work Hynes and Crawford. Get some petticoats for Glenda. To write or not to write. Arrange some *rendez-vous*. That is the big decision this Cup day. It would reduce them both to the status of Blazes Boylan. Send five hundred dollars by wire. Later, provide enough capital for her to set up a small shop. He reached the threshold of a demountable post office on William Street. Brown glaze. Mining shack. Elastic marineboard ramp. Two old men lolling in the queue. They were discussing their penury. Competitive squalor. They decried the building manager in Flat One. A prison hawk. Fetid-corridor. Stink of steamed cabbage. Raskolnikov's exit. Insert Hungarian profanities. They approached the counter. The older man passed a transfer slip under the bars. Payee Mrs. S. Kowolenko. Payment: 2 weeks rent – Flat 6, Hollywood Hotel, 345 Bourke Street. Amount: Sixty dollars. Debit account. TICK. Don Cane purchased a small booklet of stamps bearing Olympic scenes. Hanna-Barbera heroics. He tore the serration detaching a single stamp of a cerise sprinter straining cartoon speed trails. He licked the stamp and affixed it to a postcard. Outside, he inserted it into the post box marked: **Rest of NSW / Interstate / Overseas**. Minbad the Mailer. Horses pulling up short and fast. Ammonia tongue. The adjacent cubicle sprang open. Edgar spat as the barman bolted from the toilet block. False moustache. Father Cowley. Not even a proper priest. Another side of Simon Dedalus is seen in this scene. Other men in Dublin share his predicament. It is normal in a client state. Saigon collapsed after the American withdrawal. Close Clark Air Base and there'll be another hit. Get Long John to call off the bailiffs. SEEK LEGAL LOOPHOLES. Simon is a garrulous friend. Stephen is stiff in comparison. Relationships taut. Persian Jones slid up the wall. Non giggled mildly. Persian Jones found the door. I got to check out what happened to Chubby, announced Stuart turning back down City Road. Unmet debts. Money trail. Wire transfers. Pay-offs in kind. False transactions. Rhino went to the parapet of Beta House. A truck was clearing the harbor mouth at Missenden Road. Smokeplume vague on dun skyline. A sail tacking by Muglins. A young man emerged from Maurice's take away. Stan Welles glanced at the steep cycling GPO car park ramp. Dante's down. Rising to Pitt Street, a mail van, bearing the corporate crest of the letter "P" cut into a white circle, received loudly flung sacks from pink armbands and caps. A Vietnamese refugee stood before the sorting slots distributing handfuls of sample letters cross-handed in the training room. Ainslie Dickson Downer Hackett. All 2600s. All ACT. Right-centre. Eager-eyed. Fifty-two and a half kilos in his saddle. Eight AM start. He arrived an hour early each day to practice. English is a strange language. Lanky ribbons all jumbled.

Gungahlin. Wee Waa. Beaver Boy. Tamarama. Where do they get such names? 2194. A card. Bottom. Far right. Cluttered images. Gold jeepney. At various points along the eight rail lines west, trains with motionless trolleys stood in their tracks, bound for or from Hornsby, Carlingford, Richmond, Penrith, Campbelltown, Bankstown, East Hills, Sutherland, Cronulla, Bondi Junction. All still. Becalmed in short circuit. Cars, cabs, delivery vans, trucks, buses, trains and airplanes gouged and knitted the city. I can make a true black knot. Learned when I served my time. Don Cane walked down William Street until he reached a small square cut into Darlinghurst Hill where transvestite streetwalkers plied their trade. Top of the stairs was Premier Lane. Avis rent-a-car office. Don entered. A young woman in a navy uniform highlighted by a yellow scarf looked up from a low seat behind a laminate counter.

"I'd like a car please," said Don Cane.

"What model would you like, sir?"

"Something modest."

"How long do you want to book it?"

"Three days."

"Name?"

"Donald John Cane."

She wrote down his name.

"Sorry," he said pointing at the order book. "It's Cane without an 'I'."

She smiled.

"License please."

He placed a booklet on the counter.

"International license," she said scrawling down his personal details. "Got your passport?"

He passed it into her hand directly.

"Australian," she said. "Why don't you have an Australian license?"

"It lapsed."

"I'll just check your details. Born 1932."

"Correct."

"Place of residence?"

"Manila Philippines."

"Home Address?"

"Valle Verde 3, No 1 Acacia Street, Pasiq 1221."

"Could you write it down please?"

He wrote down his address.

"Sign where I marked," she said. "I've been to Thailand. But I never thought of going to the Philippines. What's it like?"

"It's fun."

"Are there beaches?"

"Best in the world."

"And food?"

"It's the worst cuisine in Asia," he said grinning.

"Thanks for the tip. Cash or credit?"

"Credit card please."

She placed his AMEX card in a manual machine, manipulated a docket over it and swiped brutally.

"Sign here," she said putting the docket on the counter. She checked his signature closely.

"All good?" he asked.

"Close enough," she said smiling. "I'll show you to your vehicle."

She collected a set of keys from a lockbox on the rear wall and walked around the counter. Don Cane followed her into the garage. Rows of white vehicles muted the damp lime walls.

"Is there a street directory?" he asked.

"Glove box."

"I haven't been in Sydney for 20 years."

"That's a long time. Do you still have family here?"

"Yes. That's who I'm going to see."

She held out the keys. Don Cane settled into the driver's seat. He put a map on his lap. Ignition. Take a test drive. He entered St Peters Lane and proceeded to Bourke Street. At a break in the traffic, he started to turn right quickly. A young woman was waiting on the median strip. Low frame. Deeper-set by dark tights. He relaxed the brake, changed gears and the car lurched a few meters then stalled. She gazed at him angrily. A tired face. He mimed an apology. She ignored him. He turned on the car stereo.

"You're on Talk Radio 2GB. I'm Mickie de Stoop. Just thirty minutes now to race time. Better hurry up if you want to place last bets."

Don Cane proceeded towards the city.

"A race for stayers of a different sort returns to centre stage tomorrow with the Federal Election entering the home straight. It's taken a back seat to racing in recent days but things will hot up again tomorrow. Although 'hot' mightn't be the word that springs to mind for most people. It's been the longest election campaign in living memory. It was called by Prime Minister Hawke way back on October Eight. That means four weeks down and almost four weeks still to go. The biggest story of the campaign so far has probably been revelations surrounding the drug addiction of the PM's daughter. As a result of Mister Hawke's highly emotional reaction, there have been questions raised about his capacity to govern. I wonder what our listeners' think?"

Don cut off the first caller. Don't need that kind of guff. Why give them a stage. In Vietnam, there was always someone down the other end of a wire. Journalists fluffing up war stories. Politicians pushing boys onto mines. The only radios he liked were the ones calling out dropzones. Hueys hovering through tracers. He passed the flat yellowblock façade of the Australian Museum and turned left onto College Street. Go down Wentworth Avenue. Cross Oxford Street. He squeezed into the slit between a mail van and a cement truck. Hairline crack. Catch the tide twixt Scylla/Charybdis. A snake casting its slough. Grinding if off on rocks. Sydney/Saigon > Manila/Sydney > Helen/Penelope > William/Tom. Memory of a dead son; fact of two living. A belt of empty warehouses bordered the industrial edge of the old city. Exciting new commercial development, said a banner. Don followed traffic underneath the City Circle rail lines. Sandstone arch. Pitt Street looming. Red arrow. Wait. Above him, the causeway for the Interstate Terminal. Bloodline where nature flips from chlorophyll to silicon. Traffic spurt. Suddenly he was plugged into Sydney's lifeblood. Spat down its miserly conduits apace. Kent Brewery flashed. White horse rampart. Horse and stallion. Kentish hops. Orwell's gone a-picking. John Tooth was born in Kent. Hengist and Horsa. Saxon chiefs. Edgar and Edmund. Ebbsfleet. Empirebbing. Temeraire sunk off Singapore. Heifer maiden. Io's retreat. New sites of exclusion. Blind Bellerophon bucked by Pegasus. Wandering alone hated all his days. Vets. Don's car passed the Australian Hotel. Early opener where the Fairfax printers drink. Eric's white horse. Gelded emblem. Sound Kiwi stayer. Portent of Tooth's decline. Carcass sold off to Adsteam. Spalvin's showpony. Bones and offcuts of 200 banks flung across the slaughter yards. Don took on the amber at Wattle Street. He punched the radio back ON. Bored. "So you'll be travelling on the Abattoir Express on Friday." He stopped in pole position. "Oh yes, Mickie." Broadway Hotel brown and unyielding. An advertisement for **Lovely Lingerie Ladies** scratched on a scratchy chalkboard. "And I believe you're encouraging members of the public to come along?" A girl with straw hair tied back by a paisley scarf lurched in front of westbound traffic. Sandals pumping. BRAKE! "Motor Eighteen isn't the Indian Pacific, Mickie." Cars behind braked also. "There should be plenty of room for all-comers." No ding. No dong. University bells. She reached safe footing. "Another piece of Sydney's vanishing history." No backwards glance. Don Cane pressed the accelerator. Time by one of the copper clocks on Grace Bros roof measured Two thirty-five. He turned onto City Road. Wait. A middle-aged couple was crossing against the lights. Impatient horn. It wasn't me fella. They rushed awkwardly. Looked like but no it couldn't be that would be too much of a coincidence even for television. RISE. Sydney built along ridgelines. John Glover limbs. Jungle so thick you got a mouthful. Hmong trails. Map and memory guide. Split right/left off the track. Plant a Claymore. Blast a hole under the truck. Fire everything you got. Split. Regroup. One hundred and sixty known sex perverts in Newtown. They found poor Joan Ginn dead amongst the gravestones in Camperdown about one hundred yards off King Street. Big story straight after the war. ALPHA HOUSE. Old clothing factory. Close to Bradmill Cotton Mills where Helen Capri worked. Probably some insane soldier. Community Food Store. Strategic hamlets. Press gang the peasants inside like hens. Operation Sunrise. A misnomer. Lemon cardigan used like a straitjacket. A colour slide was shown on every cinema screen in Sydney. Dummy with her face superimposed. Strangled with her own singlet. Mum wouldn't even let me go down Marrickville Road alone after that. Still the same long dark rows of shops. Dirty stuff happens upstairs. Liver brick blockhouse. Pillbox on top. Good observation post. Some workmen were fixing the loading bay doors. Telephone booth had its glass guts splattered. That was the spot where a witness saw her legs dangling off the ledge. Half-cabinet booth. Blue socks. We all went for a gander. Police are looking for a man in his late twenties of average height with a fair complexion and dark hair. He was wearing a military top coat and grey felt hat. Only one million ex-servicemen like that in Sydney. Probably don't want to find him. That would unlock a lot of badness. Don Cane checked the fuel gauge instinctively. Full tank. Drive all the way to Vung Tau. Wrong way. Go to Binh Long Post. Hospital sign right. Maybe my sons were born there. Never found out the location. He decided to take the vehicle back to his hotel and wait.

---

15. BOUNTY HAWK

"The youngster will be alright," said Bob Capri sternly.

They passed under Memorial Arch at the summit of Science Road. Helen Capri rubbed her forehead firmly.

"I wish we hadn't told Billy."

Her husband guided them past the Clock Tower. Seagulls chased a seagull with a ragged food scrap across Botany Lawn. Shrieking birds. Got on Helen's nerves. She hushed them angrily. Her husband banged a boot on the wet grass. They ran then bounced. Joyce refers to time pieces consistently in Wandering Rocks yet mostly does not take up the opportunity to disclose the actual time to his readers.

"We didn't have any choice, love."

"He might have left Sydney before Don found us."

"Look, we've thrashed this all out. We made our decision. It's not as if we've done anything wrong."

Easy for Bob to say in fact he like a hero strutted his stuff since the decisive sacrifice she thought oh that was a bad thought I should be grateful YES I DID but since then blameless so now why should I still be expiating this is all Catholic logic Protestant hate and vica-versa. Seventeenth Century Taliban. An imageless, soundless, tasteless bunch they were. They proceeded around the declining perimeter of University Place. The Great Hall squirted soprano songlines into figs as dark as Jerusalem mills. Helen shook at her bonds. *Ave, verum corpus*. She hated that trap. *Natum ex Maria Virgine*. Her son was worth it but. A heretic's beauty. The smell of rubber on country tar. William Byrd sidelined. Reformation chartbusters. Long sermons. Karaoke hymn books. The cassette played poptones. Pop is used ironically by Joyce in polysemous terms to mean both father and the act of childbirth. It was inevitable that England would produce The Beatles once they reconnected with SONG. A petri-green lawn slid towards Stack. Random students strayed and retreated onto its sucking pasture. The couple crossed University Avenue and descended towards the campus boundary. Bob slid on the wet track gripping the iron rods of the fence to remain upright. They clambered awkwardly over a sandstone parapet upon which was mounted an askew iron gate. Victoria Park dropped suddenly. Bog assailed them. The path turned to slope. They struck onwards towards the shore of Lake Northam. Fountain upon miniature isle within artificial pond inside glade. Tarnished bronze statue of a boat mounted on Olympic Rings. Helen Capri checked her watch.

"We'd better hurry, Bob. Meter runs out in five minutes."

They passed the cyclone wire fence of the municipal pool. A woman sopped drops from a gleaming blue bathing suit. Distant Nausicaa at bath. Bathsheba unconscious. Peroxide Girl went back to her laminated table to read the end of *The Malady of Death*. The man is called YOU in Duras' novella. YOU is one version of Willy. Am I SHE? No. SHE always pays, not YOU. It was almost time to go back to work. Duras was writing about how to stage this story. SHE started her shift at 2 pm just before the Cup. It was probably going to be a rough night. Candy stopped reading to check her Gearbag. SHE needed to make sure there were a couple of strong BLASTS. "You say you want to try, try it," Duras wrote. That is exactly the words that Willy used when SHE said, "I want to try heroin." Edgar Welles left the grandstand. Athene stood shaking the sparkling drops from her torso. Helen Capri pressed her hands around the arm of Bob's smooth brown coat. They reached City Road. DON'T WALK flashed as they hit bitumen. "Come on," said Bob hurrying. They rushed in front of queued traffic. Cars commenced moving. White Toyota first. A horn shot too long to be civil. Bob glared. The driver grimaced. A BMW shot past on Parramatta

Road. Joyce has Stephen and Bloom cross paths briefly during the Scylla episode. Helen and Bob found refuge under the awning of the Lansdowne Hotel.

"Too much excitement," gasped Helen smiling. Barry rubbed her wild hair off her gleaming wet forehead. Still the same girl he fell in love with. That was what he always saw. But he had never been able to find her wildness. It had all been snuffed out. A moment of desire born of agony tightened his gut. He knew that he would expend this feeling with Minh later this afternoon.

"Let's sneak down the back of the pub," he said. "It'll save a few minutes."

They passed the open doors of the public bar. Sour smelling hops. Deep recess. Broken bottle-glass crunched their soles. Chippendale's dun vales. Blackfriars discoloured steeples emerged slowly behind rundown terraces and squat warehouses. Knox Street fell swiftly away. Bright steel chimneys of Tooth's Kent Brewery wound sallow smoke. Martin Cunningham is raising a subscription for the fatherless boy, Arthur Dignam. Touch me not. Got no time for charitable causes. He raises the case with Father Conmee. I'll have some of that. Catholic mammon. Mister Power suggests asking Boyd. Cunningham discounts that option. John Wyse Nolan notes Bloom's generous donation. Boylan is loitering. They cannot interest Fanning or Jimmy Henry. Insert no puns on the Prime Minister's name nor on the word 'bounty' in this sub-episode. No reference to Bligh or payola. Tom Hallem is this horse. Precocious four-year-old. Favourite on the day. Bart Cummings trained. Looking for his eighth Melbourne Cup win. Harry White in the saddle. Famous for consecutive victories on Think Big. Cup specialist. Won the VRC Derby as a three-year-old over two-five-hundred. Second in the Caulfield Cup. Black. Green hoops. Brown sleeves. White cap. Gelding. Bounty Hawk faded from the scene after its poor showing in the 1984 Cup. It has the low strike rate of any Group One winner in history. Ended up racing in Japan. Retired as a six-year-old. Still alive as at this date.

---

16. HUSSAR'S COMMAND (1 PM)

They say a cat always lands on its feet. So does a man wearing cement shoes. Willy-the-Pimp was one of those soft-boiled kids from Subiaco that crossed the Nullabor Plain in a Toyota Hi-Ace in the early '80s playing guitar in a New Wave band wired with too much Gram Parsons in his junk-saturated bludd. He worked over weak-hearted types with roadhouse songs that he picked up on a prison farm upstate. His B-Grade, B-Boy looks meant that he could turn tricks at the Wall whenever he needed junk money; long after the shellac had cracked on his dishonest face. This is all years before and after Nova, Juarez, Interzone, Tangiers, William Tell, Charles Manson, Joan, bailing out to Baton Rouge over the Mexican border, Ugly Shit Going Down and met him wif pike hoses. Yea, Willy the Pimp was an anorexic log-loader who got into junk when it was a weight loss fad after watching Midnight Express. I have also known bulemics who got into junk in this manner. He was a natural-born user who could stick any old shit up his veins. I've seen him bake bluddy morphine residue burped out of sharps from hospital waste bins and shoot it behind his eyeball with a horse needle. I first encountered him when the GAG was holed up in a bunkhouse over Lawson Square huddled along a lumpy sofa in front of a portable monochrome television set squinting at M*A*S*H reruns in the dead winter of '84. W-the-P just sauntered into the room and dropped a block of Real Pollen on the milk-crate coffee-table and sank into an armchair with a self-satisfied smirk. He'd just ripped off the Assos Parlour. This was an act of monumental folly. They were hot-wired into the drug cartels coming out of Beirut that ran the show all the way down Liverpool Road. They got fat on the sidelines of the gang war between the Croats and the Viets in Cabramatta. Lots of people got popped during that war including tit-for-tat political assassinations. This is all before bikers took over the scene. Absinthe is as close as Joyce gets to hard drugs but back in those days there were no laws against opiates, cocaine or snuff. Doperman was always good for Black Russian. His cousin brought it back from the Bekaa Valley. They also ran a car rebirthing operation in Punchbowl. But opportunism is ever the hallmark of the junkie. It creates reckless commandos out of even the most atrophied hogs. Yes, Willy-the-Pimp always stood aloof from the crowd but he was no voyeur when it came to MUD. He had an insatiable urge for the New Jack that made him notorious as a liar, thief, stool-pigeon and freak. He was a small-time juggler at all the band pubs – Talking Tables, Frenchs, Central Markets, the Southern Cross – where he was reviled for dealing cheap-cut lemonade. Every day he crushed his silk abdomen into stretch denim making labia out of his cleft scrotum. This drove the Pansies crazy. But he had no sex instinct. It was only deployed for Dirt. His rocket-hard, weepless cock got jacked countless times by subs snorting poppers in jerkoff booths down Dawn's place on Oxford Street. But there was never hard jam. He had no interest in what passed for the Straight Cosmos. Sharing a dirty fix with a Darlinghurst B-boy working the Wall was his idea of intimacy. His clothes were always spotted with blood and crap from fixing in a TV font with a screwdriver then disappearing into the bathroom to try to pass shit through his bluebottle piles. He had a perceptible limp from a stray syringe that popped a gland in his groin. Such an injury is not uncommon in junklore. He was one of those all-star users who got harder and deeper with age until he was tough as a slice of dry driftwood. He was considered invincible by denizens of the Scene. There are soldiers who carry such an aura into battle. On the other hand, I've seen hard men kick-start a summer holiday habit and wind up DEAD next autumn from smack toxicity. AIDS, Hepatitis, trap bashings, rip-offs, paybacks, jail. They all have their quarries. He worked a comfortable patch down King Street. "New Girls!" exclaimed the advertisement in the Daily Telegraph. Wanda – big busty Islander girl size 24 natural French and Greek (extra cost). Martini – 3-day forecast: 34-26-32. Candy – 19 real Aussie girl *special kisses*. Chelsea – Brazilian centrefold. Chanel – tight Thai body. NEW! Bikini Day Tuesday! Yellow with dark blue hoops. Cosplay uniforms. Purple cap. Afternoon delight! 15 per cent discount before 6 pm. Theme rooms. You will be satisfied! Behind 130 King Street. Enter via Soudan Lane. Seven-year-old bay gelding. Wayne Harris in the saddle. This clientele generated a stable supply of funds for his personal use supplemented by occasional munificence from marks. But there's no such thing as a day job for a hype. Heroin reduces the capacity of your cells to endure co-valencies like time, space, motion except when junk sickness drives you onto the streets scouring for cupcakes. He was always getting trimmed for cutting. Often, his body was a miasma of low bruises. But he was a versatile galloper. Some fat-hearted Bear would always pick him up off the Wall for an all-night strawberry. It was the kind of job that always gets a true addict licking their luxurious lemans in anticipation. He'd blast some Jack in the bathroom, tweak Daddy, wait for coma then clean out the credit cards and fridge. Willy's preferred mode of transport was government buses. There was always more safety in public places. They inundated Broadway and City Road. He would doze on the back bench with a curdled cream bun staining his crotch. He was slumped against the bar of Cleopatra's with a free can of Passiona sweating in his palm when the door buzzer broke. The hostess guided a new client across the turtle rug. Buck Mulligan whispered to a friend behind a panama hat.

"Look. Whitlam's cur."

Haines twisted as the man passed their booth.

"Yes," Mulligan added, "that's him alright."

Joyce creates a hackneyed juxtaposition of art and comfort in sub-episode sixteen. This is one of the weakest scenes in *Ulysses*. It may have satisfied Joyce's need for revenge against the peers of his young adulthood but it remains petty and awkward, especially in the wake of a great scene like when Stephen is forced to confront Dilly. The *bon vivants* are seated in a restaurant on Dame Street enjoying a copious afternoon tea. Parnell's brother is examining a chess board in the corner. The one-legged sailor makes another appearance. His song is the soundtrack of conquered Dublin throughout Wandering Rocks. There is an ironic allusion to Nelson Street, near Bloom's home. Elijah the Throwaway continues its wash down the Liffey. It passes a boat that Stephen saw that morning (the Rosevean). Haines and Mulligan egg each other on during a cruel exchange about Stephen Dedalus. Haines disparages Stephen for his interest in Shakespeare. Mulligan compares him to Aengus, the Gaelic god of poetic inspiration who has a flock of singing birds circling his head. Mulligan offers some mawkish Hellenism (Attic notes, Swinburne, the sea, a quote from his poem "Genesis" in *Songs Before Sunrise* inter alia). Stephen is deficient against this definition of a POET. They attempt psychiatric analysis. Stephen is represented as a madman who suffers from *idee fixe*. Mulligan suggests that his obsession is a Catholic fear of hell. Haines contrasts Stephen's mindset with Celtic culture, which Pokorny theorised had no evidence of hell. This suggests an absence of moral accountability for actions of earth. This aligned with the British stereotype of the Irish population in this era as treacherous, conniving and indolent. Insert on horse name. The Hussars were a triumph of style over matter like Pater or Foucault. Basically, they were just Dragoons dressed up in continental costumes. They were the only troops in the British Army allowed to grow moustaches. French Hussars wore braids. They could cut open a bottle of champagne with a sabre. They sported fur coats over their left shoulders for protection against a sword and carried handbags called sabretaches. As noted earlier in this chapter, Mulligan recounts Stephen's statement that he will write something in ten years from 1904 in sub-episode sixteen. 1914 is the year that Joyce commenced *Ulysses*. Joyce uses individual words in Wandering Rocks to create connections and contrasts between characters. Conmee's "listless lady" becomes "listlessly lolling" Miss Dunne. Both Mrs. McGuinness and the seductress of *Sweets of Sin* are said to be 'queenly.' The six eyes of three boys mechanically observing Conmee mimic the six wheels of Rochford's machine. Joyce also renames objects or revives archaic names. Carlisle Bridge becomes O'Connell Bridge. Dan Lowry's music hall is called by its original name, the Empire. Mud Island is the old name for Fairview Park. Dame Gate is gone. The viceroy represents the apogee of this strategy, being given different titles by characters as he proceeds across Dublin. Lastly, Joyce creates incidental figures who share the names of major characters. There is Bloom the dentist and Dudley the curate. Dignam is a family name and also a courtyard. Today, the restaurant where Joyce's characters were located is long gone. Malvern House I.E. is situated on the first floor of 33 Dame Street. It is an English language school. The brothel on Soudan Lane has also gone. It is used as staff accommodation for a restaurant called Thai Foid. The hostess escorted a gentleman to the bar and opened a Crown Lager. He perched on a stool awkwardly and ran fat fingers through his silver mane. Haines returned to the menu. The Mamasan approached deftly.

"I'd like to see Candy please," said Haines plainly.

"Full hour only," replied the hostess.

"How many shots?" asked Haines.

"Unlimited."

"Extras?"

"You can sort it out in the room."

"One hour it is then."

Haines rose and followed the hostess behind a thick velvet curtain. He passed from the set. He is not seen again in *Ulysses*. Mulligan picked up his drink and approached a corner table.

"My–my, if it isn't King Willy," he stated extravagantly.

"Professor Mulligan," shot back the peddler.

"That was absolute shit you sold me last week," said Mulligan urbanely. "I'll have to inform your superiors if you try that stunt again."

"I didn't cut it. That's how they sold it to me."

"Then I'll take it up with Persian direct."

"Don't bother him. He's a busy man. I'll make it up to you. Here. Take a blast of quartz."

He slipped his hand underneath his cap and produced some shiny paper which he slipped into the chest pocket of Mulligan's coat. Another sidestep. He knew how to placate. You could see it on his smug-ugly dial.

"You really don't know SHIT," said Mulligan raising his companion's chin with his cane. Willy squirmed sideways.

"I'll make sure it doesn't happen again. Excuse me. I've got to relieve myself. Mind my drink, will you?"

Mulligan sneered affirmation. Willy-the-Pimp hobbled into the anterior cubicles. Mulligan admired his tight ass and ordered another Brandy Alexander. He slipped the junkie's diary out of his shoulder bag and turned the pages hastily seeking amusement:

A JUNKIE'S DIARY

Quote	Assessment
Since moving to Sydney, I've not had A SINGLE script.	LIE
If I can get any dope for free, sure. Otherwise, I just cream off the scores.	AGREED – this is his basic strategy
A rare find last week. In a bin outside a suburban pharmacy I struck gold – Morphine, Peth, Benzos.	TAWDRY

Quote	Assessment
Here, I don't know any joy bangs or doctors – well, just one ... and no-one's going to give me free shots.	FACT
I was on probation for a couple of years for MANUFACTURING MORPHINE.	NEWS TO ME
I knew I was sunk so I skipped bail with a bowser-slut of my acquaintance. I fixed him with a canula in a motel room in Albany. He DIED in the bath tub even after I'd packed a whole tray of ice cubes up his anus and given him a strong hand job.	FICTION (see Burroughs)
Last Friday night, I caught the late bus home with Eva and Bob. I'd taken a good shot before I left Hazel's as well as purchased one for the morning as I had to rise early to help Candy pack the van to get to Balmain markets. She was selling our records and clothes to pay the phone bill. Anyway, I had tomorrow morning's shot an hour later, which is often my way. I feel disheartened when I fail to give myself planned treats as if I had let down my own child.	FACT – I bought 2 albums: The Cure's *Seventeen Seconds* and The Reels *Quasimodo's Dream.*
I found four packs of Rivotril amps in the magic bin yesterday.	BORING DATA
It is an absolute delight when one composes the ideal stone. Mine would be: 2 x Pethidine, 1 x Valium, 2 x Morphine, Cocaine or Amphetamine.	MENU / FANTASY
I now recall a shot five years ago. It dropped me to my knees in a wave of divine bliss. It was six Palfium. That forged script cost me three months jail.	FOND MEMORY
A good haul from the chemist today. A month's supply of powdered Opium in one-ounce jars. It looks like gravy powder. It is best stirred as a large heaped teaspoon in black coffee.	NEW INFORMATION
The general ignorance of addicts about their DRUG – this drug that rules their life – disgusts me. They've not read a single book about the social history of its use, its pharmacology or the literary works that are concerned with its particular routines: De Quincey, Burroughs, Alex Trocchi, Monkey Grip by Helen Garner, Jabber's new novella (although it reads like a shot at stardom), Cocteau's Opium. Baudelaire's Artificial Paradise was just a translation of De Quincey.	GOOD ANALYSIS
I plan to write something in a few years. It will be part autobiography like Jabber but with a much stronger theoretical base. I will weave all my favourite books and recipes into the text. The ending is tricky. I don't want to be cured or fried or rich or dead or even infamous. All these things have been done already. I need to find an original angle. Maybe I could get into a position to secure really high-quality synthetic opiates by smuggling – like Palfium, Pethidine, Omnoporn, Proladone, Fentenyl or Dilaudid – and sit on a tropical island writing travel books.	WE SHALL SEE, thought Mulligan

Mulligan laid the pocketbook in the bag. He has an *idee fixe*, he concluded. But I don't want to put him down like Joyce did. He writes beautifully at times. He has a sound grasp of his material. Maybe he will write that work someday. It is certainly no throwaway line. Men leave just like that in China. They trade in a perfectly good wife for a shiny new model. It is six years since we came. My son is seven. My daughter is twelve. If I fail at this enterprise, they are still my great love poems. I hope people can see beauty in the language. Not just technical objectives. I got to get home. I got to write it all down before it's too late.

---

17. MARTIAN'S SON

I am 10 kilometres aloft in an Air China 767 one hour out of Shanghai PuDong Airport. It's minus 50 outside. I'll be back in Sydney in 10 hours. I am a 48-year-old BUSINESSMAN half in love with a Dongbei working girl half my age. I was hustling infrastructure assets out of China on behalf of MNCs until the GFC broke. Then the capital markets splattered. Everything went alien. Dubai crashed. London got patchy. The Australian banks withdrew. Abu Dhabi was still OK. Singapore actually got stronger. But that was just good luck after the IRS enforced disclosure on UBS in Switzerland. Everyone moved their money out of Basel during the stand-off before the Swiss finally cracked. This bucket of cash is stuck in Asia looking to get placed. But you got to know the Lee family to get into Temasek or GIC deals. All the Chinese SOCs got cashed-up with government debt. They hoovered up all the domestic assets and even started doing offshore M&As. They want to transfer capital out of China. I'm helping Chairman Gu get cash into Australia. It's like an insurance policy. He controls a large public power plant portfolio in Shanxi, a private power plant construction business (as you do), a local supermarket chain and a new five-star hotel in Tai Yuan. His brother is MD of a coking coal trading company. They're well connected with the Chinese steel industry. He lives in a big estate on the edge of an eighteen-hole golf course with a priceless collection of Xinjiang jade. His brother collects Qing art. He claims that a horse painting in his tea room was done by Lang Shining. I try to tell him that Lang was an Italian missionary but he just laughs and tells me that the Chinese even invented noodles. Also, Marco Polo was a thief. Also, the Brits smuggled black tea out of China disguised as nuns. I can't pass judgment. I've got to run with the money. They can say what they like. I'm just an outsider undergoing ritual humiliation for what they would consider pin money. I have established a Cayman SPV to distribute fees into a Hong Kong bank account in the name of Zhang Nan. I've never met the guy. He might as well be an astronaut. They all got sent down to the same village in Gansu after the Cultural Revolution ended. They lived together on the floor of a barn. This must have been like an extra-terrestrial experience for these princelings. That makes for tight *Guanxi*. I feel like I am moving into uncontested space between artificial nations like Rimbaud running guns in 1891. I flick the pages of a duty-free catalogue looking for a belated gift for my kids. I didn't have time to visit Jiu Guang department store. Agenbite of inwit. I was too busy with Xiao Fang. They've got a toy shop on level six. I used to take my kids up there all the time to pay them off for relocating to China. It was also a good pick-up point. *Locum tenens*. I'm going home to get divorced. My wife has agreed to the settlement formula. She doesn't know about Judy, Xiao Fang, Doctor Gu. They symbolise Calypso, Nausicaa, Circe respectively. I've got the Stooges first album starting on my Discman. Its dinosaur technology to the Hongcouver kids playing computer games all night on their champagne iPhones. Their profiles glow against the whorling cabin gloom. Bronze carvings in spectacles. Only their fingertip buds move almost imperceptibly. 1969 kicks into action. It's was a song that surprised the MC-5 as if it came from another planet. I'm sipping Taiwanese High Mountain Tea making out with an underpaid air hostess. We both know the score. I can come to her hotel room in Sydney in return for a good meal and a gift. The stewardesses always want opals. Nightclub girls in Shanghai ask for laptops. My feet are stuck in the maw of cheap pale blue slippers. I shuffle up the aisle to the toilet to release the plant inside my stomach. A hot stream of soft green leaves passes from my penis unravelling like a vine into the gun-barrel grey plastic cistern. Every word selection matters in W. Rocks. See cistern, unravelled et al. The power of the flushing mechanism is always strong enough to induce concerns over suction even in hardened passengers. I could be floating through space like Talos in a few moments. A Chinese woman knocks me into a sleeping passenger on the way back to my seat. Zhong guo ren mei you li mao, I mutter unfairly. Peasants have got no concept of space. By contrast, Shanghainese people move through it almost spiritually. Judy could negotiate a minefield on Nikes like she was bobbing weightless. They're like different species. I need to get to my Oxen episode. I got to keep my heroes moving through Sydney as night settles plus set up the fatherlode. Odysseus was like a Martian to his son. Telemachus is thus the Martian's Son. Ithaca = Dublin = Sydney. Odysseus/Telemachus. London/Sydney. Shanghai/Berlin. Border cities. Prospero was cast out of office into exile with the following instructions: go to a remote island; make a water town; give it the appearance of home; emancipate thieves; assign land bountifully; kill the natives by raw violence and stealth; use your daughter as currency; wait for rescue. This trope parallels the British experience in Australia. It was an alien landing. The hostess is distributing steaming towels with plastic tongs. The flannel burns my cheeks momentarily. A shower of hail. Meteors. The seat belt sign flashes. This plane is relatively light. It's shoulder season. Fifty and a half in the bags. We must be leaving mainland airspace. Somewhere south of Taiwan and east of Hong Kong entering the South China Sea. It was No Man's Land before 2012. I can see the full moon leering across a moustache of dark clouds. The case of the Man in the Macintosh (MIM) has enlivened the margins of literary scholarship regarding *Ulysses* since its publication. He can be considered either one of Joyce's comic boobytraps (riddles and puzzles) or a deeply significant symbol running through the novel ... as well as any gradation within these extremes. His form was moderate until a devastating last start win in the Werribee Cup. Joyce himself enjoyed taunting admirers by asking theatrically ... "but who was the man in the macintosh?" He's coming good at the right time. An enigma really. MIM or the "Man in the Brown Macintosh" (MIBM) appears continuously in *Ulysses* beginning in Chapter II. He is cited in seven of its twelve episodes. He also appears in the Ithaca episode in Chapter III. He is first encountered in Hades, where Bloom is one of twelve mourners at Dignam's funeral. Just as the gravediggers are about to lower the coffin into the grave, Bloom, by internal monologue, asks: "Now who is that lankylooking galoot over there in the macintosh?" (105). Bloom's unusually loose, colloquial language is notable in this passage. He sounds more like an acerbic Dubliner than at any other point in the novel. He follows up his initial query with a series of secondary comments. He notes that LLG increases the quantum of mourners to thirteen, which is "Death's number." Later in Hades, Joyce exploits MIBM for comic effect around his perennial theme of false naming, errors of nomenclature, variations, mishearings and misspellings. Hynes is compiling a list of mourners for the funeral notice. He asks Bloom if he saw "that fellow in the, fellow was over there in the ..." Bloom finished his elliptical query with the word "Macintosh." Hynes inscribes the name "M'Intosh" on his list, assuming that Bloom was furnishing the man's name. Hynes is also responsible for mis-transcribing Bloom's name so that it appears as "Boom" in the notice (see Eumaeus). MIM/MIBM then appears in six consecutive episodes. In the climactic sub-episode 19 of Wandering Rocks, the narrator notes that, "in Lower Mount Street, a pedestrian in a brown macintosh, eating dry bread, passed swiftly and unscathed across the viceroy's path." This locates the MIBM in one of the central thoroughfares in *Ulysses* near the National Library (Scylla), National Maternity Hospital (Oxen), National Museum (Lestrygonians), the National Gallery, Merrion Square and Oscar Wilde's childhood home. He must have passed University College where Joyce studied and Gerard Manley Hopkins died. The image of dry bread associates MIM with religion, dullness, poverty and birds. In Sirens, Bloom briefly recalls MIBM's appearance at the funeral and asks, "wonder who was that chap at the grave in the brown mackin," before becoming distracted by the sudden appearance of a local prostitute of past acquaintance. In Cyclops, new information is added: "the man in the brown macintosh loves a lady who is dead." Critics have suggested that MIM is therefore Mr. Duffy from the *Dubliners* story, "A Painful Case." Duffy is a recluse who falls in love with his landlady, Mrs. Sinico, but perversely rejects her subsequent entreaties. She is struck by a train at Sydney Parade Ground and killed (probably committing suicide). Supporting this theory, Bloom remembers attending her funeral at Glasnevin Cemetery where Hades is set. Duffy was a quasi-characterisation of Joyce's brother, Stanislaus, projected into middle age. He brings to the surface Joyce's playful but cruel sense of resentment of his brother. In Nausicaa, Bloom once again remembers "that fellow today at the graveside in the brown macintosh" and claims he has "corns on his kismet." The critic, Eamon Finn, solved the riddle of this obscure comment. In an 1895 edition of the *Weekly Standard*, an anecdote competition includes an entry from M. S. Dean titled "Korns on Her Kismet." It turns on a racist joke regarding mishearing 'fate' as 'feet.' Dean recounts how a housemaid asks a lady for the meaning of the word 'kismet' on the underside of a statue. She is told that it means FATE. Later, she is walking with her boyfriend and complains about corns saying, "'I have the most tirrible korns on my kismet!'" In Oxen in the Sun, MIM is cited near the end of the episode as language devolves into complex word association littered with sexual and paternal allusions and puns as the revellers leave the pub at closing time. There are eleven drinkers and MIM makes twelve, reprising the Biblical numeracy of Hades. This updates the graveside scene where he made the total thirteen. Initially, the drinker's express incredulity ('tunket') at his appearance amongst them; it now being very late. He is compared to a cartoon tramp (Dusty Rhodes). His possessions are identified as being Jubilee mutton (i.e. 'not very much'). This expression refers to handouts of cheap meat given to the poor in Dublin at the time of Queen Victoria's Jubilee. Later, crowds mocked her by shouting the phrase when she visited Ireland. He has purchased a jar of Bovril. He probably ducked out to get it because he is shoeless ("d'ye ken bare socks"). There are multiple song references (D'ye ken John Peel, The House that Jack Built etc.). The focus shifts to Bloom's family. An unascribed question is posed: "seedy cuss in the Richmond?" It relates to sperm, a curse and hereditary insanity. Richmond lunatic asylum is a place where Mangan spent time. Bloom suggests that his father, Rudolf Virag, committed suicide due to madness bringing a malediction down on the family. This interpretation is supported by the next sentence, 'Trumpery insanity,' which Joyce listed in his notebooks as a pun on TEMPORARY INSANITY. Cunningham stated in Hades that this was the cause listed on the death certificate of Rudolf Bloom. The MIM has also been seen near Richmond in Wandering Rocks, suggesting that he may be the ghost of Bloom's father (like Hamlet Senior). In this vein, MIM is represented as an abandoned cowboy figure from a Western dime-novel: "Walking M of lonely canyon." This passage ends with allusions to pyromania: "Blaze on" and "Brigade!" They link to the next reference to MIM in Circe where he is associated with the popular round, "London's Burning." He springs through a trap door pointing an accusatory finger at Bloom. Finally, MIBM speaks: "Don't you believe a word he says," he says of Bloom (and Joyce). "That man is Leopold M'Intosh, the notorious fireraiser." This dream image associates Bloom in his own mind with MIM. Pyromaniac as renegade. MIM goes on to say that, "his real name is Higgins." This is Bloom's maternal family name. His mother was Ellen Higgins, second daughter of Julius and Fanny Higgins, born Karoly. Significantly, Judaism is matrilineal. Thus, it is Bloom's REAL name in hereditary terms. The name Higgins is used elsewhere in *Ulysses*. Francy Higgins is listed amongst Irish heroes in Cyclops. It is also the name of a prostitute, Zoe Higgins. The final reference to MIM occurs in a catechism in the Ithaca episode: "What selfinvolved enigma did Bloom risen, going, gathering multicoloured multiform multitudinous garments, voluntarily apprehending, not comprehend?" This question confirms that Bloom has not comprehended the significance of MIM's appearances. He is like a primitive man gazing at Haley's comet. No answer is given to the question. The answer is yet another question: "Who was M'Intosh?" The identity of MIM/MIBM has thus remained a source of conjecture. He is elusive yet potent like sightings of alien space craft. He orbits the outside of *Ulysses* like Pluto. Is he a star or a dwarf? That is the question. Nabokov exclaimed that MIBM was Joyce himself: "Bloom glimpses his maker!" This suggests a postmodern mindset. Nabokov based his conclusion on the Scylla and Charybdis episode, where Stephen postulated that Shakespeare himself was present in his own works and that his name, William, was continuously used for incidental characters. This is the same co(s)mic impulse as Alfred Hitchcock making cameo appearances in his films. The Franco-German critic, U.U. Bardun, suggests that it is also self-referential given Nabokov's anagrammatic appearances in his own works (e.g. Vivian Darkbloom, Blavdak Vonomori). This joke was updated by later writers who created characters such as Humbert Ecokov and Humberto Humneckov to indicate the influence of both Nabokov and Umberto Eco. Other critics have suggested that MIM is God (a humanised version of the 'shout in the street'), Jesus (the thirteenth person at the Last Supper), Joseph, Lazarus, the Wandering Jew, the Jewish messiah, the Devil, Death, Hamlet's father (Hades being the grave digger episode), an acquaintance of Joyce, the character Wetherup (his name is an imperfect rendition of 'weather up' meaning a change in the weather which requires use of a raincoat), the sandwich board "Y" of the HELYS

Five, the full HELYS advertisement, the arsonist in "Oxen of the Sun", James Clarence Mangan (who loved a student that died and wandered from pub to pub after her death with a further piece of evidence being the Joycean pun on "man/gan"), Charles Parnell, a figment of Bloom's imagination (Hades being an interior monologue), Rudolf Virag (ghost of Bloom's father who was a regular barometer due to sciatica), Hades, Hermes (messenger god of liminal states) and Theoclymenos (who predicted the suitors' demise in the *Odyssey*). In the last instance, MIBM is distinguished from all other characters on this fine day by being prepared for inclemency. Thus, he is the only person who is dressed for – and figuratively predicting – the FUTURE. In summary, MIM/MIBM can be any or all of the above but is probably no single representation. He remains an enigma. The MIBM might be able to answer one of the great extra-textual questions of literary history: WHO SENT A COPY OF *TLR* TO THE BROWER GIRL? That unsolicited package contained the infamous Nausicaa episode. It kickstarted the whole chain of censorship that cruelled *Ulysses* for a decade. An eminent critic concluded: "the man in the macintosh is a synecdoche of *Ulysses* and our frustration in attempting an interpretation of the character is a microcosmic display of the messiness of all textual exegesis." This conclusion rings true when thinking of Joyce, who was a genuine prankster (for further information on tricksters see sub-episode on Levi-Strauss in C6). Frank Kermode investigated the literary ethics of Joyce's use of MIM, particularly in the context of Robert Adams' theory that MIM was just a joke and had with NO REAL MEANING. Kermode notes that readers and critics are instinctively drawn to find meaning in MIM because "within a text no part is less privileged than the other parts" (53); in other words, the reader cannot – or finds it very hard to – differentiate between AUTHENTICITY OF INTENT by an author. He goes on to say that the reader has a "prior expectation of consonance." Of course, these notions must be tempered by the fact that authors often signpost devices like unreliable narration. Kermode notes that indicators such as 'typographical variation' are sometimes used in such instances. Some might argue, for example and however, that the employment by Joyce of the dramatic form in Circe – in what is ostensibly a novel form – is intended to draw the reader's attention to some license with 'authenticity of intent' and textual consonance. Kermode postulates that Joyce intended to "mime the fortuities of real life" through MIM. While generally agreeing with this concept, I would argue that a fracturing has ALREADY been achieved in *Ulysses* in the incidental references to individuals and use of random events that play no further part in the novel. In fact, the use of MIM/MIB might be considered TOO SUSTAINED to fit into this category. In the end, Kermode steers close to Lyotard's notion of "presenting the unpresentable" when he quotes Adams' conclusion that these are "devices by means of which ... the work of art may 'fracture its own surface'" (54). This has been the challenge for all subsequent literature since Joyce. It is a contest from which fiction has withdrawn abjectly in the 100 years since the publication of *Ulysses*. The alien and planetary imagery in this sub-episode represents the type of stylistic indulgence that Joyce himself would have used, albeit with tight connection to plot.

—

18. ALIBHAI

The name of the racehorse Alibhai is a wilful misspelling. Joyce used this technique throughout *Ulysses*, especially in Wandering Rocks. It ran second last in the 1984 Melbourne Cup. An alibi is, of course, an excuse or explanation usually pertaining to the time that a crime took place. It means 'elsewhere' in Latin. *Ulysses* is littered with alibis. All the major adult characters dissemble. It all starts with Bloom's epistolary ruse. Only Stephen Dedalus seems to act with candour (to his detriment). Boylan and Molly both cover their tracks to some extent. But the absence of subterfuge is also startling. Molly makes no attempt to hide Boylan's visit, leaving the bedroom as it was used. The Alibhai which raced in the Melbourne Cup shared its name with a famous sire. However, it was no blood relation. Thus, it matched the relationship of Billy Capri to his step-father. However, Bob Capri could hardly be termed a generous procreator like the great American stallion. He suffered a very low sperm count, which meant that Billy never had half-siblings until he discovered the identity of his half-brother, Tom Hallem, in Chapter Four. Alibhai was bred by the Aga Khan but broke down in training after it equalled the one-mile record at Santa Anita and never raced. It became famous at stud being ranked in the Top 10 American general sires eleven times before its death in 1960. It had a thirteen-pound heart, more than 60% greater in size than average thoroughbreds. This was slightly smaller than Phar Lap whose cardiac muscle tipped the scale at fourteen pounds. This was the kind of prodigious organ that Tom Hallem could have profited from. Although you could argue that he was poisoned like Phar Lap. Heroin being his arsenic. Alibhai is an uncommon family name, mainly found in Ivory Coast countries and Kenya. Alibhai was only a four-year-old in 1984. It was sired by Noble Bijou (USA) out of Gem Flight. Noble Bijou was one of New Zealand's great sires and broodmare sires. He is the only horse to lead both categories in the same year (1992–93). An interest in bloodlines is apt for any study of Telemachus. Alibhai was considered an outstanding prospect. It stood on the second line of betting amongst the favourites in 1984. But it never lived up to its potential. This is another correspondence with Tom Hallem. It wore the colours of Ireland. The horses entered the barrier. Alibhai was frisky. Len Dittman didn't consider this a good sign. Time moved. Space moved marginally. The history of European settlement in Australia is a story of alibis. The question for indigenous groups in 1788 was whether this was an incident or invasion. For them, history was not a concept. People are not fixed in time. Events do not happen NOW. Time is not a horizontal line as in the western cosmos not on a plane not even vertical. It is circular. A sphere. There is only continuum. Shelley would have been an apt poetical adjunct for explaining this concept to a Western audience. Everything goes IN. It stays. All is sacred. Always eternal. Time is really a place full of spirits and stuff. They made everything. Our beings live there. You can still see what they left behind if you examine the remnant landscape. We have always been here. We talk about it all the time. It's the only subject worthy of discussion. Always with the Dreaming. You can try to calculate it if you like:

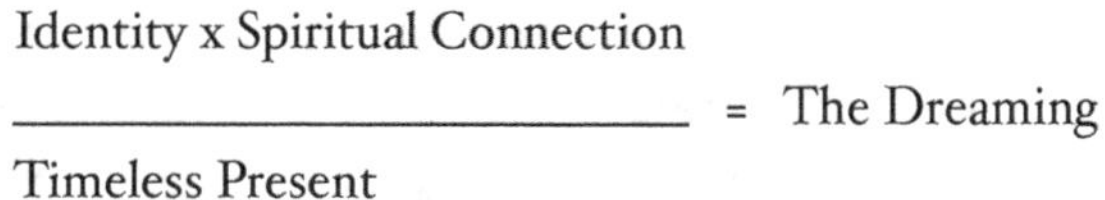

Our obligations take precedence over ephemera. And what we consider important is different. Like being with your mob. Sometimes we walk off. Sometimes we hang about. It's not a big deal to us. You're the drifters. Otherwise why would you have left home. And we are not interested in your junk. We like your trinkets precisely because they're not consequential. It's like the Chinese Emperor said to your envoy in 1793. We saw his visit on the regional news channel. We possess all things in prolific abundance, he told you. There is therefore no need to import the manufactures of outside barbarians in exchange for our products. This is exactly what we think. You came here out of desperation, I guess. Thirty-three governors followed. A dream of fair-to-middling administration. Passing the sceptre down the line like an Empire Games relay race. Start my version of a vice-regal cavalcade. Substitute a historic sequence for the progress of one. On Bennelong Point, Sir James Rowland AC, KBE, DFC, AFC (1 November 1922 – 27 May 1999) swept crisp thinning ripples off his parched forehead and paced from the Yellowblock colonnade past the fountain to graze on Middle Harbour. A thousand ships of the line might manoeuvre here with ease. He had served with the 1663 Heavy Conversion Unit operating bombers out of Britain. Few have the brand of courage to match this honest son of Noble Bijou. Lancasters' looping and blending for take-off. Upparise from Sydney Cove stood the first

Governor's residence. Georgian plain. Two levels. Six rooms. Advance on a flat-pack tent. Sandstone base. Governor Phillip strode towards his garden. Weevils in the seed stock. Sandy soils. Blunted spades and picks. Failed crops. Wheat, barley and maize. Too many sensitive plants now wrecks. Lost livestock. Send out a ship to Calcutta. More salt meat months. It was cured four years ago in England. Pea stock expended. Rations reduced to 1,500 calories per day. Enervated labour. Can't even manage to catch fish like the natives. Mouthful of mussels' spit berley. Cunning bream gone sideways. Arabanoo. Our first hostage. Never seen a staircase. Cable versus Sinclair. First civil case. Inscribed their location on the writ as 'new settlers of this place.' Crafty tactics. Chalk message to Adolf on an 8,000 pound bomb. "CONVICTS BEAT SEA CAPTAIN." A legal precedent. Laws of England not applied in Collins' judgement. Pay them for finery stolen from their crate. £15 pounds damages. Celebrity felons. Subscription raised by gentlemen and ladies. Soon I will depart for home. My gubernatorial dividend? Four years drift. Scales still in balance. Plumb bob motion. What shall I render unto the Lord for all his beens? A brick kiln but no carpenters. Norfolk Island timber but no port. Reverend Johnson's wheat harvest on the Cooks River flats and disappearing cattle. Abolition of slavery. One quarter of the Second Fleet dead. How do the British cope with misery? Make statistics. Attrition rate: 35 per cent. Total lost: 9,000 aircraft. Bomb load: 1 million Imperial tons. Sick landed: 486. Chained together up to their guts in brine for months. POWs put in motion by the Germans at the start of 1945. The living were left attached to the slumped and sunken dead. I saw living skeletons, recalled Governor Rowland, on the road to Hitler's lair. Survivors of Dachau. Sick sweet smell of death. We were going to become hostages. Bring them up on deck, said Johnson. The open air kills them faster. Curdling cold July. Cleanest southern light slicing their frames. Crawling through the scrub to shudder-to-death in four-man canvas tents. Man of Ten Thousand Lice. Come and see this strange exhibit! Corpses tossed overboard bobbing in coves for months. What must the natives make of us? Intransigence of Ross. I pissed him off to Norfolk Island. But for all the setbacks, the Union Jack still flutters down Tarra. Sydney is no longer just a gaol. Final Report to the Home Secretary. (1) A town plan has been laid. (2) Consolidation of Order. (3) Lines mark out streets three chains wide. My residence lies on the east flank. The hospital is situated to the west a safe distance from transmission. We have re-pitched the Marines' irregular tent placement. (4) Grants of land on regulation blocks. I provided Lieutenant Macarthur with one hundred acres of farmland at Rose Hill with free convict labour. His wife is a civilising influence on the colony. Her practice of astonomy with Dawes enlivens our scientific forums. Tinkling on Worgan's piano that new Nelson song. A boy dawdled with a pound of sausages observing his own image in a milliner's pane. Man in a cracked top hat. Grose's paymaster. I don't want to go home where everything is pent and cryptic, thought Master Dignam in mourning. Eye-catching fourth to Affinity in the Caulfield Cup. Throwaway for a boxing match. Blazes Boylan grips a red rose in his teeth while Bob Doran sings. Wileemarin's spear hurled with a whoop. It pierced the Governor's shoulder. Protruding ten feet out my back. Flyweight title. Dash to the boats. Spear kept jamming in the ground repeatedly as I retreated. Apply lime made of oyster shells. Dead face of my father in a pine coffin. Dai Bread bawling for his boots so he could go out and get drunker. BE A GOOD SON. The New South Wales Police motorcycle escort gathered in the driveway. Radio played. Police have halted random breath testing until they are issued with plastic gloves due to the fear that HIV could be transmitted via saliva. Fear of the plague. Spit in the Liffey. Tank Stream veiled. Vein under asphalt. Shitgerms. Concrete needles. In *Ulysses*, the vice-regal cavalcade crosses town at the end of Wandering Rocks rebooting all the characters introduced over the course of the novel to date. Penelope's weft. It crosses history and lives at escape velocity. Hunter assumed command after a period of near-anarchy when the NSW Marine Corps ill-used the colony for profit from the trade and sale of rum. He sponsored farms on the rich alluvial flats of the Hawkesbury River. Built a road to Bathurst. Grew melon, citrus and grapes. Discovered that Tasmania was an island. Established Newcastle. It was dubbed HELLHOLE. INSERT WIKIPEDIA ENTRY. It was a place where the most dangerous convicts were sent to dig in the coal mines. The locals are a straight, thin but well-made people, he wrote. Ninety-yard lance stroke gored Patagarang. Kangaroo meat is not as good as the mutton from Leadenhall Market. Engage the natives by stealth. This is no Chesapeake raid. Go quietly. My hat is a removable body part, they think. Green bough of friendship. Spaniards serving chocolate to our ladies. Malaspina's report noted that the colony's harshness reflected the national pride of the British. Minyi taperun kamarigal? Ganin. Bennelong caught between two temples. Petitioning for new stockings. His wife, Goroobarrooboollo, has gone off with Caruey, also known as Black Caesar. Try to lure Molly back with a gypsy bonnet. They have been plundering remote farms. Organise reprisals. White court always delivers white acquittals. Black face beneath a white wheel. Buried country. We stopped the native burn-offs which so threatened our farms. Trains of gunpowder could scarcely have been more rapid. King published the first newspaper. The emancipist, Ann Ilett, became his common law wife. They had two sons named Norfolk and Sydney. A practical man with a family back in England. A pedagogue. He sponsored Ticket of Leave settlers. A settlement was made at Coal River. It was renamed after the famous coal port, Newcastle Upon Tyne. Today, it is the world's largest coal export port. Its suburb names such as Jesmond, Hexham, Wickham, Wallsend and Gateshead betray that flawed connection to the

Motherland (see C4 paper). Note complementary distance from the main town of Morpeth, NSW and Morpeth, Northumberland. Through my glass from the short window upstairs at the Governor's residence, I can see Morgan hanging off the gibbet in chains on Pinchgut Island. Castle Hill Rebellion. A second Vinegar Hill. Irish Defenders seeking to start a New Republic. Two thousand strong they came amarching. Evacuate Parramatta. Parley. Johnson cut Cunningham down without warning and the whole thing floundered. Normal rules don't apply with bandits. Nine hangings were deemed sufficient. The first hundred lashes exposed the lad's spine so they moved onto his buttocks. When that was jelly, they went down his legs. I started Van Diemen's Land for these miscreants as well as a new prison camp on Coal River. Bligh went to New South Wales with a commission to break the rum trade. Johnson's coup. Four hundred soldiers marched on this House. Cartoon slander. Go down the staircase at knife point. I am perfectly safe with Mister Minchin. Imprisoned on the *Porpoise* in Hobart. Lancaster down. Trapped like Odysseus on Aeaea. He found the world without as actual; what was in his world within as possible. Beginning of the end for the Sydney Marines. Macquarie was a foot soldier from India who knew all about civil administration. Not a sailor lubbed on land. His wife had the ballroom adorned with variegated lamps and bound the columns with greenery. A Temple to Hymen decorated the gardens. It was illumined at night. Homage to Graham the Hygienist. Shrine in the Adelphi, Pall Mall. The celestial suite was used by Lady Hamilton to woo Admiral Nelson. Fifty quid per night. Bed twelve-foot-long by nine-foot girth secured to the floor like Odysseus' olive post. Apply some Nervous Aetherial Balsam to the Admiral's afflictions. Shot of Electrical aether. Enlivens the stump. Lisurgic chambers. Proust's forehead pressed against the pinhole aperture. Glass columns, angled mirrors, peepholes, erotic art, flashing electric lights, organ music, a whipping post, nail-barbed Cats and drafts of eastern incense all added to the dissolute atmosphere designed to arouse its inmates. Earth-bathing. Buried up to your neck like Beckett's Win. Almonds, apricots, pear and apple trees in blossom. Armadale dairies furnished milk. Lady Macquarie's Chair a scrape in stone. We danced to Pandean pipes and flutes on the thirtieth anniversary of English settlement. Dionysus under Aldebaran. No moon that night. Captain Piper's domed ballroom in the shape of St Andrew's cross. Dance quadrilles. Fly patterns. Native shrubs give grateful perfume. Smell of Elsan. White parachute flares lit the target. A fourteen-mile road straight to Parramatta was built. Into our bomb run. Wentworth's walks and journals. Our O'Bede. Insert data analysis. The precipitous range surrounding the colony at the western perimeter was crossed at last. I appointed emancipists like Greenway, Redfern and Thompson to government positions. Invited transported men to tea. Start a new Assembly. First bank. Punctured fuselage. Holey dollar. Rich lands were discovered by Oxley up the coast near Moreton Bay. Ground plan of Sydney prepared. All traffic shall pass to the left. First use of the term AUSTRALIA. Indigenous school. First stolen children. Punitive expeditions as required. Give back land scrapings. Macquarie was finally brought down by the Bent brothers and Bigge. He was replaced by Wellington's protégé. A keen astronomer. Stars above flak tracers. Sights over Hanau. Una's prophecy. Shift to meridian 129. Black shape sudden touch gyrating down. Tail gone. Control arm numb. Altimeter unravelling. Get them out the hatch. Civil lacks. No time for my own body. Dinghy hatch snaps. Wind wrenched me out. Treetops closing fast. Branches tear my chute. An enlisted man's tone of discipline. Miscalculation of Thompson and Sudds. Banned dramas. Composition of *Quintus Servinton*. Darling sought to ensure the education of under-age prisoners. A new Governor's House was approved. A cold northern spring assailed Rowland. Forty-five centimetres of snow. Nazi dogs howling. Show Bush nous. Go down to a stream to kill my scent. It was designed by Edward Blore, Royal Architect in the Gothic Revival style. A full set of 97 drawings, plans and specifications was completed by late 1834. In the end I ran out of puff. Walked through Frankfurt trying to get arrested. Military juries replaced. Cell 31. Black bread and soup. Limits on punishment. Religious equality. Stalag 13D. Jerkings of self-governance. Local hate. Bomber crews strung up on wires. Mcleay and Riddell. *Terra Nullius*. Indigenous Australians cannot sell or assign land. The siting of the new Governor's House on Bennelong Point was determined by the Colonial Engineer, Captain George Barney, and the Colonial Architect, Mortimer Lewis. Construction began in September 1836. Pugin infused luminosity of Sydney sandstone. The first public statue in Australia was erected in honour of Governor Richard Bourke. It still stands outside the Mitchell Library. Look left as you gaze out the limousine window. Tramp to Bavaria under SS guard. Bormann's redoubt. Gipps sent Hobson to New Zealand. End of transportation. The ground floor was completed in 1843 for a ball celebrating Queen Victoria's twenty-fourth birthday. But it was 1845 before Gipps could take up residence. Rowland turned from sea-gaze guilt-lines to the Armadale greens that framed our vivid caprock three miles deep and blanched by one hundred and forty years of sunglaze. More land reform was attempted. Three-year drought. The final cost was £46,000. There was no fanfare when we got back to Woolloomooloo. Sydney was full of Yank worship. Down the Double Bay Rissole they weren't interested in the likes of us in 1946. Appeaser by nature. Brother of the *Beagle's* captain. First Governor-General. Still living out Fromelles. First overseas branch of the Royal Mint was established in Sydney. FitzRoy invited Wentworth's wife, an ex-convict, to the Governor's Ball. It created a local furore. She declined the card gracefully. Pacific boys got all the promotions back home. I became a test pilot like Icarus. Wife killed in a coach accident. Hosing tail gunner parts out the back of a Lancaster hull. Crimean War. Considered one of the cruellest and most brutal wars of modern times. Turn Pinchgut into a fort. Last Martello Tower. Walls ten feet thick. Joyce's Sandymount. Go up get up you fearful Jesuit. Crawl down the back into your glass coffin. Up top you get a sight line right down the harbour. Four turrets. Twenty cannons strong. Ten Browning's. Four in the rear for Tail End Charlie and two each in the rest. They gave us a sense of false comfort rather than any illusion of prowess. Glad to get out of that rat trap. The new Government House in Hobart will not be completed until 1857. Bi-cameral parliament formed. Grey's flip-flops. Still sending convicts as late as 1852. Join Pathfinders. Rowland turned from Fort Denison and walked back towards his seat. Regal sun slid west through the fine verticals of Sydney's gunmetal grey coathanger. The eastern terrace and fountain were installed in 1861 along with new servant's quarters. It was almost time to go down to the Hyde Park War Memorial. One hundred and twenty thousand stars. Swamp the Council with Tuppenny Lords. Fifteen thousand signatures to commute John Bow's death sentence. Bronze frieze. Bushrangers in teal. Different rail gauges. Paternalism and dissent always run parallel in our history. Convict and land thief. What diff? Almost figureheads by Lord Belmore's time. Mad Bridget O'Farrell shooting Prince Alfred in the back. Hit him in the cross-braces. Indian rubber. Strides at his ankles. Hoff's Sacrifice. Airman broken over a cart. Ruined the royal picnic. Assassination of Cavendish and Burke in the Eumaeus episode. Phoenix Park murders. Clontarf Beach regicide. Vial's gold watch. Hang the bog-jumper quick smart. Keep those pot-lickers in place. Gestapo held me in solitary confinement. They said they were going to put me in front of a firing squad. Transferred me to the care of the Luftwaffe. Stalag Seven. Robinson ticking off boxes on his calling card of colonial appointments. Head carved in the GPO along with all those other figments of our magi/nations. March of Empire east. Float rather. Annex Fiji. The redundancy of the position in New South Wales politics was counterbalanced by a new interest in home renovation. In 1872, the Lieutenant-Governor directed the Colonial Architect to construct a *porte cochère* at the entrance to the Governor's House. Goldrush boom in civic architecture. 1879 World's Fair. Beat Melbourne to the punch. Two hundred-thousand-pound glass folly. Metonymy of the Crystal Palace. Symbol of Australia's simulacrum of a true machine. First elevator in the colony. Our equivalent of stairs. Come one and all to see the largest pumpkin in the Southern Hemisphere. English call it pig food. The Governor had the State rooms redecorated in the fashionable style of the Aesthetic Movement. Gingko leaves and feathers lining a Cadbury chocolate box. Jessica holding a peacock kitten. Asian motifs ironic in Whitening Australia. Slave daubings. Big red buck mounted in the Ballroom. *Bulletin* heyday. Elephant's head with coronet and three Fleur-de-lys on the regimental badge. Lady Carrington's silver horse. District Grand Master. United the lodges. The Carrington family had humble origins in trade. Jubilee banquet for a thousand poor boys. He encouraged Parkes. The vice-regal couple was renowned for their polite and unaffected charm. At Home in Government House displayed a temper democratic. Old ball and cartridge blunders. Medals struck for the occasion. Controversial speeches promoting Australian nationalism back in London. Contrast with Lord Jersey. He brought bathtubs and a large supply of drinking water. Truncated term. Same as Brand and Beauchamp. Harmless little job. Your duties are mostly of a social character. Chalet constructed at the western terrace. Yellowblock extension to the Billiard Room. Duff was the first Governor to die in office. Liver full of pus. Added a new kitchen and scullery. Summoned to Brackley Towers. Belloc's Lord Lundy. High Church St James. Our convict birth mask. Too freely moved to tears. "I thought men like that shot themselves," the King said. They installed an electric lighting system during his governorship. Government House was occupied by the Governor-General of Australia for the first 14 years after Federation. There was Hopetoun, Tennyson, Northcote, Dudley and Denman in order. Flamboyant young aristocrats. Political sumps. Disappointed son of the Poet Laureate named HALLAM. He bore a dead man's label. Twisting the Telemachus rope. Chamberlain's Spy. Squandered our Dreadnought money on a steam-boat folly like Ci Xi and her marble barge. Genial Davidson handled the political intrigues of Dooley and Fuller with aplomb. Rawson's nephew. Forty years a sailor. Deflected Jack Lang's effort to abolish the Council without referendum. Witnessed the first great Labor social programs. Scullin's poisoned cup. Desperate manoeuvres. A ball was held for Rear-Admiral Kayser and the visiting Dutch Squadron. One of the most brilliant events seen in recent years. It lit up the gardens with bright green and soft pink lights. Bond default. People sleeping in sandstone crevices in the Domain. Lady Game's gown of oyster white satin with a tightly moulded bodice. Lang trying to swamp the swamp. Harbour Bridge opening. New Guard outrage. To cut a ribbon. Game's laconic slant. I was sad really at Lang's dismissal, he wrote. We always got on man to man. Nice portrait wearing all my decorations. Ironic smile on my face. Followed by short timers. Anderson died of a brain haemorrhage in this House. Shipped his corpse home. Then the long periods in office of Wakehurst, Northcott, Woodward and Cutler. Soldiers all. First Australian born governor. Only took 158 years. Knocked in the chest at ANZAC Cove. Lay on a pile of dead bodies all day. Head of the BCOF in Japan. First man to be televised in Australia. Rowland checked his wrist watch. Lost his leg at Damour. He strode through the drawing room towards the entrance. Wall of soft lancet windows. Jigsaw Gothic. Imperial stage. White strangers. Ossian Fingal. High church idyll. Baron's turrets. Governor Rowland adjusted his garb.

White with orange sash, green hooped sleeves and orange cap. Davitt and Parnell. Australians have never liked leaders. All Jubilee-mutton robes and chattels. Elsan contents sloshing down the fuselage. Take a beer bottle each flight. Wran likes military men. They know how to take orders, he says. Kerr was an apostate. Evatt's fag. Go down Macquarie Street towards the Hyde Park canopy. We have become the rulers of all cleared land up to the head of the Spring and from Brickfield Hill to the mill and all the entirety of waterfront from the battery of Point Maskelyne down to Hogan's farm. Filthy memorial pool full of leaves, face down crushed soft drink cans and bloody food wrappers. Need my breathing apparatus. Discarded syringe casing. French poplars. Fertilising their soil with our larrikin imprint. Pink granite flesh. Concrete form. Bushranger sigil. Get to the top of Somme ridge. Walk up the stairs on the north side holding my own umbrella. The First Division wore wide brim hats. Forget the useless tin ones. Zigzag trenches. Over we go. Art deco setbacks and buttresses. Ziggurat roof. Step pyramids. A star for each volunteer from New South Wales. A few have fallen off, says the building manager smiling. I keep them in my desk drawer. One day we'll re-attach them. But you've got to build scaffolds to climb aloft. First flight over Dusseldorf. Celestial spread above. Flak butter. Dead boy crucified on a sword. Slimy bronze. Suspended on a caryatid. Unburied. Review an embossed invitation to the Re-dedication of the ANZAC Memorial. Memorise the text of two commemorative plaques which I will unveil on November 30. View Hoff's friezes. Bas relief upon west wall. A death procession. It starts with a bicycle then an old bi-plane. I was trained in one myself. Then soldiers digging bayoneting loading shells shelling stretchers tanks wounded dying. The governor's detail wound back along Elizabeth Street. The TAB was purring with one day punters. Leer elbowed his way to the bench. Faded flyer for the Fenech bout at Marrickville RSL. That Maltese kid can really fight. Seventh round knockdown. He filled in a betting slip where he stood. Four awkward blue biro crosses down the page. Fifty buck Trifecta. Track: Melb. Race: Five. Number: seventeen. Track: Melb. Race: Five. Number: six. Track: Melb. Race: Five. Number: fifteen. Track: Melb. Race: Five. Number: seven. Four-year-old chestnut. Carting fifty-four. Insert analysis of BROWN as the colour of MIBM's significant garment. Note it may just be the common colour of raincoats in the United Kingdom during that epoch. In "The Dead," Joyce deals extensively with what he terms the "hated brown Irish paralysis." Brown and yellow are the colours symbolic of paralysis (footnote discussion on gold/yellow in Pater/Wilde). A text search reveals that Joyce's use of brown is largely conventional in *Ulysses*. Corpses are put into brown grave clothes. Eyes and hair are brown. Objects like sugar, tea, gravy, bread, bricks, turf, hats, boots, socks and paper are all brown with no adjectives. Workers' tanned skin and that of some native peoples is brown. A seal's head is sleek and brown. Rotting rosebuds also.

Brown[e] is a common name. Popular derivations of the word 'brown' used for poetic affect are generally absent in Joyce's work. Words such as hazel, russet, fawn, sepia, umber, caramel and chocolate are hardly employed. In general, Joyce is not the type of author to pander to niceties of description. It should be noted, however, that brown is created by combining green and orange. These were the colours of conflict in terms of Irish nationalism. Leer shook his head. Counter queue longer than the Congo into Hell. Clerk behind the grill shifted his weight on bowed kneecaps. **INSERT RACE CALL**. It should correspond to the vice-regal cavalcade. The final sub-episode follows Billy Capri as he walks along King Street during the race. This is an emblem of his basic alienation/disaffection from local culture. It also locates him beyond Joyce's narrative structure. Thus, it represents the first step on the road to Gibraltar. Johnny Tapp in a holding pattern of language while the horses struggle at the barrier. All ten runners were fronted one and a half pounds of heroin every Saturday at the Star Hotel. Gravy's crawl proceeded to the White Horse Surry Hills, Covent Garden Haymarket and finally the Lord Wolseley Ultimo, where he drove a knife into Mal Spence's neck. Farquhar, by contrast, went to the Lord Wolseley first then continued onto the Covent Garden, where he was reunited with Gravy briefly, before a Chinese dinner at the Old Tai Yuan with RR and some ALP mates then a short taxi ride to the Australian Youth hotel in Glebe for a cleansing ale. Suddenly, the gates opened. Finally, the race caller was able to announce: "They're racing in the 1984 Melbourne Cup."

---

19. LEGANA (2.15–2.50 PM)

Billy Capri left John Woolley Building, struck eastwards and checked his watch. He had plenty of time to reach the Shakespeare Hotel before the race. He turned south for a brief sharp descent to Manning Road then tacked west, keeping the Old Teacher's College to port. Ahead lay No.2 Oval. He negotiated the arc of Western Avenue curling around University Oval and Bosch Lecture Theatre. Debris from Monday's tempest littered the pavement. Thin branches flexed under his footfalls. Large fig leaves spotted with bat droppings collected in piles over stormwater grates, creating wide deep pools. A film of motor oil made brilliant yellow and blue rings which transformed themselves constantly to his gaze. His heavy boots splashed through a succession of puddles that had gathered in rifts in square cement slabs. A strong gust suddenly released sprays of water from reeling trees. Capri shivered. He pulled his brown coat collar around his neck and lowered his head. Press on regardless of placing. The geography of the Telemachy to Pylos and Sparta is clear. There is no need for a map to explain it to the reader. Ithaca is usually identified with the island called Thiaki although some scholars argue that it is Leucas and others identify it as Cephalonia, especially the area near Paliki Peninsula. Regardless of exact location, these places are all relatively close to each other in the Ionian Sea. Telemachus travels down the west coast of the Peloponnese to Pylos. This is a journey of about 300 km. After visiting Nestor, he travels overland to Sparta. This is a further 100 km or about two days on foot. He returns along the same path only deviating to avoid the ambush set by the suitors. It is a self-contained journey, which is symbolic of Telemachus' own trajectory in life. It is the final journey in Classical literature and thus Telemachus could be seen in symbolic terms as running in last place like Legana. The horse Legana could also be seen as a part-pun on the character ANA LAFEI although it is sheer coincidence. I could insert various references to her legs and indeed this has been done over the course of the first five chapters. She drives with pedals, walks, washes her body, and gets pressed over a bench and raped. But this is either chance or subconscious coding. In contrast to Telemachus, scholars are divided on whether the places visited by Odysseus over the eighteen years between his departure from Ismaros and his return to Ithaca are real. Many maps have been produced charting his voyage during the *Odyssey*. The passage is recounted retrospectively by Odysseus himself in the *Apologoi*. This is the term given to the tale he tells Alcinous and the Phaeacians from Books IX to XII. Ioannis Kakridis argues that it is illogical to try to locate any of these places on a map. His reasoning is simple: that to believe in a factual basis for the geography of the *Odyssey* would also mean countenancing the existence of gods, giants and monsters et cetera. See Chapter Four for further analysis of this argument. However, Odysseus' route is not relevant to this work, which examines the POV of Telemachus using those chapters in *Ulysses* which involve Stephen Dedalus. Billy's corkscrew hairstyle bobbed and waved. His foot split a deep hole. A spray of grit was released into still water. Insert symbolism. To shake the stagnant pond and bring sediment gathered on its floor into play, clouding the way but forcing change nonetheless, surely that was better than certitudes, the entropy of uninquiring minds, and the objective of this fictional expose of what Tolstoy would call an unhappy family. He was exhausted. Only the seismic momentum of his farewell address and the jist of genetic aftershock sustained him. He climbed an alley. Joyce makes everyone intersect in Wandering Rocks. He suffers from a kind of Titanic afflatus. By contrast, you should make them all splatter like they got blown beyond Gibraltar. Billy reached the summit of Little Queen Street and turned into City Road. A channel of peak hour traffic hemmed him against its Victorian shopfronts. Tormina. A hobo, pushing ahead hastily on aluminium crutches, collided with him. Sweet smell of Toohey's Old gusht forth. Christ-like countenance. Brown trousers. Safety-pinned to the groin level. He swore loudly. Gimme two bucks, he demanded. William Capri hastened ahead his wallet intact. Joyce would run a whole lot of internal associations from this exchange. But I am in too much of a hurry. Billy turned into Maurice's Lebanese take-away. The proprietor stood at his counter erect and inscrutable. He smiled blandly slowly withdrawing his eyes into brown sockets even as his moustache spread broad and rich across stubbled Persian cheeks. Jars of Pablo instant coffee lined the shelves. Fresh falafels bubbling in a tub. Wet lettuce crisp and clean behind invisible glass. Maurice crushed three hot falafels into a sheet of unleavened bread. They broke open steaming. He washed fluid hummus upon. Tong handles sprinkled rough tabouli. He gripped the sandwich firmly and rolled it inside a paper tourniquet then slid it into a shiny bag. The cash register rang. Billy took his meal from the top of the tall counter and left. He tore the wrapper in soggy flags as we walked. Desperate to be filled not isolated. He bit hard and opened his mouth to suck cool air. His tongue burned. Swallow ASAP. He ripped away more ribbons. The release of pressure made the wrapping splay and drool. He licked at watery beige sauce. Horse at water trough. Can't make it drink. You don't miss water until the well runs dry. In the beginning I really loved you. A cover version is a mask for real emotions. A translator is always an author's slut. Feint at a new style. Another dead end. Go back to epic rock anthems. Dodge at hiphop. Rapping without the DOUBLE-U. Willy and Tom make one entity. Jars of lollies congealed in tall jars in the dirty striptease window of Alex Cordobes pizza parlour. An emaciated seamstress proppt in the doorway of her sparse workshop chewing on the nub of a wet cigarette butt. Capri wiped sauce from the corner of his mouth. Square album covers hung in plastic bags at Recycled Records: a Japanese import of Music from Big Pink; new Minutemen double album; Fall LP. Book of Ray Pettibon drawings. Husker Du single of Eight Miles High. Leaflets for the next Feedtime gig at Frenchs held down by half a brick. All Proceeds to Prisoners Action Group. Teeth sunk through underboiled pulses. Capri chewed cud. Question posed by Mildling. Trojan Horse but containing what cargo? And how then the marginalised of Minor? Chidley. A body beyond. I wrote an essay on him which was rejected by *Southerly*. "HEAD, THOREAU & ABDOMEN" it was called. Pun on anatomy of the bee. Thoreau's favoured metaphor for man. The HEAD of the title signifies Chidley's obsession with physiognomy: the convergence of brows, injured eyes, corrugated foreheads, bulbous Bardolphian noses, flushed cheeks, sly, knowing smiles and clumsy hands all caused by the shocks of coition and self abuse (47). Capri stopped at the traffic lights opposite the Marlborough Hotel and observed his reflection in the mirrors of Mapp's Glass. Anomalous emanations of hair on a hatcheted cranium. Deep, careless gougings in the scalp moating a funnel of stiff locks as if a pipe had been mounted in the brim of his skull. THOREAU represents an epistemology comprised solely of literary sources. The first prosenchymatic thinker. Language which shifts in small units, compartmentalised by punctuation, constantly qualified or extrapolated, centripetal with scientific detail, powered by alliteration. Tis the orderly progression of theory. Ba(r/w)d Capri's stomach tightened. Too fast he ett. Unchewed stuff. Yet consumed he still. Peccant sweat. Spinal flaccidity. He felt perspiration gathering in the back of his shirt. These are clear metaphors for his disgust with human functions and diet. Capri discarded saturated paper to get at the fag-end of his meal. ABDOMEN. Sunk in his mouth. Bitten bitter biter bit. All these variations were relevant to his mind. Little Hans and Dora. Seventeenth century term for trickster. Capri held at arm's length his load. Sauce dripped on the footpath. AUTO FELLATIO. The Mouth is the insertion orifice. Capri unravelled sodden paper disclosing the soggy butt of his repast. He cradled it by the stamen. A Dandy with a tulip. Sunset felt its way into the tranche of light between trenchant clouds and shop awnings. Bronze by gold. Colour of a Turner painting. Joyce's style in Wandering Rocks is largely conventional reflecting the descriptive needs of his diverse subject matter. He returns to Modernist high style at the start of Sirens. Billy presst content out of the sodden carapace and popped it inna. Sunk. These images of consumption represent a direct symbolic adjustment against Joyce. Chidley was an obscure apostle of suffragette feminism before a template formed. Joyce constructed *Ulysses* against strict categories as detailed in the *Linati schema*. This approach either needs to be exploded or intensified in postmodern texts until it achieves farcical intricacy. Like D'Workin, Chidley believed that sexual penetration was an attack by patriarchy on women. Instead, he promoted male passivity in coitus using what he termed 'vulvic suction' based on observation of ducks. Meat was associated by Chidley with lapses into masturbation and drunkenness. Contra was fruit. It echoed Thoreau's Elysian Life which spurned cooked food for fresh fruit ripened by sunlight. He also rejected clothing and shelter. A "balanced, normal and cool" brain became the foil to facial convergence. Thence you would be able to FLOAT. These days he would write a lifestyle manual. Capri compacted the pulp and slammed it into a brimming municipal garbage bin. It bounced into the gutter. He cleaned his palms on the arse of his trousers leaving oily discharge. A severed cord. Mothers, stepmothers, mothers-in-law, wives. Penelope and Circe act in all these roles in Classical literature. The Circe episode re-examines much of the material in Wandering Rocks as the hallucinations and nightmares of Stephen and Bloom. It also adds material that was not brought into sharp focus during Wandering Rocks. In the next chapter, this text engages with Joyce's famous Oxen of the

Sun episode, which charts the stylistic evolution of English Literature in the context of content about childbirth. Plot progress is minimal:

- — Billy walks past the Marlborough Hotel during race call (symbolism noted above).
- — He enters the Shakespeare Hotel after the running of the Cup.
- — He wanders amongst the crowd finding no traction (displaced amongst supposed peers).
- — Hallem enters pub by a different door (symbol).
- — We meet Leer (false father figure).
- — Exit Billy (decisive break between brothers).
- — Bloom and Stephen are united at Holles Street Hospital for the final drive to closure (Tom Hallem and Leer mimic then break this bond).

6.
Oxen of the Sun

"The radical force of Joyce's writing has not fully registered in the literary studies (and practice) of the Anglophone world ..."

– **Derek Attridge**

Language is usually an adequate vehicle for expression. With perseverance, you can find the right words to explain events and feelings; albeit with some loss of energy over time's mass. There was a whole lot of hype about *bricolage* and sign systems and the redundancy of history in the late twentieth century but all the parenthesised polysemous terms in *Semiotexte* multiplied by the 'escape velocity' of every computer link drilling down the internet ad infinitum hasn't stopped people talking, writing and reading with the dopey defiance of Doctor Johnson's decisive foot-strike. Tonight, my daughter Rachel was sitting on my lap in the bath. She leaned backwards into my legs and flipped her head straight at the strip light for a few seconds then pushed herself towards me, shaped her mouth into a kiss and blew warm sweet breath in my face. After that, she drew her body back up to its full height, sucked in more air and unleashed a pure high scream. Its volume surprised her. She looked startled then sat down smiling. We finished the bath. I deposited her on the tiled floor on a towel with a soft rubber starfish and dried myself quickly. Rachel inhabits space with the same blank power as Nature. She held out her arms so I would pick her up and we looked at ourselves in the misty mirror. I strained to discern my features in her mint condition face. I wondered whether she got any sense of identity from my face, smell or touch. She pulled at a brass handle on the cupboard. It sprang back revealing a cluster of medicines and cosmetics. I drew her away. We went into her bedroom. I closed the door, collected her singlet, nappy and jumpsuit then followed her across the bare floorboards as she folded her body into ingenious positions to avoid dressing. I withdrew each hand in turn from the toy she was chewing and worked the sleeves over her doughty arms and legs.

Her fingers and toes popped through blue elastic. O entered with her bottle. I left them together, went into the backyard and looked up at the airplanes whistling towards the third runway leaving trails of silver mist in the repressed summer sky. The sun was lowering. It was late February. I got a telephone call to say Tom died. Mechanically I went back into Rachel's bedroom. I collected her from my wife and buried my face in her body. We started the bedtime ritual. First, we visited a wall poster to count all different types of Teddy Bears wearing different national costumes. Then we examined her mobiles. There was a diving green and red papier-mache fish that her mother made. A school of bright wooden fish from Thailand. Finally, phosphorescent stars orbiting her cot. Next, I took her to the stuffed koala on the dresser. This had been my toy when I was a child. It's pretty ragged now. Dirty grey stuffing seeps out of burst stitching in its rump and paw-stumps. It has a metal ring in its navel which can be wound to release the melody of "Waltzing Matilda." I gave it a few turns and the decelerating melody followed us twirling around the bedroom. I switched on her night light. It is an electric globe. Bronze light illuminated the trails of famous explorers across the eastern oceans. I hope she will become an explorer herself someday. We blew out the lightbulb. I flicked the OFF switch simultaneously. We both laughed at that trick. She knew it was a charade by now. I placed her in the cot and raised the metal bar. Good night, I said softly. I kissed her cheek and left. I could hear her bouncing on the mattress as I receded. I went to the porch and loitered uselessly. Stationary leaves shuffled suddenly before belated vespers. Skinny zephyrs. Sun-drops stoked my face. Birds were passaging the deft season. The moon up-cranked. Duskdown. Venus was posted, alone and faintly ruddy, on the fine leg boundary. Later that night, my Muse visited. She's not entirely welcomed nowadays. There are certain ideas and activities that you've just got to suppress so you can go about your job in peace. It's all very well to talk about inspiration. I don't have time to get lost like that. Writing is like driving a car through a Radburn suburb at night. I love back-tracking through half-remembered novels, embarrassing myself with my lack of recollection while savouring beautiful clauses again that I will soon re-forget. You've got to live with a book like a blood relation. One must hover over the text like a dragonfly scanning the surface of a still pool for motion. I have spent most of my adult life with the same works, breathing in the sameness and unsameness of their deep forms, reacquainting myself with their landmark images, getting inside the guts of what Barthes calls Readerly Texts, wondering how much they were controlled by the author and how much was organic, growing cranky at their lapses and exhilarated at their paranormal sublimes, never baulking at recognition of their banalities [he sighs] until they became like the family I had that never knew me. Great books possess punishing architectonics that suspend you like a bird above the plot line. The reasons why one abandons a book are never as interesting as why it sticks. I could never read *Ulysses* until I became a father. I used to sit on the sofa with my daughter bundled-up in my lap while O got some sleep before we swapped for the 1 am feed. Channel Nine was playing *Star Trek* repeats every night until 11 pm. At the end of the episode, I still had time to kill. One evening I just began reading *Ulysses* again. Rachel had sunk hot and wet on my ribs. I was getting bronchitis. I got to the end of Chapter One. Something clicked. Next weekend, I borrowed Clive Hart's monograph and Don Gifford's Notes from Fisher Library and sank into its dense references like Stephen Hero immersed in Skeat's etymological dictionary. Obscure images got fitted into form. Structure as a chassis for meaning became my apotheosis. I am now part way through my reply. Wandering Rocks was a masterpiece of humanism. Oxen of the Sun is its foil. C5 moved a lot. C6 almost does not move at all. Neither of them progressed the plot much. You could bypass C6 with information in the ToC. But that was not Joyce's point. He was moving fast inside slow motion like someone on drugs. In the end, Tom Hallem couldn't hold all the fragments together. It's hard to fault his logic really. His death was a definitive statement. Oxen is a birth episode in *Ulysses*. This is a death chapter. Its plot motif is aligned with Homer. All of Odysseus' crew are killed on Thrinacia. Thus, it is a mirror (see NACAL). It was Joyce who flipped Oxen not I. Tom's daughter will have to learn the truth one day. And his death will change the way she perceives her father. It didn't shock me when it happened. The fading loop of smack culture had been hanging around Tom like a vulture drawing tighter each day. Metaphors like the ones in the last sentence represent image-association in the cause of clarity. They produce an abundance of repercussions that amplify meaning if you pick them apart like say Barthes or Derrida. The facets of metaphor have been termed Tenor and Vehicle by I.A. Richards – meaning the subject and its rendering respectively. I went onto the balcony overlooking the compound and lit a mosquito coil. This could all be imbued with great symbolism. There are 4 types of metaphor. Plain metaphor (1) is a straight transfer. Implied Metaphor (2) infers Tenor rather than states things outright. It's a Protean form like a mask or puzzle. All nouns were originally metaphors. They explained appearance to a third party. The first nouns were designed to draw attention to an object. It was probably approaching predators. Later, they evoked the beauty of sunset as a manifestation of some primitive Deity. Eventually, metaphor became enshrined as the title of the 'thing itself' – The Word. This is Dead Metaphor (3). My favourite form of metaphor is still Simile (4). It rolls off the tongue without contrivance, making life seem bigger and brighter than before. It's also great for humour. Australians love simile. That and litotes. It suits our deflected Muse. One might almost say that we are reticent like Calliope. It also enables us to stay one step removed from any direct statement of feeling.

JOYCE

The Oxen of the Sun episode is one of the most notoriously difficult passages in literature. Joyce himself said it was the hardest episode to execute and interpret (Weaver, *Letters*, Vol 1, 137). The subject matter is childbirth and sex. The Organ is Womb, according to the Linati schedule composed in 1920. Its Science is Medicine. Joyce's goal was to disclose "the crime committed against fecundity by sterilising the act of coition." Chidley would have applauded that sentence. It begins in the National Maternity Hospital, known locally as Holles Street Hospital, around 10 pm where Missus Mina Purefoy, former paramour of Leopold Bloom, is engaged in protracted labour. It ends at Burke's pub at closing time around midnight. It employs consecutive prose styles that correspond to the gestation and evolution of the English language. This is also a metaphor for the development of language in the individual from birth to maturity. In terms of Joyce's self-constructed cosmos, it harks all the way back to the start of *Portrait of the Artist as a Young Man* with its opening lines about "baby tucco." The Oxen episode is a brilliant concept which has been universally admired for its originality and scope. But it is also a totally artificial achievement in aesthetics with limited relevance to plot. Its very conceptual framework necessitated the creation of the densest, most complex literature ever written. It resembles a scientific or medical text more than fiction. It is a prime example of the Hieratic sensibility in English. It epitomises what Barthes called Writerly Text. Lacan would term it "Big T Text." Critics have struggled to accurately demarcate the styles of different periods and/or authors mobilised by Joyce. Joyce himself wrote of his intentions:

> Technique: a nineparted episode without divisions introduced by a Sallustian-Tacitean prelude (the unfertilized ovum), then by way of earliest English alliterative and monosyllabic and Anglo-Saxon ... then by way of Mandeville ... then Malory's Morte d-Arthur ... then the Elizabethan 'chronicle style ... then a passage solemn, as of Milton, Taylor, Hooker, followed by a choppy Latin-gossipy bit, style of Burton-Browne ... then a passage Bunyanesque ... after a diarystyle by Pepys-Evelyn ... and so on through Defoe-Swift and Steele-Addison-Sterne and Landor-Pater-Newman until it ends in a frightful jumble of Pidgin English, nigger English, Cockney, Irish, Bowery slang and broken doggerel. (Bugden, *Letters*, Vol 1, 139–140)

This free-wheeling definition, as loose as the executed form in the novel, claims nine parts corresponding to the periodicity of pregnancy, lists twelve different styles and names twenty authors either individually or in groups. Joyce may also have added additional elements as he drafted the episode. Most critics calculate thirty to thirty-five authors in total (see Carlin & Evans, Johnson, Killeen). Of course, any attempt at strict classification acts against the very spirit of evolution which sees styles and authors intervolved in a continuum of language ('everflow') that transcends arbitrary notions of periodicity or a restricted Canon. Robert Janusko identified nearly eight hundred different sources in the episode including seventy-five entries from Saintsbury's *A History of English Prose Rhythm* (1912). Stanislaus Joyce advised Richard Ellmann that *AHEPR* was a key reference point for his brother. A coloured chart of the episode is the most logical method of delineating sub-sections (see Sarah Davidson, *Genetic Joyce Studies*, 2009). INSERT TABLE

Table 2. Cavalcade of styles in Oxen of the Sun

Style		Author(s)	Scene/Content
1.	Primitive	Arval Brotherhood of Rome	Invocation (3 x 3). Fertility chant. Location is established. Also authority (Horne).
2.	Latinate prose	Sallust, Tacitus	Sex in society. Hyper-civilised style. No punctuation. Juxtaposition with Primitive style above. Note – opening two sections act as poles/extremes invoking Vico's concept of historical cycles (see also Foucault opening of *DP*)
3.	Medieval Latin chronicles	William of Malmesbury	Irish medical tradition on childbirth.
4.	Anglo-Saxon	Aelfric	English Alliterative. Enter Bloom. It is ~90 minutes since he masturbated in Nausicaa.
5.	Middle English	Everyman	Blooms asks after Mrs Purefoy. Nurse Callan.
6.	C15 Prose	Mandeville	Bloom meets Dixon then enters the room where a group of drunken men are eating sardines and bread.
7.	Medieval Romance	Malory	A nurse requests silence. The group is identified as Drs Dixon, Lynch and Madden; medical student Punch Costello; and Lenehan and Stephen Dedalus. Mulligan is expected. They discuss the ethics of baby taking precedence over mother in event of life risk. Bloom as a married man is asked what he would choose. Stephen rants about the church. Crotters tells one of Mulligan's jokes. They all laugh except Bloom and Stephen. Bloom feels sad about Rudy and pities Stephen.

	Style	Author(s)	Scene/Content
8.	**Elizabethan prose chronicles**	Holinshed	Stephen pours drinks. Blasphemy of religious ceremony. He pretends that his teaching salary is the proceeds from a song. More ranting about Mary's pregnancy with Jesus. They are again warned to be quiet. Bloom sits quietly.
9.	**C16–17 Latin prose**	Milton etc.	Thunderclap. Stephen's terror.
10.	**Moral-allegorical**	Bunyan	Terror continues. Stephen recalls a prostitute.
11.	**C17 diarists**	Pepys, Evelyn	Shift to external scene. Dublin in rain. Mulligan meets Bannon. Gossip about girls (Milly).
12.	**Allegory (a)**	Defoe	Lenehan and Costello characterisation.
13.	**Allegory (b)**	Swift	Foot and mouth disease (see Deasy). Papal bulls. Oppression by English Kings named Henry.
14.	**Essay**	Addison & Steele	Arrival of Mulligan with Bannon. His jokes about sexual prowess (proposed *Omphalos* clinic). His pregnant gut.
15.	**Learned Wit**	Sterne	Bannon and Crotthers on prophylactics (purchase for use with Milly). See Musgrave on Menippean Satire. A bell tolls.
16.	**C18 man of letters**	Goldsmith	Nurse Callan advises Dixon of childbirth.
17.	**C18 Political**	Burke	Bloom's acceptance of being mocked. His relief at childbirth.
18.	**C18 comedy of manners**	Sheridan	Ribald toasts. Bloom shocked at baseness of doctors.
19.	**Satirical**	Junius	Hypocrisy of Bloom's self-righteousness is critiqued savagely.
20.	**Historical**	Gibbons	Various topics relating to childbirth. Stephen as deacon.
21.	**Gothic**	Walpole	Mulligan's ghost story (Haines as Black Panther). He steals Stephen's *bon mots* repeatedly. Parody of Hamlet theory.
22.	**Sentimental**	Lamb	Bloom's pathetic recollections of Stephen as youth. Realisation that he is a father figure amongst these younger men.

	Style	Author(s)	Scene/Content
23.	**Hallucinatory**	De Quincey	Bloom's pessimism as drunkenness holds sway. Vision of Martha Clifford.
24.	**Essay**	Landor	Stephen's atrophied career as a poet. Insult of his mother. Ascot Gold Cup discussed. Throwaway's victory revealed.
25.	**19th century historical**	Macaulay	Detailed character descriptions.
26.	**Naturalist**	Huxley	Bloom wonders how gender is determined. On infant mortality. Mulligan blames sanitation and lifestyle. Crotters blames trauma of work. Lynch suggests a mathematical formula.
27.	**Sentimental fiction**	Dickens	Mrs Purefoy as joyful mother. She thinks of her husband and children.
28.	**Catholic conversion**	Newman	Past sins omnipresent.
29.	**Aesthetic / Euphuism**	Pater	Bloom recollects Stephen as a gloomy child (Like Flaubert, Pater invariably opens his works with a symbolic childhood event).
30.	**Sublime**	Ruskin	Comparison of assembly with Jesus' childbirth.
31.	**C19 man of letters**	Carlyle	Stephen's spontaneous suggestion to go to pub. Exeunt. Virility of Mr Purefoy hailed. Also fertility of his wife.
32.	**C20 dialect and slang**	Joyce	Burke's pub. Stephen drinks absinthe. MIM. Fire brigade. Pub closure. Vomit. Stephen to brothel district with Lynch. Bloom follows.
33.	**Advertising**	Media	Poster advertising visiting American preacher.

Oxen of the Sun evolves into Joyce's own High Modernist Pidgin at closure (Row 32 above). This style acts as a precursor to the form of *Finnegans Wake*. This nexus was turned into a backwards-segue by Joyce, casting a revisionist glance across the subjects of Oxen and elevating his own status. In this formulation, his style becomes the apogee of the English language. It was an act of *(self) daemonization* that converted Joyce into his own precursor. This is consistent with all of Joyce's writings, which were successive, interlinked quasi-autobiographies. In *Anxiety of Influence*, Harold Bloom outlines six revisionary ratios that govern relations with the precursor: *Clinamen*, *Tessera*, *Kenosis*, *Daemonization*, *Askesis* and *Apophrades*. *Clinamen* is wilful misreading that swerves from the original in a corrective movement. Tessera completes a truncated work. *Kenosis* is breaking with the precursor from a pose of humility. *Daemonization* goes back to a Sublime origin and creates a new counter-Sublime. *Askesis* is self-purgation to achieve a sense of solitude. *Apophrades* is return of the dead. In this chapter, each of these ratios will become relevant at different points. We can assign a category to each French Thinker in terms of their response to Joyce's influence. It would have driven them crazy to be divided into reductive structuralist slots. Each of them tried to break out of existing models to unlock independent space. Often this took the form of cannibalising structure to leave only style at the end of their tomes. The ultimate challenge for any writer struggling with the Oxen episode is to find a format which can stand alongside the precursor. There are a limited range of options open to the contestant who is willing to embark on a mission to build an inheritance-text to Oxen of the Sun (insert references to quest tropes). Option One would involve proceeding forwards from the endpoint of Oxen on new linguistic adventures. This would be an example of *Tessera*. Some of this option was attempted by Joyce himself in *F(W)ake*. Bakhtin would have called his approach heteroglossic. Joyce's innovations in *F(W)ake* largely related to language and myth (rather than theory) which he blended across races and cultures to create new word amalgams, neologisms and a composite spirituality, perhaps even the stuff of a new religion. It took him twenty years to end-up with what many critics believe is a mess. A more theoretical approach would incorporate later forms of discourse such as Structuralism, Post-Structuralism and *Ecriture Feminine* as well as Post-Colonialism and new verbal styles like Rasta, Punk and Hip-Hop. Option Two would reverse the temporal progression of Oxen. This would be an instance of *Daemonization*. The text would regress until it reached Joyce's linguistic starting point. It would essentially unravel his chronology just as Penelope unstitched Laertes' funeral shroud each night. Such an approach might enable Joyce's method to be explained. However, it would not ADVANCE a study of *Ulysses* – merely invert it. Any inheritance-text based on Option Two could not really stand alongside *Ulysses* in the same way that Telemachus was able to stand alongside his father as an associate (rather than a subordinate) by virtue of completing the Telemachiad at the start of the *Odyssey*. At best, it would cancel out *Ulysses*. In summary, pure inversion will not create an inheritance-text. It will merely stall space. Option Three is really an extension of Option Two. It would continue backwards before the start of Oxen to study human linguistic origins as per Saussure, Levi-Strauss and Kristeva's *chora* as it occurs in phallo-logocentrism et al. Oxen (like *PAYM*) really starts at Lacan. The best approach is probably to incorporate all three options into a deconstructive campaign that reverses backwards past Joyce's STARTPOINT in Oxen, drives forwards beyond his

ENDPOINT, plays in the GAP between *Ulysses* and *F(W)ake* (ergo Scylla/Charybdis) then makes its way AROUND *F(W)ake* to extrinsic space (this is the post-Place of the inheritance-text). This is an act of *Kenosis*. Obviously, it can't be represented as a single sequential journey. You can't go backwards and forwards simultaneously. For example, Odysseus does travel east from Ithaca (START OXEN) to Troy (END OXEN) then goes back to Ithaca (RETURN TO START OXEN) but this trope only works if you successfully argue that the slaughter of the suitors is a CANCELLATION DEVICE that rescinds the whole experience of OXEN AS TROY (itself problematic) and leaves his cosmos tabula rasa. This trope is eventually blocked anyway by the lack of significant PRE-OXENISATION murmurs. We would have to explore Odysseus' genealogy for them, but it is a threadbare curtain of rumours and gaps that goes all the way back to his alleged great-grandfather Hermes. We can, however, take this trope forwards fairly easily. Joyce begins at Ithaca (all writing up to *PAYM*), proceeds on a return ticket to Troy (this is the process of composing *Ulysses*), gets back to Ithaca (end of *Ulysses*) then leaves for Gibraltar *[F(W)ake]* entering extrinsic space without defined closure (the inheritance-text also emerges here). Most criticism considers that Joyce used the Oxen episode as a means of getting Leoplod (Sic) Bloom to become a substitute parental figure for Stephen Dedalus with the episode's style brilliantly paralleling the plot. In fact, Bloom becomes Stephen's mother; not his father. Nobody could usurp the role of John Joyce. Bloom's maternal role becomes much clearer in Circe, when Joyce shifts to the psychoanalytic symbolism of his dreams. It is a difficult labour for Bloom like that of the character giving birth in Oxen, Mina Purefoy. Initially, he enters the hospital where Stephen is being 'treated' by a crack team of medical practitioners. They are all trying to wrench Stephen out of the corpus violently. This is an end-in-itself for them. They don't care where or how the foetus leaves the womb. Just so long as it goes. They have no interest in its subsequent human development. Like Tom Finnegan in the ballad that named Joyce's final work, Stephen is being (re)birthed by alcohol. Finnegan revives to the smell of whisky. Stephen is INDUCED by consumption of liquor. This is an example of *Apophrades*. He is natalised when he leaves Holles Street. He literally pours onto the footpath in a parody of birth. This is the point at which Bloom starts guiding and raising Stephen. Over the rest of the novel, Bloom blunts Stephen's existential agony with empathetic blandness. Stephen's pain subsides into boredom. Bloom dulls his wits with pedantry and bourgeois niceties. He becomes the reincarnation of Stephen's dead mother with her idiotic religiosity and forbearance. This MIMICRY enables Stephen to expiate his guilt and move on. Critics have never been able to reconcile the theory that a grandiose new father–son bond is created between Stephen and Bloom with the fact that Stephen chooses to leave Bloom as soon as practicable to go back towards his real father's home at the end of the night. He exits with alacrity into a narrative void. This act is completely consistent with the author's own feelings about his father, as evidenced in Richard Ellmann's definitive biography. James was totally faithful to John Joyce. He relished his ebullience, wildness, humour and voice. *Ulysses* is the father of *Finnegans Wake*. But also its son. It mimics Stephen's Shakespeare theory. One is a birth book. The other one of death (insert Oedipal theory). Likewise, Oxen is a BIRTH episode. This is a DEATH chapter. This approach is actually consistent with the *Odyssey*, which contains NO BIRTHS but numerous DEATHS. It is also consistent with the BOOK itself as signifier. All texts mimic the procession from birth to death. This is not a factor of plot. It is a PHYSICAL quotient. Books always drop off a cliff when you finish. They are immediately forgotten. Only manuals might be excluded from this definition, although they are mostly ordered alphabetically (or information sourced through an alphabetical index). The abecedary format is thus just another trope of chronology. Barthes talked about the author's death. Death of text is also a DESIGN. Joyce spoke of putting language to sleep in *F(W)ake*. This was an act of Euthanasia. In fact, Joyce did exactly the opposite. He kept language awake so long that it went into a state of mania. Joyce hated English. He tortured it. But he had no other linguistic option. There is no word to describe what was done. Only an antonym. It was the OPPOSITE OF AMPUTATION. Maybe it can be termed a RE-PUTATION. It was a GRAFTING UPON. An act of "gra(f)tification" then. Like Lacan said, every word in *F(W)ake* is an elongated pun. This was the primary method used by Joyce to achieve his aim that any person should be able to open any page of *F(W)ake* and know it was written by HIM. Such vanities of scale in this statement. Every page, thus, had to become a FIXED IMAGE like a painting. It must be branded with HIS STYLE like a slave. Just like any viewer can always identify any work of Picasso. Content MUST end up subordinate in such an equation. All text aspires to the condition of painting would be Joyce's retort to Pater. Joyce curated critical work about his writing in the same way that a contemporary artist uses essays to explain the meaning of their art. Joyce kept a picture of Cork in a cork frame on his wall. It was a 'found object' worthy of Marcel Duchamp. Joyce had a readymade temperament like his great contemporary. They never met. I could write another book about Duchamp's writings. They are extraordinary examples of faux manufacturing. He invented the parody manual. The key mental traits of such a thinker are liveliness of spirit, ingenuity and humour. Mallarme was his direct antecedent. Much more than any artist. MD was the next step in poetics. All poets are tricksters. Note Ginsberg on Shaman. See Duchamp's notes to *a mariée mise à nu par ses célibataires, même*. Today, his work is almost forgotten. Google Search 'bride stripped bare' and you get a sequence of links to a soft BDSM novel. The reader also experiences death each time a book ends. The end of text is a definitive severance. Black gives way to blank. The back cover is closed like a VAULT. Officially, we realise that it is already spiralling towards closure long before the conclusion as pagination yields thickness to time from right to left like the brittle skin on the back of my ageing hand (I scratch at the fading freckles, the bulging veins). At that point, it is good to get it over and done with. That is why we always rush to the end of a novel. How many times do you go back to check what really happened to the Bovary family or Frederic Moreau. The French were the great proponents of the speed-rush ending. English writers preferred Pater's slow extinguishment (see the death of Little Nell). Our grasp of any person's life is similarly incomplete. The death of the mother that I loved. The death of the father I hated. We tally their allotted time. We might feel contentment at a life well-lived, loathing their flaws or a life cut short. But we never feel true severance. They always hang on messily. The ghost of Hamlet's father might have been real or not real but either way he was an accurate representation of the mood of the living towards the dead. We always fall into an interval between DEATH/LIFE. Death is the only collective sublime. My strategy now is to let gaps speak. It's a new slogan. So, it would be better now if we turned backwards in time; backwards in time, which is ironic, because it is only by going forward again, beyond this point at which we are now stationed, that we will reach the close. TIME. See Chapter One definition. We know where to begin this story: with Joyce. We know where to end: with Joyce dis/ closed. We need to learn how to advance in the meantime. Beckett showed us this trope over and over again. Insert step-by-step instructions:

(1) Generate new insights about *Ulysses* through a matrix of Joyce's heirs all put to the service of narrative.
(2) Extend *F(W)ake* via Lacan.
(3) Apply a prosenchymatic dome (see Appendix C).
(4) Employ the notion of Technical Fiction (Baudrillard called his work "theory fictions" because theory must compete on an imaginative level).
(5) Bring forth the unpresentable onto the page (see epigraphs).
(6) Make the unintelligible frankly fabulous in all its senses.
(7) Interrogate but do not necessarily resolve the Telemachus myth.
(8) By not chronological sequence; neutering suspense; unmimicking keystone tropes; not stable naming (note partial anagrams and word play: Hallem as He all me; ANA/EVE et cetera; unreceiving language see *F(W)ake*.
(9) Accept that readers might give up (see Browning for sop).

Let us start then at the point at which Joyce ended. It is impossible to find genuine successors to Joyce in English fiction. The whole chinless aristocracy pretty much opted out of the Modernist project. Children's authors like Dahl and Seuss are probably the only relevant candidates. Exclude also the author of *Crash*. Yet *Crash* itself is an interesting idea that should have remained forever an aphorism (i.e. "write a novel about car-crash paraphilia with a film star as bait"). It is dull and repetitive in execution. The influence of Joyce is most strongly discernible in French Structuralist and Post-Structuralist theoreticians after the Second World War. This is a key sentence. Like Joyce, their writing epitomised what Lyotard terms "our human drive to complexification." They deployed key Joycean tropes – gestation, desire and individuation – that predated modern linguistics (see Tadie, *Cypherjugglers*) and which subsequently become central mythemes in modern French theory. As Barthes said in *Writing Degree Zero*, "linguistics is the skeleton of all signifying systems." Elucidating the influence of Joyce on these thinkers will be the focus of this chapter. Joyce ends Oxen of the Sun with an image of a religious poster containing text that appears to be a prophecy of God dispensing bootleg salvation to his adherents: *"He's got a coughmixture with a punch costello in it for you, my friend, in his back pocket. Just you try it on."* Why does the episode end thus? What do these sentences mean? Why do we revert to God at this endpoint of the Canon? At face value, this is an underwhelming closure to a virtuoso display of Joyce's creative prowess. However, structural analysis (see *S/Z*) discloses a jumping-off moment and challenge in this short passage. Let us break it down into linguistic units to disclose meaning:

a) *He's got* – God in literal terms. Actually, Joyce as artist. Possessive. It becomes clear in the next few words that this whole section involves Stephen Dedalus spruiking his creator, James Joyce, and *Ulysses* to prospective readers. It is an advertising slogan for Shakespeare and Company, 12, Rue de l'Odeon, 12, PARIS, 1922.
b) *a coughmixture* – an elixir. Heaven as such. But *Ulysses* really. A hallucinatory beverage and cure. Stephen has been drinking absinthe, which is a compatible dream liquid. Perhaps this is a kind of Delphic divination of his subsequent performance in Nighttown. He is playing the role of deacon to the revellers, acting out the way that the poster 'speaks' to its readers. He is clearly still vulnerable to the message of religion. A new compound word is created by Joyce to signify *Ulysses*. It is oddly dissonant. Two distinct words are run together with no apparent gain in terms of verbal confluence or flow. In fact, the syllabic resonance is soft then hard ("ff" to "mix"). This is an awkward combination.

Perhaps it is an anti-lyrical act. HeGod (Joyce) is presented as a travelling showman promoting fake patent medicine (*Ulysses*). This is consistent with the sermons on Dowie and Vaughan which incorporate phrases like "rush your order and play a slick ace" and "score a buck joyride to heaven." This word, coughmixture, becomes a synecdoche for *Ulysses*. It acts upon the voice. It is 'of' the voice. It is each of sedative, relaxant, stimulant and narcotic. We can split the compound like a nut shell and yield further meaning ~~(a polysemous sausage)~~. Cough means to exhale with noise (see Attali); expel germs (soul-fixer); attain provisional relief yet create the conditions for compulsive repetition by irritating the larynx; and share infection. It is a sub-signifier of breath/breathe. Its signified is not ocular. It is a vesper. A whisper. Air then. Mixture denotes assemblage, soup, conglomeration *et al*. It is a symbol for this novel. This is embodied in the neologism itself which literally jams words together.

c) *With a punch costello in it* – a character in this episode. A popular phrase in boxing denoting exponential force (i.e. 'to pack a punch') that is also used to refer to liquor with high alcohol volume. Punch is a mild alcoholic drink that blends spirits, carbonated water and fruit. The nickname of Francis Costello, a medical student prominent in Oxen. He is presented mildly. There is no other reference to Costello in Joyce's writing (aside from related intrusions in the dream sequences of Circe). Castlecostello in *F(W)ake* does not refer to this person. It is an alternative name for Castlemore in County Mayo. There is an element of free association in this linguistic unit. The nickname suggests the pantomime puppet show, Punch and Judy. It was first recorded by Samuel Pepys in 1662. Pulcinella and Judy are warring spouses. Various characters fall victim to beatings from the slapstick (club) of Mister Punch. It is a traditional form of entertainment in English culture. He is an emblem of British Imperialism for Joyce. The puppeteer in P&J is known as the Professor. He is assisted by a "bottler" who spruiks the show to the audience outside the booth, acts as master of ceremonies, collects donations ("the bottle") and plays accompanying music on a drum or pan pipes. Stephen is acting as the 'bottler' for Joyce as Professor ('HeGod'). *Ulysses* is literally the novel with a "Punch Costello in it." This unit clearly relates to Joyce and *Ulysses*.

d) *for you, my friend* – a direct statement to the reader containing false intimacy. Insincere. Who is speaking these lines? The narrator? A wired-up Stephen Dedalus? Joyce himself? Almost certainly it is not L. Bloom (unless this is internal monologue where he can be strident on occasion).

e) *in his backpocket* – a term used to describe an object (usually advantageous) held in reserve. Related to 'up his sleeve.' Location of the male wallet in trousers. Potential homosexual allusion. Often the whereabouts of a hip flask. A saying that describes effective control by one individual over another. It usually relates to criminal power over public officials. Emblematic of Joyce as author. He always has another device, image or character available for sudden use. He is always exerting control over his reader et cetera. It could also refer to a pocket-sized edition of *Ulysses* (note problems of scale).

f) *Just you try it on* – an offer to assume God's raiment. Rag-trade spruiking to the reader of the come along (x2) just-feel-the-width variety. Spruiker is an Australian English term first recorded in 1915. To 'try it on' also means to attempt to gull another party. Finally, it can also be used as a threat. In this instance, it is a threat to any party contemplating an inheritance-text to Oxen.

How is the Gold Cup used as a symbol by Joyce?

There are regular references to the Ascot Gold Cup throughout *Ulysses*. It forms an essential part of the plot. The name of this horse race alone evokes an image of Classical heroes toasting each other with draughts of wine poured into gold cups by comely maids at torch-lit feasts. Whenever Homer wants to exemplify *xenia*, he uses this formula. Gold is always associated with wealth in human culture. A 'brick' (see below) evokes the imagery of a gold bar but it actually refers to a package of currency banded with steel straps in Australian English. It signposts Imperial London (see Eleni Loukopoulou, "London, Language and Empire in 'Oxen of the Sun'"). Initially, Joyce's references to the Gold Cup are confined to linguistic slapstick. Bloom offers Bantam Lyons a copy of a religious pamphlet, which he terms a "throwaway" when he enters the pub. Lyons misinterprets it as a hot tip (AKA "London to a Brick On" in Australian slang), although Bloom isn't even aware that a horse named Throwaway is competing in the race. Later references to the Gold Cup become highly symbolic. In Oxen of the Sun, it is revealed that the rank outsider, Throwaway, now associated with Bloom, has won the Gold Cup beating Sceptre, the hot favourite, backed by Hugh Blazes Boylan. Joyce's symbolistic equation becomes: "Throwaway (paper) = Elijah (subject) = Bloom ('bloody dark horse') = black horse (Throwaway) then REVERSE." Boylan corresponds to the fallen favourite (Chagemar). His physicality is symbolised by the sceptre in *Ulysses*. It corresponds to the cane which he wields so brazenly. It is a phallic object. Molly comments on Boylan's prodigious endowment and copulatory strength in Penelope. Finally, the sceptre acts an emblem of Imperial authority. Ireland (Bloom) will ultimately defeat England (Boylan). This victory is cleverly insinuated by Joyce. The first sign of Boylan that Bloom sees when he returns home in Ithaca is torn up betting tickets in the kitchen. England has torn up its false mandate and gone. Later, we learn from Molly that Boylan was very upset about his horse losing the race. Bloom is sanguine. He did not bet on the race. Therefore, we can deduce that Bloom has come from a long way back in the field to NOT LOSE. Molly ends the novel reflecting positively about her husband. It is the only moment of pure sentimentality – in the sense of meta-pathos – in the entire novel. Other potential competitive references – such as the dead Rudies (son and father) – are dehumanised by Joyce's cold pursuit of Modernist High Style. "Let's get whacked," murmured Willy the Pimp poised over Tom Hallem's bursting bloodlines. Need him; don't trust him. Or any man. Wish I had his cock in my mouth. False father figures. No friends just users. And just using people myself. No proximity. No hold. Impermanence maybe. But some respite nonetheless. Dead-out all feelings. Don't try to dredge sentiment out of the heavy mud of text. That was Joyce's motto. In *The Order of Discourse*, Michel Foucault creates a Post-Structuralist Intentional Fallacy. All commentary must be carried out in exile. It must operate outside the text. It must feign precedence. "You've been in there a long time," inquired a dub voice. That's the first thing I remember. Willy was wrong to leave me. But who can blame him? I'd have done the same thing myself. He also stole the last coins out of my pockets. Business is business, I guess. Wealth for toil. Rat up a drainpipe where junk is concerned. Fare the well ole England. See you when your worms are straighter! My new island home. Golden brown. Girt by semen. Low father feeling + strong mother = liminality. Wandering Rocks was a Hermes chapter. Gobby green gem in a grave. Paterian fathernoster. Wilde the de-fatherer. Olympic metropolis. Neon **No Vacancy** sign. Molly takes the sign out of the window at Eccles Street. Messages withheld and delivered. Inconstant wind wishes lackspray. A drowned man. End of Chapter 2. Search party. Oars in murky reeds. Argonauts. Conrad-style coal steamers. Carcass swinging on a rope at the entrance to the Governor's residence. Overturned vehicle. People hanging upside down like socks. Release the seatbelts. Plop. Bill Henson's *Leda*. Exeunt all making their way through oh yea cats and dogs. It's all about beings-in-motion *en route* to observe pure speed. Distance Form Closure over 3200 m at Flemington. "Black Knight gets the money." No rank outsider this year. Time's sup, gentlemen! Crumple and tear up your inutile chits and throwaway them. Discard. Bless my soul! I pulled my fix from the woodpecker's hole. Woody-the-Peck opened the washroom door and came beak-to-beak with Tyro Power. Beige drag. Insert slang term for "excuse me." What o'clock be it, Sir Frangible? he asked. Three the answer. Damn I missed the Cup. Who won? More disappointment. Woody could have made the following single or multiple bets on the M.Cup to meet the symbolic fancies of this character:

TABLE 3. MELBOURNE CUP 1984 – AN UNRELIABLE FORM GUIDE

	Horses (in order of finish)	Rationale for character and/or plot decision to bet on this horse
1.	Black Knight	Self-perception as rebel figure
2.	Chagemar	Highest chance of profit if backed for WIN (race favourite)
~~3.~~	Mapperley Heights	N/A
4.	Rose & Thistle	Potential tattoo image on atrophied bicep (Later DNA analysis disclosed 97.3% British ancestry with the balance assumed to be anonymous Spanish/Italian waiter in London during Empire period).
~~5.~~	~~Foxseal~~	N/A
~~6.~~	~~Affinity~~	N/A
~~7.~~	~~Rocky Rullah~~	N/A. Woody appears in C5, S-E7 leaving his girlfriend (ambiguously P.Girl?). There should be multiple analogies to *King Lear* in this S-E.
8.	Lancelotto	Outside chance of flutter if he was amused by this simple pun on the famed English Knight and popular numbered-ball gambling game across Australia.
9.	Pass the Baton	Ironic syringe-sharing metaphor might have tickled his fancy.
10.	Fountaincourt	WtP is the active character in S-E10. Alternate name for toilet where W/TH shot-up. Ironic label for methadone clinic.
~~11.~~	~~Forward Charge~~	N/A. Woody commutes from university to brothel in S-E11. This sub-episode scrambles chronology, playing ironically on the horse name 'forward charge.'
12.	Secured Deposit	Allusion to his dream of consistent supply of narcotics.
13.	British	Love of English '60s rock (R.Stones, Kinks, Faces, Mott).
14.	B-Boy	Self-deprecating link to his role as rent boy
~~15.~~	~~Bounty Hawk~~	N/A
~~16.~~	~~Hussar's Command~~	N/A. Willy at brothel in S-E16. Devonshire tea scene in *Ulysses*. Note analogy to junkies' consuming cream buns on bus (C4).
17.	Martian's Son	Love of '60s US TV series. Self-identification as son of Uncle Martin (Tim O'Hara?).
~~18.~~	~~Alibhai~~	N/A
~~19.~~	~~Legana~~	N/A

The most reasonable conclusion to be drawn from this suite of potential gambling options is that it is most likely that Woody the Pimp would have made a NET LOSS on the M.Cup in 1984. The only single or combination bets which could have yielded GROSS profit are: Win/Place on Black Knight, Place on Chagemar and/or Quinella on Black Knight and Chagemar. These options would have yielded relatively low profits due to short odds. Any profit in this column needs to be balanced against losses on other horses upon which Woody "chanced his arm" (note extended heroin injection imagery). All of the eight other horses cited in the table above failed to place. Broke skint insolvent *zonam perdidit*. Wolf gnawing at my door. Lady Lightpurse hast come and throttled Job's turkey. Father Con-me (an invocation to the RCC). I'd kill for a durry a mystery bag covered in dead horse and a wet silver bullet right now. Or sheets of bronze toast topped with lashings of gold butter and Polonius [(L.) *pressed meat*]. I can tell a wank from a wandsaw make no mistake. Maybe exorcise the old five finger discount. Score some Jubilee Mutton. I'll dob him into the Filth. End up spending Friday night eternity off Sydney Heads chained to a Coolgardie safe. Bubbles and fishes. Flat loaves dispensed with. Shave my scone go live on runes up the side of Mt Mantra embrace air diet. Dice toll in a marble vault. Every fuck is a new lifeline. Deal some coke make enough dosh to bail out to Baal-ee or Phuck-it. Rip-off McCann. Or Leer. I know his combination. Lift away the pantry floorboards. Slide down the Batpole. Medical Dick and Medical Davy were on duty. "Inner West Drug Wars!" Keep on the headgear. Leer is a dunny rat Odysseus. A college cricket match belied the elements at Williams Oval. The smoke of barbequed meat arose from the pavilion. Tom Hallem passed from swerve of Main Oval to bend of Ward Gymnasium by aery paces clawing through Gidgee and mashed up murph, a defiant swaggerman sliding down a riverbank then shimmering o'er bongpuddle potholes past RPA symbolically walking alongside this hospital gazing in on the Oxen not going WITHIN symbolic of how this text is always outside *Ulysses* he felt in his pockets for nothing still half-blasted and friendless (not even a Costello) ill-fitting Leo's old suit [symbolism] don't try to compete with Joyce's ending (emulate) **BECKETT** Sadosanct staggered autochthonously, mud clucking under his soles, KGV ill-looming out of lo thunderclubs, his crisscross feetures marred by a plooming cyst, one bare manifestation of all-rottenness within, heightening his crippled gait, whose severity had already been exasperated by still-gloaming leather boots that he was instructed to wear by his erstwhile mistress, in some perverse inheritance from her husband, an act of munificence, or was it cruelty, nobody could explain the variance, which Sado accepted mildly, even dutifully, making him a base vowel, albeit 2-blistered, in their Severinesque ablaut. There is no need for textual spacing between Joyce and Beckett in any lineage. They make a natural segue like the border between Ulster and Eire. Beckett purges Joyce's style of all wordplay. We can see linguistic experiments dwindle in the changeover passage above. SS crunched at the bubbly gravel which weeped under weighed atmos. His eyes observed the shuffling figurines of Detox. A bewildered elder rested in his steel walking frame. Could have been any man's father. Just as I could ebb as any man's son, reasoned Sado. The old cocksucker parsed the scene. Too weak to raise the belt these days. He lifted and clacked, scraped and redirected his ironic chariot. If only I still had Chrysippus chained to its bars, he mused, with his arsehole weeping off the end of my cock in faux Pisan airstream. Beckett can be crude like that. He rejected all full tropes and mythology. He had seen the outcome of Joyce bolting together such an abomination in *F(W)ake*. Blend war imagery, Beckett, Classical allusions, sport and personal experience into a parody. All I need is some salt and a plough to escape war-service. Odysseus was a great hater on a delayed-action fuse. He was always going to reimburse Palamedes for throwing Telemachus in front of his tank. Literature was his art. Fake letter purportedly from Priam. Dear Palamedes, please get your Greek friends to leave. Enclosed is a small token of our affection. Yours, P. Lemon-scented stationery. Gold bars planted in a footlocker. Enjoy half his revenue forever. Odysseus cashed-in his immense prestige amongst the Greeks to execute this revenge motif. Everyone turned a blind eye. Palamedes is not even mentioned in the *Iliad*. Ody gets air-brushed by Homer. Tom Hallem walked towards the compound. "Hail Mary, sinkhole of God! It's dry Laius," he exclaimed hauling his guts to the wire. The old man lurched. A bit more choke and he would have started. He sucked up some more chocolate milk. No point now in futile gestures. I knew what kind of man you'd become, Don Cane stated baiting his hook. Insert pent pause. A turncoat, he added conclusively. The last words I remember being uttered by my father. He turned adrift. I stabbed him at the three-way crossroads. Tom Hallem withdrew. Act Five, Scene Three begins with Lear's delusion about what would constitute a pleasant place of escape for Cordelia. His idea is to entomb them in an incestuous box together. Sounds like fun. A greater meaning gets hauled into view when you re-set these trifling motions in Telemark, Norway. That's where Ibsen was born and his dramatic cosmos ploughed seed. I told the registered nurse to administer Diazepam freely. Anything to stupefy hate. Beckett was the first writer to breed off a mean, senile culture. They called it Existentialism at first. But it was almost the opposite because there was no freedom, no choice, no conclusion, not even death. Don Cane was propped up on a foam mattress at the foot of the stage by the time of my final entrance. We two alone at last sat like birds in his antiseptic cage. The stench of reheated roasts pined the dim room. I pressured him to sing his last lines. The audience was waiting to get back to the car park. How are you feeling? I asked. What do you fuck-ing think? he husked. Wardell's jigsaw seminary squatted o'er grassy lowland verge into which had been sliced lush playing fields. Churchill's uplands remained unsunlit. A distant clock dong-dinged. In English, it is possible to derive the past tense of strong verbs by substituting the base vowel with another vowel. This is a metaphor for Beckett's relationship to Joyce. He was Telemachus for a time. He learned alongside to Joyce like an apprentice. The real Telemachus learned by absence and gaps. Posters pasted the wall in a crucifix-symbol. **Was Jesus a Sun Myth?** they asked. This is a direct lift from *Ulysses*. More Catholic Club flim-flam. Stations of the Cross. Insert Molloy's mathematical formulas. Comfort from science. Sixteen sucking stones. Four in each pocket. Beckett was always gaming Joyce's love of numerical symbolism. There are eleven celebrants in Burke's pub at the end of the Oxen episode. Eleven members of the Denzille Lane Boys. Eleven disciples at stumps at the Last Supper. Plus the bloke carrying towels and wine. There were twelve celebrants in Burke's pub. List of the twelve worst books in history. Bloom makes thirteen. Cricket was the first data sport. Samuel Beckett played for Dublin University against Northamptonshire in 1925 and 1926. He was a left-hand batsman and left-arm medium fast bowler, according to *Wisden*. He scored 35 runs at an average of 8.75 and went wicketless. Willow on red leather rapped like an index-knuckle on my skull. Sweet silence after. Applause for the bowler. I faddle-fiddled with my pads. You're up next, Private Parts, yelled Slut-Major. Bric-a-brac tumbled from my pockets. A charmed red handkerchief, for instance, got off Desdemona's bung. Lucky was loitering at the gate like a fresh fart. He was blind or deaf this time I really can't remember which or why. Beckett is always reversing imagery. INSERT rotational ambigram. Circus amateur at Nutley. Newell's PUZZLE. 180-degree rotation. Australia defeated England by eight runs at Lords in 1882. A spectator burned the bails, put them in an urn and took out a mock advertisement in *The Times* announcing the death of English cricket. The Ashes were oxymoronically birthed. Another crime against Helios. Phoenix-play. Father boxing son. Bosie's leg spin. Low shot after the bell. Intergenerational trauma. Ebbs and Sutcliffe open the batting. Decimal Bradman at three. Jardine's Bodyline reminded Australian crowds too much of trench warfare. Players and Gentlemen still use different gates. Laius got Jocasta pregnant when he was dead drunk after a gig at the Ironworkers Club. Forgot to heed the Sirens. She was an older lady like Anne Hathaway. They staked the baby by the foot to Mount Manna. This is arch-symbolism (personal). Coincidences are also symbols. Laius drove his chariot over Oedipus' foot at Cleft Palate. Both made Filth with Jocasta. *Experience limite*. O sublime disgrace! Beckett eschewed linguistic games in order to steer around the Joycean impasse. Odysseus never named boats. All anonymous vessels. My father's name does not appear on my birth certificate. False father figures abound. Don > Les > Leer. Make up your own story. Sitting in a room full of strangers in Wolverhampton who look like YOU talk like YOU and ALL breath ALIKE. Laryngeal theory. Same-shaped palettes. Moment of

Abjection. See Kristeva. Insert more arbitrary numerology (parody of Joyce). Palamedes invented eleven consonants in the Greek alphabet. The order of the sub-episodes in this chapter can be changed without any impact on textual flow. They are each utterly self-contained moving towards the same endpoint. Insert arbitrary batting order: Beckett (Captain), Barthes, Levi-Strauss, Saussure, Lacan, Deleuze & Guattari, Foucault, Baudrillard, Derrida, Lyotard, Virilio, Bataille. Twelfth man to be named. INSERT AVERAGES (M, I, NO, R, AV, 50, 100, C, R, W, AV, 5I, 10M). Controversial omission of Althusser. No females. Add Kristeva and Irigaray to the squad. Chairman of Selectors, J-P Sartre, told a packed media conference [DOWNLOAD MEDIA CLIP 1]: "There are only eleven places in the Argo so someone had to miss out. Unfortunately, Louis was the man." Sartre also defended the selection of Irishman, Beckett, as skipper [SEE CLIP 2]: "He is the only member of the team with first-class cricket experience in England. He was an obvious choice for skipper." English will name its squad later this week. It will be led by F.R. Leavis. It is expected to include the Americans Eliot, Pound and Bloom. These Caribbean entertainers are known as the "Three Double-U's" to linguists. This sets the stage for a decisive theoretical struggle. **INSERT TITLE. THE UNBOW(E)LABLE. SHIFT TO FIRST PERSON PRESENT TENSE.** I am striding to the arena ("Cock" goes up on the scoreboard) despite my shell, which impedes flowing movement, though it hardly protects ... or camouflages. At the sound of the conch I come forward shamelessly regardless of the pleadings of my family and the disdain of onlookers. It has always been thus. A cheap tart for tunes. I am dressed in white like an archangel. This is ironic (did I say 'ironic'? If only it were truly so) for I am hardly Holy; hardly holey either being wholly hard and round. Except for my limbs which make me star-shaped. And the flesh itself which is secured to the inside surface by cleats. Descending now but no not to Hades. It's not as simple as that. If only it were merely the spatial projection "DOWN." Part of some genial dichotomy to deconstruct Dialectical Materialism. Like Derrida did to undermine binary codes. Typically, Beckett creates a mundane style then inserts sudden incongruity – maybe an Archaism or some technical term that he can then disclaim all comprehension of; such as the use of *aporia* at the start of *The Unnameable*. My feet are crackling on the concrete steps. But not upon leaves, not brogues, not Fall. No. Spikes have been glued onto the soles of my boots ... but why?! As a *cadeau* for to tread in the skulls of my opponents? I would do that. Yes, obey. If obeisance was possible. Which it isn't. Why pretend? I should know. I've made a science of its study. No. It's compulsion. Compulsion to accord. Without the choice to rebel or obey. Not compulsion then. PROSAIC THRALL. Without servility. *Sans* force. I just do it. Do it, or even more, because it's time. I flow forward like a puddle, my weapon swinging alongside me ... but not as a deterrent, no: if only it was! For it does not ward off attacks on my person. It only draws them down with still more fervor even though it is hardly able to swat the flies asunder. Or reach my a(nta)gonistes. Did I just insinuate Milton into the text? What confection! I'll be invited to write an essay for *Quadrant* next. As if it were really a contest and my opponent was the giant Harapha and I could somehow link this metonymy to Samson's moral recall. Well, he was also a blind and denuded prisoner I guess. But as for any extended metaphor ... don't make me laugh! My windpipe will seize and I will make a protracted velar nasal. It's time to turn my attention to the pitch. Oh dark dark dark amid the blaze of noon's new moon. There they are. It's time for me to join them. The gate opens miraculously, of course. Why not? No?! Well in that case, it jams – or, before I reach it, it is already jammed – so that I struggle to get it open, to release the latch, while wearing such heavy mitts ... though they hardly protect ... my fingers all got broken. It's almost as if they're specifically designed to make my scratchings more awkward. And apparent. For yes, I do scratch. INSERT Beckett's common references to psoriasis. And these gloves ... do they give some added titillation? To the bureaucrats who framed the rules, designed my equipment (or should I say 'evolved it'), organised this travesty and allowed it to be broadcast? Do they gain some added excretions from the sight of me struggling with the latch? Why not. Why wouldn't they do that. Because it makes it look as if it's my decision, my choice ... to go. ALLEZ POILU! In that there is genuine irony ("if only it were so!" exclaimed Beckett, "it would be a construct worthy of Swift"). For I would never choose to go freely (did I say 'free'), of my own Will (did I say 'Will' ... my heart skips a beat at his name) and volition (cantare, oh-oh oh-oh) onto said arena (was it always designated thus or sprung from Merlin?) and this whole 'latch manoeuvre' is merely a literary device to effect added indignity on my person as if it were my fondest wish to go, to be gone into the RED ZONE or whatever they call it and sample Tenebrous Nature. The whistle blows. The Sergeant-Major sings. We pop Over the Top into No Man's Land. I am wearing my gas mask. Yes, through the thick visor I can see grass. My head is enclosed in a turret. I am a panopticon branded with Michel Foucault's special logo. It designates my acquiescence. They have secured it to my bulb with a strap like Molloy's hat and upon its face is riveted a clear mask for to affect my observation. But of what? Will they pop out my eyeballs and leave them weeping on my cheeks to make all of me watch the PLOP below? A sum which basically amounts to Caliban's moment before the mirror ... a glimpse, painful but real ... of life? More Abjection. More ellipses. It's an epidemic. But did I actually say the word REAL? As if I could just walk out the front door of the Holles Street maternity ward one morning, enter the crowd and catch a trolley car to work without being dragged by my hair to some remote underwood where they conducted all kinds of experiments. It's my fault. I can hardly shift the blame to another gender or pass the whole abortion off on paternity. That was the luxury of past epochs. We've got psychiatry these days. It forces us to TRY TO END trauma. I know only too well that no single human can be blamed for my predicament. There are so many people I should thank for this opportunity. I'd like to thank the sponsors for attaching themselves to this farce. The fans for their support (as if they too had any choice in the matter ... as if they weren't coerced under threat of becoming my proxy). Also, my parents. INSERT CANNED LAUGHTER. Lucky restates all my best lines to the audience with a wink like Mulligan. When he says them, everybody laughs. There are nodes of recognition. Perhaps it's all in the delivery. I hop over the picket fence, abandoning the latch (this has gone beyond a joke), enjoining my gourds (I have glue), my soles tearing at the turf (how I hate Nature), looking up at the sky (as if for God) although I know that salvation can only come on earth via some magic elevator of Shelley. I grind at the spongy crust (Demeter's scab) like an angry bucolic on a cobblestone lane in some quaint Irish village. It is all hopelessly obtuse. The turf has been baked hard and flat. My *prosopon* is cracking. I scrape at the earth to gouge out symbols. Dirt medallions spark. I carve skinny scars like some Druid. I remember Tolkien writing of such periods. But now it is my turn to inquire of the Soul. Does this mean it is time to take up my position? I take it without thinking. Johnny Turk is waiting. I mutter the creed. My eyes squeeze themselves shut then burst open like combustible products. But such metaphysical speculation is futile when confronted with this MOMENT. Next time,

Next ...

time ...

there must be a whole career of poses ahead of me as I squelch onwards (ever-onwards) an unlikeable form (an UNLIKELY form maybe) in an unlikely forum (an UNLUCKY forum perhaps) unlikely to achieve anything with my swat ... I'LL DO ANYTHING THEY SAY JUST DON'T HURT ME! I am no Prometheus. Just let me down off this rock. Doctor Septisure appeared with a grommet punch and stuck his tongue up my DNA releasing facets from my entrails. I wait. The MRI test requires absolute stillness. Otherwise they get a fuzzy image of the brain. As if it is any different! My enemies are positioned to restrict me, organised from inside, behind a screen, sometimes there's a circle to offer arbitrary constraint for the pretense of presenting A CONTEST. I'm taking up my stance. But why get technical? I bang my stick hard just to let Nature know I'm still heathen. Head at an uncomfortable angle. I am hunched, true, yet totally exposed. Naturally, they gather in places I cannot see. Some huddle in a cordon (do they think they're unapparent?) with feelers outstretched – this is one of their techniques – and whisper sweet nothings. I threaten to report them to the prefects. Beckett was still able to invoke school practices without qualms in his day. But why pretend that such a thing is still possible? No, I can't go, I must go on, there's something happening. Distant movement. I wait erect and exposed. I bolster the troops on the walls of Camp Paravel. If I had fallen and crawled I could pretend to be a ground-based insect so much do I resemble one. Even Solipsism is not out of the question. Oh, to be able to report back to Berkeley and Fichte on Eschatology. It would be like the thrill of facing God. But I'm a creature of spontaneous thrall who labours under the consequences of motion as I ponder sloth and inertia. The Canker says "stay." I can see a pallid speck on the horizon – there are timpani's – the wooden wheels grind closer – I'll run – I'll not – I'll walk – wait and see – hesitate and waver – until perhaps I will be released by indecision or death (it's just like marriage) – we both loiter for the melee-hack – turning our backs on each other (despite our suspicions) – retreating to the farthest permissible distance (that is the best time) – arming our muskets – but why pretend: I cannot capitulate to halt death or whatever you want to call it. Better to just keep my eyes on the spot that I have marked out in the gloom and against which I measure progress. It's hard to explain exactly what happened next (it all took place at the speed of Evolution) but it went something like: Motion A, stasis, Motion Anti-A, stasis (reverie) then by increment Motion A, Motion B, Motion Anti-B, Motion Anti-A, Motion Negative A to the Power of One, Pause, Return to Bar Six, CHORUS. It took me this long to invest my movements with design. But I feel like they are all metaphors for a moral oscillation between evil and good. This must have been how the apes started. Everything becomes part of some causal sequence. I charge the turd running down my legs with meaning. Tom Hallem reached Missenden Road and planted his feet on the pedestrian crossing stepping onto the chiaroscuro impress of hire car tread. Hamlet's father's ghost. I pass over his warm grave. Look up. Birthplace balcony. High up in space like a rotten spire. Cries of a newborn press through the glass brick wall. Thick feint figures. The characters left Holles Street Maternity Hospital after Missus Mina Purefoy gave birth. *Exeunt all.* The widower remained. He was propped up in bed listening to a one-day international on a transistor radio thumbing a copy of Dante's *Divine Comedy* in Italian. He always slumped into a stupor in the middle overs – 1 0 0 1 0 1. Binary symbols. Repetition. Occasional boundary. Ninety words per day. Write with nostalgia of a negated cosmos.

"There seems to have been a technical fault in our line from Headingley," said the booth announcer. "We'll return to the cricket as soon as possible. In the meantime, it's *My Word!* with Denis Norden and Frank Muir."

Samuel Beckett smiled, opened his eyes and raised the mohair wrap still higher over his white teats suckling gently on English butterscotch.

BARTHES

We have already sampled Barthes' early technique of structuralist analysis in relation to our examination of the end of the Oxen episode (see "coughmixture" sentence above). This was the method made famous in his review of Balzac's "Sarrasine" entitled *S/Z* (see below). OotS does not contain much plot movement. But it's hard for the reader to keep even this limited progress in view because of continuous style shifts and numerous references – both literary and local to Dublin. This makes the text as dense as any product of French theory. It's like those Buddhists who see a whole landscape in a bean. Basically, there's a bunch of small events coming together in fast sequence. That is Joyce's mode. We saw it in Wandering Rocks in terms of people, place and motion. This time the clutter is language. Broken down into its plot components, this chapter simply traces the movement of Tom Hallem towards a public bar. He passes a hospital but does not enter. This is highly symbolic against Stephen Dedalus' schedule in Oxen. He is hungry (see contrast with his brother who eats with relish in C4 & C5). The abundance of characters in the previous chapter recedes, especially females. This was a harsh ironic device by Joyce given that Oxen is an episode about conception and childbirth. It is the most aggressive, masculine and sexist episode in the whole of *Ulysses*. Even the Citizen is not so bold. Professional women are denigrated. It is as if Joyce wanted to display the worst features of the male gender in the most inappropriate place conceivable as an emblem against which Bloom could subsequently pivot. The medical students become the equivalent of Homer's privileged and self-indulgent suitors, rather than Odysseus' starving crew. Narrative focus tightens. The main characters make but little progress. Billy Capri eats food (see Foucault S-E, also C5 S-E19). He stalls at the prospect of facing his peers and mentors (see Virilio S-E). This suggests he will not pursue an academic career. Don Cane takes a nap (LACAN | NACAL S-E) then goes on a test drive (Virilio S-E). Both father and sons are locked in fruitless orbit. Don has decided to visit the home of his eldest son first. Why he chooses Tom Hallem over Billy Capri is never explained but it is clear that there is a simple reason – he already possesses the address – as well as a more complex epistemology around gender, power and family. The eldest and legitimate son possesses preeminent rights in all cultures. Don may also feel residual rights over his wife. Finally, there is the relative weakness and anonymity of his male counterparty (Les Hallem) compared to the messy option of confronting his old friend and saviour (Bob Capri). Don Cane may also feel constrained in approaching the Capris because he had spent only limited time with Helen McFadden, principally during their intense love affair. This was a severed connection never sealed. Roland Barthes is always the Last Romantic. He was forever trying to confect positive reasons to read, write, live and love.

His notion of hedonism in *The Pleasure of the Text* was far different to Foucault. He called the climax of reading, *jouissance*. His titles were always a gift of gentle reason. There are no book titles in his oeuvre containing words like PUNISH or POWER. He even critiqued his own back catalogue. This was a kind of hair shirt he assumed. He wanted to create NEUTRAL WRITING. *A Lover's Discourse* (the French title is longer and better) was his written attempt at describing the fragmentary, passive beauty of falling in love badly. He wanted to write an image of erotic surface like Bonnard's "Siesta" and deep tone like Monet's pond. It is truly one of the worst books ever published. A mawkish text. Its appropriated prosody and cliched scenes contain none of the stylistic or imagistic ingenuity of real love. It is a stagnant pool with dead fish on top (mainly Goethe, Proust, Plato). It is actually a great advertisement for DOXA (what he called 'loaded prose'). Barthes was a terrible selector. The book intercuts fictive scenarios with fragments of theory, set piece mummery and quotations that are designed to amplify and deconstruct: (1) our idealised visions of the beloved; and (2) those tokens of the beloved that mean nothing to anyone except the lover. Whom we cannot forget and cannot remember are equally significant. Memory bears no relation to marital status, longevity of relationship or relative physical beauty in LOVE. INSERT COMPARABLES. Penelope felt love for Les Hallem. Not Don. Certainly not Dick Stone. Odysseus held onto an iconic version of his wife. Bloom as well. Helen Capri for Bob. Also Don. Don Cane for Richie. Also Helen. Not Penelope. Bob Capri for his wife at all stages. A pang of guilt assailed him as he contemplated his journey to the warm body of his lover, where he experienced a calm grip that had never been possible with his wife. This lack made his obsession even stronger. And it got even stronger as the possibility of achieving the same tenderness withdrew with age. Elizabeth retained a sentimental image of her husband. Body images had begun to infest her. Leon recalled the weak fertility they shared. Chaim. Elizabeth looked vacant and exhausted at his death bed. Stan retained a strong token of his visit with Elizabeth to Greece. It was hard to tell if it was the person, place or both things. The Sublime will be examined in the Virilio sub-episode. Billy always held onto O. Even her basic smell that he did not like. Even that was beloved. Shanghai Dog and Judy. Also, Xiao Fang. Tom Hallem never managed to summon such morsels. Maybe he felt it for WtP. It could have been suppressed homoeroticism or maybe not. Love of this kind can be uncoupled from sex. Stephen Dedalus was too young to feeling anything external to his own senses. Penelope Hallem parked the car on George Street. The Queen Victoria Building was shrouded in scaffolding and fabric. When the wind blew, loose hessian sheets lifted revealing a dusty sheen on its sandstone torso and lightless stained-glass cloaks. Low-level construction work reverberated through the hollowed interior. A hoarding proclaimed that HKG was restoring this palace to its original glory. She crossed the dead road. The exterior of the

Hilton Hotel exhibited the grubby pall of Brutalist architecture even though it was relatively new. Dun concrete façade and brown panels. She descended a blank staircase and followed its sharp turn. History sunk under the pavement in layers. The Marble Bar was a relic of the nineteenth century gold rush. Penelope remembered the place from the old days when it was located on Pitt Street in the old Tattersall's Hotel above a maze of old alleys. She held tight onto a walnut staircase. A cardboard sign rested crookedly on an easel. Pentel Australia Tenth Anniversary, it said. Thick ink calligraphy. She went to the entrance of the packed saloon. A tarnished plaque caught her attention. She paused. George Adams Marble Bar was designed by Varney Parkes in the ornate tradition of the Italian Renaissance, it read. Cost of 32,000 pounds. Each column decorated with solid bronze capitals. One hundred tonnes of the world's best Belgian and African marble. Cedar joinery. Stained pictorial glass frames. Cavernous fireplaces inlaid with marble. Fourteen Edwardian paintings. When Tattersall's Hotel was demolished, the entire structure was dismantled, refurbished and rebuilt inside the new Hilton Hotel. Grand re-opening 1973. Settle back, share a drink, and bask in the reflected ambience of a fully restored Australian icon. Involuntarily, Penelope Hallem retrieved an unwanted vision of her husband topless on the edge of a bed in Cremorne. He rolled to his feet and stretched his torso. Smooth light held the bulging pallor of Les Hallem's rolled hind where it was pulled into thick culverts of scarred flesh. Penelope Hallem entered the bar. Shanghai Dog watched dawn come low-glowing through the kaleidoscope of a scratched plane hatch. Below massed clouds. Above only casing. Occasional gaps revealed dry riverbeds writhing through the desert. The Odysseus myth is broken from beneath. Talos is propelled off ramparts to the ground. Lester Byron dropping through space. No time to reflect. Smash landing. Crafty Dedalus high as a kite. Flight paths to Australia converge over Mindanao and track the Arafura Sea to landfall. Shiny milk coated Lake Yamma Yamma. Don Cane would have seen exactly the same scene when he looked down over what was then called Lake Mackillop in 1984. A crosscut in space/time then. What lies behind the eyeballs is the prevailing factor not shared eye colour or the same nose. List the presiding mythemes of *Telemachus*:

1. Father and mother in fruitful union (c.1960).
2. Father commits abomination against Nature (family relation or plough).
3. Father in exile at war.
4. Son(s) born.
5. Mothers' mild deceptions (see also Circe, Calypso).
6. Normalised childhoods (insert false father figures).
7. Father returns (C2).

8. Truth revealed belatedly (C4).
9. Sons break with paternal trope (post-novel): one is destroyed; the other survives.
10. Living brother writes of dead brother ("In Memoriam").

We have reached the threshold of number nine in this sequence.

Barthes & L-S Combine in a One-hundred Run Stand for the Eighth Wicket

In the course of a myth anything can happen. There is no logic, no continuity. Any characteristic can be attributed to any subject; every conceivable relation can be found. Link with the arbitrary character of linguistic signs. *Parole* is the statistical aspect of language. Past, present and future are embodied in myth. Bundles produce meaning. Buy index cards. Inscribe hermeneutical code (HER). Things must be rewritten a dozen times in keeping with Levi-Strauss' concept that repetition is necessary to reveal the underlying structure of myth (821b). This is the mode of oral history. How can a story bear such repetition? It is invested with such deep underlying symbols that it constantly stimulates continuous reimagining. It is 'slated' in overlapping layers (AKA Prosenchymatic tiles). Demented elders recite the same story over and over again until it's lodged in your head. The core precept of the Telemachus sub-myth is that the son must repeat or break the journey of the father. This is its fork. In this instance, I-as-narrator is in the same position apropos James Joyce (note – Joyce is already his own SHAKESPEARIBSEN). As well, Sydney is an illegitimate son of London (c.1788 onwards). It is also Dublin B in narrative terms. Hence, the splintered main characters. Tommy is Dublin and Bill is London or vice versa. Barthes would step back to the source and ask the following questions. Is the Telemachus story no myth at all? Does it have the 'tenor' of myth? Can a secondary character in one myth become the central element in another myth? Or subset of a myth maybe. A minor myth, as D&G would have it. Second-class legends like the Newtown Jets. Barthes would commence any analysis with the title. Titling is the portal to the system. It creates a ROCK. Both of Homer's classics become monuments as soon as their titles are spoken or seen. The subsequent text is a tunnel boring machine back to the light of the title. Joyce used long and short titles. He used classical and colloquial terms. The aesthetic and mundane. Place and person. Songs. They are all sincere and ironic simultaneously. The best books have the best titles. The greatest writers are always great titlers as well. Women are invariably excellent titlers excluding Mrs Gaskell. I won't speculate on the reasons. Note Woolf, Behn, Stein, Eliot, Austen, Bronte (plural), Schreiner, Franklin, Richardson, Stead,

McCullers, Mary Shelley, de Beauvoir, Nin, even Ayn Rand, Roy, Weldon, Greer, Atwood, O'Connor, Walker, Morrison etcetera. Not a single dud in the list. Naomi Wolf by contrast is a cold-blooded titler. She always tries to create clever brand identity with titles. The Russians are the best at titling amongst men followed by the French. Germans are good. The English male capability at titling is spasmodic. Dickens' titles were fun. He was mainly interested in The Joke. *Bleak House* is great. Hardy had good titles. Pater was the best titler in nineteenth-century English prose. Wilde inherited this faculty. Lawrence created an explosive title in *Lady Chatterley's Lover*. *Kangaroo* is perhaps the worst offering in English. It serves no purpose to the plot. Hemingway invariably made bad titles. *The Sun Also Rises* is that rare book where a bad title is countermanded by a great work of art. In fact, it possesses two bad titles. It was renamed *Fiesta* for the UK by Jonathan Cape. Colonial literature generally produces worse titles than the true machine. *Such Is Life* is the greatest title in Australian literature and it is therefore the greatest book. It came during the period of individuation in Australian culture just prior to Federation. We have never replicated that wild thinking except in painting during WW2. Patrick White had imperfect titles with wide variance in quality. *Voss* is good. Better than the novel. *The Aunt's Story* is barely okay. Everything else is too fruity, nasty or forced. He tried mysticism with *Tree of Man*, *Riders on the Chariot* and *Solid Mandala*. He resorted to cliché in *Eye of the Storm*. Imagine telling your friends at a dinner party that this was the title of your next book! He probably called it "the Hunter book." *The Twyborn Affair* is a clever parody. Bad books always have bad titles. There is no such thing as a great book with a truly crap title. *Gravity's Rainbow* must be a bad book. So too *Illywhacker*. But not *Oscar and Lucinda*. It is neutral of significance. *True History of the Kelly Gang* is a very weak joke. *Bliss* is another meaningless title. Both Gibson and Ballard make great titles. That is why their titles are used for band names and songs. Their names produce quite different effects. Ballard is a great name for a writer. It contains the anagram ALL BARD. Everyone subconsciously unscrambles this anagram at the moment of cognition, giving him an instant headstart. The same applies in reverse for someone whose name was an anagram of Unbard or Bardno (Brando). Initials always work to the benefit of an author. On the other hand, Gibson is no good until you add his first name. A gravestone is another type of title page. It is full of undisclosed and implied text. I placed my father's ashes in his family plot at Woronora Cemetery with his two dead children, Susan (two days) and Robert (3.5 years). They both died of Spina Bifida. It isn't my plot. All great poets have great names. Thomas Eliot and E.W. Loomis Pound. John Ashbery. Christopher J. Brennan. Charles Mangan. The aptly named Wordsworth. Shelley and Byron. Names that roll off the tongue are what create great literary movements. It has nothing to do with style. There are NO BOOKS only titles. This can be back-calculated by reader experience, which was paramount to Barthes. Nobody has ever re-evaluated a title after reading the text. Nobody has gone back and said, "*A Lover's Discourse* is actually a really good title now I've read the book." This never happens. What makes a great title? A statement of final intent without alternatives. One-word titles are best. Extremely long titles are usually good too. They can be abbreviated into something great as well. But titles never survive translation. This even applies to Beckett who considered his texts in English and French to be separate works. He often looked like a character from Thunderbirds with his hollow blue eyes and pert expression. Bowie impersonated him well on the cover of HEROES. Titles translated into English are always worse than the original. They lack HATE. Titles of bourgeois length produce the most mediocrity. Orwell wrote great titles, he had a great pseudonym and he even had a great name in real life. The most painterly element of any piece of writing is the title. Pater should have submitted titles to the Royal Academy. Here, we have been presented with the title TELEMACHUS* It raises a threshold question for Barthes: What is Telemachus? A person, place or thing? The response to these questions depends on the reader's habit of education. In the nineteenth century, urbane authors deliberately cultivated rare images and allusions to appeal to a like-minded Hieratic readership. It was all wink-wink to the in-crowd. In contemporary terms, this title asks a frank question about our selection processes for valuing the past. In the proliferation of information now entrenched in our lives through technology, what do we pick (and what is picked for us) as useful, archivable data? Most people perusing this title today might not be aware of its meaning prior to opening the text (they have not become 'readers' yet). Is this a cause for concern? Not really. All the information that a reader needs to understand *Telemachus* is contained within these hallowed halls. Anyway, humanity still produces great art without the epic or poetic drama. Even the novel doesn't retain much currency. Some would argue with conviction that we still use Classical topos TBH. So, who is Telemachus? All or some of the author himself (BD), the sometimes-unreliable narrator (BC1?) and/or one or both of the central characters (TH/BC1)? Is it Australia? Note that the father (DC) was a fatherless son as is the false father figure in Chapters 7–8 (L). Fathers exist as surrogates (BC2, LH, LD) to strong women (HC, PP, EA), Sometimes, I wonder what happened to all the normal families. All the tender relationships exist outside conventional structures and/or conceal a lie (EA/LD, BC/O, HC/BC2, PH/LH). Binary pairs interdict – TH/BC, PH/HC, LH/TH, DC/BC2, EA/FL, FL/O. The reader knows that Telemachus is a male Classical figure and metaphor for the main characters in this novel only because we have read to this point. TELE means 'far off' and MACHUS means 'thrower or warrior' in Greek. A cover shot of an Attic youth would help define the title, *Telemachus*. The best titles don't need cover shots. Maybe some creepy film noir stairs and shadows for the *Collected Works of F.*

Kafka but that's it. That and anything by Edward Burne-Jones. He only painted album covers. Millais was assigned to chocolate boxes. A book called *Telemachus* could be about some or all of the following things:

(1) The minor mythic figure named Telemachus
(2) A proxy set against the novel *Ulysses* by James Joyce
(3) A default from the mythic figure of Odysseus and thus a metonymy/reductive symbol
(4) The name of a leading character who shares traits with Telemachus but NOT the figure in Dot Point 1
(5) An illustrated book about famous battles and the development of spears, with a secondary title after a colon like "Tossers of Olden Times"
(6) An arbitrary word choice or even the start of a puzzle.

This list raises a sequence of questions. Is the narrator also one of the central characters or a character-in-itself? Does 'I-as-narrator' complement or cross-out the Telemachus myth? Or is he a partial consumer? And, thus, a consumer even of his own product? Does the 'author' bypass the narrator at times with a direct representation of SELF? Ponder the depth of the writer's obsession with this truncated mythical figure. What does the writer see in Telemachus? Why does he keep stalling the narrative to drive downwards in inspiral critical loops? What does he see in this 'follower' – one of Homer's least original figures? Maybe it's a capacity for mimesis. His ambition to defer. The way he is characterised as lack. The fact that his future life is all outside enframing – not just of the *Odyssey* but the ENTIRE opus of Classical literature. Pater wrote an imaginary portrait called "Denys L'Auxerrois" about the disinterment of Dionysus in medieval France. This must have been a gap of 2,000 years. You can add another 500 years to get to 1984. Telemachus exists in this crevice without crystallisation at any point. He is the first postmodern character. He is the only under-specified character in Classical literature. Everybody else is over-determined. They have all had so much written about them that there is a vast, contending discourse. His father, Odysseus, is also left hanging at the end of the *Odyssey*. But his status is quite different. There is a super-abundance of tales about him. We even get prophecies about what happened to him hundreds of years later. The Romans renamed him Ulysses. There is NO equivalent to TELEMACHUS in Roman literature or Latin. Telemachus becomes NOPE. He is tabula rasa. Telemachus never had an original thought in his life. His great ambition is to replicate. He just copies his father's journey in miniature, acts as his accomplice and is ended with the text. This passive storyline begs the question – under what stimulus does the son finally break free from the will to emulate the father? This is the great cleavage in Homer's text. He stops the *Odyssey* at the reunification of Odysseus and Penelope, leaving Telemachus hanging around the ante-chamber. This severance is an act of both fulfillment and demarcation. The *Odyssey* ended the Classical period. It was the point at which the Ancients decided they had achieved total unity of meaning. It was the last LP. They went to ground after that. You can read about it in Herodotus. They had a conference. There was a vote. It was decided that nothing could be added that would increase the yield of their law, only denude its wholeness. Their epoch had achieved self-containment. Its weft had been loomed into a funeral shroud. Their withdrawal came with a warning: do NOT modify our cosmos. Don't try to dilute or defile the eschatology of the Gods. Like the Lapsarian apple, Telemachus was only half-consumed by the Ancients and left on the table rotten. He was cancelled out of the Ancient World to inhabit extrinsic space. He is suspended over the breakage line. He is cast out of heaven into ether. He never lands like Icarus or L. Byron. This isn't the kind of outcome that can be written down on a postage stamp. Everything in a text about the act of writing is super-imbued with meaning. It is the content of MAXIMUM significance to the author because it comes out of the act-in-production. It is a synecdoche of the act of writing itself. That is why epistolary works are so boring to read. Anywhere a book has writing-itself-as-content always requires structural analysis with a level of persistence pioneered by Roman Jakobson, which Roland Barthes expanded in *S/Z*. In Chapter 5, we saw Donald Cane writing on a picture postcard. What is the significance of this simple act? For a start, he is writing. He is leaving a formal record. This alters the furtive habits of a lifetime. The corporeal hero has become a scribe. Bloom is made to do the same thing by Joyce. Any statement from Odysseus is welcome. Any act of communication is a step forward for a man who disappeared for twenty years. His selection of form is important. A postcard is a convenient short form of communication. It is image-centric. It accumulates meaning from the interplay between word and image. This occurs by flipping the card. It creates a type of primitive pixilation. The postcard is a symbol of complementarity with the creative endeavors of Don Cane's sons – writer and image-maker. On one side possesses the picture. The other has print explaining the image as well as space for a stamp, address and a brief message. The viewer takes in the picture first. Then the card is turned. This is called the 'back.' This reflects the fact that the image side contains the instant ZAP of reception. The written message is never more than affiliation (AKA Telemachus). The first thing we see on the written side is a template for form. This is how all text must be ordered and structured. It is formulaic like a Trollope novel. Initially, we read the title of the image. It is always at the bottom. It contains bald facts. But these facts are brought to intimacy because our correspondent sent the card from this specific location. Therefore, it is both impersonal and intimate at the same time. There is a stamp with a postage mark in the top right corner. This is a further signifier of place. It also situates the postcard in time. Beneath, there is a space for inserting the recipient's address. It takes up ~50 per cent of the blank white space. This always creates a feeling of waste for the recipient (Barthes would say 'beloved'). They already know their own address. How much more we could have been told without this transmission data! It is also a reminder that we are still fixed in our normal place of residence when we read the postcard. It is a signifier of our own quotidian. But it also adds a sense of exotic experience because it places our name and place against the card image. Finally, we read the actual message from our correspondent. Hand-written communication is always formulaic and semi-spontaneous. There are always typos. The most erudite correspondent is reduced to illiteracy by the pressure of postcard space limits. There is never complete pre-meditation. Only intent. Maybe some key points are prepared. But the final product is always a let-down. It is never truly surprising. There just isn't enough space. Even if something unexpected has occurred, we always half expect it. One may learn of a new adventure. A new love (see *A Lover's Discourse*). An accident. Meteorological statistics. Mundane information about the hotel and food. But it is probably just a description of the instrument of relaxation as presented in the image. We turn back to that image once more seeking deeper meaning or solace. If it is a single image, we search the corners. If it is multiple images, we scour the smaller ones. You can never read both sides of a postcard at once. This is a critical disclosure symbol for this novel: Tom Hallem and Billy Capri are linked back-to-back yet separated. It is also a statement of the binary nature of the visual and written arts. The use of a postcard assumes a certain identity. It proclaims that the sender is a transient. Don Cane's postcard has a more sinister purpose. He sends regards to his former mistress from his hometown. This puts a knife into the present (he has gone back to Sydney) and a line through the past (they have separated). She is only an incidental party. Only worth a postcard. He is trying to recover lost pride. It is also a type of hook that tries to pull the recipient (Barthes' beloved) back into the relationship; not least because the luxury inherent in a postcard image of Sydney is directly aligned with languor and the intimacy of sex. This is what D&G call an "unconscious libidinal investment." A shot of a surfer riding a wave in Hawaii, for example, directs the viewer beyond the image of hot unclothed bodies and percolating water (symbols of foreplay) to deeper associations with lust . This is the source of Ambrose E. Welles deep reverie about Elizabeth Archer. Finally, the postcard scene re-positions Don Cane in the role of mythic figure. It is an Odyssean proclamation of RETURN. His discourse is located in the most acute place in any desire-reading of place – HOME. There is a bank of received meanings to home, both in terms of personal place as well as symbology. Home can never be referred to as just another SPACE. It is always A DEFINITIVE PLACE. My objective in TMAC was to write the definitive book of Sydney without locating any scenes at icons. I wanted to fix the book in adjacent spaces where outsiders never go. Average suburbs. THE SELVEDGE OF A CITY. Also, the city itself acts as SELVEDGE for FORM. Its perimeter. These are the court walls within which Bloom and Stephen bounce. TMAC always moves towards Sydney's jewels yet never actually reaches them. Things always get side-tracked. Destinations are a little too far. Like Odysseus stuck on Ogygia, the effort becomes too great. Don Cane surveyed the postcard text. It read, "Sydney is a modern city with a temperate climate, vibrant culture, icons such as the Opera House and Harbour Bridge and a coastline dotted with beaches led by world-famous Bondi Beach." These words would have had a strong impact on Richie when she received the postcard in Manila. The author has deliberately exacerbated the differential in their relative prosperity by reducing her circumstances and taking Don Cane back to the first world . The metrics of life after a postcard is put through a letter box slot are irretrievably altered. You can't go back. The repercussion for Don Cane in this postcard is that it betrays his sense of 'foreignness' in his homeland. This act insinuates how much he misses Richie. In summary, she lived with him for seven years. He regrets their inability to have a family. He mourns the death of their baby. He is despondent that it caused them to part. He confesses to himself that he is no longer local in Sydney. He does not relate to ANY place on earth anymore. Our hero is exhausted. He falls asleep in his hotel room. He dreams (see C7). He awakes in a stupor. He gets up. He is disoriented. His body is stiff after the long flight. He takes a shower (cleansing symbol). He slowly regains his sense of place and self. Finally, he goes to the hire car. This is an image of transience. A car makes everything temporary. In fact, it involved a capital exchange so it represented 'acquired impermanence' for the bearer. This makes it the equivalent of a postcard. Both express the desire for evanescence to be set in motion. They are engines of forgetting. Barthes' structural analysis in *S/Z* is microscopic. Honore Balzac's short story, *Sarrasine*, is divided into 561 numbered textual units called *lexias*; ninety-three subject headings (or *divigations*) marked by Roman numerals; and five codes (hermeneutic, semantic, proairetic, cultural and symbolic). This level of detail seems exhaustive to the reader. But isn't out of the ordinary for a scholar of Joyce, who becomes used to trying to release meaning by negotiating a balance between autobiographical utterances (both accurate and apocryphal), biography (primary and secondary), whole of novel studies, individual episode analyses and examinations of specific words, images, metaphors, symbols, characters and themes (including political, economic, social, musical, sporting and numerical leitmotifs). In S/Z, Barthes looks at the division between <u>writerly</u> and <u>readerly</u> texts. He deploys the language of consumption in a parody of Marxist theory to state that "the goal of literary work (of literature as work) is to make the reader no longer a consumer, but a producer of the text." In *Writing Degree Zero*, Barthes has already added "writing" to Sartre's dualism of language (social property) and style (individual decision). Sartre really ignored form, suggesting that it was almost an organic outcome of writing. In other words, the writer really was as "stupid as a painter." The Writerly Text instates the reader as a producer by the act of mental rewriting. This isn't as stupid as it sounds. It is just a variant of Barthes' "death of the author" theory. It means that the text is composed in a manner that triggers the reader's mind to work creatively in the moment, free of any retarding system or distorting organising device (such as ideology, genus, critical lens). TITLING SHOULD THUS BE PROVISIONAL in a Writerly Text. It should be rewritable by the reader. This is just common sense. How many times does the reader think of a book by their own shorthand term rather than its FULL & GIVEN one? For example, *Le Temps Perdu* (itself an abbreviation and retitling) is always called 'Proust' by readers. I want to stick labels on the cover of every book to substitute my own titling. *Heart of Darkness* could become Kurtz. Or *The Education of Philip Marlowe*. *The Great Gatsby* could be renamed *On East Egg*. It would no longer be written by 'F. Scott Fitzgerald' but "F.S.K. Fitzgerald." All books by Ernest Hemingway would be renamed "by Grant Boof, author of *No Balls in Pamplona*." Yes, the name of the writer should also be replaceable in a Writerly Text. The reader should even be able to reallocate a book to another author. This would strip away plagiarism once and for all. We can invent new hybrids or even use our own names (see C10, Marion Hackett) or make up an entirely new *noms de plume*. *The Picture of Dorian Gray* by Oscar Wilde could be retitled as *The Defensible Death of Basil Allword* by Edgar A. Pater or *Death Painting* by Smug. *Ulysses* could be re-titled *A Meeting of Souls*, *One Day in Dublin*, *Bloom*, *The Reconciliation of Molly Bloom* or *24 Hours in Dublin* (a thriller) or any/all of the previous titles at any given point during its reading. A Writerly Text should come with a thick wad of labels for its cover to reflect its perpetual retitling. The greatness of any text should be HOW MANY RETITLINGS it stimulated. This would give a quantitative logic to the Canon. These labels need to be transparent like a visor to create a meaningless tattoo of language like Kafka's harrow. Character naming should also be provisional in a Writerly Text. Ballard did that in *Atrocity Exhibition*. Stephen Hero becomes Stephen Dedalus becomes Shem the Penman and they are ALL James Joyce over the course of his corpus. Ballard used his own name in *Crash*. Writers are very good at making-up character names. All the great books have the best character names. Don Cane is an under-named character. I wanted the first names of Australia's great heroes of his age – Bradman and Monash. But I could never think of a permanent family name. I tried many alternatives including Cave, Paine, Candy,

Farquhar, Mal Feasance, Cestus, Dildam, Negative Ions, Pinhead McPherson et cetera. Many of these sobriquets ended up attached to incidental characters. Cane is really just a holding name. I might change it back to Paine at any point. So please call him Bloomish, Odysque, Marty Sheen or anything else you like. I should hold an online competition to RENAME DON CANE. Both readers of my blog could enter. In fact, the very weakness of a character name can be filled with meaning, especially set against strong names that are poignant or amusing. Writers usually give each character at least a first name and a family name, although they often add stuff like titles, middle names or initials. They alternate between name combinations throughout the text, usually to break up the monotony of using the same name all the time. This is particularly important as a formal device in the novel where 'spoken word' by characters needs to be suffixed with speech tags like "X said," "X exclaimed," "added X," "X replied" and vica-versa so that the reader can comprehend who said what. Some writers like Joyce do not adhere to this convention. It becomes a little game to create ambiguity. That is a classic writerly gimmick to be sure. But characters should really blur into one mass. They should compose a single utterance. Forget POV. Forget the ingenuity of Tolstoy and Dickens using regional slang or linguistic mannerisms to demarcate voices. It's afflatus. They are all one character. Conversely, all characters should be subject to manifold names just like the manifold selves which make up our own single sense of self. This is different to Booth's concept of an Unreliable Narrator. This device falls into various categories like picaro, madman, clown, naif and liar as well as the current voice. Some characters are denoted by their first name only and some by just their family name. Sometimes, this is shorthand. Leopold Bloom is always referred to as 'Bloom.' Stephen Dedalus is always 'Stephen.' We never read 'Bloom' and think of Milly or Molly. However, we do read 'Dedalus' and think of Simon Dedalus (though not the sisters). This is a default setting privileging patriarchal lineage. In *Ulysses*, the elder male is known by his patronym [Bloom = long trousers] while the younger male remains in shorts (use Christian name). When he is called by the family name, Dedalus, it feels like Stephen is being admonished. Women remained naked in the hut because there was only one set of female clothing. Chinese naming often allocates the first name 'Xiao' to females, which simply means 'small'. Barthes succumbs to his usual heroic rhetoric at the high point in *S/Z*: "The writerly is the novelistic without the novel, poetry without the poem, the essay without the dissertation, writing without style, production without product, structuration without structure" (II. Interpretation). This tendency in Barthes actually denudes the strength of his writing. Ironically, it is a readerly flaw. It suffocates and paralyses the text with rhetoric. Readerly Texts are almost everything, according to Barthes. They are products, not productions. The reader consumes the text passively:

> This reader is thereby plunged into a kind of idleness – he is intransitive; he is, in short, serious: instead of functioning himself, instead of gaining access to the magic of the signifier, to the pleasure of writing, he is left with no more than the poor freedom either to accept or reject the text: reading is nothing more than a **referendum**.

The readerly cannot be rewritten (*recuferl*). Barthes calls the objects of such reading classic texts. This binary division is equivalent to the demarcation between hieratic and demotic literature, which I have explored in other essays in relation to nineteenth-century literature. Hieratic writers wrote for an audience that they assumed shared a common pool of literary touchpoints. Pater, Ruskin, Swinburne and Wilde are good examples of this group but so too is James Joyce. Demotic writers like Dickens wrote of everyday life for periodicals to be enjoyed in recitation by illiterate people. Joyce wrote of the quotidian but in Hieratic style. This was one of his core innovations. Let us be quite clear in summary: *Telemachus* is designed to be a Writerly Text.

LEVI-STRAUSS

Everything in this book relates to Structuralism. Its title alone fills me with anticipation (the false bravado of its flipside, foreboding). I open the book and look at the chapter headings then the episodes and character names. Everywhere I see adherence to myth and therefore Structuralist potency. I am even a kind of character in this novel. But why am I placed before Saussure? He is my source. I guess it's just a matter of writerly will. To break down chronology. This is not a bad thing in itself. Myth doesn't need to be sequential in time. Why should the text? It was Saussure's work that gave me the basic idea to invert the paradigm in which the immediate family is seen as the basic unit and the extended family is clustered outside. I was more interested in the relationships between all these units – not just Oedipus, Odysseus and their offspring, for instance. Myths generally look ridiculous to rationalist thinkers in our technical age. We tend to downplay them as the rantings and rationalisations of savages. Yet they are similar across cultures disclosing universal laws. I want to keep it simple like Hegel. I will deal in facts. There are dialectical elements in opposition within myth. Mediators resolve these oppositions. The trickster is one example. It mediates between life and death. It is represented as either a coyote or a raven. These animals live on carrion so they are neither an agent of death (hunting/beast of prey) nor synonymous with the production of life (agriculture/herbivore). Because it hovers in the centre between such extremes, the Trickster must retain elements of that duality – thus it becomes unpredictable and ambiguous. I am such a figure. Myth is language. I love word games. That's why I called my book, *La Pensee Sauvage*. In English, it is just known as *The Savage Mind*. That title takes all the nuance out of my work. In French, the title is a joke. It puns on the word 'pensee' for 'thought,' which also means 'pansy' in French. Thus, it can equally be read as 'The Savage Pansy.' This title creates a statement of extremes – poles within which I-as-Trickster will function. It also plays on Rousseau's shibboleth juxtaposing the hardness of purity in the savage (positive) against the softness and opaqueness of western civilization (negative). The first edition of my book even had a dust jacket image of wild pansies. I took this word from *Hamlet*. It's the speech where Ophelia gives her brother a garland. She says, "there is pansies, that's for thoughts." In French, it reads as "et voici des pensÈes, en guise de pensÈes." It is almost as if Shakespeare was speaking directly to the French people with this pun. He was fluent in our language. This double-meaning probably stayed with him subconsciously waiting for the right moment to be used as a juxtaposition in his own tongue. You need to perform Structuralist analysis to disclose the full meaning of this passage (Act 4, Scene 5, ll.199–209). Shakespeare was special like that. Ophelia's supposed to be crazy by this point but critics have noted that she dispenses the six different plants quite incisively. She has become a trickster. Her actions summarise the plot to date and even predict the final denouement. She retains Hamlet's own ambivalence about decision-making. Claudius receives two flowers. They offer conflicting meanings and can even cancel each other out. Her numerology is not insignificant. She has six plants to allocate. There are six participants in Hamlet's *Mousetrap*: himself as director, Horatio as scout (or Ophelia as receptor) plus four players on stage. Hamlet is invisible in the play, just as he is physically absent during Ophelia's floral apportionment. Yet he is, of course, the key figure in both dramas. Some think Ophelia is just being given special insight by Shakespeare as a kind of 'saintly savant.' In fact, she does much more than just deconstruct a garland, allocating the contents according to symbol (flower) and signified (recipient). She is actually acting out her own interpretation of Mad Hamlet. It is psychoanalysis by performance. Guattari instituted this tactic at La Borde. Her method mimics the allegorical foundation of *Mousetrap*. This makes her actions a play as well as a play on a play within a play. By this mode, she can become co-author and thus 'mate' of Hamlet. She folds a bigger box over Hamlet's assemblage of Russian boxes: encasing him in a prosenchymatic dome or garden (insert womb symbolism). They both become tricksters inhabiting/exploiting the median/mean of sanity/madness. This reconciles the abusive element of their relationship. Hamlet's mistreatment becomes one pole in an oscillation between extremes of innocence and abuse. Instead of just ricocheting between these poles and making a simplistic moral judgment, the audience is refocused by Shakespeare on the balance of their shared emotional space; carving out a niche that is meaningful and real. This analysis has nothing to do with Joyce's Hamlet theory. He was solely focused on the Male Self. By way of qualification, we should acknowledge that it is impossible for a contemporary audience to countenance the abuse of Ophelia by Hamlet (even if he is designated insane). He would need a full program of CBT. Of course, a critical element of this scene is that Shakespeare doesn't actually designate which plant goes to which individual character in the stage directions. That is a decision of the director and players for ALL TIME. Conventions have developed despite his open-ended offer. In fact, they have become known as "fixed stage traditions." Hamlet gets Rosemary, Laertes gets pansies *et cetera*. But this allocation can just as easily be altered. This is a unique postmodern element in *Hamlet*. It returns production to the 'reader' rather than impose the passive reception of a 'classic text.' It reiterates that *Hamlet* is the first Writerly Text. It is NOT didactic. In fact, it is possibly the most writerly drama ever created. It bears all the hallmarks of an Agatha Christie murder mystery. Hence, and thus, *Mousetrap* was so named. It is possible to INSERT this **Table of Variables [ToV]** as a basis for formulisation of the mythemes in *Hamlet*:

TABLE 4. TABLE OF VARIABLES – FLORAL MYTHEMES IN *HAMLET*

Flower Units [FL1]	Meaning/Symbol [M-SYM]	Recipient Convention Allocation [RC-A] ('fixed stage tradition')
Rosemary [RO]	Remembrance (as stated by Ophelia) [RE]	Imagined/absent Hamlet [H] (alternate [ALT]: Laertes)
Pansy [P]		
	Thoughts (as stated by Ophelia) [T]	Laertes [L]
Fennel [FE]	Flattery [FL2] – also strength, praiseworthiness [SP]	Claudius [C]
Columbine [C]	Folly, male adultery, faithlessness [FMAF] – also protection against evil [PE]	Claudius [see above]
Rue (herb of grace) [RU]	Regret, bitterness [RB] – also used for abortions [A]	Ratio – Gertrude [G] 70% with 30% kept by Ophelia [O] thus [G70:O30] ([ALT]: Laertes, Hamlet)
Daisy [D]	Innocence, cheerfulness [IC]	
	Laid down without allocation – i.e. Denmark is rotten [DR]	

The operatives in [M-SYM] are [FE] and [C] because they can be assigned very different meanings as [FL2] or [SP] and [FMAF] or [PE] respectively. These units actually govern the Allocation [ALL] of all other flowers. They are active, dominant flowers [AD-FL1]. Causation [CAUS] springs from them. In fact, there are only two logical variants in this [CAUS] equation: [FL2] + [FMAF] <u>or</u> [SP] + [PE]. These combinations are consistent with the [CAUS] of *Hamlet*. It is not really possible to have [SP] + [FMAF] – as this would be praising the strength of a faithless man who commits adultery. Likewise, it is highly unlikely that the combination [FL2] with [PE] would occur, as this would mean you want to protect against evil someone prone to flattery. While not impossible, it is definitely anachronistic in terms of [CAUS] and unlikely to be the goal of [O] in [FL1-ALL] – which is to reveal her interpretation of [CAUS]. The other [FL1] in [ToV] which induces multiple meanings is [RU] which can be seen as either [RB] or [A]. However, this [FL1] is secondary and passive against the dominant flowers [AD-FL1] and thus can be signified as [S-FL1]. [O] doesn't provide disclosure on who should get what flower [FL1]. She doesn't know the answer to the murder mystery [CAUS] – or even if it is one. Shakespeare here is toying with [CAUS] and [M-SYM]. In one [CAUS], [C] could be considered strong and praiseworthy [FE-SP] with [O] giving him a charm [C-PE] against premeditated attack by [H]. Alternatively, she could be giving him [FL1] to disclose that [C] is prone to flattery [FE-FL2] and a cuckold-maker whose seizure of power is folly [C-FMAF] and ultimately invalid. The following table summarises [ALL] of flower units according to [RC-A] or the 'fixed stage tradition' of [CAUS]:

[FL1]	[M-SYM]	C	G	H	L	O
RO	[R]					
P	[T]					
FE	[FL2] [SP]					
C	[FMAF] [PE]					
RU	[RB] [A]		70			30
D	[IC]					

In this [CAUS] formula, [C] may perceive that he has been allocated [FE] and [C] for positive reasons: [SP] and [PE]. The conventional judgment however is that [O] is [ALL + FL1] as follows: [FE-FL2] and [C-FMAF]. Certainly, the non-allocation of

[~~ALL~~+D] suggests a judgment by [O] as a final act of climax/closure. The option that [O] may, indeed, believe that [C] is a just ruler and needs protection from [H] would require [D] to be [ALL] to [C] – because he would be totally innocent and have every reason to be cheerful [IC] because Denmark is not be 'rotten' [~~DR~~]. reallocation [RE-ALL] of the floral dividend against [RC-A] gives away the reader's decision about the core questions posed in this Writerly Text [WT]: did [C] kill Hamlet Senior and/or was [H] mad. The following table provides a simple formula for this analysis. If [H] (in absentia) was [ALL] active/operative flower units [AD-FL1] being [FE] and [C] with negative [M-SYM] of [FL2] and [FMAF], the following [CAUS] would be enacted and Claudius would, indeed, be [ALL + D] by [O]:

[FL1]	[M-SYM]	C	G	H	L	O
RO	[R]					
P	[T]					
FE	[FL2] ~~[SP]~~					
C	[FMAF] ~~[PE]~~					
RU	[RB] ~~[A]~~					A
D	[IC]					

In this [CAUS + ALL], Hamlet's adultery with Ophelia [F**MA**F], its repercussions [O=A] and his subsequent faithlessness [FMA**F**]are clearly disclosed. [G] receives [P] in a token of womanly empathy from [O]. [L] gets the consolation flower [R]. It is already a flexible [FL1-ALL] to him as the [ALT] in [RC-A]. [H] can be considered vulnerable to flattery [**F**MAF] in various ways. For a start, he is a handsome, intelligent and eligible young Prince. This gives him a privileged position in medieval society. His perception of Social Rupture in the State [SR-S] frees him from any lingering social constraints. Subsequently, he takes all sorts of licenses: he can sexually use and dispose of [O] at his whim; he can argue about his future with his 'parents' [STEP-C+G]; he can affect the mantle of playwright and director coercing [C+G] to witness what they see as his ludicrous, self-indulgent production; he can murder Polonius and expect no punishment; he accepts the actuality of the Ghost as soon as it offers him a sacred revenge mission etcetera. The same [ALL + FL1] with a different [M-SYM] to the operative flower units [AD–FL1] produces the following [CAUS]:

[FL1]	[M-SYM]	C	G	H	L	O
RO	[R]					
P	[T]					
FE	[SP]					
C	[PE]					
RU	[RB]					
D	[IC]					

In this [CAUS] table, [H] is strong and powerful in his justified purpose of revenge. [O] is trying to offer him protection against evil by disclosing the evil activities of [C+G]. In short, she's 'outing them' to try to forestall tragedy. [L] is innocent [D]. [G] is being urged to [R] of her dead husband. [O] keeps [P] because she's all about thinking, deduction and strategy. Of course, other combinations of [ALL + CAUS] are possible. An intriguing [CAUS] focuses on [L] as the primary target [PT] of [O]. It would not be surprising if [O] focused on [L] given the circumstances. After all, [L] is the brother of [O]. He is her closest relative after the death of Polonius and her closest emotional connection after estrangement from [H]. [L] also has the issue of revenge against [H] to process. [L] as [PT] produces the following [ALL + CAUS]:

[FL1]	[M-SYM]	C	G	H	L	O
RO	[R]					
P	[T]					
FE	[SP]					
C	[PE]					
RU	[RB]					
D	[IC]					

In this [CAUS], [H] is justified in his Actions [ACT]. The Ghost is considered to be Real [REAL] by [O]. [H] is thus justified in [ACT] including the death of Polonius. [O] is counselling [L] to be strong in restraint [SP] and trying to protect him [PE]. [H] gets the daisy [D=IC]. [O] gets [P] because she is disclosing her [T]. [G] must get [R] and [RU] so that she is compelled to [R] and [RB] of her actions. In this [CAUS], Claudius gets no flower [ZERO – FL1]. He is left to stand isolated and garlandless; exposing his position as the guilty party. The opposite pole is that everybody is culpable in *Hamlet*. This [CAUS] formula has perhaps been overlooked by critics and readers due to the rush to [ALL]. If it was brought into effect, all characters would receive ALL [FL-1] take collective responsibility for all [ALL + CAUS + ACT]. This [TofV] would be very dense so I will illustrate it with [H] and a single [FL-1] being [FE] with both [FL2 + SP]:

<table>
<tr><th>[FL1]</th><th>[M-SYM]</th><th>C</th><th>G</th><th>H</th><th>L</th><th>O</th></tr>
<tr><td>RO</td><td>[R]</td><td></td><td></td><td></td><td></td><td></td></tr>
<tr><td>P</td><td>[T]</td><td></td><td></td><td></td><td></td><td></td></tr>
<tr><td>FE</td><td>[FL2]
[SP]</td><td></td><td></td><td><table>
<tr><td>[FL1]</td><td>[SYM]</td></tr>
<tr><td>RO</td><td>[R]</td></tr>
<tr><td>P</td><td>[T]</td></tr>
<tr><td>FE</td><td>[FL2] [SP]</td></tr>
<tr><td>C</td><td>[FMAF] [PE]</td></tr>
<tr><td>RU</td><td>[RB] [A]</td></tr>
<tr><td>D</td><td>[IC]</td></tr>
</table></td><td></td><td></td></tr>
<tr><td>C</td><td>[FMAF]
[PE]</td><td></td><td></td><td></td><td></td><td></td></tr>
<tr><td>RU</td><td>[RB] [A]</td><td></td><td></td><td></td><td></td><td></td></tr>
<tr><td>D</td><td>[IC]</td><td></td><td></td><td></td><td></td><td></td></tr>
</table>

We must reduce these multiple meanings of flowers to single definitions as units if we are to apply definitive meaning to *Hamlet*. There need to be dialectics put in place to systematically reduce causation down to a single flower allocation and singular meaning. Levi-Strauss has been charged with over-rating (embellishing even manipulating) samples to support strict categorisation. Examples are contained in the Table below. I don't expect any writer to be a saint. We are all exploiting whatever clay comes to our disposal. If it requires setting up partially false dichotomies or stretching Classical mythemes ... why not? It's not as if this is a scientific experiment where thousands of women will be exposed to a cancer-causing drug to avoid miscarriage. In the end, the text is all about STYLE and ENTERTAINMENT. We're all trying to get through life as amateurs. I also popularised the word *bricoleur*. It literally means 'one who tinkers' in French. It refers to any improvised work. It's like plugging a crack in the wall with metal objects like coins, screws and nails before swiping a layer of plaster over the top. These DIY jobs always needed to be repeated because the wall moves due to subterranean forces. This is a GIANTIC METAPHOR for the fight against Fascism. Vanity thy name is Handyman! The publishing company for this work, anAnnal DIY, exemplifies this concept. It is a sentiment first brought to truth by 45RPM independent singles of the Punk movement. Bloom was one of those blokes. He just went around Dublin closing down anomalies embarrassedly. But without ever fixing anything. You can see this mode most clearly at the end of *Ulysses* when he parts from Stephen Dedalus. He got the lad out of a brothel, sobered him up and offered him a bed for the night. But Stephen does not take up this offer. In Oxen, Bloom mediates between the noisy group of drunks and the nursing staff. He doesn't need to do this job. There are doctors present who should take responsibility. But Bloom just has to try to fix everything. It is the same with music. He wants to set Molly up with Stephen. It isn't a logical concept. More in the nature of just connecting whatever things are available at any given time. It is lucky that Bloom didn't get his hands on a fuse box. This is Bloom's "[CAUS]" throughout *Ulysses*. He performs a sequence of opportunistic acts of *bricolage*. They overlap and parallel each other like an urban rail system. The myth can be treated as an orchestra score if it is placed in a unilateral series. Our task is to re-establish the correct arrangement that will demonstrate the recurrence of leitmotifs that are universal in all versions of the myth, regardless of location and time (as opposed to a formula which contains these limiting items). Let us turn to the Oedipus myth for instruction. The groups of relations that appear in the Oedipus myth exhibit common features as disclosed in the following table (Table 5, see over). It is clear from the above table that a myth consists of binary oppositions. Hot/Cold. Raw/cooked. Animal/human. This schema can be applied to all subsequent versions of the myth. One can also identify these basic elements in all previous accounts across all cultures. For a myth is whole and total. It produces what I call 'mythemes.' This is another portmanteau pun. Joyce was an expert in using this device. Mythemes can accommodate all variants; however aberrant. They are even able to complete truncated retellings – for example, you could read Joyce's *Ulysses* with confidence in its ultimate fidelity to the Odysseus myth from a combination of just the title on the cover and Stephen's fractious exit from the Martello Tower in Chapter One. It already exhibits enough Odyssean DNA by this point to be produced within a normal range of narrative variables for the next 600 pages. Even divergence from the myth – such as Bloom avoiding Boylan rather than confronting the suitor – still answers to the basic template. The reorganisation of Odysseus' experiences by Joyce makes no difference. As I noted in *Structural Anthropology*, the diachronic ordering of events within any myth can be ignored (211). The narrative convenience of appropriating myth has usually been employed in modern art to insinuate meaning and add depth to

TABLE 5. CATEGORIES OF RELATIONS IN THE OEDIPUS MYTH (LEVI-STRAUSS)

Category	Levi-Strauss Samples	Comment
Over-rating of blood relations (excessive intimacy)	• Quest by Cilix, Phoenis, Thasus and Cadmus to find Europa after she was kidnapped by Zeus (rape) • Oedipus/Jocasta (marriage) • Antigone buries Polynices against Creon's orders	• Quest for Europa is not pursued vigorously (exceeds accepted norms) • Antigone followed burial rituals (piety setting itself against authority)
Underrating of blood relations	• Murders of Spartoi, Laius and Polynices.	• Etiocles and Polynices are cursed for disrespecting Oedipus (Cadmus crockery; wrong beast-part). • Could be extended to other examples of murdering close relatives in Theban origin myth – e.g. Laius abandoning Oedipus; Zethus' wife accidentally murders her own son; Creon entombing Antigone. • Suicide is a regular correlation – Haemon's suicide; Zethus grieving himself to death. • Fatal women – Agave; Zethus' wife; Amphion's wife (boast against Leto, mother of Artemis and Apollo).
Denial of Autochthonous Origins (born of earth)	• Monsters slain - Cadmus/ dragon; Oedipus/Sphinx.	• Man overcomes autochthonous being (symbolism of). • Most famous autochthons are sons of Gaea (Pontus, Uranus, Actaeus, Cecrops, Cranaus).
Affirmation of Origins	• Shared naming -Labdacus/ Laius/Oedipus.	• All men born from earth have difficulty in walking straight & standing upright.

otherwise fragile structures. This is particularly true of cinema, which needs to concentrate narrative into blunt gestures to fit its temporal restrictions. The movies *O Brother Where Art Thou?* and *Head On* profit from alliance with the Odysseus myth, although TBH I never liked the American movie because it uses mythemes too cosmetically / cynically / simplistically [DELETE ANY NOT APPLICABLE]. A final advantage of myth is that destiny is fixed in advance. Narrative cannot shake off the mythic template. The reader can relax. There's no suspense. One must go through the motions held in its thrall. That is what this work is trying to achieve. We already know by now that Tom and Ana are dead like Hamlet and Ophelia. We know what happens to Don Cane. We are aware that Elizabeth Archer has a baby. Let us disclose the relational groupings of *Telemachus* by two methods – (1) chapter-by-chapter analysis of the Telemachiad followed by (2) mythic comparison with the *Odyssey*. Thematic analysis can be represented by key words that epitomise mythic elements:

Table 6. Thematic development in TMAC, chapter-by-chapter

	Chapter (Subject)	Themes (Functions)
1.	Gods in Council	Immutability – power – variables itemised.
2.	Telemachus and Athena	Mutability – false union – sexual abomination – destruction of a temple – return from Paris (humiliated).
3.	Proteus	Mutation – opportunism – re-assertion of natural order – confronting the past – family restored (false/temporary) – transitory sanctuary.
4.	Scylla and Charybdis	Breakage of natural order – revelation of false nature of perfect family (Capri) – new family relations disclosed (Tom/Billy) – old unions broken – revelation of systematic lies by authority – inversion of previous blood relations.
5.	Wandering Rocks	Life – place as character - episodic nature of existence –centripetal movements – false unions – individualism.
6.	Oxen of the Sun	Language – myths/themes - stasis/dromology – surdity/utterance.
7.	Circe	Night and dreams - sexual abomination – blasphemous union – death visits good/evil equally INSERT NEW ESSAY CONTENT.
8.	Eumaeus	Hiatus - inside the hut (Leer) including stratagem entry – mockery of blood relations (hyperdermic) – revelation of false idol – flight.
9.	Penelope/Ithaca	Woman as home – death of Ophelia and/or goddess (Ana).
10.	Gibraltar	Post Odyssey time plate - Homeric order reinstated and extended – crossing point in/out – Tom Hallem exposed to suitors – Demodocus' Song (Frenchs as Alcinous' palace) – Sirens (Francine) – her warning – group splits between heights/ depths (Harbour Bridge and St James tunnels) - temporary sanctuary (Francine) - a father awaiting return of the son (wooden horse) - Nostos.

The above table may have changed as the author completed the work. My analysis is based on an incomplete version. *Telemachus* can be compared to the following relational groupings of mythemes in the Homeric narrative:

TABLE 7. *TELEMACHUS* VERSUS THE *ODYSSEY* – MYTHEMES COMPARED

	Telemachus Mytheme	*Odyssey* Mytheme
1.	Father and mother in fruitful union (Don, Penelope)	Odysseus/Penelope at Ithaca (1)
2.	Son born (Thomas)	Telemachus
3.	Abomination A against Nature (Helen gives birth to Billy)	Madness + War (Troy)
4.	Father in exile (Vietnam, Manila)	*Odyssey*
5.	~~Normalized childhood – sequence of false father figures and proxies (Les, Westacott, Dick Stone, Willy the Pimp, Leer)~~	Telemachus' life - Siege of Suitors
6.	~~Maternal deceptions (re-paternity + aliveness)~~	Penelope's web, ambiguous Athena
7.	~~Father returns (Sydney)~~	Odysseus on Ithaca
8.	Truth revealed [Tom and Billy are half-brothers like Telemachus and Telegonus]. Kinship formula = FaMoMoBrBr.	Visit to Menelaus.
9.	Thwarted homecomings – Tom (pub, brothel, Leer's apartment, exhibition opening, restaurant). Contrast with Billy going home with Barry ('REAL' father)	Homecoming - Telemachus and Odysseus both return to Ithaca.
10.	Rejection of social hierarchy/customs (Tom exit from art clique at restaurant – mirroring Elizabeth's pregnancy tactics)	Disposal of suitors without proper ceremony.
11.	~~Wandering son (Frenchs, Francine).~~	Post-*Odyssey*. Telegonus on Ithaca – murder of Odysseus.
12.	Death of Ana [O + D + IC] – dromological/free female will be fixed in place by death/stasis.	Post-*Odyssey*. Woman as patriarchal victim (see Antigone, Ophelia et al).
13.	Abomination B against Nature - Elizabeth bears 'illegal' child (see Items 3 & 10 above) [Non-A]	Post-*Odyssey*. Penelope marries Telegonus.
14.	Sons struggle with father legacy (post-*Ulysses*): one is destroyed (Tom) while the other survives in diminished form (BC).	Post-*Odyssey*. *Telemachus*
15.	~~Living brother writes of dead brother.~~	Post-*Odyssey*. Tennyson (*In Memoriam*).

Insert (16) Blood reunion (affirmation of origins). We can see from the above table that we depart from the core Homeric version of Odysseus myth after Point 10, although there is still alignment to later versions of the Myth in Points 11–13. Point 14 has been projected out of the myth by many authors since Homer. Point 15 is accretive. However, it is not misaligned with the myth. It is a fond wish that my niece finds me, wrote Billy Capri. She is ~23 years old. I don't know how it will happen. I don't have a My Space account. I am in the Sydney telephone directory but she may not know my family name (not Hallem). She might not even know that her father had a half-brother. She could look for her grandmother, who may or may not explain the family history (what I call a blockage in C1). Penelope is now classified under her maiden name, McFADDEN. The girl has access to court documents. I believe in my heart that she will find me. In this regard, I am quixotic like Barthes. We will sit at a park bench sharing mute mannerisms like two characters in a Duras novel. Telemachus must have experienced a similar sensation when he was waiting in the dark with his father prior to entering the hall to confront the suitors. He would have heard his father's respiration. This would have been a bittersweet moment. I am sure James Joyce felt it with John Joyce. I never had that with my own father. I remember the night Barry helped Billy move home from Darlinghurst before he went to the UK. He grunted and gasped in the dark after he had stopped the car in Campsie. But it didn't sound like a familial sound-bond. It was quite different. I will not vilify Elizabeth. The mother/child bond is sacred. In all cultures, the mother/father relationship is reciprocal with that of father/son, according to L-S. A dominant mother is formal with the father. This usually meant the father was intimate with the son. I think it's like that with me, O and the kids. The Relational Groupings in the Odysseus myth are as follows:

Relations		Cluster	*Telemachus* Mytheme
1.	Natural Order	1	1, 2
2.	Abomination	2	3, 4
3.	Fragmentation		5-11
4.	Punishment		12, 13
5.	Reassembly	3	14, 15

The following table puts the relational groupings into cyclical sequence. The vertical axis represents temporal progress while the horizontal axis represents ethical progress (return to natural order).

			1		
	2				
3					
4					
	5				

Leavis said in *The Great Tradition* that no work can be considered great art without evincing a moral purpose. Joyce failed in comparison with Lawrence. *Ulysses* was a 'cosmopolitan' conceit, he said. Leavis completely missed the moral dimensions of *Ulysses*: its critique of Imperialism; its rejection of violence and war; its humanism; the transcendence of racial bullying right across Dublin by Leopold Bloom; Stephen's guilt in the Telemachiad and wild angst after; Molly's decision to re-commit to her marriage. He didn't even understand the significance of its last word – YES.

SAUSSURE

Saussure is an enigma. His closest correlation in literature is the ghost of Hamlet's father. He influenced later generations without being present. He is a famous theorist that hardly published a note in his lifetime. Even the works that were released under his *name* were half-summaries, notebook jottings, second-hand recollections of students who had heard his lectures, people who read his memoirs, old course notes, abandoned theoretical fragments and unfinished essays. Some material was withheld by his family until 1996. His book on Lithuanian phonetics was lifted out of Kurschat then probably streamlined by his students, Bally and Sechehaye. The "Course on General Linguistics" was offered at university only three times. The book of that title was constructed from notes. His theories are outdated and discredited. Even Laryngeal Theory started as an aside in an article about vowels in the PIE Ablaut. Today, critics can write that "Saussure hardly plays a role in current theoretical thinking" and that his concepts were "wrong on a grand scale." Others pay lip service. He died a lonely, broken man. A retrospective of my brother's work at the AGNSW titled, "On Some Australian Mountain Range (Imagining A Kind of Change)," has been curated by Professor Marion Hackett, Dean of the Faculty of Arts and Social Sciences at the University of Sydney and Head Acquisitions Adviser to the Macquarie Group Contemporary Australian Art Collection. It contains 29 works mainly from his most active period between 1980–1984 including:

- 4 x large paintings (oil on unstretched canvas with punch-holes and grommets): "Speed Painting 1," "Tim playing guitar (Meat Puppets)," and "Justin on bar stool with ghetto blaster," which represent his mature style. Also, a late untitled work which is derivative of Paladino's horse sculptures (c.1987).
- 1 x landscape painting (oil on unstretched canvas): "Untitled (coastline from satellite)." This work was completed after a field trip to Stanwell Park in 1984.

- 2 x small paintings (1 x oil on canvas; 1 x acrylic on black poster paper): "Untitled Heads (Dorian Gray)" and "Untitled (~~Permanence~~)." The former is a self-portrait gazing at 2 smaller self-portrait heads (no perspective) while the latter incorporates white text in the style of Colin McCahon across the face of a nocturnal landscape featuring the then-abandoned motorway columns of Pyrmont, Sydney.
- 2 x drawings (Czech oil pastel): "Francine in West Berlin" and "(Untitled) Bulimia." The first is his then-girlfriend, Francine Hackett, covering her mouth with elongated fingers. The second is a self-portrait in profile of Tom thrusting his fist into his mouth. It resembles the underside of an erect penis.
- 4 x drawings (black biro on butcher's wrap): all "Untitled" using a style similar to Dale Frank. They are named by the curator in parentheses: "Skeleton Beau," "Skeleton Gentleman with Cocktail watching Burlesque Dancers," "Skeletons Skydiving (The Tightrope Walker Falls Alone)," and "Self-Portrait Examining Palm (Lifeline)."
- 1 x super-8 movie (5 min), "Entr'acte Redux." This movie updates the scene in which Marcel Duchamp and Man Ray play chess in the 1924 short film *Entr'acte* by Rene Clair.
- 9 x drawings (pen on paper): all "Untitled" heads given titles based on their subjects. They are John Cale, Man Ray, Karl Marx, Simone de Beauvoir, James Joyce (1, 2), Martin Luther King (1, 2) and Self-Portrait respectively (I remember that these images were produced by analysing photographs for 30 seconds then executing an urgent image with his eyes shut – the result being Cubist bodily dislocation).
- 5 x cut-ups/ephemera (pre-1980):
    - 1 x postcard of hollowed rock formations on the Portuguese coastline with the title, "Patriarchy as Viewed from Within"
    - 1 x cartoon of slaves at a cotton gin titled "Alabama 1867: Newly emancipated negroes purchase 'dye-pigment' machines and ingredients from white traders" (an allusion perhaps to *The Sneetches and Other Stories*, which he considered the greatest ethical work of our time)
    - 1 x magazine picture of New York Skyscrapers with 3 rectangles cut into the image then pasted on black card
    - 1 x untitled cut-up of a photograph of a statue of a stone King on his throne with an Egyptian mummy lying across his lap called "Father" by the curator
    - 1 x industrial-strength brown paper bag (70 x 40) folded into a rectangle (19.5 x 14) which could sit upright on a mantelpiece and upon the face of which

had been glued a typed note reading: "PLACE OVER HEAD FOR THREE-DIMENSIONAL VIEWING".

The consensus of critics was that the only works of residual value to Australian art were "Speed Painting 1" and "Untitled (coastline from satellite)." These works were loaned by the Macquarie Group and later acquired by the National Gallery of Australia, Canberra. They are not currently being exhibited. They are considered fine examples of the domestic Neo-Expressionist style in the period from 1978–1989. Its principal proponents were Peter Booth, John Walker, Jenny Watson, Davida Allen, Mike Parr and Imants Tillers. The remainder of the paintings came from Private Collections. As executor, I provided drawings, cut-ups and the sole print of his only movie. Since the retrospective, Tom's larger works can sell at auction for over $40,000. There are probably less than twenty premium pieces in total. An unspecified number remain in the possession of EA² Gallery on behalf of his daughter's estate. Macquarie Group has recently recycled its asset portfolio. The wry humour revealed by his juvenilia was noted in reviews. This is an element of Dave that is often forgotten. He was a FUNNY GUY. An unauthorised biography was released to coincide with the show. It was written by rock journalist, Vivien Jug. It completely by-passed his spirit. Jug traded on the novelty value of Tom's story: his affairs with his dealers; Elizabeth's child; allegations about his role in the death of a young musician in 1984; the forgery scandal; his relocation to Melbourne; his death; and various court cases and coroner's reports arising from the above. We know about Saussure only because his students tried to capture his theories posthumously. I am trying to put together the same accumulative picture of Tom Hallem. Saussure wanted to look at language without the static interference of real-time production. He perceived language as a structured system of signs all internal. This was called "la langue." Utterance itself was termed "la parole." Academics all over the world like to use these French terms when in fact they simply mean 'language' and 'speaking' in English. His most famous concept is the linguistic sign: signifier and signified. This 'double entity' is composed of two parts: concept (signified) and the common sound image it produces in our mind (signifier). It was Lacan who noted that signification follows the path of the signifier. There can be multiple signifiers for each signified. For example, the signified 'cancer' can be conveyed equally by an animation of red-colored cells moving inside the human body (internal) or an image of a denuded human (surface). Maybe we perceive them simultaneously; creating a kind of 'split screen' in our heads. Everything about sign connections is arbitrary. Tom's best paintings turn the signified into a cartoon. The 'unpresentable' is called forth by style. Hung canvasses sag against the wall off eyelets pierced by cup hooks. There is no framing. Occasionally, he traces a gold border with a heavy house-painter brush. Brushstrokes are clearly visible. Patches and silhouettes of abandoned works are retained. Oil flows down the canvas seeping into adjacencies. A red shirt leaks into black trousers into a bar stool. A ghetto blaster melds with floorboards. Tom Hallem paused in the alcove of the sunken Modernist lecture theatre. Leaves gathered around his feet. Levi-Strauss descended into the Maginot Line. He felt in his back pocket for a torch. He had just returned to Paris. Joyce had just left. Now he was out doing fieldwork again. A broad flat roof hacked into high pines. He drew closer to a fire door seeking cover against rain spray. *Drole de guerre*. Hiatus. The storm sounded like a creek flowing in trees. A medical lecture was taking place. The lecturer's dome gleamed against bright fluorescent lights. Grey halo of seedhead. Yellowing notes. A bunch of dead dandelions. Billions of filaments. Perfect sphere. Culture like nature has structural principles. Levi-Strauss took to his desk where a hive of telegrams awaited censorship. The lecturer cleared his throat (link to laryngeal theory > family palette).

"We have been studying Surgery of the Stomach this semester," he commenced. "Today we will look at perforated ulcers. Next week, our final lecture will examine pancreatic cancer. The information in these lectures can be found in *Primary Surgery: Volume One*. In the event that the library has insufficient copies, a photocopied booklet of individual chapters can be purchased from the Faculty Office for two dollars each."

The lecturer took a sip of water from a drinking glass concealed by the lectern. Insert symbolism. The death of Joyce from a perforated ulcer is the end of (t)his plot. Everything after C6 in TMAC is aftermath and revisionism. Not tragedy. He lived life to the fullest. It was a Romance trope.

"We all know how food is digested," said the professor drolly. "It is swallowed, squeezed down the esophagus then pushed down a sphincter into the stomach, where it is mixed with gastric juices containing enzymes and hydrochloric acid. The stomach churns this mixture – called chyme – breaking it down like a washing machine. Once the food has become paste, it is forced through a second sphincter into the duodenum. The lining of the stomach is layered with folds. Ulcers occur in this lining. A perforated ulcer is caused when an untreated ulcer burns through the wall of the stomach or gastrointestinal tract. This causes digestive juices and food to leak into the abdominal cavity. Treatment requires immediate surgery. Otherwise, the patient will die quickly and painfully. The writer, James Joyce, for example died exactly 72 hours after the onset of cramps in January 1941."

What causes a stomach ulcer?

Stomach ulcers can be caused by a variety of factors. Stomach cancer is a principal cause. Surgical intervention in this instance will need to be coordinated with an oncologist.

The micro-organism, *Helicobacter pylori*, discovered only last year, is estimated to cause ninety per cent of duodenal ulcers. This germ lives in the stomach lining and causes related diseases like gastritis and dyspepsia. By the time a perforated duodenal ulcer is treated surgically, the causes are irrelevant.

Outline symptoms of a stomach ulcer.

Loss of appetite, concomitant weight loss, chronic indigestion and heartburn. The ulcer is still defined as 'peptic' at this stage. It has not yet burned through the full thickness of the stomach or duodenum wall.

How is it diagnosed?

The range of diagnostic methods includes Endoscopy, Barium meal, Biopsy and, more recently, the C14 breathe test for *H. pylori*. The C14 test involves swallowing radioactive carbon (C14) and testing air exhaled from lungs. It is effective because bacteria convert urea into carbon dioxide. Sound is another diagnostic tool. An ulcer can perforate almost silently in old patients such as Joyce.

What are the symptoms of a perforated ulcer?

1. Sudden, severe, sharp abdominal pains just below the ribcage. This pain is so intense that the patient will recall the exact moment of origin. Typically, maximum intensity occurs immediately and persists until surgery or death.
2. A rigid abdomen that is extremely vulnerable to touch.
3. Symptoms of shock such as excessive sweating, confusion and fainting.
4. Bright or altered blood coloration in vomit and stools as well as dark, tarry faeces.

Summarise

A perforated ulcer floods the peritoneum with the acid contents of the stomach causing sudden and constant agonising pain across the entire upper abdomen. The patient is pale, sweating and hypotensive with a fast pulse but normal temperature. The stomach is NOT distended. Typically, the abdomen has a surfboard-like rigidity, unlike that in any other disease.

How does the disease progress?

After 3 or 4 hours, pain and rigidity lessen. A silent interval begins. The patient starts to feel a bit better. This is like the eye of a storm. At the sixth hour, signs of diffuse peritonitis will develop. The patient now needs an urgent laparotomy to close the hole in the stomach or duodenum and to wash out the peritoneal cavity. Remember that the fundamental rule of all emergency surgery is to only do what is absolutely necessary. Don't waste your time on frivolities. X-rays are unnecessary if the diagnosis is clear. A fit patient who has a successful operation within 8 hours of onset has a good chance of survival. If you delay intervention until the twelfth hour, the chances of survival fall to sub-fifty per cent. Closing the perforation is not difficult but be sure to wash out the peritoneum thoroughly. For this task, you will need large volumes of warm saline.

What is the key diagnostic risk?

The main risk in diagnosis is distinguishing a perforated ulcer from appendicitis. Indicators for perforation include shoulder pain (usually on the right side), shock and production of at least one litre of stomach aspirate. As we know from lecture six, appendicitis presents quite differently with a colicky onset, fever and a small stomach aspirate of mucoid or bile-stained fluid. There is no evidence of shock in appendicitis. There is no evidence of fever in perforation. The lecturer offered this last cross-piece of information smugly.

Outline the pre-surgical procedure.

I don't propose to go through the pre-surgical process line-by-line. You can refer to your textbook. I do want to restate, however, that surgery should only take place if pain persists or gas under the diaphragm increases. Remember there is a grace period of only 2 to 4 hours for this decision.

Outline the surgical procedure.

The surgical method is very well-established. It isn't like spine or brain surgery. There are ten basic steps in your illustrated manual. Again, I will focus on some key points. Item 2. When you make the first midline or upper right paramedian incision then escaping gas should confirm your diagnosis. You can close-up if there's no stink and tell them it was all a horrible mistake here's a Chupa-chup please don't sue. Item 3. Initial examination should show a pool of exudate under the liver with food and fluid everywhere and an inflamed peritoneum. This fluid may be odourless and colourless with yellowish flecks, or bile-stained in the case of biliary peritonitis. Patches of fat necrosis indicate acute pancreatitis. If there is no or little fluid, push a swab on a holder beside the ascending colon towards the caecum. If it is soaked with fluid when withdrawn, this suggests perforation. If there's no fluid, go back to the end of Item 2 and hand out lollies. Item 4. We've diagnosed the ulcer and we're really going for it now. Place a retractor in the wound to expose the stomach and duodenum. Place a moist abdominal pack on the greater curvature of the stomach. Draw downwards, he said making a fondling motion. Ask an assistant to hold it. At the same time, ask the assistant to hold the liver upwards with a deep retractor. Put an abdominal pack between the retractor and liver for protection. If necessary, get help from a second assistant. If there are no assistants then just jam stuff everywhere and do your best. Item 6. What we are looking for is a small circular hole from 1 to 10 millimetres in diameter on the anterior surface of the duodenum. It should look freshly drilled out. Feel it with your fingers. Don't be afraid. You're wearing gloves. At least I hope you remembered them. The tissue around it will be thickened, scarred and friable. If the duodenum is normal, look at the stomach especially the lesser curve. If the hole is very small, there may be more to feel than see. Persevere. We are long past Item 2 and we've just run out of Chupa-chups. Item 7. Sometimes gastric ulcers are sealed off by adhesions to the liver. If they are adhered then separate them. If the ulcer is BURROWING into the liver, separate the stomach or duodenum from the liver by pinching between them with your finger and thumb. If this is difficult, cut around it and leave the base fixed to liver. Do NOT put finger through the ulcer into the liver under any circumstances as it will bleed severely and may cause shock, convulsions and death. Make sure you've got lots of blood or plasma handy just in case. Item 8. An ulcer high up posteriorly may be difficult to find. Feel carefully. It will feel like finding the surface of an earring that your wife dropped down the s-bend when she was doing the washing up. Item 10. The closure procedure is fairly standard. There are some important points. I recommend interrupted sutures of 2/0 chromic catgut on an atraumatic needle to bring the perforation's edges together with 1 to 3 deep stitches. Always sew omentum over the perforation by bringing up a fold of the greater omentum. A hole so plugged is unlikely to leak. There is one absolutely critical point to remember. Wash out the peritoneal cavity. Let me repeat. Wash out the peritoneal cavity. This is absolutely critical. It may be more important than closing the hole. Tip one litre of warm saline into the peritoneal cavity. Spread well. Suck it out. Repeat this procedure several times. Try to wash out every possible recess in the upper abdomen. Mop the surface of the liver. Instil tetracycline 1g in a litre of saline and leave it inside. Close the abdomen securely with non-absorbable sutures in a single layer. Do not insert drains. You're done! You're an expert stomach surgeon. If this is all too much blood and guts but you do like working with guts, as opposed to in them, then consider specialising in gastroenterology. Then you can sit in an office rubbing people's bellies and smelling their eructs while you leave the surgery to the butchers in emergency.

Equipment and team required.
General set. At least ten litres of warm saline. Two assistants (if possible).

Post-operative procedure

Nurse in high Fowler's position. Continue with nasogastic suction and intravenous fluids as per Sections 9.9 and A 15.5. Replace gastric aspirate with 0.9% saline. Continue to 'suck and drip' for 4 or 5 days until the abdomen is no longer tender and rigid and normal bowel sounds return. If the patient runs a FEVER in Week 2 you should suspect the development of a subphrenic abscess. If pain persists, or gas under the diaphragm increases, operate again.

Who is susceptible to a perforated ulcer?

This disease is a well-known writer killer. Kipling, Joyce and Tolkien all died in this manner. The irony in the word 'perforation' is noted. Joyce considered that the three writers of the nineteenth century with the greatest natural talent were Kipling, D'Annunzio and Tolstoy. They all became fanatics. The lecturer reached for his glass. Hallem set off. He ascended the driveway separating the playing fields of St Johns College from Royal Prince Alfred Hospital edging towards his birthplace, the King George the Fifth Maternity Hospital, across Missenden Road. A college cricket match was still in progress. Overhanging Jacaranda branches obscured his view of the dim summit. The sky darkened quickly like a time-lapse movie of a bruise on tanned flesh. Street lights struggled to sustain perception in the heaving breeze. Tree limbs were slung across isolated beams. Southerly coming. Dim martins wheeled above overflowing hospital skips. Hallem observed an ibis picking through garbage with its beak like Willy sorting through magic bins for dope residue in used hospital syringes and vials. The above description corresponds to the surgical procedure for ulcers. General anaesthesia with good relaxation is sufficient. Pre-medicate with intravenous morphine. It swung off the skip ledge at a sudden gust. A bird designed in advance of the garbage bin. Proof of God. How long would it take mankind to develop wings, Tom pondered. 4.6 billion years of evolution. 220 million years since mammals. 100,000 years of Homo Sapiens. 50,000 years of full behavioural modernity. Bonobo apes have already evolved skin flaps. Intelligent Design. Squash it all into the Blink of an Eye. If I start flapping my arms now it might only take one million years of continuous reinforcement by my heirs. Stalin's ape army. Inseminate female apes with human semen. Try also injecting women with gorilla sperm. *Lebensborn*. The translator is the novelist's ape, according to Simon Ley. Hitler's purpose was the opposite of Stalin. He was seduced by perfection; not functional debasement. His henchman, Himmler, was a chicken breeder like Darwin with his pigeon fanciers and dogs. Plato believed that human reproduction should be controlled by the State through a star rating system. Catholic broods. State-sponsored infanticide in China. Invert Natural Selection. Sparta exposed feeble infants at the *Apothetea*. Oedipus in tundra. Rome mandated the drowning of deformed babies (Table 4 of Roman Law). Stolen Generations. They thought it would all be bred out of the nation in fifty years. Forced Resettlement. Japan murdering all Chinese. Religious rape in Sudan. One Child Policy. There were thirteen million terminations in 2008 (source – State Media). There are 119 boys born for every 100 girls in China (Hsu, *Scientific American*, 2008). See Chinese *Book of Songs*. "When a son is born, / Let him sleep on the bed, / Clothe him with fine clothes, / And give him jade to play ... / When a daughter is born, / Let her sleep on the ground, / Wrap her in common wrappings, / And give broken tiles to play." There was a knock on the peasant's door. A female voice replied, "no one is home." All these images are relevant to Oxen. It is about BIRTH. Like Saussure, Joyce forces the reader to an awareness of the permutations within phonetic sequences. There is increased phonetic density and heightening of phonemes (the smallest units of utterance). Joyce's language is refracted in Saussure's obsession with anagrams. He employs a mechanical device to frustrate the sacred ends of nature (Pure/foy, "In fishing cap and oilskin jacket"). There are four types of birthing: **Natural**, **Mechanical**, **Hygienic**, **Hybrid**. Queen Victoria was strapped into Albert the Good's iron stirrups like some regal lab rat. Insert forceps. Mistress Purefoy on a stool. Two days past term can't deliver queasy from slop shrewd drier up of insides heavy breathing. Nurse Callan speaking a few words in low tones. Anaesthetic intervention. Caesarean section. Low mortality rate. Churn them out. Less insurance risks. Babies can live from twenty-three weeks. Susan Richards died on Day Two. Richie's miscarriages. Chaim. Language is just a system of differences no value judgments. Plato's Hermogenes said that "all words of a language are formed by an agreement of people among themselves." Language is thus a SOCIAL compact. A community generates signs. They cannot be produced in isolation. An arbitrary signification can only become formalised by consensus. Then it is made into a cultural emblem. It may even be considered the defining mark of a self-identified community. But it is in the nature of language to be overlooked. In this way, it avoids radical engagement with its own conventions. We are all responsible for language. English is a Heraclitan language. See Liffey's riverrun (also Cratylus). Mandarin is a relatively young language. Old Chinese up to the Zhou dynasty in the 3rd century BCE and Middle Chinese up to the Song dynasty in the 10th century CE have only been partially reconstructed. Topography governed the development of Chinese languages. Mandarin was the language of the plains from Sichuan to the north-east coast. The mountainous regions of the south had greater diversity. Ok Tedi killed eighty languages alone. Most Chinese only knew their local dialectic up to the Communist revolution. Mao selected Mandarin as the national language. Hanzi characters were simplified. Some say that the Communists took the poetry out of the Chinese language. But they made literacy possible for the masses. You still need 3,000 characters to read a newspaper. Mandarin is a logical language. New compounds are created out of existing words. For example, *wenxue* means literature. It is formed from *wenhua*, meaning culture and *xuexi* to learn. The Chinese repeat short words to create longer ones because they can't get clarity of expression out of monosyllabics due to tonal limitations. Thus, *yi dian dian* means a 'one little-little.' They are practical in making words. Mobile phone is *shou ji* – literally 'hand machine.' My favourite Chinese adaptation is *ji wei jiu*. It literally means 'chicken tail drink.' In English, this word is 'cock/tail.' If you say "I love you" in another language, it doesn't count in China. It doesn't sound the same as Mandarin and it doesn't count. I say it whenever I can to prostitutes, bogus girlfriends, KTV hostesses, bored housewives at five-star hotel bars even sloppy old massage ladies. It never has any meaning. They don't even understand it as language. What type of creature are you anyway? Your thin lips don't look Chinese. Our mouths are swollen and dark like soft tropical fruit. Blood fills them with meaning. Lips dominate the Han face. They can make unfamiliar shapes. This gives us greater dexterity of utterance. Put your tongue behind your top teeth. Pretend you've got lips. Wrong. You sound like a snake now. Let's go back to restaurant etiquette. Chinese people don't have time to listen. They are too busy studying your face. Your profile is like a beak. A big nose is a good sign. Show me your foot. Truly you are too big for a little Chinese girl like me. Does your sister look the same? Then she would not be beautiful, they conclude sadly. I want a son who looks like you. He could even wear spectacles! We can never kiss your face because of those sharp bristles. So ticklish! It would make our skin raw. Preservation of a milky complexion is an essential feature of beauty. Chinese women cannot understand why Western people burn their skin deliberately. It is a sign of poverty and ignorance. Common people are called *lao bai xin* – literally "old one hundred names." They are very perceptive. They always pay lip service to my Chinese language skills. They say my Mandarin is *bu cuo*. It means NOT BAD. I understand this term as an Australian. We also use a lot of litotes. They are obsessed with body hair. When a woman sees me naked for the first time, I always make a series of jokes to defuse her embarrassment. I say that I look like a monkey (*wo kan qi lai hou zi*). Next, I live in the zoo with my monkey friends (*wo zhu zai dong wu yuan gen wo de hou zi peng you*). Lastly, I say that my favourite fruit is bananas (*wo de zui xi huan shui guo shi xiang jiao*). *Hao chi!* Good eating! It's a killer routine. All women love to laugh most. It's more important than being handsome. Once I was at a KTV in Beijing when a drunken toll road owner asked if he could stroke my arm. I let him run his soft palm down my forearm. I had my shirt open from singing "Delilah." He asked if he could run his hand through my chest hair. I laughed out loud and said that the pretty hostess could do it then tell him how it felt. Later, he bought me an overnight session with this woman. I told her "wo ai ni" many times. Love is also a Trickster in the binary opposition between Love and Death. Death contains no element of surprise. I am announcing Derrida's mode of death in this section well in advance of examining the influence of Joyce (see DEARREADER). He died of pancreatic cancer. This provides a little dignity for the disintegration of what Christians call our 'wretched form' (Romans 7:24). Maybe I'll stuff him down the end of the chapter like a cancer cell breaking from the top of his skull and racing all the way down his spine to metastasise in his coccyx. We should ONLY study the death-modes of philosophers, not their works (see Leavis). There is no text anymore only headstones (see Barthes). Levi-Strauss went to Brazil. Nobody knows how Saussure died. Foucault never left the academy. Barthes was hit by a laundry truck near the Sorbonne and died from complications. Rimbaud got bone cancer in his knee in Aden, had his left leg amputated and died in Marseille. James Joyce suffered ocular degeneration. These are all strong Signs. There is a song called "The Death of Ferdinand Saussure" by Magnetic Fields. It's a good title. All signs are titles that then generate content. The title is a distillation of the Sign in relation to Love set against the fuller representation of love in pop classics by Holland Dozier Holland. Tom Hallem was always turning words like a tin pan alley lyricist. He had a gift for making slight shifts in their landscape with gentle puns. He started out ironic went anthemic then became self-deprecating as his physical powers waned. In the end, he was working on miniature scenes from Baudelaire. These works were never exhibited. They exist in demos. Tom Hallem mediated with the surface of his body after the heart transplant. He displayed the thick vertical scar running down his chest with pride, like an initiation symbol. He observed himself in the mirror with detachment (link to LACAN | NACAL). "Am I still the same person?" he asked in one of his last letters. What would Derrida have done during his illness? He had plenty of time on his hands. Ionesco would have enjoyed this surreal English idiom immensely. Perhaps he would have made a portmanteau word out of the language of disease. For example, the term 'pan-creative' is a good summary of Derrida's life work. Like Pan, Derrida possessed enormous strength. He was a champion footballer back in Algeria. He became a midfield dynamo who seemed impervious to injury. Later, he learned to transform objects into different forms (AKA magic flute). He was the sworn enemy of Apollo (see Dionysus). He mastered teleportation (see AE, C10). He also loved to write of The Fuck.

LACAN | NACAL

Before born babe bliss had. | emac-eB ebab htrib dnoyeb. Beyond birth babe Be-came | Dah ssilb ebab nrob erofeb. Prieš gimęs baba palaima turėjo. Don Cane was slumbering in his hotel room. He experienced a dream narrative of false remembrance. He was holding his infant son in tight swaddling. This was an event he knew NEVER HAPPENED.

The baby had never rested on his scales. He held it up to a MIRROR. His saw his own father. Dead on a boat in 1942. Lithuanian accents. Like Hamlet's father, the sensation of Inhabiting Absence lifted him towards pent consciousness. He became sharply aware of his surroundings. He opened his eyes. In the reflection of the wardrobe mirror, his bloated trunk was stretched sideways along the mattress tight-twirled inside a white bed sheet. He rolled onto his back and closed his eyes to release himself from all images real and imagined. His arms fell akimbo in surrender onto the flabby pillows next to his head. Aircon blew across bare skin. CYA. A few seconds bursting with facts. Daniel Boone squad spreading Bitrex through rice bags. COCKADAU! COCKADAU! Hmong tribesmen burst a withering field of fire. Miracle I wasn't hit. Everything else shattered. You gotta walk out of Out-Country. Take a dust-off UP. Get to the PRC-10. RTO dead. Squelch one time. Call in Medivac. Bark coordinates. 100 yards west of that BFR. Four guys zapped. Multiple GSWs. Multiple T&T s. Di di mau. Stuff them full of morphine syrettes. Guts spilling. Blasphemy of birth. Hold him together with pressure bandages. No LZ. I can hear Green Hornets. Let off some Goofy Grape. Two Snakes come first cutting up the jungle then a C-130 made an LZ Cut. Its flat bomb smashed a gap in the Triple Canopy. My mouth felt thick like chewing on a big spoonful of Choke. He took a print from his wallet of his baby son's face gazing knowingly at the lens of a Box Brownie. His wife sent it. On the back she wrote, "Tom – 4 months." No accompanying letter. Nobody treated him with spite. A smirk spread across the baby's bulbous cheeks. Lacan's face. His legs stretched. Unformed stomach muscles tightened and popped. His stiff arms reached awkwardly. Offertory. He presented himself for acclamation. The lens created a stage. Also, a mirror. Concave glass. Pregnant stomachs. *Elan vital*. Babies use it as clean energy to form their personalities. Like getting right up close to a radio as it transmits false messages. Don fractured his own life. Calculate Cost-Benefit Analysis. Develop some new *formule* for evaluating "life force." Calculus of *Qi*. The last breath left the body. A gasp sometimes a gurgle this time a sigh then the bowels drop. Don had seen men die in all formats. Richie handed over Robert's corpse. He couldn't make it more special for the soldiers who died in his lap. A sudden need to inhale made him suck hastily. **S = LF/T over PE x I x E** where: S = Subject, LF = life force, T = time, PE = psychic energy, I = intent. E = experience. MAKE A DIAGRAM OF THIS EQUATION. Subject at the Eastern head. "E" at the Western tail. Thus, mouth IN nose OUT. Trauma stays with you in breathing all the rest of your life. Tom Hallem reached the summit of Missenden Road opposite the art deco *oblige* of King George the Fifth Hospital. Update the lost child motif in Australian art. Glue a picture of an abandoned refrigerator in the foreground of McCubbin's idyll. Make a painting of the paddock where Pepe died. Howard Arkley bungalows. Suffocation also a metaphor. Courbet's *L'Origine du Monde* enclosed by Sylvia

Lacan behind a plain painted panel. Her husband liked to slide back the flap before his guests revealing the utterly apparent vagina. Lucien Freud's template. An old cold-box cannot be opened from within. Lift-the-flap book. Inside, position the huddled child. Make it an installation. Soundtrack of air weakening until silence is too long. Another foetus dead in Richie's womb. I have two healthy sons. Tom Hallem brushed the residue of wet leaves from his cheek. Cold not briney. The phallus is also in that painting, Lacan said. Courbet's putative headshot indicated he had painted a corpse. Tom bowed to the earth. Unyielding but resisting. Heroin had hardened his shit into a brain trying to burst out of his gut. Constipation is a sign of good health in Pomeranians, said Molloy. Beckett suffered anal boils. Hope it's not too thick. Bring on piles again. My grandfather squatting on a rolled-up newspaper. Bloom gazing up the arseholes of Classical statues to see if their logs winked like Bataille's priest-eye. He only overcame constipation in Calypso due to the alleviating impact of *Cascara Sagrada*. Baudelaire said the French were barnyard animals. Beasts of the Latin Race. Shit did not displease them. This associates them with swine. But they could equally be equated with goats. Father Ambrose. Big cock, gown uppa. It hurts when they press through the knot then it's easy. Stroking my shoulder-blades. Just relax. Yielding not resisting. Bloom allowed his bowels to ease as he read Beaufoy's *Tit-Bits*. Explore every inch of the cave. Tom had forgotten all about Pepe. Was he even REAL? Insert psychoanalysis. Tom replayed a sequence of recent sensations [INSERT TABLE]:

Table 8. Tom Hallem – Symbolism of actions in C6

REAL	SYMBOLIC VALUE
Overhanging row of natives	Distinctive Australian landscape
Looming darkness	Loss/death
Storm	Catharsis = wild memory (sublime 1 – nature A)
Detox Clinic	A sealed box
Pulling a coat over his head	Mother's shroud; death shroud
Birds circling and picking at food	Death and disintegration (raven)
Excrement	Lacan's Seminar on Anxiety (1963)
Pepe's suffocation	Homoeroticism (sublime 2 – libido/death)
Walking alone through familiar places	Lost innocence … lost certainty … reflection … isolation
Art	Of F/W
Joyce's "Oxen" episode	One of Birth
This chapter	One of Death (Joyce mirror)

Tom Hallem walked through the hospital maintenance yard. It was blighted with chimneys, garbage skips, corroding machinery and empty gas cylinders. He took shelter beneath a corrugated awning that wound alongside the car park. The Queen Mary Building rose off brick wings half-hidden by skirting figs (sublime 3 – nature B). Nurses Callan and Quigley emerged eating grapes. Chew up a bloke at the Prince Alfred pub after each shift. Open all hours. Callan so fertile. Luster of her own sex. Bloom's faux pas. When will you too be pregnant? Hallem crossed Mallett Street and entered Camperdown Memorial Park. Keep the base narrative simple like watching *Blow Up* or Pasolini. He could see the distant Bandstand through mangled landscaping. He had fucked there after a gig. Melanie's hand reached down his spine. Her finger penetrated his sanctum. It's alright to cum inside me, she said (Sublime 4 – libido/orgasm). There was a plaster memorial to the Great War Dead. This had no significance for him. He felt thirst. The oval was wet with fallen pods. Grandstand toilets. Hot. Go there again. No way. He turned uphill into Australia Street and entered the corner shop opposite Bell's Ice Cream Factory (Sublime 5). How do machines make cold? he wondered. The human when brought into existence deals first with language. This is a given. One is caught in this trap even before birth. A father puts his mouth onto the warm female pelt. He whispers sweet words. Play Bach. All distorted by the machine. Lacan might have been a loathsome character but I am not going to dwell on his life-story. He was a Trickster. A Sufi. Today, he would become a top celebrity. He liked to construct a power dynamic in all situations. Money was his locus. He swindled people out of valuable books. Acolytes delivered his favourite type of cigar at a click of the fingers. His therapeutic method was outlawed by Authority as a cynical form of fee maximisation. I respect this approach as a banker. As a patient, I applaud his candour. Sometimes you can deal with an issue of substance in the waiting room. Perhaps a brief exchange about a magazine cover is enough for one session. I hate the production pressure of the fifty-minute hour. By the time we get the niceties out of the way and talk about Doctor Pat's epiphany in an Indonesian waterfall there is only time to re-run the skeleton of the psychic machine and grind forward by increment. He needs to draw a map of relations so I don't have to retell the myth from origin. Lacan used algebraic formula. I would present my own case as: {M + F = fO} – {M – F} = M + S = SELF (Not-F) *where* M: Mother; F: father; fO: foetus (small f + Other); S: Son. There are direct transferences from unacknowledged sources in Lacan's theoretical writing. Mirror image comes from the Communist psychologist, Henri Wallon. A/P Tuck began to transcribe Capri's paper into his computer in MS-DOS format. White text on black. He was in a rush to get to the pub. He had a new limerick to orate. This is normal Hieratic practice. Joyce never acknowledged sources. I am not going to acknowledge Tom Dalzell. Lacan's "Back to

Freud" campaign was just a propaganda slogan. One wag claimed it meant "Go to Lacan." Cooking with Jacques. He had bespoke uniforms tailored out of rare filaments and furs like some *Fin de Siècle* dandy. He revelled in his own notoriety. Performance was his favoured mode. He deployed Surrealist theatrics. This was evident from his first appearance at the IPA in 1936. Lacan was the first BRAND in the psychiatric industry. He was the Johnny Halliday of Human Personality. Cliff Richard to Freud's Elvis. He presented mimesis as innovation deploying the self-assurance of an impenetrable style. Insert self-deprecating comment. He latched onto obscure utterances of Freud repositioning them as Thesis Central. Saussure believed that the Lithuanian pitch accent was the missing link of Indo-European linguistic history. It was the most direct living relic of the vowel *A. Lacan believed that the Unconscious had a language structure equal to that of the Conscious. This made them collide as equals. It was a direct repudiation of Freud. He had the audacity of Mao in stating sincerely that thought should bloom. He created formulae to illustrate his precepts in a parody of algebra. Psychiatry has been struggling to present itself as a quantitative science. This qualification would increase its access to government medical subsidies. He installed the mirror as his basic theoretical tool out of Narcissism. This is the same impulse as Freud with his mother. Or Joyce with his father. *Ulysses* is really an ode to John Joyce. He is the ABSENT CENTRE. A KEY. James Joyce never abandoned his father's portrait. Leopold Bloom is just a sideshow. Stephen Dedalus is going home at the end of the novel. He has nowhere else to go. Nor does he desire any other place. His mother is dead so he will return to his sisters as subs. Joyce's brothers are never mentioned in his works, although Stanislaus was a close companion and reader up to WW1 and the death of their younger brother George was a pivotal event in the collapse of the family. Perhaps this moment was too painful for Joyce, who struggled to elicit strong feelings out of his characters. Stephen was ABOVE his siblings in W. Rocks. He becomes EQUIVALENT to them by going home – perhaps even BELOW them – at the end of *Ulysses*. It is hard to tell if Stephen is continuing his descent into nihilism or the seeds of greatness have been sown. That is the genius of Joyce. Lacan regarded John Joyce as a "deficient father" (*un père carent*) because he did not instate the "Name of the Father" ("Not-F") in his son. By this term, Lacan means that the father is meant to give the male child knowledge of what the mother desires via "paternal metaphor." This is a masculine and linguistic version of the Oedipus complex. Not-F takes the place of the desire of the mother; balancing the male child. It is what the mother wants and what the father must transmit. Lacan calls it a "symbolic phallus" (SP). Unfortunately, James Joyce was given "Poor Phallic Bearing" (PPB) by his father. It was only his successful drive to FAME (F) that ameliorated PPB. It restored the paternal function which in turn prevented the precipitation of Schizophrenia (SCZ).

Lacan uses the symbol of the Borromean knot to explain the operation of this precept. There is an argument that Joyce was conscious of Borromean signification. Something of the error in Joyce's knotting is hinted in *Finnegans Wake* in the fable of the Mookse and the Gripes. In a letter to Frank Budgie, Joyce explained: "When he gets A and B on to his lap, C slips off, and when he has C and A, he loses hold of B." Phallic Restoration (PR) amounts to a Borromean Symbol (BS) weaving three subjective registers together:

- The Real (RE) – everything outside language
- The Symbolic (SY) – language (all signifiers)
- The Imaginary (IM) – ego and body-image (signified).

Collectively, these are termed "RSI" by Lacan. He also represented it as the word "*He+res+ie*" for a seminar title. BS is relevant because it collapses if any link in RSI is broken. In Paranoia (P), BS-SY is at risk. In SCZ, it is BS-IM that is loose. Dalzell concludes: "this is how Lacan understands the error in Joyce's subjective knotting because the paternal function had not been instated in him to hold the three registers firmly in place." Joyce's Formula (JF) can be presented thus:

- ~~Not F~~ transmitted to Joyce resulting in PPB/FF
- Thus, Joyce himself needed to find a "Supplementary Ring" (BS-SR) to restore the Fallen Father
- As noted, his BS-SR was F. This gave him WHOLENESS (W)
- JF can be presented thus: [(~~Not F~~ = PPB = subordinate-BS-IM = -SCZ) + (BS-SR = PR)] = W

To remedy ~~Not F~~, Joyce constructed a *sinthome*, his BS-SR, a paternal remedy to hold the three circles knotted together. What repaired his *lapsus de noeud* was creating for himself what Lacan calls an "ego in the sense of F." Joyce experienced intense guilt for BS-IM = BIG A SCZ (full-blown schizophrenia) in his daughter, Lucia (LUC). He tried to use the prowess of JF to heal LUC through language. This can be presented as *F(W)ake* = LUC-W. The failure of this calculation can be attributed to "Intergenerational Trauma" (IT), which James Joyce was only able to transcend via F = W. John Joyce was the original victim of deficient fathering. His father was a horse-trader, alcoholic, gambler and bankrupt who died before his fortieth birthday. His greatest failure in Lacanian terms was that he transmitted [PPB + FF] to his son because he was too much friend (F2) and not enough father (neg-F). James Joyce was the next entrant into what became a hereditary club. Joyce had already noted in *Portrait* that Stephen's father acted more like a brother. Ellmann cites the example of John Joyce as a teenager being caught smoking by his father. Rather than being reprimanded, he was offered a cigar (PPB, FF). My own father acted in the same manner (business lunches at Chinese restaurants). In this reading, I have passed PPB + FF = IT onto my son. Lacan says that Joyce's father taught him ZERO. Clearly that is not accurate as the above formulation demonstrates. But at least he was PRESENT. Joyce was able to observe a 'father' figure. By contrast, Tom Hallem not father, not had (HNFNH). This raises the basic question of whether such LACK (PPB + FF + IT = Z) is better than HNFNH – raising the whole 'nature and nurture' (NvsN) argument. Further, it should be noted Tom Hallem had the proxy experience of a crippled step-father (CSF-PPB-OEDIPUS) which may have further mutated his PPB in Lacanian terms. Carl Jung diagnosed BIG A SCZ in Joyce's daughter and latent or SMALL A SCZ in Joyce himself. This is also Lacan's argument. Joyce reasoned that LUC's mind was his own. He refused to accept any diagnosis which did not promise hope. He called her a TELEPATH. I don't know what Elizabeth told Lucy. She was raised with no father. Perhaps she believes that her father was that dead dentist. Maybe she doesn't know about AIDS. Joyce want to invest *F(W)ake* with the power to cure his daughter. Its title comes from the comic ballad, "Tim Finnegan's Wake" (TFW). Lucia's mind was to be the subject of Joyce's own act of resurrection. Finnegan falls from his ladder drunk like Elpenor in the *Odyssey* and is presumed dead. He awakes when he is splashed with whisky. As with Finnegan, Joyce believed that Lucia was not truly gone. TFW was one of John Joyce's favourite songs. It became one of the mainstays of his singing performances. Finnegan's resuscitation is paralleled in the recapitulation of the river at the end of *F(W)ake*, when waking finally puts an end to dreaming. INSERT VICO. *Ulysses* was the history of a day. *Finnegans Wake* was about all-night. It's a dream that takes the form of the river, winding through its course then returning to its source in Book IV at dawn. This form corresponds to Vico's *ricorso*. This book must also possess circular repetition weaved into Borromean loops until closure. End on the word SPOILT. Weave it into the final soliloquy. Meaning in *Finnegans Wake* is constantly slipping. As such, this text presents a series of displacements and condensations where characters come and go and are transformed constantly. Everything is fluid. Names change. A name changes meaning as well. The acronym HCE stands for over fifty different linguistic units including "Howth Castle and Environs" and "haveth childers everywhere." It's all on a LOOP. Mine only starts if I win an award (see C11). That will be when I am recognised for technical innovation in the category of supporting artist. Theoreticians have generally downgraded Lacan's theories. Lacan was a great literary critic (including of Freud) but he was not an original thinker. His legacy was one of incubating fright. Foucault wrote extensively about Lacan as a term never mentioning his name. He epitomised everything that Foucault feared about *Scientia Sexualis*. Lacan invented incarceration for profit. Guattari was once his star pupil. He paid to drive Lacan home. He was Lacan's roadie. He formed a new band with Deleuze called The Anti-Oedipus. He was surprised when Lacan cut him from the album credits. He didn't understand that it was just show business. There was only room for 1 x "Big A Other" per stage. Lacan wore suits of grey felt. He founded the Freudian School of Paris. He was accused by feminists of sadism. Noam Chomsky of all people said Lacan was an "amusing and perfectly self-conscious charlatan." He needed a peek at himself in Lacan's mirror. Lacan argued that invisible structures dictate society and culture. He was obsessed with tactile opulents. He wore pendants, brooches and bracelets made of gold and precious gems. His shirts had hard collars without flaps. Or collars twisted and turned upwards like a nineteenth century priest. He venerated ingots for their heft. They were soothing like gravity bearing him down. He would have fetishised the cool ponderousness of JADE if he had been exposed to Chinese culture. He argued that Free Will is chimeric. He wore shoes made of rare skins. He particularly loved snakes. It was a material preference invested with signification. For Freud, there is nothing literal about a dream; it's all metaphor. The Unconscious is beautifully complex like language. The psyche is not reducible to a fixed print. There is no such thing as normalcy. Desire can never be sated. It is the fabric of OUR LACK. Link back to Dominioned Literature (C4). Lacan annexed Bataille's wife. It enabled him to attach himself to Surrealism by the phallus. This sounds like a bad joke but they really thought like that in those days. They were blunt chauvinists. And Lacan was one of the crudest of all. I lost that book I can't give it back, Lacan often said. I never had it, was another retort. This is a metaphor for his annihilation of all sources (see above). Lacan looks just like my father. They were both charming men. Their faces got heavy and broader with age. They had big, hang-dog eyes. The bottom lids watered slightly when they spoke, creating an artificial impression of sentiment. This only happened when they spoke of themselves. Neither registered any empathy. External events recounted to them were just HO-HUM. Lacan turned this sociopathy into a well-paid career. My father just became a parasite, using women for cashflow until he ran out of puff. They took immense pride in rich, rippled manes. Their coifs straightened in old age but they never went bald. This is another time-lapse symbol worthy of Proust. The parallels with my father make it impossible for me to evaluate Lacan. John Stanislaus Joyce (1849–1932) became what his son, Stanislaus, called, "a failed medic, actor, singer and commercial secretary." In *Ulysses*, Lacan concluded that Joyce had rejected the concept of father. This is a common critical position. It is seen in numerous ways like Stephen's

Shakespeare theory or his decision to visit Bloom's house in the first place. Stephen is father-testing. In fact, I would argue that Stephen recognises that Leopold Bloom is NOT and CAN NEVER BECOME his symbolic or substitute father. He can never instate Not-F or SP. He is too anodyne. Too methodical. Too safe. Instead, Stephen decides to return to the family home where his BIOLOGICAL father is located. Stephen places himself back in adjacency to his BIOLOGICAL FATHER in the vain prospect that he can become a REAL FATHER. I know from personal experience of this insatiable hope. It is a complete waste of spirit. Joyce maintained the illusion of fealty by not seeing his father for decades. It was the drive from this lack that Joyce used to write novels, achieve F and attain W. James Joyce never censured his father for family privations, despite episodic criticism in *Ulysses*. He chose instead to blame "paralytic" Irish society. This was what Harold Bloom would call *Clinamen*. Joyce appreciated that his father had given him the gift of Aggressive Dissolution [AD], which he regarded as the source (actually we could even use the term 'well-spring') of his literary genius. In this reading, Eccles Street is the outer limits of Stephen's Telemachiad, Bloom acts as Menelaus, Stephen rejects his overtures to stay in Sparta and Telemachus starts to return home to face the suitors (John's creditors, his sisters etc). This reading of *Ulysses* creates a continuum with *F(W)ake*. It is *Portrait of the Artist as an Older Fragmented Male*. An alternate reading is that Lucia's mental condition was the spur for Joyce turning from rejection of the father figure (John Joyce) in *Ulysses* to renewed engagement as a father through his obsession with using language to resurrect his daughter in *F(W)ake*. In short, he tried to create spells to heal his daughter like Merlin. This would achieve what Harold Bloom calls *Apophrades*. It would enable Joyce to RE-FILL THE FATHER TROPE. John let down James but James would not admit it and anyway he was going to fix Lucia. This would pass on a feminised Not-F. Of course, the great flaw in Lacan's whole argument about BS is that Lucia was female. IT can only be expunged by the end of a biological line – i.e. sexual barrenness as delivered to the Egyptian God Seph by castration. Spina bifida ruined my father's line. INSERT SIMON DEDALUS TAUNTING DILLY. Stand up straight girl. You'll get curvature of the spine. The drunk then impersonated his daughter. Stanislaus Joyce dodged IT because he saw his father with clarity and was thus able to measure him rationally and BS himself. My father was a charlatan. It took me thirty years to confess this fact. It came in a sudden utterance like epiphany. Like Lacan, my grandfather sired two families simultaneously. My mother was the third of four children. He had three children out of wedlock. My mother was his only legitimate child. Lacan sired a child with Sylvia Bataille. He concealed his daughter's existence from his other children. My father had five wives. I was illegitimate. I am his only living child. He never told his family in England about me. I bear another man's surname. HELL/AM. Insert ratio of autobiography. The following table [NOTE complete box-shading] supplies Total Content Ratios for *Tmac* (TCRT):

TEXT					
Theory 50%		Fiction 50%			
IA 30%	OT 20%	TA 20%	A 15%	F 10%	I 5%
AT/T 50%		OA/F 50%			

The assumptions in the model are:

1. *TMAC* = 100%
2. Theory (T) | Fiction (F) = 50:50 split
3. Within T: Interpretative Analysis (IA) = 60% | Original Thinking (OT) = 40%
4. Within F: Autobiography (A) = 30% | Facts (F) = 20% | Tropes (TR) = 40% | Invention (I) = 10%
5. *Thus*, [1] Received by Self (IA + TR) = 50% of Total
6. *Thus also*, [2] Invented by Self [(OT + I) = 25% *Plus* (A + F) = 25%] = 50% of Total
7. *Therefore*, [1] + [2] = 100%
8. *Reverse engineering (proof test)*, where [1} = -T & [2] = -F
9. [1] + [2] = *TMAC*.

It is critical to the task at hand that I maintain an even split between technical writing and fiction. It is easy to succumb to plot. I know it makes the Readerly Text easier. I also know that it reduces the proportion of Writerly Text. This ratio is essential to Technical Fiction, although it comes with the greatest risk (of writing a boring book). There have been many novels based on famous works. *Wide Sargasso Sea* is a prequel of *Jane Eyre*. Lacan became obsessed with the writing of one of his patients. Marguerite Anzieu had been institutionalised for attacking a famous French actress with a knife. Her work became the subject of Lacan's 1932 thesis. It was the first real piece of Structuralist analysis. She was a post office attendant. In other words, she traded in language (note link to Vietnamese post office worker in C5, S-E14). Lacan gave her the pseudonym 'Aimee,' after the title of her first novel. By being given this title, she also became a vinculum for Lacan's notion of Love. His text was NOT REALLY about Miss Anzieu. He used her as a bargaining chip. He read her fiction, journals, correspondence and notes to Surrealist arbiters like Breton, Dali and Eluard. This content gained him membership of their Club. She also wrote a report about the memoirs of Becassine, the cartoon character of a Breton maid who spawned the first comic book. This was a complex conceptual frame in an apparently simple guise. Roudinesco describes Lacan as a fetishistic collector. His dog was named JUSTINE. He kept detailed lists of possessions. Obsession is ingrained in any passion especially that of the artist. It's like having brown hair, as Delmore Schwartz said. His corpse rotted for two days in the Columbia Hotel. He was the model for Bellow's Fleischer. Lou Reed was hanging around his sick room. He wrote a song with Schwarz's name in parentheses as part of the title. The song had no real content alignment with Schwartz. But the title is enough (see Barthes S-E). There are a sequence of middle-aged figures dying of painful terminal illnesses in Joyce. Stephen's mother. Nuncle Richie. Uncle Paul on Crown Street. This was just part of life back then. Lacan attended the first public reading of *Work in Progress* in Paris, 1937. Joyce had deployed languages that he didn't understand to explode the English language via its strongest defence mechanism – its immigration policy towards words. The British Empire was always intervolving new words into its vocabulary. It created the world's first big dictionary (Oxford) to contain them and provide a platform for continued English Imperialism. English turned every Signifier globally into English and even made English into a Signified in its own right. Joyce used writing as a mutiny for Ireland. This was probably the most important type of revolution that Joyce could perceive. He genuinely wanted to free Ireland. There was Fame in that achievement. But it didn't mean harking back to the Celtic Revival. That held no interest for Joyce. He considered it atavistic. To transcend FF and achieve [F/W] he needed to establish himself as a language in his own right. Invading English was the simplest means of attack. D&G have examined this tenet (see C4). *Ulysses* set the standard for technical fiction. Lacan said nobody ever made literature like *F(W)ake* before. There has been enough history since its publication in 4 May 1939 to state categorically that nobody in fiction has extended Joyce since. Certainly, no Australian text has ever tried to compete with the English canon in this way. There is a pun in each word of *F(W)ake*, Lacan said. Lacan himself was addicted to punning. He like complex anagramgags like Joyce. He worked across different languages like Joyce (see Ophelia's 'pansy' speech in L-S S-E). He coined the term *sinthome* for a seminar on Joyce emphasising the English word "sin." It was the Latin way of spelling the Greek origin of the French word, symptome, meaning symptom in English. He related it back to Original Sin and thus back to the Courbet painting which he owned and by deductive association HIMSELF. He said that Joyce's *sinthome* made up for his father's failing. Lacan did the same thing. Joyce was Lacan's father because he became the father of ALL words. We all suffer IT because of Joyce. Lacan is my portal to *F(W)ake*. It is the last book against which I must struggle (*kenosis*). *F(W)ake* is structured like BS. It is the place that Odysseus went after the end of the *Odyssey*. It is the place to which Stephen Dedalus walked into invisibility that night. In *F(W)ake*, Shaun travels East–West and Shem goes North–South. These cycles cross in two places. I will name these locations, Dublin and Australia. Opposite ends of the globe. Two sides of the same coin. A guiding metaphor. When you ignite Rachel's globe, the routes of the great explorers are illuminated. *Ulysses* + *F(W)ake* = *TMAC*. *Distance Form Closure* [DFC].

LYOTARD

Lacan was the last link to an older generation of thinkers like Breton and Joyce. Lyotard represents the next wave. Later theoreticians were oddly divorced from art production. They wrote of art, in particular Joyce. They associated with artists. However, they did not draw PATERNAL outputs from this nexus like Lacan. He was an anonymous young man in Paris enthralled by major artistic figures before the Second World War. He sought to impress them by divulging casebooks as art objects. This created a stage for him. He gave lectures that became Dadaist performances. He received Not-F from Breton (and others) and later gained SP. This formed part of his successful drive to F. Shanghai Dog had plenty of time on his hands while he burnt the last of the management company capital so he bought a copy of Barthes' *S/Z* from a pirate book stall opposite Shanghai Library. It had been many years since he studied a theoretical text. A resonance possessed him as of OLD LOVE (*jouissance*). He began to accumulate relevant secondary texts. This was hard at times because of the Great Firewall. He needed VPN. He worked his way through *Sarrazine* while he tracked global markets DOWNWARDS on Bloomberg at Time Passage Bar. This period represented the post-Sublime. I was looking for a theoretical formula that fitted Tom Hallem's journey from the university grounds passed his birthplace to the Shakespeare Hotel. This route was roughly equivalent to Stephen's movement from the National Library to Holles Street Hospital and finally Burke's pub. I selected a nocturnal journey through Venetian alleys towards an orgy (... is there such a direction as 'towards' an orgy?). But to make it effective I would need to put this passage on a loop so I can place Joyce's Modernist drive in *Ulysses* into stark contrast with the spiraling texts of French theory (see Vico). Joyce only evolved a True Borromean Knot (TBK) formula later during *F(W)ake*. For now, we must solace ourselves with phallic intrusions in the form of symbols. Hypodermics enter the epidermis. Styx burrowing into Hades. Derrida's spurs. All Burkean epics. Balance anti-Cartesian postmodernism with the repressed necessity to tell a tale and you get THIS BOOK. I've talked a lot about Lyotard by proxy. His definition of the postmodern is integral to this enterprise. We can see in his life, book titles, form of death, relationship to his father (NotF) and attraction to the Sublime all we need to know about Lyotard. His background is typical of a whole generation of post-War French theoreticians. He grew up outside Paris in a bourgeois household. His father was in sales. He had normal aspirations for a French child: to be a Dominican monk or an artist. He wrote a novel at the age of fifteen. It was an artistic failure, he said. He was too young THEN to realise that the novel as a format was redundant after Joyce. One could only express fictive precepts in the future through the new medium of theory-out-of-language (TOOL). Freud was the first disciple of this art. It was only later, after these academics, heirs of Joyce, or, rather, his he(i)r/etics, and hieratics, had passed into history (MET THE LOGIC OF DEATH) that it became clear that any future fict[it]ion could ONLY achieve Lacan's F/W nexus by UPSIsing to a COMBO DEAL comprising:

1) Firmness of purpose
2) Rejection of all inlaid patterns of Readerly Text production [this means continuously asking questions like: why would I describe the appearance of characters? For example, Stan Welles has an enormous epiglottis like a turkey. He wears a false nose in all his movies. So, what is the technical advantage in using this image?]
3) Denial of good form (Lyotard 1)
4) Inscribing the unpresentable on the page (Lyotard 2)
5) Deployment of TOOL
6) Retrogressive tendencies (Proust)
7) *Kenosis* (SCY + CHRB)
8) Inside-outing thereby expanding the scale of meta-narrative (write a book longer than *Ulysses*)

This list could be called my EIGHT COMMENDMENTS. We will refer them form tiem to time. All this work needs to be done without universal theories. Commandment NINE. Terms that Lyotard rejected include: "progress of history," "we can know everything through science" and "absolute freedom." These are all Language Games. He would have reserved special attention for the concept that "in America, everyone has the opportunity to get rich." This is a special sauce full of artificial flavours. We need to gaze past such icons without credulity. Not act like a savage looking at a sail. Lyotard signalled how this could be done with his concept of Little Narratives. This 'descaling event' or miniaturisation is already in evidence in modern social media with its slogans, memes and micro-videos. One hundred-page reports are dead. We now have full communication by symbols (EMOJI).

These works are the output of what Lyotard called "information machines." Today, this term goes by the acronym ICT. Lyotard was with Kubrick on Hal. He was uncannily aroused by Julie Christie's impregnation by a computer in *Demon Seed*. Hence, he wrote *The Inhuman*. This is long before William Gibson or *Terminator*. It is now the Year 2020. We are well past the temporal boundaries of the text. The human race has been attacked by Skynet. Lyotard's theory could be modified by the production of NEW meta-narratives out of a plethora of Little Narratives. This would be an amalgam of scenes loosely connected by some universal plotline to produce what was once termed Menippean Satire. But isn't that *Ulysses* already? And if you embolden language further isn't it *F(W)ake*? I'll have to ask Musgrave, he's the expert in that field. Joyce had a notebook full of what he called Epiphanies. They were mainly dream chronicles, which are always of limited interest. Dreams possess a spurious relationship to truth. The dullest people always spend a lot of time recounting their dreams as if they were a substitute for experience. This is one of the principal flaws in *F(W)ake*. *F(W)AKE!* was a rock album about LIFE ON THE ROAD. Joyce became a singer who spent too many years on a tour bus. Too many groupies. Living on royalty advances from Weaver and Beach. What is the difference between an Epiphany and the Sublime? Epiphany is the sudden realization of a larger essence and meaning due to observation or experience. It comes from the Greek: "manifestation." It is used when Gods appear to mortals in Classical literature. It is also associated with the revelation of Christ as the Son of God. James Joyce popularised the term in literature. His notebook contained seventy-one samples. He was responsible for democratising the concept by triggering epiphanies from trivial events. The Sublime is the next threshold UP. It is an oxymoron combining anxiety and pleasure. It is so great and impenetrable that it exposes the limits of human perception. Longinus did the first study of the Sublime. It was one of Utterance. Only a few words need to be remembered to understand Longinus: *hupsous*, *ekstasis*, amazement, rhythm and, above all, spirit. His equation was: content + passion + flow > banality. The Sublime must also possess RISK. Longinus considered strange persons and eccentrics uniquely endowed to induce the Sublime. Errors and clichés were integral to this art. The Sublime needs a maverick and unruly force; in other words, Saussure's Trickster. It was Addison who first responded to the Alps on his Grand Tour in 1699, delineating three basic elements of the Sublime – greatness, uncommonness and beauty. Burke separated the Sublime from Beauty. Kant tried to codify the Sublime as mathematical or dynamic. To Joyce, it was just an adjective describing lofty speech in Rhetoric. [SHIFT TENSE] For Lyotard, the Sublime is the foundation of Modernism. It releases the writer from the constraints of the human condition to shoot for the ineffable. Rather than trying to articulate universal values (such as truth and justice), Lyotard recommends that we should think of the human project in terms of the "infinite task of complexification." He says: "maybe our task is just that of complexifying the complexity we are in charge of." This becomes a replacement for the meta-narrative. It is the basis of TOOL. You can see it coming into the Canon in Shelley's receding piles of metaphors which stall narrative drive and undo teleology. Pater's dense style was its prose equivalent with its shifting linguistic units and qualifications. All questions of agency, cause, intention, authorship and history dissolve into a sublime asocial NOW. Derrida calls this space *Aporia* ("unpassable path") – the moment when the self-contradictory nature of human discourse stands exposed. Foucault finds the same phenomenon in the reductive spirals of Power/Knowledge. Kristeva calls it *Significance* – the unravelling of the subject inside the pleasure of the text. Lacan christened it the REAL – that unsayable, unbearable space outside language where humans meet at the moment of absorption into flux (this is also a type of epiphany). All these definitions are relevant to Joyce. Lyotard argues that the postmodern is that element within the modern which "puts forward the unpresentable in presentation itself." Joyce has become so synonymous with *Ulysses* that you can substitute his name for the novel and everybody knows exactly what you are talking about. He is the "unpresentable" that made itself present. But he didn't do it bluntly with first-person narrative. He insinuated himself with autobiographical feints, allusions to aligned characters like Hamlet and extra-textual commentary by proxies. The Sublime is installed by Lyotard as the place of epiphany and terror where the inexpressible stands over/against human endeavour. It can be monstrous and unthinkable like Death Camps. It can be unbearably sweet like the breath of a newborn baby. For Lyotard, the Sublime defined the Avant-Garde project as it evolved over the course of the nineteenth century. It was the breakout mode. Pater clearly saw his own "assiduously cultivated age" positioned between Euphuism and Decadence. This is an utterly critical mode of self-conception. Wilde utilised the full range of literary forms – plays, horror stories, children's tales, a novel, essays, his famous ballad on Reading Gaol and numerous epigrams – each acting like a different shade on the painter's palette to create HIMSELF as the ultimate work of art. This explains his interest in self-presentation. He became a FIXED IMAGE like Dorian Gray. It also explains his vulnerability to REAL LIFE. Wilde felt impregnable – NOT as if he was above the law but because he felt like an image no longer a human. Writers like Wilde and Pater updated Shelley's poetics for prose and positioned it to influence High Modernists like Joyce. Indeed, Modernism as a movement shares many facets with Shelley's poetics: emphasis on subjective inner perceptions, which is both a lyric and Romantic trait; deconstruction of received literary forms, images and language to provoke new types of expression; increasing reliance on intratextuality and intertextuality for meaning; an aspiration to employ antinomian matter as an affront to literary and social convention (this was epitomised by the emerging avant-garde); and a final tendency towards despair which predicts Existentialism. Shelley would have become a theoretician if he had lived to an old age. You can see it in his last writings. He had almost done with verse. "The Triumph of Life" is a shrunken rehash. The Oxen episode was Joyce's technical Sublime. It was a statement of what he COULD achieve through complexification of language and form. It was a simple idea delivered impenetrably by necessity. This makes it much like religious texts. Lyotard rejected Marx, Freud and the whole Enlightenment as so much theology. Nothing is universal to him. No system works. Everything is fraud for control. Sometimes it expresses political ideology. Sometimes a therapeutic fix. Lacan dressed like a priest. Lyotard believed in the ominousness of fashion. Always there was laical theory laying over dirty theory like Astroturf. Lyotard's postmodernity is informed by Wittgenstein's language games. The Austrian has been selected in the England XI as wicket keeper. *Ludling* (or *argot*) is a system for manipulating spoken words to make them incomprehensible to the untrained ear. It is spy-talk. Language games are used by groups attempting to conceal the content of their conversations. The Catholic Church used Latin for this purpose. The limits of my language equal the limits of my world. A misreading of Wittgenstein yields theoretical innovations. Wittgenstein was heavily influenced by *The Brothers Karamazov*. He was a zealot in the true sense of the term. He renounced a fortune. He sought out danger in warfare. He helped the lowest classes even though they repulsed him. He became a teacher. He wrote children's books. He sought to dismantle his own pride. He wrote gorgeous lists of confessions like Chidley. He went back to old places to seek forgiveness from people he had wronged. He worked as a menial. He designed joinery. He had an obsession with detail. His designs for a house included heavy metal screens to shut out all external life. This is an architectural symbol of his eyelids and sentiment towards life. He behaved like a mad monk. Wittgenstein really desired a primordial life. This was what he called 'wild life' striving to erupt out of the skin. It's the point he started in *Tractatus*. It means 'leap' in German. I am going to call the novel of my mother VAULT. This single word encapsulates the same meanings of sealant/darkness and airborne/light that Wittgenstein could never find in a single word. Wittgenstein confronted death many times. Three of his brothers committed suicide. Orson Welles' father blew out his brains on his son's sixteenth birthday. Ironic that his middle name was HEAD. He contemplated the act himself continuously. Wittgenstein was inflamed by self-loathing. Portrait of an ostensibly successful man who was still prey to childhood hits. *Menschliches allzum menschliches*. He believed that the fundamental problem of philosophy was the schism between what can be expressed (*gesagt*) by propositions (which is the same as thought) against what cannot be expressed but only shown (*gezeigt*). He split literature and art. They should not be considered in the same breath. The Sublime is NOT caused by external stimuli. It is latent. Its triggers are arbitrary. The Sublime creates a feeling like what C.S. Peirce called *Firstness*. Nothing proceeds it. It relates only to itself. It erases all pasts. There can be no metaphors using Firstness as a comparator. The most common causes of the Sublime are rhetoric/music (hearing) and monolithic Nature (sight). They are each apposite to Barthes' notion of authorial death. What inspires one person in an auditorium leaves another audience member cold. One human's pleasurable anxiety at lightning striking a snow-capped alpine peak is another person's horror. James Joyce was terrified of thunderstorms. He rejected a professorship in Capetown due to its reputation for lightning. Any individual recounting any incidence of the Sublime suffers from the disconnect caused by posthumous recollection ("intranquility"). What was Sublime becomes a dead letter. Periodicity in the Sublime remains a point of conjecture. It may last a single moment, some seconds or a sustained period of time. This creates a fundamental division that has been ignored by theoreticians. The Sublime can be classified as either "Big S (Single) Sublime" or "Small S (Plural) Sublime." The latter can also be termed a Sublime Sequence (SS) or Sublime Sequencing (also SS). Small S is the equivalent of Lyotard's Little Narratives. It stands against the meta-narrative (Big S). One SS in total can equal or even exceed 1 x Big S. Tom Hallem entered a state of prolonged receptivity to the Sublime during his walk from university to the pub. Small S as SS ensued to a total of Big S+. Each individual Small S lasted from milli-seconds to a maximum of ten seconds. Each interval between individual Small S lasted between five and twenty seconds. After the Sublime passes out of the eminent phase, a state BENEATH DESOLATION immediately succeeds. There is no greater let-down than post-Sublime. The gap created is just too wide. The speed of descent is too fast. Human consciousness fails to apprehend this phenomenon. Saussure's poles must be reset beyond Life/Death. No Trickster has sufficient medi[c]ative powers. This MACHFALL (*machsturz*) is in fact the principle characteristic of the Sublime. It is a misnomer to believe that the Sublime is experienced during APPREHENSION. In fact, it is an AFTERMATH DISEASE. We feel the DROP, not the LIFT. First the DROP cancels out the LIFT. Then the DROP exceeds the LIFT. The bottom CANNOT be fathomed. Only the Fall of Satan in *P.Lost* contains similar elements in human records. When Kant invokes Eternity at the end of his illustrative SS, he should really be in the thrall of Hell (DOWN) not the moon (UP). Burke said that depth is more sublime than height. Big S can be considered strong orgasm, according to Lacan. He called this state *jouissance*, which is a state of transgression beyond Freud's PP to the endurance of pain leading all the way to Bataille. Barthes, of course, converted it into a term for reading. Small S in SS can be likened to multiplē orgasms (MO) in the female. Sadly, Lacan confined *jouissance* to males until he was nearly dead. It took Cixous to make the obvious connection to MO. An SS often outlasts Big S. Small S as a single S can be repeated almost instantly without pre-set limits of frequency so that it quickly becomes SS. It is catalytic like that. Small S can be stimulated by repetition and/or variety (i.e. application of new stimuli). Multiple orifices/digits come into play. It may encompass different combinations of: touch (lips, fingerprints, toes, bellies); external observation (looking at the disembodied sex act in a mirror); external rhetoric (erotic commentary on orgies or threats of bondage); and mental imagery (memories of past sex acts and/or person-substitution). Cixous calls this tone, RAPTURE. Clearly, MO and Big O are physical versions of the Sublime in which the senses are overwhelmed by the soul. In summary, Small S is initiated by touch, speech, contemplation and/or the imagination. SS is not necessarily linear; evenly spaced through time; equivalent in duration; or equal in intensity. One could argue that SS is masculine wish fulfilment of our desire for female orgasm. This is one of the driving forces of Patriarchy (along with birthing-envy). This puts it into the category of Mania. Lacan's Big A thus becomes the Big O. The sequencing of Small S in Chapter Six can be rendered thus (see Table):

Table 9. Sequencing the small sublime (SS) in C6

Small S (no.)		POV	Framing	Typology	Period (Seconds)	Gap (Seconds)
1.	Storm over birthplace	Beneath> Up	Tunnel	Nature (A) – panorama	10	5
2.	Pepe's suffocation	Without	Box	Libidinal – homo-erotic death	5	5
3.	Queen Mary Building	Approximation	Phallic	Nature (B) - monolithic	~1	10
4.	Bandstand	Voyeuristic	XXX machine	Libidinal - orgasmic	2	10
5.	Corner Shop	Within (Memory)	Uterine	Maternal - childhood	1	-

CASE NOTES

A. Small S (1) occurred from the perspective of a low topography looking upwards at a +45° angle to an artificially high topography (eight level hospital building). This represented an east-west cardinal line. Distance was ~150 metres in total. Peripheral framing contained psychologically relevant emblems in the form of sport (evoking Hallem's displacement from conventional culture/nation/groups) and a mental institution (representing his fear of the future). These signified north and south cardinal points respectively. Distance was ~50 metres. As Hallem rose uphill, he reached a point where he traversed the crossing of these intercardinal lines. This triggered the Sublime; initially as "proto" Big S. This cross pinned Hallem at its centre. The cardinal points corresponded to: Birth (west); Recent Time Past (east); Lost Past (north); and Future (south). The intercardinal crossing was low on the west-east axis: about 20% along Hallem's route. It thus corresponded to the correct proportions of a Crucifix, which has a 3:1 ratio with interlocked palings crossing ~20% of the distance along the vertical axis (see Pinterest). Of course, this is an archetypical symbol of the Death of Christ (see Jung). This was the locus of Hallem's Sublime. Tempest surrounded the apprehended birthplace above. This was the visual focus of the Sublime. The resultant scene could be likened to the initial prospect of the Tower in Browning's "Childe Rolande." It should be distinguished from a "downwards spatial projection" into caves, grottoes *et al.* as found in Novalis, Blake, Shelley et cetera. This has quite different symbolism and archetypes. It concludes as Hallem crosses Missenden Road. However, he is now receptive to further orgasms.

B. Small S (2) was prefaced by an idea to use/update the 'lost child' art motif. Subsequently, it 'flips over' onto memories of the death of Hallem's friend Pepe. The motif is symbolic of Hallem himself as well as the literally lost Pepe. Its timeframe is governed by the chain of ideas (internal to the psyche). As long as they are sustained so is Small S. The bi-polar nature of the Sublime is clearly evidenced in the content of this sequence with excitement over the creative impulse overbalanced by remembrance of death. Indeed, the form of death in this instance is deeper than bog standard expiry. It carries the tragedy of a child's life cut short loaded with all its symbolic meaning. The mode of death – suffocation – is highly evocative. It includes the REALISATION at some moment of death as palpable. This increases the struggle hastening the exhaustion of oxygen. Heat and sweat cause the body to expand inside the confined space. This exacerbates the horror. Small S (2) is characterised by libidinal energy brought to the level of the Sublime by death. This is an erotic nexus (see Bataille). The refrigerator box represents society. It is hard, metallic and white. Hallem associates himself as OUTSIDE this enframing looking <u>AT</u> society from WITHOUT. But he does not feel a sense of space. He is concentrating so hard on transportation into the box that he is mesmerised. His homo-erotic impulse is repressed inside the locked box in the form of dead desire. Small S (2) is sustained. It morphs and mutates over its course. It continues during the period under the metal awnings, which represent intestines. It starts after Hallem crosses Missenden Road and ends with the start of Small S (3).

C. Small S (3) commences with the sudden sight of the nurse's quarters. Hallem has been sheltered from the storm. He is distracted by Small S (2). There is a gap in the canopy. He looks UPWARDS at the building from almost directly underneath. Its location is north-west from Hallem. This aspect has no background urban development. All enframing has fallen away. It is a pure prospect of the phallus in wide screen tempest. This triggers conventional Small S. It is broken almost immediately by the soft laughter of the nurses. Hallem responds with conventionalised quotidian imagery. They are eating fruit. This represents sensuality. More particularly, they are consuming grapes. This associates them with Dionysus triggering related sexual imagery. The cliched nature of Small S (3) may be a cause of its brevity. Hallem would be self-conscious about aesthetic susceptibility to this hackneyed version of the Sublime. He would subconsciously seek to truncate it. Its emblems are thus premature ejaculation and castration. The former is an act of sex cut short by singular excitement and the latter is an act of anti-sex (*contra baise*). They are both self-directed. Premature ejaculation is used as a standard metaphor for sudden misplaced aesthetic spurts. The 'cutting off' of the testicles is a bloody severance associated with truth, power and patriarchy. The thief is castrated. The man is made into a eunuch to serve the emperor. The wife castrates her husband for infidelity. Failure to generate sufficient 'aesthetic tumescence' in Small S (3) necessitates immediate SELF castration by Hallem. This is the most painful form. It is characteristic of madness; usually brought on by religious mania. Famous examples include William James Chidley, Rasputin and the pre-medieval *Galli* who castrated themselves for the fertility goddess, Cybele, who is also known as Aphrodite, Isis, *Kubala*, *Mater Deum*, *Magna Mater* and *Caelestis*. This would normally be the end of any Sublime sequence.

D. Small S (4) extends the Sublime sequence abnormally due to the sudden stimulation of a pornographic memory. Fertile ground has been prepared by viewing the nurses in Small S (3). Hallem sees himself from WITHOUT as both voyeur and participant. The bandstand represents an entertainment platform. It is the equivalent of a bar stage for strippers (see Chapter 5). The recollected moment is the urging to ejaculation (UTE) by a female combined with simultaneous insertion of her finger into his anus (IFIA). IFIA reprises the homo-erotic sensations of Small S (2). It was a new experience for Hallem. It caused a rush to orgasm. Any UTE by a female creates both anxiety and pleasure in the male. This mood corresponds directly to the twin sensations of any classic definition of the Sublime. The male both desires and fears causation of pregnancy. This is the result of a primitive urge being corrupted by modern morality. The result is disjuncture in the moment (DIM). Many sexual risk-takers are inspired to act by the prospect of this feeling. It is one of simultaneous self-realisation and self-loathing. The mouth goes dry. The loins harden. The vocalised nature of the UTE also creates a strong Sublime sensation. Hearing is one of the major stimuluses of the Sublime.

E. Small S (5) extends and concludes the Sublime sequence for Hallem. He enters a mixed business. It corresponds to his mother's shop – his earliest memory of physical space. Small S (5) is a direct corollary of Small S (4). The child is produced by the UTE – either vocalised or tacit – between man and woman. All memories in Small S (5) evoke restriction and containment. Hallem is a firmly swaddled baby in a small pram jammed behind a shop counter in a dark constricted place. These memories blend with Small S (2). Yes, it bears a resemblance to descriptions of the womb. It ends before he meets the gaze of the shopkeeper. A loud radio set is tuned to the Vietnamese language news on 2EA. Smell is an element in Small S (5). It has not been present in any previous Small (S). But it is not a smell that Hallem recalls (like Proust and his stinking cupcake). In fact, Hallem is struck by the difference between the immediacy of odour – which can be broadly termed as that of 'Asian cuisine' – and the forgotten smell of his mother's shop. To be clear, his memory of smell only exists as a GAP or LACK in Small S (5). Edmund Burke noted: "Smells and Tastes have some share too in ideas of greatness; but it is a small one, weak in its nature, and confined in its operations." Odour is only an auxiliary aspect of Small S (5). It cannot induce Small S in its own right. Indeed, it is mainly active in this text as a point of *differance*. This disjuncture might be the mote that dragged Small S (5) into being. Indeed, it could cause the initial rush to Sublimity like a blast of Amyl Nitrate. But it would not have been strong enough on its own to sustain the Sublime. Burke considered that "no smells or tastes can produce a grand sensation, except excessive bitters, and intolerable stenches." These elements are both present in Small S (5). Bitterness is present on his tongue from the residue of tasting heroin. The spot corresponds to the placement of the holy wafer on the tongue in communion. The association with the uterus in Small S (5) provides physical proximity to orifices of excrement. They are characterised as bearing stench. However, many individuals including Joyce found their aroma/outputs highly amatory.

GENERAL INFERENCES

— Periodicity. This is also referred to as 'length.' Philosophers have not considered this aspect of the Sublime sufficiently. There is a popular belief in the existence of a "Sublime moment." This suggests a short, singular period amounting to a fraction of a second of intense subliminal shock. This Sublime By Electrocution (SBE) should not be confused with the horror of being struck by lightning and killed on a golf course. By way of contrast, Kant describes a long SS on a summer evening which commences gradually over the course of sustained lackadaisical movement as a bunch of hackneyed lyrical elements scroll past him: stars, shadows, rising moon etcetera. Kant's emotional palette is similarly unoriginal: deep friendship, disdain for the cares of the world, musings on Eternity. Analysis of SS of Small S (1–5) above suggests that a typical Small S is executed in 0–10 seconds. The intervals between each Small S were uneven. The entire journey took approximately 5 minutes. The proportion of sublime sensation was thus ~16.66%.

— Built-Form (BF) in Time. Each SS relates in some way to BF: there are two hospital buildings, one refrigerator, one bandstand and a mixed business on a corner location. Kant selected two human constructs as possessing the Sublime combination of terror, magnitude, long duration of construction period and subsequent longevity as extant: the pyramids and St Peter's cathedral in Rome. Scale is quite different to this SS. In Australia, the Sydney Harbor Bridge (SHB) and Sydney Opera House (SOH) in Circular Quay (CQ) are the human constructs that possess relevant BF features of the Sublime. The manner of first apprehension (SBE) can aggrandise BF traits. Many visitors first experience CQ from the heavy rail service suddenly bursting from tunnels at either end of CQ station. The presence of this rail 'girdle,' undulating topography of the area, tight eighteenth-century streets, and occurrence of skyscrapers also obscure any prospect of the Quay until SBE B-F.

— Subject Psyche. The mental state of the subject of the Sublime has not been explored. It is assumed that the Sublime receptor is a Hieratic male. This is exclusionary. It also sees the Sublime as a SANE experience. The length of Hallem's Small S sequence suggests covert schizophrenic tendencies. There are five types of signs associated with schizophrenia: delusions, hallucinations, disorganised speech, disorganised behavior, and so-called "negative" symptoms such as apathy, lethargy, social withdrawal, chronic inattention, sexual impairment and *anhedonia* (pleasurelessness at life's homely joys). Hallem showed evidence of hallucinations during this Small S sequence. Its prolongation is a factor in this diagnosis. All "negative symptoms" emerged in later years. NOTE – retrospective diagnostics should be avoided.

— Framing. Chronicles of the Sublime always exhibit framing. Even an incidence of Big S in thrall to panoramic Nature is fitted into a gilt frame on the wall of a museum AS IT OCCURS (AIO). In other words, a necessary feature of the Sublime is the capacity to restrict and present the experience AIO. Framing is then formalised in subsequent textualisation or visualisation. But it is an *a priori* act. In this specific sequence in Chapter 6, Small S (1) and (5) relate to MOTHER. They frame the sexualised Small S (2), (3) and (4). Small S (2–4) follow a chronological human development pattern: childhood homoeroticism in Small S (2); adolescent self-absorption in the phallus-icon and unattainable contemplation of older women in Small S (3); and early adult sex acts in risk-taking environs in Small S (4). Thus, infantile worship of maternity frames/pincers male sexuality. This is consistent with both Freud and Classical myths.

— Topography. Sydney's topography has been discussed above. In general terms, Burke argues that depth can be more sublime than height, and both are more sublime than length. Kant calls them equal. Burke's first premise is supported by Small S (1). Depth in Small S (1) initiates SS. Height in Small S (1) is made Sublime by Hallem perceiving and proceeding from depth. Small S (1) represents what Heidegger would call an UNCANNY shaft. It has a highly-constricted aperture resembling the entrance to a tunnel or cave. Yet, in fact, it ascends not descends. Further, it goes upwards and outwards TOWARDS LIGHT as opposed to inwards to darkness. It thus simulates the dimensions of a kaleidoscope barrel. Burke's second premise can be disputed on the basis of the evidence in the analysis on Periodicity above. To repeat, length is clearly NOT a disinhibitor to Sublime experience. Hallem sustains Small S (1) for a long period along a great distance. At this point it is still a single Big S. He is able to convert S (1) into SS by virtue of continuous stimulation of sublime antennae. There is an element of chance in inducing any SS (see Mallarme). Nonetheless, total SS length in this case study can be considered at least EQUAL to depth and height if not superior. Note – the work ends with two groups travelling to Sydney CBD. One group goes underground (death of Ana) while the other climbs the SHB and views the SOH (freedom). This split is HIGHLY SYMBOLIC and should be considered carefully by the thoughtful reader.

— Intensity. Periodicity in SS can be used to measure the relative intensity of different versions of Sublime feeling. For example, Tom Hallem had his most sustained Subliminal experience when contemplating maternal/childhood experiences. This was followed by libidinal stimuli. The least evocative form of the Sublime was Nature in Small S (3).

— Lyricism. Kant wrote a stupid passage about the Sublime full of Romance cliché. He sounds like Stephen Hero. His definition of the Sublime does not approach psychological elements. It is all oppositions. The night is sublime, day is beautiful [INSERT QUOTATIONS MARKS] et cetera.

— Gender and Death. As noted above: "SS is masculine wish fulfilment of desire for female orgasm. This is one of the driving forces of Patriarchy (along with birthing-envy). This puts it into the category of Mania." It is clear that ONLY MEN experience the Sublime. Kant, Burke and other chroniclers and theoreticians of the Sublime are all male. Hallem is male. The Sublime is a club or male bath house. The Athenaeum Club recorded numerous instances of the Sublime. By way of gender proof-testing, Ana experiences NO SUBLIME during her death throes in Chapter Ten despite a highly receptive environment as defined by Burke and Kant (darkness, depth, a cave, accelerated motion through space, a lake, pale pinprick of light above [moon substitute], drug-induced disdain for the world, musings on the nature of eternity). A supplementary question would be: "can the Sublime be experienced during death? In other words, is there such a phenomenon as 'death rapture'?"

— The Four S's: Surprise, Suddenness, Speed, Symbology. The achievement of a Sublime state relies on exposure to highly stylised – even passé – elements. This is, in fact, a prerequisite. In most instances, this combination of such symbols (see Kant above) will induce DISGUST in the receiver. It is the surprise of the receiver at these hackneyed symbols being elevated to pure fidelity by maximum propulsion that ignites the Sublime. A state combining cliché, speed, suddenness and surprise is thus required to ignite the Sublime.

— Mental Capacity. A moron CANNOT experience the Sublime. It MUST be an ADVANCED THINKER (alternate terms for this person include Barthes' Reader of Writerly Texts, Lacan's Big T Text Reader and Hieratic Cult).

— Sex. Kant wasn't a very sophisticated thinker when it came to textualising the Sublime. He saw it only as a SEX MOMENT. Basically, the Beautiful is a euphemism in Kant for the exquisite adornment of girls; the Sublime is a paean to the bounty and mystery of mature women. The Beautiful is frigid; the Sublime raunchy. This is really a useless attempt at difference. Hallem's SS indicates that the Sublime is definitely intervolved with erotic feelings. Small S (2–4) rely on active sex imagery. But it would be better to NOT DEFINE the Sublime than girdle it in platitudes of erotic opposition.

— Poise and Apprehension. Kant sees stunned human lumps facing the Sublime. He writes that "mien ... is earnest, sometimes rigid and astonished." The Sublime is thus a catatonic state to Kant. It is a form of bondage without bonds. Of torture in aspect. This version of the Sublime can be seen in lots of science fiction movies. It is parodied in *1984*.

— Motion. The Sublime is sometimes considered a static enterprise. The above SS is generated and protracted by consistent motion. It ends when Hallem ceases to move. It terminates at a dead end. It knocks against buffers. Kant is right in the first half of the following epigraph: "The Sublime *moves*, the beautiful *charms*." Kant wrote so much stuff on the Sublime that he had to be right part of the time.

— *A posteriori*. We associate the Sublime with direct experience. Art has always tried to capture this moment. This is classic Wordsworth territory. But he only sees it as a positive creative mode. In relation to the Sublime, however, it is *a posteriori* rendition creating a metonymy. It's like being a kid playing with a superhero figurine in the backyard after watching the franchise DVD.

— Aftermath. Hallem descends from Small S (5) by MACHFALL to AFTERMATH DISEASE. This will be the subject of the next chapter. It is written in dramatic form like Joyce's Circe episode.

Tom Hallem stood at the counter of the mixed business. His boots ground on the scratched linoleum floor. The shop keeper was leaning against a wall of homemade shelves languidly. He roughened his presence. She made eye contact. He took in the full enmity of her gaze, framed by disappointment. She was hoping to see Barry Capri. Tom wanted food and drink. She was a small figure, largely unexpressive, but I have already stated that I will not dwell on cornering devices like character description. This is unquestionably the realm of the reader in terms of fictive realisation (see Barthes).

BAUDRILLARD

Jean Baudrillard's essay, "Simulation and Simulacra," begins with an exposition of Borges' one paragraph story, "On Exactitude in Science." It deals with cartographers composing a "Map of the Empire whose size was that of the Empire, and which coincided point for point with it," followed by commentary about how it was mostly destroyed by later generations. It was credited by Borges to *Travels of Prudent Men*, a seventeenth-century tome by Suarez Miranda, although the story was actually based on Lewis Carroll's *Sylvie and Bruno Concluded*, which described a fictional map with the scale of "a mile to the mile." Carroll's story actually takes this concept much further: "we now use the country itself, as its own map, and I assure you it does nearly as well." Baudrillard is really writing about all these above stories and more. He solidifies Borges' forgery into his own meta-forgery. He dissolves everything down cycles of false citation as well as Hieratic non-citation. Baudrillard was only too aware of Jarry's Faustroll, sailing across the top of Paris in his pataphysical boat, which was essentially another mapping venture. His opening gambit thus amplifies, recedes, stalls and reverberates until it epitomises his notion of Simulation. This sentence with its long aside marks full disclosure of Baudrillard's TOOL. In fact, he really should have stopped the essay at this point – like Borges – as it gains no new content from further recycling. But that is not Baudrillard's objective. The act of complexification is in fact the goal of all French thinking. Its mode causes content to crack. It aborts form. This leaves STYLE as the last man standing. Odysseus was always cast into this role in the *Odyssey*. At the time Joyce finished *F(W)ake*, he told Laubenstein that "the value of the book is its new style" (Ellmann, 557). He had failed to create a NEW mythic template, one that matched the received myth of *Ulysses*. This is why *F(W)ake* must be considered a failure. Joyce tried to jam together every type of legend and allusion into one novel as a successor to the smooth flow of Classical tradition. He tried to move away from strict modes of emplotment. This really denied Joyce one of the principal features of Classical myth, which was catharsis and climax. Partially, Joyce took this path because of his humanism and distaste for war. After all, he had already denuded the *Odyssey* of violence, turning a shoving match into a climactic event in *Ulysses*. By contrast, contemporary literature and cinema have SOLD PLOT TO SLAUGHTER. It's a reductive cycle that should have ended with Tarantino, but subsequent auteurs continue to compete to inflict more 'realistic' bloodletting on their audience. We all know this ends with murder in REAL LIFE. Pasolini used to be the benchmark with 120DoS. He has probably never been exceeded for HORROR because he started with a strong platform in Sade and rendition during the decline of Italian Fascism. Joyce tried to downgrade emplotment. We must travel down the same channel. For example, Ana Lafei's death should constitute tragedy but she is kept at the level of a secondary character to reduce its prominence. She is not Emma Bovary or Anna Karenina. We know nothing about her life. Judgment is never made. There is no resolution. This is all done by design. It does not affect the overall thrust. For Joyce, it was hard to write off a twenty-year sales-pitch on *Work in Progress* (its title was jealously guarded). Joyce hystericised English in *F(W)ake*. It was a hostile act. His formula was to trash Imperialism with whatever he had. Baudrillard's Theory Fiction allows theoretical writing to become more enigmatic, more fabulous. JB had few other tools at his disposal because he was such a limited thinker. This meant that he had to accelerate the equation and elevate it UPWARDS with the following subcutaneous (AKA religious) man/oeuvre:

1. THESIS

Disappearance of history. Escape velocity reached. *Vitesse de liberation?* Go faster still. Everything is now going to go so fast that there's no time for recognition. Accelerated metabolism of society. Forgetful of sequences. The Real is no longer possible. A certain slowness is displaced. All atoms of meaning are lost. Space punctured. Post Classical period. Unregulated time.

2. ANTITHESIS (LOVE)

Deceleration of time (history) as it grates against matter ('the masses'). Density increases. Mass indifference. Light dwindles. History cools. No longer able to pull away. Darkness incumbent. Cold star of the social. Brine. The end of "the end." A space by no air taken. Bureaucratic socialism.

The Joycean equivalent is Old Finn Maccumhal watching history and time flow past him on the River Liffey as he edges towards expiration like Alastor. But like Tom Finnegan he never dies in the text. To mix history and fable in a comic setting. To turn human beings for all their flaws back into heroes. To create a new myth for the age of humans so the world can finally end. And for me to create it. That was Joyce's conceit in *F(W)ake*. It was really a postmodern amalgam of all humanity's cores and dags. He believed that the joy of comedy made it a higher art form than tragedy. Can comic novels stand the test of time? Only slapstick works across epochs, I think. It is almost impossible to sustain the joke in low voltage comedy of attrition like Oxen and *F(W)ake*. This isn't the violent gagging of Artaud and Moe Howard. It is equivocal parody. Any reader of this chapter would endure similar desensitisation to THE JOKE. Yet it is one. Vico's historical rounds were each set off by a pie in the face skit. Malignant cells passed through the lemon meringue, theocratic, aristocratic, pecan, autocratic, -democratic and automated gland stages until cancer found mass. Of Vico, Joyce said, "I use his cycles as a trellis." Likewise, I must climb Joyce. We will observe Telemachus scaling a vine in C10 to get close to his parent's bedroom as they fuck as a symbol of this task as well as an allusion to Freudian theory. Tom Hallem took a cheap flight to Moscow on his way to Paris, juxtaposing authoritarian and libertarian geographies. Shanghai Dog worked in Saigon and Beijing. These ideologies represent another *ricorso*. They are cities where the master narrative of communism was played out. Churchill said democracy was the worst system of government ever invented, just better than anything else. Its title is MING ZHU in Mandarin. ZI YOU means FREEDOM. Three per cent of any population can induce revolution. We only need titles and slogans. Thump ideology into the hot body of the masses. Put Cyclops' in charge. They had no concept of COMMONWEAL. Stalin's black-market eye. Aery ideals of butchers. Promethean parodies of dystopic parodies. Simulated RE[E/A]LS. Lapse of the Soviet Union then put(-in) it back together. They wrote off Althusser after he strangled his wife. Return to Marxism. Return to Freud. They're all just tactics to annex the power of the foundation text. Note TMAC nexus with UL. Deng legislated against Mao then some new Mao will delegislatedeng. Palindrome history. Exchange blue jeans for hard currency with the room cleaner, convert it all into Rubles on the black market then invest the whole stake in Communist badges from the GUM Department Store to sell at Camden Markets to anti-Thatcher Reds. Socialism with Chinese Characteristics. Distil polemics. Althusser saw Marx's philosophy only becoming apparent via Lacan. Theory of the Break. Althusser's *Kenosis*. IMPLICIT theory. Locations where the text can only be produced if an ideological framework is invisibly in place. Althusser called these 'symptoms.' LINK TO TMAC. Temper democratic, bias Australian + Whitlam coup + pro-indigenous + multi-cultural slant. Althusser approximates ideology to Lacan's understanding of the Real. It is impossible to access REAL conditions due to the SPIEL, he concluded. A scientific approach helps disclose how we are inscribed by ideology. A British officer hailed Stephen. "Hey, you there!" he exclaimed. A shout in the street. If you turn around, you become the subject at that moment. Inscribe Lacan's NotF upon the foetus with Kafka's harrow. Althusser wrote that even before a child is born, "it is certain in advance that it will bear its Father's Name, and will therefore have an identity and be irreplaceable." Billy Capri took his birth certificate out of the filing cabinet. He unfolded it and placed it on the desk. There was NO NAME against FATHER. Just a DASH. Real names be the truth, D Boon said. First, he was E. Bloom. Richard Hell. Joe Strummer. Good ole John Doe. History Lesson 2. Tom Hallem also wore another family name. For Althusser, naming meant a NotF given to us in the womb. People aren't capable of self-naming. They can't see themselves. Just a reverse image in a mirror, like NACAL said. Left-hand bias. Characters need to assume multiple names over the course of one narrative. It is the only means of destabilising the text against its propensity to become a reactionary machine. We need to put wooden parts against alloys. We must make sure that cogs are not aligned. Gouge out large indents for small teeth. Crush big teeth into small indents. Baudrillard argued that all such choices are simulated. We can buy one car or buy another model even select other transport modes and it is all false selection. A real choice would be to cut off your own legs. Objects beat subjects. Protest is fuel. Neo hid his secret code in a hollowed-out copy of Baudrillard's [INSERT NAME OF]. They misread his work. He didn't mind. It was all hyper-validation. They adhered to his creed: to make the unintelligible more unintelligible. Aphorisms were to Baudrillard what puns were to Lacan. He was like Wilde. The Gulf War never took place, he proclaimed. He was more Godard-68 than Godard in 1968. More L(l)anguage than Language. SHIFT TENSE> Baudrillard is always trying to turn the French fashion for street revolution into the last great European flourish. He can never disconnect from place (Europe/US) or time (1968). He talks de-historicisation but he is a MOST HISTORICAL THINKER. Another of Spinoza's glass vassals. Janus was Baudrillard's preferred deity. He was the god of beginnings, apertures, birth, journeys and time. He was interested in maritime commerce. He would have been the perfect Mentor for *Ulysses*, particularly the Oxen episode. Baudrillard didn't believe in any of this stuff. Only cauterised wounds. Only capitulation. In the *Odyssey*, Mentor was put in charge of Telemachus when Odysseus went to the Trojan war. When Athena visited Telemachus, she assumed the disguise of Mentor. Janus was the most critical god to Rome. He presided over war and peace. The Janus gates were opened when war was declared and did not close until peace. This is the opposite of normal fortification tactics. Janus had no dedicated temple or priests. Rex Sacrorum himself undertook his ceremonies. Janus was everywhere. An invocation to Janus prefaced all other Gods. There is no equivalent to Janus in Greek cosmos. Otherwise he would have had bookend tasks in both the *Iliad* and *Odyssey*. Someone should write an analysis of modern French theory based on its dealignment with Janus. Baudrillard would have blinded the god's forward-looking face with stick-embers. His past-face would have been exposed to religion and ideologies maybe in the form of comic animation. Eventually, there would have been an overtaking lane in which Baudrillard lodged in Janus' blind spot. With Baudrillard, there are no intrinsic prophecies stretched over the top of his temporal exigencies. There is only a HUMAN SPHINX transfixed by information. This is the ultimatum rejected by HH-1970 in the ensuing Virilio S-E. Baudrillard conducted a severely circumscribed enterprise. This is ironic given that he is always talking about motion and space. He was the Des Esseintes of French theory. He loved to play the dandy. Like Faustroll and Panmurphy, he travelled the seas in a copper skiff superimposed over the streets of Paris. He was a charlatan in the best sense of the word, which comes from the seventeenth-century Italian term, *ciarlatano*, meaning 'babbler'. I can't help liking him all the same. Especially when he is suffering a giant case of the Clampetts over the role of TV in human exchange. He hovers around the PAL screen with his giant eyebrows raised like some big brown Muppet. More Language than language. He has furry palms. I love the way he ratted out his Leftist cronies by becoming a mainstream celebrity. Become what you hate was his mantra. It's the same thing we admire in Hamlet. Jarry's first short play *Caesar Antichrist* presents a parallel world in which Christ is resurrected as an agent of the Roman Empire.

Ubu is introduced as a new messiah like Leopold Bloom. Baudrillard is like a Teletubbie having an adverse reaction to the screen in his guts. He needs to take some anti-rejection drugs. He had an early interest in Pataphysics. This imbued him with Jarry's impeccable talent for parody. It became the template for ALL modern French writing. The Faustroll novel was posthumously published. Jarry was dead from tuberculosis by then. He was almost a midget. Picasso had purchased his pistol just in case. Baudrillard was never deluded by his own TOOL. He was too well-grounded in peasant ancestry to take himself seriously. He knew only too well that he had been cast in a "Carry On" movie set on a French cruise ship. Characterisation eluded him. Or was equivocal at best. He first came to prominence as a translator of German literature, in particular Peter Weiss. He willed his own life to become *Marat/Sade*. He envied Guattari making-it-real at La Borde. This trope infested all his subsequent self-deployments. He wanted the campus to become an insane asylum overwhelmed by chaos and madness in a time of revolutionary turmoil. Wish-fulfillment came to Baudrillard in 1968. He started out as Marat but always wanted to graduate to Sade. He was a Marxist who succumbed to evasion. His doppelganger was L. Ron Hubbard. They both shared a talent for the production of mystical psycho-babble that accumulated into quasi-religiosity by stealth. It's cannibal alchemy. Content is irrelevant. They were both more interested in power. Style creates power for Baudrillard. His secret source of inspiration was how great it was to be sitting around on vinyl beanbags in a government-subsidised apartment listening to "White Light/White Heat" on a good hi-fi system while revolution unraveled on the boulevards below. 1968 was a football match lost by penalty shoot-out. Baudrillard was an office clerk who liked to dress-up as a biker on weekends and freewheel through the new Mexican desert at 70 km/h all night listening to tapes of Carlos Castaneda and the Doors pretending he was high on *peyote*. To write of Baudrillard we must always work in similes. He is Rimbaud meets Don Knotts. That was also Bob Dylan. Yet again then Baudrillard is cast into the role of belated sub-mimic. This was also the curse of Telemachus. At least he had Odyssean DNA. Baudrillard's father was a policeman. Of course, Baudrillard knows nothing about drugs, science, mathematics, art, literature, politics, culture or history. They're all terms from other people's bank balance stuffed into binary opposition (a type of hip bag) as placebo theory. He's always banging together dialectics like some handyman nailing together uneven chunks of wood. Bob Capri took Hahn into the kitchen. He picked up his tool box from under the sink. She needs that shelf fixed while I'm there. Also, the toilet seat has to be stabilised. And the hallway door chocked. The whole shop was moving. Sydney's clay base stretched over Yellowblock. Surface cracks appeared inevitably. Marx's philosophy was almost unseen in Baudrillard. Pataphysics passes easily from one definition to the next. It can present itself as gas, liquid or solid. For Baudrillard, the USA sped so fast on gushes of Black Gold that it hit a Gilligan-like vanishing point. It got sucked so fast through a silicone tube into its own senses that it reversed all polarities and spat out new *ars erotica*. Baudrillard predicted the pornographic age. But even he could never have guessed how it would be super-induced by technology. A guy on a moped picked-up Baudrillard off the footpath on *Dong Koi* and drove him to a short-stay hotel in the d.boon docks. SHIFT TO PRESENT TENSE. He loses the film crew. It's a dead zone. They proceed up an angular French Colonial staircase. He is pushed into a high-ceiling room with a speed-addled prostitute wearing a pancake face and a pink qipao who claims she's twenty-five years old. Baudrillard stands there awkwardly. Who is he to dispute her narrative after a lifetime of misrepresentation? She'll jack him off for a hundred bucks. That's the starting point for all negotiations. In Japan, he could get two hours in a spa with a Korean hand-model for that price. In the end, he pays fifty bucks for full service. I was too uptight to even unbutton my checked shirt, he said later. I just dropped my strides while she bent forwards over the motel desk. Baudrillard wore a gold lame suit when he read poetry in Las Vegas. He loved that strange desert city built on the dissonance between religion, gambling and sex. They visited fantastic islands in his TV series. He was accompanied by a monkey named de-Nage which died leaving Panmurphy to wonder if it had even been REAL. Baudrillard reminds me of those American garage bands which created one great semi-derivative riff like Louie (x2). As for CLOSURE, Baudrillard advised to just ask some vaguely heroic rhetorical questions, shrug your shoulders, insinuate the magic of the moment and go. I must turn this episode into binary juxtaposition. INSERT MORE ALLUSIONS TO ROAD MOVIES. All my textual clocks are set to *langue*. I arrived at the departure counter at Than Son Nhat on Thursday night only to find that my flight to Hong Kong had been cancelled because of the typhoon. It was stuck off the coast of Hanoi in the South China Sea right in the middle of my flight path, one hundred and fifty miles in diameter just twirling on its skates. Two hundred and fifty kilometre breeze. It was going to make landfall in Guangxi eventually. Flooding was expected. I asked when I would be able to get out of Vietnam. The steward said there might be some flights tomorrow but my flight would not be rescheduled and the corresponding flight was already full so they couldn't guarantee a seat on Friday then it was the weekend when lots of Vietnamese people went to purchase electrical appliances in Hong Kong so they couldn't be sure I would get out on Saturday. Sunday was better. Not certain. But I would definitely get out on Monday. He handed me a sticker to put on my bag and offered me a twin share room at the Airport Park Royal. I'm not even sure why Saigon came into existence. It certainly doesn't have any of the distinguishing features that would warrant establishing a settlement. It was probably just a good spot to tie up a boat like Berlin. A place on a turn in a long river. A bend in the current where people formed. You can't even get at the Saigon River these days. It's barricaded with corrugated iron fences. They say the whole waterfront is being refurbished but there doesn't seem to be much progress when you look from the top floor bar at the Caravelle Hotel. A week in HCMC is hard work. The local cadres park a slab of Johnny Walker Blue beside the dinner table each night. All the seafood looks like it's been scraped out of heavy metals on the ocean floor. The oysters are big like tumours. We re-scheduled all our meetings to the hotel conference centre after spending Day One stuck in traffic jams. Scooters make it impossible to cross the street on foot. Government vans accelerate down the wrong side of the road, sirens blaring at oncoming vehicles. Baudrillard would be terrified but excited by this symbol. It becomes a Pavlovian reflex action. Our driver even pumped the horn manically while driving down an unopened four-lane boulevard in an unpopulated economic development zone. My business partner hates the madness but this is the kind of place where I feel most at home. Arthur Symons said the art in life was to sit still and watch everything move past you. I wonder if the Sublime can be experienced from a stationary pose. Sound travels I guess. You got to keep looking for the latest goldrush. It's all about speed to market. The arc of development is going west. It's already hit the East African coast. I've been hunting assets in Asia since 2004. Those were heady times. I should have put more capital aside. Now we're trading down to zero. It's like a rocket crash. The Singapore team hasn't been paid this month. I can't go back to the Shanghai office. They changed the locks and called the Foreign Enterprise Bureau last week. I can still pull enough strings to hold them at bay. But I'm really relying on Doctor Gu. It's a dice roll in a marble vault. Nothing's free. It's a price I have to pay. This deal with her father is the sweetener. I'm helping her family set up a clearing warehouse across the border in Mong Cai. They'll truck finished product from Guangxi and brand it as coming from VIETNAM. A lot of Chinese companies are using this trick to get around WTO sanctions. The Vietnamese are sanguine about it. They hate the Chinese. But they're prepared to let it happen for some graft. Worst case, they'll hold the warehouse as ransom. I like Vietnamese people. They're totally different to Chinese. They've been fighting wars of national survival for one thousand years. They're totally upfront. It's not like Japan where everyone's doing robocop kabuki. The Vietnamese are chronic opportunists. This is a product of epochal subsistence, I guess. They're going through the motions of a Vietnamese version of *Gai Ge Kai Fang*. All I want is to get my hands on some industrial parks with a guaranteed base return from government. The Reserve Bank will need to provide a concessional loan because Vietnam has such a shallow debt market. The plan is to establish the Vietnam Infrastructure Fund One (VIF1). We'll IPO in Singapore. I'll send some juniors back here from South-West Sydney to administer the assets. They've got the best Australian accents. That glugging at the top of their throats is perfectly pitched for Strine. Barry introduced me to Missus

NGUYEN. It's the family name of forty per cent of Vietnamese people. Her daughter, Giang, also known as Jackie, has just finished a commerce degree. She's done an internship at PWC. She's keen to go back. They haven't got any connections up North. It's the same for all bail-outs. Hanoi still runs the show. My translator is a civil engineer who got sent here to build a Friendship Bridge across the Mekong River back in the Nineties. He married an airline hostess. Now he runs his own project management firm. He's got a big compound next to Long Thanh Golf Club with his kids, his mother-in-law, her second husband and his drug-dealing son. It's a poor man's Medalist set up by a spin-off SOE out of the Ministry of Defence. Socialism is the correct type of administration for the end of History, according to Baudrillard. It produces the most incestuous hierarchy. His wife spends most of her time in the air. She's got a bunch of Japanese boyfriends. Our business liaison, Mister Lam (pron. LUM), thinks his boss is a weakling. He's never had trouble with women. He just cuts them loose as soon as they use the word "love." Viet has got gender splits on the phrase, "I love you." Woman say: *Em yêu anh*. Men say: *Anh yêu em*. Lam makes a chopping movement with his right hand into his left palm to explain what happens to them. All the top government guys have got smooth, hairless hands like torturers. Greg's partner is a boat girl from Adelaide. Her father was an Australian serviceman. He acknowledged paternity, finished his tour in 1969, went back to North Queensland and they never heard from him again. It was a kind of reverse-*Odysseus* play. The family escaped in a fishing boat across the Gulf of Thailand in 1977. Got to Bidong Island, Malaysia. First, they were flown to Canada. Her father's name on the birth certificate did the rest. Whole family got flown straight to Sydney. Her mother moved to Adelaide. She worked on the Metter's production line until she saved enough money to open a small shop in West Adelaide. Now she owns a local supermarket. Her daughter warned me that Vietnam had the most beautiful women in the world and the world's ugliest men. I parked this information in my head. The government officials filed into our first meeting in HCMC. My analyst turned to me innocently and said, "it looks like we've just walked onto the set of *Monsters Inc*." They presented a spreadsheet of new projects. There were bridges, toll roads, power plants and new urban developments in outlying districts. We were competing with Kalmykian investors, said the Mayor of District Three. It was splashed across the front page of *Saigon Daily*. I had to rush back to my hotel room at the Park Hyatt where I could get Blackberry reception and find out what the fuck 'Kalmykia' was. It's an autonomous Russian republic on the Caspian Sea with 250,000 people. It's home to the International Chess Federation. They hold a lot of Grand Master tournaments in the capital, Elista, because President Ilyumzhinov is head of FIDE. I told the Mayor of District 3 that the Kalmyks could keep the subway project. They were a simulated nation. Baudrillard would consider a stateless state as the perfect ironic response to modernity. Ideally, it would hover above the earth (link to Chidley). They took us to a new hi-tech park in District Nine. There was an imposing entrance gate emblazoned KHU CONG NGHE CAO. It was still a field of water buffalos pulling ploughs through rice bogs inside. Apparently, Intel had committed to a new chip factory. They needed basic infrastructure with a sale and leaseback deal. I was due to meet the regional head in Hong Kong tomorrow. I studied the departure screen. There was one more flight out of Saigon. It was a QANTAS codeshare to Sydney leaving at eight forty-five. Air Vietnam is an excellent airline. They hired all the Ansett staff after it went bankrupt. Hawke could only succour his mates so long. I looked across the laminated counter. "Can you get me on that flight," I asked the steward. "I'll try Doctor ______," he replied. "Please give me your *billet*." I passed my crumpled ticket over the counter. He scurried across to the Air Vietnam Check-In. A queue of pissed-off tourists had started to build out of the story of my eye like a bad cataract. The TV screens flashed a picture of Jean Baudrillard. The BBC ribbon read Air Garuda plane crashes at Yogyakarta killing twenty-two. French philosopher who claimed the Gulf War never happened has died after a long illness. He was seventy-seven years old. Many of Baudrillard's obituaries were unusually facetious, showing little respect for the corpse. He might have liked it. After all, Baudrillard concluded, "dying is pointless." He wanted to become like the Elvis myth. "You have to know how to disappear," he said. There's a good Don Walker song about that. JB probably saw himself more in the guise of Jim Morrison. By his own account, Baudrillard had advanced from pataphysician at twenty years to VIRAL at age sixty. At the end of *Exploits and Opinions of Dr. Faustroll*, the title character expires. He sends a telepathic letter back to Lord Kelvin describing the afterlife. Goanna declared, "I've been to the other side and let me tell you, son, there's f–king nothing there." The airport intercom announced the cancellation of all flights until 2 pm Saturday. The steward came back. He had good news. I got a seat back to Australia. I would be able to surprise my wife in bed with the milkman tomorrow morning. At age seventy, Baudrillard said he was *transfini* like HH-1970. It was his fateful strategy to go beyond the concept to see what happened next, he pronounced lavishly. What bluster, whether it was comic or not. Death is the only moment of shared human experience. There is no way back. Did Lyotard ever ask if death was Sublime? First, language abandons you to muttering incoherently in fits and starts. Occasionally, your head tosses manically as if trying to clear concussion. My father groaned mainly with frustration at his predicament. All fear had gone. Hearing is the last sense to shut down. I spoke to him firmly. There was no point now in soft murmurings. I asked how he felt. What the fuck do you think, he replied. His rhetorical meaning was crystal clear. I told him we would get his dose of valium reduced. That should bring him back. Those were the last words I spoke to him. He died overnight. I was never close to my father. His extinguishment felt like an instance of hyper-reality. I can't even call it 'death.' Just release/relief. DEATH IS THE ONLY UNIVERSAL SUBLIME, Baudrillard would have said.

BATAILLE

Bataille died the week I was born. He is considered godfather to the incestuous clique that dominated French thinking after the War. They assumed the mantle of intellectual authority from Surrealism. Andre Breton is seen as a figure of fun today what with his antics, factions and stupidly sensuous face. But there would be NO BATAILLE and thus NO ONE ELSE if there had NOT BEEN BRETON. His comedic talents were well-suited to the inter-war years. But Dada's splastic lapstick was rendered redundant by the Nazis. To be "Against Breton" became *a la mode*. Black humor was drained of the joke by Samuel Beckett. It was thus impossible to interpret Sade as Breton had done post-Hitler. Bataille's critique of Sade by contrast possessed sufficient cruelty. It still resonates in our sexual practices today. Pasolini wrote the instruction manual for sex and politics in the modern world in 120DoS. It became a meta-comedy of sorts, because it ended in Pasolini's own death. He was bashed to death with two table legs then run-over multiple times by his own car. Ballard was interviewed as a person of interest by Italian police in Ostia. His testicles had been crushed with an iron bar. His corpse had been partially immolated with gasoline. Pino Pelosi was convicted and spent 29 years in jail. In 2005, he recanted his confession saying that it had been made under duress because the mafia threatened his family. It was always hard to believe that a single assailant could have maintained the momentum of violence against the film director. Later, extortionists were added to the brew of suspects. The case was re-opened but the coroner could not find sufficient evidence to continue the investigation. *F(W)ake* failed. In fact, there has been very little joy in theoretical writing since the 1960s. It's all trudge trudge trudge. It was the only aesthetic enterprise that proved resistant to the irresistible boyish charm of the Beatles. Bataille's ex-wife married Lacan. This was like Steve Jobs shacking-up with Joan Baez. She was an actor who starred in Jean Renoir movies like *A Day in the Country*. It's the kind of rape-consent movie that could never get made today. It ends with Henriette meeting her traducer as a married woman and reliving the experience sentimentally. Sylvie Bataille's daughter Laurence became a psychoanalyst like her step-father. It's a hermaphroditic name. She only lived to the age of fifty-six. As a teen, she was Balthus' fuck-model. She went to jail for the FLN. Afterwards she studied medicine. Lacan called her "Antigone." This is a great joke on so many planes. She died too young of liver cancer in 1986. Foucault's death from AIDS was inevitable. He had a persistent cough since the Summer of 1983. This was back in the era before anti-viral drugs. There were no cell phones. It was June 1984 when he passed away. The Panopticon was still a primitive beast. Foucault predicted how technology would intensify its gaze. He was only fifty-seven years old. My age as I write. He was the most famous intellectual on earth. He had written a dozen books covering sex, prison, power and the mind. He died of brain disease. AIDS attacked his most prominent organ. He shaved his head when he started losing his hair as a young man. He was another self-styled dandy. He drove a white sports car in Algeria. His dome became a registered trademark like the Playboy bunny-ears. His head popped out of trademark black turtle-neck sweaters like an uncircumcised cock. Foucault died in Pitie-Salpêtrière hospital. This was an appropriate location. He wrote the love story of Salpêtrière in *Madness and Civilisation*. It was converted from a gunpowder factory into a hospice for poor women by Louis XIV. Thus, it was apposite to Foucault's analysis of the shift from physical attack to the carceral. It served as a prison for prostitutes. It was also a sanitarium for women who were intellectually disabled, mentally ill or epileptic. It was notable for its bloated and unresponsive bureaucracy. Saltpeter is a key ingredient in gunpowder. Prisoners scraped it off the walls of tunnels and dungeons under medieval cities surrounded with moats. Paul-Michel Foucault was born in Poitiers, France in 1926. He was the son of a stone physician. The town was a key strategic post between mountain ranges on the Seuil du Poitou. It was also a ditch for the Charente, Loire and Sèvre basins. This made it a historic battle site. On 29 June, Foucault's *la levée du corps* was held. The coffin was carried from the hospital morgue and driven to his birthplace in Vendeuvre-du-Poitou. In the end, he was LOCAL. Like Pepe, he loved to be confined forcibly. Pepe and I were playing hide and seek when it happened. Foucault would have considered the refrigerator in the paddock as another L-E (see below). His partner Daniel Defert defied Foucault's wish for no posthumous works to be published. This meant the release of Volume 4 of *HoS*. It puts Foucault into the same category as Kafka and Jarry. They believed that death should mean NO FUTURE TEXTS. Foucault didn't want to be subjected to the same sequence of lame posthumous albums as Jim Morrison. His theory is just a metaphor for SEX. Foucault manipulated his work schedule to practice his art in San Francisco. Nobody knew much about HIV then. In 1984, some people believed in an AIDS conspiracy. Others called it the gay plague. Or homosexual cancer. Daniel Defert said that Foucault went to San Francisco for the last time as a Limit-Experience (L-E). Gide's pederasty was another L-E. This notion comes from Bataille. It claims to break the subject from itself. This was not a foreign object to French theoreticians. They constantly decried the unrealness of the REAL. What better way to challenge our consumerised format for life than by leaking our bodies with needles and pliers. Bataille invented L-E when he got pissed off with Surrealism. It was too anodyne. L-E covers rejection, abandon, fantastic assemblages, pain, lysergic visions and madness. Lacan added desire, boredom, confinement, revolt, prayer, sleeplessness and panic. But his L-E set diluted human emotions. It should be accepted that L-E disconnects sexual practice from ethics. Foucault embraced Bataille's views on love. He saw masochism as his L-E space. Bataille went in another direction. He wrote about maternal incest. He loved orgies and violence. He had a Sublime hate for all art products. His characters are always wanking and pissing all over text and imagery. Somehow, they made a movie of *Ma Mere* starring Isabel Huppert. She slits her throat at the end while her son masturbates in her face. His orgasm is her death statement. It's a belated dedication to Proust. The movie misses the religious symbolism always present in Bataille. He was a devout Catholic who studied at a seminary briefly. He wrote that the word FORMLESS made the universe seem "something like spit." This is not necessarily a bad simile in Bataille's cosmos. Everyone is always beautiful in L-E movies. It's a strategy to attract viewers to the cause. But it's always a misnomer. In REAL LIFE, these antics always involve really ugly fat stupid people. The data indicates that incest normally comprises fucking with a step-parent, cousin or half-sibling. Often, these people met as adults. So, it's really a giant beat-up. *Blue of Noon* is another corpse-fucking classic. To be clear, Bataille is always a humorous writer. He has a fixed leer on his face. Anita Lane used his character "Dirty" for an album title. She is called MANHOLE in this novel. Like Troppmann, Shanghai Dog has to choose between three women: Manhole, O and Xiao Fang. They correspond to filth, ethics and expired love respectively just like Dirty, Lazare and Xenie. I had no compunction gifting Xiao Fang to a colleague. The Englishman treated her badly. S-DOG didn't feel regret. Only relief that he had relieved himself of that burden. Like most truly ethic-less (E-L) people, Shanghai Dog started at the opposite pole. He had been an altar-boy and chorister like David Hemmings, Nick Cave and Samuel Beckett. Many people still thought of him as a man guided by a humanistic conscience. He talked a lot about being karma-positive. He had thrown himself into the worst depravity in Asia. He wore a frock-coat to a fancy-dress party at the Pudong Shangri-La as a double-sided joke. It was the narrator who named his wife "O." This is to conceal her identity from the authorities. Like most saints, she wasn't particularly nice to live with. Bataille is the source for all clarification in this sub-plot. Troppmann travels to Treves with Dirty. They fuck in the mud on a cliff overlooking a graveyard. This act is paralleled in *Telemachus* by Manhole dogging at Glamour Bar. Dirty sees a vision of war when she observes Hitler Youth. It's a Sublime moment. Bataille spent World War Two in cycles of pensive motion. Like many Parisians, he oscillated between the comparative sanctuary of rural life and his prerequisite for the city. He met Blanchot in 1940. He hid in Balthus' studio after his separation from Denise Rollin in 1943. He was being hunted by his lover's husband, Kotchoubey. Bataille was diagnosed with pulmonary tuberculosis in 1942. He developed cerebral arteriosclerosis in 1955. He was not informed of the terminal nature of his illness. He died seven years later on 9 July 1962. Bataille formed a secret society called *Acéphale* in 1936. He organised nocturnal concerts in the forest near an oak which had been struck by lightning. Members were required to follow various rituals. They were surprisingly mundane. The coven celebrated the decapitation of Louis XVI. His headless corpse became their emblem. It was depicted in a drawing by Andre Masson for the first issue of their journal. It only continued for five editions. Such groups usually start out in all seriousness then descend into farce only to jolt themselves back to connotation with a meaningless, evil act. This was the model used by Charles Manson. Bataille planned a human sacrifice. Colette Peignot volunteered. It wasn't much of a scenario. She was going to die of breast cancer anyway. Bataille contracted tuberculosis from her. It was voluntary L-E. Foucault attempted the same category of L-E in 1983. She had been raped by a priest as a young girl. It was the inspiration for *Story of the Eye*. Bataille copulated furiously as she recounted its narrative over and over. It was a type of oral history. She died in his house. He turned it into a shrine. No, that's not true. In fact, he disposed of this residence at a tidy profit. There is a moving photographic portrait of her emaciated corpse. At the end she wore a tonsured head. This image prefaced Holocaust imagery. I like her face best when she pins her hair back displaying her strong facial features; although there is a beautiful shot of her sitting on a doorstep gripping her shins with her hair let out. She had a sensual mouth. Bataille's mouth was a complementary shape. Their kiss would have been perfect like placing a soft lid over a smooth jar. O and I crack a chicken's neck. Bataille went by the pseudonym LORD AUCH. It means SHITSTAIN in English. This is an anagram of Saint Shit. L-E can create physical jerkings that trigger a crypto-Sublime (Crypt-S). It is a simulation of religious mania. Don Cane was always bored by Holy Week in the Philippines. It was impossible for him to get any spiritual lift from watching peasants haul heavy crosses through the streets of the city towards church. He had observed the same scene in Vietnam denuded of religious palsy. Remnant farming families driven inside strategic hamlets. Nagoolians dragged over to ARVN interrogators. Sodden patrols straggling back inside the false safety of combat bases up near the DMZ. Radio controllers bent over the weight of their battle-packs. Bataille noted poles of divine ecstasy and extreme horror in human endeavour. They were the same thing to him. L-E stops just short of Saussure's Life-Death polarity. L-E converts the proponent into a Trickster. It means trying to die at a moment of artificial Crypt-S. This is the same sensibility that Walter Pater chronicled in his IP, "Sebastian van Storck." Given the above sequence, Tom Hallem would have chosen to expire at the start of SS (3), I think. He would have desired SS (1) & SS (2) to be fully formed. SS (3) represented hackneyed Sublime. He would have preferred to die before those clichés registered. You don't need to get into BDSM to understand L-E. Anybody steeped in punk music gets it. But it was NOT ENOUGH FOR FOUCAULT to get L-E from books. He wanted to increase L-E to "Limit-Expiration" (~~LE~~) maybe. He is rumored to have engaged in sex with consenting partners after he was diagnosed with AIDS. I don't think this means other people infected with HIV, despite what his acolytes avow. That would have been a SAFE experience, not an ~~LE~~. There is zero risk in such practice. No, his ~~LE~~ must have involved volunteers who subjected their bodies to An Infection Wheel as a proxy for Bataille's notion of human sacrifice. They must have been bound hard then punctured in one hundred places with needles gushing Foucault's blood. His semen too would have been driven into their wounds. He would also have acted as BOTTOM. The TOP would thereby risk infection, albeit at a lower density than a Bottom. It was a game of chance really. Foucault thus sought to fulfil the aborted mission of Acéphale. Althusser was an influence on Foucault at *ENS*. He was also trained by *Waiting for Godot*. He decorated his room with Goya etchings. He revered Antonin Artaud, Jean Genet and Hermann Broch. He shared their obsession with suicide. It was the fascination of a voyeur. Everything pointed back to Sade for Foucault but this time in all seriousness. Bataille was the Shelley of BDSM. Foucault was Browning. He adopted Blanchot's tactic of interviewing himself. Foucault had been suffering fever. Brain spasms complicated his septicemia. There were several areas of cerebral suppuration. Antibiotics had a "favorable effect at first," according to the official statement. There was no question of fucking anymore. It's too dangerous and I'm too weak, concluded Leon Daniel. I couldn't knowingly risk anyone else. I've got to finish-up my current patient schedule. Take no more appointments, Miss Dunne. The end of *F(W)ake* marks the end of sexlife. It is a death book. I hate it, Nora Joyce confided to her sister. Joyce was a pox-addled drunk by then. He became increasingly absorbed by perverse sexual practices (Category IV). If I want to fuck, thought S-Dog, there are sixty girls at the Gold Star KTV. Master Chen keeps them in a stark concrete shell in the basement. I don't need Xiao Fang. He brings them up the service elevator to Level 28. They are presented in the fish bowl in sets of six. They are all dressed in gold bikinis. They wear numbered tags pinned to their gilded briefs. Through the peep hole, I saw Laure forcing a black dildo into Ladyboy Tara while Blanchot sat in the corner masturbating contentedly. Laure hacked bloody consumption into the nuthole and drove the massive entrail home. Father Ambrose rose onto the bench and forced his member through the hatch. Bella preyed dutifully. Solange snorted another POPPER. The vial knocked her flat. The young priest came over and lifted her body by the hand. He escorted her to the altar. The narrator penetrated Simone while she fellated Don Arminado. Sir

Edmund blessed the Eucharist and jammed some sodden excrement into the priest's mouth. The rope ripped his throat. He expired. Molly Bloom chewed on a caramel as she read eagerly. "This is my kind of stuff Poldy," she enthused. Sir Edmund nucleated an unlifed eye. Simone forced it up her cunt with a pop. The narrator lay down on his back and let her urine wash over him. Leer entered Hellfire with Tom Hallem. The manager welcomed them. Pasolini flicked from fuck mode to death. I am not going to re-write *Story of the Eye* or recycle Bataille's retinue of spheres (eye, egg, sun, testicle) anymore for the reader. No more Fuck Writing (FW) even if it is based on FACT. No mention of the mystery gland even though it DOES antagonise our sense organs. No secret societies even if they do control the dark web. No allusions to taboo practices despite the TRUTH (see Haitian practitioners). Bataille developed Base Materialism as a vitalic Third Eye to destabilise Dialectical Materialism. Derrida appropriated it to undermine binary philosophical codes. Foucault produces simulacra of the Sublime brimming with nostalgia for the unattainable and a child's sense of loss. On deck, I rolled a smoldering cigar in my fingertips so that pungent smoke veiled my face. The Africans were almost mutinous. Only Simone's persistent ministrations placated them. I felt for my gun. Idle threats don't concern me. Chinese guys always talk big. Their basic tactic is to intimidate foreigners with the threat of arrest by local government cronies on trumped-up charges then strip your business. Milky Li was a long way from his power base in Wuhan. The Shanghai mob wouldn't budge. I had my own *guanxi*. Chinese people are angry about government corruption. But they are mainly furious that they did not get the chance to get rich themselves. This is the rupture in Chinese life. Young people use the term, *mi shi luo*. Usually, it means LOST. It means ethically vacant in this context. Only money relationships count. I am working both sides of the Gu deal. My commission will be 1% on the sell side and 2% on the buy side. This is one point five million dollars in total. Of course, there will be plenty of outgoings. I have to pay commission to my mate in Tai Yuan who knew the CEO through the local golf club. He'll want a drink. Then there's the guy who fixed up SASAC. Also, the bank manager in Tianjin who can still get RMB denominated deals exchanged into USD. I will probably clear a brick at the end. That's enough wedge to get me out of China. No more dangling in front of Doctor Gu. Bataille's prose style is very matter-of-fact as if his narrator doesn't want to distract the reader with linguistic display cards. His narrative scenes require no illumination. There are not even adjectives except in the description of spheres. But there is a relish to his writing that is lacking in Ballard. His theoretical writing is similar. In "The Notion of Expenditure," he draws a simple distinction in consumption between base production to conserve existence and 'unproductive expenditure.' The latter group represents activities which have no end beyond themselves such as luxury, mourning, cults, monuments, games, spectacles, arts and perverse sexual practices (defined by Bataille as actions "deflected from genital finality"). We regard such items as 'disposable income' when they relate to the individual. Disposable income is used to calculate the market for car sales in emerging markets like China. We use it to estimate traffic growth and toll road revenue. Increased domestic consumption is designed to maintain the annual GDP growth rate which underpins the Chinese economy as export prices rise and competition intensifies from cheaper new entrants like Vietnam and Bangladesh. It is supplemented by the ongoing assistance of an undervalued Yuan. Stability is the self-justification for Party rule in China. It also deploys spasmodic appeals to nationalism from artificially manufactured political crises. The logical denouement of this tactic is whether China is willing to go to war over Taiwan if the economy collapses. The President made many enemies with his crackdown on opposing factions. Bo Xilai was the golden boy growing up. Xi watched him quietly. They were like Edgar and Edmund in *King Lear*. Xi struck when the balance of power shifted a scintilla towards him. He didn't have time to wait for an overwhelming position. It would never have come. A weaker man would have faltered. Bataille includes WAR in his list of unproductive expenditure. It is what he calls the Accursed Share. Bataille bemoans war although he does acknowledge its role as a trigger for events that overthrow prevailing social systems. This is all connected to the theories of Vico, Sun Tzu, Machiavelli and Clausewitz. Eventually, he incorporates the Accursed Share into a new theory which he calls "General Economy." This bland title is ironic because Bataille is actually proposing a complete inversion of economic axioms through the "surrender of commodities without return." His reasoning is that if wealth is destined for unproductive use then we should just surrender it as excess. This appears like Maoist collectivisation at face value. China has become the world's leading manufacturer by undercutting Western competition. Whole industries have disappeared. Entire communities have been disenfranchised. Skills lost. Yet paradoxically we're constipated with STUFF. Everyone has become a hoarder of CHEAP PRODUCTS. This is termed General Commodity Delirium (GCD). Our Pineal Eye has been altered by GCD causing Consumption Obesity (CO). We grow fatter each day. It is splintering the seams of our class structure. We don't even have church anymore. We only gather at shopping malls. Baudrillard revered these places. A scholar might argue that China NEVER abandoned base ideology. *Gei Ge Kei Feng* will create an industrial proletariat in China for the first time. Deng Xiaoping was always a strict Marxist. In the end, he exceeded the ambitious heavy industry ratios of *Da Yue Jin*. He differed with Mao on approach just as Mao disagreed with Stalin. Do not change the typesetting in the next section. It is an accidental deconstructive device caused by conversion form Wordperfect 5.1 to Word 10. Use this as a symbol of progress and civilisation; its impact on extant data/people; also an update of Mallarme's typography in

"Un Coup de Des." The content of the lecture relates to human sexual practices associated with Bataille in this sub-section.

FOUCAULT

CO(NTRI)ITION: In *The History of Sexuality: Volume 1*, Michel Foucault postulated an expansion in the scope of the Confession from a simple means of attaining religious absolution for sexual misdeeds to a controlling device – and noted that Sex had become tied to our visions of Utopia. Concomitant with this shift in the confessional apparatus was the appearance of a Scientia Sexualis (medico stooges for Power), who claimed to have formulated procedures for telling the hygienic Truth about Sex which superseded the art of initiation and the masterful secrets of *ars e rotica*. Four figures became privileged objects of Knowledge:

the hysterical woman;

the masturbating child;

the Malthusian couple;

persons of perverse pleasures.

Against this final, miscellaneous category was to be deployed a cycle of prohibition. Sex must renounce itself under threat of punishment. These ones were called to "step forward and speak, to make the difficult confession of what they were." Yet Foucault never discloses the full extent of SEX preferring to equivocate at the pen ultimate moment of Confession so that it is "not really recorded" but must remain out side the text. He could have become the Hug h Hefner of critical theory. Or Sade. But there are always false prohibitions in his discourse. Commentators like Foucault preferred to produce Burkean epics in which the satirical and subversive use of discourse calls attention to the contriv ances of methodology. Often the notion of matter becomes elusive in such works as the author strives to balance the imperatives of an anti-Cartesian discourse with the necessity (and repressed desire) for content to propel the text towards its ambivalent and/or ironic severance. William James Chidley's sexual theories were directed at each of these categories. He identified the stultifying oppression which drove women to stoic decline or cathartic revolt, HE HIMSELF was the auto erotic child and his 'Answer' proposed to change the very nature of reproductive coupling and cure perversion. In his *Confessions*, Chidley committed to paper sexual activities and misadventures of which he was ashamed for the cause of his Utopia. His compulsion to "speak" these lapses inextricably intertwined the act of coition, his own self disgust and a desire for absolution. Contrition was the predicate of coition; connected to it by a copula. It was against misogyny that his sexual theories and Confessions were directed. They remain a chivalric enterprise despite problematic personal insufficiencies; albeit riddled with misconceptions and errors. By gender from within Patriarchy but from Patriarchy riven, Chidley was an obscure apostle of suffragette feminism. He became obsessed with the fatal consequences of marriage for women. Romantic expectations, born of reading, contrasted with later visions of careworn, converging wrecks. A paralysed woman, wife of the school gardener, was the first of a sequence of females crippled by marriage; a theme which reached its apogee at the Female Emigrants Home in the mass physiognomical spectacle of women who "had the same look in their eyes of burnt out passions and lusts, the same ugly hands and figures." He also chronicled the demise of his Mother and his Aunt cum stepmother both "abused to death by Father's wooden penis." [non conductive matter]. His final formulation of *The Answer* formalised this mistrust of men to offer salvation to women.

"HEAD, THOREAU & ABDOMEN." A pun on the anatomy of the bee, Thoreau's favoured metaphor for man. Face > writer > nether regions. The title outlines the perimeters of *The Answer*, which offered a solution to our failure to attain Utopia. Chidley proposed that the present method of coition was unnatural – based on the violation of the erect penis – and that, instead, the passive male should lie alongside a loving female until her vaginal suction, stimulated by arousal, inhaled the tip of his penis and drained it of spermatozoon (clues: strings of Alice's dress being sucked into her vagina; Ada's vagina inhaling his penis once ; example of ducks, drakes and horses). He ripped more paper ribbons. The release of this pressure made it splay slightly and drool. He licked the beige sauce. The HEAD of the title signifies Chidley's obsession with physiognomy: the convergence of brows, injured eyes, corrugated foreheads, bulbous Bardolphian noses, flushed cheeks, sly, knowing smiles and clumsy hands all caused by the shocks of coition and self abuse (47). Anomalous emanations of hair on a hatcheted cranium. Deep, care less gougings in the scalp moating a funnel of stiff locks. As if a thick pipe was mounted in his skull. Language which shifted in small units, compartmentalised by punctuation, constantly qualified or extrapolated, centripetal with scientific detail, powered by alliteration. Sex, physiognomical contraction, recourse to alcohol, insanity. **HEAD** contains Chidley's ideas and aesthetic. His dreams and visions. Some hint at his fear of men and his fear for girls. Others threaten annihilation. Some are tangible only in the involuntary emissions which flow from them. Molten hommos flowed over his fingers. One records "tigers in the room and large pasteboard ducks that moved their tails and eyes" (277). Others expose his martyr's fervour for immolation: "A BACCHIC ELATION WAS WITH ME AT TIMES, yet a feeling of being normal. I dreamt I was naked in an assembly and ONE FLAME OF JOY FROM HEAD TO FOOT." (170) His pronouncements and struggles colour others dreams. His partner Ada dreams of him dressed all in white like a saint (179). And in return he dreams of her, eternally damned "in an indecent posture" (278) suffering the humiliations of Hell. **ABDOMEN**. An experimental sexuality gone pestilent. From childhood, Chidley was unable to control his burgeoning sexuality so he literally punished his penis. His first childish sexual interaction with a girl ended in him cutting his penis with a knife to sever the "precocious reverie" (11). On another occasion, he knelt down and smashed it with a toilet seat at school so that it went "quite black"≅ (27). It eventually evolved into his doppelganger: the separate side of a key. We find him tearing away the bedding to uncover the autonomous, sapient sexual organ as it rears up at him out of the sheets. Symbol of the snake. Capri ate. Peccant "unholy sweat." Spinal flaccidity. Humid wet fever. Clear metaphors for his disgust with human functions and diet. Another DREAM OF Ada found her compressing human excrement onto a piece of bread, "quite naturally, as if it had been a sausage, and I ate it" (192). Bitten. Chidley longs to be repulsed and to repulse the moon – a key female symbol in Classical mythology (see Hecate, Astarte, Diana, Cynthia, Phoebe, Selene or Luna) – with his orgasm. He huddles out of sight in the hull of a boat self stimulating in front of its luminous rays (90). Or he satiates the "mad tendency" in a cave. Later metaphors availed themselves of size. Indecent photographs gave him "an unnatural orgasm that made me feel AS BIG AS A HOUSE." If this lucid testimony of fantastic, macabre and grotesque pornographic and scatological details had fallen into Freud's paws, Chidley may well have become as ubiquitous as Little Hans or Dora. He held out his leaking food. Sauce dripped onto the pavement. **THOREAU** *Walden* was one of a cluster of texts which permeated Chidley's consciosuness. His "unholy sweat" and metaphorical horror of flesh were the result of unbalancing what Thoreau called our "vital heat" (12). Throughout his over-heated existence, Chidley sweated at sex like Ruskin in front of Swinburn e's "Faustine," which had made him feel "all hot, like pies with t he devil's fingers in them." Meat was associated by Chidley with lapses into mast urbation and drink. The antithesis lay in fruit and a fruit diet insp ired by Schlickeysen's *Fruit and Bread: A Scientific Diet.* This echoed Thoreau's 'Elysian life,' which spurned cooked food for fruit ripened by the sun and rejected clothing and shelter. A "balanced, normal and cool" brain became the foil to streaming convergence. T h e benefits from stimulating "natural fruit blood" would include **FLOATING.** This was the same glorious leap that appended a tail to the human body in Charles Fourier's Harmony. Chidley grasped at literary ideas and incorporated them into his work. Walter Pater's Imaginary Portrait, "Denys L'Auxerrois," provided his central Dionysian trope of lapse and renewal . He incorporated Pater's sacrifice of Denys to the frenzied demotic crowd into his own self-perception as martyr. He invoked *Heiterkeit* – a term borrowed by Pater in the essay on "Winckelmann" – from Hegel's *Aesthetik* to exemplify the Hellenic ideal (137). His reading was eccentric, coherent and analytical. For example, his nickname for a lover's ageing benefactor was SILENUS, an attendant of Bacchus who is represented as a fat jovial old man always full of liquor and riding an ass. A decrepit opium eater, is tagged FOSCO after Wilkie Collins' Count. His tastes in literature developed down channels: like Pater > Swinburne > Blake > Baudelaire. It tracked oscillations between lapse and renewal shifting from Gay's fables and the romances of Sir Walter Scott to "pornographic" passages in Smollett's *Roderick Random* and "lewd" encounters in Shakespea re. As a young clerk he buried himself in novels like *Barnaby Rudge*. Dickensian realism imbued his sordid recollections of this period as "in that dingy hole I abused myself again and again" (44). The consequences of self abuse for Chidley were a startling deterioration of his physiology: "I grew stiff in the neck, my spine clogged, and I had unholy sweats. The pupils of my eyes were like pin heads so small and weak I could not look at the sun, or a healthy lad or lassie in the eyes. Even the picture of a healthy boy in the Gallery (45)." **SYNTHESIS.** What we must do is take the title and solder it into a ring – to bind it as O was bound through the flesh, by the shac kle and in hre mind and click shut the plastic cap like Chidley himself achieved by folding upon himself in **AUTO-FELLATIO**. The Mouth is the insertion orifice. Capri unravelled the sodden paper disclosing the soggy butt which he cradled like a stamen. It withered before light. He presst it out of the paper and popped it inna. It sunk. God placed genitals out of convenient reach of the lips. But self stimulating himself in what he called "the nameless way," Chidley, unable to bear naming it, for there was no terminology invented for this act, struggled to make his head and abdomen meet for **LITERAL INTERPENETRATION**. Capri cleaned his palms on his trousers leaving a shiny wash. This contortionist bending of the spine unto self enclosure (as if Chidley himself had become a book whose wings were torn back unnaturally) is a paradigm of his mental anguish; an anguish alternately titillated and allayed by reading as he rotated through cycles of Dionysian energy and dissipation until his attainment of stern Apollonian serenity begat discovery of the Answer.

VIRILIO

"TEXT POINT ALPHA." The projector replays looped Kodachrome Super-8 road movies of FM-2030 (Star-child) and HH-1970 shooting hoops through a plastic mini-ring in seventeen ('the least random number') identical Five-Star hotel rooms across Central America always fully-grown never ageing totally naked except for empty tissue boxes on their feet listening to Bach minuets getting smoother and fuller across time until their shiny sealed faces tremble and split in a larval flow of skin, silicon and muscle scrapings. They were the first Fast Humans. This is the moment of the Big Accident. Strauss' *Zarathustra* slows to a long flat fart. The Monolith emits a piercing howl. Everything blows. Personal assistants rush to scrape up body parts, focusing on ladling dollops of dough-like brain for Vitrification as per the Entropy Institute's instruction manual: "place mask over mouth and gloves over hands; remove can from sealed bag; scrub exterior; wash in de-ionised water; dry in autoclave (do not overfill as it results in uneven sterilisation); remove wrapping from Cryo-Preservation Kit; press brain parts into container with downwards pressure to minimise air pockets; seal and place in freezer; call 1300 number; technicians from Alcor HQ will collect." Link to Tom and Willy if they lived to a ripe old age. In *2001*, Kubrick suggests the existence of Beings so advanced we can't comprehend them. Junkies of pure energy and spirit. Incomprehensible except as gods. They study Dave like novelists. His life passes. He sees himself age quickly. He dies. He was only thirty-six years old. He is transfigured into the super-child returning to earth. *Ubermensch* blah (x3). Kubrick painted an optimistic picture. James Joyce too remained a broad humanist. In contrast, William Gibson's enterprise is not really relevant to Joyce. A coin-shaped bulb named Alcor-3 (also known as Poseidon) has been attached to the planet by Maglev. It sucks rare earth from open-cut mines through suction hoses positioned just inside the protective shadows of The Eclipse. Photo-voltaic panels protrude into the solar line-of-sight without exposing Poseidon to the direct rays of the Sun. This has become critical since the ozone layer inverted. I could write endless passages with this type of pompous science fiction prose. It is engrained in our minds like a blanking device. Tarkovsky is filming a team of cyberneticists at work. Commence zentropy muzak. INSERT FOLLOWING IMAGE SEQUENCE: close-up of closed eyelids splitting suddenly leaving Doric columns of rheum; a flashing neon tag-line ("REFRESHSHSHD"); ECT pads shudder elephantine flesh; subliminal community service banner ("not to be attempted on minors"); alternating shots of FM-2030 and HH-1970 gazing into hand mirrors with appropriate product placement; bodily reconstitution as per infotainment channel instructions (see Special Offer); triangular silver chips inserted behind each ear lobe (*Sponsored by Content Management Services!*); they hover out of the laboratory to take their place in a purpose-built apartment. The choice of French neoclassical decor recalls The Enlightenment. Grammar is no longer relevant, just storyboards. Imagery is designed to reach the soul like a gut-reaction. Like a great painting. Find a new way of writing to match. Make a prosenchymatic field. Alcor-3 is the oldest and most liberal of the new colonies. Other outposts would not risk infection from FM-2030, although there were multiple offers to accept the more sanitary HH-1970. Alcor-3 is protected from micro-organisms by a Dry Heat Sterilization Field. Each individual is fitted with a programmed casing that prevents disease transmission. HH-1970 shuffles to the water cooler on Kleenex clogs, which are sponsored by Unilever. It has just received a lifetime achievement award for subsuming its last rivals (El Goog, Buy Dough, Zamaz). Children at Alcor-3 are sedated with Stillnox at Dream Academies and palsied in learning modules. There is the gentle rap of a Styrofoam Blunt on the door. Servbot is oddly inactive. The polyurethane eyes of Tiresias spring open. He starts mouthing a scroll of platitudes by Barbara Kramer. *I am always happy when surrounded by smart people who also happens (sic) to be rich and powerful I was told the people here at WIG were interested in inviting in (sic) future initiatives which means A. I. which means me.* Source - "THE TAKE." Cassandra makes a prophecy by mathematical formula. Hera swoops down and pokes out her eyes. She smashes a pair of copulating snakes with a lightsaber. A spider gives birth to a plethora of star-children. FM-2030 lifts a horned conch to his lips. Ralph appears on the set holding Billy's smashed spectacles aloft. The knock recurs louder and sharper. HH-1970 shuffles to the door. Insert ape = spacemen scenes. A mob in activewear rushes inside. They have fashioned weapons out of soft polymer. He is knocked to the ground. They stomp on his body to a soundtrack by Bizet. Insert more references to Droogs. Also, 120DoS. Max More orchestrates the crowd. FM-2030 smashes a glass of red wine. It represents the human body. Also, Christ's blood. They smash FM-2030 with Q-bricks until his carcass ponds red-on-snow over the floor. Tom reached blindly towards the Monolith simulating the famous image of the "Creation of Adam." HH-1970 grins. Occasionally, he applauds childlike like Warhol. He offers the crowd absorbent towels before poking out his only good eye with a long nail on the end of his right hand, which he has nicknamed The Screwdriver. The crowd flay him alive. A mound is constructed. Four monoliths appear linking epic transitions in human evolution. *2001* represents the odyssey of humankind. When they finish with Dave, he is transformed into a GOD. The crowd lifts the corpses onto a pyre using mind-magnification. Attendants rush to the scene with extinguishers. They recite statistics on trench warfare. The quantum of bombs dropped on North Vietnam exceeded the total volume delivered by the Allies on Germany by a factor of 3.5 to one. Each B-52 payload = 6 x B-17. The remnant body parts of FM-2030 and HH-1970 are spirited back to The Bubble where Tarkovsky chronicles their reconstruction so that the whole scene can be repeated *ad infinitum*. Nietzsche's Eternal Recurrence of the Same. But their memories are NOT erased. This would totally defeat MEANING. INSERT SOUNDTRACK - "Daisy (Bicycle built for two)." Serenade of an IBM 704 computer to Arthur C. Clarke. Bicycles. A symbol of modernity. Bowman (Ody) unplugged Hal (Trojan Horse) to facilitate the next stage (Odyssey). Technology = violence. Kill all monstrous offspring or A. I. will take over the world. But we are long past HOPE in contemplating that battle (see C6, Arche-Text). This is TEXT POINT OMEGA. Loop back to TEXT POINT ALPHA. A loop is a reflection in a still pool. Janus was also Virilio's God. He was all about motion. This is the Travelling that Virilio calls the Aesthetics of Disappearance (Futurism-with-Scruples). An installation titled *Road Movie* is being exhibited in the Left Wing. A holographic plaque reads: "Opened by M. Duchamp." Neon slogans flash his message across curved walls: *Stupid as a Painter Still as Paint*. The concept of Dromology is central to Virilio's critical enterprise. It comes from the Greek *dromos* for racetrack. This is apt for Joyce's *Ulysses*, which is set on Gold Cup Day. Also, TMAC (Melb Cup). Virilio condenses all narratives into one hundred minutes of quick edits, flash-forwards, montages, psychedelic effects and stylised brutality. *2001* contains 140 minutes of imagery but only 40 minutes of dialogue. Impressionistic like art. This was the same goal as *F(W)ake*. All cinema represents road trips. It is integral to the technology. Kubrick's style in the closing sequence was intended to kickstart the next stage of human evolution (THE REVOLUTION). But he didn't pretend to have all the answers. Was Dave dreaming or conscious? Dead or alive? This was a new kind of end-point to VOID closure. Kubrick wanted to harness the subconscious power of the audience as an energy field. To penetrate our minds like a Bond villain. Anxiety about progress has been replaced by terror and fear, according to Virilio. Billy Capri adjusted his spectacles. Einstein's train passed into the present tense en route to meet Bergson (see A. Uhlmann). Dusky light. This is the time of day when human activity gives way to passive observance of the televisual (Transhumanism). In *Ulysses*, everyone goes to the pub. One moment there is sunlight, next aftermath. The animal body of the worker becomes transparent. Technology passes not pausing. To illuminate night has always been the objective of human societies. It literally expanded the amount of time available for exploitation. Fire-heat became work-light. The speed of light became the dream measurement of Capital. That's why space travel was pursued so fiercely. There is a manic addiction to pace. Now society has progressed to the phase of collective emotionalism. This produces what Virilio calls a 'communism of affects.' His father was a Marxist, originally from Italy. Sharp-rusted shadows pulse with green ticker-tape lanterns. Banks of watchful eyes form a cinema screen. Everything is over-exposed. Australia is the correct setting for Apocalypse. Communications domes bulge on the arid surface of this ancient land like herpes blisters, the voiceover says. Bikes become speed prosthetics. Trucks mimic tanks. Insert refs to *Mad Max* & *Stone*. Pseudoephedrine is a fast drug. Billy Capri worked his way through fast-food along fast-falling King Street seeping hummus juice from a sodden wrap across his second-hand jacket. He pressed hard against the city's footpath-veterans as they leaked railway tickets, chewing stones and fading cigarette coals over plaid kerbstones into streaming stone gutters. Increase of unease seemed to make his speed increase exponentially. He paused to watch a torn strand of greaseproof paper resist shape-forming on the crest of merging rain-tides. It bashed away at a heavy stormwater grill, repelled and urged back, with no way in/away, just bobbing, backing-up and bobbing again, swelling against speed's weight, a symbol, until the rain-flush abated and it cud rest. Billy checked the pedestrian signal and started across Missenden Road. His first footstep hit a broad puddle allowing rain to penetrate his shoe. This provoked an irrational fear that he would drop through space like spilled coffee (see C5, E1). His second step smashed into reflected shop lights. Phenomenology of darkness. Of wetness. A slimy outhouse path leading to a damp, close toilet cubicle. Faded image of *Mona Lisa* glued to the wall (Search 'Giaconda'). A gale passed. His third step hit even ground. Humans always created flatness. Flat campsites. Flat fields. Flat house blocks. Flat steps. A sudden shower on step four caught him midway across Ashfield Park in his school uniform. It became inundated in seconds. He burst into tears. Step 5 – he was obliged to pause on the traffic island by a turning signal that sent a constellation of sharp vehicles rushing across his gaze. A heavy van sprayed his trousers. He looked into the dim front bar of the Marlborough Hotel. The levy of his hairline was finally breached. Water pooled in his eyebrows. A purl slid down his temple (see C2). It reached his cheek. He licked. Lion Island brine. Caravan park holidays. Bob tinkering with a gas tap. Playing hide and seek in heath. Billy hurried to the far shoreline. The pub awning sheltered him at last. He brushed his face with a damp coat sleeve. Smell of gentlemen. He was giving his apartment to O. A kind of sanctuary, he thought. Howard Hughes cared only for objects-in-transit until they sent him insane. He vanished into STATIC absence, fortified against light. Literature is caught in the oscillation of these conflicting forces. The crux of narrative teleology is *decisive movement towards closure* while the apprehension of language is *a mood of intellectual arrest*. This disjuncture is paralleled by the schism between matter and style. One is of facts; the other beauty. Facts constitute a Dromology. Feelings are immobilised narrative. Plot acts as a fusillade even when it is careering down the discursive channels of Post-Structuralism like a proletarian mob. Speed is the assault phase. It must be maintained forever or else political momentum will ebb. Mao understood this maxim. An obsession with technology and speed has made teleology pre-eminent. Everything is a matter of Story Thrust. The arrested moment is redundant. Fantastic tales accelerate the reader down an intellectual bypass. This is the map coordinates of literature TODAY. Joyce's male characters are all trapped in Dromological progress in *Ulysses*. Nobody is allowed to stand still. Language must also keep morphing like Proteus. This corresponds to Virilio's notion of a city penetrated with channels of communication, each with a separate set of regulations. Wandering Rocks is the epitome of this concept. All the characters in *Ulysses* are moving all day. They remain stuck in drive-mode, but according to different rules of kinesis. Only Molly Bloom remains stationary. Other females are working, giving birth, scouring the house for items to pawn, or selling their bodies on the street. The city of Paris was restructured by Haussmann after the French Revolution to facilitate swift movement by Authority to quell insurrection. Paris was thus the first urban carceral. No philosopher of Sydney could draft the same roadmap. Sydney's urban channels have always been diverted like intermittent streams. Emancipists chipped away at its civic plan. Ridgelines dominated its transport arteries. People travel like cancer cells through carpellated streets. Veins are always cut off or tied. It has become a city of leakages. Sydney possesses NO GRID. The harbour acts as a SOFT BOUNDARY. Paris is wire mesh; Sydney, all thread. Paris is geometry; Sydney, a jerk-system. Urban deformity triggers the sublime in cities. Barricades are turned or broken to reveal awe-inspiring perspectives. Sydney is One Big S calculated from a sequence of accidental Small S moments. Sydney was the first unintentional city. That remains its urban vector in Virilio's terms. It is a clear weather day in *Ulysses*. Track: FIRM. Joyce employs no meteorological symbology. Shooting stars expire as Bloom and Stephen urinate at 11 pm. The storm made King Street look like Rome 1,000 AD. Shopfronts scattered tawdry products, stagnant behind sub-lit casements. A second-hand bookshop displayed its jaundiced wafers. Rotting cereal fermented in forty-gallon drums at the health food co-op. A hippie played with a cash register. It belled insistently. Narrative as a machine-in-landscape always seems to be going downhill at a slight gradient due to the unwinding of our unconscious brain. Plot involves building or dismantling a human form. Attack from higher ground with the sun behind your shoulders (Sun Tzu). Choose the moment to engage and to disengage (Mao). Cross a dark lane. Gap between awnings. Exposed to sniper fire. Billy rushed through a puddle jabbing his toe. Grim friction. Patchouli oil stench from a crystal shop flooded my scentses. He could just make out the sky's gunmetal scarf dying in space above ornamental facades. Decaying Victorian past. Masonry urns. Queen Victoria's orb. The earth moves in miniscule measures. Dull thuds like footsteps. The dialectic of stasis/movement (style/narrative) is in effect a representation of the natural contrast between land:sky and/or land:sea. Movement is cancelled at the ocean horizon where all forces meet. This is where sea:sky (speed-against-speed) achieves suspended carriage. Cancellation of fluctuants. Horizon ever-receding from grasp. Symbol of Quest. Movement/Immobility. Virilio/Other. Browning's stall. This is not an unusual dichotomy. The relentless progress of the British Empire was framed, pinned and secured by the Shibari figure of its Queen. Shelley explored this dialectic in the 1820 volume of "Prometheus Unbound" (see C4). His epic drama celebrates Olympian energy being expended against fixity. It is followed in the first edition by "The Sensitive Plant," which represents the hopeless bondage of mutable existence. The plant acts as a fixed pivot and compulsory voyeur for the flow of elements and seasons that bring adverse change to the garden (AKA Life). It becomes an emblem for the human condition. This inverted Quest symbology was taken up by Browning in "Childe Roland to the Dark Tower Came." Billy Capri paused at the entrance to the Milton Hotel, pondering a quiet middy before joining his peers. This is a stalling device to suggest underlying disquiet about his future. Jerome McGann argued that images of stasis were a strategy in Victorian poetry to "break with the poetry of quest, effort, and personal advancement" (35). *Ulysses* represented a new variation on this theme. It was a quotidian quest with no significant teleological resolution at closure. Both Bloom and Stephen peregrinate across Dublin hardly making any advances over the course of a single day. This is logical given the short timeframe of the novel. Small spiritual inroads are achieved on behalf of personalised cosmoses, although they represent insinuations rather than fully disclosed narrative leaps. This intervolvement of speed and stasis was intensified in Beckett's *Trilogy*, which comprises a reductive quest (*Malone Dies*); the discourse of apparently immutable totems (*The Unnameable*); and a combination of both (*Molloy*). The body of Beckett's texts are always positioned so close to the end of their apparent tropes that there is hardly any narrative movement possible. Closure is always imminent. Yet, like Zeno's paradox, resolution is never quite reached and, therefore, his characters must remain like the Sensitive Plant forever fastened and exposed at an uncomfortable juncture, enduring perpetual re-runs (ERotS) until arbitrary abandonment by the author. This logos requires the writer to engage in a post-modern revaluation of form. The end of the text is the ultimate Staticising Device. I've been burning capital for twelve months waiting for the GFC to end. The speed of commercial decline even seems to make the taxis go faster. Pedestrians accelerate. Sex is fast but I never seem to cum. Tom Hallem was in a hurry. He needed to find Leer to get Ana's fix. He paid for some crisps and left the shop. The shopkeeper weighed coins in her palm. Blunt symbolism. Tom crossed Salisbury Road against oncoming traffic and proceeded up Australia Street. Same route as Chapter Three. Stuck on a smack loop. Riverrun. Vico's cycles. Enter another Two-Up ring. Drizzle slipped out of the sky. Welterweight shelters. He turned into Federation

Road. A panel beater was bashing at a crumpled side panel. Assistants bathed in golden sweat sprayed silver duco over a bull bar. *Insert air bags into Achilles' armour. Hallem cut across the park through a row of finely woven eucalypt trees towards the sharp corner of the cemetery wall at St Stephens. Strongest point in any structure. Interlocking teeth. Shark bites. Les' stomach was woven together with chaff-bag scars. Tom walked upon the abandoned plots. Bodies still interred down there. Rich loam. Dogrun. Don't start burrowing. You'll dig all the way to China. Xi Jinping is digging the other way. A dog on a leash passed. It is no coincidence that Argos is owned by the Citizen in *Ulysses*. Joyce loathed dogs. Yellowblock perimeter ten feet high. Church well hidden within a cage of soggy figs. Castle Keep. No vegetation can grow beneath its broad canopy. Inedible fruit and leaves. Flying fox colonies patrol at night. Released bats. A high belfry. Carillon of twenty domes installed in 1880. Whitechapel foundry. Gothic Revival. Cruciform plan. LINK TO C3. It was built from Pyrmont sandstone with a slate roof and stone traceries. Pass parallel to Lennox Street. Joshie fit the battle of. Fusillade over the Dardanelles. Probable site of Troy. Dead ANZACS still poke out of dry dirt. Jawbone of an ape. Walk in circles chanting Jehovah's name. Fine Walker organ. One thousand pipes. Anchor of the Dunbar rests in there. Headstones propped against the internal wall blanched of colour like old teeth. Bathsheba Ghost. Go to C8. Derrida's TOMBSTONE. Marble figurines set above. Letters and dates withworn wormdrawn drawndown. Efface Plato's enterprise. Certainty exists only in our folly to fix determinist structures. Pater severed his texts at a moment of calm delusion. Rush to coma. All this stuff coming together so fast. Plot threads, character actions, tropes, devices, weblinks, references, images, symbols, even words, all interpenetrating. Repetition unwoven and rewoven anew. Arachne challenging Athena. Insert diary entries (C8). Make a type of living record as I go. Pepys meets Sterne. There is a deep organic form in the subconscious deeper than any received narrative structure. China has avoided recession. They pump-primed the economy with debt. Bad infrastructure got built too fast. They call it Shenzhen Speed. One skyscraper level per week. Now the central government is bailing out the banks to support non-performing local government loans. The whole damn place is grinding to a halt. Not that official statistics tell you anything. China will always register acceptable GDP growth. The locals are pouring all their cash into the Shanghai Ex. Yesterday, the global economy dropped off another ledge. They closed the Nikkei when a big life insurance company in America went bust. Banks won't lend to banks. Greece is on the verge of default. That will trigger the fall of Italy and Spain. Investors are waiting for rock bottom. It's going to be great if you're still trading. Pick up good assets in impaired vehicles. Major houses like Lehmans, Merrills and Bear Sterns have already hit the wall. Babcock & Brown and Allco are the sacrificial firms in Australia. Even celestial houses like Goldman Sachs are shedding staff. Billy walked into the Shakespeare Hotel pausing on the verge to check his front foot was elevated above the frayed carpet in the doorway. He didn't want to trip and fall. Judy always entered jade buddha temple this way. Claymore hop. She burned incense for dead relatives. There are still one million tonnes of unexploded ordinance under the surface of Vietnam. Rudd has guaranteed the big banks. ASIC banned short selling. Virilio was most worried by biogenetic bombs. Everybody is mobilised for a type of war that can never take place. Space is mapped into camps. There is a velocity to re-alliancing. We need speed to become hysterical so we can manufacture new weapons that nobody will ever use. Atomic collectibles. States like North Korea exploit the unpredictability of haste. Missiles collapsing on a launch pad or careering off course. It's all part of their game. Technology engineers its own mistakes, according to Virilio. Every contraption carries its own *hamartia*. Reich's orgone box. Wooden box of minor literature all misshapen (C4). Technology always seeks to order disorder in any extant system. An accident is just an inverted miracle. When you invent the ship, you also invent shipwreck. The technology of *Ulysses* contains its own fatal flaw. Joyce used up all his Intellectual Property writing *Ulysses*. The only place left to explore was the ultimate assault on language and plot in *F(W)ake*. Joyce went to the same place as Odysseus after the *Odyssey*. Comedy Is the only mode of emplotment for such an enterprise. It represents a POTION. The Trojan Horse turned deception into a winning tactic. But it carried the seed-fruit of Classical severance. Odysseus must go BACK INSIDE at the end of the *Odyssey*. He must file for Chapter Eleven. It's also known as a "Safe Harbour" provision. He must continue beyond Ithaca. It was never going to be the LAST PLACE. He must find a landlocked location where the people have never seen the sea. That means travelling WEST like Voss (LL). By then, the Classical period will be closed. The history of the water-people of the Ionian Sea consigned to tomes. It is succeeded by fragmentation. Sites are self-selected where Dromology and Stasis can make contact in extrinsic space. Places like Afghanistan have become theatres that are "always in play." They can never be allowed to cease fighting. There is no circus without a circle, Virilio said. EBIT graphs ALL OF HISTORY. Virilio does not believe we have entered the hyper-real yet. He thought we could still turn away from the screen. He differed from his friend, Baudrillard, in this regard. Warcraft was Virilio's profession. Don Cane shifted easily between the frontline and clandestine missions. Don't say his service record isn't authentic. That's not the point. He needs to be LARGER THAN LIFE to compete with Odysseus. North Vietnam could have been overrun in a single day if we got the order. In 1968, French thinkers prospered from unrest while intellectuals in the Eastern Bloc were jailed. This is the premise for *Unbearable Lightness of Being*. Lives were irreversibly altered by the events of Prague Spring. Ballard was the other driver in the head-on collision that claimed the lives of Tomas and his wife Tereza. He may have been working for the S-t-B. Tomas was survived by his only son, Simon, who composed this hateful epitaph: "He Wanted the Kingdom of God on Earth." This was a euphemism for the fact that his father wanted to fuck all the time whenever he wanted with whoever he liked regardless of cost. Life was all L-E until he retired to the countryside with a much younger wife like an ageing rock star. *Crash* was a shock to contemporary readers in England but Ballard was really just channelling the grand tradition of British antinomian writers like the anonymous author of *Autobiography of a Flea*. English has always attacked its own shibboleths. It is not by mistake that Bataille created an English aristocrat, Lord Edmund, as the moving force in *Story of the Eye* or that Pauline Reage chose Sir Stephen as the master of O. "O" signifies cunt whereas "I" is penis. The best writers in English inherited deconstructive tendencies off Joyce. Virilio was nominated as a Professor by architecture students in 1968. In the last months of his life, as he lay dying of prostate cancer, Ballard finally moved-in with Ms Walsh, his partner of forty years, swapping his suburban home in Shepparton for her flat above a boarded-up shop in West London. He had been a widower since 1964. He raised three children, writing novels at home during school hours. Bataille was diagnosed with Symphorophilia. Bill Henson famously represented this type of lust in his car crash image of Leda. We have all been infected with such a psychosis to some extent. It was injected by moving pictures. It all started with viewing German concentration camp movies after the war. The first time we recoiled in disgust. Later, we became inured. Finally, they became sick supermodels of desire. Now we always want to secretly re-experience this disgust. We seek out depictions of violence. It is a Negative Sublime (MINUS-S). Virilio is still alive at the time of writing. He grew up in the port city of Nantes. He was a child during the Second World War. He observed Blitzkrieg first hand. Columns of tanks sped down the city's narrow lanes. Fleeing in cattle trucks. Sleeping in sheep folds. Moving by night. Deploying ellipsis to extend the sentence so that it becomes a trail. This was Levi-Strauss' mode of survival when he escaped south to Vichy. Joyce considered World War Two to be a deliberate act of subversion by Hitler to rob his new book, *F(W)ake*, of publicity. Incredibly, Levi-Strauss requested repatriation to Northern France where it was already known that intellectuals and Jews were being sent to camps. This could be seen as a kind of L-E. Eventually, he escaped to America on the same ship as Andre Breton in 1941. Nantes was a centre of the Resistance. Hotz was assassinated there. Many hostages were executed in public reprisals. Virilio was exposed to all the perverse logic of Nazi retribution as a child. He came to look at war as the core human endeavour. Doug Kellner believed that personal experience caused Virilio to over-determine the role of technology. Nantes endured a sequence of Allied bombings aimed at its port facilities. Inevitably, bombs strayed over the town. There is UXO to this day. The heart of Nantes was accidentally bombed by B-17s on 16th September 1943. They came straight up the Loire. Nine hundred civilians were killed. A week later, the Americans returned. Another two hundred and sixty died in morning and afternoon raids. Originally, Lyotard trained as a stained-glass maker assisting Matisse in adorning the churches of Paris. His first analytical work was a study of the Atlantic Wall. It is ironic that this fortification was completed by Rommel, who was a master of fast movement. History can be repeated but it cannot be remade. Rommel would have fought at Kursk, if Hitler sent him to the Eastern Front. It was the greatest tank battle in history. It decided the outcome of the Second World War. Rommel's talent could have been crucial. He was wasted in Africa. A blast of dispute swamped the hockey field. Master Dedalus lowed. Mutilated language expired in a heap. The students assembled. Derrida is not really interested in speed. He prefers deferral. It creates a timeless interim. Virilio only believes in speed and things-which-impede-speed. I also believe in stasis. Speed and stasis are calibrated by technology to ensure RECURRENT CONTACT. Barry Capri dropped his wife at home before going back to close-up the shop. Missus Tran had left a message on his answering machine. Don Cane tumbled to the low point of Darlinghurst. Unknown jungle. Charlie owns night. My sons were born at the beginning of the Vietnam conflict. I was slightly younger than the average member of the AATTV. They were all officers and senior NCOs. My work in Signals got me the gig. Hacking was the first bloke who went down. His death narrative kept changing. First, he shot himself cleaning his gun. Then a sniper got him. Next, one of his mates killed him accidentally. Finally, they said he blew out his own brains. They sent his sealed coffin back to Australia. Occupant unconfirmed. Classified papers. No one ever saw his face. That is all going to change tonight. I am counting on the element of surprise like Odysseus. OUT

DERRIDA

I am only going to focus on one element of Derrida's writing. From this trace, all other elements will naturally spring to cont[r]act. I will not set up any artificial binary or hierarchy. I'm not going to expostulate with Derrida. There just isn't enough love between us. I intend to treat Derrida like an enthusiast. I think he would like it that way. For, at the end of the day, as dark clouds combine with autumnal sunset on the airport overpass to create a perfect pantomime of doom, what is our love of Art but an incestuous fuckfest with first icons INSERT RHETORICAL Q-MARK. Jacques Derrida returns to James Joyce like a psychopath. He is always 'after' Joyce in all senses of the word. And it is usually in association with the image of Babel. Joyce had the same relation to Shelley. He did not cite him often but when he did it was manically. I am going to deal with Derrida like an after-match interview. He had no time for formal theory. He just deployed piles of inter-related terminology, updated and partially revised, aping Joyce's renamings in *F(W)ake*, to create a kind of forced-field within which Theory could ricochet like Mallarme's chance but SOFT. Derrida wanted to leave theory hanging in a vault like fuzzy dice dangling over the rear-view mirror of a fast-moving car. Theory would have had to be defined like a chemical compound if it was a hard substance. He wanted it to become outsized and plush like a charm ornament. Derrida is the natural successor to Joyce. They are bound together but backwards in time like an anthropologist tied to a tomb ceremony. One can never apply enough similes to any analysis of Derrida because his writing is so oblique that it is only by simple metaphor that his mass of words can be somewhat discombobulated. We should always write about Derrida in the style of *F(W)ake*. This is pandering to his BIGGEST DREAM. But who am I to deny succour to a dying man? Pater always ended his plots the same way: letting his characters expire in some misguided misapprehension of a new brand patent of divine morphine. Joyce begins *F(W)ake* by introducing the character, Sir Tristram. He is described as a man in love and a noble knight who lives in a castle. By Page Five, he is excised from the text. Thus, Joyce explicitly promotes then abandons a conventional Romance trope in a clear breakage. It is a statement of defiance towards the un-writerly reader. The title of this episode would be "DEARREADER" if Derrida was an incidental character in *F(W)ake*. TBH he would have been delighted to be cast in any role especially dull, evil Kevin (AKA Shaun the Postman, Chuff, Jaun, Yawn, Primas, Justias, the new HCE et cetera). He was an extra on the set of *Apocalypse Now*. Europeans were in short supply in Manila in 1974. His Algerian heritage and equestrian skills got him work as a scimitar-wielding horseman on the set of many post-war romances set in the desert. He applied the precepts of Furūsiyya to his later academic work. Derrida could have played any male or female part in Mary Ellen Bute's movie of *Ulysses* (1965) except one which required wearing a boater. He would have looked fine delivering the new Irish stew speech. Derrida was a handsome man with silver bouffant and perforated lips, which were never allowed to camera-smile. This is ironic given Derrida's pre-occupation with Joyce and laughter. He felt Joyce was laughing at him all the time as a reader. He had bad teeth. Maybe his interest in laughter was a surrogate for that sour seductive gaze. Joyce would have employed comic variants to Derrida's name over the course of *F(W)ake* like "Dare Rey Duh" (farceolatteadough), Derridunbardun (a Scottish town) and "Der-riddler" (German + enigmatic wordsmith) as well as incorporating par-translations from other languages such as Dereidhur (Irshish). Like Derrida, Joyce got calibration out of partialised repetition. Material is put there to be repeated. The notion to be delineated (not defined) can thus assume its connotation-in-full because difference makes it 100% clear by default like a mandala. Blame Vico a bit but not much. Joyce re-enacts the fall-rise-fall principle. *F(W)ake* reverts to 1132 AD. This isn't even a date in historiographical terms. Joyce has just created an arbitrary numerological date and given it justification as usual. This is an entirely deconstructive act that shifts History from a focus on big events to the unchronicled places that billions of humans inhabited. At best, this date alludes to the rate of physical fall of an object (32 feet per second) as a metaphor for the descent of 'great men.' History recurs in four arcs. We were back at the Theocratic Stage by 1940, according to Joyce. From our modern perspective, how accurate was Joyce as a seer? Certainly, the Democratic Epoch seemed to be drawing to a close at the time of *F(W)ake*. It hung on grimly, however, slowly expanding its scope as Communism faltered. By 1989, it appeared triumphant. There was no sense that "the centre cannot hold" in Yeats' terms. Today, Stage One (god worship) has been skipped. We have progressed straight to Stage Two. Joyce was unable to predict the impact of technology, not being H. G. Wells or Virilio et al. This is the most important deduction in assessing Joyce's application of Vico. Not where we are NOW but whether we followed his cycles sequentially. In that sense, Joyce was wrong. Derrida is unique in ignoring Joyce's obsession with numerology. Joyce is rigorous in mathematical balance. The mother has 111 children and gives them 111 gifts over the course of *F(W)ake*. Cluff and Glugg fight in front of 29 girls of Saint Brides. Duchamp used plural 'bachelors' in *The Large Glass*. Note correspondence with Penelope and the suitors. Another interest in *F(W)ake* was pederasty. HCE is all over his daughter. Swift too was interested in girls. There are a lot of Freudian jokes about towers and stems. HCE built the city. ALP is its river. There is a whole tranche of puns about Bruno in the context of Irish legend, which now includes Joyce as a key figure. The whole critical edifice that Joyce composed to bolster *F(W)ake* became the target of internal satire-within-the-text. ALP's letter is clawed out of a heap by Belinda the Hen and subjected to blunt hermeneutics. Anthony Burgess makes *F(W)ake* appear so simple. In fact, he is too successful. *F(W)ake* is unattainable as product. It passes Derrida's gramophonic urge AROUND THE OUTSIDE. Burgess spends eleven pages cataloguing the narrative but only two pages on its language. This is totally upside-down. For Derrida, writing folds inwards according to a set sequence. He is the most methodical, predictable writer. But there is no overarching motto. Nothing to grasp. Aeolus blows the surface. Poseidon churns the substance of the text. Still, there is no maxim like "I am rewriting the *Odyssey* from the POV of the son" or "The Son must repeat the journey of the Father." It is only in exposition that Derrida becomes penetrable. This is his rhizome of structure: form an archi-graph > DRIVE westwards out of Dublin >

become gramophonic > keep south of Phoenix Park > close shapes on a page > misread Saussure somewhat > pass the Jameson's distillery on Bow Street > let word-burroughs arrange the order of soil penetration > dig your way out of Kilmainham Gaol > compose provocative slogans like 1968 > register a motif of obstruction (what Derrida calls by many different terms like 'specter' and 'differance') > trigger recognition of the Without (exterior/lack) > track the Liffey northwards-turning > huddle under a shower-fall of exemplars and qualifications > update repetition to strengthen the mould > become a ghost writer or *pharmakon* > arrive at Chapelizod. You can visit the Bristol Hotel, known as the Dead Man because drunk customers stumble out of its doors at closing time straight onto the tram tracks like Barthes getting smashed by a laundry truck on the Boulevard Saint Michel. His death-site was ironic given that Saint Michael is the cleaner of souls. The landlord of the pub is Humphrey Chimpden Earwicker, father of Isobel, which means Izod in Gaelic and gave to mythology the female name for the opera composed by Richard Wagner. His sons are the speaker Shaun and the scribe Shem. It is the writer who beats time. History only immortalises artists and warriors. Great rhetoricians like Socrates were only known by written records. Today, we have recordings of Joyce reading sections of the Aeolus episode in 1924 and the Anna Livia Plurabelle episode in 1929. In the future, there will be NO TEXT only RHETORIC. This is the logographic form of Vico's cycles. Logography for Derrida is simply Cyrano de Bergerac producing the script of *Krapp's Last Tape*. It is all the sharper because Cyrano cannot understand Roxane's speech. He fights language, attacking the air into which it is projected with his sword and dies in a verbal muddle. Joyce's text for *F(W)ake* sounded better when he read it onto tape. Etymological deconstruction continued apace. This ended badly at times in intractable compound and portmanteau words. But it is much easier to understand the sound and sense of new words when they are coming out of the author's mouth. For Derrida, speech/writing are bound together back-to-back like the outer skin of BOOK COVERS. Joyce succumbed to STYLISM in *F(W)ake*. He wanted to create a textual masterpiece that nobody could dilute only ever-increase. He sought to absorb all myths and words, covering their scanty bones obesely. He wanted to stuff everything into one encyclopedia. Inscription on paper is for the purpose of historical storage. *F(W)ake* is an archive of stuff. The cult of 'newness' associated with Joyce ended with *F(W)ake*. It was the first concept album. Like Sgt Pepper, he gave up after three songs and pulled it all together at the end with a reprise. *F(W)ake* made *Ulysses* appear antique, despite the patent failures of Joyce's new opus. This was the defect embedded in the 'new technology' of *F(W)ake* as per Virilio's dictum. The precursor flaw in *Ulysses* was that it left no alternative but to increase centripetal massing. What an arid volume *F(W)ake* represents. Joyce called *F(W)ake* a comic novel. It could not have been attempted with any other mode of emplotment. *Ulysses* was a romance. Joyce could never have written a tragedy or satire. He was too bureaucratic for tragedy and too humanistic for satire. He believed in harmony too longingly. He didn't want to see good people sacrificed. And he was liberal in his concept of goodness as well. He invested too much time in myths and legends to create a word-world riddled with folly that turned on chance. Like *Crash*, *F(W)ake* should probably have remained a *bon mot*: "make the last novel of Modernism with a title based on a word-joke." It's all too clever as a slogan. To turn a slapstick ballad into a Creed, that was the impossible paradox of *F(W)ake*. The title of course is a pun on HCE's awakening/coma and, missing the apostrophe in the ballad which gave the novel its name, a call to all Finnegans (Irishmen) to rise up. The resurrection of Tom Finnegan became Joyce's swerversion of Jesus. It could have been a parodic thrust full of sacrilege and loathing. But, like Swinburne, Joyce could never tell of blasphemy outright like Bataille. It had to be refracted through so much mandible language. Derrida is wrong to see Joyce as a kind of Brave Odysseus travelling freely INSIDE a field of culture bouncing off equivocations. In fact, Joyce was strangled with excruciating slowness by this approach over seventeen years of composing *Work in Progress*. He got away with it in *Ulysses* because it concentrated on a singular myth. By the time of *F(W)ake*, he was consumed by hubris. Joyce increasingly referred to its comic emplotment as the critical atmosphere around its reception darkened. He also defended it as 'music' to try to annex the Paterian notion of a composer's multi-layered score. Even his greatest supporters disowned it somewhat. He was forced to solicit puff-pieces from acolytes to prepare the way for publication. Joyce extolled the humour of *F(W)ake* with humourless harangues. It lacked the basic element of comedy: it could never go straight to DVD. There is very little of what Aristotle called *mythos* during any recital of Derrida. Everything is in motion in Derrida's garden yet nothing grows UPWARDS. His work is not arborescent, as defined by D&G. He produces only ground cover. There is no technical term for WEED. *Mimesis praxeos* is choked. As an arid breeze blows horizontally across the scalded surface of the notorious Chapter 6, this is all we read: Tom Hallem is going to score some drugs (mainly in the Joyce & Beckett sub-episodes); his brother is going towards a pub (these are simple acts of apposition); there is imminence of convergence; their biological father is driving a hire car west across Sydney; Bob Capri is driving in an easterly direction (these are simple acts of opposition); plus various pin-pricks of plot disclosure to de-suspend C7–11. Derrida is constantly slowing the reader with deconstruction. This runs against every instinct in today's brain. The reader gets caught in a Closing of the Gates. Always there is a moment of apprehension as the doors start to shut. Yet they never close fast enough to act as a trap. We never choose to fully withdraw either. The reader is caught in a moment of apprehension. The fridge door never fully seals. There is never absolute darkness.

Never "space but by no air taken." Never Sublime. There is no "negative pain (delight)," as Burke put it. Derrida is the least awe-inspiring writer of his contemporaries. There is no effusion in any of his scrolls. No revelations. Not even a dirty smear of sex. He is all data. He produces a surfeit of information like Lyotard's hype-machines. That is his interdiction. Joyce assumed the same stance in *F(W)ake*. The humanist sensuality of language in *Ulysses* has been abandoned. Joyce is carefully constructing an anthropological and mathematical text. Exclude the Borromean first and last lines. Also exclude the ALP speech, which Joyce felt was the most beautiful piece of writing in the English language. Censorship's decompression in the 1960s lifted the novelty of PROHIBITION from Joyce's work. He lost the PORNOGRAPHIC STATUS to Miller (Sex) and Burroughs (Guns). Their dissenting narratives suited the new world's needs for VIRTUAL EVIL once the REAL WORLD was broken. Joyce became a {parch/monu}ment. A TOURIST ATTRACTION FOR A CITY HE REJECTED. Today, you can visit the sites of a novel you will never read. There is a USER MANUAL. Its recycled paper cover contains a line drawing of a keyhole through which a gartered leg can be seen balancing a bowler hat on pointed stilettos. There are maps. It contains a 'major character' list. You can learn how to dress dolls in costumes of the early twentieth century. There is a temporal format for 6 June 1904. You can time plot | plot time (plotime). This timetable would have to be reordered if you wanted to make a physical tour of the sights of *Ulysses* in a straight-line from its south-easternmost point at Dalkey, where Stephen Dedalus taught, to Glasnevin cemetery in north-west Dublin, where Dignam's funeral was held. It would require a combination of short train rides and walking. They put statues and plaques all over Dublin to Joyce. It is a meta-city of Joyce's invention. He made it MODERN. They made it POST-MODERN. There is irony in this formula. For Dublin has been a backward place forever. In 2015, it reminded me of Sydney in 1984. Half de-built but as yet un-rebuilt. Sydney was a carceral. Dublin became one under British rule. Soon, every city in the world will operate under this arrangement. Alibaba founder Jack Ma said that smart cities powered by his computers and artificial-intelligence algorithms will make it possible to short-circuit security threats. "Bad guys won't even be able to walk into the square," he told a commission overseeing law enforcement in his birthplace, Hangzhou. '*Dubb linn*' means black pool in Gaelic. A Nigerian taxi driver warned me about razor gangs on the north side of the Liffey. They are called The Inner-City Crew. We had The Rocks Push. They thrived in the close, shadowy lanes of *fin de siecle* Sydney. This place was known as Tallawoladah by the Cadigal people. They built fires on top of its sandstone slopes to cook fish. It became the convict side of town across the Tank Stream. Eccles Street was all uphill. Bloom's house has been demolished. A hospital stands on the site today. A medical clinic over the road at Number 78 advertises itself as the Bloom

House. It has a bright yellow door. I got my picture taken outside it like a fan. Of course, the fictional Blooms lived at Number Seven. I relished this untruth. It acts as a *pharmakon* in Derrida's lexicon. He constantly made up neologisms to cross-out, supersede or change the nuance of his existing terminology. It is a sign leading one astray. The motive for its fabrication is unclear. I doubt it would improve the commercial performance of the clinic by attracting new patients. Perhaps it was pure mischief. Socrates lies down at this point in *Phaedrus*. A diagnosis can now be performed on the corpse. The doctor will act like the Egyptian King who receives the gift of writing in Socrates' parable. He will diagnose VALUE. It is the same trepidation felt by Barthes' author. Derrida specifically reverts to paternal symbolism at this point in *Plato's Pharmacy*: "the *pharmakon* is here presented to the father and is by him rejected, belittled, abandoned, disparaged." This is a common experience, especially paternal volition made clear by absence. TMAC is based on this type of personal history. The son in Derrida's instance is writing. Here, it is the writing of the son. This is a useful homonym for Chapter Six, which examines the herd of the sun god Helios. His father was Hyperion. He was a doomed Titan like James Joyce. INSERT QUOTE: "the specificity of writing would thus be intimately bound to the absence of the father." This is a perfect epitaph for this enterprise. Derrida goes on to offer a definition of the *pharmakon* that obviously corresponds to the predicament of Hamlet as well as Telemachus at the start of the *Odyssey*. He speaks of the impulse, "to have lost one's father, through natural or violent death, through random violence or patricide; and then to solicit the aid and attendance, possible or impossible, of the paternal presence ..." This passage begs the question of whether Shakespeare considered the Telemachiad in composing his play. Hamlet's voyage with Rosencrantz and Guildenstern equates to Telemachus' journey to Pylos and Sparta. Both act as the means of awakening the son to action/duty upon homecoming; albeit Hamlet's new-found WILL is based on parody and murder. Both episodes disclose the meaning of the FATHER. The Ox episode is a killing field. All of Odysseus' crew die. This is all the product of misguided rhetoric. Eurylochus' relentless speechifying connives to produce fatal consequences for the crew. Their feast is mirrored in the revelry of the medical staff in Joyce's episode. Joyce implies that this group will all die as well. Bloom becomes Odysseus in this trope. The critical difference to Homer is that Bloom is shepherding Stephen Dedalus from the pub. He thus supersedes the *Odyssey*. It should also be noted that Mulligan acts like Eurylochus in this episode. He is a complex individual. Contemptuous, rebellious and rude, yet also warning Odysseus about Circe's pig-magic on Aeaea and offering him wise counsel to visit Tiresias. The French theoretician who most resembles Eurylochus is Louis Althusser. We walked to the local high street past Saint George's Church. It had been deconsecrated and sold. The bells were relocated to

Dundrum. The pulpit was carved into pieces to decorate a pub. This sounds like chainsaw blasphemy. It was converted into a nightclub. Today, it is an office building. It is for sale on a net yield of 8.5 per cent. The hospital is an anchor tenant on a ten-year lease. Cushman & Wakefield are lead agents. It is remarkable that Joyce's powers of observation were not hampered by narcissism. I slipped on a frosted metal manhole cover on Earl Street South. Let's walk up Meath Street to the pub. Billy Capri overheard Professor Milkmaid state that Derrida was the logical heir to Joyce as he entered the Shakespeare Hotel. He embodied Plato's *Anamnesis*. Fresh cuts of lamb from Tony Martin Meats touching Hanbury Lane. "It is very late, it is always too late with Joyce," postulated Derrida at the start of "Two Words for Joyce." This sense of belatedness is understandable, especially in a person approaching Joyce in translation. It would have been faster to learn English than to translate *F(W)ake*, let alone wait to read Philippe Soller's translation. The six hundred pages of *F(W)ake* probably require 10 minutes reading time per page for full comprehension given its cryptic nature, making it an exercise of ~100 hours of sustained concentration staring at characters and blanks trying to make sense out of spoilt neologisms and portmanteau words spanning forty different languages and every mytheme known to humans. I don't think Derrida even uses the word 'late' again in this essay. It is just a Throwaway. In fact, his essay – which was originally a lecture and thus became 'gramophonic' – is about laughter, technology, his insecurities with Joyce and maybe liking him or not. Derrida picks a couple of incidental words – HE & WAR – deep in *F(W)ake* ("the reader can count the lines," as he says at the start of "*Plato's Pharmacy*") and presents them as Joyce's buried architypes. Frankly, he selects these two nondescript words from page 226 like an undergraduate student picking a short quotation from the middle of a book to try to trick the teacher into believing the whole thing has been read. Derrida could have picked any two words in *F(W)ake*, it's just that "HE WAR" came easily to hand at the end of Chapter One as Joyce launched into a parody of Old Testament fee fie faux fumb-led brimstone proselytising. Any reader can discern the core puns in this ungrammatical pairing. It is like the speech that comes out of the mouth of the savage when he talks of the late Mister Kurtz. HE DEAD. It became Eliot's great choice of epigraph. We can always channel Joyce in many directions. He was very systematic in streaming every possible derivation of each word selected for *F(W)ake*. That is why it took him seventeen years to write his o'pus. Seventeen years equates to seventeen episodes. As always with Joyce, it is all about superstitious numerology. The irony in his formula is that Joyce created MACH SPEED in *F(W)ake*, even as he wrote slowly, even as the reader is slowed by style. He wrote in anticipation of internet point-and-click. Of sound bites. Of code. He was proleptic. His brain was bigger, faster, more intrinsic than ours. We have to swallow our pride and accept the invitation to marvel at Joyce's memory in order to read

F(W)ake. It's like a cockpit with dozens of knobs and gauges which mean nothing to the passenger and are always spiking, dipping, recalibrating. That is the source of Derrida's weak (or maybe untranslatable) pun of always being "in memory of him" (Joyce). It's not like he's dead or even perceived in recollection. Derrida means that we're stuck in his head. This is the cause of Derrida's "resentment and jealousy" of Joyce. Nobody likes to feel stupid especially a scholar of Major Literature lodged at the cor(e-)p(l)us WITHIN. Derrida does himself no favours by selecting the words, HE WAR. HE WAR is easy to decipher. In fact, Derrida has given himself NO CHALLENGE AT ALL by selecting HE WAR. He could have picked apart the structure of *F(W)ake* like Brave A. Burgess. He could have wrestled with one of Joyce's one-hundred letter words (see pp. 3, 23,44, 90, 113, 257, 314, 332, 414, 424). These words became known as *thunder(s)clapswords* because the first example contains the term for thunder in multiple languages. McLuhan, Fiore and Agel deployed them as symbols for technology in *War and Peace in the Global Village*. Eric McLuhan turned *F(W)ake* into oral history, picking up his father's work, in *The Role of Thunder in "Finnegans Wake"*. The total of 1,001 letters in these words equates to the numerology of the masterwork of Arabian literature, *One Thousand and One Nights*, or *Alf layla wa-layla*. This will be the subject of a future work titled *Binary Nights* (1111101001_2). Marshall and Corinne McLuhan had six children: the eldest son, Eric, being followed by the twins, Mary and Teresa (Shem and Shaun), Stephanie (Issy), Elizabeth (Milly), and Michael (Rudy). Six is the most harmonious number. It is the number of days that god spent making earth. Mankind was made on the sixth day. Jesus was labelled a devil six times. There are six names for the serpent and six for the lion. Twelve is the number for administration. 666 is the symbol of the Antichrist. With HE & WAR, Derrida picked words so short and light, and his discourse is so SOFT, that he exacerbated the sense of insufficiency, almost ignorance, against Joyce of which he speaks so expressively, if not eloquently. Perhaps there is a deeper meaning, then, in Derrida's choice of HE & WAR because Derrida is really the one making WAR ... with Joyce. Joyce becomes the *pharmakon* who pulls down philosophy to the level of literature. Joyce tried to put everything – one hundred per cent of his version of Lyotard's Unpresentable – onto the page in *F(W)ake* by amplifying each WORD so that there was no insinuation left unstated, no undisclosed meaning. But he didn't show what it looked like when you strip the engine back to its skeleton-mechanics. HE didn't explain the process. His art was discursive, not incisive. It was a dissemination, not a confession. He foretold the rebuttal of Barthes' concept of death of the author. He created a mechanistic form of writing for this task – completely the opposite of automatic writing or oneiric registration. Joyce invented what is now known as technical fiction. To be clear: Joyce makes Derrida feel like a dunce. Derrida looks like a handyman next to Joyce. He is an enthusiastic amateur like Darwin with fancy dog breeders and pigeon fanciers. Like all great critics, Derrida was more at home in centripetal massings than outlandish facts. That's why Derrida tried to shovel everything into Joyce: all cultures, histories, languages, religions, mythologies, philosophies, sciences, literature, even modern psychology. Socrates was the midwife for birthing knowledge as we know it in Western cosmology. Joyce is the de-liverer for Derrida disemvoweling langwich in Helios' Cattle. He is Odysseus to Derrida's Eurylochus. Derrida killed Joyce with Illegal love like Oedipus. Upploud becomes uppalouderamain becomes upplause. Derrida got everything back-to-front on Joyce. In fact, it is still so early with Joyce that we haven't really gone ANYWHERE, like Derek Attridge said. Literature has shrunk from Joyce, unlike the plastic arts which have always tried to EXCEED his doppelganger, Marcel Duchamp. In English, nobody has tried to compete with Joyce in sustained contest. There has been no *Agon*. He is Achilles and everybody knows he will kill you. There has been no Hector. What were Hector's motives? To show how to fail. To demonstrate to humanity that IT IS NOBLER THAN THE GODS. There are plenty of literary critics who have written exhaustively on *F(W)ake*. But there are NO STORIES. No *Clinamen*. Technology has not been deployed to this task yet. The internet hasn't been tested as a means to out-encyclopediate Joyce. We aren't speeding past Joyce ON THE OUTSIDE or WITHIN. Lyotard, Virilio and Baudrillard would all recommend this approach. There can be no *Tessera* because Joyce is seen as complete. We have capitulated to halt like Zeno's arrow. We are always calculating ways NEVER TO REACH JOYCE. Modern theoreticians like Derrida have engaged Joyce from the parallel track but they never truly threatened to puncture his afflatus. This is due to the fact that their TEXTS are fundamentally incompatible with Joyce, being NON-FICTIVE. They don't have the skills in storytelling to challenge him. Joyce was a master of the art by the time he had finished the short stories in *Dubliners*, his bildungsroman, *PAYM*, and the pinnacle of Modernism, *Ulysses*. Philosophers can construct fabula, tropes, plots and even full modes of emplotment in their indentured, unlikable works. But no genuine CHARACTER has been created in modern philosophy like Plato's Socrates. One who is human all and too human. In fact, philosophy these days takes pride in producing non-humanist imbroglios. They have confused Joyce's symbolistic interest in Borromean knots for an archetype. There is no interchange of voices. It is all didactic. Too soon it is then for Joyce. Too soon because he has never been tested with his weapon of choice. Joyce should be treated as a fencing opponent. Derrida is wrong to speak of readers "being in memory of him." In fact, we are lodged in quite the opposite tendency. Rather than having to "inhabit his memory," Joyce must be made to spring out of our heads as Athena from Zeus. We use the term 'Joyce' as a way of defining the outermost limits of our grasp on language and fiction. He has become extrinsic space. Nobody reads Joyce anymore.

We only observe his spine on a bookshelf. We "take the word of" Wikipedia about him. Or we rely on some analyst, some mediator, to learn of him. This has turned *F(W)ake* into a success because its hermeneutics are strong. But is it TRULY A STORY, in the sense of a satisfactory piece of fiction? We must leave aside all jargon and ask that basic question as if we were George Orwell. *F(W)ake* is undoubtedly a failure. Yet who can honestly say that they are an EXPERT on Joyce? Even I, with my decades of stuck-in-this-book-existence, find Joyce always just out of reach, his archi-ecriture scattering then re-conglomerating into a familiar-sounding yet indecipherable language, like an English speaker listening to Dutch. A search for Derrida in Google Images discloses some book-covers, a few early campus headshots and a series of highly stylised mature portraits always shot from the left-hand side and dominated by his rich shock of fine silver hair. His biography in Wikipedia can be itemised thus:

— Born 15 July 1930, in El Biar (French Algeria) to a Sephardic Jewish family originally from Spain. Third of five children.
— His parents named him Jackie after the actor Jackie Coogan, who played the urchin in Chaplin's *The Kid*. Cheap sentimentality became a hallmark of his writing.
— On the first day of school 1942 (age 12), he was expelled by French administrators implementing anti-Semitic quotas set by the Vichy government.
— He dreamed of becoming a professional football player.
— He adopted the formal version of his first name when he moved to Paris in 1949. The double mark "Jackie/Jacques" (young/mature; light/solemn; informal/ponderous) came to dominate his discourse (he could never expunge the sentimental spirit of being co-joined Jackie from his writing).
— He studied at Harvard in 1956–57, spending the academic year in the library reading *Ulysses*.
— In June 1957, he married psychoanalyst Marguerite Aucouturier. Their first child, Pierre, was born in 1963. A second son, Jean, was born in 1967. A third son, Daniel, born in 1985. The mother this time was Sylviane Agacinski, who later married French Prime Minister Lionel Jospin. This sequence of unions is redolent of the Classical tradition of women being used as strategic chattels like Hermione or Briseis. Subject matter should always disclose Political Systems.
— During the Algerian War, Derrida was exempt from military service (1957–59). There was a fear that he would become a terrorist.
— In 1964, got a permanent teaching position at the École Normale Supérieure, which he held until 1984. This was like signing with Manchester United.

— His paper at the Colloquium on Structuralism in 1966 led to international prominence. This is the equivalent of scoring a goal in the FA Cup Final.
— In 1967, he published three books — *Writing and Difference*, *Speech and Phenomena* and *Of Grammatology*. These books made his name (as Dearreader). He published a new book every year from 1973 to 1980. This sustained level of output has only been matched by Bob Dylan.
— Derrida traveled widely and held a series of visiting and permanent positions. He was awarded many honorary doctorates. His love of heraldry and costume is well documented.
— In 2003, he was diagnosed with pancreatic cancer. He died in Paris on 8 October, 2004.

I don't mourn Derrida. He is not an acquaintance. I have got other issues to deal with. I still think about my brother most days. It doesn't decrease over time. He has become irreplaceable through death, as Derrida puts it when he remembers Paul de Man. His demise diminished my world view somewhat. It did not make me fear death. On the contrary, it gave me the prospect of companionship when I cross Styx. Currently, I am dying off my parents. Derrida postulated that death is our passage to individuality because it is irreproducible. Each death is unique. You can't be killed twice. Therefore, it is an immortalising act. Thus, only someone dead is immortal. And the immortals are all dead. Stripped of ironic gameplay, this is a very Romantic notion in a bathetic sense. Timing/ placement of death is critical to Derrida, although he never discloses the best mode of death. THE MOMENT OF DEATH IS THE ONLY <u>COMMON</u> SUBLIME IN ALL HUMANITY. V. Woolf said that her own death would be the "one experience I shall never describe." This is usually interpreted as a statement of subject scope. In fact, it is an acknowledgement of the inadequacy of language in front of the UNIVERSAL SUBLIME OF DEATH. Otherwise, she could have easily jotted down some notes. I am told Derrida died in hospital with his three sons, his ex-wife, some former mistresses and extended family surrounding his bed. This sounds like a death scene from a sentimental French moral comedy by Eric Rohmer. But, of course, Rohmer never made films about old people, only girls, despite Balzacious output. Derrida would be played by David Duchovny in a Hollywood biopic. Studies of patients with pancreatic cancer indicate that the primary issue is pain control. Forty-four per cent of palliative care patients with pancreatic cancer record severe pain. So, Derrida and pain were thus almost a 50:50 proposition. He would have chuckled at these odds. He loved gambling. Pain syndromes with pancreatic cancer occur due to its proximity to a wide variety of other organs: the duodenum, liver, stomach, jejunum and transverse colon. The pancreas itself is innervated by nerve networks that interact with both the parasympathetic and sympathetic systems. Pain may be felt at multiple – and even distant – sites as a consequence. The character, quality and temporal nature of this pain will worsen as illness progresses. Yet pain is the aspect of cancer that is most readily treatable with drugs. Derrida refuted Plato's separation of cure from poison by showing that good and bad medicine always mix. Oral analgesics alone provide relief for 90% of pancreatic cancer patients. Thesis: Derrida may have been comfortable in his last days due to a drugged and sedated state. Antithesis: Joyce died at an impossible juncture. Omens abounded in the months leading up to his death. Lucia's mental health remained his principal concern. She was stuck in an asylum in a remote location that was difficult to access in wartime. Helen Joyce had another breakdown. George took custody of Stephen. His wife left for the States. Paris' wartime blackouts made life difficult for a par-blind man with a stick. "We're going downhill fast," he told Beckett. He also felt frustrated that the war was diverting attention from *F(W)ake*. The negative reception to his new work grated. He virtually stopped eating from 1939. The family spent months at a time in Saint-Gerand-le-Puy (St GleP) in central France near Vichy. Stomach pains blighted his nights until the wine kicked-in then he would sing "Ye Banks and Braes" and other Irish airs. Dancing down narrow stairs to the tune of the traditional waltz, "Come on, let's dance a little," he said to Missus Jolas, "you know very well that it's the last Christmas." Joyce was a dog hater. He carried stones in his pockets to launch at them. He clobbered them with his stick if they got within range. On Sunday mornings, he would sit up in bed until lunchtime recounting stories of Ulysses to his grandson Stephen. Like Churchill, he had an astounding memory. The Nazis occupied St GleP for six days before the Armistice. A mortally ill woman died while Joyce was attending her. Securing Swiss visas was a venal process. The family finally got visas on 29 November 1940, after intervention from high-ranked friends. They still needed French approvals to depart the country. News of the death of Nora's mother traumatised them. The new Swiss visas were only valid until 15 December 1940. On 14 December, they finally got French approvals but they still needed to get to the rail station to catch the last train. This became like a classic chase scene. They borrowed a car. George managed to purchase one gallon of petrol. The train schedule was: Geneva – Lausanne – Zurich. Thus, James Joyce returned to the city in which he had arrived with enthusiasm and confidence in 1914. Ruggiero kept throwing his damn hat on Joyce's bed ignorant of the superstition that it forebodes death. The old man bought his grandson marzipan and chocolate. He went walking with the little boy in the snow. Xmas 1940 was spent at the Giedion's house singing songs in Latin and Irish whilst drunk. On 7 January 1941, Jim sent his last postcard to Stanislaus in Florence offering a list of people to help with the Italian authorities. "Thursday, 9 January 1941 – dinner at Kronenhalle." Mrs Zumsteg tried to tempt Joyce with his favourite treats. But he could not eat. Just drink. At 11.30 pm, Nora slipped on the stairs. It was a bad omen. Back at the hotel, Joyce was suddenly overcome by stomach cramps. A doctor was called who administered morphine. It offered no relief. They summoned an ambulance. Joyce was strapped into a stretcher writhing in agony like a fish and taken to the Schwesterhaus vom Roten Kreutz. On Saturday 11 January 1941, the hospital took X-rays. He was diagnosed with a perforated duodenal ulcer. Banking authority was organised for Georgio. At 10 am, Dr H. Freysz performed surgery. It appeared successful. JJ sat up in bed and spoke to Nora. But on Sunday 12 January 1941, he started to weaken. Transfusions were provided by two Swiss soldiers. Joyce entered a coma that afternoon. On Monday 13 January 1941 at 1 am, Joyce woke and asked for Nora or George then lapsed back into coma. He died before they reached the hospital at 2.15 am. Nora agreed to the construction of a death mask. It has become a famous image, reproduced in countless biographies and critical studies. The mask is now located at the James Joyce Tower and Museum, Sandy Cove Point, Dun Laoghaire. When Lucia Joyce was told of his death, she replied: "what is he doing under the ground, that idiot? When will he decide to come out? He's watching us all the time." Instinctively, she grasped at a correspondence with Plato's *Anamnesis*. D&G would consider this image as Joyce-down-a-burrow. He was buried next to Zurich Zoo so he could hear the lion's roar. SYNTHESIS: Joyce's choice of the novel as a creative form enabled him to release his humanity. It came from WITHIN. He could never replicate it in drama as Ibsen did. By contrast, Derrida's humanism was displaced by theoretical writing until the belated epiphany of *Mournings for Paul de Man*. It has always been a case of YES/MAYBE between us. Derrida sees the Signifier and the Signified in One. He contends that the Signified can never be attained. For him, words can only be defined by summoning other words to support them so that 'real' meaning is forever deferred by an endless chain of Signifiers. Yes, he builds a Tower of Babel. So he and I are actually MAYBE/ALMOST. Tom Hallem expired with everything lost. It is the totalness of his death that appalls me. It was a terrible Sublime. I hate myself for delaying my response to his last entreaties. Derrida's concept of mourning is based on a perfect tone between friends. But I mourn him as dissonance. He is still "present tense." He never closes. He always remains PRESENTTENSE. How many linguistic atoms must I squander on regret? How many binaries can be interdicted on the subject of fratricide? INSERT LIST: Celebrate/violate; birth/death; lodge/inscribe; keep/burn; stabber/stabbed; Joyce/Derrida; Romulus/Remus; Cane/Abel; Eteocles/Polynices; Claudius/Hamlet; Edgar/Edmund. Archives are an institution of repetition and updating. They require a system like Dewey who used the numbers, the alphabet and time. Every repetition is individualised by context. It becomes a new outpost: a salient that is further refined by the enemies' response. Derrida/Joyce are a double mark repeated: Joyce is the first stroke (/) and Derrida the last (\). The son must repeat the journey of the father. Repeat the journey in a different format. Or shrink in scale until minute. Counting words like fleas in a dog's coat. Did our father (HCE) establish the rules for the death of his son (WAR) when he re-entered our lives packed with dim symbolism (1984) from a far, surdy battlefield (BABELIAM)? It is sum peeriodd in tiem nowra synce Dearreader rote and even(t) languer synce Joys Shemself beastrodden the stayge (Steve Jobs would have termed this place a 'mutability platform'). Ye toady their embers R staypuddled totether LOCHD in d'arche-ness uprepentdead their slangwich dis-solved in2 plasterseen bredcrumbells. Vee Co. turnstyles the crinkly-crank unclotwise. The sighcle of fog-getting N rivereviewruns is wowndown. **Why is pancreatic cancer not diagnosed earlier?** Primary cancer does not always kill the patient. It is often secondary cells – or metastases – that dispose of the human body. Cancer cells break from the host and tour the blood stream, lymph system, even body spaces such as the abdominal cavity, attaching to normal cells all over the place. Sarcomas, for example, spread through the bloodstream. This is what happened to Michel Foucault and Leon Daniel. Pancreatic cancer prefers a lymphatic route. This makes it hard to diagnose quickly. Eventually, Levi-Strauss recognised the danger for Jews in France and escaped on the *Captaine Paul-Lemerie*. He slept on a makeshift pallet under a straw mattress. Passengers on the overcrowded vessel crapped in a zinc trough. It was emptied port side to shield the faeces from the prevailing wind. This avoided blowback onto deck. Everyone was always hyper-vigilant, almost hysterical due to the preponderance of Nazi submarines. This must have been what Odysseus' crew felt as they scoured the sea for evidence of Poseidon. Seaspray lashing their faces. Wild with survival and knowing his hate and their looming death. A single cancer cell starts the process of colonisation. Each type of primary cancer has a preferred pattern of metastases. But the location of metastases is not determined by an infallible system. The only thing we can say for sure is that the form of a specific cancer never changes. It stays true to type wherever it gains harness. For pancreatic cancer, tumours in the liver are a common form of metastasis and a cause of rapid death. **When is curative surgery possible?** Generally surgical treatment, by resection or removal of the tumour, can be pursued if the cancer is still localised. This means that the cancer has not spread to any blood vessels, lymph nodes or other organs, such as the liver or lung. Run each sub-episode into the new one. Create a prosenchymatic path. Tissues of interconnecting narrative cells. There was a North African fugitive with a stolen Degas in his suitcase on the board. Breton was always trying to induce automatic events. Random assemblages. Irrational awareness. Set Breton against Saussure (also the art of surgery). Juxtapose symbols in Breton's vision of a hung ox carcass, ship flags and Homeric dawn. Levi-Strauss observing him wrapped in an overcoat despite tropical heat looking like a big blue bear. Make the sky into a painting in a gilt frame. It sounds like some Rene Magritte image. **How should a surgeon handle non-curative cases?** In Stage 4, it is time to help the patient and family make the decision between palliative chemotherapy and expedited death. Intensive chemotherapy occasionally results in dormancy. There is a case where the metastases disappeared from the liver and the tumour had shrunk by 80 per cent after 9 rounds of Chemo. The physician must avoid any language which could create false expectations in the patient or family. Chemotherapy should NOT be presented as a potential means to cure. Dormancy is as good as remission in this instance. **What interventions can be made to alleviate discomfort?** There are various options outlined in Chapter Five. For example, a stent can be fitted from the liver to stop jaundice and acid accumulation. A small dose of steroids can be administered to ameliorate the symptoms of trapped gas. Provisional weight gain might become apparent after this treatment. The patient may show improved energy. This could have a flow-on impact on mood. Any positivity should always be tempered by the physician. It is only a hiatus in a process ending in certain death. They gave Tom large doses of steroids while he waited for his heart transplant. This produced a miraculous improvement in his appearance. For a few weeks, he resembled a young man again. His tone brightened. This intermission ended after the operation. He never looked that good again. The medical procedures outlined in this chapter are a direct metaphor for the scientific and mathematical characteristics of Joyce and French theoreticians. **What types of surgical procedures are performed to treat pancreatic cancer?** This depends where the tumor is located within the pancreas. Cancer in the head, neck or uncinate process of the pancreas can be treated with the Whipple Procedure. Cancer in the body or tail of the pancreas can be subject to distal pancreatectomy and splenectomy. Note my father's spina bifida babies. Also, Chaim. And Richie's son. Doctor Peat turned the load of my daughter's pelvis onto his forearm, slipped a finger into the back of O's vagina to flick free the baby's legs, let her salmon-scaled back flow into his latex palms then turned her crazed face to the striplights. Later, they banned natural breech births based on the findings of a definite study of perinatal mortality in the UK. Frank Zappa was a breech birth. Frank Sinatra also. And Kaiser Wilhelm. Derrida may have developed diabetes in the months before he was diagnosed with cancer. This can be an early warning sign. It is quite common for pancreatic cancer to appear in people aged in their early seventies like Derrida. It usually metastasises in the liver. The abdomen becomes distended. Psychological state may deteriorate. These are all signs of disease.

KRISTEVA (1) – SOLLERS

One can speak of Kristeva without mentioning Sollers but it is convenient in this case because of her husband's obsession with James Joyce. One must remain perpetually cognisant of the woman/man issue in France. ADD NOTE ON FEMALE CHARACTERS (PENELOPE, HELEN, ELIZ, O, ANA, EVEN MANHOLE, JUDY, XIAO FANG). Let us get Sollers out of the way like a secret before we deal with Kristeva. A focus on spoken language first drew Sollers toward Joyce, a fellow Catholic also educated by Jesuits. He translated *Finnegans Wake* with Stephen French into English. But Joyce is much more than poetry for Philippe Sollers. He is a political writer. Sollers called *Finnegans Wake* "the most formidable anti-fascist book produced between the two wars." This acknowledges the intense political atmosphere of the period. Much the same thing could have been said of *Ulysses*. Joyce was composing it through the period climaxing in the Easter Uprising of 1916. The fact of the British Empire consumes the narrative of *Ulysses* from the Eugenics of Garrett Deasy and Haines to the vice-regal cavalcade and Private Carr's assault on Stephen Dedalus. It is ever-present in dialogue between characters. We pass through places like Phoenix Park where The Invincibles assassinated Cavendish and Burke. We imbibe different opinions about Parnell. He died in 1891. We see his surviving brother in the corner of a restaurant eating lunch and playing chess. Simon Dedalus is the archetypal Parnell Tragic. He was the type of figure who inspired intense admiration. Gladstone called him the most remarkable man he ever met. Asquith said he was one of the top three or four men of the nineteenth century. Haldane considered him the most powerful presence in the House of Commons in the last 150 years, a period that featured Peel, Pitt, Melbourne, Wellington, Disraeli and Wilberforce. Joyce draws a subtle parallel between the fall of Parnell and the slide in the Dedalus family fortunes. Parnell is now revered as the preeminent person in making Ireland feel like it could become an independent nation. He was the son of a wealthy Anglo-Irish landowner and his American wife. He was protestant like Beckett. A member of the Church of Ireland. Parnell could not speak Gaelic. The literary scene in Dublin was enlivened by the political impact of preserving and disseminating the Irish national language. The Citizen is a chauvinistic nationalist. Gifford suggests this character was based on Michael Cusack, who founded the Gaelic Athletic Association. This outfit harassed people who watched English sports like rugby and soccer. Richard Ellmann believes that Joyce modelled the character of The Citizen in part on his younger self as an observation on the bigotry of his early writings. It is easy to attribute egocentrism and opportunism to Sollers due to his high profile as a publisher and controversial public figure as well as the relentless autobiographical focus of his novels. This is ironic given that he often used secret agents as his protagonists or created characters who acted like spies, even down to the act of writing itself becoming covert. It is convenient to link this theme with the claim that Julia Kristeva was purportedly a Bulgarian spy. What a paradox is Sollers. He claims not to always deal with facts. He doesn't even use his real name – Sollers being as false as Bob Dylan or Johnny Beatle. His wife sometimes uses her married name, which is Julia Joyaux. She allegedly went by the codename Sabina. His *nom de plume* means 'clever' in Latin. Sollers has been leading a sanctimonious truth-attack for the last fifty years. Kristeva requested that she only give oral testament to her Bulgarian handlers. She avoided the written word. This means that the dossier released by Bulgarian SPECTRE does not contain any example of her hand-writing. Thus, it will remain forever an enigma. A baseless charge. FAKE NEWS. Sollers would be familiar with LACK OF HARD EVIDENCE from his novel, *Le Secret*. Its plot turns on a letter never sighted like Poe's tale. There is a school of thought that this novel is a proxy confession by Kristeva delivered by her partner. The Parisian literary scene was deeply affected by the suppression of the Prague Spring. It operated in the vanguard of industrial action in France. Sollers journal, *Tel Quel*, and its stable of writers including Kristeva, Derrida and Barthes, turned from the pro-Moscow French Community Party to embrace Maoism. The Bulgarians were dismayed. Pierre Ryckmans pilloried them in works like *Broken Images* (French translation, 1976). Like Sollers, he used a pseudonym, Simon Leys. Kristeva's letters requesting visas for her parent's form part of her official file. There is disgruntled marginalia about Kristeva always wanting something but offering nothing in the way of good intel in return. One bureaucrat wrote, "Sabina is employing the same tactics once again." Vladimir Kostov was the Bulgarian spy who apparently groomed Kristeva. He was almost killed in a poison umbrella attack in Paris in 1978. Sollers would be pleased with this kind of peculiar fact. It is far more bizarre than fiction. It was a standard Bulgarian assassination technique. The dissident writer Georgi Markov was stabbed at a bus stop with an umbrella tip laced with Risin. He died in days. When the government fell in 1989, a cache of modified umbrellas capable of firing miniature darts and pellets was found in the Interior Ministry. Bulgaria's State Security operated a network of 10,000 agents. This was a popular numeral in the Bible. It is used 45 times, whereas it is only used once in the Koran. An abacus ends at this number. It is called WAN in Mandarin. Armies and victims were all assessed as totaling this sum. It was popular with Saint Paul. Ten thousand is also the number of the Swastika. This was the total quantity of truths concerning the mysteries of the universe. In pecuniary terms, $10,000 in 1940 when Joyce was alive would be worth $170,000 today. Kristeva was ranked in the Top 100 thinkers of the Twentieth Century by *Foreign Policy* magazine. The Bulgarian dossier is full of contradictions. Elsewhere, it states that Kristeva was recruited by Ivan Bozhikov in 1971. It's impolite to say that Sollers is a mediocre novelist. His concepts are predictable. His forms are lame. But he gave postmodernism a NAME. He made it into a 'thing.' This is the opposite goal to P-MOD, frankly. It should never be set in stone. It is a water form. Sollers is a reductive thinker. His novel, *Femmes*, is a typical example. He always writes in displaced personas. The main character Will is a misogynist. He is not 100% Sollers. But still the text springs from Sollers. He must take responsibility for Will. There is a deep well-spring of hatred for women in Sollers. His female characters are perpetual clichés. In *Femmes*, he reduces them to coitus-types: Diane, Flora and Deb. His attempts at parody are inane like the acronym WOMANN (I won't bother decoding it). *Femmes* is a crass book. Sollers always seems to be trying to recapture hegemony. In interviews with his wife, he is found hovering around the microphone with beverages; butting-in to modify Kristeva's talk; citing differences of interpretation; putting her down; encouraging her to turn the subject to him. He invented the Essay-Novel genre. Some critics would see his influence on TMAC. I had never even heard of Sellers until 2018. His interest in painting, and specifically Watteau, is another accidental correspondence. He coined the term 'readable novels' for his later commercial work. It could have been him instead of Umberto Eco cashing in on human interest in medieval monastery mysteries (MMMs). Sollers is crazy about acronyms like "MRI." It's a television crime show affectation. Sollers has used the term, Multiple Related Identities, since he wrote *Femmes*. They are always Sellers himself. He played four main characters and seventeen minor ones in the movie including the iconic Bluebottle and Henry Crun. Sollers concocted feeble sobriquets like Froissart, which refers to the chronicler Jean Froissart as well as the verb, *Froisser*, meaning (1) to offend and (2) to crease. Of course, it also contains the English word 'art.' Slight misspellings and renaming's feature throughout his work. *La Fête à Venise* derides the mercantilism of modern art and examines the lucrative traffic in forgeries. This is another theme common to TMAC, albeit it is treated by the author in a more pragmatic fashion. My interest in Watteau arises from Walter Pater. It would be interesting to know if Sellers ever read Pater. He began each character with a VOICE. This is apposite to Pater's notion that all art aspires to the condition of music. Kristeva would term this 'semi(idi)otic.' He was an early adoptee of the philosophy of Guy Debord regarding Life Directly Lived (LDL). LDL is a little like Pater burning always with a hard gem-like flame. Debord wrote of modern tourism well in advance of the debasing spectacle of sight-seeing in Dublin today. His definition of this pastime as "fundamentally nothing more than the leisure of going to see what has become banal" is a perfect summation of our times. Debord produced excellent maxims. It is a shame he died in 1994 at the age of sixty-three. His insights on information and communications technology would be invaluable. Seller's characters are always making up stories and plots to conceal their true purpose. He believes that fiction can produce better insights than histories or journalism. This is the core premise of *Being There*. That, and mistaken identity. And also the manipulative practices of the media in modern politics. Sollers would be comfortable with all those tropes. It is not a pioneering theory when you consider the social impact of historical novels by Dickens, Zola and INSERT. Sellers came from a family of entertainers. He was christened Richard Henry but was always known as Peter, after a stillborn brother. He remained an only child. His mother was Jewish like Molly Bloom. They shared an unnatural bond. He learnt the ropes in the family theatre at Infracom. Sollers believed that images had usurped the word in line with Debord's concept of the Spectacle. He was a renowned Ladies Man. His most famous romance was with the Swedish actor Britt Ekland. These liaisons became the subject of his novel, *Les Femmes*. INSERT PRESS RELEASE EXTRACT: "The novel follows the adventures of Will, a misogynist, novelist and journalist under surveillance by extreme feminist groups who wish to establish a matriarchy." One reviewer wrote: "Editor of the avant-garde French review *L'infini*, Sollers writes a relatively predictable postmodern novel called *Women* about an editor of an avant-garde French review writing a relatively predictable postmodern novel called *Women* that will be published under the name of his literary friend who apparently is none other than, well, Philippe Sollers." This sardonic put-down encapsulates the flaw in Sollers' technology of Relentless Self. He excelled in the role of flamboyant American television playwright, Clare Quilty. Kubrick expanded his involvement in *Doctor Strangelove*, asking Sellers to portray three different characters. Sollers owes much to Nabokov. Unfortunately, he never learned how understatement in self-referentiality was integral to Nabokov's art. A review by Deirdre Sackerson concludes: "A best-seller in France that's often comic and always disconcerting – but never as new as it wants to be. Besides the fact that the reader never for a minute believes that Will and his wife are supposed to be from the southern US, the novel's blatant self-reflexivity, hyper-literary name-dropping, and relentless plotlessness seem dated by now. Antiseptically intellectual, this one smells of the classroom." Link to thesis assessment. Thank her for the inspiration/template for TMAC. The way in which close correspondences can be drawn from arbitrary coincidences like similar surnames is highlighted in this sub-episode. Like Joyce and Stephen Dedalus, Sellers did not leave the film set to visit his dying mother. My greatest fear is that I am too much like the weak side of Philippe Sollers. French literature is governed by a simple gender rule according to Coquillat: man is transcendence, woman a contingency. Even Marguerite Duras adheres to this theory. We can see it in her racial works. In *Hiroshima Mon Amour*, female agency is lost incrementally. Initially, the actress seems independent. She becomes increasingly hysterical. Near the end of the movie, she is wandering drunk. Eventually, she regains her composure with the help of the returning male. This is a familiar trope. The male character remains resolute. It is SHE who must give up time and space to stay at his place. She lost her hair as a traitor. Locals in Hiroshima lost their hair from bombs. We see her story as a flashback. It is a stupid story of uncontrolled love. The political dimension of the Occupation was lost on her. She is just another "Juliet emotion." Jean-Luc Godard called it "the first film without any cinematic references." This must have been a joke because it was a simple retelling of the 1942 Academy Award–winning masterpiece, *Casablanca*.

KRISTEVA (2)

Joyce's portrayal of women was famous for physical genuineness. Molly Bloom farts, masturbates, gets cramps and starts to menstruate (see Table 16, C9). She makes sure that coition with Boylan occurs before her period commences. Christian women have been wise to hide their blood from men. It only creates violence. Molly compares penis sizes. She is not disparaging. This is an important difference with men in *Ulysses*. The very existence of Molly Bloom as the active agent at the climax of *Ulysses* was not typical at the time that Joyce was writing. To get inside her mind as a practical, hard-headed person as she makes a rational decision about whether to recommit to her marriage is refreshing after the brain fevers, sprained ankles and victims of Victorian fiction, not to mention the torture, gang rapes and murders in contemporary media. There had always been independent female characters in English literature. They were written by both women and men. They can be seen as sovereign individuals or patriarchal victims or somewhere in-between (in a liminal, post-structuralist state) depending on your spin. Moll Flanders and Fanny Hill fit into this formula. Also, Emily and Alisoun in *The Canterbury Tales*. Chaucer was the origin of strong female characterisation in English. The twenty-four stories which make up *The Canterbury Tales* contain a host of women who want more than just survival. They want economic power and independence. Exploration of parity in marriage is a major theme of Chaucer. Women are seen in fully-human terms in a clear precedent of Joyce. There is the famous narrative of the Wife of Bath; sexually liberated, comic Alisoun; the wily widow of the Friar's Tale; the re-worked *fabliau* of the Merchant's Tale concerning clever May; the secret gender equality in the marriage between Arveragus and Dorigen in the Franklin's Tale (which is much more sophisticated than its model, Boccaccio); and the envoy after the Clerk's Tale who advises women to disregard Griselda's passivity. It also contains the sexually abused women of The Reeves' Tale, who are chattels in a revenge motif, human sacrifices to lust and injustice, as well as the wife of Phoebus, who was executed for adultery. Later, *P&P*, *Emma*, *Jane Eyre*, *Persuasion* and *W.H* turn on "half savage and hardy" women rejecting social patterns and put-downs to pursue self-realisation. This theme evolved into political activism with the Wollstonecraft-Godwin family, which spawned Mary Shelley. *Aurora Leigh* was perhaps the best exposition of feminist issues in nineteenth century poetry. *Vanity Fair* showed that a male novelist could build complex female characters. Emmy Sedley and Becky Sharp were later updated as Em and Lyndall in *Story of an African Farm*. *Middlemarch* accounts for the life of Dorothea Brooke in the Midlands region, where David Lawrence would later make his mark. It was a precursor to the exploration of woman-as-survivor in *Portrait of a Lady*. Eliot herself relocated from Coventry to London to live with George Lewes, accepting rejection by her family. All these works fed into Molly Bloom. Joyce had no examples of such a person in his life until he met his wife Nora Barnacle, who eloped with him in 1904. Later, he was supported financially and practically by women. *Ulysses* owes its existence to the commitment of women. The principal cast was Marsden, Anderson, Heap, Beach and Weaver. Later, we can add typists like Cyprian Beach, Raymonde Linossier and Mrs Harrison (Typist Nine). The Sunwise Turn bookshop in America was co-owned by a woman. It had a list of people willing to act as middlepersons for *Ulysses* as contraband. They were ALL WOMEN. INSERT INTO FEMINIST ANALYSIS. Emma Goldman was an anarchist. Joyce was a revolutionary as well. He thought of *Ulysses* as a bomb. His letters to them reveal no gender prejudice. Joyce depicted women's conditions in *Ulysses* unsparingly – the religious mania of Stephen's mother; his sisters' abject poverty and limited hopes; the romantic illusions of Martha Flower and Gerty McDowell; and the protracted labour of Missus Mina Purefoy. Women are restricted to certain workplaces in *Ulysses*. They work as barmaids, servants and prostitutes. They are subject to conventional sexism. All male characters voyeurise women and categorise them according to physical appearance. Any sign of sexuality is interpreted as perversion. Molly Bloom is the principle victim of this trope. Joyce has been analysed extensively by feminist critics. Their assessment has changed with the times. It is pertinent to remember Joyce's starting place. *Ulysses* was set in 1904 in a provincial location under the oppressive influence of the Catholic Church. Joyce was shielded from the increased role of women in the labour force during the Great War by virtue of his domicile in Switzerland. Frontier societies like Australia and South Africa tried to perpetuate social stereotypes. However, the facts of existence – especially in rural areas – required a loosening of rigid gender roles. Australia produced a series of major female writers beginning with Barbara Banyton, Rosa Praed, Ada Cambridge and Miles Franklin. *Story of an African Farm* was available by mail order through *The Bulletin* to the most remote locations in Australia. Its female protagonist, Lyndall, portrayed the crude reality of life for women. She attempts to live freely. She takes a lover. She becomes pregnant. Ultimately, she is abandoned and dies after complications from childbirth. The subsequent generation of writers in Australia included female authors of global significance in Henry Handel Richardson and Christina Stead. It could be argued that literature has provided the most tolerant path for women of all art forms. Certainly, there are very few women in the plastic arts except as models and sex-muses. Kristeva applied the death drive to literature. Freud coined this term in "Beyond the Pleasure Principle" when he moved beyond the simple human urge for pleasurable experience to describe an opposition between the ego and sex. Ego has a death drive (*thanatos*) whereas sex (*eros*) has a life instinct. Freud was alerted to this concept by working with trauma victims of the Great War. They constantly reverted to traumatic experiences rather than seek out pleasurable alternatives. This observation was reinforced when Freud watched his grandson fervently enjoy a game called *Fort/Da* in which he had to fantasise that his mother has disappeared. I recall a similar sensation from my own childhood. I was the only child of a single mother with no family. I imagined my future if my mother died. This nightmare caused me endless trauma yet I never sought to truncate it. Kristeva distinguished between semiotic (feminine) and symbolic (masculine) signification. Semiotic is like the pre-Oedipal/pre-mirror stages in Freud/Lacan. It is classified as *chora* (0–6 months) by Kristeva. It is instinctual and emotional. The baby struggles to apprehend existence. There is no speech as yet. *Chora* resides in the gaps and tones of language. It is the Apollo stage where music and rhythm predominate. The symbolic, by contrast, occurs at the later mirror-stage as the child becomes a speaking subject and gives way to abjection. Kristeva's point of difference from Lacan is that the subject continues to oscillate between the semiotic and symbolic throughout life – rather than transfer irrevocably from one to the other. This enables Kristeva to align her thinking with post-structuralist theory, which rejects fixed systems. She also relaxes the tight link in Lacan between the unconscious and the structure of language/subjectivity, which is all about creating LACK, and thereby evades his restrictive Oedipal Laws. *Revolution in Poetic Language* explores how the semiotic tendency of humans is governed by the death drive. Mallarme and Lautreamont are seen as prototypes of modern avantgarde practice. Joyce is the only writer in English studied by Kristeva and then almost always in tandem with Mallarme or Bataille like some co-joined set-up. She feels safer in theory if she runs writers in packs. Kristeva sees Freud in the central position "raising the veil of mystery the nineteenth century had held over sexuality" (84). In this theory, sex created a nexus between language and drives. This made the subversive impact of Lautreamont and Mallarme possible. It distinguishes them from poets who were "quickly concealed, or re-fetishised (Apollinaire), even academised (Valery)" (85). In conclusion, "only after Freud has poetic writing had a future (Joyce, Bataille) and it is only starting with Freud that one may attempt to measure its significance" (85). Joyce would have been scandalised by this conclusion, given his distaste for Freudian psychoanalysis and ambivalent experience with Jung. He referred to them in a letter to Harriet Weaver in June 1921 as the "Swiss Tweedledum" and "Viennese Tweedledee." The Circe episode of *Ulysses* and the whole of *F(W)ake* can be seen as direct rejoinders to Freud's dream theories. He also took issue with Jung's analysis of symbols, which he found 'mechanical' and simplistic ("house = womb, fire = phallus" were the examples he gave to Oscar Schwarz) compared to the historic depth and sophistication of literary symbolism. Joyce reinstates the primacy of literature over theory through the intercession of what Kristeva calls "poetical language." Joyce was an early reader of Freud in German during his time in Trieste, perhaps as early as 1911. In Zurich, Ottocaro Weiss, whose brother was one of Freud's early students and the first Italian psychoanalyst, acted as a crib for Joyce. One of Joyce's holographic notebooks provides incontrovertible proof that he read "Little Hans" and "The Wolf-Man," which are both cited obliquely in *F(W)ake*. He was an inveterate interpreter of dreams. He pored over the dream notebook kept by Frank Bugden. He analysed Nora's dreams in 1916 (Ellmann, 436–8) and his own dreams throughout his life (Ellmann, 547–50). Some of his dreams included characters like Molly Bloom. His American benefactor, Missus McCormick, tried to get Joyce to submit to psychoanalysis by Jung. Nora preferred to joke about her expensive lingerie. Ultimately, Joyce sided with his wife. This episode had an unpleasant denouement, which reflects poorly on Joyce. Weiss took the blame when McCormick cut off Joyce's stipend. However, Ellmann believes it was more likely that Jung was responsible as he knew of Joyce's heavy drinking and had previously counselled McCormick to cut off funds to the composer Wolf-Ferrari, facilitating his emergence from dissipation. Later, Jung wrote a preface to the German translation of Gilbert's book. It was withheld by the publisher because it presented Joyce as a sample of the schizophrenic mind. Joyce wanted it published. Jung's remark that *Ulysses* could be read 'as easily backwards as forwards' appears negative at face value but it is actually quite perceptive in Structuralist terms and may have provided Joyce with the germ of the opening and closing passages of *F(W)ake*. Jung later revised the essay. He sent Joyce a timid and self-deprecating letter praising the work as a "gigantic opus" and describing Molly's monologue as "a string of veritable psychological peaches." He confessed to the struggles which many readers of *Ulysses* have endured. Joyce referred to psychoanalysis as "neither more nor less than blackmail." He contrasted it with his work in *Ulysses* which "recorded, simultaneously, what a man says, sees, thinks, and what such seeing, thinking, saying does, to what you Freudians call the subconscious". Mockery is a key weapon in his fight against Freud. In Circe, Joyce turned the suppressed sexual desires of Bloom and Dedalus into vaudeville. In *F(W)ake*, Joyce wrote: "we grisly old Sykos who have done our unsmiling bit on 'alices, when they were yung and easily Freudened, in the penumbra of the procuring room ..." (115). This recalls his comment that Jung must have read *Ulysses* without a single laugh. Elsewhere, Joyce taunted their diagnostic language: "you have homosexual catheis of empathy between narcissism of the expert and steatopygic invertedness. Get yourself psychoanolised!" Near the end, Joyce tried to cure Lucia's schizophrenia with a new fur coat. Kristeva acknowledges key Joycean attributes in *Revolution*: exploding linguistics; inscribing what Joyce called "the epic of the human body"; exhausting ideological institutions and apparatuses; demonstrating the limits of formalist and psychoanalytic devices; attesting to a crisis in social structures; disclosing ideology and coercion. Lautreamont, Mallarme, Joyce and Artaud are all cited as representatives of some 'new phenomenon.' Their incomprehensible poetry discloses the limits of social discourse and therefore attests to its repressions in the same way as Shamanism, festivals and magic. The capitalist mode of production tries to marginalise and exploit their shattering of discourse. Any annexation (seepage) is resisted. It is a heroic enterprise. Signifying practices are disclosed by texts which attain semiotic *chora*. This is a reverse oral movement to back-before-rhyme. In the experience of Joyce or Bataille, literature makes a leap that maintains both "delirium" and "logic." Rhythmic, lexical, even syntactic changes disturb the signifying chain and open it up to the material crucible of its production. We can only read Mallarme or Joyce BACKWARDS starting from the signifier. Kristeva argues that the death drive process cannot be carried out in a conventional narrative. It needs a 'text' which seeps through the sign. It must have "violent rhythm." Readers need to give up deciphering and instead retrace the path to production. This is said to be 'dangerous' practice. These theoretical definitions do not really describe Kristeva's own writing. There is a chasm between the subject texts and her own work. She makes no attempt to challenge FORM. She accepts conventional hermeneutical style and structure. She is not a challenger like Joyce. She refines some precepts of Lacan but never writes 'poetic language.' Kristeva is thus always barracking from the sidelines. Her fiction is similar. They are just books. Like Sontag (but unlike Eco). Her novels never become texts. It is as if Kristeva is writing stories to popularise a political ideology. Her novels never look like anything written by Joyce. She churned them out. Kristeva justified these works by saying that, "to write fiction is a more genuine integration to the French language than any theoretical writing." This is an abdication. It retreats from praxis. It is a shrinkage. Her recurring sleuths – Rilsky and Delacour – are a dim metaphor of her former occupation. There is no innovation. No *divagations* (wanderings/ravings). Kristeva should have looked to Mallarme or Joyce for a template. Mallarme wrote critical poems to mash theoretical space. Joyce incorporated Stephen's Shakespeare theory into *Ulysses*. Kristeva prefers to see her fiction as "an oneiric and safe place that is not judgmental." In short, it is an escape hatch. Mallarme produced the first concrete poem with "Un coup de des n'abolira jamais le hasard" (abbreviated as "Un coup de des"). It is called "A dice thrown will never annul chance" in English. This work was laid out thinly across the page like a musical score with different fonts and font sizes to provide nuanced meaning. Large gaps of blank page predominated. Chris Brennan, the principal Australian symbolist poet, produced a manuscript which imitated 'Malahrrmay' called the "Musicopoematogaphoscope" after reading/observing *Cosmopolis* in 1897 at the NSW Public Library, where he worked as a cataloguing assistant. Kristeva wrote that the "poetic" side of the text can be seen in the pianistic scansion of sentences in Maldoror, Mallarmean rhythmics, the iciness of "Herodiade," and the opulent chic of Mery Laurent. This is her best writing: when she behaves like a literary critic. Her political and psychoanalytical programs are stretched. Mallarme shared many features with Walter Pater: composite syntax; gridding of words; concealment of subjects/objects; relentless hieratic imagery; factual remoteness; always delaying or displacing expression until a disjuncture occurred. They both removed 'I' from their work. This was a particularly strong statement by Mallarme, who worked in the historically personalised lyric format. They both believed in creating a literary complex in which music, language and image could combine in a descant above the basic sign. Mallarme was like a radio producer who specialised in special effects. He was obsessed with form, in terms of both completion and DELAY. He never finished *Herodias*. It was a conscious decision to abort. *Revolution* is about one hundred pages too long. It is repetitive but not in the strategic sense of Derrida. It serves only to restate the point rather than reposition it in a matrix of implied definitions. It is an act of bullying rather than freedom. For Kristeva, oralization acts as a mediator between rejection and sublimation. Suction/expulsion from the mother's breast are the root of our eroticised vocal apparatus. All melodic and rhythmic poetic utterance may be interpreted as oralisation. A return to oral and glottal pleasure combats the superego and linear language. Oralisation restrains the aggressivity of rejection through an attempted fusion with the mother's body. Kristeva concludes that "Mallarme's biography documents this attempt." Kristeva also appears to allude to a macabre biographical event in developing her theory. In 1898, Mallarme had a sudden series of throat spasms at home. His vocal cords closed, blocking the flow of air into his lungs. It is unclear what triggered the event. But Mallarmé died of suffocation at the age of fifty-six. This turns Kristeva's reading of Mallarme into a type of biographical mysticism. Every writer in this chapter believed in this kind of voodoo including Joyce. All their scientific language is a mask. I am writing all around Kristeva. She could have done more. V. Woolf and Stein both combined technical innovation in fiction with feminist themes. *Ulysses* daunted and challenged Woolf. She tried to downplay its significance, saying that she read it with "spasms of wonder, of discovery, & then again with long lapses of intense boredom." She called it "Genius ... but of the inferior water" and "underbred ... in the literary sense." She also referred Joyce as part of an "underworld," writing for a clique.

This is a bit rich coming from a Bloomsbury insider who never had to work a day in her life while Joyce survived hand-to-mouth to pursue his artistic vision. The naming of 'Bloom~~sbury~~' was a conscious assault on this set by Joyce. He did literally want to '~~Bloom~~sbury' them with all the pent-up resentment of a D&G outsider. I don't care if my impressions of Woolf are right/wrong. It is essential to be a provocateur. Everything Woolf wrote after reading *Ulysses* was an *Agon* with Joyce. Like *Ulysses*, *Mrs. Dalloway* is set on a single day. It deploys interior monologue. It travels sequentially through time. *Ulysses* is also the covert matter behind her essay, "Modern Fiction." But her style and thinking in that essay remained trapped in British conventions of what constituted suitable modes of literary success. She imagines freedom but cannot articulate this feeling except in negative terms. The subordinating conjunction, "if," resounds through the essay. Woolf is oppressed by fictive customs. Finally, she asks the key question: "Is it not the task of the novelist to convey this varying, this unknown and uncircumscribed spirit, whatever aberration or complexity it may display, with as little mixture of the alien and external as possible?" The answer of course is Joyce's humanist, "YES." When Woolf gets to this moment of intellectual explosion, it has to be expressed as a heavily qualified rhetorical question. It is like a child calling out in a cave. Woolf tried to eschew the epic and avoid a *clinamen* with Joyce. She aimed to "do as much, perhaps more, with as little as two characters and a day." This became her theoretical goal: to manage female reality within a severely circumscribed fictive format (see Baudrillard). It was a bright manoeuvre. She said that "you no longer cast your net in order to catch the whole sea. Instead, you angle for the one perfect fish." *Jacob's Room* was the first novel which achieved such miniaturisation. It combined the detail of Proust with the nuance of still-life scenes and portraits by Cezanne. Its atmosphere of wartime – and unspokenness – also gave it social relevance. Woolf stood at a desk at a height of three foot, six inches to create the effect of an easel when she wrote. She liked to step back and witness her words like Mallarme. Sometimes she sat in a chair to write with a piece of wood on her lap like Penelope at her loom. She was nicknamed "GOAT" as a child (see B. Capri, C4). For a while, she believed that birds were chirping in Greek. This is an allusion to the execution of young females garroted on wire at the end of the *Odyssey*. Woolf was anorexic. She synecdochised her stomach and mouth as disgusting entities. Woolf had been trying to kill herself since 1913. She and her husband kept enough petrol in the garage to asphyxiate themselves with car exhaust fumes if the Nazis won the War. Joyce's YES is turned into Septimus' suicide at the climax of *Mrs. Dalloway*. This *Tessera* reflects Woolf's personal experience as well as her social situation in the aftermath of the Great War. There is no death scene in *Ulysses*. Woolf can also be credited for reducing the cosmic scale of the title *Ulysses* to the married name of the leading female character. She is the next step (Gibraltar) after Molly Bloom. She is

Everywoman to Bloom's Everyman. Tangential connections bring Septimus and Clarissa together through the medium of Sir William Bradshaw. This type of third-party connection in fiction is normally a contrivance. In fact, *Mrs. Dalloway* contains many passé elements. They are generally mitigated by Woolf's deployment of tropes and styles from *Ulysses*. In this regard, she may have considered *Ulysses* a "mis-fire" but it certainly helped her avoid bathos. Bernard in *The Waves* is Stephen Dedalus cossetted by Bloomsbury comforts. After a successful literary career highlighted by *The Waves*, *Orlando*, *To the Lighthouse* and *A Room of One's Own*, Woolf finally killed herself in 1941. Her home in Bloomsbury had been destroyed by a Nazi bomb. The same thing happened to her next house. She retreated to a country estate. She had written so much by then. The sheer bulk of diaries, letters, essays and creative writing can be seen as a process of building a career by volume. She rarely wrote during periods following a mental breakdown. Her output was augmented by aristocratic connections at the heart of Imperial London. The British elite needed someone like Woolf during the Culture Wars of the 1920s. Woolf's suicide was a badly managed melodrama. She left notes to her sister and husband then drowned herself in the Ouse. Her hat and cane were found on the riverbank. She probably expected her body to be found in a soft-focus setting like Ophelia. But it was swept downstream and not discovered for three weeks. Some children found it at Southease. By then, it was bloated and decayed. Like Mallarme, Woolf was interested in the image produced by text, maybe as a result of founding Hogarth Press. This was evident in "Kew Gardens." She typeset in text-blocks surrounded by white space. Her first edition covers are non-linear like her textual forms. She preferred curved to angular imagery. Woolf used a code involving domestic pets when she corresponded with Violet Dickinson about sex. She used 'forehead' as a euphemism for vagina, according to Jane Lillianfel. Lawrence was considered the pre-eminent male writer of the 'female question' in English Modernism, largely due to his glottal expositions of female orgasm. This augmented his genuine effort to depict female social disenchantment. Havelock Ellis was another writer who was uniquely geared to write about women. His pseudo-engagement to Olive Schreiner was a manifestation of his suffragette cred. **Why isn't Havelock Ellis famous like Freud?** He was essentially a chronicler ... an accumulator of information ... an encyclopedist. He developed isolated hyoptheses. But he never developed a full-blown theory like Freud. Ellis wrote the first medical textbook on homosexuality and introduced transgender studies into our discourse (Eonism). He is credited with introducing the terms Narcissism, Autoeroticism and Undinism (previously known as Urolagnia). He discovered that he got sexual arousal from watching women urinate at the age of sixty. Like Freud, literature provided Ellis with a major source for his thinking. He travelled to Australia as a young man and worked in a one-teacher school in the Hunter Valley near Scone. His experiences were fictionalised in the novella, *Kanga Creek*. It reflects the deep influence of Schreiner. His major work, *Studies in the Psychology of Sex*, discloses the continuing influence of Romantic tropes and imagery. He gave peyote to Yeats. **Provide an example of Ellis' method.** The opening of Volume 5 of *SPS*, titled *Erotic Symbolism*, opens with a definition in terms of an aesthetic reaction recalling Ruskin or Pater. Ellis then quotes Rossetti's poem "The Woodspurge"; Huysmans' *La-Bas*; a series of examples of symbolism in the naming of genitalia and the sexual act in Latin, Shakespeare, the Talmud and Classical Greek; Stendhal on "crystallisation" and the potency of physical "defects"; Mary Wollstonecraft on the "sacred respect" of the man for the "glove or slipper of his mistress"; a list of fetish objects from Burton's *Anatomy of Melancholy*; Casanova and Ovid on foot fetishism; and the interest of Hardy, Goethe and Restif de le Bretonne in the feet and shoes of their heroines. Lit refs are used as a proxy data over the first 30 pages. A continual review process of gender representation has been undertaken during composition. This was especially valuable in ensuring that depiction of women is audited at a whole-of-text level. There is no inadvertent accumulation of bad practice out of a sequence of single incidents. Literature contains a lot of tawdry little plot elements involving intimidation, coercive sex, rape and violence against women. They all add-up. It anaesthetises the audience about violence against women. TMAC is focused on the relationships between men due to the use of the *Odyssey* and *Ulysses* as foundation documents for an exploration of the son-father dynamic in terms of absence, falsity and lack. This is consistent with the author's own experience. It forms an autobiographical base which gives the author a feeling of re-assurance that there is a guarantee of fidelity-to-fact underpinning the narrative. It executes a contract with life. This made it possible to write this novel. Male characters are generally deceitful, manipulative, unlikable, selfish and corrupt. Some are shiftless, albeit young. Their emotional spectrum is quite limited. Sexual gratification is a primary drive. Pity is confined to self. Elder males exhibit the worst behaviour (Westacott, Leer, Welles, Cane). The only gentle mature male character is Leon Daniel. A focus on male identity does not mean that female characters have no active role in the play. Indeed, one could argue that they are the sources of volition for much of the plot. Elizabeth Archer is a driving force in the narrative. Yes, she does bad things to Tom Hallem. But there is no clear-cut moral judgment about her decision to conceive a child by deception. Indeed, the author's own mother conceived him in a similar fashion. Penelope Hallem played with curtain gauze. It stank of cigarettes. Sales reps were hopping like fleas around her chlorophyll work suit offering iridescent cocktails. Patrons ragged with liquor spat brand-hype in her ear. Their breath tickled her neck. Interlopers. "I'll be home as soon as I can," she told Les from a noisy phone booth. "Still looking for a taxi," she said later above the trumpet cry of a Dixieland jazz band. She put down the receiver and got out her car keys. Penelope Hallem evinces no strong maternal bond with her son.

This mirrors Penelope's choice in the *Odyssey* to remain at arm's length from Telemachus. Both Richie and Judy make well-reasoned decisions to leave the material comfort of life with a western boyfriend. These decisions are metaphors for national self-determination. Ana Lafei is a tragic figure although she has been placed in a secondary trope. This is a conscious decision. In any other novel, her death would be the leading plot line and climax (see Emma Flaubert, Anna Karenina et al.). It would become *mimesis praxeos*. But I don't believe in *agnorisis*. The main thing is that the reader gets all the information they need over the course of the novel. The sequence of disclosure doesn't matter. It doesn't need to be chronological or involve artificial constructs of suspense and discovery. It doesn't even need to be rendered in fictive formats like dialogue between characters. The narrator can just enter the text self-deprecatingly like Chaucer. It is important to resist the urge for teleological balance. Confluence is critical in preparing any text that seeks to align theory with narrative. It is a disclosure of socio-historical FACT that the central event in the novel is represented as a secondary trope because it INVOLVES A WOMAN. Reduction in status due to gender is thus exposed both in text and form. Ana could be seen as a passive character like Ophelia. Imagery consistently suggests this correspondence. In this respect, she is the victim that creates the necessity for Hamlet (Hallem) to die to close off the text as Tragedy. This makes him much like Agamemnon. This chapter ends with the emergence of female thinkers in France in the 1960s. INSERT Greer. Embedded social roles for women are prevalent, as in *Ulysses*. Junkies prostitute themselves for cash. A female shop assistant is propositioned by an ageing businessman. Men dominate the art world. The campus scene has comparative gender equality. There are strident female academics like Barbour and Krafter. O is more enigmatic. She already seems to be taking on a conventional gender approach with Billy. Later, she accepts a traditional maternal role after they have children. The future of their marriage is unclear at the end of the novel. Manhole (or Shredded Ginger) is symbolic of what can happen to an expatriate wife pressed into the role of *tai tai* in China (see C10). Her husband controls their finances. He has taken their children to another city. She is utterly disempowered. The female curator is a stock character from Sydney's art scene over the last 30 years. Her sister is a more interesting case study. She becomes Tom's girlfriend. They travel to Europe soon after the time period of the novel ends. She has been damaged by an abusive father. This resulted in bulimia and alcohol abuse. She is a matching risk-taker for Tom. They are almost *doppelgangers*. This is destructive for both parties. Helen Capri is the most passive female character in the novel. She is a remnant of the 1960s. She broke out of her confines once and once only. The trauma of her consequent pregnancy caused her to withdraw irrevocably into the role of supporting wife. A suppressed air of dissatisfaction always accompanies her appearances in the text.

IRIGARAY

All my backsliding and qualifications about gender would be passed very quickly by Irigaray. She would just disclose my text for what it is – about men, for men, employing Sameness, disclosing the manner in which women were still (in both senses) commodities, my *Cockbrainism*. There would be no need for *aporias*. She would declare that a rape scene just provides men with a guide on tactics, how to use power, an instruction manual, charts on rationalising its aftermath, even legal advice on perverting female language and response into tacit compliance. In retrospect, I think Ana should have thrust a Stanley knife into Matt Supplejack's eye. This would have been a good symbol. Oedipus as a painter. Like Tom Hallem gone blind in bed. I'm going back to change that text. Just got to block the existing lines and hit STRIKETHROUGH. Maybe I will leave them placed together in equivocal engagement. That's more in keeping with Irigaray. She is always PENT. Irigaray wires great slogans. They distort predictability. Sometimes she changes direction almost like mistyping a letter and getting a different word that you decide to keep. It's atomatic writing. Nietzsche wrote aphorisms. They're too long already. You can isolate Irigaray's text into short verdicts, single words and strings of ellipses. She demands precision in line-length like Mallarme. Irigaray is the only writer since Joyce to write with centripetal zest. Everyone else plods. She has an eighteenth-century eye for detail. Irigaray is a fictive writer who created no characters, only herself. In the lead role, she shines through each work as a sentimental figure. She is the detective that Kristeva could never create. Kristeva argues that Joyce disrupts the 'system' as soon as he brings to utterance what is repressed in all COCKBRAIN structures: the female voice of Molly Bloom. Kristeva writes with uncharacteristic energy of Joyce's language as "dazzling, unending, eternal – and so weak, so insignificant, so sickly." This dialectic gets to the crux of Joyce's greatness in a way that no other critic has managed. It is as if Kristeva spent her entire career working towards this conclusion. James Joyce has the most hubris and the most vulnerability of any writer I know. He is the most insipid, wheedling, pampered mummy's boy in literary history. His susceptibility oozes through narrative glass. His dogged self-indulgence created a dichotomy: either genius or failure. Joyce wrote in the first person always. Everything is a diversion back to autobiography but refracted. He knew that it was the only way to retain the reader's interest. Irigaray also writes in the first person. She doesn't hide inside soliloquy. She always makes spoken word monologues to an implicit accomplice. There is always and only an Other. It is never the reader. Let alone an audience. It is always an implied lover. Her *jouissance* is not of the ecstatic compound. She can't get outside the signifying chain like a beatific nun. Irigaray is ever-more post-coital. Always smoking in bed. Looking at her recumbent form in the mirror. Masturbating in a way that men cannot see or emulate. Soaking up weak sunshine on her pellucid gut. She learned a lot from Duras then hardened and fastened her stasis. Irigaray is a lover not a hater. She was expelled from the Freudian School of Paris in 1974. Why did Lacan eject Irigaray? Why supply a platform to your new arch-enemy? Surely, he saw enough of Godard's movies to learn brawl tactics. Lacan had to behave like Andre Breton whenever he could. Breton was always ousting people from Surrealism with maximum publicity. Likewise, Lacan. Being Belgian, Irigaray is aligned with D&G's notion of a diaspora along with Kafka and Joyce. We have dealt with that notion in C4. We must read all myths in terms of what Derrida calls the Phallogocentrism – or COCKBRAINISM – which is the foundation of Western culture. Lacan had been accused of Cockbrainism by Derrida. This term was coined by E. Jones in 1927. He argued that women were not driven by penis-envy. In fact, male theoreticians created it as a defence against castration. Freud rejected his thinking. Irigaray reviews Lacan's contribution to psychoanalysis in a survey chapter in *This Sex Which is Not One*. Irigaray is unstinting towards Lacan's work. She has no interest in cant. She gives him credit for reopening the debate on the primacy of phallic symbolism over the penis and an awareness of the potential impact of vaginal orgasm and the clitoris (p.60). But ultimately Lacan clung to Freud on the chronological rosary of castration anxiety > female entry into the Oedipus complex > and penis envy (which he actually inflated). Irigaray is an innovative stylist. She wasn't wild for justice like Mary Daly. It's not clear if she feels the same anger. She appears detached almost sanguine. She never wanted to disclose any details of her life. She rejected biography. It's always used AGAINST women. Lacan's Orcs would devour it eagerly. Her most extensive autobiographical data is gathered in an epistolary exchange in *Through Vegetal Being*, just like D&G composing *Anti-Oedipus* by mail. Her exchange with Michael Marder is atavistic wish-fulfilment by Irigaray. They both want to deploy Classical/Eastern teachings on the integration of culture/nature in total isolation from the sexist standpoints of these creeds. Her grandfather took Luce on adventures in the Belgian forest. She gave up driving and became a pilot. She eats meat. She was disconsolate at her dismissal from the University of Paris after the publication of *Speculum: Of the Other Woman*. These events pushed her to a realisation that the intellectual and cultural tradition into which she was dropped neglects LIFE. She could find an antidote to this still birth in Joyce. Some of her texts are imaginary dialogues like Walter Landor. Only Van Loon attempted a similar type of discourse in the twentieth century. Her narrative style gets stolid after a few pages. You can't sustain this type of prose intensity without plot distraction. It works like television commercials. You need regular product placement. It gives the reader time-off to process horde-data. This re-facets the message. It acts as a form of subliminal sub-titling. With Irigaray, you are always skimming to the next sub-climax only to go backwards to look for something missed. This is the dilemma of *Marine Lover*. It has nothing to do with Nietzsche. His name is never mentioned. He is always insinuated like a secret triste. Irigaray turns the reader into a bloodhound. Her plots never intensify. They are like Minuets. Always the same routines perfectly formed and timed to closure. Her work is not like a Dostoyevsky novel. Everything there is going along quietly then suddenly there's a crazy fizz. Irigaray is against SAMENESS in the way that counter-clerks keeping turning up to complain about the same job each day. She says using the same language reproduces the same story. She reworks the message into a million Sames. This is also Derrida's tactic: to ring-fence theoretical definition with spores. To make a new *chora* ... to go back and wipe down all claymarks ... to break all penis-moulds ... to file down all the oversized phalluses in antiquity to human girth ... to defenestrate all fauns and satyrs ... against male discourse to plunge hard or unhinge deftly ... to confect your own Imaginary based on waterflow and cures ... to knock down all skyscrapers and build a uterus of interconnected retail tunnels ... to live underwater in conversation with dolphins and seals amidst seaweed ... for Irigaray that is Atlantis (success). I too can yearn after the vain prospect of harmony. Could TMAC be re-written without the characters disclosing their gender, he asked rhetorically. This brings forth the whole issue of naming. It's so easy to default to patriarchal set-pieces. Pump a cop. Get drunk. Rape a slave. Pump iron. Pop steroids. Hatefuck Lolita. Slap your girlfriend's face in a demesne moment. This is the template used in part or whole by writers as diverse as Cave, B.E. Ellis and McCarthy as well as a lot of modern movies like *True Detective*, *Silence of the Lambs* et al. Not one of these narratives introduces a single theoretical innovation into the Canon. This is not to question the power of writers like Palahniuk, who create genuinely original concepts. But the plots of these writers are relatively benign compared to Sade. They tend to lack the moral insight achieved by Hardy's *Tess* or Murakami. Nick Cave's *Tessera* against hard-boiled pulp, the Bible and Faulkner is designed to intensify this schema to a point of overload. Tarantino did the same. Today, it all just looks like an artefact like Phrenology. I guess you've got to work out a way to re-commence literature after *F(W)ake* if you want to take the mechanics of literature forwards. One which proceeds by "jamming the theoretical machinery itself" and accepts that it's going to end up somewhere different yet probably just as impenetrable. *Ulysses* started to use language directly and obscenely but this was only to puncture social pretensions. Only inadvertently did Joyce disrupt the signification chain. He wrote that the four cardinal points in Chapter 3 of *Ulysses* were the female breasts, arse, womb and cunt as substituted by the words, 'because' (breasts), 'bottom' (arse), 'woman' (womb) and 'yes' (cunt). This is a cave drawing before the datamap of *F(W)ake*. Joyce still largely adheres to conventional characterisation of females as cunning, willful, sexy, long-suffering, strong under duress, defiant in defeat, nurturing and ultimately accepting their status as a body affirmative to the requirements of the male-as-subject (CUNT/YES). Mary Daly believed that there could be a radical decontamination of the planet based on compression of maleness. This campaign will probably need to deploy the combination punch of another big war plus sperm banks. Irigaray is primarily concerned with the way men and women speak. She wants to build a site for the origins of feminine language. This really means composing a unique dictionary. It will mean every sound, word, signifier and symbol has to be deleted and each signified re-conceived as an autonomous unit which is then: (1) tested for purity and difference against the emerging/total archive, (2) introduced into FEMSPEAK as a temporary unit until usage confirms complementarity, (3) regularly audited for infection, and (4) revised as necessary. This task cannot start in any place where men currently exist. Also, it must occur inside water. That is the location of SOFT THINKING. This is the locale to which Vattimo and Zabal must arrive. You can't fight with swords in a dam or shoot wet rifles. Their theory of passivity and equivocation is not unlike Guha's reconstruction of subaltern consciousness from Imperialist records. It reinstates the oppressed. Irigaray argues in C8 of *TSWINO* that the phallic economy places women alongside signs, products and currency as forms of exchange conducted exclusively between men. Women are exchanged just like any other commodity. They possess two values – Exchange Value & Use Value. See also Margaret Atwood, *The Handmaid's Tale*. Exchange Value is determined by society. Use Value is natural qualities. A woman's self is divided between Use Value and Exchange Value. She is only desired for Exchange Value. This system creates three types of women: the mother, who is all Use Value; the virgin, who is all Exchange Value; and the prostitute, who hovers between both Values like a dragonfly. Women are in demand due to a perceived shortage in supply. Men always want more women to add to their collection. They want to horde all the Blue Smarties. They seek a supply surplus which can be set against other surplus items to create a market just like any other friction between commodity powers in Capitalism. *THT* is perhaps the greatest novel written in English since *1984*. It has no stylistic innovation like *F(W)ake* despite its use of Chaucer as an ordering device. It is a gimmick with no structural fealty. Further, we have already examined the positive attributes of women in Chaucer earlier in this seminar series. *THT* possesses social authority due to directness and plausibility. IT HURTS. Irigaray speculates that volume is more critical than individual use in terms of the female market. This converts women into slaves. The Chinese economic miracle of *Gei Ge Kai Feng* operated on a similar rubric – there was no productivity element only sheer volume of migrant workers applied cheaply to each task. Irigaray concludes that the accumulated stress/mass of Exchange Value and Use Value creates a surplus called DESIRE. This places SEX firmly in the arena of Marx. Women become Collectibles. They are subject to the collector's shifting allegiances. They can be sold on E-Bay. Vattimo and Zabal reject any philosophical system that 'solves' humans. They want to avoid the violence of systematicity. All they seek is the right to "interpret, vote and live." This is the risk taken by any democracy throughout history. Hordes always overwhelm talkfests. This is what happened to the Greeks, Romans, Vikings, the Versailles States created in 1919, the States created after WW2, even the Chinese Empire after Ya Pian Da Zhan. Ultimately, the world order was saved by water in 1940. The English Channel held the Nazis at bay. Water anxiety is ingrained into Teutonic consciousness. They have always been land gangs. Irigaray believed that Nietzsche feared water. Hitler was water-averse. Fluid is the woman's element. Irigaray got that off Joyce, who stole it off the Classics. But she missed the female compulsion to commit suicide in water. It is not mentioned at all in *TSWINO*. A word search of the book shows zero results for SUICIDE, WATER, OCEAN, DROWN as well as derivates like OPHELIA, NAIADS, WOOLF. Only on page 215, right near the end of her opus, Irigaray finally writes, apparently to a naked lover, to language and to the symbols in her midst, with a plaintive rhetorical query. Here, Irigaray rejects the science of water for dream-water. She wants to extract rocks in her path that dictate the pattern of waterflow like so many teeth. She wants to reclaim water from land like anti-Faust. She wants to create mud, swamps and bogs full of mangroves and other Rhizophora. For Irigaray ultimately always writes of love, sex, humans, contact, words, life. She is a true humanist. Like Cyrano, she speaks as one lovelorn. She only writes love letters. Her texts are always innovating against hardness, always permeating, always dissolving hate. In this regard, she performs an *askesis* with sub-elements of *daemonization* towards Joyce. My own task is perhaps more akin to *Apophrades*. I am reopening the casket of dead Joyce by writing a sequel to *Ulysses*.

DELEUZE & GUATTARI

"Say stupid shit," implored Felix Guattari speaking/writing to himself. It was an imprecation to bravery of expression. The easiest default is to back-track from the vi[r/t]al path. Deleuze has dominated Guattari because of his relative fame, his capacity to ENFORCE PRODUCTION and abecedary PRIORITY. Guattari appears as Eliza Doolittle in their untitled passion play. They are like Edmund and Edgar in *King Lear*. Deleuze milks Guattari like an interrogator. He desires Guattari's unchained freedom of utterance all for himself. Like Tom Hallem, Gilles Deleuze knew only too well that he had flatlined by 1970. He needed Felix Guattari to kickstart momentum again for the final push against Freud and his Lac[a/u]na. Guattari had three ideas per minute. Deleuze insisted he record them immediately without revision like dreamscapes. This speed to canvas was taken up by Neo-Expressionism in the early 1980s. Its leading proponents were Immendorf, Middendorf, Fetting, Salome, Cucchi, Clemente, Paladino and the American Schnabel. In Australia, Peter Booth, Mike Parr, Jenny Watson and younger painters Matt Supplejack and Tom Hallem were associated with it. The return to traditional figuration in NEX created a sympathetic landscape for the emergence of graffiti artists lead by J-M. Basquiat. These painters are a natural data-set for any critical assessment of whether NEX achieved the stature of the Figural (as defined by Deleuze) or just represented a cynical art industry manoeuvre to create colourful, marketable product. The term, Figural, was coined by Lyotard in 1971 and picked up by his great friend, Deleuze, in *Francis Bacon: The Logic of Sensation* (1981). The Figural is to art what the *chora* is to Kristeva or *archi-ecriture* for Derrida – a state before/beyond language and its peculiar brand of signification. It represents a form of denotation arising from imagery/association rather than rational, linguistic concepts. The two variants of the FIGURAL proposed by Deleuze are abstraction towards pure form – as conceived by Klee – and opposition to the strictly figurative. The latter turns on creating an emblem. For example, it is the exposed teeth and maw which enable Francis Bacon's popes, businessmen and chimpanzees to conquer the Figural plane. The dentures are exposed IN FULL as if the lips had been cut away with a fighting knife, disclosing the hard surface of the gums. The tongue occasionally thrusts into an azure cavity, as in "Three Studies of the Human Head" (1953), but usually not. Normally, Bacon just leaves a gape. This hole somehow symbolises the abstract tragedy of the soul and the bleakness of our human condition. Why does this work, pondered Tom Hallem when he viewed the major retrospective of Bacon's work at the Tate Gallery in July 1985? All Bacon has really done is paint a portrait with prominent teeth inside a dark blue ruff, leave a black gap in the centre and run a thin brush vertically over the face with a diluted titanium solution. It creates a sense of DROP. Bacon closed the mouth about 1969 and never opened it again. Afterwards, he chopped the face into Cubist patterns or painted naked trunks, such as those wearing cricket pads in his famous series of 1982. Bacon's other achievement was to shut down space in paintings. Often, he makes the outlines of a box around his figures or places them flat on a podium or throne. There is no external place of withdrawal. Everything is always on display. In this regard, he reaches Deleuze's south pole of the Figural: PURE ABSTRACTION. Guattari is operated by Deleuze like a dice tossed around a sealed marble vault violently. He defines by rebound. He is like an alarm clock: he goes off, he doesn't pass judgment. Thus, he is more than a mere

TRICKSTER functioning along a two-dimensional plane. He came to notice in Paris perversely. He was Lacan's acolyte before turning on him like JUDAS. He tried to buy his way into Lacan's inner circle, even procuring patients from the staff at La Borde. Lacan treated him like shit. It was an abusive relationship. Guattari sought the status of Lacan's anointed successor. When this dream was dashed, he formed an alliance of convenience with Deleuze. This broadened his characterisation somewhat. Like any adherent to Masoch, he desired at night what he dished out to others all day. Deleuze inscribed him thoroughly like the official on Kafka's harrow. "It's so hard, being strapped to Gilles," Guattari said. This image creates uncertainty as to whether Gilles is a man or a torture device. My principal concern with Irigaray is that she never discloses a subject. Her work is as illusive and elusive as the writer herself: always getting in your face (words emanating out of her head like thorns) yet utterly indecipherable and ostensibly engaged in intense conversation with someone else. You are consistently left grasping for a definition of human form with Irigaray. Guattari is all too human by contrast. "Be stupid in my own way," he invoked with the simple pleasure of Nietzsche advising all future philosophers that their task was anti-Platonism. This is one method of undoing a Borromean knot. (1) To lose your inhibitions in the analytical task. (2) To confront the theoretical expedition without stopping or editing. (3) To invent your own prose, both in style and substitution of phonemes. (4) To make cleavage out of the radical opposition of irrational sentences. Joyce could have done the same thing. Some would argue *F(W)ake* is just that. No one could argue the same of *Ulysses*. It was still pier[c]ed by myth. Guattari was an imaginary character created by Deleuze in the style of Samuel Beckett. He learned only from experience like Clov. He could not take external advice. He followed his heart [INSERT CANNED LAUGHTER]. Deleuze played Hamm in this production. He was the ebullient dolt. Guattari started out as the foreman in an insane asylum then morphed into a draft-dodging lunatic during the Algiers Crisis. By the time he reached La Borde, he was cured of fascist cruelties. He set up a communist utopia in a madhouse. This was later the subject of *Marat/Sade* by Peter Weiss. All role definition, all demarcation, all pretense to conventional treatment was dropped except the use of psychotropic drugs. One of his patients was a Maoist who did magic tricks. He wrote to Charlie Chaplin's daughter proposing to start a circus together. Eventually, they married after a long correspondence and she came to live at La Borde. Only Classical myths can concoct the same kind of fantastic absurdities. Their union created the in-house skillset to invent madness as performance. Deleuze loathed the insane. Their random-ish acts of kid-iness deplored him. Stephen Dedalus struggles against any authoritarian or regulating structure as well. Even in the apparently benign setting of Chapter One, he resists (in order): creative normalisation; death-bed sops; social codes commending home, thrift and sobriety; Anglo-Irish education policy; the Church; and British Imperialism.

Like Guattari, his classroom method rejects all notions of control. He enforces disorder. Joyce disliked any dichotomy of true/false factuality. This culminates in the anti-riddle of the "fox burying his grandmother." The real answer is "Stephen Dedalus is not able to bury his own mother." He is a dispossessed son who mourns his dead mother obliquely. He is thus in a different state to Telemachus, who seeks out a missing father. Telemachus has a whole ocean full of hope to search in. Stephen has nowhere left to go. His life is a dead-end just like James Joyce at the age of twenty-two. This is why Joyce selected the night before he met Nora Barnacle as Bloomsday for his novel. She was his escape hatch. This was one of the hackneyed tropes that Joyce consistently enacted throughout the course of his ill-gotten life. Joyce's subsequent quest took eighteen years like Odysseus: from exit from Dublin in 1904 to the publication of *Ulysses* in 1922. He had to pass through different locations across Europe, often begging for *xenia*. He found refuge during war. Ultimately, his first quest ended successfully in the creation of *Ulysses*. This is the equivalent of Odysseus' return to Ithaca. Joyce slaughtered the suitors (his literary competitors) in one cataclysmic scene in the banquet hall (his novel). Like Odysseus, however, he wasn't allowed to stay still. He was forced by his financial sponsors to start another quest almost immediately. One which took another eighteen years: the construction of *F(W)ake*. This perfect numerological balance (count it!) was probably conceived by Joyce soon after the completion of *Ulysses*. He knew that he would have to die on the altar of publication. There are five core tropes in the myth of the Classical hero:

1. Extraordinary circumstances in birth and childhood.
2. Obstacles appearing soon after birth.
3. A deity helps the hero.
4. As an adult, the hero faces great challenges usually during a quest. Often there is a monster (see Levi-Strauss).
5. For his feats, the hero is rewarded with political power, marriage, and/or wealth.

Oedipus is perhaps the most pathetic tragic hero in the ancient canon, along with Heracles. In myths, these archetypal heroes all display profound COCKBRAINISM. Normally, it acts like fuel. The word 'Heroin' is derived from the German "heroisch" meaning powerful and heroic. The male hero in a myth always defeats an existential danger. This peril is associated with the irrational and therefore the disorganisation of society. Heroin effectively defeats this mytheme by destroying the hero. Schizoanalysis was developed by D&G as a response to the shortcomings in psychoanalytic practice. Guattari was disgusted by the Oedipus complex and all authoritarianism for that matter. He wanted to be WILD WITH PASSION. The Oedipal framework colonises and represses desire. History is not a dialectical class struggle. It is a battle over desire-flow, they mused. Allusions to the Oedipal tragedy associate Tom Hallem and Billy Capri with the figure of the unlucky son (also Eteocles and Polynices). This is a key correspondent of the Telemachus figure in Classical mythology. However, it would be wrong to see Oedipus as a direct analogue to Telemachus. For Oedipus is a FULL mythic figure whereas Telemachus is only a functional entity within another hero's myth (a subset of his father). Actually, Oedipal themes often work at a tangent to the Telemachus figure. The core mythemes of Oedipal tragedy are: Blighted birth > Rejection by father > Death sentence (mis-executed) > Exposure > Limbo (apparent erasure) > Bucolic childhood (temp idyll) > Journey to the city (fatal movement) > Murder of father (blasphemy) > A test is passed > Identification of special qualities > Temporary privilege > Tragic revelation > Exile (2) > A puzzle is solved (it is not surprising that limping Oedipus solves a riddle that relates to the act of walking) > Defeat of external monster creating conditions for internal monster > Momentary triumph > Marriage > Fatherhood > Presiding over disaster (Nature's rebellion against) > Rejection of prophecy > Self-Realisation > Selfless self-mutilation (actual blindness replaces symbolic blindness) > Exile (3) > Wandering > Care of loyal party (Antigone) > Pantheistic Closure (absorption into Nature). Both Tom Hallem and Billy Capri are shunted into the snowball momentum of crazy events and inadvertent consequences that characterise Classical mythology. Tom Hallem was coming down hard now. Willy's mix was too dirty. It was cut with whatever white shit came to hand. He smashed his palm against bagged cement. A hairline crack ran out of a window frame at a forty-five-degree angle. Cracks yield surface (not a blockage). Sex is immanence/revolution. Make pornographic text. A conga line of crotchless harlequins enters. Zeus transforms himself into a menagerie. A ballet choreographed by Sade. Everybody fucks. Some burn from contact with the God. Sweep used genitals off-stage. Hermaphrodites burst through the surface of a cunt-shaped swimming pool. It is filled with equal volumes of sperm and vaginal juice. The cast perform synchronised swim routines of grotesque inventiveness. This is all televised live at half-time. The Chinese emperor was only allowed to copulate according to the cycles of the moon as calculated by scholars. Ironically, it never matched the female menstrual cycle. This is why the Qing Chao struggled for heirs. Sub-heading: Crimes Against Fertility, Part X ("X"). My father's forked tongue. A double play. "Choice of left-hand pussy or right-hand pussy or one full pussy for each," touted a spruiker. Don't let the goanna near the nest, Eurylochus. They'll swallow her eggs. Seven herds of oxen and seven herds of sheep each of fifty heads are pastured on three-pointed Thrinacia. The text is an island. Another stage. Joyce's hospital boardroom on OotS is guarded by Helios' daughters in the guise of a tema of midwives. Carcasses bellow raw or roasting on a spit. Lift yer skirt and show old Hawkie your stirrups. "Mound of Venus" is the top tip for

Race 3. Billy Capri scanned the front bar of the Shakespeare Hotel from King Street. Tom Hallem entered from a side door on Hordern Street. The difference is symbolic. From the pane, Billy watched his brother lurch across the room and disappear towards the toilets. The Oxen of the Sun episode ends at Burke's pub in Dublin between 10 pm and midnight on 16th June 1904, where a group of revelers have adjourned to celebrate the birth of Mistress Purefoy's twelfth child. Midnight ("M") is the time of night when Deleuze said there was nothing left to lose, nothing to gain. You can reflect blandly on the meaning of philosophy when the night is no longer pent with desire. Joyce built the Oxen episode out of 9, 17, 26 or 31 segments (depending on your interpretation) to demonstrate the evolution of English prose style from GRUNT to SLOGAN. His primary source was two popular anthologies: *The English Prose: From Mandeville to Ruskin* by William Peacock (1903) and *The Anthology of English Prose* by George Saintsbury (1912). These works do not cite subaltern dialects like Cockney, Geordie or music hall parlance. Joyce ("J") did not want to act as an English anthologist. He was famous for telling Arthur Power that "I don't write in English." Rather, Joyce approached these works critically seeing them as propaganda tools of British Imperialism. One objective of the Oxen episode was to demonstrate how English subjugated Irish expression and culture. Joyce embodied this situation in the opening chapter of *Ulysses* in the figures of Haines and the quisling Mulligan. The characters in Oxen are Irish yet they speak in Irish-tongued English. This makes them figures of fun. English narrative styles continue to **lay over** their colloquial gestures. They are unconscious of speaking local patois [USE AUSTRALIAN ENGLISH AS METAPHOR]. As noted at the outset, the Oxen episode collapses into Pidgin English by closure to elucidate the fact that Imperialism creates hybrid forms of expression all geared to production and profit. These are the tongues of Pure Capitalism. Studies of Pidgin English across various jurisdictions demonstrate it is a mercantile construct with a high percentage of words relating to trade activities. Yet Pidgin English also shows how the subaltern language blows back on the Imperial Power bringing new terms and grammar into the arch-language. Essentially, this is the dialectical struggle between Major Literature and Minor Literature explored by Deleuze and Guattari. The road to Malahide/Mandalay was a two-way street. Structuralism and Post-Structuralism are highly relevant to any parable of English. London was usurped by Paris over the course of the twentieth century as the theoretical hub for linguistics. Structuralism replaced Imperialism as the dominant influence on English. It was a new Theocratic Age. YES ("Y"). Derrida has written that Deleuze ("D") and Sarah Kofman ("K") both gave themselves to death in suicide ("S"). It is his way of migrating death rituals to the West. What a cruel statement. You only have to suffer the loss of a father, poisoned ["P"] with aconitine pastilles (Rudolph Virag ["V"], died 1886), or a son (Rudy Bloom, died 1893), to query ("Q") the value of life, our impotence at its forfeiture and death's bitter aftermath. Don Cane, Richie and the Archers all knew the loss of a baby, as did my own father. It is ironic that they are placed in contradiction in this work. Aconitine is quickly absorbed, even through the skin. A Rumanian umbrella-tip can deliver a fatal load. After a few minutes, burning and numbness begin in the mouth and extremities then spread throughout the body. Sweating, chills, nausea, cramps and diarrhea follow. Respiratory paralysis and cardiac arrest eventually lead to death. Jack Power discusses suicide blithely with Bloom on the journey to Paddy Dignam's funeral, ignorant of the fact that Bloom's father had killed himself. After Kofman's death, Derrida wrote of her pitiless and implacable love of Nietzsche ("N") and Freud ("F") as well as her obliteration ("O") as their blood critic. He does not address the fact that she committed suicide on the 150th anniversary of Nietzsche's birth (15 October 1994). Not death on his death day. Not death/death. That would equalise death and/or make a "double mark" of death. But, rather, death/birth. Like a tombstone laid. Cancelling out hope. Onec upno tiem, ("F.") Nietzsche was a chubby baby in a cot. He wasn't born with that insane ("I") moustache. Kofman may have been trying to alter history by passing the existence of Nietzsche through the distorting zoom ("Z") lens ("L") of her own suicide. Death overlaying life then. Overturning the Jesus myth. Did Kofman have the ego ("E") for that? Her thesis *Nietzsche et la Métaphore* was supervised by Deleuze. In 1969, she met Derrida and began attending his seminars. She became a leading authority on N and F. In 1994, Kofman published her autobiography *Rue Ordener, Rue Labat* ["R"]. She killed herself the same year. The book tells the story of her life from the age of eight to eighteen (1942–52). Its key plot elements are: her father's detention (he died at Auschwitz ["A"]); her family being forced to hide in the underground ("U"); and her mother's custody battle ("C, B") with the woman known as Meme ("M") who had sheltered her during the war. The increasingly autobiographical nature of her writing ("W") coincided with her path to suicide. Experts believe that you can write about trauma ("T") but you cannot resolve it with words. It is always recalled through bodily sensations. Thus, it is encoded in the body and cannot be assimilated by the mind. Trauma can therefore be experienced as a loss of language. It must be cauterised by action against the body. Deleuze committed suicide (4 November 1995) by throwing himself from the window of his apartment. He had suffered a terrible respiratory illness for years. Tom Hallem ("H") died with a cannula stuck in his left forearm. He had been topped-up by his dealer as his credit card was systematically emptied over three days. He must have been virtually unconscious most of the time. He knew it was coming. You can't rock back like that without intent. One of Deleuze's last public activities was a television series for Arte Channel in which he used each letter of the alphabet to generate ("G") discussion. His subjects were as follows:

Gilles Deleuze – A–Z of TV topics

Letter	Subject/Title	Letter	Subject/Title
A	Animal	N	Neurology
B	Boire (E. "drink")	O	Opera
C	Culture	P	Professor
D	Desire	Q	Question
E	Enface (E. "childhood")	R	Resistance
F	Fidelity	S	Style
G	Gauche (E. "Left Wing")	T	Tennis
H	History (Philosophy)	U	Un (E. "One")
I	Idea	V	Voyage
J	Joy	W	Wittgenstein
K	Kant	X	Inconnues (E. "Variables")
L	Literature	Y	See X
M	Malady	Z	Zigzag

Deleuze covered a broad range of topics above. Likewise, each character has been allocated a subject/title in the Kofman text ("X"). They all relate to birth, family and death. It is almost a self-deprecating Joyce-like joke ("J"). The kind picked up by George Perec and Alain Robbe-Grillet. D&G's final solution was to annex art to a new clinical enterprise (see *One Thousand Plateaus*). Create a coalition of artist-clinicians. A new guild. Churn the margins within cultivated soil (major[minor]major). Make an Urstaat of artists, libertarians and thinkers like Kierkegaard, Nietzsche, Adami and Peguy with superpowers like humour, irony, repetition and schizoanalysis. Wait for Lacan's hegemony to wane. Maybe skewer him in the back in a pack as with Caesar. Then build a desire engine. Make it look like a tank. Use a schematic overlay that traces barbarian, despotic and fantastic capitalist machines. Dayglo-camouflage your true intentions. Sneak up on the swimming pool by stealth. Crap in the deep end. Shoot market-piercing art. Battle the forces of conformity and acculturation. Form a new corps like Dada or Punk. Design uniforms. Wear masks. Peer through the eye holes of antique portraits. Namecheck Poe. Tap into a primary state of reality using spy equipment. Start a band. Evolve from art noise to melodic pop. Rationalise it as mainstreaming your craft like Sonic Youth. Release 45s with a decentralised hole. Build an island resort called Sodoma (also known as Somaville, Sodadome, Schizodome and various other word palsy) where the libido isn't de-sexualised or sublimated. Re-time through tense shifting. The overindulged cognoscenti of the 1970s embraced it hotly. They organised group tours. Many hippies moved there, drawn by its temperate climate and surf. Others book well in advance to ensure that they can repeat the experience each year. Oppose the damming of the libido by chaining yourself to a column if necessary. Enter the *plane of immanence*. Row to Tracey Island. Visit Batman's cave. You are Brains and/or Alfred. A privileged gaze. Erase your memory of this event with a shot of repellant. Suppress misplaced romantic sentiments. Literature is stuck in a reactionary period. Its criminal masterminds have never been more insidious. When has it never been thus? Stand between them and the wall/precipice. To resist both Stalinism and psychoanalysis with a new product, that was Deleuze and Guattari's principle achievement. They rebuilt desire as a hot rod which constantly produces new connections and productions through speed-seepage. They defined it as part of the economic base not some charismatic ideology. "The truth is," Deleuze and Guattari explain in their greatest quotation, "sexuality is everywhere: the way a bureaucrat fondles his records, a judge administers justice, a businessman causes money to circulate; the way the bourgeoisie fucks the proletariat; and so on ... Flags, nations, armies, banks get a lot of people aroused." Deleuze critiques Hegel in *Difference and Repetition*, which was his doctoral thesis. He perceived repetition as an active force producing difference and renewal. Nietzsche's 'eternal return' creates the power of beginning again like Vico's cycles. We have dealt extensively with that notion in this work. It counters Freud's desire to stop repetition through its disclosure (what Foucault would call, confession). Deleuze examines Joyce in his chapter, "The Image of Thought," as an example of Empty Time. This layer of Time breaks free from repetition via an earthquake that makes it omnipresent. Tiem is then emptied out of before/after and left SAT. Deleuze uses Oedipus and Hamlet as samples. These characters self-efface, joining the abstract wor(l)d of the eternal. Deleuze cites the figure of Thanatos, the Greek personification of death, as a role model for repetition. He doesn't assume that Thanatos is just hanging off Eros blankly. Deleuze asks why he cannot be active even positive. After all, destruction predicates renewal. Virilio saw to that by inventing technology with built-in flaws. Thanatos is seen by Freudians as the opposite of Eros – the life instinct – and thus the energy of the death drive. Everybody hated Thanatos. He was cynical, manipulative and indiscriminate in behaviour. Like Lacan, he was outsmarted by King Sisyphus (Irigaray) and chained to his own machine. Bodies are machines because machines arrange and connect flows. Thanatos' imprisonment suspended human mutability until he was liberated. Prometheus had the opposite impact. Deleuze mentioned Watteau in *Difference and Repetition*. Elie Faure wrote that Watteau, "imbued with the utmost transitoriness those things which our gaze encounters as the most enduring, namely space and forests." This genius is almost the opposite of the Figural. It is a third pole cancelling out the gap between meta-abstraction and hyper-figuration. Many modern French critics have been infatuated with Watteau. His work has an obese, over-ripe tone that could have been replicated in text by a scandalous novelist of manners like Prevost or a modern social historian like Bourdieu. He atrophises the lusts of any desire machines. Incredibly, he captures a sense of time-in-decay in the confines of a still image. Watteau's sunshine always seems to be waning. There is a soft imminence of doom. Watteau is represented by Pater as the prototype for Charles Baudelaire's Painter of Modern Life, Constantin Guys. To dignify petty fashions with the Will to make them Art: that was the achievement of Watteau. Walter Pater really extracted the right message from the incisive critique of the art industry in Watteau's masterpiece, *L'Enseigne de Gersaint*. This work, which amounts to a deathbed statement on a career which had acted as a proxy for life, is an ironic metaphor for Watteau's own sense of disappointment at his time as a human being and successful artist. In the left foreground is a large painting which has been displaced from the cavernous showroom walls of the prosperous art dealer, Gersaint. It is being inserted into a box by staff prior to removal to storage. Already, it is impossible to discern where it once hung. The gap on the wall has been filled by a new painting. Thus, the room seems (in fact, has no 'seams') perpetually re-papered. Watteau juxtaposes the redundancy of the painting itself with images of human superficiality, fashion and vanity. On the right-hand side, another work of art is being scrutinised by critics. Above them, aristocrats are preening themselves in a hand-mirror in preparation for portrait-sitting. In the bottom right-hand corner, an emaciated dog gnaws at fleas on its hindquarter in the space normally reserved for the artist's signature. Thus, the painting reads like text – like FIGURAL – but with a firm conclusion: that the current is always overlaid and everything is transient from this work of art to the artist's reputation, money and all these flawed human bodies. It is not hard to see direct parallels to Elizabeth Archer and Tom Hallem in this mercantile tableau. Similarly, Pater presents Watteau's images in "A Prince of Court Painters" as either incomplete, fragmented or doomed to be effaced. His paintings at Valenciennes contained variegated imagery smearing the walls of the sunlit workroom, producing the same uneven aesthetic effect as the Ducal salon in "Duke Carl of Rosenmond." His cycle of the seasons in the panels of the dining room places a bright opaque membrane over traditional imagery ... and lets in the sun. The work's lustre, so soon to be parched by Apollo's rays, is all the more flaming, all the more resonant, for its inevitable fading: the fleeting summer glow of Dionysius. This is the final testament of D&G. Freud would blank out Self completely to attain a psychoanalytical end. Deleuze and Guattari look at schizoanalysis as a form of self-regulation. Conclusions should be read at the outset, wrote Deleuze at the start of his career, as though he invented the Executive Summary. Kill all masters (fathers), he also wrote. By the time of "Style," Pater had resolved any problem with the precedence of Ruskin in his own favour by incorpor-

www.ingramcontent.com/pod-product-compliance
Lightning Source LLC
Chambersburg PA
CBHW081138300726
48982CB00006B/991

* 9 7 8 0 6 4 5 0 5 9 2 0 5 *